2004
PUSHCART PRIZE XXVIII
BEST OF THE
SMALL PRESSES

EDITED BY BILL HENDERSON
WITH THE PUSHCART PRIZE EDITORS

Note: nominations for this series are invited from any small, independent, literary book press or magazine or online journal in the world. Up to six nominations—tear sheets or copies, selected from work published, or about to be published, in the calendar year—are accepted by our December 1 deadline each year. Write to Pushcart Press, P.O. Box 380, Wainscott, N.Y. 11975 for more information, or contact us at w.w.w.pushcartprize.com

Acknowledgments

Selections for *The Pushcart Prize* are reprinted with the permission of authors and presses cited. Copyright reverts to authors and presses immediately after publication.

The Pushcart Prize Fellowships is pleased to announce substantial recent gifts from The Katherine Anne Porter Literary Trust, Bernard Conners, and Elizabeth Richebourg Rea in support of The Pushcart Prize and our endowment campaign.

Distributed by W. W. Norton & Co.
500 Fifth Ave., New York, N.Y. 10110

Library of Congress Card Number: 76–58675
ISBN: 1–888889–36–5
          1–888889–37–3 (paperback)
ISSN: 0149–7863

INTRODUCTION

by BILL HENDERSON

In memory of
Oliver Gilliland (1948–2003)
and Leslie Fiedler (1917–2003),
a Founding Editor of this series

THIS GLORIOUS COLLECTION OF FICTION, poetry, memoirs and essays from the authentic publishers of our time should give us all faith that in the age of American Empire—when money, machines and machinations seem to rule—the still quiet voice of inspiration and individuality is alive and thriving. These sixty-two selections from forty-three presses are all the proof we need.

The publications and editors that contributed nominations for PPXXVIII exist because many before us fought battles against cultural oppression and indifference. Thomas Paine issued *Common Sense* in 1776 with his own press because the newspapers of his time spurned him. Walt Whitman became the one-man publisher of *Leaves of Grass* in 1855 (writing some of the best reviews himself) because society thought him perhaps dangerous and at best a lunatic. "Walt Whitman is as unacquainted with art as a hog is with mathematics," said one reviewing wag (presumably not Whitman himself). Sylvia Beach published James Joyce's *Ulysses* from her Paris bookstore when the novel was an international scandal and US customs officials were confiscating parts that appeared in *Little Review* and slapping hefty fines on its editors.

The list of ancestral small press heroes is too long for this brief space, but I do want to note the recent passing of two of those giants, both of them Founding Editors of *The Pushcart Prize* series—Leslie Fiedler and William Phillips.

Leslie Fiedler, who died in January, 2003, joined our editorial board in 1975. He was everything a small press person ought to be. "I long for the raised voice, the howl of rage or love," said Fiedler. All his life he was proud to be identified with the counter culture that thumbed its nose at prevailing powers. His visceral book of criticism, *Love and Death In the American Novel* (1960), brought him a lot of heat from proper academic circles, which he gleefully answered: "I have to admit a low tolerance for detached chronicling and cool analysis".

When he died at age 85, he had taught at the State University of New York at Buffalo for two decades never ceasing his contrarian and questioning stance. In 1997 he received the National Book Critics Circle Ivan Sandrof award for lifetime achievement.

Fiedler got his start in the publication of another Pushcart Founding Editor, William Phillips of *Partisan Review*, who died in September of 2002 at age 94. Fiedler's seminal essay "Come Back To the Raft Ag'in Huck Honey", the basis for *Love and Death*, first appeared in *Partisan Review* in 1948. Over the sixty-six years that William Phillips and others published *Partisan Review* it discovered and encouraged not only Fiedler but writers like Delmore Schwartz, Wallace Stevens, Lionel Trilling, Sydney Hook, Edmund Wilson, Norman Mailer, Elizabeth Hardwick, Susan Sontag and hundreds more.

Sadly, just as this edition of Pushcart goes to press word arrives that Boston University, sponsor of *Partisan Review*, has decided to close it forever. Thus dies, along with its co-founder, what critic Morris Dickstein called "one of the four or five greatest magazines in America . . . the most brilliant intellectuals America ever produced."

Partisan Review leaves as its legacy the hundreds of small journals that followed its example over six decades. Not all of them—few in fact—came close to its impact but many carry its flame, among them the late George Plimpton's *Paris Review* which, against all odds, has just celebrated its 50th Anniversary.

In previous Introductions, I have expressed my personal gratitude to George Plimpton for not only inspiring the naming of Pushcart Press with his participation in Project Pushcart in 1972—Plimpton and a battery of authors disgruntled with commercial publishers paraded with their books for sale from pushcarts through New York City streets—but also for his personal hospitality and generosity to Pushcart and his dogged, gritty determination to keep *Paris Review* alive. *The Paris Review* has provided a venue for many authors among them W.H. Auden, Ernest Hemingway, William Faulkner, Elizabeth Bishop, Toni Morrison, and Rick Moody. Our next edition will feature tributes to Plimpton.

So many editors, perhaps less celebrated than Plimpton and Phillips, keep our small press culture alive. They know that writers are not mere "content providers" hired to fill in the spaces around advertisements in commercial rags. The proprietors of the forty-three presses reprinted here—and hundreds more celebrated in our "Contributing Small Presses" section, refuse to believe that we are mere passive consumers, that our only business is consumption. They continue to insist on the sacredness of the writer's voice uncorrupted by bucks.

In PPXXVIII, truly one of the best volumes ever (I know I say that every year, don't remind me), two first-time-in-print authors are honored: Margaret Luongo for her story "Pretty" (*Tin House*) and Valerie Laken for her tale "Before Long" (*Ploughshares*). We also welcome five journals that have never before been represented here: *Spillway, Hotel Amerika, Literary Imagination, Mizna, and Brain,Child.*

In assembling this mighty volume I have been honored by the suggestions of 226 Contributing Editors listed in the "People who Helped" section and also by Monica Hellman, Jack Driscoll and David Means who helped me read the fiction, and by Tony Brandt, essays editor, plus Hannah Turner, who processed the 8000 nominations with skill and terrific handwriting, and by PPXXVIII poetry coeditors Martha Collins and Carol Frost.

Martha Collins is the author of four books of poems. Her most recent, *Some Things Words Can Do*, was published by Sheep Meadow in 1999, and included a reprint of her third, *A History of Small Life on a Windy Planet*, which won the Alice Fay Di Castagnola Award and was published by the University of Georgia in 1993. Her first book, *The Catastrophe of Rainbows*, was published by Cleveland State in 1985 and reissued in 1998; her second, *The Arrangement of Space*, won the Peregrine Smith Prize in 1991. A large selection of her poems, translated by Maria Grazia Marzot, was featured in the Italian journal *Poesia* last year.

Collins herself co-translated *The Women Carry River Water*, a collection of poems by Vietnamese poet Nguyen Quang Thieu, which was published by the University of Massachusetts in 1997 and won an award from the American Literary Translators Association in

1998. Her co-translations of poems by Vietnamese poet Lam Thi My Da, *Dedicated to a Dream*, will appear soon from Curbstone.

Collins' awards include fellowships from the NEA, the Bunting Institute, the Ingram Merrill Foundation, and the Witter Bynner Foundation, as well as three Pushcart Prizes. She recently returned from a Lannan Foundation Residency in Marfa, Texas, where she was working on a book-length poem.

Collins founded the Creative Writing Program at the University of Massachusetts-Boston, and since 1997 has taught at Oberlin College, where she is Pauline Delaney Professor of Creative Writing.

Carol Frost is the author of two chapbooks and nine full-length collections of poems, including the Academy of American Poetry's Poetry Book Club selection *Love and Scorn, New and Selected Poems*, in 2000; *Venus and Don Juan*, TriQuarterly Books, 1996; *Pure*, 1994; *Chimera*, Peregrine Smith, 1990; *Day of the Body*, 1986; *The Fearful Child*, Ithaca House, 1983; *Cold Frame*, a chapbook from Owl Creek Press, 1982; *Liar's Dice*, Ithaca House, 1978; *The Salt Lesson*, a chapbook from Graywolf Press, 1976. Her newest collection of poems, *I Will Say Beauty*, appeared in the spring of 2003.

Her work has garnered her two fellowships from the National Endowment for the Arts and awards from the PEN Syndication Fiction award committee, the Elliston Prize committee, and the Poets' Prize committee. She has also received the Cohen Award for poetry from *Ploughshares*, and a Readers' Choice Award from *Prairie Schooner*, and residencies at Chateau de Lavigny and Yaddo.

Her essays and poems appear in *The Atlantic Monthly, The Writer's Almanac* (Minnesota Public Radio), *American Poetry Review, Kenyon Review, Michigan Quarterly Review, Paris Review, Poetry Daily*, and the *New York Times*. Anthology publications include *Contemporary American Poetry* (Houghton Mifflin) and several appearances, as winner and honorable mention, in *Pushcart Prize* volumes.

I am deeply honored that Martha Collins and Carol Frost have guest-edited our poetry nominations this year.

And I am just as grateful to the late Oliver Gilliland, national sales manager of W.W. Norton Company, who represented our prize for decades, and to the hundreds of Pushcart Contributing Editors and small press editors who continue to participate in this amazing commune of spirit, intelligence and light.

THE PEOPLE WHO HELPED

FOUNDING EDITORS—*Anaïs Nin (1903–1977), Buckminster Fuller (1895–1983), Charles Newman, Daniel Halpern, Gordon Lish, Harry Smith, Hugh Fox, Ishmael Reed, Joyce Carol Oates, Len Fulton, Leonard Randolph, Leslie Fiedler (1917–2003), Nona Balakian (1918–1991), Paul Bowles (1910–1999), Paul Engle (1908–1991), Ralph Ellison (1914–1994), Reynolds Price, Rhoda Schwartz, Richard Morris, Ted Wilentz (1915–2001), Tom Montag, William Phillips (1907–2002), Poetry editor: H. L. Van Brunt.*

CONTRIBUTING EDITORS FOR THIS EDITION—*David Plante, R.C. Hildebrandt, Daniel Orozco, Richard Tayson, E. Shaskan Bumas, Pamela Painter, Joan Swift, Rick Bass, Naomi Shihab Nye, Joy Williams, John Kistner, Rebecca Seiferle, Jody Stewart, Marie Sheppard Williams, Karl Iagnemma, M.D. Elevitch, Karl Elder, Monique de Varennes, Stephen Dunn, Katherine Min, Kenneth Gangemi, Marianna Cherry, Natasha Trethewey, Michael Bowden, Alice Mattison, Bradford Morrow, Joseph Hurka, Jane Hirshfield, William Wenthe, Stacey Richter, Richard Garcia, Ron Tanner, Anthony Hecht, Elizabeth McKenzie, Carol Potter, Dan Masterson, David Baker, Eleanor Wilner, Cyrus Cassells, Ted Deppe, Dorianne Laux, Richard Kostelanetz, Diann Blakely, Bonnie Jo Campbell, Meredith Steinbach, Julie Thacker, Arthur Smith, DeWitt Henry, Edward Hoagland, Mark Wisniewski, Virginia Holman, Beth Ann Fennelly, Lucia Perillo, Wally Lamb, Mike Newirth, Elizabeth Graver, David Zane Mairowitz, Kent Nelson, Michael Waters, Salvatore Scibona, Katherine Taylor, Gary Gildner, Andrea Hollander Budy, Maxine Kumin, H.E. Francis, Jim Simmerman, Philip Levine, Jim Moore,*

Paul Maliszewski, David St. John, Robert McBrearty, Kristin King, Nancy Richard, Michael Palma, Janet Burroway, Jeffrey Hammond, D.A. Powell, Robert Phillips, Ted Genoways, Jessica Roeder, Michael Parker, Daniel Henry, Joan Murray, George Keithley, Joyce Carol Oates, David Jauss, Maura Stanton, Mark Irwin, Rosellen Brown, Renée Ashley, John Allman, Ed Falco, Philip Dacey, Caroline Langston, Colette Inez, Janice Eidus, Julie Orringer, Thomas E. Kennedy, Lance Olsen, Sherod Santos, Donald Revell, Jim Daniels, Brenda Miller, Nancy Lord, Gerry Locklin, C.E. Poverman, Christina Zawadiwsky, Kay Ryan, Chris Forhan, Philip Appleman, Melanie Rae Thon, Paul Zimmer, Robert Cording, Lee Upton, Timothy Geiger, Rachel Hadas, Madison Smartt Bell, Claire Bateman, Grace Schulman, Tony Quagliano, Debra Spark, David Kirby, Tony Ardizzone, Glenna Holloway, Kim Barnes, Kevin Prufer, William Heyen, Melissa Pritchard, Jennifer Atkinson, Antler, Michael Martone, Len Roberts, Gibbons Ruark, Elizabeth Spires, Christopher Buckley, Kathy Callaway, Arthur Smith, Ladette Randolph, Carl Dennis, Ron Carlson, Cathy Song, Mark Halperin, Josip Novakovich, Jean Thompson, Michael Martone, Ranbir Sidhu, Richard Burgin, Jana Harris, Sharon Solwitz, Sylvia Watanabe, Laura Kasischke, Laurie Sheck, Aimee Bender, Ralph Angel, Judith Taylor, Joshua Beckman, Kim Addonizio, Sharon Dilworth, George Evans, Alan Michael Parker, Robert Wrigley, Molly Bendall, Claire Davis, Dan Hoffman, Fred Leebron, James Reiss, Carolyn Alessio, Kathleen Hill, James Harms, Alice Fulton, Nancy McCabe, Dara Wier, Kathy Fagan, Richard Jackson, Charles Harper Webb, Donald Platt, Bruce Beasley, Stuart Dischell, Jack Marshall, Rita Dove, Marianne Boruch, Stephen Corey, Roger Weingarten, Gary Fincke, Karen Volkman, Reginald Gibbons, Susan Hahn, John Drury, Margaret Gibson, Rachel Loden, Linda Gregerson, Jeffrey Harrison, Wes McNair, Judith Kitchen, David Rivard, Matt Yurdana, Cornelia Nixon, S.L. Wisenberg, Ed Ochester, Erin McGraw, Christian Wiman, Andrew Hudgins, Vern Rutsala, Tom Filer, William Olsen, Michael Heffernan, Bob Hicok, Lynne McFall, Chard deNiord, Gerald Shapiro, Carl Phillips, Bert States, Emily Fox Gordon, Jane McCaffery, Jeffrey Lockwood, Jean Thompson, Maureen Seaton, Robert Boswell, Katrina Roberts, Marvin Bell, Linda Bierds, Michael Dennis Browne, Kirk Nesset, Christopher Howell, Robert Gibb, Pinckney Benedict, Barbara Hamby, David Wojahn, Mark Cox

9

CONTENTS

THE
PUSHCART PRIZE, XXVIII

ELECTION EVE

fiction by EVAN CONNELL

from THE THREEPENNY REVIEW

Proctor cyril bemis, emeritus C.E.O. of the securities firm that bore his name—Proctor Bemis, grossly fat, not yet altogether bald, cheerful when undisturbed by gout, sat beside the fire as a fat man likes to sit with fingers laced across his belly, jowls at rest, and thought about Costa Rica while his wife sorted the mail. He thought he would enjoy a visit to Costa Rica. Sunshine, gentle waves lapping sugar-white beaches, palm fronds dipping in the breeze, carioca music or whatever it was, pretty girls smearing oil on their legs, deepsea fishing, rum, ocean-fresh lobster—oh yes, Mr. Bemis thought, twirling his thumbs on his belly. No drizzly, threatening overcast. No winter storm watch. No schoolboys in black trenchcoats gunning down classmates. No lunatics blowing up federal buildings. No hillbilly militia. No politicians braying platitudes. Costa Rica ought to be just fine, yes indeed. He dropped one hand into the silver bowl of cashews, scooped up a handful, and tossed them into his mouth.

How many people want money? he asked.

His wife looked at him over the top of her spectacles and he thought she was going to say something about the cashews. Then she turned to the envelopes.

Democratic National Committee, addressed to you. HOPE. CARE. Bread for the World. Alligator Refuge. I think that's all, except bills.

How many bills?

One, two, three, she said. Three. No, here's another.

My God, said Mr. Bemis.

Here's a note from Robin. I do hope they're enjoying the trip. Let's see, what else? This looks like an invitation from the Wibbles.

He watched her open the envelope. I don't want to go, he said.

Now isn't this tricky! A masquerade party the night before election. They'll have presidential masks. George Washington. Lincoln. Eisenhower. Nixon. Jimmy Carter, who wasn't one of my favorites. Harry Truman. Gerald Ford. You can take your choice.

No, Mr. Bemis said. No.

You could be Grover Cleveland. He weighed three hundred pounds.

I don't weigh three hundred, Mr. Bemis said. I won't go. Absolutely not.

She opened the envelope from their daughter. Well, my goodness! Mark won a prize at a carnival.

What did he win?

A statue of Donald Duck. He loves it. Melanie skinned her elbow. Ed has a touch of flu. Oh, my word! Somebody broke into their car and stole the radio. They'll need to see the insurance company. Otherwise, everything's fine.

I'm glad they're having a good time, Mr. Bemis said. Now listen, Marguerite. I am seventy-three years old. My knees hurt. My back hurts. I don't want to stand around listening to Thornton and Stu and Betsy and Cliff and all the rest. I know their opinions on everything from school vouchers to nuclear bombs. Let's go to Costa Rica.

You were seventy-five last March. I'm going to phone Renée and tell her we'll be delighted.

I will throw up, Mr. Bemis said. I will kick their damn Siamese cat.

Ooma isn't Siamese. She's Persian. She's just adorable. And you needn't have a fit. The party isn't for another month, three weeks from Monday.

Monday? Mr. Bemis asked with dismay. That's football night. I think the Chiefs and Broncos are playing.

I'll be right back, she said.

Mr. Bemis threw a cashew into the fireplace and wondered how he might talk her out of it. He remembered going to costume parties when he was a child. He had worn a red devil mask and remembered looking through the eye holes. Witches, goblins, clowns, all sorts of games—pin-the-tail-on-the-donkey, blindman's-buff, spin-the-bottle— little girls shrieking, balloons popping, parents watching, candied apples, licorice whips, paper hats, ice cream. It had been fun. However, those days were gone. I don't want to bump into Charlie Hochstadt wearing a Reagan mask, he thought. Lord, what have I done to deserve this?

Reagan. Mr. Bemis threw another cashew at the fire. Why hadn't the man been dragged out of office by the heels? Ollie North funneling weapons to the Contras from the White House basement but El Presidente knew nothing about it. Smacking his lips when he was questioned, pretending to think. Let me see, now, that must have been some time back, some time ago. Smack. Yes, sir, a while ago. Smack. Well, now, I'm afraid I don't quite recall.

Mr. Bemis grunted and opened the newspaper. Oil prices rising. Electricians vote to strike. Light planes collide. Drought in Oklahoma. Post-office worker shot dead. Charlton Heston looking less and less like Moses, more like Madame Tussaud's lover. Another religious cult swallows poison. Mutual funds merge.

He glanced up when his wife returned from the telephone.

Renée and I had the most delightful chat. Everyone is excited. It's going to be gobs of fun.

Somebody will put on a Truman mask and play the piano, Mr. Bemis said. Somebody will be FDR and wave a cigarette holder. Some jackass will do Nixon, hunch the shoulders and give us that V sign. Let's go to Costa Rica. Call that nice young woman at the travel agency and book us a flight.

I cannot bear it when you behave like this, she said. Will you please stop whining.

I only whine if there's a reason, Mr. Bemis said. I'm not as fat as Grover Cleveland.

Stop eating those cashews. All you get from now on is grapefruit juice.

Mr. Bemis glared at his left foot, which had begun to ache. He thought about the palm trees and sandy beaches and pretty girls in bathing suits. He looked out the window. It was raining, almost snowing.

As they were being chauffeured to the party on election eve he remembered how much he despised Reagan. The man had spent the war in Hollywood and never heard a live bullet but he could not stop saluting. He saluted and saluted and saluted. He would snap off that Hollywood salute to a flagpole or a fireplug. He would salute a dachshund if there was a photographer nearby.

Proctor, stop that, his wife said.

Stop what? he asked.

You're grumbling.

I'll keep it to myself, he said.

How long have we been married?

Mr. Bemis thought about this. Why do you want to know?

I know perfectly well. But even now, after so many years, I cannot for the life of me understand you. At times you might as well be a complete stranger. She leaned forward. Phillips, do you have trouble seeing the road?

Phillips answered in his pleasantly neutral voice. No, Madam.

You will be careful, won't you?

Phillips replied that he would be careful.

Mr. Bemis watched snowflakes dissolve on the window and thought about trying to explain, but it would be difficult. She had voted for Reagan. She voted for Bush and Dole and Nixon. If she had been old enough she would have voted for Landon and Hoover and the Whigs. She hated Kennedys, all Kennedys, including wives and fifth cousins, and thought they contaminated whatever they touched. She disapproved of modern art and welfare and foreign aid. She did not like immigrants. She subscribed to newsletters warning that liberals had weakened the armed forces. The United States could be destroyed at any moment. Crazed, malignant letters oozing poison. Absurd theories. Libelous charges. Implausible conspiracies. Rhetorical questions. Secret societies. Jewish bankers. Communist armies in Montana. Letters concocted of hate and fear. Doomsday letters. Nourishment for the paranoid.

We'll have oodles of fun, she said, patting him on the knee. Just you wait.

I do not intend to wear a mask, he said. I like who I am.

Renée told me that several husbands objected. You can be yourself. I wouldn't expect anything else.

What about food?

There'll be a nice buffet.

Itty-bitty pinkie sandwiches and cheese dip, Mr. Bemis said. I wish we were going to Costa Rica.

However, the Wibble buffet was sumptuous, imperial, a whopping tribute to an exemplary bourgeois life. Mr. Bemis gazed with satisfaction at the roast beef, sliced breast of duck, venison, platoons of shrimp, a giant salmon, lamb-chops sprinkled with herbs, prosciutto,

20

crisp little sausages, and more. Rosy red tomatoes stuffed with something creamy. Butterfly pasta. Mushrooms. Mr. Bemis gazed at the
beautiful mushrooms. Asparagus points, juicy pickles, Gargantuan
black olives. Nor was that all, oh no. Desserts. An absolute regiment
of alluring desserts. Lemon tart. Mince pie topped with hard sauce.
Blue and white cheeses. Chocolate mousse. Peaches. Pears. Melons.
Petits fours. Nuts. Strawberries. A silver compote of mints. Fancy
bonbons individually wrapped in gold foil. Nor was that all. Mr. Bemis clasped his hands.

Good to see you! boomed a familiar voice. Mighty good! I am
counting on your vote, sir!

There stood Quint Huckleby disguised as Abe Lincoln.

Hello, Quint, said Mr. Bemis.

Lincoln is the name, sir. Abraham Lincoln. May I take this oppor-
tunity to remind you that our great nation stands at a crossroads. To-
morrow we decide. Shall we permit ourselves to be hornswaggled?
Or do we fulfill our grand and glorious destiny with the Grand Old
Party? Should I be fortunate enough to earn the confidence of the
American public I shall propose to Congress that we chase those
Democrat scalawags out of town. Tar and feathers, sir! That's the
ticket!

Huckleby shuffled into the crowd, bowing to ladies, clapping men
on the shoulder.

Mr. Bemis looked around and saw Marguerite chatting with the
Vandenhaags. He looked again at the buffet. An olive, perhaps? One
or two little sausages? What harm could there be in a slice of duck?

He noticed Speed Voelker loading a plate. Voelker never seemed
to change. Year after year a bulky, menacing presence in a tailored
pinstripe suit. Broken nose. Massive, sloping shoulders. Neck like a
tree stump. Diamond ring. Hair slicked back like a hoodlum in some
gangster film. Big as a water buffalo.

I hear you and Dodie went to Europe, Mr. Bemis said.

Voelker nodded. The whole shebang. Tower of London. Norway.
Copenhagen. Swiss Alps. Berlin. Venetian gondolas. You name it.
Europe costs like the elephant these days.

Uncle Sam gave me a tour, Mr. Bemis said. Didn't cost a cent.
France, Belgium, Rhineland. Mostly on foot.

Voelker grinned. I was a lieutenant in Patton's outfit. Like to froze
my nuts off. Mud, rain, C rations, bugs. I saw that old fart once, close
enough to touch.

21

I saw Ike, Mr. Bemis said. He drove by in a Jeep.

McCarthy deserved a medal. Ike didn't do squat about those Commies at State.

Yankee Doodle and all, Mr. Bemis thought.

Voelker pointed his fork at the dessert table. Eisenhower was reaching for a chocolate mousse.

He ought to be here. Straighten out the lefties.

They watched Eisenhower pick up a handful of bonbons.

Tomorrow we kick butt. Dump the goddam liberals. They ought to move to Russia if they don't like the U.S.A.

Enemy headquarters, Mr. Bemis thought. He watched Voelker stab a slice of beef and tried to remember how long they had been acquainted. Norman Voelker. Star athlete. Captain of the high school football team. Honor roll. Class president. Speed to his friends. And what was I? Corridor guide. Nothing else after my name in the yearbook. I didn't know how to catch a football and if I tried to jump a hurdle I'd have broken my neck. He never spoke to me. Not once. Not once in four years did he say hello. Now here we are, high-priced attorney and ex-stockbroker, members of the same country club, almost equal. Almost. Not quite.

Jerry, Voelker said.

And there he stood, jaw protruding, vacuous, amiable, shaking hands with Lucy Waldrop.

He played at Michigan. Pretty good lineman.

Mr. Bemis munched a spear of asparagus and thought about Ford pardoning Nixon. Twenty-five flunkies went to jail, maybe twenty-six, but not Tricky Dick. Everybody thought the republic would collapse if Richard Milhous wore prison stripes. In fact, the republic would be better off if Nixon had spent a couple of decades mumbling and raving in the jug. No man is above the law, we told ourselves. What a lie. The time has come to put this matter behind us, declared his faithful subordinate who by the grace of God and a terrified Congress inherited the office.

Those eighteen minutes of tape. What skulduggery did they preserve? Jimmy Hoffa. Mr. Nixon, high priest of law and order, scourge of corrupt unions, pardoned Jimmy Hoffa, who strolled out of prison and dropped from sight as if he had walked the plank. Was he squashed inside an old Chevrolet? Why did Mr. Nixon intervene? Rosemary Woods deserved a medal for loyalty, if nothing else, trying to demonstrate how she accidentally erased those eighteen minutes, almost twisted her back out of joint. Meanwhile the world's greatest investigative body, the FBI, couldn't figure out what happened.

Mr. Bemis grunted, heard himself make some disrespectful remark and observed Voelker light up with rage.

Norman! Marguerite exclaimed. What a pleasure! It's been ages! You look marvelous! Ida Mae tells me that you and Dodie treated yourselves to the Grand Tour. That must have been a thrill. Did you see the fountains of Rome? Proctor and I are so jealous.

She went on talking while Mr. Bemis considered the situation. People were gathering around Voelker. They wanted to be seen chatting with him. That being so, why not slip away to the buffet? Nobody would notice. Why not two or three of those tasty little shrimp? Prosciutto? Of course. Mushrooms? Yes, indeed. Another pickle? Maybe a soupçon of pasta?

He found himself at the table. He spoke cheerfully to the Armacosts, recommended the mushrooms. He said hello to Woody Schenk, discussed the Wyandotte Hills Country Club renovation. He nodded to Virginia Tyler, whom he did not like very much, spread anchovy paste on five crackers, reached for some olives, and moved along. He walked around the table for another slice of duck. Then he paused.

Missouri Waltz, he said.

Sure enough, Harry was thumping the piano. Beside him stood Jimmy Carter theatrically beating time.

He thought about Jimmy's struggle with the rabbit. Nobody except Bosch or maybe Lewis Carroll could have dreamed it up—March hare bent upon murder swimming crazily toward the President, planning to bite his ankle. Jimmy in that canoe flailing away with a paddle. The rabbit finished him. Inflation got out of control, which was serious. And that hostage fiasco, American helicopters on a cloak-and-dagger rescue mission lurching around the desert like injured bats, that was humiliating. But the rabbit did him in. The President fighting a loony rabbit, that was too much.

Nancy Reagan should have been there, he thought as he slipped a cracker into his mouth. The newspapers said she carried a pistol, itty-bitty derringer or some such. Whap! No more bunny. Mr. Bemis stopped chewing. Why did she carry a pistol? He tried to remember if she had been in any of Reagan's films, maybe the dance hall girl in some Wild West horse opera. What could happen in the White House? He imagined her leading a gaggle of tourists. They pause to

23

admire a portrait of John Adams when out pops the masked intruder from behind a marble bust of Spiro Agnew. Stick 'em up! Your purse or your life! But the First Lady is prepared. Not so fast, young fellow! Just you wait till I find my derringer. Let's see. Kleenex, aspirin, nail file, sun glasses, eye shadow, lipstick, mascara, brush, comb, tweezers, cold cream, lotion, scissors, hair spray, compact—I know it's here someplace.

He thought about Charlton Heston brandishing an eighteenth-century musket for the benefit of photographers and gung ho patriots. Moses defending life, liberty, and his Beverly Hills mansion from the redcoats. Why not an assault rifle? Why not wave a Saturday Night Special?

I do believe, murmured a voice from the past, I know this handsome dog.

Mr. Bemis turned around and there beneath a ragged brown toupee resembling a smashed bird nest, decades older than when last seen, was Howie—the same Howie Price-Dodge who got so drunk he tried to climb the Spanish-American War memorial and served heroically in the OSS and married a Chicago stripper and demolished the family fortune.

Get yourself a plate and let's talk, Mr. Bemis said. In fact, I'll join you.

Howie explained that during the Vietnam War he went back into service. He had been a liaison officer stationed at the Pentagon. He knew McNamara. He attended high-level briefings. He shuttled between Washington and Saigon and learned quite a bit. He knew Westmoreland. He had ridden in helicopters while enemy soldiers were interrogated and saw them pushed out.

This world is no place for idealists, he said.

On the contrary, said Mr. Bemis.

Howie squinted, adjusted his toupee, and went on talking while Mr. Bemis thought about the days when they agreed upon almost everything from politics to women to beer. It was strange that so much time had gone by. He looked around the room at familiar faces and it occurred to him that this was where he belonged. Yes, he thought, I'm one of these people. I've lived a solid Republican life. I earned money the good old-fashioned way selling stocks and bonds, lots of money. I joined the best country club. Marguerite and I have a couple of fancy cars and a very expensive home. I drove myself to the office for at least a hundred years while Marguerite took care of

24

everything else. We've done our work, toted that bale. We deserve what we have. Yes, I belong here. The trouble is, I feel like an Eskimo.

Howie was explaining that America could have won the war if it hadn't been for draft dodgers and the liberal media. And while Mr. Bemis listened to Howie justify Vietnam he remembered the ugliness. Even now, after all this time, it festered like the Nixon pardon, provoking arguments, refusing to heal. The flesh of the nation was raw. The photograph of that naked child seared by napalm running toward the camera screaming in agony, that image would not fade. And he reflected that he had frequently touted E. I. Du Pont, which manufactured napalm. Du Pont, as everyone knew, was a substantial corporation with good earnings, a secure dividend, and offered the likelihood of capital appreciation. A dollar invested with Du Pont was a dollar prudently invested.

Mr. Bemis examined his plate. Celery. Two olives. One radish. Not much. Howie was interpreting the disaster, explaining why the security of the United States depended upon Southeast Asia. Mr. Bemis munched an olive and looked around. Next to a flattering oil portrait of Cope Wibble in a huge gold frame stood Emmajane Kathren, Democrat, chatting with the Altschulers while holding a shrimp impaled on a toothpick. Beneath the glowing chandelier stood Monte and Lorraine Fordyce, Democrats both, listening to Joslyn Upshaw. We're not many, he thought. Oh, not many. What's to become of us? Half a century from now will we be extinct? And as he considered this it did not seem implausible.

Is that Speed? Howie asked.

Mr. Bemis nodded. Voelker was holding DeWitt Simms firmly by one elbow while talking to his wife.

Lord God, Howie said, I'll never forget the way he flattened that Rockhurst defensive back. Everybody in the bleachers whooping, then you could hear a pin drop. What was that kid's name?

It happened sixty years ago, Mr. Bemis said. McNabb, McNee, McGee, one of those names.

Paralyzed, Howie said. Just a kid. Hell of a note. I still see that ambulance on the field.

They watched Simms try to pull away. Voelker ignored him.

Built like a piano. Give him the ball and Katie bar the door.

Harry Truman was plunking out Sewanee River. A woman laughed insanely. Voelker—arrogant as a Babylonian king—held Simms captive, demeaning the man in front of his wife. A Texas voice boasted about upholding law and order with a noose. Two masks collided and all at once it seemed to Mr. Bemis that he had entered a madhouse where the inmates were performing a macabre dance.

Voelker approached casually but rapidly, sapphire-blue eyes fixed on Howie. Almost at once they were discussing Vietnam, why it was necessary, how the war could have been won.

Voelker gripped Mr. Bemis by the elbow. What about you, sport? Tell us what you think. Did you support our troops?

I mistrusted the government, Mr. Bemis said.

Tell us about it, soldier. We want to know what you think.

You want to know what I think? I remember how Ike tiptoed into that swamp and Kennedy followed. The best and brightest had no more sense than Hogan's goat. And I remember LBJ plunging ahead like a goddamn rhinocerous. I remember Nixon after everybody got sick of the war telling us he had a secret plan for ending it. He told us delicate negotiations were under way. My grandfather's banana. Nixon kept it going past election day because he wanted another term in office. You want my opinion, lieutenant? I didn't salute.

Mr. Bemis jerked his arm away from Voelker.

He had addressed the office staff on various occasions, but this was different. It occurred to him that he should have chosen public life. He saw himself on the floor of the Senate addressing misguided colleagues, instructing, ridiculing, exhorting, convincing. Persuasive arguments came to mind, burning rhetoric, soaring imagery.

No doubt you gentlemen recall the domino theory. No doubt you recall the days when half the citizens of this country thought we should turn Hanoi into a parking lot because if we didn't stop the Communists over there we'd have to stop them on the beaches of Hawaii. Do you remember when schoolchildren were taught to crouch underneath their desks? Keep away from windows. Pull down the shades. Do you recall the backyard bomb shelter? Of course you do. We were advised to dig holes in the ground. Furnish the hole with toilet paper, matches, bottled water, spinach, dehydrated beef, graham crackers. Newspaper delivery may be suspended. Magazines and phonograph records may help to pass the time. Moon-struck madness, gentlemen, if I might borrow a phrase from the great John Milton.

Mr. Bemis discovered that he had an audience. People were staring. Obviously they wished to know more.

Ladies and gentlemen, while destitute citizens rummage through garbage cans and prowl the streets, what does our government do? It sheathes the Pentagon in gold. I submit to you that we could at this moment vaporize whatever creeps, crawls, flies, walks, hops, slithers, or jumps. I submit to you that we could do this thirty times over. Meanwhile, Republicans wring their hands, claiming we are defenseless, ill-prepared, at the mercy of two-bit tyrants. In fact, no eight countries on earth allocate as much to the splendid science of war as we do, yet conservatives argue that we need a Maginot Line in the sky. As Mr. Reagan explained it, a missile shield will protect us from nuclear attack just as a roof protects a house from rain. The simplicity of such logic astounds us, but let it pass. Will a magic roof suffice? Of course not. We are surrounded by godless enemies from Zamboanga to Uttar Pradesh.

Mr. Bemis realized that his voice had risen. He patted his brow with a handkerchief.

May I remind you that when Isaac Newton was president of the Royal Society he caused a newly designed cannon to be rejected. Why? Because, Sir Isaac said, it was a diabolic instrument meant only for mass killing. Our culture, ladies and gentlemen, is a culture of death.

What do people in other countries think of us? he asked. How do they regard us?

This was a provocative question so he paused significantly before continuing.

They see a nation steeped in righteousness where guns are as easy to buy as lollipops. A nation that executes criminals without losing a drop of blood. A nation of lecherous hypocritical preachers with the brains of pterodactyls and politicians who would sell their daughters for a vote. But I digress. Let me say a few words about our teflon President. He informed us that pollution is caused by trees. Many of us did not realize that. He told us that a Nicaraguan army could march from Managua to Harlingen, Texas, in two days. Quite a march, yes indeed. Honduras, El Salvador, Guatemala, Mexico. And once across the Rio Grande what would these Nicaraguan Communists do? Burn the Harlingen Country Courthouse?

Folks, I'm just getting started. Dutch opened his presidential campaign in Philadelphia, Mississippi. He did that for a reason. He went to that town where three civil rights workers were lynched and declared that he stood for States' Rights. Every good ol' boy from Tallahassee to Kalamazoo got the message. Hey, the big guy says it's okay.

Nor should we forget those Marines in Beirut. The Joint Chiefs advised pulling out of Lebanon. Mr. Reagan knew better. What happened? Some Lebanese kid drove up to Marine headquarters in a truck loaded with TNT. Two hundred and forty-one dead Marines.

It occurred to Mr. Bemis that he might have talked long enough, but there was so much to be said.

Ronald Reagan attempted to overthrow the elected government of another country and what did Congress do? Renamed the airport in his honor. Fifty years from now people will wonder what kind of dope we were smoking. Ladies and gentlemen, the emperor has no clothes.

Mr. Bemis took a deep breath. He felt encouraged. People were attentive.

He heard himself speak of George Bush whose nose kept growing—longer, longer, and longer. He spoke of the oil in Kuwait, of April Glaspie. He spoke of Jesse Helms, of Joseph McCarthy, J. Parnell Thomas. He pointed a finger while speaking of the National Rifle Association. Ladies and gentlemen, he said, some things about this country turn my innards upside down. Politicians claim they trust the judgment of ordinary people. Well, sir, I do not. Athenian citizens condemned Socrates to death. So much for the perspicacity of John Q. Public. Did I mention Roman Hruska?

He noticed that his audience was dwindling. He looked around for his wife. There she stood, her face a deathly mask, arms crossed.

Are you satisfied? she asked. Dodie and Norman left in a huff. Norman was livid.

Mr. Bemis felt tired. It was late and his knees ached. He wanted to go home. He saw that it was snowing and wondered if they might have trouble on the Sycamore hill.

All at once people stopped talking because somebody outside had fired a gun. Several men walked uneasily toward the windows.

On the way home Marguerite suddenly threw up both hands like an opera singer. I do not believe, she said, enunciating each word, that ever in my life have I felt so embarrassed and ashamed.

I thought I did quite well, said Mr. Bemis.

Proctor, what in the name of sense? What on earth? I cannot imagine what got into you. Oh, I could simply expire.

It just happened, he said. It felt good.

That speech was utterly incomprehensible. April Glaspie! J. Parnell Thomas! Nobody had the faintest idea what you were talking about.

I did, said Mr. Bemis.

Roman Hruska! I haven't heard that name in fifty years.

I didn't like him, Mr. Bemis said. There were a lot of people I didn't get around to. J. Edgar Hoover. Thurmond. Rusk. Laird. I could think of plenty.

Proctor, do you realize what you've done? We won't be on anyone's guest list. Never again. Never! Never! Never!

That wouldn't be the end of the world, said Mr. Bemis.

She put one hand to her forehead. Oh, this has been a perfect nightmare! I can just see Eunice Hupp telling everyone under the sun. And let there be no mistake, Proctor, I certainly want the United Nations out of our country. Foreigners have no business telling us what to do. If those foreign bankers get their way they'll take every cent we have. Every last cent. Furthermore, you know quite well that the Trilateral Commission is bent on enslaving America.

We've gone through this a hundred times, said Mr. Bemis.

I think I'm going to cry. It was such a nice party. Socrates! I have not the remotest idea what goes on inside your head. There are times when I think I married an alien.

That's interesting, Mr. Bemis said. That hadn't occurred to me.

Everybody was having so much fun. I'm just sick. Honestly, I wanted to sink through the floor. Phillips, she said, raising her voice, are you able to see the road?

Yes, Madam, Phillips replied.

It looks awfully snowy. Shouldn't we take Leimert?

I believe we can make it up Sycamore, Phillips replied in the same neutral voice. We could take Leimert if you prefer.

Mr. Bemis grinned. Phillips didn't want to lose his job. Who are you pulling for? he asked. The elephant or the jackass?

In tomorrow's election, sir? Both candidates seem qualified.

He's afraid I'll fire him, Mr. Bemis thought. I wish he'd speak up. All of us had better speak up.

Phillips looked straight ahead, gloved hands on the wheel, attending to business.

29

I know who I'm voting for, Mrs. Bemis said. I am unbearably tired of scandal. One thing after another. It's time we restored decency to government.

Mr. Bemis considered mentioning Nixon, but that was a long-dead horse. Decency in government. What an oxymoron. Both candidates seem qualified. Ha! One of them can't remember how to button his shirt and the other would lick dirt from a voter's boots.

As he reflected upon the evening he felt pleased with himself. I blew that party to smithereens, he thought. Hoisted the Jolly Roger—not that it will do any good. And the shot. Sooner or later everybody will find out that Speed blasted a snowdrift or a tree or punched a hole in the sky. Nobody will be able to make sense of it. Ha!

What a blessing Ronald Reagan wasn't there, she said as they waited for a traffic light.

That fake, Mr. Bemis said. I needed another twenty minutes.

Ronald Reagan was a President we could admire and trust. He won the Cold War and cut taxes and set us on the road to prosperity. He made us feel good about ourselves and he brought back morning to America when many people thought we were on the verge of night. Those tax-and-spend Democrats want to give our money to black people.

She heard that on the radio, Mr. Bemis thought. Some right-wing gasbag. She believes whatever they say. She's a true believer and she's terrified. She gets up in the middle of the night to pray.

I just hope the Republicans win, she said.

Mr. Bemis folded his hands across his belly and considered the invasion of Grenada. A sleepy tourist island near Venezuela. Reagan ordered the attack without consulting Congress, probably without consulting anybody except Nancy's astrologer. Why? Because the Prime Minister was liberal and the airport runway was being extended. Soviet bombers would be able to land and refuel en route to the United States. True enough, if they flew the wrong direction a couple of thousand miles. Reagan never looked at a map in his life. If he did, he couldn't understand all those numbers and squiggly lines. So what happened? U.S. Navy planes bombed the Grenada mental hospital. They didn't mean to bomb a hospital but they did. An international court of justice at The Hague condemned Reagan. Nobody cared. Millions want his face on the ten-dollar bill. Millions want him on Rushmore. All right, there's room enough if we get rid of Lincoln.

People forget, he said. They ought to be reminded.

You certainly don't forget. And I do not wish to be reminded of anything else. I have heard more than enough, Proctor. More than enough.

She had almost divorced him because of Vietnam so he decided to keep quiet. He thought about Howie, who seemed a bit uncomfortable with himself. Years at the Pentagon. Policy wonks. Alice in Wonderland briefings. Light at the end of the tunnel. Somewhere along the way they got him.

Now what are you grumbling about? she asked.

I wasn't, he said.

I thought you would never stop eating. I was so humiliated. You made four trips to the buffet.

Three, Mr. Bemis said, holding up three fingers.

Eunice Hupp was watching me while you made a fool of yourself. Oh, Proctor, how could you do such a thing? I'll never live it down.

I took one small step for mankind, said Mr. Bemis.

I do not understand what possesses you. We have so much to be thankful for. We have a nice home in the loveliest neighborhood. We have everything we could possibly want. Everything.

She was right, of course. And yet, he thought, she's wrong. Is there anything I want, he asked himself, that I don't have? I don't know. I'm a success. I ought to feel satisfied.

Phillips drove carefully up the Sycamore hill. Streetlights through falling snow reminded Mr. Bemis of a village in France when he had been a private in the Army. He tried to recall the name of the village but it was gone. He touched the window with one finger. The glass was warmer than he expected and the snow was turning to slush. He wondered how he could be seventy-five years old when he had been a young soldier just yesterday.

Marguerite, he said, I'm hungry.

What little of her face could be seen above the collar of the fur coat proved that he had not been forgiven.

You are imagining, she said. You couldn't conceivably be hungry.

That was an hour ago, he said. What's in the fridge?

She refused to answer.

He thought affectionately of the buffet—gorgeous black olives, anchovy crackers, lamb chops, venison, duck, salmon, lemon tart— and heard a familiar rumble in his stomach. He considered the evening while Phillips drove them homeward and something from

31

Aristophanes sifted like a snowflake through the years. What heaps of things have bitten me to the heart! A small few pleased me, very few.

That was not the whole of it, but he could not remember what came next. For now, that was enough.

Nominated by Katherine Min, Jessica Roeder, Salvatore Scibona, Threepenny Review

F.P.

memoir by MYRA JEHLEN

from RARITAN

A FRIEND DIED and asked in her will that her ashes be divided between two places. She was French, so one place is in France, under a tree in the field behind a house in a village of the Charente-Maritime. The other is in the U.S.: a cemetery up a dirt road in Vermont. We who were to do this two-part burial asked the undertaker to give us her ashes in two urns but he said he was not allowed to divide bodies: "le corps," he said, "est indivisible." We wondered at this; that a corpse can be divided harmlessly is, after all, one of its defining traits. But the undertaker was adamant, so we said one urn was fine, and to one another said we would do the dividing ourselves.

I looked up the law the undertaker had invoked, which turned out to be a ruling by the court of the city of Lille which, in 1997, added a provision about ashes to a regulation it already had about bones. The occasion was a suit brought against a widow who had removed her husband's ashes from the cemetery to her house, making it very hard for his sister, who didn't get along with the widow, to visit his tomb. The sister claimed the widow had violated the law against removing bodies from their burial places. The judge, observing that an urn wasn't, like a tomb, a permanent refuge, but a container for ashes whose vocation, as he put it, is to be scattered, ruled the widow could move the urn wherever she wanted. The undertaker had it wrong, or hadn't kept up with recent rulings: it's not ashes but bones that you can't divide. I hadn't thought before about the opposition between burying a body and burning it: by the first, you fix it forever in place, or mean to. But by the second, you transform it into something that flies off with every breeze. The urn is a way to temporize between the two, I suppose. I know several people who have the ashes of their fathers or of their mothers in closets, unsure whether to bury or scatter them. Parents being where you leave from, it's hard to imagine them more adrift than you. My friend, who had been born on the left bank of the Seine and never considered living anywhere else, imagined herself dead becoming part of places that alive she would only consider visiting; as if in her life she'd rehearsed leaving and then in death gone and done it.

The cremation was at the Père-Lachaise cemetery, which has the only crematorium in Paris. One crematorium is not enough, and there is a crush. Each burying party gets a half-hour in an underground room beyond which, visible through a window, is the place where the coffin will be set on rails to carry it into the furnace. The cemetery personnel call the furnace, the device (*l'appareil*). But before it goes into the device, there is a ceremonial half-hour during which the coffin is in the room with the mourners. It's laid on a wheeled cart in the middle of the room and surrounded by eight chairs. The chief mourners or the oldest sit, and everyone else stands because the room is too small to accommodate the average party sitting down. At the head of the room, the end with the window on the rails, there is a platform on which people who want to speak or have been designated to speak stand up facing the coffin.

There were four people speaking at my friend's funeral, representing stages of her life. She was just coming of age in 1968 and for the next decade she did sixties things. One of these she carried over into the eighties, when she ran her own very small publishing house, which was not an unlikely occupation though fairly heroic. Actually she was not herself heroic, only ironic, but she kept her house going and proved to be commercially shrewd about writings most people thought commercially impossible. When eventually she moved on to a larger publishing house, she turned out to be remarkably good at navigating the mainstream too. Personally, she held steady where she'd always stood, a yard to the side of everything. The four people spoke well, became interested in their arguments, almost forgot she was dead. We listened carefully.

We had already asked that the speeches be short, but, to move things along just in case, the Père-Lachaise provides a master of ceremonies, a young man who keeps his head reverently bent even when speaking directly to you. I'm not sure whether we could have refused his services, but anyway, at the moment, we didn't have the presence of mind to send him away. Apparently not remembering the last names of the speakers, he called them Michel, Françoise, Geneviève, and Boris, like in California. At the beginning and again at the end, he urged us to mourn our dead friend and wish her well. Then two young cemetery attendants (all the attendants were in their twenties) wheeled the coffin out of the room through a side door and the master of ceremonies told us to stand and face the window for the dispatch into the fire, the *mise à la flamme*. Some people did, most didn't; it was confusing because a shade had been dropped over the window while the coffin was lifted onto the rails and the shade stuck, so that the coffin had begun to move forward by the time it became visible again. It disappeared and the attendants were guiding us out. Another party was already coming down the stairs and there was some of the awkwardness of rush hour on the subway. The social services in big cities are always overburdened.

The next day we went to collect the urn, which was to be delivered to a local branch of the funeral parlor. (We hadn't waited because a cremation takes one and a half to two hours.) The urn hadn't arrived due to the heavy traffic. In Paris the traffic is called *la circulation*. The circulation was bad that day and they asked us to return in a half hour. I would be coming back alone and the man recommended I bring a bag, possibly the one I used for shopping. When I arrived, he insisted I sit down and told me that, amazingly, the urn had gotten there not ten minutes after we'd left. Then he went into a back room and came back with a blue satinate sack tied around the neck with a cord in a darker blue. The outline of a box was visible through the sack. Inside, the man said, was a certificate of cremation. I know, he said, that these ashes will be traveling. I wondered how he knew but then remembered we had told him about our friend's wish. When you travel with the ashes, he urged, be sure to bring the certificate with you. If you are stopped by the police, they will consider that you are transporting a body and you must be able to show them everything is legal.

I was surprised by how heavy the urn was. I had to keep changing hands as I carried it home. By the weight, I could well believe my friend's body was all in that box. I thought how much I would have liked to tell her the story of trundling her ashes along the rue St. Jacques, and how as we, she and I, passed the church of the Val de Grâce, the bells were ringing and I looked in the courtyard and saw a hearse. My friend was neither Christian nor religious, nor am I, and

I didn't go in. When I arrived home, I put the ashes in the corner of the living room, next to a ficus she'd raised from a cutting, and sat down to think what to do next.

This was self-evident: next was the will. She had left a will written in ballpoint on two sides of a page of French graph paper. It was eloquent and elegant, and it conducted masterfully for the last time the ensemble of a complicated life. It was also a sad will, written in a moment of despair. Legally, however, it was not much. Fortunately it was handwritten, dated and signed, so it was valid. In the U.S., a will has to be witnessed to be valid. In this matter, France seems to value vows over contracts, so a will is valid so long as it clearly denotes personal wishes. My friend's will, being in her handwriting, met this requirement, but it was lacking in other ways. She'd written it logically, thinking of her possessions singly and giving them away singly. There weren't many: she left her apartment to one, to another some furniture and a few paintings, and a third was to choose an object or two. But the notary said she wished my friend had called her so she could have told her a will should never be a series of gifts, but a universal donation; you should designate a single person to distribute this to that one and that to this. Otherwise, anything not named in the will goes to a default heir, a blood relative who also becomes the executor. My friend had forgotten that she had two small bank accounts, as well as death benefits from her job, odds and ends, *des poussières* in French, dust. Her only relatives were a nephew and a niece, children of a brother now dead and long estranged, and she had written in the will that they were not to inherit. They therefore wouldn't, but their small children could, which came to the same thing. It wouldn't be much of an inheritance by an accountant's reckoning, and it would be still less minus the French sixty percent inheritance tax, but symbolically who inherited mattered very much.

Henceforth she was all symbols, and these of the will had meanings she had assigned herself. It was essential that her symbols not be revoked by her relatives. Between us, we referred to them generically: *the* nephew, *the* niece. They were *the* children of *the* brother. She had loved her mother wholly, her father not so much, and her brother, after a bad time, not at all. Now that she was dead these distinctions vanished: mother, father, brother . . . her family. In addition, they were all dead, mother, father, brother; but still they were an official family more powerful than any relations her life had bred: the nephew and the niece, banished from her life, could now become the crux of who she remained. The family, I thought, gets a lot of its meaning, most of it maybe, from death.

She had written her will as if a child, in drawing a fence around her picture of a house, had forgotten to extend the line all the way round. She hadn't said the nephew and the niece mustn't inherit her bank balance, the miles on her American Express card, the security deposit on her rented apartment. So they would. I imagined the stuff of the law flowing in over the place in the world where she no longer was, like water closing, cloth knitting, a hole filling, erasing the perturbations of her ways of living. Strange, no? that a person's absence should restore wholeness? Yet she wasn't a disruptive person, not difficult to work or live with and no more critical than comes with a sense of humor. Maybe not quite a member in good standing, a pillar of society. I thought that it happens like this: willy-nilly the dead become pillars of society.

We knew what she would have felt about the nephew and the niece transforming her into their aunt and decided that we couldn't let them. We said we'd get a lawyer, we swore we wouldn't let them. Then, in the midst of swearing, I lost the thread of fierceness. All this about the will was crucial to our keeping faith with our friend, I thought, but it was also beside the point. A few months before she died, I saw a child born. The hours it took were incandescent with consciousness, concentration, fear, hope, work, curiosity. In the room, everyone was supremely present. Except the child: at the center of all the sounds of his coming into life, there was a great silence. He made no sound, and for all that his presence was overwhelmingly impending, I could only sense his absence. When I thought that keeping faith with our friend's will was perhaps necessary but also irrelevant, I remembered the silence of the unborn child cutting it off categorically from the world of our anticipation. While we were swearing we'd not let the nephew and the niece get away with it, our friend was silent the way the unborn child had been. So, in the middle of it, I fell silent because I saw my swearing on her behalf was nonsense. Literally without sense which is another word for connection, when there's no connection, no continuity or relevance, between life and death. There's nothing to understand about death, not even that it exists. Epicurus said death was nothing to us, since, as he put it, where we are, death is not and where death is, we are not. It's well to remember that birth bursts in on a long silence, so as to be prepared for the bursting into silence of death. It's not a diminuendo, it's the absence of all sound.

At first, I wanted burying my friend to be a diminuendo. I was glad she'd asked us to divide her ashes because it was a way for us to continue the story of her life, to add another episode, under her direction. Then I lost my train of thought and, instead of what she had asked us to do, I heard mostly her silence and I found this silence intolerable, and excessive. It was what they call in French English, "too much," by which they mean not a relative but an absolute muchness.

I find myself objecting to the excess of her death. At insignificant moments, crossing the boulevard, putting the milk back in the refrigerator, spraying the cactus, I've spoken to her aloud. The last time I spoke so strangely that I heard myself: I was saying all right, that's enough now, *ça suffit*, it's time you came back, really it's time. I said before that I'm not religious. I don't think there is an afterlife, and certainly not that the dead walk the earth. Yet I meant it when I told her it was time she returned, and I was annoyed that she stayed away. I'd not have been surprised if she'd appeared and I'm disappointed that she hasn't. I'd have told her that this thing she asked us to do with her ashes was more complicated than she'd realized; she'd have said forget it; I'd have said, no, it was turning out to be very interesting and we wanted to do it, now that she'd mentioned it. I can imagine this conversation very easily. What I can't imagine is that she's dead.

I don't blame my imagination. Death is not a subject for the imagination. Literature, painting, and music only talk around it. Two weeks after my friend's death, I went to hear Haydn's *Orfeo ed Euridice* about a man penetrating alive into death. Orpheus just will not accept that he can't have Eurydice. She's taken from him once alive, and he gets her back by dint of his music. Then, the fool, he leaves her unguarded and she's taken from him again. This time, fleeing her abductor, she's killed. The question is whether Orpheus's music can bring her back to life. Most people would say no. At the funeral, we played Chopin études to acknowledge my friend's death, not to dispute it. Once death has happened, there is nothing to say. All the living can do is show the flag, make a show of force the way a nation might march its army up to the border of an enemy state. The force of the living is in nonetheless giving shape to the world they don't transcend. So when they see death rising up at their borders, they go out and demonstrate this power to give shape. Hence ceremony, and music, the most formal of the arts. A funeral ought to be the most formal of ceremonies, for, there being nothing to see in death but dissolution, a funeral has nothing in view but form.

Orpheus, however, mistook a flexing of muscles meant to keep up your spirit in the knowledge of ultimate defeat, for having a fighting chance. He was misled by his music's wondrous power over nature and man into thinking it transcendent. Haydn's librettist Badini invented the character Genius who tries to explain to Orpheus that the best answer to death is philosophy, which, having walked the metes and bounds of life, accepts the limits of the estate in return for getting to furnish it. But Orpheus will have none of such trades and, for a little while, he seems to be right, since Genius now tells him that after all he can regain Eurydice, on one not very difficult condition. Which he can't fulfill: the great puzzle of the story of Orpheus is why he turns back to look at Eurydice knowing he'll lose her for it. I thought, watching the opera after my friend's death, that Orpheus had a greater ambition than reviving Eurydice, which was to breach the underworld. He had to see Eurydice while she was still on the ground of death for, if he saw her again only after her return to life, his invasion of death wouldn't be realized as such. It would have had consequences but no reality of its own. Persuading Pluto to annul Eurydice's death is not enough for Orpheus. What he really wants, what the living want, what I want, is to see with my living eyes the world of death; and, by seeing it, to overcome its discontinuity, to make it another condition of life, so I can go on, or can imagine going on, even though dead. Sight is the most important sense. Emerson insisted that what you see you possess. Orpheus, for his glimpse of the world of the dead, for thinking he could make the dead Eurydice his, was torn apart by the forces that rule that world, the forces of disorder and the antithesis of the force with which he makes his music. Pluto's prohibition is simple and absolute: you can't with your living mind know death.

Eurydice just faded away from Orpheus's sight, but in real life the way it becomes evident that death is a closed matter feels like mockery. We were in the other room, talking, when my friend died. I went in to check on her and couldn't see her breathing. The doctor came and said she was dead. Then quickly there were other people. The doctor recommended a funeral parlor and they said they'd come in two hours. This seemed too fast but, it being Friday, it was then or not until after the weekend. They said to choose clothes in which they would "prepare" her. I thought, having had to die, she shouldn't have to undergo being prepared and said I would dress her, not knowing how difficult it is to dress a dead person. To begin with, I couldn't pull out the intravenous tube that still connected her to a morphine drip. The tube had been inserted into a catheter through which she had been undergoing a chemotherapy. When I tried to pull out the tube, blood seeped from the opening of the catheter. So instead I cut the tube and so doing saw that she was dead. I had wanted her to wear a favorite gray cashmere turtleneck, but I couldn't put it on her. She was too heavy, although she weighed less than eighty pounds, and too stiff, so I dressed her in a shirt and pants. She looked terrible, yet fully and definitively herself. You're never so wholly incarnate as in death.

When I was dressing my friend, I expected her to help. The utter stillness of her arms and legs filled me with hopelessness. In French, there are two words that look like despair but the second means hopelessness: *désespoir* and *désesperance*. It's useful to have despair and hopelessness look alike; they correct one another, so that *désespoir* is less sentimental than despair and *désesperance* less childish than hopelessness. The feeling I had when my friend didn't raise her arm even a little so I could slip on her sweater was *désesperance*: there was nothing anymore to hope for in relation to her.

This feeling had an unwonted finality. I wasn't used to despair. She had been sick a long time and I knew she would probably, nearly inevitably, die of the disease. But such an eventuality never seemed immediately relevant. Ten days before she died, we went to Nantes where she had been invited to visit in a course on book editing. She didn't seem strong enough to go alone, so I went with her. We took the TGV and arrived in the rain. I walked with her to the place where she was to talk, stopping on the way to get her some coffee and a raisin bun for strength. Later, the talk having gone very well, we ate at a fish brasserie from the turn of the century, and shared a big platter of shellfish. We were to return to Paris the next morning but instead we stayed over one more day. It was no longer raining, and we turned the trip into a holiday. We rented a car and, because my friend had passed the summers of her childhood on the Atlantic coast, she knew a place she wanted to go, near Pornic. We drove, in fact she drove, and it all started to come out right. After a while, on the left was a long driveway down to a parking lot on a beach. We parked and walked down to the water. The sky was mostly gray but a bright gray, an ocean gray with white seagulls. It wasn't cold, not cold enough to make the mist uncomfortable. We walked down to the water. The tide was coming in and, to go all the way to the water, you had to be ready to jump back. She stayed farther up the beach and I went down to the water. A perfect seashell floated in on a small roller and was left behind still cupped upright, the only one on the beach (I checked) that was hollow side up. I told her it was definitely bringing something. Superstitious only to the degree that connotes a proper sense of your own understanding's limits and the infinitude of possibility, still, we took it as a sign. So to drink to the sign, we entered the beach cafe, which was called Bahia and decorated with plastic parrots two feet tall hanging from the ceiling on round swings. The African owner made us impeccable hot chocolates.

I'm stuck in that day. And I'm simultaneously stuck in the night before she died. She wasn't conscious. I didn't have a view about her unconsciousness. For the moment, I only thought of the night. I lay down beside her. I talked to her and told her she should rest tranquilly, we were there and were taking care of her. I said, *On te soigne.* Sleep. It's all right. I'm stuck in the day on the beach and in that night. Being stuck I suppose is a way of dying with the dead by stopping when they do. Yet the mother of the child I saw being born, in whose silence I had sensed a universe outside of life, said, when I told her I was stuck in the night of my friend's death, that she was stuck in the night of her child's birth. You get stuck, then, when you meet up with something that makes the limit of your perpetual motion just too obvious.

Stuck, you turn back. My friend didn't appear to me, so I made her appear: one night, I dreamed she had come back to life, or rather that she hadn't died. At first, in my dream, she was as she was in the moments before she died. But, in the dream, as I bent over to see how she was, she grew better and better, until, in the dream, I called out to the doctor to do something, since something could be done.

Nominated by Raritan

SIDEREAL DESIRE

by ELEANOR WILNER

from SPILLWAY

Star struck   following this latter-day   Aphrodite
as she clatters   down the street   high heels
with gold glitter   on her tired feet   sparks thrown
from the friction   of dream   against the rough stone
of the real   daylight   having its way
of showing the dark roots   of even the brightest
blonde   these days   the lights stay on
there's the cool glare   of publicity   veils torn off
the body of desire   just spotty
flesh   pubic hair   shaved legs
stretch marks   a fine film of glistening
sweat   look how the stars have fallen

tonight   when she leans over the bridge
                    eyes brimming with water   tired
from the constant exposure   from trying to arouse
even the memory of desire   (in times like these)
        when she stares down   eyes filling
into the dark water   on which a galaxy or more
        of stars have fallen   why   there it is again

the veil!   a glowing scrim of shifting moiré silks
        silver asterisks set in motion by a wind   a blur
of stars   like a stir of bright wings in a dark air
        and the water   that was once a mirror
                is now a swirl of veils again

the stars   the gods   are taken back into the stream
   what wore our faces in an old design
drawn down   return once more to the elements
     that called them forth—
          are whirled along, a silver thread, a starlit river
in a canyon seen from air, then gone . . . until the pause
     some other place   a million years downstream from here
        and there the fleeting forms take shape again
          though not like ours   or anything we knew

Nominated by Marianne Boruch, Spillway

A JEWELER'S EYE
FOR FLAW

fiction by CHRISTIE HODGEN

from THE GEORGIA REVIEW

The times are strange, and the ways we kill ourselves even stranger. In the course of a year we receive letters from our missing fathers—men who have worked their whole lives as lumberjacks, gravediggers, butchers, fishermen, ambulance drivers, marines, and garbage men—but now these fathers send word they're recovering from strokes in government-funded rehab centers, and it's nothing but oatmeal dribbling down the chin, elastic bands cinched around the upper arm, serums shot into blown veins, the glorious state of bedsores and perpetual pajamas. They write this with their left hands, their script wild and slanting across the page, like lost kites. In the course of a year there are whole factories of workers laid off from their jobs. Our families change. Broke and hopeless, our mothers give up on the tired and maddening routine of child care, all the scolding and straightening, and they seek refuge in dummies. They become ventriloquists, and start speaking to us through our childhood teddy bears, which they wave amicably in front of our faces, making the bears talk to us in high, girlish voices, even allowing the bears to turn cruel, to say what our mothers themselves have always thought but never voiced, that we'll never amount to anything but homeless whores. In the course of a year a boy at our high school attempts three suicides, lighting himself on fire, slitting his wrists, and swallowing pills. All year he wears the scars of his efforts with a spooky stateliness, and we watch his every move. We spread rumors, saying that he keeps a rope coiled like a poisonous snake in his hip pocket, that he plans to strangle the first person who speaks to him. We are trapped in high school's interminable final year. We are still young enough to believe that these troubles are temporary, to believe the promises of politicians in this election year as they talk into television cameras about economic recovery and personal responsibility, and we think we see, in the slender gleam of their tie clips, an end to this suffering, this staleness, this strife. All of this happens over and over again, in slightly different forms, in every suburb of every failing industrial city. We are, as everyone is happy to remind us, nothing special.

Ever since my father took the car and started north, looking for work, my mother and I walk a mile every Wednesday to the grocery store. We fight in the fluorescent-lit aisles, comparing the merits of each brand of chocolate-covered marshmallow cookie, of frosted cereal and canned ravioli, of bargain diet soda and frozen pizza.

"I must have my Pecan Sandies," my mother says, waltzing with the shopping cart. Her long gray hair streams behind her like a cape. She is the superhero of shortbread, swooping down to rescue five bags of homeless cookies. A former music teacher, she is the kind of person who makes theatrics out of the most ordinary desires. She holds up a bag of cookies like Scarlett O'Hara with the raw carrot in the famine scene from *Gone With the Wind*. "As God is my witness," she says, "I'll never go hungry again!" She tosses the cookies in the cart. "Pecan Sandies," she whispers, "I'm going to eat you alive."

We pause, as we do every week, to survey the many brands of hair color that my mother is considering buying. She has debated for months the benefits and detractions of hair dye. "I don't want to look like a hooker," she says this week. "You remember what your grandmother looked like, right?" I am unmoved—a sulker and a moper, an eye roller. Although I can't help but smile when, on the walk home, my mother points out a conspicuous van stopped at a red light. "Joe's Bolt and Screw" is painted in red letters across the side of the van. "Funny," my mother says. "Usually Joes screw and bolt."

This is, my mother reminds me, the trail of tears: take only what you can carry. We walk home with our awkward bundles, stopping every hundred yards to shift our grip on the grocery bags. It is late fall. The sky is dark by six and the grass is stiffened with frost. The trees are bare, their lost leaves blowing from lawn to lawn. This is the season that always gives the impression that time has stopped. I fear that the semester will go on forever, that I will chant for all eternity conjugated verbs in Spanish class, that I will spend the rest of my life stuck somewhere in the depths of *Middlemarch*, that I will deliberate infinitely which colleges to attend without ever completing an application, that I will evermore play my clarinet in the second row of my high school concert band, knowing without question that nothing I do or fail to do will be noticed or even heard.

"Stop sulking," my mother says. "Other kids your age have fun. They enjoy life. They live a little."

My mother refers to a group of teenagers who have just run past us, whooping and laughing and carrying large pumpkins. "We rock!" one of them yells. "We fucking rock!" They howl. There are five of them, dressed identically in black unitards. I don't notice until one of them turns around that the fronts of the suits are painted with glow-in-the-dark bones, that these five kids my age are having fun, enjoying life, living a little, while dressed as skeletons.

"We forgot the fucking candy," my mother says, and sighs. It is Halloween, a detail escaping both of us until now.

"I completely forgot," I say.

"Me too." She looks dejectedly into her sack of groceries.

"You can give out Pecan Sandies," I say.

My mother straightens to her full height, appalled. "Watch your mouth," she says. Just then I hear footsteps. Someone is running toward us. And when I turn to look back something brushes my shoulder, someone's chilly white bedsheet, someone's Halloween cliché, someone's lousy costume. It clings ever so briefly to my shoulder, then whisks away, the tail of a speeding ghost in black combat boots.

"I think that was James Woodfin," I say to my mother. "I think those were his boots."

"How's he been doing?"

"Okay," I tell her. "He's got scars on his neck and all up one side of his face."

"Poor thing," says my mother. Her mouth is full. She has already broken into one brilliant yellow bag of Pecan Sandies. "Never forget," she tells me, "I named you after the thing I love most in the world."

"I know," I say. My name is the worst name in the world, stomach turning, sickly sweet.

"Watch out, Sandy," says my mother, too late. I have stepped on a patch of smashed pumpkin, and I slip on a heap of squash and seeds. Canned pasta and frozen waffles and marshmallow cookies fly out into the street. I gather them up, imagining the evening exactly as it will unfold: how my mother and I will sit in the dark in our living room, afraid to turn on the lights or even the television, listening to the approaching feet of eager trick or treaters, and the hollow ding of the doorbell, and the shuffling and chatter and the eventual disappointed retreat of those who are turned away unsatisfied.

James Woodfin, the Suicidal Maniac: this was his official title at Brown High School. Last summer James sneaked into the garage of his house at three o'clock on a Saturday morning, doused his shirt in gasoline, and lit a match. His burns were severe. He crawled back into his house, half blind, and struggled down the long, dark hallway to his parents' room. When the police and ambulance and fire department came it woke the whole neighborhood. We stood in doorways with our arms folded in the glare of the red and blue lights of five emergency vehicles. Many of us assumed that James's father, Mr. Woodfin, had at last suffered a heart attack. He was a pink-faced man with a bulging stomach and a flair for violent outbursts. Hourly Mr. Woodfin could be heard cursing the family dog, a giant Dalmatian, who liked to stand in the Woodfins' backyard, on their picnic table, facing the house, barking loudly and rhythmically for hours on end. "Jesus Christ, Dildo," Mr. Woodfin would yell. "Shut the fuck up, you spotted sack of shit!" No one suspected that James, the Woodfins' only child, would have done something so noteworthy. For years he had lived in that house and shuffled through our town's public schools and delivered the morning paper at five o'clock each weekday morning, buzzing through the neighborhood on his moped. For years he had done all of this in nearly complete silence. No one knew him.

James was friendless, and therefore the victim of rumors. Some said that James was in the habit of cutting himself every time he fought with his parents, and that his chest was like a quilt. Others claimed to have seen James walking alone in the city, late at night, in dangerous and suggestive proximity to groups of streetwalkers in their fishnet stockings and ratty fox stoles, all of whom were making a better living than the rest of us. The only thing we knew for sure about James was that he was tall and lanky and gray-eyed, that he kept his black hair long enough that it covered his eyes, and that he

47

stuttered. He had suffered horribly in grade school. When he was forced to answer a question in class, he would grip the edges of his desk, and his head would jerk. Veins bulged in his neck, and his eyes would roll back. Eventually, in our childish versions of politeness, we simply stopped speaking to James.

Because I was James's next-door neighbor, I knew something of his life at home. I knew that Mr. Woodfin was ashamed of his son, that he yelled at James most evenings, telling him to be a man, for Christ's sake, just once in his rotten miserable life. "Wha-wha-wha-wha-*what* did you say?" Mr. Woodfin mocked, every so often, when James stormed out of the house, letting the screen door slam. "You can go fa-fa-fa-fa-*fuck* yourself!" I never told anyone in our class about Mr. Woodfin, about James's suffering. I wondered if he knew that I kept his secret, if he thought of me at all.

And so in a surprising and brilliant protest to his father, his home-town, his isolation, James had set himself on fire. When school started up in the fall, James began the year as though nothing had happened. He walked the halls with impeccable posture, his head held high, gazing dreamily past the stares of his classmates. In class he sat up straight and took notes in a tiny, intricate script. The only thing different about James that year was that every day he wore a black trench coat and combat boots, which did a good job of hiding his scars. But he couldn't entirely cover his neck, which was pink and wrinkled, like worms, and he couldn't hide his face, the red, oval-shaped patches, like slices of rare roast beef, that had been grafted to his cheeks.

It wasn't until Halloween, when James dressed as a ghost, when his white bedsheet brushed against my shoulder on the walk home from the grocery, that James displayed the slightest strange behavior. On the day after Halloween, James showed up at school in his cos-tume. Our teachers pretended not to notice the ghost sitting up per-fectly straight in their classrooms, taking detailed notes. A week passed. We admitted to no discomfort when the ghost, already so far out of season, passed us in the hall. James could see us without being seen. Whatever regrets we suffered over James and his solitary life, the agony that we developed and carried around in our minds, even our dreams—this was the revenge of the meek, the lonely, the dead.

Weekday afternoons I return home to the madness of my mother's il-legal day-care service. She keeps two neighborhood children while their parents are at work. Maxwell—a blond, plump terror whose parents both work at McDonald's—can be heard yelling a hundred yards from the house.

"Sandy, Sandy," he says, this day like any other. "The Beach is home."

"Sandy the Beach!" cries my mother. It is her clever pet name, her underhanded and diabolical version of humor.

"Hello, Lydia. Hello, Maxwell," I say, hunched miserably under a backpack full of books. I have walked home through rain in soggy shoes, sniffling, wiping my nose with my mitten. I am playing for sympathy.

"Maxwell has something to tell you," my mother says, placing her hand on his blond head.

"Sorry, Sandy. Sorry, sorry, sorry, sorry, sorry."

"Sorry for what?"

"For your room," he says, and giggles maniacally, turning his face into the skirt of my mother's housecoat.

"I couldn't stop him," my mother calls after me. "He's an animal!"

I have seen worse. In my room, for the hundredth time, I find drawers pulled out from the dresser, underwear flung about, socks separated from their happy marriages. My bed, which I straighten and tuck every morning with military precision, is stripped of its blankets. The fine tips of my sharpened pencils, which I keep in a mug on my desk, have been snapped off. Worst of all, I find my aloe plant overturned and oozing, its soil scattered on the carpet.

"I'm going to kill you, you little shit," I call, stomping out to the kitchen, where I find another round of absurdity. Pilar—the six-month-old baby whose parents are first-year surgical residents at the city hospital, parents who drop her off at four in the morning and pick her up at midnight—is screaming in her high chair. Maxwell stands before her with one of my childhood teddy bears, Benjy. "Baby, baby, baby, baby," Maxwell says, making the bear talk in a squealing voice, thrusting it in Pilar's face. "Poor little foreign baby!" My mother is nowhere to be found.

"Quit it, Maxwell," I say, grabbing the bear out of his hands. But the baby is beyond repair. She has the scream of a bald eagle. I move to stroke her hair but she flinches, screams even louder.

"Okay, Pilaf," my mother says, suddenly appearing. "Don't cry. Only a few more years of this and your parents will be rich." My mother takes the baby from her high chair, and the baby calms. She

49

clings to my mother's chest, latches onto my mother's housecoat with clenched fists. My mother is Pilar's mother, more so than anyone wants to admit. Pilar's parents are at the hospital so much that the baby has ceased to react when they pick her up. "Where's my girl?" Pilar's mother says each night, all excitement. But Pilar sits nonchalantly in her chair, yawning. It is too embarrassing to stand. Pilar's mother thrusts a wad of cash into my mother's hand, gathers her baby, leaves without another word.

"Let's make you some bacon," my mother tells the baby. My mother has been forbidden to feed the baby meat, and doing so is her secret joy.

"Mom," I say. "You're not supposed to."

"She loves it!" my mother says. "You know, you're turning into a real drag, Sandy. You're more like your father every day." My mother takes Benjy from my hands and turns him on me. "Let's see some more Mozart," she has the bear say to me. "Less Beethoven."

My mother was a music teacher at the local junior high for fifteen years, but she lost her job after a series of layoffs in which all teachers of supplemental subjects, such as art and music, were let go. Only the essential faculty remained, including gym instructors. The gym teachers—recent graduates of junior colleges—kept their jobs with full benefits, an irony which made the already significant torture of playing indoor dodge ball even worse.

My mother has grown strange in the months since she lost her job. She spends her free time in our damp, unfinished basement watching television and eating entire bags of Pecan Sandies. The smell of them is always on her breath, their crumbs caught in the folds of her clothes. On rainy afternoons she is fond of turning up the volume full blast on her organ and playing the kinds of frightening chords popular in vampire movies. They shake the house in bursts. Each time I hear one I see a vision of my mother as Dracula, spinning around to face me, her teeth bared, a cape flapping magnificently behind her. Lately my mother even dresses gloomily, in a black velour housecoat. Her hair, which had been dyed black for years but which is now almost entirely gray, hangs wearily down her back. She is defeated. Music had been her life. She was the kind of music teacher who wrote letters on special stationery that was lined with G clef staffs. She dotted the *i* in her name, Lydia, with an eighth note.

In my mother's opinion the world is filled with and ruled by idiots.

Her defeat in this situation, knowing that she is hopelessly outnumbered, has had the effect of almost entirely silencing her. Her only friends are children. In public she barely speaks and suffers insults without protest. She sighs when the supermarket scanner gyps her out of an advertised sale price, sighs when propositions pass which she has voted against, sighs when happy, youthful couples walk past us in the mall, we the jilted wife and daughter of a luckless raconteur. Only now and then her wit slips out, a sign of protest. Every so often she mutters asides under her breath, like W. C. Fields. "Never give a sucker an even break," she is fond of saying. Or, "Children should be neither seen nor heard."

The longer my father is gone, without sending money or even a word of his whereabouts, the more my mother and I grow sheepish, awkward, strange. Some days now my mother will only speak to me with the help of an inanimate translator, Benjy. Benjy's fur is matted, mangy. His body is flattened in places and bulging in others, his stuffing having shifted under the force of gravity and the occasional pile of books he has been trapped under for weeks at a time. Benjy is also marked by the drool and gnawing of Pilar and Maxwell. One of his eyes, a brown button, hangs miserably from a thin thread. My mother likes to wave the bear playfully while it talks. It only speaks in an exaggerated girly voice, like Betty Boop. "Oooh," Benjy says, when I come home from school, "Mommy's *late*. And she looks like she's in a *bad mood*." I glare at the bear whenever it speaks to me, and try to rip it from my mother's hands. Sometimes I grab it by the throat and throw it on the floor, step on its back. "Don't hurt me!" the bear screams. The bear's chief complaint is that I am leaving for college in a few short months, and it wants to come along. "Oh no, Mommy," the bear is fond of saying, "I'm *naked*! I need some new clothes for school."

The closer I come to leaving for college, the more my mother takes refuge in the bear. Lately she has begun caring for it like a baby, like her second child, sitting him in a high chair next to the dinner table, extending forkfuls of potatoes and green beans to its mouth before taking a bite herself, having long conversations with the bear, making it proclaim its everlasting love and devotion for her, taking it to bed, brushing its fur, and ironing each morning one of a whole wardrobe of satin ribbons to be tied around its neck and, bothered by its dangling eye, buying and altering a pirate's patch to slant across its head.

51

"More Mozart, less Beethoven," the bear says again.

"Mom!" I say, but she won't look at me. She waves the bear tauntingly in my face.

"She's not talking to you," says the bear. "I am."

Though it is raining, and nearly dark, I walk out to the backyard and take shelter in my father's slanting toolshed. The shed is poorly made out of old, rotting lumber, and there are wide gaps between the boards. My father's tools hang from hooks. A shovel and a rake lean in one corner. There is a shelf on the back wall, stacked with rolls of duct tape, paintbrushes, jugs of turpentine and gasoline, and old coffee cans filled with nails and bolts. Also on the shelf is a pack of my father's cigarettes, Lucky Strikes. I take the cigarettes and hold them up to my nose, wanting some memory of my father, but the smell is faint.

I drop the cigarettes when I hear the scurry of a rodent at my feet. It is a small brown field mouse, no more than three inches long. Its whiskers twitch. Merciless, petty, I grab the shovel from the corner and bring it down on the mouse, wishing, before I am even through with my swing, that I had walked away and left it alone. I consider leaving the mouse on the floor of the shed, its head flattened, bloody, and unrecognizable. But I go out into the rain, into our dark patch of back lawn, and dig a hole by the fence behind the shed. When I finish burying the mouse I stand over its grave, leaning on the handle of the shovel. I try to concentrate on a kind thought to help usher the mouse from this earth—a comforting verse about nature or the food chain or reincarnation as a higher entity, perhaps a squirrel. But I am aware, dreadfully, of a faint scraping a few feet away, in the Woodfins' yard. When I turn to look I see a blur of white, a ghost bent over his yardwork. James is raking the lawn in the rain. He works slowly, methodically, gathering the wet leaves together in small piles. I face James and raise my hand up, and keep it there, as though taking an oath. I don't know if James sees me or not, for he gives no sign. The rainfall is heavy, and James's sheet clings to him. He is rail thin, a ghost of a ghost. I wonder if he feels the rain on his skin, the cold, or if his scars have dulled for him even the sensation of moving through weather, through space, through time.

We are behind the times, this failed industrial city. Our factories are empty, useless, outdated. We produce nothing. Our only functioning facility is a state-of-the-art trash incinerator, perched atop a high hill. A dozen counties send their garbage here. Their trucks, giant donkeys burdened with trash, grumble past our houses, gears grinding, brakes wailing, toward the incinerator, where a flame rumored to burn at eighteen hundred degrees swallows tons of garbage a day, a flame so fierce, we're told, that it can reduce a sofa to a handful of ashes in under thirty seconds, and so well engineered that the smoke it releases through the stacks—though black—is entirely refined of pollutants. The smoke rises and swirls, rises and swirls, all day, stretching out over our houses, darkening our windows with the ashy remnants of the unwanted—the sleeper sofas, dining room tables, kitchen appliances, tennis rackets, encyclopedia sets, LPs, patent leather shoes, photo albums, and board games of our friends and neighbors.

My neighborhood is settled in a valley between two small hills—one the site of our infamous incinerator, and one the site of White City, a commercial sprawl, acres of neon, a collection of the city's best resources—gas stations, grocery stores, ice cream parlors, pizza places, tire and lube and muffler garages, windowless government offices, doughnut shops, and vocational high schools. This is a neighborhood of two-bedroom, single-bath homes with wood-paneled walls and unfinished basements. Each plot of land is bordered by a chain-link fence. It is a neighborhood populated by plumbers, carpenters, truck drivers, telephone operators, cashiers, bank tellers, fast-food restaurant managers, and retired military men. There is a hunched hatchback or a shamelessly hulking station wagon in every driveway. And on nearly every set of cold, crumbling front steps there is a man staring down into a coffee mug, steam circling slowly toward his face, or there is a man whittling with a jackknife, smoking a cigarette, or a man uprooting a political sign in his front yard—signs in favor of failed candidates who promised jobs, jobs, jobs, as full-time factory workers with benefits and dental, jobs as manufacturers of military equipment and nuclear weapons, state-funded jobs as policemen and firemen and construction workers. These are my neighbors, the men trying to escape the house. But having no money and nowhere to go, they choose the front steps and the chill of autumn. They have watched leaves change and fall, the grass wilt. They have been waiting for jobs since spring.

We, their children, wear the marks of their shame. We wear their palm prints. As teenagers we endure the humiliation of our parents, a sickness which can unleash itself at strange, unexpected moments. Our parents have drunkenly burst into our rooms late at night while we are sleeping, turning the lights on and ripping the covers from our beds, and have told us to get the hell up, start earning our keep in those godforsaken houses, and at three in the morning we have found ourselves scrubbing kitchen floors on our hands and knees, listening to our parents' stories of hardship, the brutal conditions they endured at our age. We fight back with silence and sarcasm, and have cigarettes put out on our backs. We are kicked in the pants, slapped across the face. And after we have scrubbed the floor or washed the dishes or shoveled the driveway or raked the leaves, our parents have cried to us, great miserable sobs of regret and apology, and what grows in us more than any other desire is the desire to sleep. To return to bed, the dark solitude of our small bedrooms, to sleep it off through the morning, through daylight, through the winter until the summer of our eighteenth year, the season of our imminent escape. We want to get out, to move on. We want, at the very least, to suffer somewhere else.

My father left after just such an evening. He had woken my mother and me at four in the morning and demanded we stand trial in the kitchen while he listed our offenses. He swayed in the kitchen's bright light, its yellow wallpaper, its yellow linoleum floor. His eyes were blurry and red, his hair slicked down on his forehead. He had walked home two miles through rain, sick and drunk, because we couldn't be bothered to get out of bed to answer the phone. He had called us for a ride, goddammit, fifty times if he'd called us once, and now his boots were water-logged, ruined, like the love he had once carried for us blissfully, lightly, effortlessly, in his giant goddamned heart.

The next morning my father announced that he was taking me to his favorite place, the dog track. We sat in the bleachers among ruthless patrons, who threatened the dogs with beatings and even death if they didn't for Christ's sake run faster. We sat next to men in fedoras and polyester pants, men with stubby cigars and rotting teeth and bulging veins, men with thermoses full of whiskey, men who cried at the tops of their lungs for their number thirteen dog to run, goddammit, for the sake of the rent, the leaking roof, the stalled car, to run for the sake of doubling their last severance check, for the sake

54

of baby's perpetual new pair of shoes. Watching the dogs circle the track, I recognized for the first time a horrible truth about myself: that I had worn for sixteen years, without knowing it, the face of a greyhound. Bony and fierce, slight, with wet, bulging eyes, a long nose, and the expression of something recently beaten. This was my face. The resemblance was so obvious to me that I grew sick with embarrassment, as though I were naked in front of the crowd. I asked to leave but my father insisted on dispensing advice. This was his fatherly swan song, though I didn't yet know of his plans to leave. He left me with a handful of harsh facts, most surprisingly the revelation that a pig going to market wasn't the same thing as a pig sent out with fifty bucks for the week's groceries.

He left that night, leaving behind only the gray suit bought for his father's funeral, which hangs now in the coat closet so far to the right that we usually forget it is there, with its useless buttons on the coat sleeve, three of them, matched with holes already sewn, never meant for a single moment to close a gap.

The time moves slowly. I am stuck forever in the middle of *Middle-march*, the subject of my term paper. Our teacher requires us to compose a list of questions about the book, things which we would like to answer in a ten-page essay. "Why is the main character so stupid?" I write. "Why doesn't she just book a seat on the next flight to Milwaukee?" Before turning in our drafts, we are each paired with another class member for peer review. James and I are assigned to one another. We sit in a corner of the classroom, a ghost and a hoax. He reads about my frustrations with Dorothea Brooke and George Eliot, about not knowing when to rent a car and get out when the getting is good. James has written twenty-five pages on Dostoevski's *The Idiot*, and his paper is a brilliant treatise on the importance of outcasts. I write three pages of confession to James, unburdening myself, saying how I've always cared for him and wondered about him, asking him about his plans after graduation, offering to serve him coffee and ice cream for free if he ever wants to visit me at my job at Friendly's Restaurant, weeknights from six to eleven.

I wait for James's reply. Thanksgiving comes and goes. I watch the Macy's parade with my mother and Pilar, both of them gnawing mercilessly on legs of turkey. Soon after, the first snow falls. The sky will remain cloudy, colorless, for the rest of winter. The black smoke clouds of the incinerator stand out best in this cold season. They seem to keep their shape in this weather, and seem always to float in the direction of our house.

I still wait for James's reply. I work nights and weekends scooping ice cream and serving hamburgers, slogging through my shift without looking anyone in the eye. An autistic savant sits nightly in my section in a yellow rain slicker, drawing cathedrals on napkins and drinking cups of coffee loaded with sugar. Each night he leaves a scratch ticket on the table, as a tip, and each night I return home with luckless traces of silver under my nails. "Gramma and I waited for you to come home all day!" screams Benjy, when I walk through the door. "Where the hell have you *been*?" I give the bear the finger and head for my room. "Don't worry, Benjy," I hear my mother saying. "Gramma still loves you. Even if Mommy doesn't. Even if Mommy's turning into a snooty college bitch." My mother cradles the bear in her arms, and rocks it frantically.

I wait for James's reply. Finally, just before Christmas, our neighborhood is wakened once again by police sirens. I watch from my bedroom window as James, having lost a liter of blood after slitting his wrists, is carried from his house on a gurney, as short men in white uniforms lift him into the back of an ambulance. "Do you think he's dead?" I hear my mother say, her voice soft and blank. She is standing in my bedroom doorway. All I can see of her is the shining silver of her long hair. I realize that she could be talking about either James or my father. I realize it is the first time she has spoken to me, without the help of Benjy, in weeks.

James does not return to school after Christmas break. We are told that he is recovering at home, and finishing his coursework there. My English teacher reads James's paper on *The Idiot* to the class, her eyes brimming with tears. She looks up from the paper now and then, staring at us accusatorily. She repeats the final paragraph of the paper three times, so that we understand its importance. "We neglect the potential of our surroundings. These days most of us are jewelers in search of flaws," James had written. "We are in the habit of examining each gem through such a powerful scope that we fail to see its beauty." I consider knocking on the Woodfins' door that day after school, and every day afterward, but I am deterred by the bark of their Dalmatian, by the sound of Mr. Woodfin yelling, by the cheeriness of television advertisements blaring in the living room. Sometimes I make it as far as the door, my knuckles poised for knocking, before turning back. And sometimes I simply stand in the snow by the chain-link fence that separates our yards, staring at James's house, at the dark window that I suspect is his.

Spring: my mother decides to fill the circular above-ground pool in our backyard. The pool has been empty for years, but my mother now sees its potential as a kind of playpen. "I'll strap some floats on those kids and let them splash around all day," she says. "I'll just sit in the lawn chair eating cookies and reading magazines." But my mother neglects to treat the pool, and its surface turns marshy. A fine moss settles over the water, a tapestry of fungus and fallen leaves and drowned insects. By the time it is warm enough to swim, the pool is hopeless.

It is a season of indecision. I have won scholarships to two colleges after writing devastating personal essays about the economic recession and its impact on families. I mention my poor, poor mother, laid off from her life's work, and I mention the sad, longing music she plays on her piano when she thinks no one is listening. I mention my hard-luck father, traveling the country looking for decent work, his skin so calloused from hard labor that his potential employers know from the first handshake that he is a man out of his league. I have a choice between two schools, one in California and one in my hometown, which my mother assumes I don't have the gall to abandon.

I return home from one of my last days of school to the usual daycare circus.

"Quack, quack, quack," Maxwell says, flapping his arms and walking in circles around the kitchen.

"Quack," says Pilar, sitting as always in her high chair, sucking on a strip of bacon. Her brown eyes are beautiful, and always wet with tears.

"Quack," says my mother, appearing from the living room, where she has been watching soap operas. "My dear, there are baby ducks trapped in the pool. And we're going to watch you save them."

There are indeed five baby ducks trapped in the pool, too small to fly themselves to freedom. How they made it into the pool is a mystery. Regardless, they have been swimming in circles for hours, possibly days, without stopping. I hear their mother quacking somewhere in the yard. "She's been doing that for hours," says my mother. "If I had a gun I'd shoot her."

57

"Kill her, kill her, Benjy," cries Maxwell, and he runs off in search of the mother, making the bear growl.

The idea is for me to lean over the side of the pool, reach out with my arms, and usher the ducks into a large pot. I move for them, but they circle away. I lean further in, balancing on my stomach. The mother bird honks miserably. I hear her coming closer, and then all at once there is a flurry of wings, and she is flying straight for my face. I lose my balance and fall headfirst into the pool, into the filth and slime that has collected there for weeks. My mother, Maxwell, and Pilar are thoroughly entertained. Chest high in filth, I gather the ducks into the pot, climb out, and release them. They strut away behind their mother, nonchalant.

"I hate you," I yell at my mother, who is still laughing. "And I hate you," I tell Maxwell. "I hate everyone in this whole town and I hope you all die." It is the first time I have raised my voice to my mother. She takes Benjy from Maxwell and chases me into the house. "Oh no," cries the bear. "Poor mommy needs some *anger management*. Maybe mommy should get some *professional help*."

"Fuck off!" I tell the bear, swatting at it.

"Oh no," says the bear. "Mommy smells like a *hooker!*"

I decide that day to commit to California. I walk to the nearest mailbox, pull at its moaning door, and mail my acceptance. I decide not to tell my mother, to let her continue to believe that I plan to enroll in our city's pitiful satellite to our state university.

All summer James fails to emerge from his house. I watch for him, spend time lurking by the fence in the backyard, but he never appears. Once I desperately called out to Mrs. Woodfin, who was hanging clothes on the line, asking if she wanted me to trim back the branch of one of our trees that extended into her yard.

"What?" she said, turning toward me. Her gray hair was set in curlers, her feet tucked in slippers.

"How's James?" I called.

"What?" she said, cupping her hand behind her ear. She was utterly surprised to be spoken to, and looked at me with fear, as if I were a talking bear.

"Nothing," I said. "Never mind."

A week before I was to board the Greyhound for college, I received a letter from my father, who always had a knack for timing. He wrote that he was in a rehabilitation center in New Hampshire, recovering from a stroke. He wrote how strange it was to lounge around all day with nothing but thoughts for company. He wrote he was sorry. He wrote he had worked his whole life at tough jobs, lumberjack, butcher, and now he was stuck there in the unfamiliar stiffness of clean sheets. He asked to be visited, and included a list of contraband indulgences I might bring along. Cigarettes, a fifth of Jack. He also complained that he missed the pleasure of sucking meat off chicken wings. He missed the sight of a pile of small, helpless bones on his plate after each meal. In closing, my father mentioned the daily torture of a blinking neon sign visible from his bedroom window. "Cold Ice Cream," it said. What he wouldn't do for a milkshake. "If you can't come see me it's okay," he wrote. "Although I do miss having a radio, which you could bring me."

That night, after work, I undressed and stood in front of my mirror. I was a mess. So thin, all ribs and hip bones, and so pale. My skin was bluish white, like skim milk. There was ice cream smeared on my arms and face. I hadn't noticed any of this, hadn't really looked at myself in months.

"Sandy," someone called, in a loud and sure and commanding voice. Someone was in the backyard. I went to the window, pressed my face against the screen, squinted.

"Goodbye," said the voice. And then I saw a slight figure, retreating into darkness.

"James!" I called. "Wait!" I pulled on a T-shirt and ran from the house into the yard. "James!"

What took me by surprise at first was the smell, an overwhelming sweetness, like I was walking through a grove of grapefruit trees. And then from the corner of my eye I saw a burst of whiteness, a whole circle of light. It was the pool. It was its usual four-foot-tall circle, but the dark water was gone, the horrible smell of rot, the mass grave of spiders and crickets, the layer of scum mixed with fallen leaves, all of that was gone. The pool was choked with flowers. James had floated dozens of magnolia blossoms on the surface of the water. I took one in my hands and held it, brought it to my nose, took in its sweet, sweet smell. I imagined James spending the afternoon climbing trees in better neighborhoods, those tall, magnificent trees with their glossy leaves. He must have collected the white blossoms in a sack, then floated them one by one in the pool's dark water. It must have taken him hours.

These were the first flowers I had ever received. I stood, staring at them for a long time, hoping that James would return. When he failed to emerge from the darkness as I had imagined it, as I had seen in films, I thought about knocking on his door, but it was too late. Tomorrow, I said.

James left the next day. I was still asleep when he loaded his suitcases into his parents' car and drove off. I had no idea where he had gone. A week later I walked to the bus station, leaving a note for my mother with my new address and phone number. "Call me in a week," it said. "Love, Sandy the Beach." The last I saw of my mother, she was slouched in her armchair, staring vacantly at the television, one hand buried inside a bag of Pecan Sandies.

After a month of college, when I finally decide to call home, Benjy answers. "Hello?" he cries, more Betty Boop than ever.

"Hi Mom," I say.

"It's my mommy!" cries Benjy. "We've been waiting and waiting by the phone!"

"Mom?" I say.

"She's not home," says Benjy. "She's out on a hot date." There's something in Benjy's voice, a new enthusiasm that sounds truly crazed, as if Benjy has wandered off too far from my mother's mental leash, never to return.

"Mom," I say. "What if it wasn't me calling? And you answered the phone like that?"

"I said she's *not home*," says Benjy. "Cripes! So you'll never guess who called looking for you!"

"Who?" I ask, thinking of my father.

"I guess the Navy thinks it's okay to enlist *suicidal maniacs*," says the bear.

"James called? He really called me? From the *Navy*? Did you give him my number?"

"Yes. And don't get so excited," says Benjy. "He's sailing the South Seas, a million miles away. It's not like he called for a date. Besides, what am I, chopped *liver*?" This is classic Benjy, one of his favorite questions.

"No. *I'm* a chopped liver," I say. "James is a chopped liver."

"What the hell are you talking about?" Benjy demands.

"Nothing," I say. "Forget it."

"How's school?" says Benjy. "Do you hate it? Do you miss me?"

"Well," I say, and trail off.

"Yes?" says Benjy.

"Can you keep a secret?"

"Can I! Of course I can."

"Don't tell my mother," I say.

"Never!"

"Okay. Here goes." I pause.

"Tell me!" cries Benjy. "I can't take the suspense!"

"The secret is that all her worst predictions are true." I pause again.

"What do you mean?"

"I mean I love it here and I'm never coming back." For once, Benjy says nothing. "I have a million friends. And I'm so busy giving blow jobs to professors that I can't see straight."

"Shut up!" Benjy screams. "Don't say that. Just shut up!" Benjy is hysterical now, like a girl in a slasher movie.

"Mom?" I say. "Talk to me." A group of girls wanders by, headed to the lounge. They are dressed in pajamas and head scarves, and they are dissecting each other's strategies for sorority rush. They walk past without looking at me. I am huddled deep in the dark phone booth, the glass door pulled shut. There is such a long silence that I think I might have been cut off. The girls pass, and I hear their laughter trailing off.

"Talk to me, Mom," I say. "Please."

"She's not home," says Benjy, in a girly whisper. "I told you a million times."

Sometimes we miss our connections. We run frantically after buses, hailing them, knowing the driver sees us growing smaller in his mirror. When James finally called me, a few weeks later, I ran down the hallway to the phone booth. I was the only person who used that phone, for the rest of the girls on the hall had lines in their rooms. The ringing was fierce. When I answered the line there was only a strange humming. "Hello?" I said again, and waited. Just as I went to hang up I heard my name, faint and mechanical, followed by a click. "James?" I said.

"It's ship to shore," said a voice, followed by another click.

"What?"

"Ship to shore," came the answer, five seconds later.

"James? Where are you?" I said.

"Don't say anything," said a voice, after a pause. It sounded faintly like James. "I want to see you. Can I see you?" Every time James spoke, the sound of his voice was followed by static. I couldn't tell when to speak. There was a long silence. "You're my only friend in the world," said James, and then the line was taken over with squeals.

"James!" I said. "Yes. Please." But the line was dead.

Our conversation was strangled by the strange technology of ship-to-shore, which I hadn't understood. We spoke over each other's words, impatient to be heard and answered. Something had cut us off, some loose wire, some crashing wave, and we never spoke again.

Weeks later I received a newspaper clipping from my mother. It was Jame's obituary. He had swallowed a bottle of sleeping pills, stowed in a ship somewhere in the Pacific. The newspaper had printed a picture of James in uniform. He wore a stoic expression under his ocean-liner shaped cap. I could just barely see his features, his scars.

I knew that James had died without ever hearing my answer, that I wanted to see him. I knew that we might have saved each other. Instead James had escaped, had simply fallen asleep, tucked in his bunk, lulled by waves. When I thought of him I choked, wondering about that dark, narrow corner in which he died, and whether he was calm, or scared, or lonely. Or perhaps, finally, at peace.

There was no escape for me. I thought constantly of James. I thought of my mother, who I imagined playing her organ late into the night or absently stroking Benjy's fur, staring at the television. I thought of my father half-paralyzed in a nursing home, looking out the window, expecting someone, wanting a milkshake, wanting a radio. It was nearly impossible to bear, this burden of adulthood, which James had understood all his life. Sooner or later, finding ourselves alone, we all came to appreciate the importance of outcasts.

Nominated by Joyce Carol Oates

ECCLESIASTES

by KHALED MATTAWA

from MIZNA

The trick is that you're willing to help them.
The rule is to sound like you're doing them a favor.

The rule is to create a commission system.
The trick is to get their identification number.

The trick is to make it personal:
No one in the world suffers like you.

The trick is to make it local:
We have branches everywhere.

The rule is their parents were foolish,
their children are greedy or insane.

The trick is that you're providing a service.
The rule is to keep the conversation going.

And when they say "too much"
give them an installment plan.

The rule is to make them feel they've come too late.
The trick is that you're willing to make exceptions.

The trick is to sound like the one teacher they loved.
The rule is to assume their parents abused them.

And when the say "anger" or "rage" or "love,"
say "give me an example."

The trick is they feel you have all the time in the world.
The rule is to get them signed up as soon as possible.

The rule is everyone is a gypsy now.
Everyone is searching for his tribe.

The rule is you don't care if they ever find it.
The trick is that they feel they can.

Nominated by Alan Michael Parker

THE DYSTOPIANIST, THINKING OF HIS RIVAL, IS INTERRUPTED BY A KNOCK ON THE DOOR

fiction by JONATHAN LETHEM

from CONJUNCTIONS

THE DYSTOPIANIST DESTROYED the world again that morning, before making any phone calls or checking his mail, before even breakfast. He destroyed it by cabbages. The Dystopianist's scribbling fingers pushed notes onto the page: a protagonist, someone, *a tousle-haired, well-intentioned geneticist*, had designed a new kind of cabbage for use as a safety device—the *"air bag cabbage."* The air bag cabbage mimicked those decorative cabbages planted by the sides of roads to spell names of towns, or arranged by color—red, white, and that eerie, iridescent cabbage indigo—to create American flags. It looked like any other cabbage. But underground was a network of gas-bag roots, *vast inflatable roots*, filled with pressurized air. So, *at the slightest tap*, no, more than a tap, or vandals would set them off for fun, right, *given a serious blow such as only a car traveling at thirty miles or more per hour could deliver*, the heads of the air bag cabbages would instantly inflate, drawing air from the root system, to cushion the impact of the crash, saving lives, *preventing costly property loss*. Only—

The Dystopianist pushed away from his desk, and squinted through the blinds at the sun-splashed street below. School buses lined his block every morning, like vast tipped orange juice cartons spilling out the human vitamin of youthful lunacy, that chaos of jeering voices and dancing tangled shadows in the morning light. The Dystopianist was hungry for breakfast. He didn't know yet how the misguided safety cabbages fucked up the world. He couldn't say what *grievous chain of circumstance* led from the *innocuous genetic novelty* to another *crushing totalitarian regime*. He didn't know what light the cabbages shed on the *death urge in human societies*. He'd work it out, though. That was his job. First Monday of each month the Dystopianist came up with his idea, the *green poison fog* or *dehumanizing fractal download* or *alienating architectural fad* which would open the way to another ruined or oppressed reality. Tuesday he began making his extrapolations, and he had the rest of the month to get it right. Today was Monday, so the cabbages were enough.

The Dystopianist moved into the kitchen, poured a second cup of coffee, and pushed slices of bread into the toaster. The *Times* "Metro" section headline spoke of the capture of a celebrated villain, an addict and killer who'd crushed a pedestrian's skull with a cobblestone. The Dystopianist read his paper while scraping his toast with shreds of ginger marmalade, knife rushing a little surf of butter ahead of the crystalline goo. He read intently to the end of the account, taking pleasure in the story.

The Dystopianist hated bullies. He tried to picture himself standing behind darkened glass, fingering perps in a lineup, couldn't. He tried to picture himself standing in the glare, head flinched in arrogant dejection, waiting to be fingered, but this was even more impossible. He stared at the photo of the apprehended man and unexpectedly the Dystopianist found himself thinking vengefully, hatefully, of his rival.

Once the Dystopianist had had the entire Dystopian field to himself. There was just him and the Utopianists. The Dystopianist loved reading the Utopianists' stories, their dim, hopeful scenarios, which were published in magazines like *Expectant* and *Encouraging*. The Dystopianist routinely purchased them newly minted from the newsstands and perverted them the very next day in his own work, plundering the Utopianists' motifs for dark inspiration. Even the garishly sunny illustrated covers of the magazines were fuel. The Dystopianist stripped them from the magazines' spines and pinned them up over his desk, then raised his pen like Death's sickle and plunged those dreamily ineffectual worlds into ruin.

The Utopianists were older men who'd come into the field from the sciences or from academia: Professor this or that, like Dutch Burghers from a cigar box. The Dystopianist had appeared in print like a rat among them, a burrowing animal laying turds on their never-to-be-realized blueprints. He liked his role. Every once in a blue moon the Dystopianist agreed to appear in public alongside the Utopianists, on a panel at a university or conference. They loved to gather, *the fools*, in fluorescent-lit halls behind tables decorated with sweating pitchers of ice water. They were always eager to praise him in public by calling him one of their own. The Dystopianist ignored them, refusing even the water from their pitchers. He played directly to the audience members who'd come to see him, who shared his low opinion of the Utopianists. The Dystopianist could always spot his readers by their black trench coats, their acne, their greasily teased hair, their earphones, resting around their collars, trailing to Walkmans secreted in coat pockets.

The Dystopianist's rival was a Utopianist, but he wasn't like the others.

The Dystopianist had known his rival, the man he privately called *the Dire One*, since they were children like those streaming in the schoolyard below. *Eeny-meeny-miney-moe!* they'd chanted together, each trembling in fear of being permanently "*It*," of never casting off their permanent case of *cooties*. They weren't quite friends, but the Dystopianist and the Dire One had been bullied together by the older boys, quarantined in their shared nerdishness, forced to pool their resentments. In glum resignation they'd swapped Wacky Packages stickers and algebra homework answers, offered sticks of Juicy Fruit and squares of Now-N-Later, forging a loser's deal of consolation.

Then they were separated after junior high school, and the Dystopianist forgot his uneasy schoolmate.

It was nearly a year now since the Dire Utopianist had first arrived in print. The Dystopianist had trundled home with the latest issue of *Heartening*, expecting the usual laughs, and been blind-sided instead by the Dire Utopianist's first story. The Dystopianist didn't recognize his rival by name, but he knew him for a rival instantly.

The Dire Utopianist's trick was to write in a style which was *nominally* Utopian. His fantasies were nearly as credible as everyday experience, but bathed in a radiance of glory. They glowed with wishfulness. The other Utopianists' stories were crude candy floss by comparison. The Dire Utopianist's stories weren't blunt or ideological. He'd invented an *aesthetics* of utopia.

Fair enough. If he'd stopped at this burnished, closely observed dream of human life, the Dire Utopianist would be no threat. Sure, heck, let there be one genius among the Utopianist, all the better. It raised the bar. The Dystopianist took the Dire One's mimetic brilliance as a spur of inspiration: Look closer! Make it real!

But the Dire Utopianist didn't play fair. He didn't stop at utopianism, no. He poached on the Dystopianist's turf, he encroached. By limning a world so subtly transformed, so barely *nudged* into the ideal, the Dire One's fictions cast a shadow back onto the everyday. They induced a despair of inadequacy in the real. Turning the last page of one of the Dire Utopianist's stories, the reader felt a mortal pang at slipping back into his own daily life, which had been proved morbid, crushed, unfair.

This was the Dire One's pitiless art: *his utopias wrote reality itself into the most persuasive dystopia imaginable.* At the Dystopianist's weak moments he knew his stories were by comparison contrived and crotchety, their darkness forced.

It was six weeks ago that *Vivifying* had published the Dire One's photograph, and the Dystopianist had recognized his childhood acquaintance.

The Dire Utopianist never appeared in public. There was no clamor for him to appear. In fact, he wasn't even particularly esteemed among the Utopianists, an irony which rankled the Dystopianist. It was as though the Dire One didn't mind seeing his work buried in the insipid Utopian magazines. He didn't seem to crave recognition of any kind, let alone the hard-won oppositional stance the Dystopianist treasured. It was almost as though the Dire One's stories, posted in public, were really private messages of reproach from one man to the other. Sometimes the Dystopianist wondered if he were in fact the *only* reader the Dire Utopianist had, and the only one he wanted.

The cabbages were hopeless, he saw now.

Gazing out the window over his coffee's last plume of steam at the humming, pencil-colored school buses, he suddenly understood the gross implausibility: a rapidly inflating cabbage could never have the *stopping power* to alter the fatal trajectory of a *careening steel egg carton full of young lives*. A cabbage might halt a Hyundai, maybe a Volvo. Never a school bus. Anyway, the cabbages as an image had no implications, no *reach*. They said nothing about mankind. They were, finally, completely stupid and lame. He gulped the last of his coffee, angrily.

He had to go deeper, find something resonant, something to crawl beneath the skin of reality and render it monstrous from within. He paced to the sink, began rinsing his coffee mug. A tiny pod of silt had settled at the bottom and now, under a jet of cold tap water, the grains rose and spread and danced, a model of Chaos. The Dystopianist retraced his seed of inspiration: *well-intentioned, bumbling geneticist*, good. Good enough. The geneticist needed to stumble onto something better, though.

One day, when the Dystopianist and the Dire Utopianist had been in the sixth grade at Intermediate School 293, cowering together in a corner of the schoolyard to duck sports and fights and girls in one deft multipurpose cower, they had arrived at one safe island of mutual interest: comic books, Marvel brand, which anyone who read them understood weren't comic at all but deadly, breathtakingly serious. Marvel constructed worlds of splendid complexity, full of chilling, ancient villains and tormented heroes, in richly unfinished storylines. There in the schoolyard, wedged for cover behind the girls' lunch hour game of hopscotch, the Dystopianist declared his favorite character: *Doctor Doom*, antagonist of the Fantastic Four. Doctor Doom wore a forest green cloak and hood over a metallic, slitted mask and armor. He was a dark king who from his gnarled castle ruled a city of hapless serfs. An imperial, self-righteous monster. The Dire Utopianist murmured his consent. Indeed, Doctor Doom was awesome, an honorable choice. The Dystopianist waited for the Dire Utopianist to declare his favorite.

"Black Bolt," said the Dire Utopianist.

The Dystopianist was confused. *Black Bolt* wasn't a villain or a hero. Black Bolt was part of an outcast band of mutant characters known as *The Inhumans*, the noblest among them. He was their leader, but he never spoke. His only *demonstrated* power was flight, but the whole point of Black Bolt was the power he restrained himself from using: speech. The sound of his voice was cataclysmic, an unusable weapon, like an Atomic Bomb. If Black Bolt ever uttered a syllable the world would crack in two. Black Bolt was leader *in absentia* much of the time—he had a tendency to exile himself from the scene, to wander distant mountaintops contemplating—what? His curse? The things he would say if he could safely speak?

It was an unsettling choice there, amidst the feral shrieks of the schoolyard. The Dystopianist changed the subject, and never raised the question of Marvel Comics with the Dire Utopianist again. Alone behind the locked door of his bedroom the Dystopianist studied Black Bolt's behavior, seeking hints of the character's appeal to his schoolmate. Perhaps the answer lay in a storyline elsewhere in the Marvel universe, one where Black Bolt shucked off his pensiveness to function as an unrestrained hero or villain. If so, the Dystopianist never found the comic book in question.

Suicide, the Dystopianist concluded now. The geneticist should be studying suicide, seeking to isolate it as a factor in the human genome. *The Sylvia Plath Code*, that might be the title of the story. The geneticist could be trying to *reproduce it in a nonhuman species*. Right, good. To breed for suicide in animals, to produce a creature with the impulse to take its own life. That had the relevance the Dystopianist was looking for. What animals? Something poignant and pathetic, something pure. Sheep. *The Sylvia Plath Sheep*, that was it.

A variant of sheep had been bred for the study of suicide. The Sylvia Plath Sheep had to be kept on close watch, like a prisoner stripped of sharp implements, shoelaces and belt. And the Plath Sheep escapes, right, of course, *a Frankenstein creature always escapes*, but the twist is that the Plath Sheep is dangerous only to itself. *So what?* What harm if a single sheep quietly, discreetly offs itself? *But the Plath Sheep*, scribbling fingers racing now, the Dystopianist was on fire, *the Plath Sheep turns out to have the gift of communicating its despair.* Like the monkeys on that island, who learned from one another to wash clams, or break them open with coconuts, whatever it was the monkeys had learned, look into it later, *the Plath Sheep evoked suicide in other creatures*, all up and down the food chain. Not humans, but anything else which crossed its path. Cats, dogs, cows, beetles, clams. Each creature would spread suicide to another, to five or six others, before *searching out a promontory from which to plunge to its death.* The human species would be powerless to reverse the craze, the epidemic of suicide among the nonhuman species of the planet.

Okay! Right! Let goddamn Black Bolt open his mouth and sing an aria—he couldn't halt the Plath Sheep in its *deadly spiral of despair!*

The Dystopianist suddenly had a vision of the Plath Sheep wandering its way into the background of one of the Dire One's tales. It would go unremarked at first, a bucolic detail. Unwrapping its bleak gift of *global animal suicide* only after it had been taken entirely for granted, just as the Dire One's own little nuggets of despair were smuggled innocuously into his Utopias. The Plath Sheep was a bullet of pure dystopian intention. The Dystopianist wanted to fire it in the Dire Utopianist's direction. Maybe he'd send this story to *Encouraging*.

Even better, he'd like it if he could send the Plath Sheep itself to the door of the Dire One's writing room. *Here's your tragic mute Black Bolt, you bastard!* Touch its somber muzzle, dry its moist obsidian eyes, runny with sleep-goo. Try to talk it down from the parapet, if you have the courage of your ostensibly rosy convictions. Explain to the Sylvia Plath Sheep why life is worth living. Or, failing that, let the sheep convince you to follow it up to the brink, and go. You and the sheep, pal, take a fall.

There was a knock on the door.

The Dystopianist went to the door and opened it. Standing in the corridor was a sheep. The Dystopianist checked his watch—9:45. He wasn't sure why it mattered to him what time it was, but it did. He found it reassuring. The day still stretched before him; he'd have plenty of time to resume work after this interruption. He still heard the children's voices leaking in through the front window from the street below. The children arriving now were late for school. There were always hundreds who were late. He wondered if the sheep had waited with the children for the crossing guard to wave it on. He wondered if the sheep had crossed at the green, or recklessly dared the traffic to kill it.

He'd persuaded himself that the sheep was voiceless. So it was a shock when it spoke. "May I come in?" said the sheep.

"Yeah, sure," said the Dystopianist, fumbling his words. Should he offer the sheep the couch, or a drink of something? The sheep stepped into the apartment, just far enough to allow the door to be closed behind it, then stood quietly working its nifty little jaw back and forth, and blinking. Its eyes were not watery at all.

"So," said the sheep, nodding its head at the Dystopianist's desk, the mass of yellow legal pads, the sharpened pencils bunched in their holder, the typewriter. "This is where the magic happens." The sheep's tone was wearily sarcastic.

"It isn't usually *magic*," said the Dystopianist, then immediately regretted the remark.

"Oh, I wouldn't say that," said the sheep, apparently unruffled. "You've got a few things to answer for."

"Is that what this is?" said the Dystopianist. "Some kind of reckoning?"

"Reckoning?" The sheep blinked as though confused. "Who said anything about a reckoning?"

"Never mind," said the Dystopianist. He didn't want to put words into the sheep's mouth. Not now. He'd let it represent itself, and try to be patient.

But the sheep didn't speak, only moved in tiny, faltering steps on the carpet, advancing very slightly into the room. The Dystopianist wondered if the sheep might be scouting for sharp corners on the furniture, for chances to do itself harm by butting with great force against his fixtures.

"Are you—very depressed?" asked the Dystopianist.

The sheep considered the question for a moment. "I've had better days, let's put it that way."

Finishing the thought, it stared up at him, eyes still dry. The Dystopianist met its gaze, then broke away. A terrible thought occurred to him: the sheep might be expecting *him* to relieve it for its life.

The silence was ponderous. The Dystopianist considered another possibility. Might his rival have come to him in disguised form?

He cleared his throat before speaking. "You're not, ah, *the Dire One*, by any chance?" The Dystopianist was going to be awfully embarrassed if the sheep didn't know what he was talking about.

The sheep made a solemn, wheezing sound, like *"Hurrrrhh."* Then it said, "I'm *dire* all right. But I'm hardly the only one."

"Who?" blurted the Dystopianist.

"Take a look in the mirror, friend."

"What's your point?" The Dystopianist was sore now. If the sheep thought he was going to be manipulated into suicide it had *another think coming*.

"Just this: how many sheep have to die to assuage your childish resentments?" Now the sheep had assumed an odd false tone, plummy

72

like that of a commercial pitchman: *"They laughed when I sat down at the Dystopiano! But when I began to play—"*

"Very funny."

"We try, we try. Look, could you at least offer me a dish of water or something? I had to take the stairs—couldn't reach the button for the elevator."

Silenced, the Dystopianist hurried into the kitchen and filled a shallow bowl with water from the tap. Then, thinking twice, he poured it back into the sink and replaced it with mineral water from the bottle in the door of his refrigerator. When he set it out the sheep lapped gratefully, steadily, seeming to the Dystopianist an animal at last.

"Okay." It licked its lips. "That's it, Doctor Doom. I'm out of here. Sorry for the intrusion, next time I'll call. I just wanted, you know— a look at you."

The Dystopianist couldn't keep from saying, "You don't want to die?"

"Not today," was the sheep's simple reply. The Dystopianist stepped carefully around the sheep to open the door, and the sheep trotted out. The Dystopianist trailed it into the corridor and summoned the elevator. When the cab arrived and the door opened the Dystopianist leaned in and punched the button for the lobby.

"Thanks," said the sheep. "It's the little things that count."

The Dystopianist tried to think of a proper farewell, but couldn't before the elevator door shut. The sheep was facing the rear of the elevator cab, another instance of its poor grasp of etiquette.

Still, the sheep's visit wasn't the worst the Dystopianist could imagine. It could have attacked him, or tried to gore itself on his kitchen knives. The Dystopianist was still proud of the Plath Sheep, and rather glad to have met it, even if the Plath Sheep wasn't proud of him. Besides, the entire episode had only cost the Dystopianist an hour or so of his time. He was back at work, eagerly scribbling out implications, extrapolations, another illustrious downfall, well before the yelping children reoccupied the schoolyard at lunchtime.

Nominated by Joyce Carol Oates, Conjunctions

GATE C22

by ELLEN BASS

from THE MISSOURI REVIEW

At gate C 22 in the Portland airport
a man in a broad-band leather hat kissed
a woman arriving from Orange County.
They kissed and kissed and kissed. Long after

the other passengers clicked the handles of their carry-ons
and wheeled briskly toward short-term parking,
the couple stood there, arms wrapped around each other
like satin ribbons tying up a gift. And kissing.

Like she'd just staggered off the boat at Ellis Island,
like she'd been released from ICU, snapped
out of a coma, survived bone cancer, made it down
from Annapurna in only the clothes she was wearing.

Neither of them was young. His beard was gray.
She carried a few extra pounds you could imagine
she kept saying she had to lose. But they kissed lavish
kisses like the ocean in the early morning

of a calm day at Big Sur, the way it gathers
and swells, taking each rock slowly
in its mouth, sucking it under, swallowing it
again and again. We were all watching—

the passengers waiting for the delayed flight to San Jose,
the stewardesses, the pilots, the aproned woman icing
Cinnabons, the guy selling sunglasses. We couldn't
look away. We could taste the kisses, crushed

in our mouths like the liquid centers of chocolate cordials.
But the best part was his face. When he drew back
and looked at her, his smile soft with wonder, almost
as though he were a mother still

opened from giving birth, like your mother
must have looked at you,
no matter what happened after—
if she beat you, or left you, or you're lonely now—

you once lay there, the vernix
not yet wiped off and someone gazing at you
like you were the first sunrise seen from the earth.
The whole wing of the airport hushed,

each of us trying to slip into that woman's middle-aged body,
her plaid bermuda shorts, sleeveless blouse,
little gold hoop earrings, glasses,
all of us, tilting our heads up.

Nominated by Beth Ann Fennelly, Carol Potter, The Missouri Review

A MEASURE OF ACCEPTANCE

memoir by FLOYD SKLOOT

from CREATIVE NONFICTION

THE PSYCHIATRIST'S OFFICE was in a run-down industrial section at the northern edge of Oregon's capital, Salem. It shared space with a chiropractic health center, separated from it by a temporary divider that wobbled in the current created by opening the door. When I arrived a man sitting with his gaze trained on the spot I suddenly filled began kneading his left knee, his suit pants hopelessly wrinkled in that one spot. Another man, standing beside the door and dressed in overalls, studied the empty wall and muttered as he slowly rose on his toes and sank back on his heels. Like me, neither seemed happy to be visiting Dr. Peter Avilov.

Dr. Avilov specialized in the psychodiagnostic examination of disability claimants for the Social Security Administration. He made a career of weeding out hypochondriacs, malingerers, fakers, people who were ill without organic causes. There may be many such scam artists working the disability angle, but there are also many legitimate claimants. Avilov worked as a kind of hired gun, paid by an agency whose financial interests were best served when he determined that claimants were not disabled. It was like having your house appraised by the father-in-law of your prospective buyer, like being stopped by a traffic cop several tickets shy of his monthly quota, like facing a part-time judge who works for the construction company you're suing. Avilov's incentives were not encouraging to me.

I understood why I was there. After a virus I contracted in December of 1988 targeted my brain, I became totally disabled. When the Social Security Administration decided to re-evaluate my medical condition eight years later, they exercised their right to send me to a doctor of their own choosing. This seemed fair enough. But after receiving records, test results and reports of brain scans and statements from my own internal-medicine and infectious-diseases physicians, all attesting to my ongoing disability, and after requiring 25 pages of handwritten questionnaires from me and my wife, they scheduled an appointment for me with Avilov. Not with an independent internal-medicine or infectious-diseases specialist, not with a neurologist, but with a shrink.

Now, 12 years after first getting sick, I've become adept at being brain-damaged. It's not that my symptoms have gone away; I still try to dice a stalk of celery with a carrot instead of a knife, still reverse "p" and "b" when I write, or draw a primitive hourglass when I mean to draw a star. I call our *bird feeder* a *bread winner* and place newly purchased packages of frozen corn in the dishwasher instead of the freezer. I put crumpled newspaper and dry pine into our wood stove, strike a match, and attempt to light the metal door. Preparing to cross the "main street" in Carlton, Ore., I look both ways, see a pickup truck a quarter-mile south, take one step off the curb, and land flat on my face, cane pointing due east.

So I'm still much as I was in December of 1988, when I first got sick. I spent most of a year confined to bed. I couldn't write and had trouble reading anything more complicated than People magazine or the newspaper's sports page. The functioning of memory was shattered, bits of the past clumped like a partly assembled jigsaw puzzle, the present a flicker of discontinuous images. Without memory it was impossible for me to learn how to operate the new music system that was meant to help me pass the time, or figure out why I felt so confused, or take my medications without support.

But in time I learned to manage my encounters with the world in new ways. I shed what no longer fit my life: training shoes and road-racing flats, three-piece suits and ties, a car. I bought a cane. I seeded my home with pads and pens so that I could write reminders before forgetting what I'd thought. I festooned my room with color-coded Post-it Notes telling me what to do, whom to call, where to locate important items. I remarried, finding love when I imagined it no longer possible. Eventually I moved to the country, slowing my external life to match its internal pace, simplifying, stripping away layers of distraction and demands.

Expecting the unexpected now, I can, like an improvisational actor, incorporate it into my performance. For instance my tendency to use words that are close to—but not exactly—the words I'm trying to say has led to some surprising discoveries in the composition of sentences. A freshness emerges when the mind is unshackled from its habitual ways. I never would have described the effect of a viral attack on my brain as being "geezered" overnight if I hadn't first confused the words *seizure* and *geezer*. It is as though my word-finding capacity has developed an associative function to compensate for its failures of precision, so I end up with *shellac* instead of *plaque* when trying to describe the gunk on my teeth. Who knows, maybe James Joyce was brain-damaged when he wrote "Finnegan's Wake," built a whole novel on puns and neologisms that were actually symptoms of disease.

It's possible to see such domination of the unexpected in a positive light. So getting lost in the familiar woods around our house and finding my way home again adds a twist of excitement to days that might seem circumscribed or routine because of my disability. When the natural-food grocery where we shop rearranged its entire stock, I was one of the few customers who didn't mind, since I could never remember where things were anyway. I am less hurried and more deliberate than I was; being attentive, purposeful in movement, lends my life an intensity of awareness that was not always present before. My senses are heightened, their fine-tuning mechanism busted. Spicy food, stargazer lilies in bloom, birdsong, heat, my wife's vivid palette when she paints—all have become more intense and stimulating. Because it threatens my balance, a sudden breeze is something to stop for, to let its strength and motion register. That may not guarantee success—as my pratfall in Carlton indicates—but it does allow me to appreciate detail and nuance.

One way of spinning this is to say that my daily experience is often spontaneous and exciting. Not fragmented and intimidating, but unpredictable, continuously new. I may lose track of things, or of myself in space, my line of thought, but instead of getting frustrated, I try to see this as the perfect time to stop and figure out what I want or where I am. I accept my role in the harlequinade. It's not so much a matter of making lemonade out of life's lemons but rather of learning to savor the shock, taste, texture and aftereffects of a mouthful of unadulterated citrus.

Acceptance is a deceptive word. It suggests compliance, a consenting to my condition and to who I have become. This form of acceptance is often seen as weakness, submission. We say *I accept my punishment*. Or *I accept your decision*. But such assent, while passive in essence, does provide the stable, rocklike foundation for coping with a condition that will not go away. It is a powerful passivity, the Zen of Illness, that allows for endurance.

There is, however, more than endurance at stake. A year in bed, another year spent primarily in my recliner—these were times when endurance was the main issue. But over time I began to recognize the possibilities for transformation. I saw another kind of acceptance as being viable, the kind espoused by Robert Frost when he said, "Take what is given, and make it over your own way." That is, after all, the root meaning of the verb "to accept," which comes from the Latin *accipere*, or "to take to oneself." It implies an embrace. Not a giving up but a welcoming. People encourage the sick to resist, to fight back; we say that our resistance is down when we contract a virus. But it wasn't possible to resist the effects of brain damage. Fighting to speak rapidly and clearly, as I always had in the past, only leads to more garbling of meaning; willing myself to walk without a cane or climb a ladder only leads to more falls; demanding that I not forget something only makes me angrier when all I can remember is the effort not to forget. I began to realize that the most aggressive act I could perform on my own behalf was to stop struggling and discover what I really could do.

This, I believe, is what the Austrian psychotherapist Viktor E. Frankl refers to in his classic book, "The Doctor and the Soul," as "spiritual elasticity." He says, speaking of his severely damaged patients, "Man must cultivate the flexibility to swing over to another value-group if that group and that alone offers the possibility of actualizing values." Man must, Frankl believes, "temper his efforts to the chances that are offered."

Such shifts of value, made possible by active acceptance of life as it is, can only be achieved alone. Doctors, therapists, rehabilitation professionals, family members, friends, lovers cannot reconcile a person to the changes wrought by illness or injury, though they can ease the way. Acceptance is a private act, achieved gradually and with little outward evidence. It also seems never to be complete; I still get furious with myself for forgetting what I'm trying to tell my daughter during a phone call, humiliated when I blithely walk away with another shopper's cart of groceries or fall in someone's path while examining the lower shelves at Powell's Bookstore.

But for all its private essence, acceptance cannot be expressed purely in private terms. My experience did not happen to me alone; family, colleagues and friends, acquaintances all were involved. I had a new relationship with my employer and its insurance company, with federal and state government, with people who read my work. There is a social dimension to the experience of illness and to its acceptance, a kind of reciprocity between self and world that goes beyond the enactment of laws governing handicapped access to buildings or rules prohibiting discrimination in the workplace. It is in this social dimension that, for all my private adjustment, I remain a grave cripple and, apparently, a figure of contempt.

At least the parties involved agreed that what was wrong with me was all in my head. However, mine was disability arising from organic damage to the brain caused by a viral attack, not from psychiatric illness. The distinction matters; my disability status would not continue if my condition were psychiatric. It was in the best interests of the Social Security Administration for Dr. Avilov to say my symptoms were caused by the mind, were psychosomatic rather than organic in nature. And what was in their interests was also in Avilov's.

On high-tech scans, tiny holes in my brain make visually apparent what is clear enough to anyone who observes me in action over time: I no longer have "brains." A brain, yes, with many functions intact, but I'm not as smart or as quick or as steady as I was. Though I may not look sick, and I don't shake or froth or talk to myself, after a few minutes it becomes clear that something fundamental is wrong. My losses of cognitive capability have been fully measured and recorded. They were used by the Social Security Administration and the insurance company to establish my total disability, by various physicians to establish treatment and therapy programs, by a pharmaceutical company to establish my eligibility for participation in the clinical field trial of a drug that didn't work. I have a handicapped parking placard on the dashboard of my car; I can get a free return-trip token from the New York City subway system by flashing my Medicaid card. In

80

this sense I have a public profile as someone who is disabled. I have met the requirements.

Further, as someone with quantifiable diminishment in IQ levels, impaired abstract reasoning and learning facility, scattered recall capacities and aptitudes that decrease as fatigue or distraction increases, I am of scientific use. When it serves their purposes, various institutions welcome me. Indeed they pursue me. I have been actively recruited for three experimental protocols run by Oregon Health Sciences University. One of these, a series of treatments using DMSO, made me smell so rancid that I turned heads just by walking into a room. But when it does not serve their purposes, these same institutions dismiss me. Or challenge me. No matter how well I may have adjusted to living with brain damage, the world I often deal with has not. When money or status is involved, I am positioned as a pariah.

So would Avilov find that my disability was continuing, or would he judge me as suffering from mental illness? Those who say that the distinction is bogus, or that the patient's fear of being labeled mentally ill is merely a cultural bias and ought not to matter, are missing the point. Money is at stake; in our culture this means it matters very much. To all sides.

Avilov began by asking me to recount the history of my illness. He seemed as easily distracted as I was; while I stared at his checked flannel shirt, sweetly ragged mustache and the pen he occasionally put in his mouth like a pipe, Avilov looked from my face to his closed door to his empty notepad and back to my face, nodding. When I finished, he asked a series of diagnostic questions: Did I know what day it was (Hey, I'm here on the right day, aren't I?), could I name the presidents of the United States since Kennedy, could I count backward from 100 by sevens? During this series he interrupted me to provide a list of four unconnected words (such as *train argue barn vivid*), which I was instructed to remember for later recall. Then he asked me to explain what was meant by the expression "People who live in glass houses should not throw stones." I nodded, thought for a moment, knew that this sort of proverb relied on metaphor, which as a poet should be my great strength, and began to explain. Except that I couldn't. I must have talked for five minutes, in tortuous circles, spewing gobbledygook about stones breaking glass and people having things to hide, shaking my head, backtracking as I tried to elaborate. But it was beyond me, as all abstract thinking is beyond me, and I soon drifted into stunned silence. Crashing into your limitations this way hurts; I remembered as a long-distance runner hitting the fabled "wall" at about mile 22 of the Chicago Marathon, my body depleted of all energy resources, feeding on its own muscle and fat for every additional step, and I recognized this as being a similar sensation.

For the first time, I saw something clear in Avilov's eyes. He saw me. He recognized this as real, the blathering of a brain-damaged man who still thinks he can think.

It was at this moment that he asked, "Why are you here?"

I nearly burst into tears, knowing that he meant I seemed to be suffering from organic rather than mental illness. Music to my ears. "I have the same question."

The rest of our interview left little impression. But when the time came for me to leave, I stood to shake his hand and realized that Avilov had forgotten to ask me if I remembered the four words I had by then forgotten. I did remember having to remember them, though. Would it be best to walk out of the room, or should I remind him that he forgot to have me repeat the words I could no longer remember? Or had I forgotten that he did ask me, lost as I was in the fog of other failures? Should I say *I can't remember if you asked me to repeat those words, but there's no need because I can't remember them?*

None of that mattered because Avilov, bless his heart, had found that my disability status remained as it was. Such recommendations arrive as mixed blessings; I would much rather not be as I am, but since I am, I must depend on receiving the legitimate support I paid for when healthy and am entitled to now.

There was little time to feel relieved because I soon faced an altogether different challenge, this time from the company that handled my disability-insurance payments. I was ordered to undergo a two-day "Functional Capacity Evaluation" administered by a rehabilitation firm they hired in Portland. A later phone call informed me to prepare for six and a half hours of physical challenges the first day and three hours more the following day. I would be made to lift weights, carry heavy boxes, push and pull loaded crates, climb stairs, perform various feats of balance and dexterity, complete puzzles, answer a barrage of questions. But I would have an hour for lunch.

Wear loose clothes. Arrive early.

With the letter had come a warning: "You must provide your best effort so that the reported measurements of your functional ability are valid." Again the message seemed clear: *No shenanigans, you! We're wise to your kind.*

I think the contempt that underlies these confrontations is apparent. The patient, or—in the lingo of insurance operations—the claimant, is approached not only as an adversary but as a deceiver. *You can climb more stairs than that! You really can stand on one leg like a heron! Stop falling over, freeloader! We know that game.* Paranoia rules; here an institution seems caught in its grip. With money at stake, the disabled are automatically supposed to be up to some kind of chicanery, and our displays of symptoms are viewed as untrustworthy. Never mind that I contributed to Social Security for my entire working life, with the mutual understanding that if I were disabled, the fund would be there for me. Never mind that both my employer and I paid for disability insurance, with the mutual understanding that if I were disabled, payments would be there for me. Our doctors are suspect, our caregivers implicated. *We've got our eyes on you!*

The rehab center looked like a combination gym and children's playground. The staff were friendly, casual. Several were administering physical therapy so that the huge room into which I was led smelled of sweat. An elderly man at a desk worked with a small stack of blocks. Above the blather of Muzak, I heard grunts and moans of pained effort: a woman lying on mats, being helped to bend damaged knees; a stiff-backed man laboring through his stretches; two women side by side on benches, deep in conversation as they curled small weights.

The man assigned to conduct my Functional Capacity Evaluation looked enough like me to be a cousin. Short, bearded, thick hair curling away from a lacy bald spot, Reggie shook my hand and tried to set me at ease. He was good at what he did, lowering the level of confrontation, expressing compassion, concerned about the effect on my health of such strenuous testing. I should let him know if I needed to stop.

Right then, before the action began, I had a moment of grave doubt. I could remain suspicious, paranoia begetting paranoia, or I could trust Reggie to be honest, to assess my capacities without prejudice. The presence of patients being helped all around me seemed a good sign. This firm didn't appear dependent upon referrals for evaluation from insurance companies; they had a lucrative operation independent of that. And if I could not trust a man who reminded me of a healthier version of myself, it seemed like bad karma. I loved games and physical challenges. But I knew who and what I was now; it would be fine if I simply let him know as well. Though much of my disability results from cognitive deficits, there are physical manifestations, too, so letting Reggie know me in the context of a gym-like setting felt comfortable. Besides, he was sharp enough to recognize suspicion in my eyes, which would give him reason to doubt my efforts. We were both after the same thing: a valid representation of my abilities. Now was the time to put all I had learned about acceptance on the line. It would require a measure of acceptance on both sides.

What I was not prepared for was how badly I would perform in every test. I knew my limitations but had never measured them. Over a dozen years, the consequences of exceeding my physical capabilities had been made clear enough that I learned to live within the limits. Here I was brought repeatedly to those limits and beyond. After an hour with Reggie, I was ready to sleep for the entire next month. The experience was crushing. How could I comfortably manage only 25 pounds in the floor-to-waist lift repetitions? I used to press 150 pounds as part of my regular weekly training for competitive racing. How could I not stand on my left foot for more than two seconds? You shoulda seen me on a ball field! I could hold my arms up for no more than 75 seconds, could push a cart loaded with no more than 40 pounds of weights, could climb only 66 stairs. I could not fit shapes into their proper holes in a form-board in the time allotted, though I distinctly remember playing a game with my son that worked on the same principles and always beating the timer. Just before lunch Reggie asked me to squat and lift a box filled with paper. He stood behind me and was there as I fell back into his arms.

As Dr. Avilov had already attested, I was not clinically depressed, but this evaluation was almost enough to knock me into the deepest despair. Reggie said little to reveal his opinions. At the time, I thought that meant that he was simply being professional, masking judgment, and though I sensed empathy, I realized that that could be a matter of projection on my part.

Later I believed that his silence came from knowing what he had still to make me do. After lunch and an interview about the Activities of Daily Living form I had filled out, Reggie led me to a field of blue mats spread across the room's center. For a moment I wondered if he planned to challenge me to a wrestling match. That thought had lovely, symbolic overtones: wrestling with someone who suggested my former self; wrestling with an agent of *them*, a man certain to defeat me; or having my Genesis experience, like Jacob at Peniel wrestling with Him. Which, at least for Jacob, resulted in a blessing and a nice payout.

But no. Reggie told me to crawl.

In order to obtain "a valid representation" of my abilities, it was necessary for the insurance company to see how far and for how long and with what result I could crawl. It was a test I had not imagined, a test that could, in all honesty, have only one purpose. My ability to crawl could not logically be used as a valid measure of my employability. And in light of all the other tasks I had been unable to perform, crawling was not necessary as a measure of my functional limits. It would test nothing, at least nothing specific to my case, not even the lower limits of my capacity. Carrying the malign odor of indifference, tyranny's tainted breath, the demand that I crawl was almost comical in its obviousness: the paternal powers turning someone like me, a disabled man living in dependence upon their finances, into an infant.

I considered refusing to comply. Though the implied threat (*You must provide your best effort . . .*) contained in their letter crossed my mind, and I wondered how Beverly and I would manage without my disability payments, it wasn't practicality that made me proceed. At least I don't think so. It was, instead, acceptance. I had spent the morning in a public confrontation with the fullness of my loss, as though on stage with Reggie, representing the insurance company, as my audience. Now I would confront the sheer heartlessness of The System, the powers that demanded that I crawl before they agreed temporarily to accept my disability. I would, perhaps for the first time, join the company of those far more damaged than I am, who have endured far more indignity in their quest for acceptance. Whatever it was that Reggie and the insurance company believed they were measuring as I got down on my hands and knees and began a slow circuit of the mats in the center of that huge room, I believed I was measuring how far we still had to go for acceptance.

Reggie stood in the center of the mats, rotating in place as I crawled along one side, turned at the corner, crossed to the opposite side, and began to return toward the point where I had started. Before I reached it, Reggie told me to stop. He had seen enough. I was slow and unsteady at the turns, but I could crawl fine.

I never received a follow-up letter from the insurance company. I was never formally informed of their findings, though my disability payments have continued.

At the end of the second day of testing, Reggie told me how I'd done. In many of the tests, my results were in the lower 5–10 percent for men my age. My performance diminished alarmingly on the second day, and he hadn't ever tested anyone who did as poorly on the dexterity components. He believed that I had given my best efforts and would report accordingly. But he would not give me any formal results. I was to contact my physician, who would receive Reggie's report in due time.

When the battery of tests had first been scheduled, I'd made an appointment to see my doctor a few days after their completion. I knew the physical challenges would worsen my symptoms and wanted him to see the result. I knew I would need his help. By the time I got there, he too had spoken to Reggie and knew about my performance. But my doctor never got an official report, either.

This was familiar ground. Did I wish to request a report? I was continuing to receive my legitimate payments; did I really want to contact my insurance company and demand to see the findings of my Functional Capacity Evaluation? Risk waking the sleeping dragon? What would be the point? I anticipated no satisfaction in reading that I was in fact disabled or in seeing how my experience translated into numbers or bureaucratic prose.

It seems that I was only of interest when there was an occasion to rule me ineligible for benefits. Found again to be disabled, I wasn't even due the courtesy of a reply. The checks came; what more did I need to show that my claims were accepted?

There was no need for a report. Through the experience, I had discovered something more vital than the measures of my physical capacity. The measure of public acceptance that I hoped to find, that I imagined would balance my private acceptance, was not going to come from a public agency or public corporation. It didn't work that way, after all. The public was largely indifferent, as most people, healthy or not, understand. The only measure of acceptance would come from how I conducted myself in public, moment by moment.

With laws in place to permit handicapped access to public spaces, prevent discrimination, and encourage involvement in public life, there is general acceptance that the handicapped live among us and must be accommodated. But that doesn't mean they're not resented, feared, or mistrusted by the healthy. The Disability Racket!

I had encountered the true, hard heart of the matter. My life in the social dimension of illness is governed by forces that are severe and implacable. Though activism has helped protect the handicapped over the last four decades, there is little room for reciprocity between the handicapped person and his or her world. It is naive to expect otherwise.

I would like to think that the insurance company didn't send an official letter of findings because they were abashed at what they'd put me through. I would like to think that Dr. Avilov, who no longer practices in Salem, didn't move away because he found too many claimants disabled and lost his contract with the Social Security Administration. That my experience educated Reggie and his firm and that his report educated the insurance company, so everyone now understands the experience of disability or of living with brain damage.

But I know better. My desire for reciprocity between self and world must find its form in writing about my experience. Slowly. This essay has taken me 11 months to complete, in sittings of 15 minutes or so. Built of fragments shaped after the pieces were examined, its errors of spelling and of word choice and logic ferreted out with the help of my wife or daughter or computer's spell-checker. It may look to a reader like the product of someone a lot less damaged than I claim to be. But it's not. It's the product of someone who has learned how to live with his limitations and work with them. And when it's published, if someone employed by my insurance company reads it, I will probably get a letter in the mail demanding that I report for another battery of tests. After all, this is not how a brain-damaged man is supposed to behave.

Nominated by Andrea Hollander Budy, Richard Burgin,
John Allman, Robert Gibb, Creative Nonfiction

THE GIRL IN THE BACK SEAT RETURNS TO PITTSBURGH

by JULIA KASDORF

from IMAGE

Now I see the statue at the traffic circle is not
a talk between Satan and some poor lady who
doesn't know her dress has fallen past her waist.

Lyre in one hand, the other waves witlessly
in the wind as her breasts float for all the world
to see; he doesn't care, too busy leering

at the girl in the back seat who hates
his lips and curly hair, gumdrop horns, and those
horrible hooves stuck on the ends of his legs.

The clammy glass rooms at Phipps Conservatory
make the girl woozy in her winter coat,
studying the textures of tropical tree trunks.

Only the chrysanthemum's acrid scent
clears her head. An ancient docent intones
It is the dark that makes them bloom.

Relentless budding forces yellow mums huge
and round as a girl's head, so heavy their stems
must be tied to sticks. Where the mills along 376

used to shoot lavender flames is only sky
and water now. I can't breathe, driving through
the Squirrel Hill tunnel, until I remember

the balloon cheeks of the girl in the back seat,
how I sucked and held my breath at times like this.
But it's great to breathe,

even in tunnels. Great to sit up front and drive
my own Chevrolet. Great to be able to read
the statue's inscription after all these years:

> *A Song to Nature—Pan the earth god*
> *answers to the harmony and magic tones*
> *sung to the lyre by sweet humanity.*

Amazing finally to see humanity figured
as a careless woman, singing; great to see earth
as a goaty man, such a relief to find this bald

fact cast in bronze: the woman must be
immodest—and never seem to mind at all—
if she wants to hear Pan answer her song.

Nominated by Image

HE AIN'T JESUS

fiction by MALINDA MCCOLLUM

from EPOCH

GREEN BOUGHT the one-room bank building on the outskirts of Des Moines for himself. An air mattress inflated in the vault, a candle in a jar of sand, and all that was left was to pick up a girl and a few bottles. In the morning, sun came through the bank door's ox-eye window and made him and the girl and the room red and holy. No, he thought, taking it all in, nobody knew everything about him yet.

He dropped off the girl and went home to his wife in town. Nora was sitting with his brother, Roy, at the kitchen table, biting toast and drinking coffee. The sight of them filled him with a rage both over-sized and misdirected, but he didn't resist it. These days he'd follow anything to wherever it led.

"And?" Nora said when she saw him.

"First this one unexpected thing happened," he said. "And then another thing and before you knew it, boom, it's dawn." He poured himself a cup of coffee from the percolator on the counter. "Plus traffic."

His wife picked up her cup and walked by Green, spilling coffee onto his shoe. She made it to the living room before he heard her begin to cry.

"A single lie is more convincing than a lot all at once," Roy said. "Asshole." He took hold of his brace, straightened his leg, and stood. He was younger than Green, but looked older, hair fine and thinning, nose copper, eyes set low in his face.

"There are enough good times in the world for us both," Green said. "No need to be jealous and call me mean names."

90

"So you're flying high," said Roy. "Well, here's something to bring you down. Butcher's skipped on his rent again." A year earlier the brothers had broken into real estate with a small profit from their engraving business. They assumed a loan on a house, and Green found a tenant who rented with the option to buy. Max Butcher was a self-employed contractor, and in the summer things were fine. But in the winter his jobs disappeared, and now he hadn't paid rent in three months.

"He's playing," Roy continued. "We need to boot him."

"Five kids," Green said. "I'm no sap, but he's got five kids and winter's here. Where's he going to go?"

"His daddy's a minister in town. Let the little lamb wander home."

Green agreed to talk to Butcher. But he went to Nora first. He sat beside her on the couch, and she let him dry her face with his thumbs.

"I was out all night hunting for teeth," he said, attempting fancy. "A dead person's teeth are a powerful ingredient in a potion for love."

"You hate me," she said. "How did I end up with a person who hates me? I always thought I loved myself better than that."

"I'm here now."

"Funny," she said. "I don't believe you."

His fingers were still on her face. He studied them. "I love you."

"Lucky me," she said.

He wished she could see herself, how good she looked angry, eyes darker, skin righteous and pink. He said, softly, "We've got time."

"Super," she said. "It's not over."

"It was a bad night." He took his hands away. "No more, no less."

"Here's what I want to ask," she said then and leaned forward, her contempt coming at him like a fist. "Do you ever get the urge to talk to me like a real person?"

He shouldn't have, but he made his face blank. "Real person?" he said. "Where's one of those?"

The house they rented to Butcher had a simple facade marred only by a strip of ornate fretwork—completely unsuited to the house—which a previous owner had carved badly and attached above the front door with nails. The same owner had replaced the house's serviceable concrete sidewalk with large fieldstones sunk into the lawn in an irregular path. The path had been recently shoveled, and

Green stepped over it surely. Standing on the porch, he could see the house's double-hung windows were lined, on the inside, with foil.

"I'm remodeling," Butcher said, opening the door. Since Green's last visit, Butcher had grown a soft dark mustache which nearly hid the tension in his lips. His skin was pebbly as an avocado's.

Green stepped through the door. Inside, pale light everywhere teased him. Dust hung in the air. A ladder up against the far wall rose to a top floor window. But the top floor itself had disappeared.

"Yeah," Green said, blinking, "I remember when this was a two-story house."

"More like one and a half, with those slanted ceilings." Butcher pointed to the low-pitched gable roof. "I couldn't abide that short little half-story. So I decided to lower the floor, to have more headroom up top. Had to tear out the staircase to do that. Had to tear out the existing floor."

The house looked useless. For the first time in a long time Green realized the importance of ceilings and walls.

"I have to say the house this way has its own kind of charm," Butcher said. "Like a big church. You know my daddy's a minister?"

Green walked through the house's first, and now only, floor. Gray chunks of plaster rested on the ground like geodes. It was so cold his breath condensed into steam when he asked, "Where's he preach?"

"You're not going to call the cops, are you?" Butcher had moved into the small kitchen, next to the stove, one hand on the unlit range.

"You think I should?"

"Naw, of course not. Hey, help yourself to a beer." He waved to the refrigerator.

Green joined him and removed a beer from the refrigerator's dark and lonely interior. "How long do you think this remodeling is going to take?" he asked carefully, sipping.

"Well, I started the job, but now with winter I'm not working. I don't have the cash to get what I need to finish. And that's where my trouble lies."

But there was no trouble in his voice. The lack of it made Green nervous. He took another drink. "Max," he said, "you're already behind on the rent. We've cut you a break these last few months, and I know you got a wife and all these kids."

"Wife's gone." Butcher cleared his throat. "I thought, when I married her, that she was a Proverbs 31-type girl. But I came to find out there wasn't much Bible about her." He touched his eyes, then wiped his fingers on his shirt. "Anyway, I'm doing this work for free. I hope you'll put that into consideration when I exercise my option to buy. Maybe work the price a little."

"Where's your daddy preach?" Green asked again. "Somewhere in town?"

"Look here," Butcher said. "Let me speak clearly now. Do you always get what you pray for?"

The abrupt switch required of Green just one moment. Then he thought of the things he prayed for: small steps toward wisdom, occasional moments of serenity, effortless achievement and fame.

"I guess I don't," he said.

"Does that mean that God's a liar? He's selling you a bill of goods?"

Green realized it was the kind of conversation in which he was supposed to be silent and let the other person expound.

"No, God answers your prayers. But it's not like going into the grocery store, picking out your bananas, taking them up to the stand. Praying's like casting a seed. You sow it, then you wait. It blooms on down the line. But you got to wait first."

"Are you telling me I need to wait?"

"I'm telling you to sow the seed. Prime the pump, my man. Then you can wait."

There was an expansiveness about him that Green suddenly suspected arose from some outside source. "Are you on something?" he asked Butcher. "What exactly are you taking?"

Butcher laughed, then came over and laid his hands on Green's shoulders. His breath smelled like gasoline. "There is what I'm supposed to be taking," he announced, "and then there is what I do, in fact, take."

Green nodded and shrugged off Butcher's hands. He could see it. Inside that gap, big things might be revealed.

From another place in the house a child moaned. Green followed Butcher into the living room. Homemade toys were scattered throughout the room—socks with buttons stitched on to make puppets, pieces of painted wood cut into smooth shapes. Three kids slept on a plaid sleeping bag unzipped in front of the fire. The littlest one wore fuzzy pajamas and a pair of Moon Boots.

"You're just dying to wake them up, aren't you?" Butcher said,

93

voice low and fond. "Sometimes I have a hard time letting them sleep." He walked over to the littlest child and nudged her sweetly with his foot.

"Wait," Green said. "Don't go and wake her up for me."

"For you?" Butcher laughed as the little girl made a small noise and stretched up her arms. "You think this is for you?" He lifted the girl and swung her through the air like a sack of flour.

Green started his car three times before the engine took hold. He watched Butcher's house diminish in the rear view mirror and then turned his attention to the snow-crusted roads leading home. When he passed the drive-through Chinese restaurant on Merle Hay he made a left turn and headed back. A line of cars waited, engines running, alongside the pink building overhung with a billboard that read EGGROLLS AND MILKSHAKES DONE RIGHT HERE. Green pulled into the line. When he advanced to the speaker and placed his order, he sensed in the voice that responded to him a boundless hostility, the very thing he was attempting, temporarily, to avoid. Was his complicity in all things fucked-up that apparent? Could people hear it in his voice? He drove home, melancholy, a bag of eggrolls warm in his lap.

Roy and Molly and Nora were in the basement, working on a big trophy order for a men's club on the south side. There was another order to engrave a message on the inside of a wedding band, but they saved expensive items like that for Green because—and it was a surprise to all of them—he had the steadiest hand. Nora set type the fastest, and that's what she was doing, laying new letters into the tray after Roy finished engraving each nameplate with the double-armed engraver. Molly sat at the end of the line, assembling the trophies, screwing tennis players onto marble bases and then attaching nameplates to the bases with two-sided tape.

Roy had started engraving in high school when their father thought it would be a good way to make money without straining his polio-stricken leg. He bought Roy an engraving machine, and Roy built up a small business doing trophies and plaques. Later he brought in Green, and eventually, their wives, who assumed more responsibility as the brothers made their foray into real estate. In addition to the house they rented to Butcher, they had purchased an apartment complex called the Coronado, the management of which consisted mostly of repair work on the building's washing machines which tenants jammed with wooden tokens that were almost quarter-sized.

Green set the bag of eggrolls on the ping-pong table in the center of the room. Roy and Molly and Nora stopped working and gathered around the food.

"What did Butcher say?" Roy asked, untying the bag.

"He was giving me lots of Bible talk. I think he's sunk way in."

"Remember that time I picked up his check last summer?" Molly said. She spoke in a high whispery voice that Green tried to resist but couldn't. "He told me weak-wombed women can conceive, but can't bring forth a child."

"He was talking about your womb?" Roy said.

Nora didn't say anything. She carefully unpeeled an eggroll, picking out slivers of mushrooms and pork. Green watched her. What else could he do?

"He told me I needed to sow some seeds," Green said. "Sow seeds and then sit around and wait."

Nora snorted. "He sounds like a wise man. Next time you meet one of those, take advantage of it and ask him a question." She flicked a piece of meat at Green.

He decided to ignore her. "You know Butcher plans to buy the house," he said, "but he wanted the second story to have more headroom. He's ripped out the second floor so he can rebuild it lower. But now he's run out of money."

Roy let his eggroll fall to the table. "He's gutting the house?"

"I figure it this way. We want to get the house back in shape, whether he buys it or not. Our best option is to give him the money for the materials to finish the work."

"You're so soft." Roy shook his head.

"You're a marshmallow," Nora said. "You're a mouse."

"Our other option is to evict him and hire a contractor to fix everything. Then we have to pay for materials and labor, which is where the real money comes in."

"I never should have let you talk to him," Roy said. "You don't know people. You don't know who is who."

"His wife left him and he has five children. We have a wrecked house. I don't know what else we can do."

"Oh, he doesn't know now," Nora said. "But he'll learn." Molly sighed and covered Nora's hand with her own.

Sometimes her bitterness impaired him. But he wouldn't let it tonight. Buoyed by a sudden swell of self-regard, he found the wedding ring in the file cabinet where orders were stored. The ring was a simple gold band which fit easily into the vise beneath the double-armed engraver. He made the necessary adjustments to the machine and laid a line of Italianate type into the tray. Taking a tool in each hand, he first set the tracer to the grooves of the type and then the engraver to the ring. Only then did he catch the room's mood, the uprising of ill will. They were hoping he'd ruin the ring, even though they'd have to replace it, even though the jewelry store would never use them again.

Well, he knew his role was to disappoint. He engraved the letters into the band, unfastened the ring, and held it to the light. It was perfect.

"*A greater love hath no man,*" he read.

"Fuck you," Nora said.

Green established an account for Butcher at the lumberyard with a limit. A few days later, the lumberyard called to say the limit was reached, and Butcher was trying to charge more. The clerk put Butcher on the phone, and Green agreed to meet him at the house. When he arrived, Green could see the difference immediately. The partition that had shielded the kitchen from the dining room had been torn down. In the dining room, the carpeting had been un-tacked, and much of the flooring was pulled up, leaving beams exposed. Green half-expected to see flowers growing wild through holes in the floor.

Butcher took his arm quickly and led him into the living room, which was empty of furniture. Two of his kids slept on blankets in front of the fire, and Butcher lifted one of them onto his lap to make room for Green.

"Let me tell you the truth," Butcher said right away. "Most of the stuff I bought from that yard is gone. I resold it discounted to friends so I could buy my kids food.

"I'm not proud of it," he continued, "but listen to this. See that over there?" He pointed to a ladder leading to a top-story window. "The other night I climbed that ladder and spent a long time looking out. Not up at the sky either. Down, at the ground."

The kid in his lap exhaled happily.

"I opened the window. I took off my shirt—I can't remember why

I did that—then I leaned out the window. I thought about doing it. I really did."

"That's a fixed window," Green told him.

"How do you mean?"

"It doesn't open."

Butcher stared with a face full of wonder. "Do you think I'm lying?" he asked. "Do you think I'm not in a bad way?"

For a moment, Green attempted to imagine the house as Butcher imagined it. Instead, he had a vision of his own future, laid out neat. There were no surprises waiting for him. The heady life he'd once hoped for was a joke.

"You're going to have to leave," he said.

"Hold on," said Butcher. "You're losing me." Clutching the child, he stood slowly and left the room. When he returned, he carried the kid and a bottle of off-brand tequila. He handed the bottle to Green and then resumed his position on the blanket.

"If you're not busy this weekend, I'd like to invite you to my daddy's annual barbecue. He likes to do it in the dead of winter." Butcher broke into a slow, dirge-like song: "*In the bleak midwinter, when the lakes are stone . . .*" He stopped singing. "That man can flat-out lay down some Q," he said.

"I'll come by this weekend," Green said, "and we'll talk about a moving plan."

"We'll talk," Butcher said. "Beyond that, who can know?"

Green passed the bottle. The boy in Butcher's lap turned over. When the fire flared up, he could see the boy had a black eye.

"How'd that happen?" he asked.

Butcher sighed. "I always tell him, never attack anybody. Only strike if you're struck first. Well, these boys jumped him. He started swinging. He's a good kid, but he ain't Jesus, if you know what I mean."

"I know what you mean," Green said, though he didn't.

Butcher lifted the boy and gave him a gentle shake before standing him on his feet. "You got a club in your hand," he cooed. "You'll tear up anything that gets in your way."

The child, dozy, stumbled to Green and climbed into his lap to fall back to sleep.

"He's so sleepy he thinks you're me," Butcher said. He smiled and fingered his mustache. "That's kids for you. They don't even care."

Green put his hand in front of the boy's mouth, and felt the kid's breath on his palm, cool and weak.

Outside, full-on night. But his time with Butcher had filled Green with an irresponsible energy, and he wasn't ready to go home yet, to shoulder the weight that waited for him there.

He drove to the Quik Trip to buy cigarettes. Inside, a skinny girl stood in front of an open wall cooler, money in her fist. She sucked a lollipop aggressively. He listened to it clack against her teeth.

"Bird or Train?" she asked, turning to him when she felt his eyes. "Up to you, biggie: Bird or Train?"

He moved behind her and together they looked at the brown and green bottles. "Both," he said finally. "On me." He pulled a bottle of Thunderbird and a bottle of Night Train and handed them to her, then lifted a twelve of Budweiser for himself.

In the parking lot the girl gave the bottles to another girl who held a raccoon on a leash. Taking it all in, Green was overcome with a sudden, fierce hope.

"Awful cold," he said to the girls, not going anywhere just yet.

"The cold keeps the bad people away," said the girl with the raccoon. She put the bottles in her backpack.

"You know of anywhere where's there's no bad people?" drawled the girl with the lollipop in her mouth. Clack, clack. "Are you aware of anywhere like that?"

"I know some places," he said. The girls didn't have a car, so it was easy to get them into his. He drove them along the train tracks leading out of the town to his one-room bank. He'd driven the same way a month earlier when he'd first spotted the OPEN HOUSE sign pasted to the bank's face. The building was low-slung and sided with weather board and had a round red-glass window in the front door. That day he'd stood at the window and watched the trains stop at the neighboring elevator to unload grain. He'd considered buying the building with Roy, but when he discovered the cut-rate price and the owner's desperation, he bought it alone. Across the tracks was a sod farm, and though it had already gone brown, he knew it would be different in the spring.

The girls arranged themselves on the air mattress in the vault while he lit the candle and plugged in a portable heater. He offered them blankets from a cache he kept in a garbage bag near the front door, then dragged a folding chair to the edge of the mattress, set the case of beer on the seat, and lowered himself to the floor.

"It's so nice being out of that boring town," the girl with the lollipop said, opening a bottle.

"Dead Moines," said her friend. "That's what I say." She hiked up her skirt and crossed her thin blue ankles. She pulled an apple from her pack and gave it to the raccoon, who seemed subdued. Green wondered if she had broken his spirit or just fed him some kind of pill.

"It's such a wonder," the girl with the lollipop said. "Like here I am, holding this bottle right here in my hands, and then a second later it's inside me, making me all warm and wise and everything."

"That's a lie from hell," her friend said. "Alcohol has no effect on you."

"Don't you talk to me like that. Don't you look at me all superior," the girl said. "Professional jealousy," she explained to Green. "From one fuck-up to another."

"Ah," he said. "Yes. I see." He reached for the bottle the girl was holding and took a long drink.

"Just wait until you kiss her," her friend said. "She's got a tongue exactly like leather."

"Will you shut up?" the girl said. "I like him." She turned to Green. "I like you. I do. I can see you know how to say farewell to all this. To everything. You'll be able to say good-bye when the time comes."

"Goodbye," he said.

"Oh, no, no," she said. "Time hasn't come yet." She stood and shrugged off her blanket, then turned away and lifted her shirt over her head. She bent to untie her boots. Her spine was a stack of dark nickels.

Still watching her, he reached above his head for a bottle of beer, but his fingers weren't working, and he knocked it to the floor. He tried to sweep up the broken glass with his hands and immediately cut himself. He wrapped his hand in the tail of his shirt.

"Oh, no, no," the lollipop girl said. Her breasts shone. "You have to touch the injured part to the thing that injured it."

Her friend unbuttoned her shirt and removed it. "It'll heal better."

The lollipop girl made him press a piece of bottle to the cut. Blood came over the glass, sweet and slow. Then the girl moved away from him and took hold of her friend. The girl began to hum. His eyes were wet.

"I feel like I'm always wrong," he said.

The girls moved together. Things were hazy, thick, but he could sense some design in their motion, in their soft and synchronized breath. His hot face disturbed him. Looking away, he noticed the peculiar position of the raccoon on the floor, its limbs misaligned, its relative tension and slack incorrect.

"I believe the raccoon has died," he said.

The friend rose quickly from the lollipop girl and crawled across the air mattress to the animal. "Sometimes things that look dead are actually alive," she said, annoyed. She gave the raccoon a hard poke. The raccoon convulsed, then somehow gathered itself, rose, and took a step before collapsing. "See?" the friend said. "What did I say?"

Green decided he had to get home before morning. The girls said they'd sleep in the bank and hitchhike back to town with the dawn. He didn't care. He wrapped a blanket around his shoulders, climbed into the car, and turned the key. Driving, he suddenly realized how old he was getting, his night vision already on the wane. Traffic lights presented themselves blurrily, like flowers in a storm.

When he entered his house they were all there, awake in his kitchen, sitting fast in their collective grimness: Roy and Molly and Nora. Always Nora.

"So what you been up to?" she said brightly. She crossed her arms on the kitchen table, then uncrossed them and put her chin in her hand.

"It's been a bad night," he said.

"For once he's telling the truth," she said. "And he doesn't even know it."

"It's been a bad night," he said again. He went to Nora, actually knelt before her. "You know what I mean, don't you? Don't you?"

"He means he was out fucking," she explained to Roy and Molly, with a lovely, delicate sweep of her hand.

"I feel like I'm always wrong," he said to Nora.

"You stink of wine," Molly said, behind him, gently. "You have blood on your shirt."

"I feel like I'm always wrong," he repeated.

"You do seem to have an instinct for ruin," Nora said. "Sometimes it's hard for me to believe you were made by God." She smiled benevolently. Then the smile was gone. "What are you here for?" she asked. "What do you intend to do?"

If he didn't move, she might see there was possibility in him. If he was quiet, she might hear him change.

"Green," Roy broke in, "our boat is sinking. While you were out doing nothing or everything, the Coronado burned. It's uninhabitable. Completely trashed."

It was like it had been written down somewhere. He'd spend his whole life in a basement, scratching letters onto fake gold.

"Did anyone die?" he thought to ask, slightly dazed.

"People are fine. Building's shot," said Roy.

"It was really more smoke than flame," Molly said. "But it ended up bad."

It always seemed to, didn't it? He was still on his knees.

Roy drove. Green was in the back seat, next to Nora. She sat silent. He stared out the window. A car with no hood passed them by.

When they arrived at the Coronado, no one moved to exit the car except him. "Aren't you all coming?" he asked.

"We've seen it already," Roy said, exasperated.

Nora said, "We were here as it happened."

He left the car and walked toward the apartment. The air closed around him. Snow fell carelessly, without any real effort. The fire had left the complex featureless and turned its siding black. In front, tenants' burnt belongings were piled high under a blue tarp and gave off a wet, heavy odor like rich soil. He didn't know then that the odor would linger for weeks, even after Butcher killed himself, even after Roy and he dissolved the real estate partnership and split the insurance, even after he sold the one-room bank building to an independent travel agent at a loss.

He glanced back at the car. The dome light was on and Nora leaned between the front seats. Roy stroked her hair. Twenty years ago, when Roy was first diagnosed with polio, he was put in quarantine. Every week their parents would take Green to the hospital where Roy was, and they would stand on the lawn and look up at Roy's window through binoculars. Eventually his parents were allowed to visit Roy in person, but it was too risky for Green. He stayed on the lawn. Through the binoculars he'd see his brother, ashy and thin at the lighted window, his parents behind him. They were all as far away to Green as the moon. They were all as strange to him as Europe.

The first thing Green noticed, pulling up to Butcher's place that weekend, was the absence of the garage. Where it used to stand, a slew of boards lay in disarray, as if they had just washed up on land. When he rang the bell, one of the older children answered. He was saucer-eyed and skinny, with black hair that had been cut, Green could tell, by a man.

"Daddy's sleeping," the boy told him. Green stepped inside. He didn't know how it was possible, but the house was emptier and more cold. The rest of Butcher's kids were marching in front of a small fire in the living room fireplace, plastic bags stuffed into their shoes. The littlest girl had a towel wrapped around her head.

"Did the furnace break?" Green asked. "Where's your dad?"

"We don't have a furnace," the boy said.

"Of course you do," said Green, and headed for the boiler room. But the kid was right. Butcher had cut the pipes and hauled the furnace away.

"Dad sold it a long time ago," the boy said, beside him. "At the start of winter. We've been using the fires to stay warm. We have to have a fire all the time."

"I don't believe it," Green said, pacing in the space where the furnace used to be.

"Look at our house!" the boy said, voice rising. "Dad ripped it all up and burned it! The walls, the stairs, the floors!"

"He was burning everything he took out?" Green stopped, in momentary admiration of Butcher's ingenuity and resolve. You had to admire the people that fooled you, he knew, or you were even more foolish than you had been before.

"Yesterday I helped him get down the garage," the boy said. "It should last us a while."

"I need to talk to your dad right away," Green said.

"I told you he was sleeping."

Green pushed past the boy. He found Butcher in what used to be the first floor bathroom. The double-swing door had been removed, and the toilet too. The towel racks had been unscrewed from the walls. On the wall above the sink, where a mirror used to hang, was a perfect white circle. Butcher was zipped into a sleeping bag in the built-in tub. Green could see only a fistful of hair.

"Wake up, Max," he said. "Talk to me."

Butcher said nothing.

"I'm not playing now. This is too much." He knelt over the tub and moved the bag away from Butcher's face. Butcher was on his side, eyes half-open, teeth out in the air. Green touched his cool check with his thumb.

It was over. The house would never be repaired. Green saw the future: someday he'd die too. He covered Butcher's face and backed out of the room.

Butcher's kids stomped in front of the fire with the earnestness of a marching band. When Green lifted the littlest one into his arms, the rest fell in and followed him from the house to his car.

The streets were near-empty, and everything seemed whiter in the morning's cold, revelatory light. They drove over the Des Moines River to the city's east side.

Butcher's kids directed Green to their grandfather's apartment, where he set aside a room for his church. The apartment was over a sign-painting business the grandfather owned, and a wooden sign hung in the store's front window: CLOSED SUNDAYS IN HONOR OF OUR LORD.

The kids led him around the building to a fire escape. At the top was a small landing where an old man in a down jacket attended a Weber grill with a long-handled fork. The kids scrambled up the fire escape in front of Green, hugged the old man, then crawled through an open window. When he reached the top, Green could see a dozen people inside, milling around a big table laid with platters of deviled eggs and brownies and cubed cheese. Butcher's kids stood at the end of the table, mechanically eating potato chips out of a stainless steel bowl.

"I think something might have happened to your son," Green said.

Butcher's father stood easy, fork dangling at his side, an oven mitt on one hand.

"I'm sorry," said Green. "I wish I had different news."

The man smiled, faint and knowing. That smile on some people would have infuriated Green, but it looked right on Butcher's father, like he had earned it, like he had moved beyond this place to some easier world.

The old man opened the grill. The odor of sweet, wilting onions nearly brought Green to his knees. When you find a wise man, you should always ask a question. His poor teacher had instructed him thus. So he did.

"Maybe you know," Green said. "I don't understand. I feel like I'm always wrong. Is that how everybody feels?"

Butcher's father took a bottle of barbecue sauce from the window sill. "My old fingers," he said. "Could you?"

Green opened the bottle and gave it back.

Nominated by Daniel Orozco, Epoch

SHRIKE TREE

by LUCIA PERILLO

from AMERICAN POETRY REVIEW

Most days back then I would walk by the shrike tree,
a dead hawthorn at the base of a hill.
The shrike had pinned smaller birds on the tree's black thorns
and the sun had stripped them of their feathers.

Some of the dead ones hung at eye level
while some burned holes in the sky overhead.
At least it is honest,
the body apparent
and not rotting in the dirt.

And I, having never seen the shrike at work,
can only imagine how the breasts were driven into the branches.
When I saw him he'd be watching from a different tree
with his mask like Zorro
and the gray cape of his wings.

At first glance he could have been a mockingbird or a jay
if you didn't take note of how his beak was hooked.
If you didn't know the ruthlessness of what he did—
ah, but that is a human judgment.

They are mute, of course, a silence at the center of a bigger silence,
these rawhide ornaments, their bald skulls showing.
And notice how I've slipped into the present tense
as if they were still with me.

Of course they are still with me.

They hang there, desiccating
by the trail where I walked back when I could walk,
before life pinned me on its thorn.
It is ferocious, life, but it must eat
then leaves us with the artifact.

Which is: these black silhouettes in the midday sun
strict and jagged, like an Asian script.
A tragedy that is not without its glamour.
Not without the runes of the wizened meat.

Because imagine the luck!—: to be plucked from the air,
to be drenched and dried in the sun's bright voltage—
well, hard luck is luck, nonetheless.
With a chunk of sky in each eye socket.
And the pierced heart strung up like a pearl.

Nominated by Maura Stanton, Dorianne Laux

AT FIVE IN THE AFTERNOON

fiction by GEORGE STEINER

from THE KENYON REVIEW

M. IS REPUTED to be the most dangerous town on earth. The weekly average of homicide runs between twenty and thirty. The blast of a car bomb, the rattle of automatic weapons hardly elicits notice. Some corpses are booby-trapped and left to rot. Most are shoveled off at sundown without further bother. What persists is the odor of blood. Very occasionally, women and children are caught in the cross fire or by the shards of hot metal catapulted from an eviscerated automobile. When that happens a tremor of embarrassment does occur. But it comes out of a past of civilities and safety long lost. In the baked air above M. the vultures have multiplied. After a killing they cluster, like soberly garbed tax collectors, at the edge of rooftops. Sometimes they cast their beaked shadow even before gunfire can be heard.

The killers and the killed are of a family. They have grown up together and intermarried. Their names are almost indistinguishable. They have been recruited, often by hazard, by the roll of a dice, into cartels. These are clans for narcotics and murder. They are meant to be territorial. They are designed to exploit specific backland areas, to run the chains of harvest, refinement, and shipping which connect the coca plantations in the interior to the clandestine distilleries in the forest and the slash-and-burn airstrips from which the stuff can be flown out. But lines of demarcation, of access to middlemen and buyers, grow blurred. Greed spawns new appetites. Complicities, negotiated arrangements between cartels, fray and break down. Whereupon the killings resume. Profits and blood-feuds are interwoven.

There are, to be sure, gendarmes, military and paramilitary narcotics units, *federales*, and American enforcers heavily armed. From time to time, a plantation is sprayed or uprooted, a jungle laboratory torched. Surveillance helicopters and even gun ships can be heard like drowsy hornets. It has been known for a cartel to be driven underground, for its god-fathers to be jailed in luxury. But the forces of law are themselves a cartel. They are mined by informants and avid for each other's booty. Inevitably, a police officer, a lieutenant in the snatch-squad, a reconnaissance pilot, will be bought. The bribes are spectacular. Killings occur inside law enforcement agencies. Investigators, judges, have wives and children. These have been found on urban garbage dumps with their throats slit or eyes gouged out. Cartels knit temporary alliances; they observe an armistice when danger looms from the capital or the Green Berets who are, themselves, more often than not, addicts.

But make no mistake. Life goes on in M. There are weddings, christenings, and even funerals of a natural provenance. The cinemas are crowded on spring and summer evenings, particularly when a horror film or crime epic is being featured. Football is played with unbridled passion. The municipal swimming bath booms with the cries and laughter of children. Dance halls pay protection fees. Cafés are often full, though at certain imperceptible signals, almost barometric, their clients will melt away. The brothels of M. are justly renowned and have, until now, been immune from assassinations other than of a strictly private order. Up and down their ornate stairs *pistoleros* brush past each other with unseeing indifference. There is wealth in the town and the Holy Mother Church reaps its tithes with resigned melancholy. On festive days there are fireworks above the Piazza Bolívar so loud that, on one remembered night, their cannonades and arching hiss drowned out an exchange of small-arms fire which left six cadavers. Indeed, daily life in M. has its sardonic advocates, and rumor has it that there have been tourists (a North American package tour caters for "The World's Most Dangerous Trouble Spots: Cambodia, Afghanistan, Colombia"). The hills around M. are the home of rare orchids.

The origins of the project remain obscure. Mexico City teems with writers' workshops, little magazines, and poetry readings. Like a tightly strung bow, poetry seems to be one of the rare instruments capable of keeping in balance and of energizing the polarities of the Amerindian and the Hispanic-Catholic legacies. It spans the gaps of remembered violence between ethnic dark and light, between the snows and the jungle. Poetry modulates, like some humane twilight, between the knife-sharp pressure of the sun in its cobalt sky—four suns blaze in the Aztec heavens—and the abrupt fall of night. It disarms some of the ideological, factional collisions, some of the social rage which simmers in this volcanic land. The poem glides, as if by nature, into Mexican song, into the dialects of the dance. When a ranking poet dies, the city mourns.

The reading circle met on Tuesday nights in the café of the Eagle and Serpent (strong coffee goes with Aztec glyphs). It gathered in a back-room sonorous with the intermittent hum and cough of refrigeration. The *circulo* numbered roughly a dozen men and women, though attendance varied. Poems were recited, discussed, collectively tinkered with and amended. Like the cigarette smoke, voices, particularly during the night hours, meandered and took on unexpected contours. Who was it who had brought up, knowing it to be one of the commonplaces, one of the clichés of the claims of poetry to power and everlastingness, the matter of Orpheus? Who had voiced the shopworn, exultant proposition that poetry and the poet's incantation could master the natural world, however brutish, however ferocious, that it could pierce mute stones and make the ravening wolf dream of lilies? The conceit is as hoary as poetry itself. Francesca, more than a touch embarrassed, knew her Ovid:

> Tale nemus uates attraxerat inque ferarum
> Concilio medus turba uolucrumque sedebat.
> Ut satis impulses temptauit pollice chordas
> Et sensit uarios, quamuis diuersa sonarent,
> Concordare modos . . .

Cardenio, the self-appointed populist and bard of the common (Trotskyite) man, insisted on translation. "Oh you know," breathed Francesca. "Orpheus gathers the wild things of the forest around him. Birds thrill to his art. Rocks and trees bend closer to hear him. The fox nestles beside the rabbit."

109

"Petrarch adapted that passage, as did Shakespeare and Rilke and Neruda": Roberto Casteñon had the privilege of pedantry; he was a school-master and wrote sonnets.

"If only it was true"—Jimenez's contribution was offered in a near whisper—he found smoke irritating and was only a sporadic participant. "If only it was true." And then—was it he who posed the question, was it Rosaria?—"When has a poem ever stopped a bullet?"

"It is worse than that," ruled Casteñon. "Not only can a poem not prevent a killing, it often adorns it. It beautifies murder and makes it more bearable. The slaying of Lorca is made somehow inevitable, ceremonious, and nobly memorable by his poems." Cardenio made a fist of his scarred hand and rapped the table: "Abstractions. Always abstractions. The obscene fact is that many competent, even great poets have been on the side of death. They are fascists or sing hymns to Father Stalin. Señor Aragon wrote an ode to the GPU. Poetry is, perhaps it has to be, perfectly useless. Beyond good and evil."

"Yet there are those of us, and here tonight, for whom it is just about the only thing that can make sense of life" (Francesca, wiping her glasses with nervous vehemence).

Junio Serra was the oldest among them. He had published. He had his brief entry in the dictionary of Mexican biography. His eyesight was no longer dependable, so he molded his sentences with his fingertips, testing their weight: "*Niños*, isn't that the whole point? Only what is useless can make existence endurable. Poetry, music, the work of art. We stumble through our short, often wretched lives pursuing what is useful, putting a price on everything, asking 'What will it do for me?' The treadmill of common sense . . ." (He was quoting from his poem "The Blindness of Reason," which he had first recited in this very room a year before.) "Only art and poetry liberate us. By saying 'No' and 'No' to what is necessary, to the despotism of the fact and the balance sheet. A poem is the most potent of secret agents. Was it Brecht who called poems 'the high explosives of hope'?"

"I believe it was Comrade Mayakovski," opined Cardenio. He worshipped Serra but distrusted his rhetoric.

Afterwards no one could recall who had put the question: "Has anyone ever tried?"

"Tried what?"

"Tried to stop bullets with poems."

"Legend has it," offered Casteñon, "that in the First World War an

110

infantryman's life was saved when a volume of Keats in his breast pocket deflected a bullet."

"You know that's not what I mean" (it *must* have been Rosaria Cruz who insisted, whose mezzo voice brought them to attention). "That's not what I meant at all. Have poets ever tried, really tried, to interpose, to stop a murder by the force of a poem?"

Junio sang out: "They tore him limb from limb, those mad women of Thrace. They drank Orpheus's blood. Only his head was left, floating down the river."

"But singing still, the singer's tongue unquenched," added Francesca, her own lips moving to Ovid's beat.

"Isn't that the whole point? If death can't silence poetry, can poetry silence death?" Osvaldo rarely spoke. He would not read aloud. Only occasionally, when everyone was on the point of leaving, would he distribute a poem carbon-copied on flimsy sheets. Now Osvaldo leaned forward, his hands fluttering. "Stronger than mortality. The poet, the artist overcomes death. His ode will outlast the city to which it is addressed. It will, via translation or imitation, outlast the language in which it was written. It is stronger than midnight. That's what we have been taught to believe. Like a litany, like a sort of insurance for the ransacked house of the spirit. But it *isn't* so, is it? Books are burned, poets are done to death like everyone else. Where were the Muses in the time of the concentration camps? Mandelstam's epigram brought him a hideous end; it didn't impede Stalin for an instant." Osvaldo stopped, incredulous of his sudden eloquence. He coughed a dry, sad cough. Only the moribund cooler spluttered in the back corner, next door to the toilet.

But Rosaria would not be denied. "Hope means getting things wrong."

"That's not such a bad line of verse," interjected Cardenio. "Property is theft. I'll steal it."

"Be serious, I beg you. Of course hate has more power than grace." (Even in her lyrics, Rosaria avoided the word "love," uncertain whether ordinary human beings have any right to it.) "And greed is more powerful still. The police will always be happy to kick our teeth in. I know all that. Of course most lives are lived in shit. In almost complete indifference to beauty. Any idiot knows that . . ."

"And poets make pathos of it," murmured Serra. "That too, I know perfectly well. But am heartily sick of it! Sick up to here . . ." Rosaria's gesture was terminal. "But suppose that for once in our little lives we tried to make poetry *act*, to hammer words into deeds. To do so publicly, with immediacy, like a fist between the eyes."

"And just how do you propose to do that?" But there was no rebuke or mockery in Cardenio's tone.

Rosaria spread her hands in sorrow and self-judgment. "I don't know. I simply don't know. And shouldn't make speeches."

It was Osvaldo, his palms sweating, who unfolded the newspaper he had bought on his way to the Eagle and Serpent. The picture had made him nauseous. He was not sure he could bear to look at it a second time, let alone pass it around the table. Two women lay dead on the street, their legs splayed; next to them a child, its face like trampled cabbage but streaming with blood. At the edge of the gutter crouched a mongrel, its snout glowing with the filaments of blood and brain scattered on the pavement. The photograph had been shot in brilliant weather, the light pure and unbounded over the rooftops. The caption read: *Another Day in Medellín*. The article explained that the victims were the family of a minor drug runner suspected of being an informant. His wife had been pregnant. "Poems?" It was all Osvaldo could say.

Francesca stared at the picture. She spoke with the concentrated lucidity of a sleepwalker. "Yes, poems. Read, sung in the street. To whoever will stop and listen, in that very street. Before they hose down all the blood. Poems placed in the hands of the dead. In those of the killers. Flowers for the dead *and* the living. Especially for the living. Poems against murder. To add, however little, to the weight of life in such a place. Poems with a rage for life stronger than that of the assassins. The anger of love in a poem . . ." She broke off even more embarrassed than by Ovid. The newspaper rustled from hand to hand. Osvaldo would no longer touch it.

"Do I have to be the spoiler?" asked Cardenio. "Beloved Francesca, use your head. Do you know what would happen? The police would arrest us and charge us either with lunacy or disturbing the peace. Or the thugs who work for the cartels would beat the living hell out of us."

Serra added: "And what's worse, not even that poor dog would stop to listen."

Casteñon heard his own voice as from a distance. "Still, it might just be worth a try. It might achieve something. I don't honestly know what. But even trying could be important."

"Can you imagine the headline," Cardenio's shoulders heaved with forced laughter, "Minor poets kidnapped by drug barons. Not worth ransoming."

Rosaria conceded: "The whole idea is *loco*, totally crazy."

"But that's the point, don't you see?" Osvaldo had not uttered as many words in several weeks. "A pure madness. Useless. Perhaps hopeless. But immaculate." The word spun around the table like a roulette ball, bounding from hand to hand till Francesca snared it. "Immaculate. Dear Osvaldo. That's exactly right. An immaculate lunacy. As immune, as invulnerable as hopelessness." Cardenio pursed his lips and noted the phrase. Francesca was now caught up in the whirl of her argument: "What have we to lose except our supposed dignity?" A certain brand of nonsense can dance in one's head.

"Dear, dear girl, what we can lose is our lives. Look again at that photograph." Casteñon was right, of course.

A spinning top teeters, ready to fall either way. Rosaria had finished her last cigarette and was shredding the pack with a vengeance. Then Osvaldo spoke up. His was, perhaps, the grayest presence at the coven. He ran a very small bookstore, part avant-garde literature, part curiosa and esoterica. He knew that his verse was wholly derivative but cherished the conviction that practitioners of manifest indistinction helped put the true masters in a sharper light. "Octavio would surely want us to go. He would go himself if he could." To those present, to Mexican poets wherever, reference to Octavio Paz was talismanic. It provided the litmus paper for integrity. Paz's example was non-negotiable. "You're right. Octavio *would* go," affirmed Cardenio. Further debate seemed a discourtesy of heart. "He would want us to go," added Rosaria unnecessarily. What more was there to say?

It was only at the door of the café, under the sudden stars, that Junio Serra asked dreamily: "And precisely where is Medellín?"

"Pablo Escobar? You want to know about Escobar? He was a turd. A mother-fucking turd. You know who built him up, who made of Escobar a fucking superstar? It was shitheads like you. *Gringo* journalists. That's who it was. The man only needed to fart and you'd be all over him begging for a sniff. Escobar, the *imperador* of cocaine. The sadistic mass killer. Escobar, the guardian angel of the shantytowns, the benefactor of the destitute. Who gave money for slum schools and playgrounds. Who bounced little girls on his knees and popped ice lollies in their mouths. It was the goddamned media who hyped Escobar. Right to the time he lorded it in jail, in his million-naire suite with Jacuzzi and air-conditioned patio. Holding press conferences and photo sessions in his purple pajamas. Escobar? I'll tell you what he was. . . ."

The Informant drained his tumbler and snapped his fingers for another. Toby Warren (*Philadelphia Inquirer*) knew that expenses were mounting but edged a new cassette into his tape recorder. The interview in that flophouse of a hotel in Bogotá had been difficult enough to secure. It had taken weeks of tortuous diplomacy and tips to intermediaries. What now mesmerized Toby was the man's belly, folding like lava over a tooled snakeskin belt. It looked sodden and flabby. But the reporter sensed that if he ventured a punch, even as hard as his fist could make it, he would ram into something like granite. His hand might fracture. An intuition which almost distracted him from the Informant's sandpaper voice.

"Escobar was a small-time hood out of Cucuta. Which is a shit-hole. He ran a numbers game, fixed cockfights, and beat up whores when the spirit moved him. I don't know how he became a runner for the Bucaramanga outfit. That's where one began hearing about him. He was smart, I'll grant you that. Putting the powder into pig's bladders, burying it in piles of fertilizer which stank so much that no agent or border patrol would burrow in them. What put Escobar on the map was the way he used kidnapping. Kidnapping had been an industry in Colombia. Escobar saw that it could be combined with running drugs. Kidnap a man and shoot him up with cocaine. Then tie him to a hook in a meat house and let him sweat. Till he screams for the stuff. Till he offers to screw his own kids for a refill. That's how Pablo Escobar recruited. His men, women too, were addicts, blown out of their fucking brains, totally dependent on the dirty needles which the great Escobar allowed them. Then came the Manizales fuck-up." The mere recollection made the Informant rock with pleasure and pluck at his crotch with renewed vigor. "A large shipment was coming through Manizales. Really big. Forty million dollars worth on the Yankee market. The *federales* had been tipped off. They were watching. They roared in just as the boys were carting the merchandise to a local airstrip. Things turned nasty. Escobar was one of the few who got away. He was wounded, slightly. He accused old Gonzalo Santo of allowing a spy, a double agent right at the heart of the firm. He swore he'd flush him out. He put a man's balls in a carpenter's vice till he confessed. No one ever knew whether it was the right man, but the poor shit went crazy and Escobar had him strangled. After which he took over from Santo. But even then he would have been nothing without Gacha, without Gonzalo Rodriguez Gacha. Now *there* was a hard one!" The Informant whistled softly through his brown dentures and rolled his eyes heavenward in a mien of true reverence.

"Gacha was totally fearless. He could tear a raging cat into small pieces with his bare hands. He could throw a knife so fast you'd swear it was still in its sheath. When he looked at a woman she'd wet her pants. Gacha was a king. I've never understood why he put up with Escobar, why he was satisfied to be Escobar's second-in-command. Maybe it was out of contempt. He knew Escobar wasn't worth a bucket of hot spit. But let the media swarm all over the mighty Pablo while he, Gacha, got on with the job. It is said that between the two of them they set up fifteen hundred killings. Medellín became the hot spot for murder when the Ruiz Valencia bunch horned in, when they began roasting some of Escobar's *peones* over slow fires. A cartel lives by the protection it can guarantee its suppliers and traders. So the war was on. But Escobar was a coward. Gacha did the fighting. He planted the car bombs and would stroll past as if on a Sunday walk. When the Miami Police Department sent down its ace snooper, it was Gacha who stalked him. The lieutenant was found in a latrine with his prick up his own ass. He had died slowly."

Toby checked the tape. He would not be shocked. Zero on the Richter scale of shockability. He focused instead on the ornate patterning of the Informant's boots. "Can there be any excuse for this butchery?"

The Informant's mien glazed over. He brushed his stubbled chins as if he had been smacked with a wet fish.

"And you're the Last Judgment?" Not really a question. A hiss, rather. "Excuse, fathead? As if you and the likes of you knew what you're talking about. You don't, *amigo*. You don't know from shit. Ask the farmers upcountry. If it wasn't for the coca plantations they'd starve. They'd be chewing dung and skinning rats. Before the cartels safeguarded the seeding and the harvest, before the *peones* had a regular payout, those poor sons of bitches didn't live past thirty-five. The kids had swollen bellies like knocked-up rabbits. Grow other crops? That's what the fucking relief agencies and the U.N. sightseers preached to them. Absolute crap. When there's no market for anything else. When the soil isn't right. Till our boys came along, the starving shits out there had never seen an electric light bulb. When the rains failed they drank their own piss. What the fuck do you know about hunger, Señor Warren? Hunger has a smell. You didn't know that, did you? It hung over those valleys." The Informant twirled the last ice cube in his glass.

"Excuse?" The inanity of the word soured his gut. "Let me tell you who needs excuses. And make sure you take it down, that your machine gets it right." Toby checked the spool. "It's the motherfuckers in your own country. It's the millions from Laredo to Chicago who use the stuff. Who shoot themselves up in every stinking alley or shithouse. It's the rich and the not-so-rich who hand out reefers and pills at every party. Who start out with a sniff and go on to the needle. It's your teenagers who meet the dealers at the school gate. It's the parents who slip low-grade narcotics between their kids' lips to keep them quiet and happy. Millions of you blowing your own fucking minds to smithereens. Taking that overdose in the motel. And the craving for more eats your bowels out like a scorpion. Snow. Acid. Speed. Any grade, any filthy mixture. To stop the craving, the chainsaw inside you. American bitches—I've seen them—offering anything, anything, do you hear me, *amigo*? 'Put it up my ass. Let me suck you. Let me suck the sweat off your balls.' Anything for the next fix. 'Shoot it up me, honey. O baby, O. . . .'"

The Informant shivered almost delicately, the laugh rumbling in his opulent entrails. Now he hunched forward, addressing the recorder in a stage whisper. "If you motherfucking North Americans weren't devouring drugs, if you weren't lapping them up like rabid dogs, the whole cesspit would dry up overnight. No more coca leaves. No more labs in the jungle. No more couriers, no more mules shifting bags of the stuff after getting across the border. No more killings in Medellín. *Kaputt. Nada*, my young friend. Have you got that straight?" Warren caught something like a scent of scorched rubber in the Informant's breath. "Do you understand, scribbler? Fucking Americans preaching, asking for excuses while they snort heroin up their noses."

"Do you believe that any of the countermeasures will work?" The Informant snapped his fingers for another drink.

"For a smart boy you ask some pretty dumb questions. The cartels know about every move before the assholes in Washington or the Miami bureau or the cops in Mexico and Bogotá have even thought of

116

it. Buying agents is like robbing a piggy bank. They ask to be bought. From the cop at the border right to the top. To Noriega's CIA controllers, to the wife of the American military attaché in the embassy. When there's a stubborn one—it happened in Monterrey not long ago—when there's a brave fucker who thinks he'll change things, we grab his children, pretend to shoot heroin into their veins and mail him the video. The hero's begging for a new posting before he can wipe his ass. And who the hell tells you that Uncle Sam wants to stop the trade? There are payoffs all the way up the line. If they weren't spaced out on drugs, the blacks in your inner cities would start torching. Narcotics give an easy excuse for a military presence south of the border, for counter-insurgency training and the wasting of supposed Marxist or Maoist guerrillas. How naive can you be, little man? The big boys from Washington, from Houston, from Miami meet regularly with the cartel bosses. They have much to talk over."

"Where do they meet?"

A chortle dry as deadwood. "It wouldn't do you any good to know that, believe me. But they do meet."

Warren fumbled with the new tape. The Informant scratched his groin. The tequila was beginning to mist his cold eyes.

"Anyway, *amigo*, things are changing. Women are taking over. *Women*. Would you believe it? The bosses have gunned each other down, or been betrayed. Also among us there are informants." No irony in the voice, only a rasp of contempt. "After Gacha's death things were never the same again. The 'Black Widows' took over— that's what we call them. They say that Mery Valencia handled more than twelve thousand kilograms of cocaine in one year. It took more than a hundred agents to corner Gacha's woman, Gladys Alvarez. If you really want to know what goes on in Medellín, find 'the Godmother.' Began as a six-year-old pickpocket. The cops took her in when she was nine. Told her they'd let her go if they could sodomize her, right there in the fucking cell. She became a whore. Then a drug runner. They say she's been a party to two hundred executions. She became *capo* when Manuelito's arms and legs floated out of a blocked sewer. If Gladys doesn't like the way you fart, she'll have her boys drip sulphuric acid down your throat with an eyedropper. 'Doctor Blanco's remedy for winter catarrh.' But I've talked enough." His bitten nails hovered over the recorder. "I've given you more than you paid for. I've been good to you, shithead." The Informant seemed to uncoil out of his own bulk with surprising adroitness. Toby did not

117

even glimpse the signal with which the Informant summoned his bodyguard from behind an adjacent potted palm. The two men were eclipsed in a shadowy instant. The tumbler stood empty.

Toby Warren packed his gear. He stashed his tapes and notebook under a layer of soiled laundry in his duffle bag. It was only then that he noticed the bizarre group—he could make out two women and three or four men advancing on the hotel reception. They were carrying what seemed to be placards wrapped in town newspapers. Toby couldn't help but notice that they were Mexican papers.

The drive to Bogotá had been punishing. Rosaria's epithet was "vomitive." In the third-hand rented doormobile, she had been car sick at predictable intervals. The stink hovered. Osvaldo, who insisted on coming along, having, after all, composed and mounted the posters, developed piles. His apologetic stoicism was insufferable. The sextet had camped out wherever feasible, but flogging rains had forced them into motels of truly epic filth. They arrived in the capital rancid and bone-weary from the constant juddering of their vehicle. Cardenio seemed to speak for all of them when he suggested that they should jettison the lunatic venture and head for home. Somehow, they would whip up the train fare for martyred Rosaria. The thought of pressing on to Medellín over the Cordillera Central seemed like a black joke. "And what would we find in that hellhole? Who, in God's name, would come out and listen to us?" Even Ovid now failed Francesca, who felt light-headed at the thought of a proper shower, of scouring the muck out of her matted hair. Serra's aging muscles ached loudly as if someone had planted nails in the small of his back.

To the irritation of his accomplices, Casteñon had kept his balance. Even in the rains, he had found the landscape intriguing. "We've managed the worst of the journey. We'll have a night's sleep and think it over."

"The worst?" challenged Cardenio. "Do you have any idea what the roads will be like inland? Already we've taken twice as long as we reckoned. I say 'cut our losses'." Francesca had read somewhere that tiredness could bring on hot tears. She blew loud into a twisted handkerchief and was embarrassed to see how gray, how sweat-soaked it had turned in her pocket. Osvaldo's sudden volubility brought them up short. They had brushed against a live wire.

118

"I haven't come all this way only to turn back now. I haven't given that thief Ernesto the keys to my shop for nothing. Or sweated blood over those placards" (which were leaning against one of the hotel's ornate cuspidors, their wrappings peeling). "All that fine talk about poetry being a shorthand for hope. About Dr. Paz's presumed wishes and example. The lot of you can turn for home. I'm making for Medellín if I have to hitchhike. I'm going to put up those posters. Just give me the Xeroxes. I'll find a way to hand them out. Somehow. But I'll be damned if I turn tail now." Osvaldo wiped the spittle from his lips, dismayed by his own presumption, by his unprecedented oratory. "*Adiós* and *bon voyage*, but count me out." It was a superfluous flourish, delivered with a chivalric, mildly scornful wave of the hand which astonished Osvaldo as much as it did his fellow travelers.

Almost under his breath, Junio Serra echoed: "He's right, you know. It would be pretty abject if we turned back now."

But Casteñon insisted: "We'll sleep on it. We can't start out tonight in any case." And they shuffled towards the hotel counter, pressing the bell and listening to its tinkle, thin as dust. Lovingly, Osvaldo gathered his posters. He caught himself humming "Flowers for the dead. . . ." It was a ballad long out of fashion. He had heard it, when he was a very young child, outside his mother's window in Cuernavaca. Rosaria caught the lilt and joined in. Soon they were all humming it, the four men and the two women, persuading the night clerk as he doled out room keys that he was dealing with a troupe of penurious vocalists in search of work. And there was the guitar.

When they reassembled at breakfast, discussion seemed at once indispensable and pointless. Should they leave their dented vehicle in the parking lot and proceed by train? Cardenio regarded that as a waste of money and culpably self-indulgent. He muttered the word "*bourgeois.*" Rosaria pledged that she would throw up, if at all, in the fields and at condign remove. Osvaldo mouthed insincere apologies for his prepotency the night before. His beard combed, his eyes alight like the new moon, Serra told of drafting a new poem in the pit of the dark. Osvaldo's imperiousness had inspired him. Cardenio, with whom he shared quarters, had heard nothing of the spidery rush of the pencil. But then, friend Cardenio's snore . . .

Casteñon spread out the road map. The Magdalena river bisected it like a blue snake. After which came the brown of the mountains and the spiraling descent through Envigado. There was no way of telling whether their wretched transport would be up to the local roads, some of which were marked as under construction. "The chariot of Apollo, the prancing team of the sun-steeds," recited Francesca, shaking her wet hair and allowing Serra to complete Quevedo's celebrated couplet. The water in the hotel sink had been brackish, the flies irremediable. But she felt reborn. It was late morning before they set out, sensing their itinerary through Bogotá's interminable slums, under a copper sky. Rosaria pressed to her mouth a Kleenex, humid with what was left of her precious cologne.

🍏 🍏 🍏

On the afternoon when they reached Medellín, the sky had turned to a milky wash. They threaded their way into the town on the look-out for cheap lodgings. The clutch was in audible pain and Casteñon nursed it gingerly. He felt himself stiffening and becoming a *voyeur*. He stared through the grimed windshield and swiveled his head at corners. Looking for what?

He was uncertain, yet almost hysterically alert. An occasional passerby returned his stare or paused at the sight of the wheezing door-mobile and its Mexican plates. An old woman grinned through broken teeth. At one point a motorcyclist overtook, gunning his engine. Casteñon flinched and was ashamed. Dogs were no mangier than anywhere else. Did people seem to hurry as they crossed in front of him, did they defy traffic lights any more than in Monterrey?

Nosing towards Calle San Martin, Casteñon glimpsed blown-out shop windows and taped cardboard where there had been glass. Or was that just an ordinary building site? Twice—Francesca nudged his shoulder—he saw or thought he saw a bunch of flowers at the base of a lamppost. Once he registered from the corner of his eye, like the filament of slime secreted by some outsized snail, a dark stain on the pavement. Which might be rust or spilled lubricant. There was a queue lengthening in front of the Cinema Vasco. Casteñon's straining ears could make out the yawp of heavy metal, the patter of fruit machines from a nearby arcade. Was it that the streets appeared to empty somewhat as the travelers approached the center? Or was that perfectly normal, given the late afternoon hour? *Entre chien et loup,* "between dog and wolf"; Casteñon had long cherished that French idiom for the coming of the dark.

Not a wolf in sight, not even two-legged. The invasive odor was one of industrial grime and accumulated garbage. Had Casteñon really expected to smell terror in the air, to catch the sweet foul smell of the public abattoir? His exhaustion, seven hours at the wheel on gutted roads, took on an edge of diappointment. He fought down an intimation of ridicule, of self-dramatization. Letters were missing from the neon sign of the motel. Unbending from the driver's seat, the only reek of which Casteñon was certain was that of clogged drains. All too familiar from Mexico City. He paused, trying to get the circulation back into his aching thighs. So this was "the murder capital of the Americas"?

Just before morning the windows rattled and a shiver went through the thin walls. The explosion rumbled on like retreating drums. Rosaria surged into the corridor, her eyes white with shock.

🍒 🍒 🍒

The invocations of the Saviour and of his distinguished Mother during the exchanges with the assistant to the deputy chief of police were, on the part of the sergeant, so frequent and reiterated as to suggest some archaic litany. The expletives *"Jesu,"* *"Jesu María,"* and *"Madre di Dios"* punctuated every sentence or were, quite simply, the sum of his response. The sergeant tugged at his uniform collar, he struggled for air, he rocked his chair till the springs whined. *"Jesu María,"* "Mother of God"—it was all too much. Who in Christ's name had wished this visitation on him? Who were these deranged folk crowding his stinking cubbyhole of an office, their voices more insistent, more grating than the splutter of the fan, one of its blades cracked. Diverse conjectures scrabbled in the sergeant's aching head like rats' feet. His callers had decamped, collectively, from an asylum, from some hospice for the mentally enfeebled. They were the flotsam of a foundered musical band or road show gone bankrupt. The four men and two women, one of them dismayingly flat-chested, were swindlers, confidence artists up to some novel, twisted scam. But most likely they were beggars, seeking to leach the famously compassionate heart of Medellín—and without a proper license! *"Madre di Dios,"* should he arrest them on the spot? A dark truth had made his bowels shift. This flea-bitten pack was some species of subversives, of anarchists, or anarchosyndicalists (he remembered the term and warmed to it). Urban guerillas out of red Mexico. Should he have their doormobile examined for concealed weapons or traces of Semtex? Should he have the two whores stripped and searched? Should he put his cigarette lighter—nobly embossed "for twenty-five years of loyal service"—to the old man's beard (the

121

sergeant sensed that anarchosyndicalists wore beards)? Or would it be smarter to let them put on their fucking show, to find out, "*Jesu María*," just what shit they were really up to? The sergeant loosened his belt and feigned interest.

"And how much will you charge for your stuff?"

"Not a *peso*. We'll hand it out free to anyone who cares to have it. That's the whole point." Cardenio spoke as to a partially deaf but dangerous child.

"You'll hand the crap out free? *Jesu María*. And what's in it for you? Propaganda is it? Inflammatory tracts? The little red book?" The sergeant savored his perception.

"Nothing of the kind." Francesca put forward her best smile. "Just poetry. We'd be honored if you and your chief had a look." She began extracting a handful of sheets from her knit, Mayan-patterned shoulder bag.

"I'll tell you when we want to examine your trash. Put it away. And just what, Holy Mother of God, makes you suppose we'll let you peddle it? Just how brainless are you to come to Medellín to make some kind of shitty spectacle of yourselves and hand out subversive garbage? How dim-witted are you? Just tell me that."

"You may well be right, sergeant. But poets are often a bit queer in the head. They almost have to be. Take Orpheus, take Blake, or Rimbaud . . ." Osvaldo's voice was at once low and intensely focused. The sergeant, involuntarily, leaned forward, trying to make out the little fag's pronouncement (of course he was a fag, the sergeant's antennae were, in such matters, reputed as infallible). But he could locate none of those named by Osvaldo in his inner file of known agitators, of clandestines, and *Sentiero Luminoso* offshoots. Obviously these vagabonds had contacts and the names might, to be sure, be encoded. Close vigilance was called for.

"And who do you imagine will come and listen to you?"

"Perhaps no one. Perhaps one or two with time on their hands. Passersby, the out of work. But you are right, sir," (the honorific seemed to Rosaria worth a dangle) "most likely there'll be no one. Not a living soul."

"Just what do you propose to do then?" he inquired between clenched jaws. He felt in command. "What the fuck will you do then?"

"Leave our poems on a park bench and head for home." Serra had

122

answered with such sweet tranquillity that the sergeant smelled a trap.

"Leave your shit in a public place? In the *jardino municipale? Jesu María*, we have ordinances here. I'll have you up for loitering, for vandalism before you can . . ." The verb eluded him. The old fart's tone needled him—like a long forgotten but unnerving cadence out of an unrecuperable past. The goddamned conversation had gone on for too long.

The praetorian edged out of his seat. "And suppose anyone does show up to listen to your *merda*," he flashed the word at the two women, "what then? What are you really aiming at? I want the plain truth. I'm warning the lot of you." He tapped his holster.

Roberto Casteñon's could be considered a prepared statement:

"Honored assistant deputy commissioner, we understand that there are difficulties in Medellín. The life expectancy in this esteemed city is not always what it should be. Poetry is no use against bullets and car bombs. We know that. You will say that poems are useless, a sort of litter. But that, you see, is our point. It is their uselessness which contains their power. This is, I grant you, a contradiction, a paradox. But there are human crises in which only the perfectly useless can help. The most honorable authorities in your community are no doubt doing their best to lower the death toll. No doubt that you can boast devoted hospitals and a caring church. How can we be so foolish, so arrogant as to believe we can be of any help? Only by offering something so useless, so seemingly ineffectual that it will surprise the heart. Something as powerless as a bunch of fresh-cut flowers, as starlight. What we hope to accomplish here is to remind our listeners—oh, I do agree with you that no one may turn up—of the sound, even of the taste, if I can put it that way, of pure pleasure, of laughter. I imagine we strike you, dear sergeant, as peddlers or worse. Perhaps we are. But what we peddle is a drug more addictive, more mind-blowing than cocaine. There are all sorts of names for it. Some call it 'dreams,' others 'hope.' I myself think of it as having a magical impact on time. It stops normal time, which is that for murder and kidnapping and child abuse. Poems waste time. Not as do pinball machines. It's not easy to explain. They waste it by making it brimful. Of wonder, of renewal. Poems are breathing spells, breathing exercises for the worn spirit. Do let us try, friend sergeant."

The sergeant stared at the ceiling with its spreading cracks. The annoyance in him had veered to something more threatening. There was a taste of rage in his mouth, but also a strange, sad pride. He aimed to keep his voice under control.

"You don't understand, do you? You don't begin to understand with all your fancy talk. Why the hell don't you put on your fucking flea-circus in Tijuana? I hear they kill people there almost as often as they do here and cart their bodies across the border. Medellín is special. What the fuck do you know about it? *Nothing*." His throat was on fire. "You know nothing about Medellín, about the way we do business here. I don't care a fart about any of you, you can believe me. But why should the municipality pay for your funeral? If *they* take offense at your garbage, you won't outlast sunset. Perhaps you heard the explosion last night. When the driver came home and locked his car, he found a puppy tied to the garage door. The kind of cute puppy his little daughter kept asking him for. The animal was whimpering with thirst or fear. So the cretin bent down to stroke it. Mother of God, they had sown the dynamite into the dog's belly. That's what life and death in Medellín are like. And you really want me to believe you'll make an ounce of difference with your fine chatter, with your poetry-pills?"

Listening to himself, the sergeant sensed that the whole lunatic situation was sifting out of his hands. There was no air in the room and Rosaria kept a tissue pressed to her gagging mouth.

"So get out of here while you can. If I catch you loitering, I'll impound your van—it's probably not road-worthy anyway—and arrest you. Do you hear me, my fine friends? Stop clowning and clear out of Medellín. In this police station we strip-search. Unfortunately we have no women on the squad." The sergeant gave a metallic laugh and kept his eyes on Rosaria, who was close to passing out. "Medellín is very special."

The sergeant realized that he was repeating himself. That too made him both angry and sad. It was a sadness he couldn't put his finger on. It oozed deep inside him, like stagnant syrup. Again, those desolate memories of childhood which these crazed comedians had no right to uncork.

They were shuffling to the door. Specters smelling dimly of fear and unwashed travel. Had he made perfectly clear to them that no freak show would be allowed in any public place, that it was high time for them to decamp? Should he lunge after their retreating shadows and spell that out so that even they would understand? Instead, his hands faintly unsteady, the sergeant sank back into his chair and picked up the phone.

Ordinarily, Two-Fingers—the other three on his right hand having been hacked off with a blunt saw by enforcers who had failed to note that their victim was left-handed, an oversight which subsequently cost them dear—would have slammed down the receiver. The sergeant's mumblings and heavy breathing were those either of a drunk or of one high on the marijuana which, as Two-Fingers was aware, cocooned the Medellín police station in a brown fug. But one word on the phone had hooked into Two-Fingers' supine brain: *Mexico*. The sergeant had muttered "Mexico." The fucking mountebanks had come all the way from Mexico. The drug dealer spat meditatively into his stunted hands and began sounding alarms.

The various organizations had synapses, agreed snake pits where vital warnings could be traded. No one could accurately map the reticulations, the choking yet delicately twined web which extended from the half-dozen bosses at the summit to the most abject of pushers at the bottom, which connected the coca fields in the highlands to the derelict alleys of the South Bronx, to the patios in Malibu or the Nevada casinos. Pulsing fibers of communication and supply, of price fixing and money laundering, of political-judicial bribery and sadistic retribution. Pluck at the web at any seminal crossing and the labyrinthine fabric would start quivering all the way down the line. Mexico was, of course, a nerve-end of absolutely cardinal significance. It was via Mexico that Colombian cocaine flowed towards the hysterical appetites of the U.S.A. The points of transit, via light aircraft, speedboats or individual couriers, the *bourses* on which shipments were negotiated and futures weighed, were in Cuidad Juárez, in Tijuana, in Cucuña, in clandestine depots along the permeable border. Diplomatic relations with the Quintero outfit in Guadalajara, with the Arellano mob in Tijuana, with the specialized heroin and methamphetamine merchants and refiners who operated out of a disused marshaling yard outside Monterrey, had to be sustained and strengthened. Whatever involved Mexico called for prompt attention.

Two-Fingers passed the word. The advice from one of the tacticians for the Cali cartel was succinct: "Grab one of the two bitches and put a hot wire up her cunt." Characteristically, the Guadalajara reflex was more circumspect: "Find out what the clowns are up to. Who sent them? Cool it." The Tijuana contact had this to offer: "See whether one of them has a limp. There's an agent out of the Miami bureau who has a limp. We tried to pick him up near the border. The snatch was fucked up. Middle-aged, with a limp." Two-Fingers took it all in, as through a bent straw. The problem now was Medellín itself. A major shipment was imminent. The Alvarez whore had certainly got wind of it. Two of her scouts had been seen nosing around the airport. Could there be some connection? Two-Fingers was responsible for order in Medellín. He loathed anarchy, and the car bomb had not been of his doing. Violence must have its etiquette; even torture has conventions. Otherwise, the world would be fit only for scorpions. Amateurs were the blight of Two-Fingers' vision. Spying on the six Mexicans was wholly beneath his dignity, beneath his rung in the hierarchy. He would send Emilio. No genius he, to be sure, but observant. A man to blend with the crowd (what crowd?). The entire affair might be no more than the hallucinations of a bored cop stoned out of his asshole mind. Two-Fingers raised what was left of his hand in Masonic benediction. A private joke in the San Tomé clan. He eased the gun into his belt and went out to find Emilio.

Toby Warren had a problem. Madame Alvarez was inaccessible, out of any bounds. Tarantulas nest deep. So where was his story? True, there had been the car bomb. Yet despite its ghoulish scenario, the slaying had elicited little, if any, interest. The victim belonged to the louche end of real-estate operators and his wife was rumored to be a Brazilian Jewess. The local constabulary had been less than welcoming. *Gringo* reporters were no better than horseflies to be swatted. The neighbors had closed their doors in his face. Though he hinted at a condign bribe, Warren's visit to the mortuary had proved fruitless. What business had he snooping? What little was left of the dismembered cadaver would not even be exhibited to the dolorous widow. "These things happen, you know, Señor Warren. Unfortunately." Toby had written down the mortician's epitaph. Now he tore out the page. The two whiskeys, too early in the day, were getting to him. The air felt like cheesecloth, covering his mouth with dull warmth.

There *might*, there just might be something worth extracting from the Informant's harangue. But it was, in the main, stale stuff, already covered by those who had made of the narco cartels and of North American addiction their lurid beat. The Escobar saga had spawned *reportages*, more or less fictive interviews and even books. Toby's feet felt as if encased in sand. That upper molar would need attention as soon as he got back to base (a grotty, one-bedroom apartment in a Philadelphia condominium peopled by the recently divorced). Meanwhile his tongue brushed and brushed again over the raw edge of his tooth. The very best thing would be to pack his bag and go. This, in fact, had been the bored advice proffered by the barman in the empty, virtually unlit *bodega*.

Toby Warren was on his way to the motel (he would remember the fleas) when his eye caught the poster.

FREE. ABSOLUTELY FREE. A READING OF PO-
ETRY. A SINGING OF SONGS. BY THE MINSTRELS
OF THE FOUR SUNS. PLAZA MUNICIPAL. *A LA
CINQUE DELLA TARDE*. FREE!

At the next corner a second poster. In the shape of a new moon, the letters printed between its cheery horns.

POETRY IS THE DRUG OF HOPE. BRING YOUR
LOVED ONE. BRING YOUR CHILDREN. AB-
SOLUTELY NO CHARGE!

And once more the time and place. The third placard had been fixed to a scaffold just outside the motel.

POEMS ARE THE ALCOHOL OF JOY. COME LIS-
TEN. BRING US YOUR OWN. A POEM CAN
HURT NO ONE. FLOWERS MAKE GOOD
THINGS HAPPEN. ADMISSION ABSOLUTELY
WITHOUT CHARGE. PLAZA MUNICIPAL. AT
FIVE IN THE AFTERNOON.

That refrain, "At five in the afternoon"; Warren had heard it some-where. It signified more than it said. But what? He stood in front of the poster, strangely unsettled. Another night in Medellín might be an investment. What he needed was a photographer. From the local

127

newspaper or press agency. As he turned his back, Toby heard a tearing. A little boy was trotting away. The slash had bitten into the lettering. Toby found himself laboring to mend it. Two cats watched him, their eyes as flat and indifferent as gold.

☙ ☙ ☙

Rosaria was sure she would wet herself. Fear always started in her wretched bladder. How would she mask the fetid stain? The ashtray at her elbow was overflowing. Francesca's calm, the nerveless attention she was bringing to bear on the poem she was rehearsing, seemed to Rosaria detestable. The thought of declaiming to some empty square or worse—the sergeant's warning was loud in her head—made Rosaria choke. When her turn came, she would stand there, incapable of uttering a coherent sound, and piddle. She had been out of her senses to come on this cursed venture. "We must find a way of explaining about Orpheus. Without patronizing. I suppose they will know something about Lorca?" Francesca's inquiry, her cool voice, left Rosaria helpless. "O great God," was all she could manage. Francesca looked up, inquisitive: "You don't think they know about Lorca?"

"Who the hell cares? Don't you realize? The gangsters here slit your throat to pass the time of day. Do you have any idea how many women have been raped here in broad daylight?" Rosaria's voice reminded Francesca of a cherished grandaunt dying of a cancer of the larynx.

"O come now, it isn't quite as melodramatic as all that. Most people do seem to lead quite ordinary lives in Medellín. Most likely not a living soul will bother to show up. Or there'll be a downpour." Francesca took a long look at the fading light. When she turned from the window, she found the door open and could hear Rosaria's sandals tapping down the corridor to the lavatory.

Osvaldo's amazement at his own panache knew no bounds. He, the mouse-man, had managed to post half a dozen placards in exposed places. Osvaldo, the bookworm, known for his ineffectual timidity and spinsterish ways. Up to this day his existence had been a celibacy of soul and flesh, a blenched avoidance of any risk, be it intimate or public, bodily or mental. As if life itself was a dangerous puddle to be skirted in galoshes (Osvaldo's had been bequeathed to him by his father, dim years ago), and here he was in the lions' lair of

Medellín putting up defiant notices. He had felt naked, waiting to be mugged or even liquidated. He rolled that ominous term on his tongue. And realized that he was happy. The tremor of happiness inside him was a novelty, like the chime of an exotic bell. He bent his ear.

Cardenio was trying to be practical. "If no one shows, we must wait for a time. Or start our readings till someone stops to listen. The trick is to capture attention. Infernally difficult when there is no amplification. Nothing but our own voices. We must begin by reading or reciting what we know by heart. Only if anyone stops to listen can we do our explaining. Your sermon on poetry and hope. On the drug of the useless." Hearing himself mimed, Casteñon smiled. He was at ease in Cardenio's fraternal derision, in the impatient warmth of the man pacing up and down between their rumpled beds. He smiled again when Cardenio muttered something about being wholly defenseless. Should they not, in the name of common sense, have an unloaded weapon to hand? "There are women, you know."

"Probably less frightened than we are. Francesca, certainly . . . If anyone is out to make trouble, to arrest us, read them your ballad of the angry parrot."

Cardenio countered with a relaxed snort. "So long as it doesn't pour."

But Casteñon was impregnable: "We can bring an umbrella. Rosaria has one. In lilac silk."

Junio Serra prayed with unguarded vehemence. To whom? The aging rhapsodist had pondered the question since childhood. The notion of God at the other end of the line made him queasy. What demented arrogance it was to presume any such auditor! Titular saints or demons at some humbler switchboard struck Serra as beneath his dignity. To whom, therefore, did he address himself with such articulate need? For whose ear did he interweave prayer with poetry, *desiderata* with lament? Serra had come to intuit that prayer was a schizophrenic exercise and discipline. He was in dialogue with another self. Not even, perhaps, a purer or more potent self. Rather an intimate otherness, indefatigably attentive to every nuance, to the hidden but turbulent pulse of meaning between the lines. A close yet also detached familiar alert, beyond his own conscious decoding, to the concealed intent, to the evasions, to the truths outside paraphrase, obscurely resonant as in music, in his invocations. "Let us not make fools of ourselves. Or let us indeed make fools of ourselves, even cowards, if that is what is required. May I not forget my cough drops. Let the wings of felicitous angels keep out the rain."

As they trailed out of the hotel, a watcher was following them. He felt no need for covertness. If one's gait can proclaim indifferent contempt, Emilio had mastered the art.

☙ ☙ ☙

They proceeded single file. Like children, reflected Francesca, playing Red Indians. She had dug out of her disheveled bag a neckerchief, a lover's token given to her many years before and not worn since. Now its brave motif of yellow roses and caracolling unicorns seemed talismanic. Catching sight of one of the posters, Casteñon tipped an imaginary hat to Osvaldo. But should he have let him come along? The little man's face was ashen.

Casteñon took in the plaza at a glance. There seemed to be six or seven souls gathered near the plinth, scarred by graffiti, from which they hoped to read. An elderly man was clutching the torn half of one of the posters indicating time and place. There was a young boy, almost a child, smoking, a blind man askew on his white cane, as if in a sudden wind. And two or three women, two with bulging shopping baskets, shifting impatiently on their tired feet.

It took a moment, in the wavering light, before he saw the others (Cardenio had nudged him). There was their attendant shadow, now leaning against a bicycle rack and spitting on his boots with ostentatious disdain. A policeman, in the arcade which led to the Calle San Martín, a mobile phone swinging from his wrist. "Like a hanged man," imagined Rosaria. And oddly out of focus, at a first-floor window, an observer in a beige silk suit, a handkerchief blossoming from his breast pocket. Intermittently, the gentleman appeared to emit a vivid flash. Casteñon realized that their guest was wearing a massive ring; when he moved, it caught the late sun. "More than we dared expect," breathed Serra. Casteñon made a welcoming motion. "Ladies and gentlemen, do step nearer." No one moved, and the gendarme spoke into his portable.

"Ladies and gentlemen, we thank you with all our hearts for having come to listen to us. We realize that it may not be easy or convenient for you to do so. That you may well have better, more urgent matters to attend to. My name is Roberto Casteñon and I want to say

130

again how grateful to you my colleagues and I are." At which point a beggar hobbled into view, pulling a dun-colored mongrel after him.

"My friends, if I may call you that, you know why we are here. To read to you, to read *with* you some of the great poems in our beloved tongue." (Osvaldo brandished the sheaf of Xeroxes, picturing himself as one who lifts on high an oriflamme in some chivalric, lost battle.) "But as you must know, *amigos*, poets are vain creatures, peacocks. So we do hope that you will also allow us to read to you some of our own verse." One of the headscarfed women—was she Indian!—nodded with enigmatic vigor. "What are we trying to achieve?" Good question, mouthed Cardenio to himself. "What we are trying to accomplish is at once very small and very big. We understand that life in Medellín—I beg you to forgive a stranger for saying it—is sometimes difficult." (Casteñon had pondered the word, and its possible rightness, all the way from Mexico.) "That there is much despair and death in the streets of Medellín." The ring in the window gave off an icy flash, as if signaling. "We hope to bring you an hour or two of beauty, of the kind of forgetting which is also a remembering." O Mother of God, thought Cardenio, Casteñon the mystic, the sophist. But the blind man looked up, cupping his ear. "Poetry can take us out of ourselves and our miseries. It makes us dream wide awake. It tells of things which are fantastically real but not of our every day. Of things which will endure when our present worries and bewilderment, however burdensome, will be long gone." The blind beggar gave vent to a high-pitched cackle and Casteñon was, for a moment, at a loss. "Go on," shouted the blind man with patronizing largesse, "Go on!"

"Poets even believe, or some of them do at least, that a truly great poem is stronger than death. Because it outlives the span on earth not only of the man or woman who wrote it but of their listeners and readers. In certain cases, the poem outlives the language in which it was first composed. A truly astounding fact if you think of it!" Casteñon was smiling to himself, almost rid of the flutter in his bowels. "That, my friends, is why we have come to Medellín to share joy with you and the most potent narcotic known to man, which is hope. And that is why we want to begin with a poem which, no doubt, you are already familiar with. A poem that overcomes death."

Junio Serra's eyes encompassed the square as if a multitude was waiting. Momentarily, his lips seemed speechless. Then he began:

131

A los cinco de la tarde
Eran la cinco en punto de la tarde
Un nino trajo la blanca sábana
A los cinco de la tarde . . .

The somber splendor of Lorca's lament for the *torrero* Ignacio Sanchez Mejias beat the air like a gong. The echo from the surrounding walls and arcades rang unmuffled. Serra was declaiming the opening section only. When he came to the image of the death trolley and of the strange funereal piping, his voice faltered:

Un ataúd con ruedas es la cama
A los cinco de la tarde.
Huesos y flautas sucnan en su oído . . .

It was the gentleman with the torn poster and the carnation in his buttonhole who came to the rescue:

El toro ya mugía por su frente . . .

He had rolled the paper into a megaphone. The choking groan of the bull was unmistakable. And his voice joined Serra's at the lacerating close:

Eran las cinco en sombra de la tarde.

At this motion of sympathy and alliance, warmth flooded Casteñon's hammering heart. He bowed to the chorister while Osvaldo circulated, pressing copies of the poems on the hesitant public. He traversed the plaza to press a sheet into the hands of the stalker and that of the policeman. Only the sharer at the window remained out of reach.

Francesca stepped forward. She read from the work of Homero Aridjis and from that of Gabriel Zaid, introducing each poem with a helpful word and telling of these poets as if they too were present. The boy had stopped smoking. "Now we want you to hear a poem by one of us, a kind of song waiting for music. Written especially for Medellín." Casteñon signaled to Rosaria Cruz. She stood rooted. She knew she was leaking. Would there be a betraying smell? Cardenio plucked her by the wrist and edged her forward. "I can't hear you,"

132

barked the blind man. Rosaria began again, and the woman with the large basket nodded: "That's better":

> There are no cities of death, *de la muerte*
> There are no midnights for ever
> The heart is a suburb of hope
> A first stop at the border.
>
> To live is to cross into life
> It has hardly begun.
> Who will be born here tonight
> And bring morning
> As does the fledgling eagle
> When it gives orders to the sun?

Had the man at the window belched or emitted a stentorian guffaw? Other folk had trickled into the square as Rosaria recited. There were now a dozen or more, and a bearded listener had taken his hat off and applauded. Again, Casteñon stepped forward.

"We have come here among you because of the spirit and example of Octavio Paz. It is not only that Octavio was Mexico's greatest poet. It was because he was a shining example of courage, of the passion for justice and mercy. He would have urged us to go to Medellín, to bring poetry to all who will gather strength and consolation from it. So we want to end this reading with one of Octavio's most magical poems." Cardenio's bass-baritone carried effortlessly:

> Luz que no se derrama, ya diamante,
> detenido esplendor del melodía,
> Sol que no se consume ni se enfría
> de conizas y fuego equidistance . . .

As he launched that closing verse, Cardenio flung his arms wide, embracing the unconsumed and diamond ardor of that sun, its equidistance from all created things. There followed a rustle of hand claps and, from the outer rim of the growing assemblage, something like a cry of thanks.

Now the guardian of the law elbowed his way through. "Where is your license?" No answer. "Do you really believe you can mount a public spectacle without a permit?" He reached for what was left of the sheets to be distributed. "These are confiscated." He gave to the word a menacing volume as if addressing all those gathered. "You will follow me to the police station. We don't allow vagabonds in Medellín. We don't need Mexican beggars here. We have enough of our own." Again, he seemed to turn on the bystanders.

Their unwanted minder had materialized out of the gloom. He bent close to the policeman's ear. Did he keep an eye on the watcher at the window and his flashing ring (*va diamante*, thought Francesca). A second whisper, fiercer. The ministrant of law and order appeared to hesitate. Then he shrugged his shoulders in morose acceptance, restored the bundle of Xeroxes to Osvaldo, cleared his throat loudly, like a ruminant out of breath, and sauntered away.

The whisperer caught Casteñon's eye. He made a barely perceptible sign in the direction of the motel. A thin rain had begun to fall. Serra lifted his face to it. *De conizas y fuego equidistante. . . .*

🐛 🐛 🐛

As they entered the lobby, it was the voice of the man waiting for them which they would remember. Velvety and cloying like hot treacle. A voice altogether at odds with the speaker's bulk and the cruel blaze of his ring.

"I liked that bit about the eagle. 'Ordering the sun about,' or something like that." Rosaria flinched, imagining he would reach out and touch her breasts. "Robles, Camillo Robles. But you can call me 'Pepe.' Almost everyone does." And Robles shook his head in wonderment. "Did you make that up? Did you just take that out of your head, little lady?" A brief pause. "I want you to write a poem for me." He nodded at their shock. "What was it called? A *llanto*, a lament, like the one for the bullfighter." Francesca was riveted by the man's belt, ponderous with tooled silver, by his suit of pale linen, by the crocodile-skin shoes. "I'll pay, of course. Pepe is a generous fellow. Ask anyone in Medellín." Cardenio smells the money in the man's voice, in the bulge of his stomach. The wicker chair creaked under his relaxed weight but Pepe did not invite the travelers to sit down. He knew and savored his edge on them. "Like the one for the *torrero*, but even better!" He frowned at Serra like a vexed schoolmaster.

His throat parched, Casteñon managed a question: "A lament, Señor Robles? But for whom?"

Pepe seemed pleased. He toyed softly with his ring and breathed a

134

voluptuous sigh. "Just so. A good question." He motioned to the desk clerk. Tequila for his guests. "And not the goat-piss you usually serve. Understood?" The clerk scurried to the pantry. "A *llanto* for Jesu Soto. Known as 'Paco the Wildcat'." Rosaria found herself sitting, absurdly, on the floor, at Robles's feet, trying to catch every word from that suffocating voice.

"Believe me, my friends, Paco was my best man. The very best. He saved my life when the fucking Green Berets and their helicopters jumped us outside Cartagena. When they sprayed petrol over the road and turned on the flame throwers. I was beginning to fry alive when Paco dragged me clear and beat out the flames with his bare hands. Without him . . ." Pepe inched back a trouser leg with delicate deliberation. The scar was livid and spidery. "Without the Wildcat I was done for. Roasted alive." Robles made every pause tell. "Or the time we were unloading the stuff at the airport in Maguana and Gacha's motherfucking hoodlums had set an ambush. Animals, that's what they are. Somehow Paco had spotted them in the dark even before they started forward. In the pitch dark. The bullets swarmed like mosquitoes. The Wildcat was hit in the arm, then in his ribs. But he wouldn't go down. Kept firing back and yelling so loud that the cowards turned tail. And when we carried Paco to the van, blood all over him, Jesu kept saying: 'I have bullets left. Let's not waste them'." Señor Robles's eyes watered at the memory. "That was Paco the Wildcat for you. 'Let's not waste them'." He drained his glass and waved for more.

"About six months ago, I sent him to check out a cache outside one of our plantations. Top grade stuff, almost ready to travel. Paco knew that trail like the back of his hand. He moved mostly at night. Did one of the shit-eating Indians give him away? What the *federales* did to him I shouldn't even tell you. Not with ladies present." Robles shifted his weight in faint deference. "They sent me photographs. They had gouged Paco's eyes out and stuffed his balls in his mouth. 'While he was still alive.' That's what the fucking torturers wrote on the back of the pictures. 'While he was still alive'." Pause. "My best soldier. Had a woman and two kids in Yarumal. And a parrot. With corral-pink eyes. O that parrot, how Paco loved him." Pepe's intonation hovered between distant pleasure and sorrow. "Now you know, ladies and gentlemen, why I want you to write 'A Lament for Jesu Soto, better known as Paco the Wildcat.' And I want you to recite it on the square and put up copies on the walls. No expenses spared."

Even the rain had fallen silent.

Somehow, Cardenio managed a marmoreal air. "Esteemed Señor Pepe, we are, all of us, most honored, most flattered by your proposal. We appreciate it greatly, I assure you. But how could we compose a *llanto* for the late Señor Soto? As you must know, dear Sir, we have come to Medellín in grief for what is going on here, in horror of the killings and mutilations. You will know, far better than we do, what lies behind these events, in what ways," (for an instant Cardenio's lips froze), "in what ways your enterprise, your profits, are involved in these sad matters." Robles's eyes never left Cardenio's face; they had gone flat and smoky like antique pewter. "We are not here to judge, Señor Robles. How could we? We are without any power. All we hope to bring to the people here is a spark of pleasure, a small gust of new air to those who may want to hear our poems and to reread them. To recall to them places of fewer deaths, a kind of life in which children do not get blown to pieces or dogs have dynamite sown in their living guts." Cardenio bent closer. He could not hide the trembling in his hands or the sweat. "That's all we hope to achieve here. How then could we compose and recite a lament for your friend the Wildcat? Surely a man of your attainments must see that that would be impossible."

Camillo Robles had half risen out of his chair, then thought better of it.

"What fine speeches you do make, *amigo*. Like sucking sweets. 'A gust of new air.' Is that what you said? Poor old Pepe doesn't know how to use words that way. So let him tell you plainly." His voice had dropped, forcing them closer. Serra cupped his hardening ear. "You're talking balls. You're nothing but a shithead who juggles big words. But you don't have a clue, do you?" Robles shook his head as if addressing backward children. "Do you know who's doing most of the killing hereabouts? Well, let me tell you. And pay attention. Pepe doesn't like to repeat himself. The real killers are the army and the *Fuerza Armadas Revolucionarias*, the crazy Reds. It is they who are trying to control the coca fields and the roads to the south. It we didn't help the *campesinos* with the harvest and show them how to make pasta of it so it can be shipped out, they would die of hunger. As it is, they pay protection to the fucking Marxists. Not to us, my smart-ass friend. The Indians have been chewing coca for two thousand years, to blunt their hunger, to stay in their dream world. Otherwise they would go stark mad with misery. When the Yankees spray

136

defoliant, everything dies, everything. You didn't know that, cretin, did you? That way the price goes up and the American agents and the American military take a bigger cut.

With a viper's darting speed, surprising in so grossly rotund a man, Pepe seized Cardenio by the collar. Their faces were inches apart. "I don't touch drugs. I never have. Can you get that through your thick skull? But millions of others crave the shit. They go insane without it. They'll whore and beg and kill for the next dose. They can't even wait for us to get it across the border. They cram the fancy hotels in Boca-grande panting for our deliveries. They piss in their pants when they see us coming. I hear that there are one hundred and thirty thou-sand acres of coca under cultivation, a billion dollars' worth a year. Only because they ache for it in North America, in Europe. If they stopped using the *merda*, what you call our horrible business would close down. Do you get my meaning, Señor poet?"

Robles loosened his grip. Cardenio straightened up, shaking. When Pepe resumed, his voice came as from a distance, with seren-ity.

"You'll write that lament for Paco. You won't forget to mention that he saved my life. That there was no better shooter or runner anywhere, in any fucking cartel. You've got that straight, the lot of you? He would wade through fire for me, would Paco the Wildcat. Since his death, I have sour dreams." Robles had risen. "You'll put on your circus tomorrow. A *los cinco de la tarde.*" His leer was very nearly infectious. "I can promise you a large audience. O yes, I can guarantee you that. And some music. We fancy bands and good tunes in Medellín. From you I want best quality stuff. Nothing shoddy or secondhand. Have I made myself clear? Now to work, *amigos*, to work." Receding at an unhurried, somewhat royal pace, Pepe let drop into Rosaria's lap a wad of bills.

Neither he nor the hirelings heard the click of Toby Warren's tape recorder from behind the rangy rubber plant.

🌶 🌶 🌶

They could hear the fanfare as they left their motel. The sound came hot and yellow like a sheen of fire in the air. It made Osvaldo's skull-skin prickle. The pounding march of the bullfighters entering the ring. Francesca rocked to the beat. All around them people were hurrying towards the plaza. Some with children perched on their shoulders. The brassy prelude had shifted into a pop hit. It reverberated from walls and balconies. Involuntarily, Casteñon's feet took up the rhythm. The six performers had to elbow their way through the crowd. A proper stage had been carpentered in front of the plinth. Festooned with the national colors, equipped with a microphone and loudspeakers, state of the art. In the surrounding jacaranda and from the lampposts, balloons bobbed up and down like over-ripe fruit. As Casteñon and company came closer, a flashbulb started popping and the cameraman padded backward, like a disjointed grasshopper in retreat. Now the band was thumping away at a tango.

From a balcony, the mayor was waving amiably, his sash and chain giving off merry sparkles. The chief of police seemed enveloped by a foliage of gold braid and decorations. Osvaldo looked hard for Señor Pepe but could not locate him and felt uneasy. The nameless watcher of the previous day was testing the microphone. At every tap, raucous static boomed through the square. An abrupt silence unfurled: the national anthem. After which the bandsmen put down their instruments and emptied bottles of mineral water from under their seats. Was it a gesture from the mayor which unleashed the applause? As the visitors climbed onto the stage, it grew to a tumult. The platinum blond immediately behind the chief of police blew a kiss. The boy who had been there the day before emitted a piercing whistle. And there was the blind man, his mouth open as if drinking in the festive clamor.

Reaching for the mike, Casteñon felt at once afraid and exultant, "like a man lamed yet set free," wrote Toby Warren on his notepad. Casteñon raised his hands, palms wide open, in a plea for quiet. When the calls and plaudits subsided, he made a bow to the potentates and a salute of fraternal regard to the musicians. The tuba player waved back. A flock of choughs spiraled low in the half-light of afternoon. Rosaria was straining to count them as if her life depended on getting the sum right.

"Esteemed Mayor, your Excellency (the chief of police's epaulets, large as cabbages, seemed to solicit no less), ladies and gentlemen of Medellín, my colleagues and I are deeply honored and moved by your welcome. It warms our hearts." A robust "bravo" from somewhere in the crowd. "We are ordinary folk and have come to you with simple hopes. Your presence here this afternoon and yours, Sir" (another bow to the balcony), shows that we have not come in vain." As at a flourish from some hidden conductor, applause rippled. "To express our gratitude, we have prepared a new poem for this occasion. But before I ask our Francesca to read it to you, allow me a word of introduction." A nearby church bell marked the quarter hour with a gentle cough. "This poem, like the one we began with yesterday (can it really only have been yesterday? wondered Osvaldo, perspiring) is a sad poem. It tells of the death of a friend. Why should we have written a sad poem, a lament, for so joyous a gathering? Why sing of death when we intend to wake life and good hope?" The attention of the audience was like a weight suspended in the air. "Just like music, serious poetry is never either totally happy or totally sad. It aims to be like life itself; it seeks to sound the note of sorrow in our joys and of joy in our sorrows. It would remind us of death at even the brightest *fiesta* and of rebirth even at the blackest midnight. It is a terrible thing to lose a close friend; it is a wonderful thing trying to remember him, to know that our remembrance will keep him alive within us. Now Francesca will speak and sing for you a *llanto* for Jesu Soto, who died young."

Casteñon could have sworn that he had glimpsed the harsh flash of the ring. But from where in the plaza or on the balconies had it come? Francesca stepped forward, her eyes half closed. Cardenio could not but notice that under her blouse, with its Peruvian motif, her nipples were erect.

> The eyes of the wildcat are fire
> When they look at the thornbush
> It smolders.
> They know neither fear nor mercy.
> But the world is full of devils
> And the wildcat will never betray.

The smoke was clearing from Francesca's throat. She sang out bell-clear.

> Who are we in the tangled branches
> Of the thornbush
> To say what is evil?
> Friendship is stronger than love
> It holds even in hell.

Osvaldo could scarcely believe the new force, the soaring in her voice. The square was brimful with its power.

139

Farewell friend Paco, *adiós*,
You carried messages of death
Like the eyes of the wildcat
You kept faith with the night.

Francesca had flung her arms wide. The light ebbing behind the mountains enveloped her. She sang of desolation with exultant joy. Rosaria saw the birds career skyward as in a silent wind.

Adiós, friend Paco,
Walker through fire.
May you find peace
Like the wildcat at sundown
Like the wildcat at sundown.

It was then that the first shots rang out.

Nominated by Philip Levine

BABY

by JANET SYLVESTER

from SENECA REVIEW

Baby, for a long time, has been reading
A Short History of Modern Philosophy.
It doesn't console her. Marxism's lasting
value doesn't console her. The death
of timelessness into history
can't console her self, self, self,
aware, alienated, realizing. She accumulates,
like surplus value, years recorded
on a driver's license. Too much
wonderful self to go around,
she goes around, a fit of pique
and torque. She hopes for a modish personality
disorder and, *poof*, her wish is granted.
Her shrink, forgiveably, yawns. The sound
of Baby's love's a ticking escalator
in an empty airport somewhere in Bahrain.
Now Baby yawns. The sound of her love's
the infinitesimal wrinkling of a teabag
drying in a saucer in the 12th Arrondisement.
The sound of her love's the whirling death
of a moth in a web strung between branches
of sagebrush in Utah. Baby doesn't want to:
a) Change. b) Not change.

A blue, not cerulean—ultramarine—
deepens her. The sound of her love

is the glide of notes in the throat of a thrush
beside an abandoned barn in New Hampshire.

Listen up, boys: Baby
is not a Mommy; Baby's a baby.
She puts the entire world into her mouth:
she tastes a leaf, the satin glide
of taupe in a nightgown, the moss
and rust of light, thirst, which is closed,
hunger's blood-tinged tongue
and beating heart. *Why* is Baby's word.
She yelled it out the window of the car
when she was eight. Naked in morning sun
in an arroyo, she slid it into a rattlesnake.
She stroked it into the small of the back
of every man she loved, breathed it
on the eyelid of her stillborn daughter, caught it,
catches it still, between her teeth
at academic meetings. She's filled with the surplus
value of this feeling. Hours of unpaid labor
accumulate with textile slowness, lengthening
like Bruges lace, a halo of candle flame
illuminating her as she yawns.

The sound of her love is one dark look.
It could go on and on.
Baby considers object-relationships.
Baby considers the wing and the blade.
Rain-soaked, she's marked, the curve of an ache.

The sound of her love is astral dust.
The sound of her love is molecular water
caught in salt in a meteor billions of years ago.

This, by the way, is not a love poem.
Love's expensive, she says,
Love is just way too expensive.
When she's in it, she's a pig in dirt.
When she's in it, she's a wagonload of devils.

Poor baby.
A mirror teardrops onto Baby's brow,
across her cheekbones, into the indent
above her upper lip, along her hands.

Once upon a time's hidden geometry,
which Baby intuited rather than knew
in the endless deferral system called her mind,
Baby met a stranger. She shook the stranger
up and down; she tapped its sternum;
she listened at its head (which rattled slightly);
dog-like, devoted, she dragged it like a doll
by one arm, back and forth,
back and forth. She dragged it
into a village built around a garden.
Svelte with tears, she laid it down.
Weak with power, she opened and closed
its eyes, smoothed its fingers, kissed
its little hands. "Ein Mann
und eine Frau," the tune wafted
out of a summerhouse near Prague.
She crossed the song, a metaphor, a footbridge
giving up its distance. She kept
walking. It was a sing-along. She sang:
Spit and sinew, gauze on water,
the law of beauty rude in a world of kitsch.

The doll, which she had almost forgotten,
took on weight. It sweated at her effort,
pulled her to her knees. She aimed
one well-placed slap
at its painted face. It aimed one
well-placed slap at hers.
Counter-weights, they used each other.
They rose. Oh dear, it was much,
much taller than she, now
a man where they played at statues.
Baby spun and froze, hands on her hips.
The man continued to spin. A spinning

penny, he defined one edge.
Baby, not a dissimulator, hoped:
a) He'd save himself. b)
In the parking lot of the Mall of the Emotions,
he'd sink forever into spewy asphalt.

He stopped. The thought he thought she thought
was not the thought she thought she thought.

Why, said Baby. He watched her:
not with the gaze of an infinite number
of eyes (which Baby was growing used to),
not with the gaze of the eyes of many friends
(those she would recognize),
not with the gaze of one in love
(that's presence), but with the gaze of one
who's absent (who lives in imagination).

Baby, used to being top banana
in the shock department, waited.
She was at his mercy; he, at hers.
In me thirsts, he said.
Starved out, Baby bathed
in the fog of the phrase. *Talk English,*
she complained. At this, he smiled
like a Czechoslovakian novel. *Why?*
said Baby. At this he smiled like a Roman
pastry powdered with gold. Baby
was no longer yawning. At this
he smiled like an Aztec priest jacklit
by luxury.
                 And so, dear listener,
our tale concludes at its decisive moment
on a dirt lane in a foreign country
under trees studded with leaves large
and star-shaped, beside a fountain
weeping gardenias into the fizzy
early evening air. Baby
is a fresh horse on a lead line.
Baby's a wagonload of language.

Baby is your surplus in a world
of labor hard and unremarkable.
Baby is what's left over,
when you go home. The sound
of her love is your sleep.

Nominated by Donald Platt, Seneca Review

NEAR-EXTINCT BIRDS OF THE CENTRAL CORDILLERA

fiction by BEN FOUNTAIN III

from ZOETROPE: ALL-STORY

> *"I extended to the comandante the opportunity to walk the floor of the exchange*
> *with me, and he seemed reasonably intrigued."*
> —Richard Grasso, Chairman, New York Stock Exchange
> Bogotá, Colombia, June 26, 1999

No WAY Blair insisted to anyone who asked, no self-respecting bunch of extortionist rebels would ever want to kidnap him. He was the poorest of the poor, poorer even than the hardscrabble campesinos pounding the mountains into dead slag heaps—John Blair, graduate assistant slave and aspiring Ph.D, whose idea of big money was a twenty-dollar bill. In case of trouble he had letters of introduction from Duke University, the Humboldt Institute, and the Instituto Geográfica in Bogotá, whose director was known to have contacts in the Movimiento Unido de Revolucionarios de Colombia, the MURC, which controlled unconscionable swaths of the southwest cordilleras. For three weeks Blair would hike through the remnant cloud forest, then go back to Duke and scratch together enough grants to spend the following year in the Huila district, where he would study the effects of habitat fragmentation on rare local species of parrotlets.

It could be done; it would be done; it had to be done. Even before he'd first published in a peer-reviewed journal—at age seventeen, in *Auk*, "Field Notes on the Breeding and Diet of the Tovi Parakeet"— Blair had known his was likely the last generation that would witness scores of these species in the wild, which fueled a core urgency in his boyhood passion—obsession, his bewildered parents would have said—for anything avian. Full speed ahead, and damn the politics; as it happened they grabbed him near Popayán, a brutally efficient bunch in jungle fatigues who rousted all the livestock and people off the bus. Blair hunched over, trying to blend in with the compact Indians, but a tall skinny gringo with a big backpack might as well have had a turban on his head.

"You," said the *comandante* in a cool voice, "you're coming with us."

Blair started to explain that he was a scholar, thus worthless in any monetary sense—he'd been counting on his formidable language skills to walk him through this very sort of situation—but one of the rebels was into his backpack now, spilling the notebooks and Zeiss-Jena binoculars into the road, then the Leica with the cannon-barrel 200x zoom. Blair's most valuable possessions, worth more than his car.

"He's a spy," announced the rebel.

"No, no," Blair politely corrected. "*Soy ornithologo. Estudiante.*"

"You're a spy," declared the *comandante*, poking Blair's notebooks with the tip of his gun. "In the name of the Secretariat I'm arresting you."

When Blair protested they hit him fairly hard in the stomach, and that was the moment he knew that his life had changed. They called him *la merca*, the merchandise, and for the next four days he slogged through the mountains eating cold *arepas* and sardines and taking endless taunts about firing squads, although he did, thanks to an eighty-mile-a-week running habit, hold up better than the oil executives and mining engineers the rebels were used to bringing in. The first day he simply put down his head and marched, enduring the hardship only because he had to, but as the column moved deeper into the mountains a sense of possibility began to assert itself, a signal too faint to call an idea. To the east the cordillera was scorched and spent, rubbled by decades of desperate agriculture. The few mingy scraps of surviving forest were eerily silent, but once they crossed the borders of the MURC-controlled zone the vegetation closed around them with the density of a cave. At night Blair registered a deep suck and gurgle, the engine of the forest's vast plumbing system; every morning they woke to piha birds screaming like pigs, and then the mixed-species flocks kicked in with their contrapuntal yammerings and groks and crees that made the forest sound like a construction site. In three days on the trail Blair reliably saw fourteen species on the CITES endangered list, as well as an exceedingly rare *Hapalopsittaca fuertesi* perched in a fern the size of a minivan. He was amazed, and said as much to the young *comandante*, who eyed him a moment in a thoughtful way.

"Yes," the rebel answered, "ecology is important to the revolution. As a scholar"—he gave a faint, possibly ironic smile—"you can appreciate this," and he made a little speech about the environment, how the *firmeza revolucionaria* had banned the multinational logging and mining "mafias" from all liberated zones.

The column reached base camp on the fourth day, trudging into the fortified MURC compound through a soiling rain. They hauled Blair straight to the Office of Complaints and Claims, where he sat for two hours in a damp hallway staring at posters of Lenin and Che, wondering if the rebels planned to shoot him at once. When at last they led him into the main office, Comandante Alberto's first words were:

"You don't look like a spy."

A number of Blair's possessions lay on the desk: binoculars, camera, maps, and compass, the notebooks with their microscopic Blairian scribble. Seven or eight *subcomandantes* were seated along the wall, while Alberto, the *comandante maximo*, studied Blair with the calm of someone blowing smoke rings. He resembled a late-period Jerry Garcia in fatigues, a heavy man with steel-rim glasses, double bags under his eyes, and a dense Brillo bush of graying hair.

"I'm not a spy," Blair answered in his wired, earnest way. "I'm an ornithologist. I study birds."

"However," Alberto continued, "if they wanted to send a spy they wouldn't send somebody who looked like a spy. So the fact that you don't look like a spy makes me think you're a spy."

Blair considered. "And what if I did look like a spy?"

"Then I'd think you were a spy."

The *subcomandantes* hawed like drunks rolling around in the mud. So was it all a big joke, Blair wanted to know, or was his life really at stake? Or both, thus a means of driving him mad? "I'm an ornithologist," he said a little breathlessly, "I don't know how many ways I can tell you that, but it's true. I came to study the birds."

Alberto's jaws made a twisted, munching motion, like he was trying to eat his tongue. "That is for the Secretariat to decide, all cases of spying go to the Secretariat. And even if you are what you say you are, you will have to stay with us while your release is arranged."

"My 'release,' " Blair echoed bitterly. "You know kidnapping is a crime in most countries. Not to mention a violation of human rights."

"This isn't a kidnapping, this is a *retención* in the sociopolitical context of the war. We merely hold you until a fee is paid for your release."

"What's the difference?" Blair cried, and when Alberto wouldn't answer he came slightly unglued. "Listen," he said, "I don't have any money, I'm a student, okay? In fact I'm worse than worthless, I owe twenty thousand dollars in student loans. And if I'm not back at Duke in two weeks," he went on, his voice cracking with the wrongness and rage of it all, "they're going to give my teaching-assistant slot to somebody else. So would you please save us all a lot of trouble and let me go?"

They scanned his passport photo instead, then posted it on their Web site with a $5 million ransom demand, which even the hardcore insurgents knew was a stretch. "Sixth Front gets the Exxon guys," Subcomandante Lauro bitched, "and we get the scientist with the holes in his boots." He became known around camp as "John Blair," always the two names together, *Johnblair*, but *John* got mangled in the depths of their throats so that it came out as the even more ridiculous *Joan*. In any case they couldn't seem to speak his name without smiling; thirty years of low-intensity warfare had given the rebels a heightened sense of the absurd, and Blair's presence was just too fertile to ignore, a gringo so thick, so monumentally oblivious that he'd walked into the middle of a war to study a bunch of birds.

"So tell me, Joan Blair," one of the *subcomandantes* might say, pointing to a manakin spouting trills and rubatos or the tanagers that streaked about like meteor showers, "what is the name of that species, please?"

He knew they were testing him, nominally probing for chinks in his cover, but more than that they were indulging in the fatuous running joke that seemed to follow him everywhere. Which he handled by coming right back at them, rattling off the Latin and English names and often as not the Spanish, along with genus and all the natural history he could muster before the rebel waved his arms and retreated. But an implacable sense of mission was rising in Blair. He eyed the cloud forest lapping the compound's walls and knew that something momentous was waiting for him.

"If you let me do my work," he told Comandante Alberto, "I'll prove to you I'm not a spy."

"Well," Alberto answered, "perhaps." A man of impressive silences and ponderous speech, who wore his gravitas like a pair of heavy boots, he had a habit of studying his hands while he spoke, slowly turning them back and forth while he declaimed Marxist rhetoric in the deep rolling voice of a river flowing past giant boulders. "First the Secretariat must review your case."

Always the Secretariat, MURC's great and powerful Oz. In the evenings the officers gathered on the steps of their quarters to listen to the radio and drink *aromática* tea. Blair gradually insinuated himself onto the bottom step, and after a couple of weeks of Radio Nacional newscasts he understood that Colombia was busily ripping itself to shreds. Gargantuan car bombs rocked the cities each week; judges and journalists were assassinated in droves; various gangs, militias, and guerrillas fought the Army and the cops, while the drug lords and revanchists sponsored paramilitary *autodefensa* squads which seemed to specialize in massacring unarmed peasants. In their own area Blair could hear shooting at night, and the distant thud of helicopters during the day. Rebel patrols brought in bodies and bloody *autodefensa* prisoners, while U.S. Air Force planes gridded the sky overhead, reconnoitering the local coca crop.

"Where," Blair asked during a commercial break, "is this Zone of Disarmament they're always talking about?"

"You're in it," Subcomandante Tono answered, to which Lauro added with a sarcastic snarl, "*You mean you couldn't tell?*"

Some evenings Alberto joined them, usually when one of his interviews was being broadcast; he'd settle onto the steps with a mug of tea and listen to himself lecturing the country on historical inevitability and the Bolivarian struggle and the venemous strategies of the World Bank. After one such broadcast he turned to Blair.

"So, Joan Blair, what do you think of our position?"

"Well," Blair said in his most formal Spanish, "of course I support these things as general principles—an end to poverty, an equable education system, elections where everyone is free to participate." The officers murmured patronizingly and winked at each other; amid the strenuous effort of articulating himself Blair barely took notice. "But frankly I think you're being too timid in your approach. If you really want to change society you're going to have to start thinking in more radical terms."

Everyone endured several moments of intense silence, until Alberto cleared his throat. "For example, Joan Blair?"

"Well, you're always going on about agrarian reform, but face it, you're just evading the real issue. If you really want to solve the land problem you're going to have to get away from the cow. They're too big, they overload the entire ecosystem. What we have to do is forget the cow and switch over to a diet of mushrooms and insects."

"Mushrooms and insects?" Lauro retched. "You think I'm risking my ass out here for mushrooms and insects?"

But Alberto was laughing. "Shut up Lauro, he gave an honest answer. I like this guy, he doesn't bullshit around—with a hundred guys like him I could take Bogotá in about two weeks."

During the day Blair was free to wander around the compound; for all their talk of his being a spy the rebels didn't seem to mind him watching their drills, though at night they put him in a storage hut and handcuffed him to a bare plank bed. His beard grew in a dull sienna color, and thanks to the high-starch, amoeba-enriched diet he began to drop weight from his already aerodynamic frame, a process helped along by the chronic giardia that felt like screws chewing through his gut. But these afflictions were mild compared to the awesome loneliness, and like all prisoners he spent countless vacant hours savoring the lost, now-clarified sweetness of ordinary days. The people in his life seemed so precious to him now—*I love you all!* he wanted to tell them, his parents and siblings, the Biology Department secretaries, his collegial though self-absorbed and deeply flawed professors. He missed books, and long weekend runs with his buddies; he missed women so badly that he wanted to gnaw his arm. To keep his mind from rotting in this gulag-style sump he asked for one of his blank notebooks back. Alberto agreed, more to see what the gringo would do than out of any humane impulse; within days Blair had extensive notes on countersinging among Scaled Fruit-eaters and agnostic displays in Wood-rails, along with a detailed gloss on Haffer's theory of speciation.

Alberto fell into the habit of chatting with Blair whenever they happened to cross paths in the compound. He would inquire about his research, admire the sketches in his notebook and generally smile on Blair like a benevolent uncle. It came out that Alberto was a former banker, a *burgués* city kid with advanced degrees; he'd chucked it all twenty years ago to join the MURC. "It was false, that bourgeois life," he confided to Blair. "I was your typical social parasite." But no matter how warm or frank these personal exchanges Blair couldn't shake the sense that Alberto was teasing him, holding back some essential part of himself.

"You know," Alberto said one day, "my grandmother was also very devoted to birds. She was a saint, this woman—when she walked into her garden and held out her arms the birds would fly down and perch on her hands."

"Amazing," said Blair.

"Of course I was just a kid, I thought everyone's grandmother could do this trick. But it was because she truly loved them, I know that now. She said the reason we were put here on earth was to admire the beauty which God created."

"Ah."

Alberto's lips pooched out in a sad, nostalgic smile. "Beauty, you know, I think it's nice, but it's just for pleasure. I believe that men should apply their lives to useful things."

"Who says beauty and pleasure aren't useful?" Blair shot back, sensing that Alberto was messing with his mind again. "Isn't that what revolutions are ultimately about, beauty and pleasure for everyone?"

"Well," the *comandante* laughed, "maybe. I'll have to think about that."

So much depended on the rebels' goodwill—whether they lived by the ideals they so solemnly sloganized. Blair knew from the beginning that their honor was the best guarantee of his life, and with time he began to hope that he'd found a group of people with a passion, a sense of mission, that was equal to his. They seemed to be authentic *concientizados*, fiercely committed to the struggle; they were also, to Blair's initial and recurring confusion, loaded with cash. They had the latest in laptops and satellite phones, fancy uniforms, flashy SUVs, and a potent array of high-tech weapons—not to mention Walkmen and VCRs—all financed, according to the radio news, by ill-gotten gains from the cocaine trade.

"It's a tax!" the rebels screamed whenever a government spokesman started going on about the "narcoguerrillas" of the MURC. "We tax coca just like any other crop!" A tax which brought in $600 million a year, according to the radio, a sum that gave Blair a wifty, out-of-body feeling. On the other hand there were the literacy classes and crop-rotation seminars, which the rebels sponsored for the local campesinos, who looked, however, just as scrawny here as in the nonliberated areas. So was it a revolution *a conciencia*, or just a beautifully fronted trafficking operation? Or something of both—Blair conceived that the ratio roughly mirrored his own odds of coming out alive.

The notebook became his means of staying clued to reality, of ordering time, which seemed to be standing still or maybe even running backwards. The only thing the guerrillas would say about his ransom negotiations was that Ross Perot might pay for his release, which Blair guessed—though he could never be sure—was some kind of joke. A group of the younger rebels took to hazing him, *los punketos*, ruthless kids from the city *comunas* who jittered the safeties of their guns whenever Blair walked by, the rapid *click-click-click* cascading in his wake like the prelude to a piranha feed. Sometimes he woke at night totally disoriented, unsure of where or even who he was; other nights it seemed that he never really slept, sinking instead into an oozing, submetabolic trance that left him vague and cranky in the morning. One night he was drifting in just such a haze when a *punketo* burst into the shed, announcing through riffs of soft hysterical laughter that he was going to blow Blair's head off.

"I wouldn't recommend it," Blair said flatly. The kid was giggling and twitching around, literally vibrating—hopped up on *basuco* was Blair's guess. He'd probably been smoking for hours.

"Go fuck yourself," said the kid, jamming his gun into the notch behind Blair's left ear. "I'll kill you if I want."

"It'll be thrilling for a minute, just after you pull the trigger." Blair was winging it, making it up as he went along; the main thing, he sensed, was to keep talking. "Then it'll be like having a hangover the rest of your life."

"Shut up you cocksucker, just shut the fuck up. Shut up so I can kill you."

"But it's true. I know what I'm talking about."

"*You?* You never killed anybody in your life."

"Are you kidding? The United States is an extremely violent country. You must have seen the movies, right? *Rambo? Die Hard?* Where I come from makes this place look like a nursery school."

"You're a liar," the kid said, though less certainly.

"Why do you think I'm here? I have so much innocent blood on my hands, I was ready to kill myself I was so miserable. Then it came to me in a dream, the Virgin came to me in a dream," he amended, remembering how the rebels fell to their knees and groveled whenever the Spanish priest came to say mass, and the *punketos* were always the worst, weeping and slobbering on the padre's ring as he walked among them. " 'Follow the birds and you'll have peace,' that's what she told me in the dream. 'Follow the birds and your soul will know peace.' "

And Blair talked on in the most hypnotic, droning voice imaginable, cataloguing the wonders of Colombian avifauna until the *punketo* finally staggered off into the night, either stupefied or transcendent, it was hard to say which. But when dawn broke and Blair was still alive a weird peacefulness came over him, along with the imperatives of an irresistible conviction. As soon as the cuffs came off he strode across the yard to Complaints and Claims, brushed past the guard and walked into Alberto's office without so much as a knock. Alberto and Tono were spreading maps across the *jefe's* big desk; when the door flew open they went for their holsters, a reflex that nearly got Blair's head blown off.

"Go on," he dared them, stepping up to the desk. "Either let me do my work, or shoot me."

There was a heat, a grim fury about Blair that most people would associate with madmen and fanatics. The *comandantes* eyed the gringo at a wary slant, and it occurred to Blair that, for the moment at least, they were actually scared of him.

"Well," said Alberto in a cautious voice, "what do you think, Tono?"

Tono blinked. "I think he's a good man, Comandante. And ecology is important to the revolution."

"Yes," Alberto agreed, "ecology is important to the revolution." He tried to smile, to inject some irony into the situation, but his mouth looked more like a fluttery open wound.

"Okay, Joan Blair, it will be as you wish. I give you permission to study your birds."

Blair was twelve the first time it happened, on a trip to the zoo—he came on the aviary's teeming mosh pit of cockatoos and macaws and Purple-naped Lories, and it was as if an electric arc had shot through him. And he'd felt it every time since, this jolt, the precision stab in

154

the heart whenever he saw Psittacidae—he kept expecting it to stop but it never did, the impossibly vivid colors like some primal force that stoked the warm liquid center of your soul.

He'd known a miracle was in these mountains, he'd felt it in his bones. For five rainy days he tramped ever-widening circles out from the base, traversing ridges and saddles and moiling through valleys while the armed guard followed him every step of the way. Hernan, Blair guessed, was another of the *comandantes'* jokes, a slight mestizo youth with catlike looks and a manner as blank and flaky as cooled ashes. By now Blair knew a killer when he saw one; Hernan would as soon shoot a man as pinch off a hangnail, but as they trudged through the gelatinous drizzle together Blair began to get the subtext of the *comandantes'* choice.

"So how long have you been with the MURC?" he asked.

"Always," Hernan replied in a dreamy voice.

"Always?"

"That other boy," Hernan said in a gaseous hum, "that other boy died. I have been a *revolucionario* my whole life."

Blair studied the youth, then went back to scanning the canopy. Alberto had returned the binoculars but not the camera.

"So I guess you've been in a lot of battles?"

"Yes," Hernan said in his humming voice, and he seemed to reflect. "Yes, many," he added."

"What's it like?" Blair asked rudely, but the kid's catatonia was driving him nuts.

"Oh, it's not so bad. Once the shooting starts everything's okay."

Which Blair took for a genuine answer; five days through some of the most beautiful, rugged country in the world and the youth showed all the emotion of a turtle. It might not matter what you hit him with—a firefight, a bowl of stew, a trip to Disneyland—Hernan would confront each one with the same erased stare, but when Blair passed him the binoculars on the fifth day, pointing down a valley at a grove of wax palms and the birds wheeling around like loose sprockets, Hernan focused and gazed in silence for a time, then burst out laughing.

"They're so silly!" he cried.

And they were, Blair agreed, they were delightful, this remnant colony of Crimson-capped parrots whose flock notes gave the impression of a successful cocktail party. There'd been no sightings of the Crimson since 1973, when Tetzlaff et al. spotted a single breeding pair in Pichincha, Ecuador. CITES listed the species as critically endangered, though the more pessimistic literature assumed extinction; that first day Blair counted sixty-one birds, a gregarious, vocal group with flaming crowns and chunky emerald-green bodies, their coverts flecked with blues and reds like glossy M&Ms. Sixty-one birds meant that God was good: not only was there a decent chance of saving the species, but if he lived and made it home with his data intact Blair was going to knock the ornithological world on its ass. He and Hernan built a blind of bunchgrass and palm fronds, and Blair settled into the grind-it-out fieldwork mode. He charted the foraging grounds, the potential nest holes, the roosts and flyways across the valley; he identified the mated pairs within the flock and noted the species' strong affinity for wax palms—*Ceroxylon andiculum*, itself endangered—and surmised a trophic relationship. They talked constantly, with complex repertoires of sounds, chattering in an offhand, sociable way as they clambered about the canopy or sputtered from tree to tree, their short shallow wing beats batting the air with the noisy ruction of windup toys.

Within weeks Blair had a basic ethological profile. In exchange for the privilege of fieldwork he had to do camp chores every afternoon, which was nothing—three years of graduate school had inured him to slave labor and subsistence living. In some ways this was better than school: he got room and board, worked with minimal interruptions, and was furnished a local guide-bodyguard free of charge. Hernan proved adept at tracking the birds on their feeding rounds, leading Blair through the forest as they listened for debris tumbling through the leaves, then the fuddles and coos that meant Crimsons were overhead. At the blind he usually lay back on the grass and dozed, rousing from time to time to say amazing things about himself.

"I had a girlfriend," he once confessed to Blair in a sleepy voice. "She wouldn't let me kiss her, but she'd bite me on the ear."

In the same vacant drone he told all manner of terrible stories: battles he'd fought, prisoners he'd executed, patrols where his column had come across peasants burned to death or babies nailed to planks. The stories were so patently nightmarish that Blair wondered if Hernan was talking in his sleep, channeling the dreams that rose like swamp gas out of his wounded subconscious. His own family had been killed when he was twelve, their village wiped out by *autodefensas* for electing a former insurgent as mayor.

"Sometimes I see them," Hernan murmured in a half-doze, one arm thrown over his eyes, feet crossed at the ankles. "Sometimes I'm lying on my cot at night, and I look up and all my family's standing there. And it's like I'm lying in a coffin, you know? My family's alive and I'm the one who's really dead, and they've come to my funeral to tell me good-bye."

Blair was so horrified that he had to write it all down, the baroque, spiraling cycles of murder and revenge mixed with his notes on allo-preening among the mated Crimsons and the courtship dances of the unattached males, the way they minced around like fops doing a French quadrille. *Sickness* he wrote in the margin of his notes, *there's a sickness in the world*, along with *parrots the most intelligent and beautiful of birds, also the most threatened—a clue to the nature of things (?)*. He wrote it all because it all seemed bound together in some screamingly obvious way that he couldn't quite get. Tramping through the woods, he and Hernan kept coming across giant cocaine labs, the thuggish workers warning them off with drawn machetes. The coca fields around the camp kept expanding; radio reports of the fledgling peace talks took on a spectral air, with the MURC insisting on pre-negotiation of themes which might be substantively negoti-ated at a later time. Every few weeks Hernan would go off on a mission, and after three or four days he'd drag in with the other survivors, skinnier, with corpse-like shadows under his eyes but oth-erwise the same—the next dawn he and Blair would be at the blind, watching the birds greet the day with gurgling chatter. In March the males began to hold territory, and when the females developed brood patches Hernan offered to climb the trees for a look at the nests, a job they both knew was beyond Blair. After a year in the mountains he was a rashy stick figure of his former self, prone to fevers and random dizzy spells that made his head feel like a vigor-ously shaken snow globe. Sometimes he coughed so hard that his nose bled; his bowels were papier-mâché, his gums ached, and the sturdiest thing about him seemed to be his beard, which looked pos-itively rabbinical.

"Go for it," Blair answered, and in a flash Hernan was seventy feet up the tree, relaying information while Blair wrote. Clutch, two; eggs, white; nest, about the size of a Guambiano water jar. Hernan had left his rifle propped against a nearby tree; Blair eyed it while al-lowing an escape fantasy to float through his head, a minivacation from the knowledge that if he ran they'd catch him before the day was out. Still, the rifle raised a nagging question: how could he leave, now, in the middle of his research, even if he got the chance? But not to leave might be a slow form of suicide. Sooner or later something would get him, either sickness, a swacked-out *punketo* or an *autodefensa* raid, or maybe the Secretariat would decide to make a point at his expense. The hard line had lately crept back into the MURC's rhetoric, which Blair guessed was part posturing for the peace talks, part exasperation at the trend of the times. The Soviet Union had imploded, the Berlin Wall was gravel, and the Cuban adventure was on life support, and yet the MURC insisted it would soldier on.

"Some say the end of history has come," Alberto intoned to the journalists. "We can all have different interpretations about what's happened in the world during these very complex years, but the fact of the matter is that most things haven't changed. Hunger, injustice, poverty, all of the issues which led the guerrilla of the MURC to take up arms are still with us."

True, thought Blair. He wanted to believe in the Revolution, in its infinite capacity for reason and justice, but the Revolution wouldn't return his camera for one day. All of his research would be deemed hypothetical unless supported by a photo or specimen. No photo, no dissertation, and he'd sooner burn every page of his notes than take a specimen.

"I could steal the camera back for you," Hernan offered. "I think I know where he's keeping your stuff."

"What would happen if they caught us?"

Hernan reflected. "To me, nothing—I can just disappear. To you?" He shrugged. "They'd probably cut off your fingers and send them to your family."

Blair considered for a second, then shook his head. Not yet. He wasn't that desperate yet.

When the chicks hatched Hernan went up again, checking out the nests while the parents and auxiliaries seethed around his head like a swarm of belligerent box kites. One egg would hatch, then the second a few days later; Blair knew the second hatchings were insurance, doomed to die unless their older siblings died first, and he sketched out a program for taking the second chicks and raising them in captivity.

The Crimsons had saved him, in a way; maybe he'd save them in turn, but he had to know everything about them first. "There's something wrong with us," he told Hernan one day. He was watching the nest holes for the soon-to-fledge chicks and thinking about the news, the latest massacres and estimates of coca acreage. The U.S. had pledged Colombia $1.6 billion in aid—advisers, weapons, helicopters, the whole bit—which made Blair wonder if his countrymen had lost their minds. There was a fire raging in Colombia, and the U.S. planned to hose it down with gasoline.

"Who?" Hernan answered, cracking open one eye.

"Us. People. The human race."

Hernan lunked up on one elbow and looked around, then subsided to the grass and closed his eyes. "People are devils," he said sleepily. "The only *persona decente* who ever lived was Jesus Christ. And the Virgin. And my mother," he added.

"Tell me this, Hernan—would you shoot me if they told you to?"

"Anh." Hernan didn't bother to open his eyes. "They'd never ask me."

"They wouldn't?" Blair felt an unfamiliar surge of hope.

"Of course not. They always put the new guys on the firing squads to toughen them up. Guys like me they never bug for stuff like that."

Over the next few days seven chicks came wobbling out of the nests, and Blair set himself the task of tracking the flock as it educated the youngsters. Back in the shed he had notebooks and loose papers crammed with data, along with feathers, eggshell fragments, and stool samples, also a large collection of seeds with beak-shaped chunks gnarled out of them. Occasionally Alberto would trek up the mountain to the blind, checking in on Blair and the latest developments with "the children," as he'd taken to calling the parrots. He seemed relaxed and jolly during these visits, though his essential caginess remained; he would smile and murmur noncommittally when Blair lobbied to start his captive-breeding program. "Get with it, Alberto," Blair pressed one day. "It would be a huge PR coup for you guys if the MURC rescued an endangered species. I could help you across the board with that, like as an environmental consultant. You know we're really on the same side."

Alberto started to speak, then broke off laughing as he studied the wild gringo in front of him. Blair was dressed in scruffy jungle fatigues—his civilian clothes had worn out long ago—and with his gaunt, weathered face and feral beard he looked as hardened as any of the guerrillas. New recruits to the camp generally assumed that he was a zealot from the mythical suicide squad.

"Joan Blair, you remind me of a man I once knew. A man of conviction, a real hero, this guy. Of course he died in Bolivia many years ago."

"Doing what?"

"Fighting for the revolution, of course!"

Blair winced, then shook off the spasm of dread. "So what about my captive-breeding program?"

Alberto chuckled and patted Blair's shoulder. "Patience, Joan Blair, you must learn patience. The revolution is a lot more complicated than you think."

"They're negotiating you," Hernan said a few weeks later. "Some big shot's supposed to be coming soon."

"Bullshit," Blair said. The camp was a simmering cesspool of rumors, but nothing ever happened.

"It's true, Joan Blair, I think you're going home."

"Maybe I'll stay," Blair said, testing the idea on himself. "There isn't an ornithologist in the world who's doing the work I'm doing here."

"No, Joan, I think you should go. You can come back after we've won the war."

"What, when I'm eighty?" Blair chewed a blade of grass and reflected for a moment. "I still don't have my photo. I'm not going anywhere until I get that."

The rumors persisted, gradually branched into elaborate subrumors. Just to be safe Blair got all his data in order, but it was still a shock to see the helicopters come squalling out of the sky one day, cutting across the slopes at a sassy angle and heading for camp. Blair and Hernan were walking back for afternoon chores, and if there was ever any doubt about Blair's intentions his legs resolved it for him, carrying him down the trail at a dead sprint. At camp the helicopters were parked on the soccer field, two U.S. surplus Hueys with the sky-blue Peace Commission seal on their hulls. Campesinos and guerrillas were streaming into the compound; Blair had to scrum his way through the crowd to get a view of Complaints and Claims, where some kind of official moment was taking place on the steps. Several distinct factions were grouped around a microphone: Alberto and the *subcomandantes* were on one side, along with some senior *comandantes* whom Blair didn't recognize, while to their right stood a sleek delegation of civilians, Colombians with careful haircuts and tasteful gold chains. Blair spotted the American delegation at once—their smooth, milky skin was the giveaway, along with their khaki soft-adventure wear and identical expressions of informed concern. Everyone was raked toward the microphone, where a Colombian was saying something about the stalled peace talks.

Why didn't you tell me? Blair almost screamed. A Tele-Nacional crew was filming the ceremony; photographers scuttled around like dogs chasing table scraps. *What about me?* he wanted to shriek, *say something about me!* He tried in vain to make eye contact with the Americans, who'd arranged themselves into distinct pairs. The two middle-aged men stood farthest from the action, robust, toned, country-club types; the other two Americans stood close to the center, a tall, older gentleman with a shrinking hairline and sharp Adam's apple, then the sturdy young woman who was glued to his side, short of stature, hyperalert, firecracker cute. *The international community's show of support,* said the speaker. *A message of hope from U.S. financial circles.* Blair felt one of his dizzy spells coming on, his eyes clouding over in a spangly haze. He slumped and let the crowd hold him up; Hernan had vanished somewhere along the trail. When the delegation began to move inside Blair watched them disappearing as if in a dream, then roused himself at the last moment.

"Hey!" he yelped in English, "I'm American! Hey you guys, I'm an American!"

Only the woman seemed to hear, flashing a quick, startled look over her shoulder, then continuing inside. Blair started to follow but a guard blocked his way.

"*Alto,* Joan Blair. Only the big shots go in there."

"Who are those people?" Blair asked, craning for a look through the door. Which abruptly shut.

"Well," the guard said, assuming the manner of someone schooling a particularly dense child, "there is Señor Rocamora, the Peace Commissioner, and there is Señor Gonzalo, the Finance Minister—"

"But the Americans, who are they?"

"How the hell should I know? *Peces gordos,* I guess."

Blair didn't dare leave, not for a second, though he could feel the sun baking all the juices out of him. The crowd in the compound absently shuffled about, disappointed without really knowing why. *Fritanguera* ladies set up their grills and started frying dough; a King Vulture scraped lazy circles in the sky. After a while the American woman stepped outside and walked down the gallery to speak to the reporters. Blair brushed past the guard and was up in a second, intercepting the woman as she walked back to the door. Out of instinct she started to dodge him; he looked wild with his castaway's beard and grimy jungle fatigues, but his blue eyes beaming through the wreckage brought her up short.

"Oh! You must be John Blair!"

He could have wept with gratitude. "Yes, I'm John Blair! You know who I am!"

"Of course, State briefed us on your situation. I'm Kara Coleman, with the—" A scissoring blast of syllables shot off her lips. "Wow," she continued, eyeing him up and down, "you look like"—*hell*, she barely avoided saying—"you've been here awhile."

"Fifteen months and six days," Blair instantly replied. "You're with the State Department?"

"No, I'm with the—" She made that scissoring sound again. "I'm Thomas Spasso's assistant, he's leading our group. Thomas *Spasso*," she repeated in a firm voice, and Blair realized that he was supposed to know the name. "Chairman of the Nisex," she continued, almost irritated, but still Blair didn't have a clue. "The *Nisex*," she said as if speaking to a dunce, "the New York *Stock* Exchange."

Blair was confused, but quite as capable as anyone of rationalizing his confusion—he knew that fifteen months in the Andes might have turned his American frame of reference to mush. So maybe it wasn't so strange that the king of Wall Street would turn up here, in the jungly heart of MURC territory. Blair's impression of the stock market, admittedly vague, was of a quasi-governmental institution anyway.

"Right," he said, straining to put it all together. The unfamiliar English felt like paste on his tongue. "Sure, I understand. But who, I mean what, uh—why exactly are you here?"

"We're here to deliver a message from the financial community of its support for the current peace initiative. Foreign investment could do so much for this country, we felt the MURC might be more flexible if they knew the opportunities we could offer them. And Mr. Spasso has a special interest in Colombia. You know he's close personal friends with Ambassador Moreno."

Blair shut his eyes and wondered if he'd lost his mind. "You mean," he said in a shattered whisper, "this doesn't have anything to do with me?"

"Well, no, we came chiefly with the peace process in mind. I'm sorry"—she realized the effect she was having— "I'm truly sorry, I can see how insensitive that must seem to you right now."

Blair was sagging; all of a sudden he felt very, very tired. "Isn't there something you can do for me?" he softly wailed. "Anything?" Kara touched his arm and gave him a mournful look; she wasn't heartless, Blair could see, but rather the kind of person who might cry in movies, or toss bites of her bagel to stray dogs.

"Mr. Spasso might have some ideas," she said. "Come inside, I'll try to get you a few minutes with him."

She led Blair through the door, down a short hallway and into the big concrete room where the *comandantes* mediated peasant disputes every Tuesday and Thursday. The delegates were sitting in the center of the room, their chairs drawn in a circle as if for a group therapy session. Thomas Spasso was speaking through an interpreter, and in seconds Blair formed an impression of the chairman as a ticky, nervous guy, the kind of intractable motormouth who said the exact same thing no matter where he was. "Peace will bring you huge benefits from global investors," the chairman told the *comandantes*. "The capital markets are lining up for you, they want to be your partner in making Colombia an integral part of the Americas' economic bloc." He rattled on about markets and foreign investment, the importance of strong ratings from Moody's bond-risk service—the rebels sat there in their combat fatigues and Castro-style hats smiling and nodding at the chairman's words, but Blair could see they were barely containing themselves. It was so close that they didn't dare look at each other, but the real challenge came when the chairman invited them to visit Wall Street. "I personally extend to each and every one of you an invitation to walk the floor of the exchange with me," Spasso said, his voice thrumming with heartfelt vibrato. He clearly thought he was offering them the thrill of their lives, but Blair could picture the rebels howling on the steps tonight—*Oooo, that we should have this big honor, to walk the floor of the bourgeois exchange with him.* Even now the *comandantes*' eyes were bugging out, their jaws quivering with the strain of holding it in, and it was only by virtue of supreme discipline that they didn't fall out of their chairs laughing.

Spasso, ingratiating yet oblivious, talked on. "He's very passionate," Kara whispered to Blair, who was thinking how certain systems

163

functioned best when they denied the existence of adverse realities. After a while the Peace Commissioner got to say some words, then the Finance Minister, and then Alberto, who limited his comments to an acknowledgment of the usefulness of market mechanisms, "so long as social justice for the masses is achieved." Then some aides circulated a proposed joint statement, and the meeting dissolved into eddies and swirls as each group reviewed the language.

Kara waited until Spasso stood to stretch his legs. "Mr. Spasso," she called, hustling Blair over, "this is John Blair."

Spasso turned, saw Blair, and seemed to lose his power of speech.

"The hostage," Kara said helpfully, "he's in your briefing kit. The guy from Duke."

"Oh yes, yes, of course, the gentleman from Duke. How are you, so very nice to see you."

Nice to see you? Fifteen months in hell and *nice to see you?* For Blair it was like a curtain coming down.

"Sir, John and I were discussing his situation, and while he understands the limited scope of our visit he was also wondering if we could do anything with regard to facilitating his return home. At some possible future point."

"Well," Spasso said, "as you know we're here in the spirit of a private-sector exchange. Though your name did come up at the embassy this morning." He paused as one of the other Americans approached, a fellow with silver-blond hair and a keen, confident look. "Working the final numbers," he told Spasso, waving a legal pad at the chairman. "Then we're good to go. Thanks so much for setting this up, Tom."

Spasso nodded and glanced at his watch as the American moved off. People were milling about the big room, talking and bumping shoulders.

"Uhhh—"

"John Blair," Kara prompted.

"Mr. Blair, absolutely. I'm afraid your situation is rather problematic. There are laws"—he looked to Kara for confirmation—"apparently there are laws here in Colombia which prohibit private citizens from engaging in kidnap negotiations. Am I correct on that, Kara?"

"Unfortunately yes, sir."

" 'Aiding and abetting a kidnap negotiation,' I believe those are the words. We're to avoid any action that could be construed as aiding and abetting a kidnap negotiation, those are our strict instructions

164

from the State Department. Which I know must seem rather harsh to you—"

Blair had groaned.

"—but I'm sure you can appreciate the bind this puts us in. Much as we'd like to help, our hands are tied."

Blair wanted to hit this fool, or at least shake him hard enough that some air got to his brain. "Look," he said in his most determined voice, "they're threatening to kill me, they've accused me of being a spy. They could take me out and shoot me as soon as you leave."

"I'm certainly aware of the seriousness of your situation." *Señor Spasso*, someone called from across the room. "Believe me, I am most sympathetic. But any goodwill we foster here today will redound to your future benefit, I'm sure."

Señor Spasso, we're ready.

"Be right there! People are working for your release, I can assure you. Top people, extremely capable people. So hang in there, and God bless."

Spasso joined the general push of people toward the door. "I am so, so sorry," Kara said. She reached into her satchel and pulled out a handful of Power Bars. "Here, take these," she said, passing them to Blair. "I'll talk to you before we leave."

Kara melted into the crowd. Blair allowed the flow to carry him out to the gallery, where he leaned against a column and closed his eyes. He could not comprehend what was happening to him, but it had something to do with the casual cruelty of people who'd never missed a meal or had a gun stuck to their heads. Out in the yard the press was forming ranks for another photo op. Spasso and company gathered around the microphone; while they made the same speeches as two hours ago Blair ate his Power Bars and discretely wept, though in time he pulled himself together and resolved to make one last plea for help. He scanned the yard and gallery for Kara, then entered the building, where he found her in the big concrete room. She and the other two Americans were sitting with Alberto and one of the senior *comandantes*. They were speaking in quiet, reasoned tones, their chairs so close that their knees almost touched. Blair was struck by their visible ease with each other, the intimate air which enclosed the little group.

"Oh, John!" Kara cried. "Maybe John can help," she said to the others, waving Blair over. "John, we're having some trouble with the language here, maybe you can help us out."

The blond American stood with his legal pad. "All those years of high school Spanish," he chuckled, "and I don't remember a thing."

"John's American," said Kara. "He's in graduate school at Duke."

"Super!" The man pulled Blair close. "Listen, we're trying to work out the numbers here and we can't seem to get on the same page. I'm offering thirty-five hundred per fifty unit, fifty thousand board feet in other words. Think you could put that into Spanish for me?"

Blair eyed the scribble of numbers on the pad. "Thirty-five hundred . . ."

"Dollars, U.S."

Blair kept scanning the pad, the numbers teasing him; it seemed important to make sense of the mess. "Board feet . . ."

"It's the standard unit in the industry. One square foot by one inch thick."

"Of board," Blair said. "You're talking about lumber."

"You bet."

"Who are you?"

The man stuck out his hand. "Rick Hunley, Weyerhauser precious woods division."

"You're going to log this area?"

"That's the plan, if we can close this thing."

Blair turned to Alberto, who gave him a squirrelly, sullen look. The honks and woofs of the press conference drifted through the door, and that, Blair realized, was simply a show, a concoction of smiles and talking heads. Whereas the deal was happening right here in this room.

"Alberto," he cried in bitter, lancing Spanish, "how could you? How could you even think of doing such a thing?"

Alberto shrugged, then turned away as if he smelled something bad. "Running an army is expensive, Joan Blair. The revolution doesn't survive on air, you know."

"Christ, look at all the coca out there, how much money could you possibly need? You're going to wipe out the parrots if you log up here."

"We have to save the country, Joan Blair."

"What, so you can turn it over to these guys?"

"Enough."

"You think there'll be something to save when they're done with it?"

"Enough, Joan Blair, I mean it." Alberto flicked his hand as if shooing a fly. "Get out of here, I'm tired of listening to you. Beat it. Where are those son-of-a-whore guards—"

But Blair had rounded on Hunley. "There's a parrot up here," he said in very fast English, "an extremely rare species, these are probably the last birds of their kind in the world. If you guys come in here logging it's a pretty sure thing you're going to wipe them out."

"Whoa, that's news to me." Hunley and his partner exchanged dire looks; Hunley turned to Alberto. "Comandante, I can tell you right now if we get bogged down in any environmental issues then we're outta here. We don't have time to mess around with that stuff."

"Is not a problem," Alberto said, emitting the gruff sort of English that a bear might speak.

"Well according to your interpreter it is."

"Not a problem, no, for sure, no bird problems here. Forget the birds."

"I won't stand for this," Blair stated flatly. "I don't accept it. You people can't do this."

Alberto's lips cramped inward, holding back a smile, though Blair could see it surface in his eyes well enough, the near-lethal mix of pity and contempt. "Okay, Joan Blair, why don't you stop us," he mocked, but something skittish and shamed began to leak into his eyes, a grey, mizzly vapor that snuffed out all the light. Alberto tried to stare him down but couldn't, and at the moment he turned away Blair knew: the revolution had reached that classic mature stage where it existed only to serve itself.

"Okay," Alberto said, reaching for Hunley's legal pad, "I think we can make the deal." He circled a number on the pad and handed it back to Hunley. "For that, okay? For this price we make the deal, but one more thing. You have to take this guy with you."

"No way," Blair said, "forget it. You aren't getting rid of me."

"Yes, yes, you are going. We are tired of feeding you, you have to go home now."

"Go to hell Alberto, I'm staying right here."

Alberto paused, then turned to the Americans. "This man," he said stiffly, pointing to Blair, "is a spy. As a gesture of goodwill, for the peace process, I am giving him to you, you may please take him home. And if you don't take him home, today, now, he will be shot. Because that is what we do to spies."

Kara gasped, but the worldly lumber executives just laughed. "Well, son," said Hunley, turning to Blair, "I guess you better come with us."

Blair wouldn't look at them, Spasso, Kara, the others, he wouldn't acknowledge the smiling people in the seats around him. He kept his face turned toward the helicopter's open door, watching the dust explode as the engines powered up, the crowd waving through the storm of rotor wash. The chopper throbbed, shuddered, shyly wicked off the ground, and as it rose Blair glimpsed Hernan in the crowd, the kid dancing like a boxer as he waved good-bye. In the chaos of loading he'd slipped through the muddled security cordon and shoved a plastic capsule into Blair's hand—film, Blair had known without looking at it, a thirty-five-millimeter cartridge. The film was tucked into Blair's pants pocket now, while he clutched to his lap the backpack with its bundles of data and artifacts: the first, and very likely the last, comprehensive study of the Crimson-capped Parrot. He hung on as the Huey accelerated, trapdooring his stomach into empty space as it slammed into a sheer vertical climb. The world fell away like a ball dropped overboard, the torque and coil of the jungle slopes diminishing to finely pebbled sweeps of green. The craft pivoted as it climbed, nose swinging to the east, the Crimsons' valley with its fragile matchstick palms sliding past the door like a sealed tableau—from this height Blair could see how easy it would be, nothing at all to rub out the faint cilia of trees. Easy. The sheltering birds just so much incidental dust.

How does it feel? Spasso was shouting in his ear. *How does it feel to be free?* They were rising, rising, they might never stop—Blair closed his eyes and let his head roll back, surrendering to the awful weightlessness. Like dying, he wanted to tell them, like death, and how grieved and utterly lost you'd feel as everything precious faded out. That ultimate grief which everyone saves for the end, Blair was spending it, burning through all his reserves as the helicopter bore him away.

Nominated by Zoetrope: All Story

COMMERCE

by MICHAEL WATERS

from THE GETTYSBURG REVIEW

Niagara Falls, 18—

Some half-wit Barnum, amateur Noah,
fashioned an ark—a salvaged, broken barge—
to populate with creatures trapped or bought:
black bear, wolverine, a fox like a flame,

peacocks, possum, hogs, raccoon, wailing tribe
of forsaken dogs, weasel, skunk, even—
according to eyewitness reports—six
silver monkeys shipped by rail from New York,

God's mange-thumbed menagerie chained to planks
that would have floated three runaway slaves
had not abolitionists threatened court.
Then Noah bid his bestiary good-bye,

the raft of lamentation set adrift,
its creatures more confused than crazed, almost
calm as the ark spiraled toward the maelstrom,
the waters' vast uproar drowning weak cries,

white mists like shrouds enveloping the crew
while spectators whooped and scrambled both banks

and newsboys shilled beer a nickel a glass
till it perched midair on the precipice. . . .

Folklore swears the bear survived, pummeled ashore
where men beat her with clubs and muzzled her,
then dragged that rough beast saloon to saloon
where drafts of whiskey were chugged down her throat.

By morning she lay a rank heap on State—
schoolchildren leapfrogged the raggedy corpse.
Then one cat was found, eyeless, legs broken,
so for the next decade tramps tortured strays

to sell them to tourists, farm boys, and Poles
as The Cat Swept Over Niagara Falls,
singular souvenir, His living hand,
New World miracle—only one dollar.

Nominated by William Heyen, Andrew Hudgins, Robert Gibb

THE HIGH ROAD

fiction by JOAN SILBER

from PLOUGHSHARES

MY WHOLE LIFE, it always made me crazy when people weren't sensible. Dancers, for instance, have the worst eating habits. I can't begin to say how many anorexic little girls I used to have to hold up onstage, afraid they were going to faint on me any minute.

I myself was lean and tight and healthy in those days. I went out with different women, and I married one of them. I don't know why she married me, I was never kind to her, but women did not expect much then. She was probably a better dancer than I was, too. I left her, after a lot of nasty fights and spite on both sides, and I went and had my life with men. It was a dirty, furtive, sexy life then—this was before Stonewall—but it had its elations. Infatuation, when it happened, could be visionary, a lust from another zone. From the true zone, the molten center of the earth. I was in my twenties, listening to a lot of jazz, and I thought in phrases like that.

Andre, my lover, was in fact a musician, a trumpeter with a tender, earnest sound, sweet like Chet Baker, although he would have liked to have been as intense as Miles. Well, who wouldn't? I had been with men before him, but only one-night pickups, those flickering hallucinations that were anything but personal. When I met Andre, we were not in a bar but at a mixed party, and we had to signal each other cautiously and make a lot of conversation first. Andre was no cinch to talk to, either. Other white people thought he was gruff or scornful, but actually he was really quite shy.

When we went home together, after the party, we got along fine. For a shy person, he was confident and happy in bed (I was the rough and bumbling one). I could still recount, if I had to, the sequence of things we did that night. I have done them many times since—there isn't that much variety in the world—but the drama was particular and stunning just then. In the morning I made him a very nice breakfast (my wife had been a terrible cook), and he ate two helpings of my spinach omelet, as if he could not believe his good luck. He had a dry sense of humor, and he was quite witty about my makeshift housekeeping and my attempts at décor, the white fake-fur rug and the one wall painted black. We put on music, and we hung around, smoking cigarettes and reading the paper all afternoon. Just passing the time.

I was working in a show on Broadway, skip-skipping across the stage in cowboy chaps and swinging my silver lariat, and he came to see me perform. I suppose the other dancers knew who he was to me. Backstage everybody shook his hand and asked him if it wasn't the dumbest musical he'd ever seen. The girls told me later how nice he was. And sometimes I was in his world, when we went to hear music in the Village or once up to a club in Harlem. Anyone who saw us probably thought I was just some white theater guy wanting to be hip. Had we been a man and a woman, we would have had a much harder time walking together on the street.

Andre stayed with me more nights than not, even if he didn't live with me. But he had to go home to practice. A trumpet is not an instrument that can be played casually in someone's apartment. His own place, up in Morningside Heights, was in the basement (a great cheap find), and he had rigged up a booth lined with acoustic ceiling tile and squares of carpeting for his hours of practice. His chicken coop, I called it, his burrow. I never stayed over with him, and I only visited him there once, but I liked to imagine him hunched over his horn, blowing his heart out in that jerry-built closet.

He wasn't getting gigs yet, but sometimes he sat in with musicians he'd met. To this day, I couldn't say whether he was a great player or not. When he was playing with anyone, I worried like a parent—I looked around to see what people thought. He was okay, I think, but so modest and unflashy that he could be taken for a competent dullard. But he had a rare kind of attention, and sometimes, the way he worked his way in and the way he twisted around what they'd been playing made the other players smile. He was just learning.

In the daytime, he worked as a salesman in a men's clothing store in Midtown. Once I walked in the door and pretended to be a grouchy rich man who needed an ugly suit to wear to divorce court.

172

Something hideous, please, something you wouldn't wear to a dog-fight. This cracked Andre up. He laughed through his teeth, hissing softly. That's how bored he was there. He introduced me to the manager as his crazy friend Duncan, this lunatic he knew.

He was quite a careful dresser, from working in that place. A little too careful, I thought, with his richly simple tie and his little handkerchief folded in his pocket. I used to tell people he ironed his underwear, which he stoutly denied. For Christmas he bought me a silk shirt that probably looked silly on me but felt great. We had dinner that day with two of Andre's friends, Reg and Maxmilian. I made a goose, a bird none of us had ever had before. We kept goosing each other all night, a joke that wouldn't die. Reg got particularly carried away, I thought. Andre teased me about the ornateness of my meal—the glazed parsnips, the broccoli *polonaise*—wasn't there a hog jowl in anything? He wanted the others to be impressed with me, and they sort of were. Andre asked me to put on the record of *Aida* he liked, the one with Roberta Tebaldi.

"Renata Tebaldi," I said.

"Rigatoni Manicotti," he said. "What do I care what her name is?"

But I took to calling him Roberta after that. Just now and then, to needle him. Pass the peas, Roberta. Like that.

We were at the Village Vanguard with a couple he knew when I said, "Roberta, you want another drink?" He turned his beautiful, soft eyes on me in a long stare and said, "Cool it."

I did cool it then, but not for long. He was sleepy in the club, since he had been working at the store all day, and at one point he slumped back in his chair and dozed. Anyone who noticed probably thought he was on drugs. I sang into his ear in a loud, breathy falsetto, "Wake up, Roberta."

The week after this, he refused to take me with him when he went out with his friends. He announced it at breakfast on Saturday. "You don't know respect," he said. "Stay home and study your manners."

He wouldn't say any more. He never got loudly upset as my wife had. I couldn't even get a good fight going.

"Go," I said. "Get away from me, then."

But that night, when the show let out, I took off my satin chaps and rubbed away the greasepaint, and I went walking up and down Bleecker Street, checking out all the clubs that Andre might be in. I just wanted him to be sweet to me again. I wanted to make up. I walked through dark, crowded cellars, peering at tables of strangers who were trying to listen to some moody trio. I must have looked like a stalking animal.

What if he never came back to me? He wasn't in four places I tried, and at the fifth, I sat at the bar and drank a Scotch, but I couldn't stay still. I walked all the way to the river, close to tears. I had never seen myself like this, wretched and pathetic. I could hardly breathe, from misery. I just wanted Andre to be sweet to me again. I couldn't stand it this way.

On the pier I picked up a guy, an acne-scarred blond in a baseball jacket. I didn't have to say more than hi, and I brought him home in a cab to my place in the West Forties. He was just a teenager—the luxury of a cab ride impressed him. I could see he was less excited when we got to my neighborhood with its hulking tenements. My block looked gloomy and unsafe, which it was.

And there on my stoop was Andre, waiting. I was still in the cab paying the driver when I saw him. The boy had already gotten out.

Andre's face was worn and tired—perhaps he had been sitting there a long time—and the sight of us seemed to make him wearier still. He sighed, and he shook his head. I put my arm around the boy, and I walked him past Andre to my front door, where I fished for my key without turning around.

I could hear Andre's footsteps as he walked away—east down the street, toward the subway. I did not turn my head at all. What control I had, all of a sudden. I who had been at the mercy of such desperate longing, such raging torment.

When I got the boy inside, I made him some pancakes—he looked hungry—and then we fooled around a little, but I wasn't good for much. He fell asleep, and I got him up at dawn and gave him some money. He didn't argue about the amount, and he understood that he had to leave.

And what did I do as soon as he was gone? I called Andre on the phone. How sleepy and startled his voice sounded. I loved his voice. When I said hello, he hung up.

And then I really was in hell, in the weeks after that. I woke up every morning freshly astonished that Andre was still gone and that my suffering was still there, the dead weight in my chest. When I phoned Andre again, I got him to talk, and he was rational enough, but he wasn't, he said, "very interested anymore." His language was tepid and somewhat formal. "Not about to embark on another disas-

174

ter" was a phrase he used in a later conversation. That time I told him he sounded like a foreign exchange student.

So we stopped talking. Even I could see it was no use. But he was never out of my thoughts, he was always with me. I would be on the subway and realize I had shut my eyes in dreamy remembrance of a particular scene of us together, Andre on his knees to me in the shower. How languorous and smug my expression must have looked to riders on the A train. How disappointed I felt when I saw where I was.

I might have gone to find him at work, but I knew how he would be with me. If he was frosty over the phone, he would be a parody of polite disgust in the store, trying to flick me away with noble disdain. I hated the thought of actually seeing him like that, and I didn't want to hear what I might say back.

I didn't really have many friends to talk to. I was late getting to the show a few times, from not really caring and from sleeping too much, and I was fined and given a warning. I was very angry at Andre when this happened. He didn't care what he had done to me. I went down to City Hall, to the Buildings Department, and I looked up the deed to Andre's building to see who the owner was. I phoned the realty company to complain that someone was playing a trumpet very loudly at all hours of day and night. I phoned again and gave them another name, as a different angry neighbor. I phoned again.

On the last of these phone calls a secretary told me that the tenant had been advised he could remain in the apartment only if he ceased to be a noise nuisance, and he had chosen to leave, without paying his last month's rent. I was quite satisfied when I heard this—how often does anything we do in this life attain its goal? And then I remembered that I didn't know now where to find Andre. I didn't have his home phone number anymore.

I wanted to howl at the irony of this, like an anguished avenger in an opera. How had I not known better? Well, I hadn't. There was no new listing for him in any of the boroughs. And he was not at his job, either. Another salesman in the store thought maybe Andre had gone back to Chicago, where his family was. I didn't see him anymore, not on the street, not in clubs, not in bars. Not then, not later. Perhaps he became famous under another name. Who knows how his playing got to sound? Not me.

All these years later, I don't know if he is still alive. A lot of people aren't, as it has happened. But it may well be that he settled down—

he was like that—and a long and sedate monogamy would have kept him safe, if he found someone early, and he probably did. I wasn't with any one person, after him. I didn't even look for such a thing. I went to bars and took home the occasional hot stranger, and I kept to myself a good part of the time.

For a decade or so I got work pretty steadily on Broadway. Those weren't bad years for musicals, although there was a lot of junk, too. I was hired to slink around as a thirties gangster, to be jaunty with a rake in my hand as a country yokel, and to do a leaping waltz as a Russian general, clicking the heels of my gleaming boots. Only a few male dancers got to be real stars, like Geoffrey Holder or Tommy Tune, and I suppose for a while I thought I could be one of them. I had a strong, clean style, and I was a great leaper. Nothing else anywhere did for me what that sensation of flying did. But my career never made its crucial turn, and then I got older than anyone wanted for the chorus line.

Which was not even that old. I was surrounded, however, by lithe and perfect young boys. Quite vapid, most of them, but decently trained. I was not even attracted to these children, as a rule. Probably I looked like some evil old elf to them, a skinny, brooding character with upswept eyebrows.

For a while I tried teaching in a dance studio, but I didn't get along with the director. She gave me the beginners' classes, and the students really didn't want any grounding in technique, they only wanted someone assuring them they could be professionals overnight. "Ladies," I would say to them, "get those glutes tucked in before you practice your autographs."

I didn't last that long at the school. In the end I gave up the whole idea of teaching, and I got a job in an agency booking dancers for clubs. Go-go girls, in spangled underwear and little white boots. I was the man the girls talked to after they read the classified and came into the office, nervous and flushed or tough and scowling. I sent them to clubs in the outer boroughs, airless caves in the Bronx with speakers blaring disco and red lights on the catwalk. My temper was so bad that people did what I told them, which was the agency's idea of sterling job performance. I was a snarling jerk in these years. Contempt filled my every cell; I was fat as a tick on contempt.

These were not good years, and my drinking got out of hand. One night in a bar, a man threw a chair at me and split open my head.

When I missed two weeks' work, the agency hired someone else while I was gone, and there wasn't much I could do about it. It was not a clean or soft business. With my head still shaved and bandaged, I went back to the bar, itching for more trouble, but instead I ran into a dancer I used to know in my Broadway days. We were too old to want to pick each other up, but when I complained of being broke, he told me about a job at the union, answering phones and filing, if I didn't think that was beneath me.

I did, but I took the job, anyway. I used to say the work was bearable because of all those pert young boys who came into the building, but in fact I was in the back offices, hovering over ledgers and, in later years, facing a computer screen. It was a painless job, a reasonable thing to do until I found something else, and then it became what I did.

I didn't go to bars after a while. We knew at the union how many people were dying, even before the epidemic unfurled its worst. Cruising had not been full of glory for me, anyway, so I stayed home and counted myself one of the lucky ones. Staying home suited me. I read more books, and I had a few regular outings. I had brunch once a month with a few theater people I still knew. Through the union I got tickets to plays and sometimes operas. And I helped out backstage at some of the AIDS benefits we sponsored.

In the early years a lot of big names pitched in at these benefits, but later, too, there were people who were impressive in rehearsals. I stayed extra hours one night to listen to a tenor with a clear, mellow voice—he was singing a cycle of songs written by a composer who had just died of AIDS. The accompanist was an idiot, and they had to keep repeating the first song over and over. The singer was a puny, delicate boy, with pale eyebrows and colorless hair in a crewcut. He closed his eyes as he sang—not good form onstage, but affecting nonetheless.

During the break I told him to keep his eyes open, and he said, "Yes, yes. You're right."

"Your Italian sounds good, though," I said.

"I lived in Rome for a year," he said. "It was my idea for Jonathan to set these poems."

The composer had been his lover—I knew this, someone had told me—and the tenor sang with a mournful longing that was quite beautiful. *Amor m'ha fatto tal ch'io vivo in foco,* he sang. Love has

177

made me live in ceaseless fire. I myself had Xeroxed the text for the programs.

His name was Carl, and he was young, still in his twenties. Recent grief had crumpled his face and left a faint look of outrage around his eyes. I began to bring him glasses of water during his break and to keep advising him. *Look at the audience. Watch your diction.* He was quite professional about the whole thing, and he only nodded, even when I praised him.

He let me take him out for a drink after the next rehearsal. We were in an overpriced bar in the theater district, full of tourists. He ordered a Campari and soda. "Isn't that a summer drink?" I said. It was the middle of February.

"It makes me happy to drink it," he said. "It makes me think of Italy."

As I might have guessed, he had gone there to study voice, and he had met his lover Jonathan there. "The light in Rome is quite amazing," he said. "Toasty and golden. Too bad it's so hard to describe light."

He was a boy romantic. Every day he and Jonathan had taken a walk through a park with a beautiful name, the Dora Pamphilj or the Villa Sciarra or the Borghese Gardens, and they had poked around in churches to gaze at Caravaggios or had sat eating gelato in front of some ravishing Bernini fountain. I knew only vaguely what all this was. He glistened and pulsed liked a glowworm, remembering it. I did not think any place could be that perfect, and said so.

"It's not," Carl said. "It can be a nightmare city. Noisy, full of ridiculous rules and only one way of doing things, and those jolly natives can be quite heartless. But because Jonathan is dead, I get to keep it as my little paradise."

"*Il paradiso,*" I said, dumbly, in my opera Italian.

He asked me if I had ever toured when I was a dancer. "Only to Ohio and Kentucky," I said. "Nothing exotic. I just remember how tiring that road travel was."

"What keeps me going," he said, "is poetry. I make sure to have a book with me at all times."

I pictured him reading a beat-up paperback of Whitman while everyone else slept on the tour bus. But his favorite poet, he said, was Gaspara Stampa, the Italian whose sonnets I had heard him sing. "She's sort of a 1500's version of the blues," he said. "Love has done her wrong, but she's hanging in there. She thinks all women should envy her because she loves so hard."

I was an undereducated slob, compared to him, but one thing about being a dancer is you know how to pick things up. "I like that line you sing," I said, "about how I'll only grieve if I should lose the burdens that I bear."

"Yes," he said. "Exactly."

I went to more rehearsals. I didn't scold or correct, and I said *"Bravo"* or *"Stupendo"* when he was done. I patted him on the arm, and once I hugged him. We talked about Verdi, which I at least did not sound like a fool about, and about the history of New York office buildings, and about what he had to do to keep his voice in health. I did not ask, really, about his health.

"I am all fire, and you all ice," he sang. I told him they were torch songs. "Gender reversals of the traditional Petrarchan sonnet," Carl said. "A woman bragging about her unquenched longing. Very modern." What a swooner he was, how in love with pure feeling. And he was a huge hit at rehearsals. He had a theory about this, too. "No good words are said anymore," he said, "on behalf of torturing yourself for love. Everybody's told to *get over it.* But a little bleeding is good."

I had noticed that hopeless passion was still in high style in certain corners of the gay world, but I kept this observation to myself. "The pianist needs to practice," I said. "You know that, right?"

I wanted to cook for him, this flimsy little Carl, and I got him to come for dinner on a Sunday night. "Whoa," he said, when he saw my tenement apartment, which had been carved out of the wilderness almost thirty years before. "You've got everything packed in, like a ship." For supper I fed him beautiful food that was good for his vocal cords, no dairy or meat, only bright and cooling flavors. Blue Point oysters, cold sorrel soup, prawns with pea shoots and fresh ginger, purslane and mint salad. Everything vibrant and clarifying. Golden raspberries and bittersweet chocolate for dessert. I had knocked myself out, as he could not fail to notice.

The food made him happy. He said that when he first came to New York, he had been so poor he had eaten nothing but tofu and Minute Rice. Even now I had to show him how to eat a raw oyster. I felt like his uncle. That was not who I wanted to be.

179

"This is as good as food in Italy," he said. "In my Surviving Partners Group there's a guy who's a chef. I'm sure his food isn't better than this."

"Surely not," I said.

His Surviving Partners Group met every week. It was a great group, he said. But for him personally what was most helpful was meditation.

"Eating is good, too," I said.

"Yes," he said. "I forgot how good it was."

A beautiful suspense hovered around the table when he left for a minute to go off to the bathroom. When he came back into the room, I stood up, and I put my arms around him. He was so wispy and slight, much shorter than I was. He ducked his head, like someone sneaking under a gate, and he slipped right out of my arms.

He did not mean to mock me, he had only been embarrassed. Neither of us moved. I felt old. A vain old queen, a self-deluded old fruit.

I asked if he wanted coffee, and we sat down and drank it. He praised my espresso so lavishly that I couldn't tell if he only felt sorry for me or if he was trying to be friends nonetheless, if such a thing were possible with a grotesque old lech like myself.

At the next rehearsal Carl waved when he saw me. He came over and told me about how much better he sang ever since he'd eaten my dinner. "When I do my vocal exercises now," he said, "my voice is so good I move myself to tears." I thought he did like me. And perhaps I had not allowed him the time that someone like him needed. Perhaps the situation was not entirely hopeless.

When I went home after rehearsal, I lay in bed musing about what might happen between us after all. If I were patient. He had not been with anyone since his lover died, and I had not been with anyone in years. I had underestimated the depth of the enterprise, the large and moving drama involved. He would probably have to make the first move. He would surprise me, and we would laugh at my surprise.

In the middle of the night I got up and looked at the condoms in my night table drawer to see if the dates printed on the packets showed they were past safe use. I threw out the one that was expired. I sat on the edge of the bed in my underwear, hunched over, with my head buried in my hands. I had never asked Carl what his HIV status was. I was ready to go to bed with him without any protection at all, if that was what he wanted. All those years of being so careful I wouldn't risk going out of my own living room, and now I would have bargained away anything to have Carl. I was beyond all reason.

At work the next day the phone rang, and it was Carl inviting me over for brunch on Saturday. He was ashamed to cook for me, he said, but he could buy bagels as well as the next person.

He lived in a remote and dull section of Queens, on a street full of what had once been private houses. He had a nice little back apartment, with a view of the yard. "Welcome to my monkish cell," he said.

It was not cell-like—it was quite cozy and bright—but I was spooked by the shrines in it. On a small table, spread with a white linen cloth, was a collection of photos of his dead lover, who was a pleasant-looking young man, dark-haired and stocky. Jonathan waved from a deck chair on a beach, he stood in front of a Roman ruin and a bright blue sky, he laughed against Carl's shoulder at someone's birthday party. In another corner was an altar to the Buddha, with a stone statue of a thin, pigeon-chested Buddha facing into the room, and a fatter, calmer Buddha embroidered into a square of fringed brocade hanging on the wall. A single deep-blue iris, pure and wilting, stood in a vase. I did not like any of it.

But Carl had clearly wanted me to see it. He gave me a tour of all the photos, naming every guest at the birthday party. He gestured to the Buddhas and said, "Those are my buddies there." He told me that he did Vipassana meditation, adapted from what they did in Burma and Thailand, but that was a Tibetan *tangka* on the wall. "Very nice," I said. "It's the medicine Buddha," he said. "That's his healing unguent in the bowl in his hand." I chewed my bagel and nodded.

I gossiped about the rehearsals, just to get us somewhere else. "Did you see," I said, "how Brice is ogling that first violinist in the quartet? I expect him to drool all over the man's bow any minute. It's not subtle." Brice was the show's organizer.

"I missed it," he said. "I'm bad at noticing who's after who."

"Brice is so obvious."

"What can I tell you?" he said. "I'm away from all that. It's not in my world."

What world was he in?

"People don't think enough about celibacy," he said. "It hasn't been thought about very well in our era. It has a long history as a respected behavior. It has its beauty."

I knew then that he'd brought me here to say this, with the fittings of his cell as backdrop. "The Buddha never had sex?" I said. "I thought he had a family."

"That was before he was the Buddha."

"Don't get too carried away. You know you'll want someone sometime."

"I don't think so."

"It's *unnatural* at your age."

"I'm not unhappy."

Oh, honey, I thought, I didn't tempt you for a second, did I?

"A sexless life will ruin your voice," I said. "I'm not kidding. You'll sound like some wan little old lady. You already have to worry about that."

"Oh," he said. "We'll see."

"You already have some problems in the lower register."

"Oh," he said.

"You'll sound like a squawking hen in a few years."

"No more," he said. "That's enough."

I was depressed after this visit, but lack of hope didn't cure me, either. I didn't stop wanting Carl, and what I wanted kept playing itself out in my mind over and over. At home I would sometimes be slumped in an armchair, reading a book or watching TV, and not even know that I was lost in reverie, until I heard myself say out loud, "Oh, honey." It was terrible to hear my own voice like that, whimpering with phantom love. I was afraid I was going to cry out like this at my desk at work, with other people in earshot, but I never did.

We were civil with each other at the last rehearsal. Actually, Carl was more than civil. He made a decent effort to converse, while the string quartet was busy going through its number. "I read," he said to me, "that Rome is all different now because they've banned cars from parts of it."

"You know what I read?" I said. "I read that there was a man who was very high up in a Buddhist organization who went around sleeping with people and giving them AIDS. Lots of young men. He knew he had it, and he didn't tell anyone he slept with. He thought he could control his karma."

182

"Oh," Carl said. "That happened years ago. When did you read it?"

"A while ago."

"Why are you telling me now?"

"Those are the guys you want to emulate," I said. "Those are your shining models."

"No," he said. "That was one guy."

"Lust crops up," I said. "Can't keep it down."

"That's not what that story means," he said. "It's about arrogance and delusion, not lust. He could have used condoms."

"Right," I said. "Sure. You'll be like him. You'll see."

He reddened then. I'd forgotten that his HIV status might be positive, for all I knew, which did deepen the insult. He shook his head at me. "Oh, Duncan," he said, sourly.

On the night of the concert, I dressed very nicely. I wore a slate-blue shirt, a beautiful celadon tie that Andre had once given me, a stone-gray sports jacket. I hadn't looked that good in years. I sat with some other people from work in a chilly section of the orchestra seats. The string quartet was first, playing a stodgy piece badly. I really did not hear anything until Carl walked onstage to sing Jonathan's songs. He looked pale as marble, an angel with a shimmering crewcut.

He had a few intonation problems at first but sounded lovely and sure once he got going. Jonathan had written him easy music, except for a few jagged rhythm changes. "*Viver ardendo e non sentire il male,*" he sang. "To live burning and not to feel the pain." Wasn't it enough that I suffered at home? Did I have to come here and hear my beloved wail about the trials of the rejected? I wanted to shout in protest. I should not have come, I saw. Who would have cared if I hadn't come?

Then my protest and exasperation fused with the plaint of the songs, with their familiar trouble, and I had a bluesy ache in my chest that was oddly close to solace. I felt the honor of my longing. This idea did quite a lot for me. My situation, ludicrous as it was, at least lost the taint of humiliation.

When the songs were over, I was surprised when the applause did not go on for hours, although people seemed to have liked the pieces well enough. I was still in a faint trance when the concert broke for intermission. I stayed alone in my seat while the others milled around. The second half was a woodwind quintet I had never liked, and they did three numbers. When they were finally done, I moved through the crowd and found Carl in the lobby, surrounded by people clasping him in congratulation. *"Bravissimo,"* I said to him. "Really." He gave me a sudden, broad smile—praise from me probably did mean something to him—but he was busy thanking people.

I stayed around long enough to get pulled along with a group that went out for drinks afterward. I did not ask if I could come, and perhaps I wasn't welcome, but no one said so. We sat at a big round table in a bar with peach-tinted walls. The accompanist, whose playing hadn't been as bad as I'd feared, kept leaning toward Carl with an excited attention that looked like a crush to me.

Carl himself was busy introducing everyone to a slick young giant of a man who turned out to be the chef from his Surviving Partners Group. "My very good friend," Carl called him. "Duncan, you should talk to Larry about his food. You're the one who'll really appreciate what he does."

"Oh, I will?" I said.

"I like food," someone else at the table said. "I like it all the time."

I was about to say, "Cooks who are fans of themselves tend to show it," but then I didn't. I decided to shut up, for a change. There was no point to my baiting anyone at the table just for fun, in front of Carl. No point at all now.

But it was hard for me. I stayed sullenly quiet for a while, sulking and leaning back in my chair. When Chef Larry told a funny story about his poultry supplier, I didn't laugh. When Carl talked about a production of *Wozzeck* that he was about to go on tour with, all through Canada, from Quebec to Vancouver, I didn't ask when he was leaving or when he was coming back. I didn't say a word. But then when the pianist said he had been practicing too much in a cold room, and he complained of stiffness in his elbow, I gave him a very good exercise he could do at home. I explained it without sarcasm or snottiness or condescension. I was at my all-time nicest, for Carl's sake, for Carl's benefit. I don't know that he, or anyone, noticed.

Carl went on tour for six months, as I discovered from his phone machine when I called him later. It didn't surprise me that he hadn't said goodbye—I was probably someone that he wanted out of his life. Still, I dreamed of his return. How could I not? When he came back, I would tell him how I had begun to think of myself as a celibate, too, that I had moved toward a different respect for that as a way to be, and perhaps we could be friends now on a new basis. It made me happy to think of our new comradeship, his easy and constant company, his profile next to me at operas and plays. But I knew, even as I imagined our lively and natural conversations on topics of real interest to both of us, that my reasoning was insincere, only a ruse to win Carl to me in whatever way I could.

But since I could not talk to Carl, who was off singing to the Canadians, I was left with my own recitation of why I treasured austerity running in a loop through my mind. I was the captive audience for what was meant to disarm Carl. This was not the worst speech to be trapped with. It made the tasks I did in solitude—my exercises, my errands—seem finer.

The exercises were a particular annoyance to me. I had done exercises all my life (except for some goofing off during the booking-agency years), but now I had arthritis, plague of old athletes and dancers, in my knees and just starting in my hips. All that hopping and turning and high-kicking had been hard on the cartilage. I had to go through a full range of motion every day to keep the joints flexible, which they did not want to be anymore. Some of this hurt, and I hated being a sloppy mover. But now, swinging my leg to the side, I felt less disgraced by it. My routine, performed alone in my bare bedroom, had its merit and order. An hour in the morning and stretches at night. I had my privacy and my discipline.

Every Tuesday evening I went to a guy named Fernando for bodywork. I lay on my stomach while he bent my knees and hooked his thumbs into my muscles. The word ouch did not impress him. He had been a dancer once, too. "Stay skinny, that's important," he said. "Good for arthritis, good for your sex life."

"Good for what? I can't remember what that is."

"You can remember, Dunc. You're not that old." Free flirting came with his massages.

"I don't know," I said. "I like my quiet. A life of abstaining isn't as bad as people think."

"So they tell me," Fernando said. "I do hear that."

"See?" I said. "There's a lot of it going around. It's an idea whose time has come."

"For some. Maybe."

185

"I think I'm happier. Do you believe that?"

"Yes," he said. "That I believe."

I had never been able to throw away the program from Carl's concert, and it lay on a small table near the door, where I saw it whenever I came in or went out. I would read over his name with a ripple of intimate recognition. A ripple or a pang, depending on my mood. The very casualness of its placement on the table pleased me.

I knew from the message on Carl's phone machine that he was returning from Canada at the end of September. Once he was home, I would call him, and at the very least there would be friendliness between us. The wait seemed very long. Thirty days hath September, and in the last week I went to movies every night to keep busy. I saw too many bad, raucous comedies and bloody cop movies. The only thing I liked was a biopic about neurotic artists in the twenties.

When I came out of it into the lobby, there was a crush getting to the doors, and a man in front of me said, "No one pushes like this in Toronto." I took it as a good omen to hear some word in the air about Canada. The man who spoke was not bad-looking, either, nicely muscled in his T-shirt, and he held another man by the elbow to keep from getting dragged away by the crowd. It took me a second before I saw that the other man was Carl. His neck was sunburned, and he had let his hair grow longer.

And Carl saw me. "Hey! Hello!" he said.

He acted perfectly happy to see me. Once we were all out on the street, he introduced me to his companion. Josh, the man's name was, and they had met backstage in Windsor, Ontario.

"And then what could I do? I just packed up and went with him on the rest of the tour," Josh said. "I have heard *Wozzeck* performed more times than any other human being on the planet. Berg is not that easy on the ears, either."

"I like him," I said.

"It was great to have company on the road," Carl said. "You know how the road gets. You and I talked about that."

"Yes," I said.

"I had fun hanging out with the tour," Josh said.

"Are you back here for good?" I said.

"We're looking for a bigger apartment," Josh said. "I like Queens, though. It's not how I thought it would be."

"Some people like Queens," I said. "Certain timid types like Queens."

"Don't mind Duncan," Carl said.

"We'll invite you over when we get settled in," Josh said.

"Whenever that is," I said.

On the subway ride home I was too angry to sit still. All those sweet-faced declarations, and look how long Carl had lasted as a holy soldier of celibacy. I felt that he had tricked me and that he'd had the last laugh in a way that made me writhe. *A respected behavior*, my foot. And I had been ready to tread the same path. I who had never taken the high road in my life.

When I got back to my apartment, I went to the phone and dialed his number. I wanted to ask him: Don't you feel like a fucking hypocrite? Do you know what a pretentious little jerk you are? The two of them weren't back yet, of course. They were probably at the subway station still waiting for the N train to Queens. The phone machine said: Carl and Josh aren't home right now.

I breathed heavily on the message tape for a minute, just to leave something spooky for them to listen to. And what would Carl have said to me, anyway, if I had been able to hammer away at him with hostile questions? *I took my chance when it was offered. Anyone would do the same.* There was nothing else to say.

I had a shot of bourbon, which did not calm me down. It made me want to kick something, but I wasn't ready to throw out my knee from an action that stupid. I had more bourbon, but I might as well have been drinking water. I sat there with my hand pressed against my chest, the way a dog paws its snout if it has a toothache.

I understood, after a while, that there was nothing to do but go to bed. I got out of my clothes, and I went through the set of stretches I always did before sleeping. I felt confused, because for so many months these had been like a secret proof that I was worthy of Carl. I had been consoled and uplifted by the flavor of his ideas mixed in with them.

Stress was bad for my bones, and I woke up very stiff. My knee locked when I tried to get out of bed. *Look what love has done to me.* I felt like a ham actor playing an old man. I had a hangover, too, and it was still very early in the morning. I wanted to phone Carl, but in disguise as something menacing, a growling wolf or a hissing reptile. I was good at making different sounds. Let him be terrified, just for a second. But then he would know who it was. He would say my name, and I would keep growling or hissing. Duncan, he would say, is that you? Stop, please. Sssss, I would say. Sssss.

I was too old to do that, too old for that shit. Instead I ate my simple breakfast and had my simple bath and went out to do my simple errands. A plain and forthright man. I was so calm at the supermarket (who ever heard of someone with a hangover being calm while waiting in line?) that I wondered if the attitude I had developed in Carl's absence was now going to stay with me and be my support.

Perhaps I was going to beat him at his own game (or what had been his game) and become so self-contained that I never spoke to anyone. I could work at my job without much more than nods and signals. I could move through the streets and be perfectly silent, quiet as any monk with a vow. Then Carl would know just who understood the beauty of a principled life.

Oh, in the Middle Ages someone like me might have been a monk, one of the harsh and wily ones, but dutiful. I could be a monk now, old as I was. (I had been raised a Catholic, although not raised well.) I could take orders the way forsaken young women used to, when they were jilted by lying men and wanted only to take themselves out of the world.

I don't know why these thoughts were such a great comfort to me while I waited at the supermarket with my cart of bachelor supplies. But I got through the day, and the rest of the weekend, without doing anything rash. At work on Monday I went about my business in my usual curmudgeonly way. I was in pain, but I wasn't a roiling cauldron. I thought that once the worst of getting over Carl was done, his influence would linger in this elevated feeling about aloneness, just as Andre had left me with a taste for certain music, for Bill Evans and early Coltrane. I was doing well at the moment, better than I would have thought.

A month later I knew differently. I was tormented by longings for Carl night and day. I hardly saw anything around me—sunlight hitting the windows of a building, a man sitting on a park bench, a kid walking in time to his boom box—without superimposing on it the remembrance of Carl and things he had said to me, the most ordinary things. In Sunday school when I was a boy, one of the sisters had told us that the Benedictine rule said to "pray always." I had a good understanding now of how such a thing was possible.

This can't go on, I would say to myself (how many billions of people have said that?), but it went on for a long time, for months and months. Sometimes I called Carl's apartment, to see if the machine still announced he was living with that twinkie from Canada, but it always did. Fernando the masseur told me that the only way to get over him was to find someone new. I picked up a man in a bar who wanted money to be with me, and that made me feel much worse.

Since I had not really known Carl that well, after a year his face did begin to lose its vividness in my mind—I had only a few shreds of encounters to hold on to. But it would not be true to say I forgot him. He was like a hum that was always in my ears. He was something that was not going to go away.

I never thought I would end up the sort of person who hoarded some cruddy Xeroxed program as if it were an artifact from Tut's tomb. As if it were my job to keep the faith. I had become a fool for love, after all. You could say this served me right, but it wasn't the worst thing that might have happened to me. Not by a long shot. No, I was better for it. I understood a number of things I hadn't had a clue about before. Why Madame Butterfly believed Pinkerton was coming back. Why Catherine's grave was dug up by Heathcliff. The devotion of these years improved me, and it burnt off some of the dross. I was less quarrelsome with other people and clearer with myself. My longing stayed with me, no matter what. Who could have known I was going to be so constant? It wasn't at all what I expected, and I had some work getting used to it.

Nominated by Alice Mattison, Rebecca Seiferle, Kathleen Hill, Alan Michael Parker

SONG OF THE LITTLE ZION BAPTIST CHURCH

by BRUCE SMITH

from FENCE

It takes a mule to get to Tishibee
       The light's double exposure, the heat's animal presence
it takes becoming a mule
       and human complaint, being of two minds
with no sense of the Sabbath or depravity
       one mind Northern, nostalgic, cold, can't dance
or the judgment or the fire kindled in wrath
       one mind Southern, curried, warm, stirred together
it takes the mule's lineage and hard use
       the way the victim is the spleen of the killer
and the pull from the hollow where woodsmoke
       and the killer is the worm of the corpse
rises since Dixie. On this spot in 1850
       on this spot in January 1996
a brush arbor built of wood milled in the hollow
       the church burned to the ground
and hidden against the master
       even his forgiveness singed
and a roof put up so they could sing unheard
       the joyful noise, impossible not to hear
the planks dragged and mauled and churched up
       then *rebuilt and rededicated to justice*

under the leadership of Burnett Smith
>   *and god, with grace, love, and labor*
the name of slaveholder and slave, the call and response
>   *of Quakers, members, and volunteers*
my name is another skin
>   splinters of the burnt church rise through the new
I nose around in the graveyard
>   black asphalt. My quiet is their hosanna
I eat the bindweed and the briar

Nominated by Michael Martone, Chard de Niord, Katrina Roberts

IDLEWILD

fiction by PAUL WEST

from WITNESS

1 *Shrop*

WHEN I AT LAST lose consciousness, it will not be to regain it. Can it really be me who, with one foot planted firm on the scaffold, wriggles his other in the exposed tripes of the man just beheaded, my big toe tapping the liver, the bearded head having rolled away, wearing a drastic grin? Who cut the belly open for me to disturb his innards in so imperious and sloven a way? I will always hear that squelching sound, even though not always find myself in the seventeenth century, will I? To have been an unwarranted me in so many places is sickening, as if history were making repeated assaults on me, anxious to claim and denounce me century after century whereas, in truth, I am not such a bad lot after all. Whence, then, this wholehearted guilt? I think I was once a philosopher, who now can remember none of his concepts or precepts. I may, dimly, have been a swimming pool attendant, though I have no dream of drowning anyone, or one of those worthies who leads a parade twirling an enormous baton around his neck, faultless juggler equal to the high throw. Little of either job survives, but more than what I thought in that peculiar habit of philosophers who *think* for a living. I am a haunted man, victim of appalling dreams, both night and day variety. No, it is an optical illusion: I stand behind the headman's brawny arm as it roams about in the body cavity while the other holds aloft the wretch's heart.

"On."

Ever the obedient blackguard, I do as I am told. I am not here in this room of opaque glass to say nothing, to lapse into silence while, God help his parents, Quentin Montefiore del Patugina ("Quent" or "Tin" I call him, presuming on a long friendship that has repeatedly failed the test of time but passed the test of need) hears me out, far out, then dismisses me until next time, even if only to urge me with his callous-seeming "On" or "And then." He has heard it all before, but hopes to find something in the disparities of telling, some incongruous facet I let slip. Better, he once told me, than hovering or dawdling in the downdraft from the chapbook, whatever that meant. He seems at his greatest ease when hearing me. I wonder why. Surely my babbling rocks him and unnerves him, but on he sits, open to anything I say, neither commenting nor clearing his throat. He once swam in a pool I ministered to, stark in yellow trunks of bright yellow sailcloth that rattled and snapped.

Then he would shout, "Come on in, the water's fine."

And I would answer, "So's the air. No fear."

Did he seriously expect me to plunge into all that slop?

It was enough to keep it clean and ogle its blue dialysis. It was always more lucid than I was.

"On," he says again, a touch snappier, and I obey, chastened into new babble.

He could be writing a book about me, his tape recorder stashed safely in the bookcase, his literary aspirations couched in my own rattled language, his plot and style wholly in my own hands as I recount my miserable career, his memory become the vacancy mine is, but helping himself three times a week to whatever scenes and opportunities my mind throws up. In truth, I am his ghost writer, over whom he has no control. I pay him to listen. I pay him extra because, he says, there is more than one of me to contend with. All the bills that arrive at my hovel show me his Ph.D., flashing it a bit needlessly I think, whereas my own poor beleaguered name, Shropshire, echoing a certain famous lad, I suppose, though he never an immigrant, always has a look of sapped sunlight. Had I been unluckier at Immigration, I'd have ended up Shropshin or Scrapsir, but no, I was a lucky lad all right, wondering if on the isle of detention I'd run into some congeners such as Hampshire and Herefordshire, all the home counties, but I never did. What, I always wondered, was a Shrop.

"Good morning, Shrop," he'd say, which I never answer, not knowing what a Shrop might have been in the days when I knew things. "Shrop up, and let's get started." We did, he pressing me forward from "On" to "On, On."

I had begun, back then, to link my loss of memory with the sudden erosion of what we fancifully called our infrastructure: first the mails, going from hand to hand throughout the republic, then the money and the newspapers, followed logically by the hospitals already teeming full. So, while amid the fever and fret of making retaliatory war against the assassins for a series of atrocities, as for a more recent series of gentler-seeming biological sorties, we were busily bombing them into their caves so that we could then seal them in with mortar, rocks, and concrete, almost borrowing from the old Christian myth of the entombment to get even. Deep within the belly of the mountains, the assassins could starve, scream, and finally drop dead. The only trouble had been that the assassins yet among us, some of them committed to suicide missions, wreaked biological havoc on all our precious ways of life, on the lares and penates, the banks, the public toilets, the very food.

I ask you, then, if a man might not lose his head in such circumstances, deprived of his rational contacts, his toys and tricks, his salaried validation? How hold on when all was lapsing into a lethal menace, with banks and restaurants turned into hospitals or emergency clinics?

"On," he says again, voicing his habitual goad, as if all I was telling him was a novelty, data about another society he was concerned with.

I even heard him chortling when I told him, as often, that I had arrived fresh from the toilet, cleansed by a touch of what was left to us, a Cottonelle of fresh folded wipe that (and here I quoted) "let you feel cleaner and fresher than dry toilet paper alone, anytime, anywhere," alcohol-free, great for the whole family, convenient when traveling, flushable, sewer- and septic-safe. Also available in tubs and resealable travel packs. Visit our web site. Who could want anything more? Indeed, this was one of the things that got us attacked. We had the cleanest rear ends in the solar system, and assassins, doomed to a regimen of leaves and desert sand, envied us our wipes. Hence the hijackings that began it all, just when my memory began to fail.

On, he was murmuring; he had heard it all before. He wanted new pablum. He wants. I oblige. He claims not to have lost one jot of *his* memory, which means my response to events differs from his. We are not alike. He, he claims, can help me, but not I him. That much is clear. I grope for a word, relic of something cerebral from my earlier days, perhaps such a word as "ideal," to which I must have attributed some special force, but the word's associations had fallen away from it like ribbons from a baby's rattle. I made do with "deal." Now, for no good reason, I mentioned Rachmaninoff's *Suite for Two Pianos*, an old favorite, but remembered only the title. It must at some time have been an object of love, like so much else.

Again bidden to resume, I used what little brain I'd salvaged to suggest to him that, since I no longer had any direction, there was no longer any point in my trying to tell things in any kind of rational order. "It is no use even trying to move forward," I tell him. "Panic has wiped out the best of me. Do you not know how stress abolishes memory?" He does, as his grunt proves. On I go then, explaining how it all began, what I call the vastation, from the very first day of my amnesia, the first thing to go being whatever philosophy I had come up with after thirty years of pondering. My skull felt shrunken. I no longer felt inclined to respond to anyone, never mind what they said. A low-grade shiver invaded my system, followed by pins and needles across my shoulder blades. Headaches, yes. Arthritis where I'd never known it before, yes. Weird fluttering touches along my legs as of invisible ants, yes. I could feel the entire daily structure breaking down: no more three meals a day, faintly evoked in that old expression "three-square meals and found." Or have I got it wrong, as I often do? No matter, I tell Quent. Who cares? Take a bus? No, no schedule. Drive a car? No, anthrax in the gasoline. Only the internet remains unpolluted, and the telephone (which will be a goner any day soon; they leave it for us to bemoan our fate with, not out of kindness).

"The safest way to communicate with anyone in your own household," I am telling him, "is electronically, each with a personal screen. That's the safest, even to tell them what you have noticed about how anxious people walk, when they hardly dare breathe or touch, their shoulders hunched forward as in some forgotten last fling of a discus, their legs rigid from the thigh, their heads half-averted from what they dare not look at: the future. You've no doubt seen those films of prisoners in the camps, as they stagger out of their infested huts to greet the just-arrived Americans and kiss them repeatedly? Well, it's a similar movement, except, being the most adept technologically nation there is, we move a little better, more portly, say, and by now—what is it, three years?—chubbier from not getting out so much when you have to stay home to concentrate on the needlepoint, crocheting and quilting. How does an anal retentive walk? Like a Bulgarian. Sorry. On. One way, I suppose, of settling the hash of the assassins among us, once you catch them, is to cram their mouths with wet concrete, as with the caves and tunnels. Stuff them up see, until, next day, they can't breathe or eat. Then they won't be so slick at communicating with each other in all the civilized countries. Have to ferret them out, even if it takes years.

He excuses himself to get a glass of water, without which he would be better off; but Quent is a risk-taker, or he would not be giving me the time of day. If I am not one of the walking wounded, with my heartbroken memory of succinct phrases on clear cold days, I must be one of the stumbling sane.

"Don't you recall," I ask him, "how, of all the music we've heard, you and I, especially when sunbathing in the best days, the noblest feel came from Elgar and Sibelius, the former in love with sweet fat privilege and royal pageantry, the latter raised in a harsher society full of sleet and depression?"

He is looking at me in a very odd way, as if I have just left some bad stench between us by evoking those early years when I was to intellect as he is to psyche.

"Or Villa-Lobos," I add, determined to please him. "Just as noble. I would dearly like to devote the rest of my life to exactly pinning down the concept *noble*. What can it mean in a society as shredded as ours, the ancien régime in tatters, kids scared to go to school, technicians afraid to venture out to work the TV stations. No planes, trains, few cars. A glorious inspissated silence has taken over the poisoned land, and I am sometimes glad of it. The amnesiac thrills to the new Blitz. It might be worse, Quent, it really might. What better for the mind washed clean than to start again from scratch? What do you think? I am on edge."

With one hand he motions what I say backward, then like a commissionaire or a traffic cop motions *me* onward again, applying what I sometimes (knowing him and his mannerisms as well as I do, Columbia men both) describe as the poultice of quiet. He is here to hear me out. Then, when I haven't a single idea left, when I have milked my mind, he will come and hug me for holding nothing back. Does he care that much or had he wearied of me and my mental contortions? All I can ever do is try him again, in both senses of that word.

"Are you there?"

"Are you listening, Quent?"

"Hearing me all right?"

I construe his silence as invitation and launch again into the chilly stratosphere. "We were talking about the mind wiped clean and that being a good time to teach it the old tricks all over again. Have I ever told you before about being in England and studying aeronautics, eventually cooking up a tiny jet engine they attached to the tips of a propeller? If I had been brighter, I'd have seen that, having come up with the jet, I no longer needed the propeller. It's a nightmare, really, wondering why I was so foolish, so unobservant. Too green, I suppose."

2 Quent

I wonder if he's doing any worse than the rest of us, anxious, shaken, spavined, no longer in the first paroxysm of terror, but adjusted to prodigious uncertainty as one by one our toys and triumphs get turned against us by an enemy who seems always to be there, never quite stamped out. I doubt it. What makes him different is that, whereas most of us have lost our cherished routines (going to the mailbox, putting the garbage out, cloaking the hose-pipe sockets for winter), he has lost that entire system of ideas he took such pride in. Key concepts have gone, and he remembers none of the reasoning that took him from place to place. Such is the fate of the oral philosopher, with no more permanence than the balladeer of old. Such papers as he published and can get his hands on show him little, as if the current no longer runs through them. He is a stilt bird walking gingerly from one lily pad to the next, murmuring *Did I really think that?* It does not help him either that, having to make do in the yard with traps to catch birds, coons and squirrels, now that the canned goods have given out, and then cooking such roadkill, the taste irks him. He thought best when he was responding not at all to the taste of his food; it went down like a baby-paste, a slime to be converted into its approximate equivalent. He has, as they say, lost it, meaning not one thing only, but all of everything. He used to have a grid that made sense of life; now he has nothing of the kind.

Is his the nagging fright of the commando landed on an alien

197

beach, deathly afraid of the bullet that's aimed right at the bridge of his nose, out of nowhere with a fast lisp he does not even hear? If, as at the beginning, there were noise as the topless towers of Ilium bit the dust, but now it is all surreptitious according to a menu of horrors, from discarded diseases to maliciously disguised talcum powder. Is it anything like walking in quicksand, or blindfolded on a cliff's edge? With so much to worry about, even if you elect never to go out, we endure a kind of blind man's bluff as, hidden away in fake identities, they watch us dither and twitch, bit by bit losing the civilization lovingly assembled since the time of the ancient Egyptians. This is no doubt why, after having called him many things during our long friendship (such nicknames as Shrop), I now in my private files have come to refer to him as the Chaos Attractor, special in that he just doesn't put up with the horrors; he finds them coming toward him, fangs bared, the taste of him already familiar. They want him, he whose system was the most meticulous, so much so that in his present disheveled state he cannot remember it, and nobody else needs it. Raw importunity assails him at every corner, and life is a jigsaw puzzle with no interlocking pieces. He takes it all on the chin.

How can it be that the very things we have evolved to soothe us— Bach or Ravel, the over-dry Martini, Matisse or Samuel Palmer—no longer speak to us? The things we used to love have become as wormwood, and people are all we have left to cling to. The blind lead the blind just because we have been wounded, chronically disrupted for three years or so, living in a ghastly ruined landscape, or, as I used to say, all from having been geographically raped out of the blue. What's to be done when those who hate life devote themselves to destroying it year after year, never happier than when being swallowed up in the atrocity themselves? I suppose most of us still take some pleasure in atmospheric phenomena: rain, wind, sunsets, whereas the taste for literature seems to have gone out the window. We have no ideas, and the one thing we dread is being singled out for having an interior of some kind. Pavlov's dogs have had more *nous*.

So I say to him, off-duty: "Doodle on a pad just to see if any of the old ideas come." No book from him, which is why he cannot find himself in the reference works, and why, in some perverse fit of self-regimentation he goes to the encyclopedia and filches from it the volume titles on the spine, from *Freon-Hölderlin* and *Melange-Ottawa* to *Excretion-Geometry* and *Number-Prague*, carefully avoiding *Reti-Solovets* and *San Francisco-Southern*. No Shr—of course.

"Nihil," I say to him, "it's all about nihil, isn't it? There's *all this*, meaning Creation with capital C, and the urge to turn it all to dust, even for those who like it, and the related desire of the destroyer to have no life at all. Where did I read—how's it go?—whoever kills one innocent person has killed the whole of mankind?"

"There is the old Emily Brontë position," he says in a welcome moment of recapture. "She says the prospect of death dismays her so much that she wants to die. Well, even with all that on our minds, the most wuthering of heights surely, we somehow manage to hang on as long as we can. And we do not in the least understand the demons who want to lose their lives in taking ours, by whatever means. It's that sort of stuff that has immobilized what I used to know. Damnit, there were times when even I liked having ninety-something channels to surf on, however pointless the yield. Now, all we seem to see is walls and windows collapsing as if some deadly elevator has passed through them. Thousands mauled in an instant or two. And then the preposterous image of an entire nation's police forces looking for someone *who might have mailed a letter!* Maybe we don't deserve to survive after cutting so stupid a figure."

"Oh fui," I say agitatedly.

"Steady now, Shrop," he says. "Are we here to right a public wrong or to get you back on an even keel, spouting at us those vital words of yours, that only you can come up with? I would prefer you to remember them for yourself. Or, rather, their special meaning for you, their pith and skewed tenor. Did you realize that an entire population has suddenly begun making its wills? Here we are, menaced by a tiny regime as small as the Nazi party once was, who permit no kites to be flown and no snowmen to be built. To eat ice cream, which no doubt has more ice in it than cream, their women have to reach under their veils to let the spoonful pass. We have put men on the moon, to Borges the most outstanding human event of his time, and we allow a pack of madmen to turn our loveliest inventions against us, with money and newspapers to follow. Oh, you've heard me go on about this already. Sorry. *You* are the patient, I'm the listener. On!*"

I provide him with my wannest grin, the rictus of one who walks the tundra incessantly. "The problem is to get the system back, if system it was, and then somehow apply it—the grid that makes sense of things, like the rules of baseball or hockey." From where I lounge, I can see his keys dangling from a drawer, making against the wall the perfect shadow of a perching tsetse fly: a bit of leftover, unannulled civilization. "What is wrong with me," I ask him, "that I can do nothing with phenomena? They just tumble all over me, like grains of sand, I who used to sort them out real fast and bundle them away into groups. What's wrong with me?"

"Part of your mind's become unhinged."

"Say again."

"Overload," he says. "Flooding, a metaphor we steal from grief control. Too bloody much, old friend, Kübler-Ross."

"And one mind, presumably uninjured, can minister to another, more injured."

"*Ming yi*: brilliance injured," he exclaims. "The I *Ching*."

"I once read it."

"You will again," he tells me. "But not now."

"What then?"

"Shattered mind."

"It feels more like being numbed," I say. "Spiritual inanition."

"*Accidie* or *akedia*," he answers, "as with all those heartsick medieval monks."

"Do you think I need to start illuminating letters?"

"Whatever works."

"Tell me, Quent," I ask him, "do the Irish have a word for *mañana*?"

"Yes," he answers, "but it lacks the urgency of the original Spanish, and don't you try out your old gingersnaps on me."

"No more golden oldies," I whisper, alluding to the sprightly give and take of our long friendship. "How sad."

"The trick," he is saying, "is to come up with a better punchline, saying haste or hurry to begin with, and then, maybe, panic or sleepy intonation. See?"

"Too difficult for me."

"Well then, what about fitting little jet engines to the tips of the propeller blades? And not realizing, so long ago, that you had turned your back, as a onetime student of aeronautics, on a great discovery? You walked right past it and went away somewhere to study math."

"With Roselli, at Cambridge."

"Good God!"

"What?"

"No, not Roselli. It was an exclamation at the—er, fatuity of it. Straight to math after passing up the jet engine as a complete source of power in its own right, long before Whittle, Heinkel, and the rest."

"Well, we eventually reached the point at which he said he'd taught me all he knew. It was time to move on."

"You always know."

"I have to do it, I suppose."

"You always used to."

"A river vessel attached to the Austrian army."

"You're older than you look."

"I know what would be better, Quent."

"Do say."

"Waiting till my complex or syndrome had come full circle, was full-blown, and then come to see you."

"Ah, so you can grovel to the max."

"No, not come to you half-hatched, so to speak."

"No, I'll take you at any degree of hatch, but the sooner the better, when there aren't as many causes to have effects."

"Well, screw that."

"You're more than halfway gone already, dear friend. May we please get back to the riverboat and the Austrian army. I see that we have already deserted aeronautics and the jet."

"Alas."

"But bully for old Whittle."

"Whoever."

"Captain Steignitz was a bully."

"Kicked you around somewhat, eh?"

"All of us. Captain of vessel, not the rank between lieutenant and major."

With his mouth, somewhere in the side, he makes, almost, the sound of an Austro-Hungarian-German soldier clicking heels.

"A lout, a drunk, a slime."

4 *Quent*

He makes as if to stammer, but assumes control of the movement, as one can. Once again he is searching for some pat formula that will impose order on the proceedings: breakfast in New York, lunch in Rome, crow in Istanbul. Like that. Only the design he has in mind is not strong enough to hold things down. He misspeaks, saying contin-

201

gency for contingent, and the shaking of his face evinces the disruption he always feels, horrified beyond measure by a double dose of the impossible, beginning, as he puts it, with an avalanche of rubble bigger than any mountain has produced. The first precedes the second by a little while. Flying low and fast, a jet swings into the first tower and actually seems to fly through it, slowing of course, slowed by walls and doors, bodies and tables, but matchstick flummery to a missile travelling at over five hundred miles an hour. Inside the tower, it has been sedate and purposeful up to now, but suddenly amid an inferno of noise and fire the disintegrating fish-nose of the fuselage munches toward them in a fairly straight line, idealess and melting, but intact enough to engulf all before it amid inaudible screams, fans of smoke, gusts of flame, arms and legs and faces all of a sudden rendered soft as baby-dick, and then the mess has moved onward, carving ever lower, heedless of floors and folk.

It is this, and comparable devastations, that dog him incessantly, an incendiarist's abattoir dreamed up by some mild-mannered suicides. He hadn't thought of it, and even after seeing it he cannot fix it in his mind, next seeing in the downward moraine of wreckage the tailplane gliding along more or less intact, somehow tilted and twisted, riding what it has destroyed, but vanishing as the deluge from above smothers it, smashing it to bits. He will never see it again, but he will never forget the newsreel version. It is as if God has failed an examination in decorum and should instantly be reexamined just to keep people's hopes up. *All fall down*, he whispers for the sake of anything to say, an elderly nebbish recovering childhood cries (a different society from this) such as *Bags I*, verbal part of a shout demanding precedence at a game, or, similarly, *"fog"* and *"sec"* for first and second, the memory of them shaken loose by broken masonry and unseen bodies lapsing into the vast pour. Not unsophisticated by any means, or unread (his time as a poolman and a parade leader having given him ample time for self-improvement), he now knows that Thomas de Quincey, in an earlier century squinting through Lord Rosse's telescope at something too gruesome to endure, also frightened himself to death, not half to death, but wholly, mainly because such a thing just could not be, but also because a human had no means of coping with it except to shriek *No* and gibber into madness.

Which he does not do, not quite, but the very sight of an amputated tailplane gliding down amid a tide of dust and stone is, to his mind, forbidden. He thinks of how a box of tissues suddenly drops when one is plucked out from above; there is a momentary hang-fire and then the join between folded tissues and the selected one fails, and Mister John Wheeler's gravity takes over, downing the box, which dangles longer only if one or two tissues remain and the box appears to float, the body freed of its bulk and swept into the overall scheme of shadow and poxlight. Now he knows, he confesses, how to throw a Nuremberg egg, his mind having flinched off into the unknown regions for a little allusive privacy.

"Honest, Quent," he gasps. "A lance-corporal salutes the Milky Way." I know how to take him, after a while anyway, having spent years accommodating my rather staid mind to his baroque excesses, before his trauma, about which I am trying to keep calm as I see my friend edging toward yet another abyss, someone having taught him years ago that life made sense, otherwise why have an educational system, school to university, at all?

"The likes of me," he exclaims. "The likes of me!" That is how you have to take him, raw and intractable, if you aim to do him any good. Without the double crash, he would have gone on living a semi-normal life, listening perhaps to Saint-Saëns's piano concerto, *The Egyptian*, composed in Luxor. There used to be a German doll, before Hitler, with three heads for different moods. Perhaps he intends to initiate himself into the literature of pain, shoving his nose into dread and atrocity until he can honestly say he does not mind, convinced he is responsible for everything, like a sailor watching a clear sky. He talks of ancient mummies being burned in modern locomotives and mummy bandages being used for brown wrapping paper. *His* fault. There is going to be no limit to his savvy self-deprecation. "Look, Quent," he says, raising his mug to eye level and squinting at me over it, "I see history as it affects, impresses, me, not as it was. But I am beginning to think they're the same thing, the impact and the as-it-was. It's like being shipwrecked on Jupiter, if you see . . ."

Of course I see. I have to. Now, what's actual is the one and only subjective. He claims he's developing a lazy eye that lags behind, rolls and floats, making him virtually monocular, and that (as if pursuing the brace image further), when he wrote to a friend consoling him for having lost a testicle to cancer, he said how sorry he was that the world was the way it was, and there would be the usual ribaldry. The friend never wrote back. Such events persuade him there is no guiding principle in the universe, no charitable reflex, and I am just amazed he got this far thinking otherwise. *Rock on*, I whisper. *On.* Whatever he comes up with will be part of a mirage.

So, in his disheveled way, he begins to tell me about being on the riverboat, hearing the unmilitary gurgle of the engine, extolling the times when one boat or another leaned sideways in the silt, giving him exactly the right angle to loll at. I formed the impression that he was not a very energetic or shipshape sailor. Hearing him talk about rivers and riverboats was almost like hearing him talk about Mörbisch am See, the last village on the western shore before the Hungarian border. Whitewashed houses with beflowered porches and outdoor staircases, clumps of maize hanging from the walls. He talks of passports and bicycles, crossing the border into Hungary, a summer festival on a floating stage where Hungarian and Austrian operettas are staged next door to the marshes and reed beds. It is as if a fantasy from a child's storybook has overlaid his raw experience, and they have become interactive. Having heard him several times prate about Mörbisch and especially the lake, *Neuslieder See*, it graces, I formed the impression that, just like the lake itself, evaporating and flooding (dry from 1868 to 1872), the image in his mind waxed and waned according to his emotional needs, some of the time cloudy, shallow, warmish, at other times almost a dry bowl. Hence his addiction to the theme of a boat grounded, awaiting heavy rain or the melting of heavy snows. Even more is his languid evocation of the lake's odd behavior, the water level falling with a strong wind, then resuming its former depth as the wind drops. The only tributary, the Wulka, is similarly capricious, evaporating four times faster than it fills. I sensed in his water memoirs, spoken with irresistible candor, a fluctuating emblem more related to childhood than to military experience, but always valid whenever he wanted to recoup some aquatic image he could relate to pool-skimming, for instance, or time spent in wintrier climes such as Skjolden in Norway. His lake, which I sometimes decipher as his amalgamation of rivers and channels (all his waters scooped up), has a melancholy quality he attributes to Austro-Hungarianism, to the fact that Austrian steppe begins so close to Hungarian puszta. He finds the waters brimming with pain, four-fifths Austrian, one-fifth Hungarian, shallow as a tearing eye. No doubt it reminds him of the Danube Delta. In one of the observation posts that dot the reedscape, he has watched whinchats, little ringed plovers, black-tailed godwits, purple herons, penduline tits, avocets, and white-spotted bluethroats at their ceaseless tasks, giving himself over to a domain or dimension of birds amid a pandemonium of dwarf irises, king's candle, and luscious salmon asters, to which collusion of taxonomies he brings all his riverboat memories, dilating them to fill a beloved region he tends to call Pannonia. Leisure boats now replace the boats he remembers: those of reedcutters and fishermen and the flat-bottomed craft of wildfowlers. He often ends his rhapsodical reveries with a favorite joke, culled from colder waters and some film he has seen, when a trio of marooned women find themselves paddling about in chilly waters off Sumatra, and one recommends to the two others, "to spend a penny" for its temporary warming effect. This he says with childlike gusto, perhaps wondering to what portion of his shattered life he can relate so mild an impropriety.

You can see how his almost feverish insistences pluck one in, most of all those you have heard before, because you sense that in one of the variants you might find the key to him and his lost ideas. I, at any rate, listen to him with cautious zeal, on the *qui vive* for flubs and slips that might become useful later on, rendered back to him as the keys to the lost kingdom. Besides, I am being paid, even as he skips from river duty to a stint in an artillery workshop and then, a couple of years later, in a howitzer regiment on the Russian front as an artillery spotter, where he was decorated for bravery, quite lost for a time his memory of birds. His martial career, as he likes to call it, was taking off and, if anything, becoming too appetizing for a man so cerebral.

My question to him would be, often is: Is this a natural progression of a gifted youth or merely a clutch of patches? How often do we pretend to ourselves that our onward advance has both method and aim when, in truth, it's more ragged and haphazard than an old holed fishing net? Perhaps, even then, he was a marvel at harmonizing the disparate, melding the discordant; the pattern he showed to the outside world; the higgledy-piggledy he kept to himself like the irritation in the oyster. If only, I used to think, he would admit to being a hodgepodge of aeronautical engineer, poolman, baton twirler, riverman, artillery spotter and lake lover. Maybe one of these was the key to the others, and brought them all into symmetry, converting a Dalmatian into a Tintoretto. You have always to wonder about someone who comes to you early in life for therapy, lacking, oh, an even flow, a coherent career. He really came to me to find out if his own private self-integration was a success, or was he fooling himself? A man apart as distinct from a man of integrity? All I had to do with someone so adroit at self-coordination was demonstrate his virtues to him, agree, and send him on his way. Indeed, it was a pleasure to find him so well meshed, easily the master of whatever outlandish thing he undertook. There seemed to be nothing he could not adapt congruously into his arsenal. He was the opposite of the literary student who hates to be told to go read the dictionary, look up in it any unknown words, thus assigning to literature the thinnest, most anonymous nature. He craved only to be led far afield so as to show off his expertise, readily joining balloonist to Wichita lineman, glassblower to pediatrician, not that he embarked on all these callings; you just knew he was on their brink, ready to enroll.

How different then his disintegration, his loss of philosophy's vocabulary or of the meanings of its words. I soon began to suspect he was improvising professions, callings, to drop into the gulf where philosophy used to be. Almost a Jack-of-all-trades or a snapper-up of unconsidered trifles like Shakespeare's Autolycus in *The Winter's Tale*, he used to need none of that, only too readily making sense of things and assigning them, hinged into the album of taxonomy by a supreme philatelist. How swiftly the debris of one's daily life fell into shape under his analytical glance, "worried" to death by a cerebral terrier. Teaching here and there, always with grand éclat and affable discipline, he wandered about like an old-time troubadour or trouvere, tidying up the mental landscapes of his spellbound hearers before he moved on. Was he a poet then? Of the explicit, yes. And to cool his soup wherever he stopped off, he filled his mouth and squirted it back into his bowl. "Soupositor" he sometimes called himself and when sighting through a host's telescope often made fun by aiming at the yellow lamp on a neighbor's porch, crying out, "I have him, he's beautiful! *Mars!*"

Such this man had been, now flensed by the atrocities of terrorists who had somehow wrecked the harmonies of his erratic being, causing him to extol something by calling it the berries, phrase he'd picked up from Virgil Thomson the composer, or to put something uncouthly after the fashion of TV anchorpersons: "A French possession since the nineteenth century, I had no idea of Bora Bora." Or mulatto pidgin invaded his correct speech ("I done stole," "Gimme a pig foot") while observations of telling specificity made people look again at what surrounded them, as when he called attention to the tiny stretching bird inside the thermostat. Perhaps, as he became

206

more and more forgetful, he became more poetic, espousing finesse instead of géometrie. For a while he began to speak Japanese, rather slangy, never having seemed to learn it—*karoshi* for death from overwork, *yakitaori-ya* for eatery, and *gaijin* for clumsy foreigner. His mind became a spray rather than the single spurt of a water pistol, no doubt his idea of homage to fragmentation, shrapnel, chaff, and to the principle or precept of no longer combining like things. No more universals, he said; but it was plain he was losing heart.

5 *Shrop*

The theory is all very nice: I present myself to my old friend, Bouvard to Pécuchet or vice versa, and pour out my heart, or at least such of it as remains. From this avalanche he is supposed to figure out what ails me, and how to put me right, meaning what I think I might have forgotten. At least he is not bogus, like the Dr. Marcelle Bergmann, Assistant Professor, University of Akron State, in the newspaper offering a lecture or an ass-wipe on "Creating Communities of Reform Images of Continuous Improvement Planning Teams," whatever any of that means. You have to be careful of which imbecile you traffic with. Has he, I wonder, the variety of experience needed to cope with so scattered a person as I? Is he not too much by nature a mechanic, a tinkerer, than an originating thinker? Most of all, after jets made over into streaking bombs, anthrax contaminating the hands and envelopes of an entire nation, the American way denounced by cave dwellers, he doesn't seem to have lost his way, his backbone, or his professional memory. Indeed, quite simply he might foist upon me another man's career in place of mine, I being none the wiser. He claims I was a philosopher of some kind, but refuses to go into detail; so I might have been a Leibnitz whom he replaces with a Hobbes. You see the problem. It could end up a matter of fancy and preference. I would be nobody at all, a changeling, almost a performing fool.

But, *soft* as they used to say in blank verse plays, I came to him to be put right, or merely to rant; *he* did not come in search of *me*, having heard his old friend was rambling quite out of character. So we must be careful. I clean the pool and try to rub a certain splotch away, but find it is only a mote wafting around in my eye. That kind of thing. Or claiming *Carmen* is an opera to which few men would take their wives and no men their daughters. What kind of clue would such an assertion give him? I miss the keening, weeping, music in old movies, the permanent sentimental backdrop to the forlorn elements in the action. A dead giveaway? Or, as he claims in one of his few onslaughts on my manner of presentation, what he calls my jussive vocatives, I hector the listener with too many come-ons, such as "Will the listener please explain to her that . . . ," "This alone explains his subsequent acts," "You, silent listener," "You are to remember," and so forth: not leaving the auditor to make up his or her own mind. "You overreach," he tells me, "telling the other person what to think before you have told him anything. So, don't."

"I am in too much of a hurry to regain myself," I tell him.

"You are being previous."

"Nowadays, naturally a time of depravity, they say proactive."

"Just so," he scoffs. "Here, we will strive to be correct."

He has my first passport photograph in hand, a face of teeming innocence, so vulnerable and sensitive and high-strung as to make immigration officials blanch and wonder why they should admit so evident a patsy, at Chiasso, Tokyo, New York, and a hundred other places as the tender visage hardened on the rivers, in the aero-engine shops in Manchester, beside the artillery in the Austrian army, up in the Norwegian fjords, in the military jaws of a howitzer regiment, then as an artillery officer with several decorations for bravery "AND," I scream at him, "the facial torsion and chronic agony of working day by day at complex problems of logic and philosophy!"

"You were having a life," he says. "A *real life*."

"In spades."

"Which no longer recurs?"

"Which no longer recurs."

"*Zut!*" Ancient French oath of his.

"Yes, screw it. I want the whole thing back, and, most of all that skein of ideas with which I reduced the world to common sense. How would you like it, dear Quent, if you had discovered penicillin and then, with no other records, forgotten the whole thing? I discovered the source of the Nile, but cannot find my way back to it."

"And never will."

Again I catch that sly, pawnbroking look of his. He is wondering if I went bonkers before the attacks on the twin towers, heralding the end of civilization, or if after them. What I consider my tangential allusions he finds superfluous fireworks. If I have genuinely lost something and no longer recognize it, nor can tell what it was from something else of somebody else's, he finds me manageable, but not if I sound off at all angles, gladly recovering and reciting scraps of knowledge from hither and yon. He's a bit puritanical about his patients, does not like them double-barreled. Perhaps I am consulting the wrong man, the wrong one among many wrong ones, but it's friendship that draws me, the desire to hear the awful news from a friendly mouth. Trouble is, though, as I've said, he could equip me with someone else's system. Or, worse, reequip me with my own without my ever recognizing it. Perhaps a few hints from my own system, proffered by him, would bring the whole thing back to me, as if you were to whisper "thrown" to Heidegger or "monad" to Leibniz. Not necessarily so, but worth a chance. And at once the rest of their system would spring forth, lucid and contained as a map of the London Underground with key names like Bank and Shepherds Bush springing into the light like startled hares. I wish it might be so with me, but Quent's efforts so far have failed.

6 Quent

As any rational person might, he wonders who are these people, human antibiotics, who hate the very idea of life and by whatever means undertake to kill it, with smallpox, nerve gas, anthrax, or the suitcase that contains a nuclear bomb. They have always existed, but have never needed to massacre because the dread diseases of human history have done their work for them: the Black Death, the 1918 flu epidemic, AIDS. Their mandate, however, goes over and above such blights and calls into question, on presumably moral grounds, the right of humans to persist. As they see it, the planet would be better off without both their human targets and themselves. Kamikazes they may be, but ranged against the entire civilian population simply because it is there. He had heard from varying sources that these nihilistic fundamentalists come in various kinds: paupers who loathe capitalism; sons of plutocrats who ape Mick Jagger and other rockers; religious purists to whom women are filth. He has even heard that Taliban means "students," but he isn't sure of this, and he has a sneaking suspicion that something Quaker thrives in them, and that they have joined up so as to have something to belong to. It is Eliot, he reminds me, who in one of his essays suggests that a human only joins the universe when there is nothing else to join, which leads Shrop to comment that joining the universe is mere vacuous pretension, a nihil gesture, but that all that is not universe isn't worth joining either, not even the US Airways Club or the Red Cross. In other words, his peculiarly sensitive psychology seems to demand only the most meaningless of organizations—Dada, Surrealism, Oulipo. Cleverly testing out shades of meaning, he favors a harmless nihilism over a harmful one. There is within him a touch of the fundamentalist, the purist, as Roselli had noted when he commended Shrop's "intellectual purity to a quite extraordinary degree." All the same, he is nobody's chump; his purity is not a minimalism but only something that is not anything else, like pure lunacy or pure arrogance. And he thinks along these lines only because he has lost his philosophical memory, any vestige of what his philosophy was—so much so that I suspect he no longer recalls what *anybody's* philosophy was. In a word, he has forgotten philosophy and the claptrap, all the verve, that accompanied it. Perhaps it was worth forgetting, as so much bull, and ranked well below such a chore of contemplation as the price of cabbages from the Dark Ages to 1789. All of which has led me to arrive privately at the following conclusion: he was predisposed to damn any fundamentalism other than his own, and it is this that has driven philosophies from his head. He does not want to fell the topless towers of Ilium or anywhere else, he wants to purify the dialect of the tribe. He wants us back to basics: to handwriting, bush telegraph, cooking over an open fire, bow-and-arrow hunting. A Luddite, yes, but also sharing Lear's version of the bare, forked animal as something to cherish. Only this evacuation of the mind would have made room for his idea of clearing things out, emptying philosophy down the toilet. So he may be said to have connived against himself while, on the other hand, denouncing fundamentalists both pure and murderous. Was this a useful, worthwhile mental transit? Only if you came back from it, or so I thought. If it required slaughter, then no, of course. If not, then to come there was surely a rich harvest of god-given things. Confronted with the plenty or foison of the universe, who would gladly reduce human life to minimums? No one but a madman, which he is not, not yet, not quite.

He comes close, though.

He is beginning to be someone else, without trying, without recognizing the degree of impersonation in all he says.

Perhaps he will get a glimpse later on, even granted the embellishments he contributes to the other life he appears to be taking over. By and large it will be someone else whom he knows or knows about, and whose life he recalls in a peculiar way. Who are you? I ask, but he only says he will soon know. "Plums are quite special," he ends up telling me in his inconsequential fashion, "but they gotta be organic."

7 Shrop

Whenever I take stock of him, not always for professional reasons, I have to remind myself that, fixed as he is, he has more time for reading than others do. An unshrinking soul stationed between two bicycle wheels he never propels by hand, he has seen more of life and death than many of us. Not merely a *mutilé de guerre*, he is an officer of the peace, a justice of it. Spoiled for later life, in a rice paddy while descending from a chopper, he quickly slid in between layers of living, as I suppose a volunteer would. He was much younger then, not given too much hope of achieving a ripe old age, and so has done well in lasting until the new millennium, cheerful and popular, with as few clients as he can manage, and no one feeling sorry for him (all *that* went out with the twentieth century). With his one eye, he has been a Cyclops beacon flashing upon works of literature and psychology he'd previously neglected. He used to tell me stories of grunt life, none of them in any way embellished, and I in my full-memoried way would make erudite comparisons, long before I became a man who could remember only losing his memory confronted by a man who seemed to forget losing his legs and eye. True, certain stark reminders leapt at me from immediate circumstances: how he'd been injured, how hospitalized and cared for, but not much more than that. Every now and then he talks to me of Mozart's nineteenth quartet, the "Dissonant," or the third movement of Beethoven's fifteenth, and I receive this information like a man in a mist, wondering what it happens to be an echo of, ever dogged as I am by the misheard—the phrase "returnal home" instead of "eternal home," in that old hymn, which we sometimes falteringly try to sing together. "Fats Waller," he says, and I think it's an echo of "Fat Swallow," whoever that can have been. He tells, in his bizarre way, of ostensibly free checks that arrive in the mail, come-ons from his credit card bank but with his account number imprinted thereon for all to see, so he tears them up, not owning a shredder, and dismembers the bit bearing his number. The debris he then drops in the toilet bowl and flushes away, an event he describes lovingly as a group of deer static and at rest, then spinning away as they flee downward. I wish I always remembered his analogies as well as just now, which has cost me some effort. Only rarely can I bring him something novel I remember from reading; only my delight at encountering something unusual. As once, when I tell him, managing to recover something graphic from a sliver of newsprint, "Did you know, Quent, that the SR 71 Blackbird, originally called Archangel, left smoke rings behind it?" A major effort for me.

I am ever colloquial. I'm like, "Wow." He goes "Hot-dog!" It's only a pose of two old salts talking younger than their years, but it does sometimes break the tension that can build up between us, so we relax into a mistaken version of the National Anthem, while he peppers me with questions I can never answer: "Who was Carleton Palmer? Who was Craven Cottage? What was Hitler's art like? Can you quote the Eton Boating Song?"

No use. It used to go on for hours, when we met for play and gossip, but now that I see him professionally he sees no point in posing questions I can never answer, unless, as sometimes when you are reading an eye chart, one letter or even an entire line comes clear, a memory or the engram of it swims into the open and I become all remembrance as on Veterans' Day or Poppy Day as the English call it.

He watches me float around amid the flotsam of recall. I tie a knot in my handkerchief (obsolete folkway, I know, I know), but cannot remember what it was for. He uptips himself from his wheelchair in a gesture of romantic aversion and invites me to take his place while he lounges on the rug as if coming up from the depths for air, his lower half still at sea. "To jerk your memory loose," he says. I try it without success, then lift him back, noting how he always seems lighter, eternally doing without.

There are so many flubs and blotches in my telling that I am tempted to repeat all this in front of a mirror, so that I can at least see myself in the act of doing it. As it is, I write "he told" or "he tells" with a dizzy awareness that the moment is already gone and therefore not to be remembered; I would be better off writing "he is telling" and then break off before he finishes, or even write "he is telli—" so you can grasp the evanescence of what I'm telling. But then I recognize that to know words, any words at all, is to give the game away, or rather call the whole enterprise into doubt: "To be the way he is, you'd have to have lost language too, wouldn't you?" So, it's all a compromise, with me suggesting an impossible loss through imperfectly couched sentences, which of course is not what's happening at all. Rather than remember something, I should *dismember* it, trusting in the reader's good heart, getting him/her to say: He remembers as little as he can just to express his loss of memory. Truth told, it is only the shape, paradigm, and language of my contribution to abstract thought that eludes me, as Quent ever the noticer has told me. And no amount of refresher brings it back, even as I somehow recall the life that went along with it. So with regret, I am *Yours:*

Nominated by H.E. Francis, Joyce Carol Oates

CAIN'S LEGACY

by RICHARD JACKSON

from CRAZYHORSE

You can't stop the boxcars of despair.
You can't stop my voice from hiding out
like a virus inside your words, their knives
clamped between your teeth. You can't stop
the dogs gnawing on the bones from mass graves.
Thus your mirrors holding other faces. Thus your lungs
filled with someone else's words.
The eyelids of the heart closing. The sky drunk
on vapor trails. Otherwise, a few packages of conscience
to the refugees. You can't stop the sounds
of exploding stars as they approach you.
The anxious triggers. The land mines of idealism.
You can't stop Dismay from stumbling
out of the trenches of your dreams.
You can't stop these ghosts sitting around your table
gnawing on the past. Their candles burn down
to shimmering wounds in their cups.
Everyone holding their favorite flags like napkins.
The sound of bugles spilling from the room like laughter.
I know, you kill what you love just to hate yourself
all the more. You put on the cloak of distance.
A wind that blows away the weeks. The lovers' wilted embrace
that was your only, your last hope.
Everyone his own Judas. After a while
even the moon is just an excuse not to look too closely.

You can't stop the past boiling up in the heart like lava.
Otherwise, a history written by shadows.
For example, someone says the universe is expanding,
more anxious optimism, but where would it expand into?
There's only the vacuum that's always inside us.
There's Stephen Hawking saying the past is pear shaped
but that doesn't feed anyone. You can't stop the brain
of the starving child turning into a peach pit,
not his body terrorizing itself for food,
not his face wrinkling like the orange you leave on your table,
his liver collapsing, the last few muscles snug
over his bones like the tight leather gloves of your debutante.
Otherwise your old lies yawning to wake in the corner.
You can't stop the pieces of the suicide bomber
from splattering all over the café walls.
You can't stop the walls the tanks crush from rising again.
Otherwise a few tired rivers, a few fugitive stars.
The seasons that ignore us. The cicadas giving up on us.
Hope's broken antennas. Love trying to slip out of the noose.
The betrayed lives we were meant to live.
You can't stop that town from turning its soul on a spit,
not the light chiseling away desire, the morning
wandering dazed through the underbrush of deception.
You can't stop these sails of tomorrow hanging limp
from their masts. All you have are these backwaters of touch,
this voice spinning like a broken compass,
this muzzle made from your own laws.
But you can't stop the bodies piling up.
You can't stop the deafening roar of the sky.
You can't stop the bullet you've aimed at your own head.

Nominated by Christopher Buckley, David Jauss, Ralph Angel, Dara Wier, Gary Fincke,
Roger Weingarten, Bob Hicok, Crazyhorse

LOSING MY RELIGION

essay by TRACY MAYOR

from BRAIN, CHILD

W HEN MY SON LOST HIS INNOCENCE in the back seat of our beat-up Volvo station wagon, I never dreamed he'd take me down with him. I'm not talking about his virginity—he's only eight. I'm talking about the Big Guy in the red suit.

"Come on, Mom," he said one afternoon in the dwindling days of the year, having just observed that everything Santa had brought fit perfectly, was the right color, and had appeared item for item on his wish list, all without benefit of a single flake of snow falling to the ground. "It's you and Dad, isn't it? It's just doesn't make sense the other way."

No, it doesn't make sense, not by the time you're in the second grade. I swallowed, met his glance in the rearview mirror, and bravely gave my little speech. Santa was something his father and I did as a present, a little magic at a dark time of the year, a lark, not a lie. After a few more questions (did we actually *pay* for all that stuff? We went to the store and just *bought* it all for him and his brother?) and a few bittersweet seconds of silence, he put his hands over his ears and wailed, "Am I going to be able to forget about this by next Christmas?"

It's hard watching your firstborn reach the Age of Reason.

From there, of course, the clock was ticking on the whole childhood fantasy trip. "Easter Bunny?" he mouthed at me at breakfast a few mornings later when his little brother was distracted dissecting an orange. I made a slashing motion across my throat. "Tooth fairy?" he asked a couple of nights after that as I was shooing him into bed.

216

"Sorry, dude." Would he still get the money when his teeth fell out, he wanted to know. Yes, he'd still get the money.

"Anything else?" he said, a little sharply, pulling up the covers. I did a quick mental survey of all the unmagical truths he still has to uncover on his own: that his father sneaks cigarettes late at night on the back patio, that the Red Sox might never win the World Series, that there's very little we can do to keep him truly safe in the world. "No," I said. "That's it. I swear."

That's not true, though. There is another Big Guy who's taking the fall in our house these days, the one who wears white robes: God. As I watched my son parry and counter and feint and finally attack the Santa story head-on, I was trying to impose some logic on my own perception of the world, but coming up short every time.

The stories that tripped me up weren't about elves or reindeer or nighttime circumnavigation of the globe, but news stories, mother stories, stories so unimaginable to me as a parent that they hit the brain and bounced off again, rejected, before burrowing in deep.

Stories like the Bosnian woman forced onto her hands and knees by soldiers and raped repeatedly in front of her children before being burned alive along with them. Stories like the Kurdish mothers, one gassed by Iraqi helicopters along with her family, who all die from the poison; another who watches from the window of an ancient, overcrowded prison as wild dogs tear apart the body of her six-year-old son. The starving Afghani couple, unable to get their extended family across a freezing mountain pass, who finally decide to abandon their young children in favor of their elderly parents.

And that's not even counting the stateside stories, the planes and the towers, the children abducted or abused or drowned by their own mothers or left to die the most trivial kind of death in a hot car in a beauty-salon parking lot.

Are all these suffering people bad? The Croatians, the Kurds, the Israelis and the Palestinians, the Rwandans, the New Yorkers—are they being punished? And the people who live in my town, many of them my friends, with the Land Rovers and the leg waxes, horses in the barn and granite in the kitchen and money in the bank (real money, not the stock-option kind), are they good? Or is it rather that everything that happens to us is just fucking dumb luck?

Where is God in all of this? Truly, for the first time in my life, I can't say, not for sure.

217

Call it the Age of Reason, Part II. Just as my son had no choice but to admit, finally, that you can't make brand-name toys in the vast void of the Arctic and that mammals don't fly more than fifteen feet at a pop, I can't stop wondering if God isn't just a childish response to the staggering random cruelty of the world. Sing along, everyone: "He sees you when you're sleeping, he knows when you're awake, he knows if you've been bad or good . . ." I am afraid I know already how this story ends, in the back seat of a car with your hands over your ears, trying to forget.

Believe me, this is not where I expected to be in the middle of my life. I've always thought of myself as a "rowing toward God" kind of girl, to borrow a phrase from the poet Anne Sexton, someone who would naturally grow closer to God in a more intense and personal way as an adult. And certainly motherhood upped the religious ante for me, with its miscarriages and forceps deliveries and those woozy first few hours postpartum, the holiest times of my life, when pain and joy and Percoset and pure gratitude toward the Almighty course in equal cc's through the veins.

But now? Only the shock of suddenly coming up empty-handed, or maybe more exactly, empty-hearted. It's lonely with no God to be grateful toward, it's disheartening to think there might not be justice any more divine than what we get right here and now, and it hurts me to admit that I'm not the best person to be answering my own children's existential questions, not right now at least.

To be specific: Santa Boy's little brother, a dreamy, philosophical four-year-old, wants the lowdown on the Higher Power—how does God know we're being good? Can he see? Does he have eyes? What color? And most urgently, if God loves him, why won't God pick up his bicycle and drop it down in the library parking lot so he doesn't have to pedal all that way himself?

On and on it goes, with me thinking guiltily of the parenting books that brightly encourage readers to "State your values!" to their off-spring. What if your values are nothing but a big muddy mess at the moment? After a chat session with his mom, my poor kid is left thinking of God as some combination of Mother Nature, Lady Luck, and the Statue of Liberty who watches impassively as we scurry over the face of the Earth like bugs.

This is not good. I leave him for now to the safety of his Episcopal preschool, with its easy-to-take, Jesus-loves-me-that-I-know cate-chism.

218

My own catechism is a bit more of a problem. I know I need to read the believers and the doubters and the born-agains and the late converts, sift through Bonhoeffer and Freud and Lewis and Merton and Nietzsche and Pascal and work through all this. And I know I'm not the first person on the planet to have these doubts: Humans have tortured and murdered one another, and people have questioned the existence of God, since the world began.

As my friend Walter (cultural Jew, current atheist, practicing Unitarian, former philosophy professor, father of two) diplomatically puts it, my big spiritual crisis is completely trite by even undergraduate standards. What's more, he points out, only those who once believed in a personal, intercessionary kind of God can mourn his absence. So I might think about choosing a new religion altogether on the premise that my problem isn't with God but Christianity and its insistence on a sympathetic, human divinity.

Of course, I could give up religion altogether. History is filled with examples of intelligent, ethical people who lived lives of moral human decency without believing in a greater power. But then I'd have to give up the New Testament stories that I really do love, and I'm not ready for that, any more than my son wants to stop listening for the sound of hoofs on the roof.

The nativity is one hell of a good story, whether you're a believer or not—the frightened, unwed, pregnant teenager, the angel at the door, the bureaucracy, the poverty, the animals, the shepherds, the star. My sons' birthdays bookend the Yuletide, so I spent Christmas one year sitting in the pew on a pile of stitches with a tiny newborn in my arms and another, a few years later, being viciously kicked in the ribs by a fully grown nine-month fetus. It's hard not to feel a little closer to donkey-riding, stable-birthing Mary—the woman or the myth—after you've had a few babies yourself.

From there, it's not a big leap to internalize Mary's anguish as the grieving mother of a torture victim. And, weirdly, it's that image that finally offers me some sort of temporary peace as I agonize for the women of the world and all the pain they endure watching their children suffer and die, suffer and die, over and over.

It seems that when it happens, you can go mad, you can kill yourself, or you can try to change the world in your child's memory. So maybe Mary, always annoyingly painted as the quiet, uncomplaining woman in blue at Jesus's feet, maybe Mary chose the last option. Maybe Christianity started not with an unbelievable rising from the dead but with a mother's entirely understandable search for meaning in her son's murder. Think about it: Mary as the first Million Mom marcher, the prototypical Mother Against Drunk Driving, the godmother of victim's rights.

So what if religion is nothing more than a way for mothers to insist some good come of their children's suffering, a way for humanity to pay respect to the fierce human spirits that have gone before us? That's enough. I don't know about God, but mother power? That's one story that still works for me.

Nominated by Brain, Child

WHEN I DIED,

by MARK IRWIN

from HOTEL AMERIKA

I saw a man tearing down a blue house

but inside the blue house a green house

slowly appeared as the man motioned

toward me, suggesting I enter, opening

a white door where the man became

a woman in a yellow field with snow falling

upon so many people walking toward

a blue house, and they were telling each other

they had never seen anything so green,

not even the grass under the red sky of their names.

Nominated by John Drury, Hotel Amerika

MINES

fiction by SUSAN STRAIGHT

from ZOETROPE: ALL STORY

THEY CAN'T SHAVE THEIR HEADS EVERY DAY like they wish they could, so their tattoos show through stubble. Little black hairs like iron filings stuck on magnets. Big roundhead fool magnets.

The Chicano fools have gang names on the sides of their skulls. The white fools have swastikas. The Vietnamese fools have writing I can't read. And the black fools—if they're too dark, they can't have anything on their heads. Maybe on the lighter skin at their chest, or the inside of the arm.

Where I sit for the morning shift at my window, I can see my nephew in his line, heading to the library. Square-head light-skinned fool like my brother. Little dragon on his skull. Nothing in his skull. Told me it was cause he could breathe fire if he had to. ALFONSO tattooed on his arm.

"What, he too gotdamn stupid to remember his own name?" my godfather said when he saw it. "Gotta look down by his elbow every few minutes to check?"

Two names on his collarbone: twins. Girls. EGYPT and MO-ROCCO. Seventeen and he's got kids. He's in here for eight years. Riding in the car when somebody did a drive-by. Backseat. Law say same as pulling the trigger.

Ten o'clock. They line up for shift between classes and voc ed. Dark blue backs like fool dominoes. Shuffling boots. Fred and I stand in the doorway, hands on our belts, watching. From here, seeing all those heads with all those blue-green marks like bruises, looks like everybody got beat up big time. Reyes and Michaels and the other officers lead their lines past the central guard station, and

222

when the wards get closer, you can see all the other tattoos. Names over their eyebrows, teardrops on their cheeks, words on their necks, letters on their fingers.

One Chicano kid has PERDÓNEME MI ABUELITA in fancy cursive on the back of his neck. Sorry my little grandma. I bet that makes her feel much better.

When my nephew shuffles by, he grins and says softly, "Hey, Auntie Clarette."

I want to slap the dragon off the side of his stupid skull.

Fred says, "How's your fine friend Tika? The one with green eyes?"

I roll my brown eyes. "Contacts, okay?"

I didn't tell him I saw Tika last night, at Lincoln Elementary. "How can you work at the youth prison? All those young brothers incarcerated by the system?" That's what Tika said to me at Back-to-School Night. "Doesn't it hurt you to be there?"

"Y'all went to college together, right?" Fred says.

"Mmm-hmm." Except she's teaching African-American studies there now, and I married Ray. He quit football and started drywalling with his uncle.

"Ray went with y'all, too, didn't he? Played ball till he blew out his knee?"

The wind's been steady for three days now, hot fall blowing all the tumbleweeds across the empty fields out here, piling them up against the chain-link until it looks like hundreds of heads to me. Big-ass naturals from the seventies, when I squint and look toward the east. Two wards come around the building and I'm up. "Where you going?"

The Chicano kid grins. "TB test."

"Pass."

He flashes it, and I see the nurse's signature. The blister on his forearm looks like a quarter somebody slid under the skin. Whole place has TB so bad we gotta get tested every week. My forearm's dotted with marks like I'm a junkie.

I lift up my chin. I feel like a guy when I do it, but it's easier than talking sometimes. I don't want to open my mouth. "Go ahead," Fred calls out to them.

"Like you got up and looked."

Fred lifts his eyebrows at me. "Okay, Miss Thang."

It's like a piece of hot link burning in my throat. "Shut the fuck up, Fred." That's what Michaels and Reyes always say to him. I hear it come out like that, and I close my eyes. When I get home now, and the kids start their homework, I have to stand at the sink and wash my hands and change my mouth. My spit, everything, I think. Not a prayer. More like when you cool down after you run. I watch the water on my knuckles and think: No TB, no cussing, no meds. Because a couple months after I started at Youth Authority, I would holler at the kids, "Take your meds."

Flintstones, Mama, Danae would say.

Fred looks up at the security videos. "Tika still single, huh?"

"Yeah."

She has a gallery downtown, and she was at the school to show African art. She said to me, "Doesn't it hurt your soul? How can you stand it?"

I didn't say anything at first. I was watching Ray Jr. talk to his teacher. He's tall now, fourth grade, and he smells different to me when he wakes up in the morning.

I told Tika, "I work seven to three. I'm home when the kids get off the bus. I have bennies."

She just looked at me.

"Benefits." I didn't say the rest. Most of the time now Ray stays at his cousin Lafayette's house. He hasn't worked for a year. He and Lafayette say construction is way down, and when somebody is building, Mexican drywallers get all the business in Rio Seco.

When I got this job, Ray got funny. He broke dishes, washing them. He wrecked clothes, washing them. He said, "That ain't a man—that's a man's job." He started staying out with Lafayette.

Tika said, "Doesn't it hurt you inside to see the young brothers?"

For my New Year's resolution I told myself: Silence is golden. At work, cause me talking just reminds them I'm a woman. With Ray and my mother and everyone else except my kids. I looked at Tika's lipstick, and I shouted in my head: I make thirty-five grand a year! I've got bennies now! Ray never had health care, and Danae's got asthma. I don't get to worry about big stuff like you do, cause I'm worrying about big stuff like I do. Pay the bills, put gas in the van, buy groceries. Ray Jr. eats three boxes of Cheerios every week, okay?

"Fred Harris works there. And J.C. and Marcus and Beverly."

Tika says, "Prison is the biggest growth industry in California. They're determined to put everyone of color behind a wall."

Five days a week, I was thinking, I drive past the chain-link fence and past J.C. at the guard gate. Then Danae ran up to me with a

224

book. They had a book sale at Back-to-School Night. Danae wanted an *American Girl* story. $4.95.

Tika walked away. I went to the cash register. Five days a week, I park my van and walk into the walls. But they're fences with barbed wire and us watching. Everything. Every face.

"Nobody in the laundry?" I ask, and Fred shakes his head. Laundry is where they've been fighting this week. Black kid got his head busted open Friday in there, and we're supposed to watch the screens. The bell rings, and we get up to stand in the courtyard for period change. We can hear them coming from the classrooms, doors slamming and all those boots thumping on the asphalt. The wind moving their stiff pants around their ankles, it's so hard right now. I watch their heads. Every day it's a scuffle out here, and we're supposed to listen to who's yelling, or worse, talking that quiet shit that sets it off.

All the damn heads look the same to me, when I'm out here with my stick down by my side. Light ones like Alfonso and the Chicano kids and the Vietnamese, all golden brown. Dark little guys, some Filipino, even, and then the white kids, almost green they're so pale. But all the tattoos like scabs. Numbers over their eyebrows and FUCK YOU inside their lips when they pull them down like clowns.

The wind whips through them and they all squint but don't move. My head is hurting at the temples, from the dust and wind and no sleep. Laundry. The wards stay in formation, stop and wait, boots shining like dark foreheads. I hear muttering and answers and shit-talking in the back, but nobody starts punching. Then the bell rings and they march off.

"Youngblood. Stop the mouth," Fred calls from behind me. He talks to the wards all the time. Old school. Luther Vandross-loving and hair fading back like the tide at the beach—only forty-two, but acts like he's a grandpa from the South. "Son, if you'da thought about what you were doing last year, you wouldn't be stepping past me this year." They look at him like they want to spit in his face. "Son, sometimes what the old people say is the gospel truth, but you wasn't in church to hear." They would knock him in the head if they could. "Son, you're only sixteen, but you're gonna have to go across the street before you know it, you keep up that attitude."

Across the street is Chino. Men's Correctional Facility. The wards laugh and sing back to Fred like they're Snoop Doggy Dogg: "I'm on my way to Chino, I see no, reason to cry . . ."

225

He says, "Lord knows Mr. Dogg ain't gonna be there when you are."

The Chicano kids talk Spanish to Reyes, and he looks back at them like a statue wearing shades. The big guy, Michaels, used to play football with Ray. He has never looked into my face since I got here. My nephew knows who he is. He says, "Come on, Michaels, show a brotha love, Michaels. Lemme have a cigarette. You can't do that for a brotha, man? Brothaman?"

Alfonso thinks this is a big joke. A vacation. Training for life. His country club.

I don't say a damn thing when he winks at me. I watch them walk domino lines to class and to the kitchen and the laundry and the field. SLEEPY and SPOOKY and DRE DOG and SCOOBY and G DOG and MONSTER all tattooed on their arms and heads and necks. Like a damn kennel. Nazis with spiderwebs on their elbows, which is supposed to mean they killed somebody dark. Asians with spidery writing on their arms, and I don't know what that means.

"I'na get mines, all I gotta say, Auntie Clarette," my nephew always said when he was ten or eleven. "I ain't workin all my life for some shitty car and a house. I'na get mines now."

I can't help it. Not supposed to look out for him, but when they change, when they're in the cafeteria, I watch him. I don't say anything to him. But I keep seeing my brother in his fool forehead, my brother and his girlfriend in their apartment, nothing but a couch and a TV. Always got something to drink, though, and plenty weed.

Swear Alfonso might think he's better off here. Three hots and a cot, the boys say.

We watch the laundry screens, the classrooms, and I don't say anything to Fred for a long time. I keep thinking about Danae's reading tonight, takes twenty minutes, and then I can wash a load of jeans and pay the bills.

"Chow time, baby," Fred says, pushing it. Walking behind me when we line everybody up. They all mumbling, like a hundred little air conditioners, talking shit to each other. Alfonso's lined up with his new homeys, lips moving steady as a cartoon. I know the words are brushing the back of the heads in line, the Chicano kids from the other side of Rio Seco, and I walk over with my stick. "Move," I say, and the sweaty foreheads go shining past like windshields in a traffic jam.

"Keep moving," I say louder.

Alfonso grins. My brother said, Take care my boy, Clarette. It's on you.

No, I want to holler back at him. You had seventeen years to take care of him. Why I gotta do your job? How am I supposed to make sure he don't get killed? I feel all the feet pounding the asphalt around me and I stand in the shade next to Fred, tell him "Shut up" real soft, soft as Alfonso still talking yang in the line.

I have a buzzing in my head. Since I got up at five to do two loads of laundry and make a hot breakfast and get the kids ready for school. When I get home, I start folding the towels and see the bus stop at the corner. I wait for the kids to come busting in, but all the voices fade away down the street like little radios. Where are these kids? I go out on the porch and the sidewalk's empty, and my throat fills up again like that spicy meat's caught. Ray Jr. knows to meet Danae at her classroom. The teacher's supposed to make sure they're on the bus. Where the hell are they?

I get back in the van and head toward the school, and on Palm Avenue I swear I see Danae standing outside the barbershop, waving at me when I'm stopped at the light.

"Mama!" she calls, holding a cone from the Dairy Queen next door. "Mama!"

The smell of aftershave coats my teeth. And Ray Jr.'s in the chair, his hair's on the tile floor like rain clouds.

My son. His head naked, a little nick on the back of his skull, when he sees me and ducks down. Where someone hit him with a rock last year in third grade. The barber rubs his palms over Ray Jr.'s skin and it shines.

"Wax him up, man," Ray says, and I move on him fast. His hair under my feet, too, I see now, lighter and straighter. Brown clouds. The ones with no rain.

"How could you?" I try to whisper, but I can't whisper. Not after all day of hollering, not stepping on all that hair.

The barber, old guy I remember from football games, said, "Mmm-mmm-mmm."

"The look, baby. Everybody wants the look. You always working on Danae's hair, and Ray-Ray's was looking ragged." Ray lifts both hands, fingers out, like he always does. Like it's a damn sports movie and he's the ref. Exaggerated. "Hey, I thought I was helping you out."

I heard the laughing in his mouth. "Like Mike, baby. Like Ice Cube. The look. He said some punks was messin with him at school."

I go outside and look at Ray Jr.'s head through the grimy glass. I can't touch his skull. Naked. How did it get that naked means tough? Naked like when they were born. When I was laying there, his head laced with blood and wax.

My head pounding when I put it against the glass, and I feel Danae's sticky fingers on my elbow. "Mama, I got another book at school today. *Sheep in a Jeep*."

When we were done reading, she fell asleep. My head hurt like a tight swim cap. I went into Ray Jr.'s room and felt the slickness of the wax.

In the morning I'm so tired my hands are shaking when I comb Danae's hair. "Pocahontas braids," she says, and I feel my thumbs stiff when I twist the ties on the ends. I stare at my own forehead, all the new hair growing out, little explosions at my temples. Bald. Ray's bald now. We do braids and curls or Bone Strait and half the day in the salon, and they don't even comb theirs? Big boulder heads and dents all in the bone, and that's supposed to look good?

I gotta watch all these wards dressed in dark blue work outfits, baggy-ass pants, big old shirts, and then get home and all the kids in the neighborhood are wearing dark blue Dickies; Ray is wearing dark blue Dickies and a Big Dog shirt.

Like my friend Saronn says, "They wear that, and I'm supposed to wear stretch pants and a sports bra and high heels? Give me a break."

Buzzing in my head. Grandmere said we all got the pressure, in-herited. Says I can't have salt or coffee, but she doesn't have to eat lunch here or stay awake looking at screens. Get my braids done this weekend, feels like my scalp has stubbles and they're turned inside poking my brain.

Here sits Fred across from me, still combs his hair even though it looks like a black cap pushed way too far back on his head. He's telling me I need to come out to the Old School club with him and J.C. and Beverly sometime. They play Cameo and the Bar-Kays. "Your Love Is Like the Holy Ghost."

"What you do for Veterans Day? Kids had the day off, right?" he says.

"I worked an extra shift. My grandmere took the kids to the cemetery." I drink my coffee. Metal like the pot. Not like my grandmere's coffee, creole style with chicory. She took the kids to see her husband's grave, in the military cemetery. She told Danae about World War II and all the men that died, and Danae came home crying about all the bodies under the ground where they'd walked.

Six—they cry over everything. Everything is scary. I worked the extra shift to pay off my dishwasher. Four hundred dollars at Circuit City. Plus installation.

I told Ray Jr., "Oh, yeah, you gonna load this thing. Knives go in like this. Plates like this."

He said, "Why you yelling, Mama? I see how to do it. I did it at Grandmere's before. Ain't no big thing. I like the way they get loaded in exactly the same every time. I just don't let Daddy know."

He grinned. I wanted to cry.

"Used piano in the paper cost $500. Upright."

"What the hell is that?" Ray said on the phone. Hadn't come by since the barber.

I tried to think. "The kind against the wall, I guess. Baby grand is real high."

"For you?"

"For Ray Jr. Fooled around on the piano at school, and now he wants to play like his grandpere did in Baton Rouge."

Ray's voice got loud. "Uh-uh. You on your own there. Punks hear he play the piano, they gon kick his ass. Damn, Clarette."

I can get louder now, since YA. "Oh, yeah. He looks like Ice Cube, nobody's gonna mess with him. All better, right? Damn you, Ray."

I slam the phone down so hard the back cracks. Cheap purple Target cordless. $15.99.

Next day I open the classifieds on the desk across from Fred and start looking. Uprights. Finish my iron coffee. Then I hear one of the wards singing, "Three strikes you're out, tell me what you gonna do?"

Nate Dogg. That song. "Never Leave Me Alone."

This ward has a shaved black head like a bowling ball, a voice like church. "Tell my son all about me, tell him his daddy's sorry . . ."

Shows us his pass at the door. "Yeah, you sorry all right," Fred says.

The ward's face changes all up. "Not really, man. Not really."

Mamere used to say, "Old days, the men go off to the army. Hard

229

time, let me tell you. They go off to die, or they come back. But if they die, we get some money from the army. If they come back, they get a job on the base. Now them little boys, they go off to the prison just like the army. Like they have to. To be a man. They go off to die, or come back. But they ain't got nothin. Nothin either way."

Wards in formation now. The wind is still pushing, school papers cartwheeling across the courtyard past the boots. I check Alfonso, in the back again, like every day, like a big damn Candyland game with Danae and it's never over cause we keep picking the same damn cards over and over cause it's only two of us playing.

I breathe in all the dust from the fields. Hay fields all dry and turned when I drive past, the dirt skimming over my windshield. Two more hours today. Wards go back to class. Alfonso lifts his chin at me, and I stare him down. Fred humming something. What is it?

"If this world were mine, I'd make you my queen . . ." Old Luther songs. "Shut up, Fred," I tell him. I don't know if he's trying to rap or not. He keeps asking me about Ray.

"All them braids look like a crown," he says, smiling like a player.

"A bun," I say. He knows we have to wear our hair tight back for security. And Esther just did my braids Sunday. That's gotta be why my temples ache now.

"They went at it in the laundry room again Sunday," Fred says, looking at the screens.

I stare at the prison laundry, the huge washers and dryers like an old cemetery my grandmere took me to in Louisiana once, when I was a kid. All those dead people in white stone chambers, with white stone doors. I see the wards sorting laundry and talking, see J.C. in there with them.

"Can't keep them out of there," I say, staring at their hands on the white T-shirts. "Cause everybody's gotta have clean clothes."

At home I stand in front of my washer, dropping in Danae's pink T-shirt, her Old Navy capris. One trip to Old Navy in spring, one in fall all I can afford. And her legs getting longer. Jeans and jeans. Sometimes they take so long to dry I just sit down on the floor in front of the dryer and read the paper, cause I'm too tired to go back out to the couch. If I sit down on something soft, I'll fall asleep, and the jeans will be all wrinkled in the morning.

Even the wards have pressed jeans.

In the morning, my forehead feels like it's full of hot sand. Gotta be the flu. I don't have time for this shit. I do my hair first, before I wake up Danae and Ray Jr. I pull the braids back and it hurts, so I put a softer scrunchie around the bun.

Seen a woman at Esther's Sunday. She says, "You got all that pretty hair, why you scrape it back so sharp?"

"Where I work."

"You cookin somewhere?"

"Nope. Sittin. Lookin at fools."

She pinched up her eyes. "At the jail?"

"YA."

Then she pulls in her chin. "They got my son. Two years. He wasn't even doin nothin. Wrong place, wrong time."

"YA wrong place, sure."

She get up and spit off Esther's porch. "I come back later, Esther."

Esther says, "Don't trip on Sisia. She always mad at somebody."

Shouldn't be mad at me. "I didn't got her son. I'm just tryin to make sure he comes home. Whenever."

Esther nodded and pulled those little hairs at my temple. I always touch that part when I'm at work. The body is thy temple. My temple. Where the blood pound when something goes wrong.

The laundry's like people landed from a tornado. Jean legs and shirt sleeves all tangled up on my bed.

"You foldin?" I say. Ray Jr. pulling out his jeans and lay them in a pile like logs. Then he slaps them down with his big hand.

"They my clothes."

"Don't tell your daddy."

"I don't tell him much."

His hair growing back on his skull. Not like iron filings. Like curly feathers. Still soft.

Next day Fred put his comb away and say, "Give a brotha some time."

"I gave him three years."

"That's all Ray get? He goin through some changes, right?"

"We have to eat. Kids got field trips and books to buy."

Three years. The laundry piled on my bed like a mound over a grave. On the side where Ray used to sleep. The homework. Now piano lessons.

Fred says, "So you done?"

"With Ray?" I look right at him. "Nope. I'm just done."

"Oh, come on, Clarette. You ain't but thirty-five. You ain't done."

"You ain't Miss Cleo."

231

"You need to come out to the Comedy Club. No, now, I ain't sayin with me. We could meet up there. Listen to some Earth, Wind and Fire. Elements of life, girl."

Water. They missed water. Elements of life: bottled water cause I don't want the kids drinking tap. Water pouring out the washing machine. Water inside the new dishwasher—I can hear it sloshing around in there.

I look out at the courtyard. Rogue tumbleweed, a small one, rolling across the black.

"Know what, Clarette? You just need to get yours. I know I get mines. I have me some fun, after workin here all day. Have a drink, talk to some people, meet a fine lady. Like you."

"Shut up, Fred. Here they come."

Reyes leading in his line and I see two boys go down, start punching. I run into the courtyard with my stick out and can't get to them, cause their crews are working now. The noise—it's like the crows in the pecan grove by Grandmere's, all the yelling, but not lifting up to the sky. All around me. I pull off shirts, Reyes next to me throwing kids out to Michaels and Fred. Shoving them back, and one shoves me hard in the side. I feel elbows and hands. Got to get to the kid down, and I push with my stick.

Alfonso. His face bobbing over them like a puppet. "Get out of here!" I yell at him, and he's grinning. I swear. I reach down and the Chicano kid is on top, black kid under him, and I see a boot. I pull the top kid and hear Reyes hollering next to me, voice deep as a car stereo in my ear.

Circle's opening now. Chicano kid is down, he's thin, bony wrists green-laced with writing. The black kid is softer, neck shining, and he rolls over. But then he throws himself at the Chicano kid again, and I catch him with my boot. Both down. Reyes kicks the Chicano kid over onto his belly and holds him. I have to do the same thing. His lip split like a pomegranate. Oozing red. Some mother's son. It's hard not to feel the sting in my belly. Reyes's boy yelling at me in Spanish. I kick him one more time, in the side.

I bend down to turn mine over, get out my cuffs, and one braid pulls loose. Falls by my eyes. Bead silver like a raindrop. I see a dark hand reach for it, feel spit spray my forehead. Bitch. My hair pulled from my temple. My temple.

My stick. Blood on my stick. Michaels and Reyes take the wards. I keep my face away from all the rest, and a bubble of air or blood or something throbs next to my eyebrow. Where my skin pulled from my skull, for a minute. Burning now, but I know it's gon turn black like a scab, underneath my hair. I have to stand up. The sky turns black, then gray, like always. They're all heading to lockdown. I make sure they all see me spit on the cement before I go back inside. Fred stands outside talking to the shift supervisor, Williams, and I know he's coming in here in a minute, so I open the classifieds again and put my finger on Upright.

Nominated by Zoetrope: All Story

LITTLE TEXT

by BETTY ADCOCK

from SHENANDOAH

east Texas

1.

One needle from a longleaf pine
leftover from logging, one
needle falling through green
shade, through warp and shimmer of
September sometimes
      end over end will
turn as if marking the passing
air with form, circumference
as of time's real motion or
the approximation of, say,
a face.

Which way the needle rests,
possum or coon or wildcat
may pick up, taking on
this compass with its freight
of indication and
      downturning
invisible incident. It will be

passenger only until shed
onto brier or buttonbush, being only
a downed, straitened angel,
pin and linear argument,

line of prophecy flattened letterless
whose browning measure
                              beneath notice
points both ways at once—
though its done, erratic circle
(like the aftermath of water around
a thrown-in pebble) may widen
likewise to horizon
where it could shine the way
scripture shines, or spider's orb
or the water-drop
                    tinctured with sky.
It could be shining.

                    2.

I may have come for just this,
so long gone I can't remember bare
footlogs across the gar-infested creeks
or the heron thrust up white for magic,
for instructions
                    hidden
in the hollow wingbone.

And the scissortail has cleft this light
with journeys all my distant life.

Under a stranded palmetto,
the armadillo's metal is unzipped,
the flesh burst toward that further
wandering in earth where move
the multitudes,
                    and into air
where memory breathes its midge-cloud.

Thus unstitched, time will wander,
and the pine needle (beneath, now,
a boot) has left on air a print
of the suddenly upstanding huge
guessed-at virgin tree

and a feather, drifting, says
bird in a small stir
against the cheek,
                    barn swallow
hawk-snatched from the sky, redtail
gone, gone by.

3.

It all happened, it happened
all in glass-clear air.

And now? This present chainsaw-battered
earth, town-rent, tracked and fired
with pitiful need,
                    this water displaced
and broken into use?

The air smeared with smoke, with
gunpowder, history, the obsolete
intentions of factories, with a grease
redolent of human hope. Air here
might hold faintly, as on a fading
photographic plate,
                    a naked
walking child, bark-colored women
with baskets woven of grass and pine
needles, roots in the basket—
                              and not far,
a battle wearing
          clay
and berrystain and bearfat. There
a cougar rises to threaten the two-footed
fighters, our feet
              in those tracks.

4.

What am I but the visible door
onto that corridor incarnate with the ache

of cypress and ty-vine, raccoon and fox,
bat and buzzard, hanged man, red child,
world flesh sutured with our small past,
inscription after inscription missed
or grasped dreamlike in the unsteady
sensing the body is. And the body is
already arcing backward, describing,
darkening into path.

Nominated by Robert Wrigley

LOST CITIES

essay by RACHEL COHEN

from THE THREEPENNY REVIEW

I. Clerks

THERE IS A CERTAIN KIND OF POET who is a clerk during the day. It seems to be necessary to have mundaneness, which must involve paperwork, the long, slow soporific afternoons at an office, the sedateness of security, a regular paycheck, a bit too small, but reassuring, nevertheless, a boss, goodhearted, but not sensitive, also reassuring in his way. What does this do for the poet?

The Portuguese poet-clerk Fernando Pessoa wrote business correspondence in English and French in various offices for years; the Greek poet-clerk Constantine Cavafy translated letters for the Third Circle of Irrigation, an office of the British colonial administration in Egypt, in the same office every day for thirty-three years. Both were helped by this in an obvious financial sense. As Cavafy pointed out, the writer who does not rely on his writing for his living "obtains a great freedom in his creative work."

Pessoa and Cavafy both published only a handful of poems in their lifetimes, leaving behind countless drafts of other work. Cavafy revised continually, but he did self-publish in manuscripts he carefully bound together, so there is some sense of what he felt to be the final versions. Pessoa, on the other hand, kept all his manuscript pages in a trunk, where multiple undated versions of the same work appear next to each other, so that there's no knowing which he felt to be complete, or if he wanted them to be complete.

Pessoa wrote in dozens of different voices, each the representative of a person wholly formed, though a resident of his imagination. He

238

was a maritime engineer with a passion for Whitman and a monarchist exile who wrote only Horatian odes; he was a hunchback woman who wrote love letters to a steelworker; and an accountant who admired Omar Khayyam; he was a baron fallen on hard times; and he was an astrologer. One of these persons (whom he called heteronyms) was Bernando Soares, a dusty gray man and assistant bookkeeper with evening light in his soul. Soares was like Pessoa in many ways (Pessoa called him a semi-heteronym), not least in the way that each maintained a double allegiance to the office and the writer's study. Soares's prose writings are as close as we will get to Pessoa's autobiography. These meditations, called in English *The Book of Disquiet*, have been selected and translated into English by at least four different people. A slightly different Soares emerges from each one.

Many of the fragments begin with the mundane: the account books, Soares's boss Vasques, his occasionally foolish colleague Moreira, the delivery boy, the clock and calendar on the wall. Then there is the feeling of the office when the sky outside darkens in a storm. Anxiety comes with the storm, a sense of menace, and Soares is glad for the company of the office, the joke of the delivery boy, the protection and comfort of this undemanding company. This is the shape of his world in the day and it frees him for the night. In the evening, he walks the streets of Lisbon and returns home to write perfect crystalline meditations on depression, insomnia, nostalgia, memory, the city's geography, anonymity, and mortality. It seems that this work is only possible in his straitened conditions. The city wanderings must have their dusty contrast, must play in relief.

The contrast, the relief, these were also necessary for Cavafy. In the evenings, walking the streets of Alexandria or sitting at his desk working by lamplight, he makes his escape into love, art, history, and memory. He writes and he dreams; he dreams and he writes. He begins to lose a little bit his sense of what is real and what is imagined. In his poem "Morning Sea," he writes to himself,

> Let me stand here. And let me pretend I see all this
> (I really did see it for a minute when I first stopped)
> and not my usual day-dreams here too,
> my memories, those images of sensual pleasure.

> (*Cavafy, "Morning Sea," 1915, tr. Edmund Keeley and Philip Sherrard*)

He tried to keep them separate, perhaps not to sully the dreams, not to succumb to their temptation all the time, or perhaps because the dreams were richer if the fussy details of quotidian life were not intermingled.

Cavafy must have daydreamed at the office, too. He did not like going to work, and was always at least an hour late. He had the clerks who worked under him organized to explain his absence to his superiors. He was meticulous, correcting correspondence for several offices, and writing and translating letters into and out of English, but the work cannot have been especially demanding. After Cavafy's death, one of the other clerks who worked in the office, an Egyptian man named Ibrahim el Kayar, was interviewed by Manolis Halvatzakis, and the interview is quoted at length in Robert Liddell's biography of Cavafy. The interview was conducted in French and English, and some Arabic; just who wrote the English version is a little unclear. Ibrahim el Kayar describes how, for Cavafy, poetry sometimes interrupted translation:

> On very rare occasions he locked himself into his room. Sometimes my colleague and I looked through the keyhole. We saw him lift up his hands like an actor, and put on a strange expression as if in ecstasy, then he would bend down to write something. It was the moment of inspiration. Naturally we found it funny and we giggled. How were we to imagine that one day Mr. Cavafy would be famous!

The poet-clerk is certainly ridiculous, the relationship between his tedious office work and his moments of inspiration clear only to himself at the time. Cavafy found his poetry in the action of barricading office and home against the encroachments of the Third Circle of Irrigation.

Pessoa and Soares entered into an even more extreme arrangement: their poet-clerk is an impossibly unified being, completely interior, with no delineations at all.

> I write attentively, bent over the book in which with my entries I jot down the useless history of an obscure company; and at the same time, with the same attention, my

thoughts follow the progress of a nonexistent ship as it sails for nonexistent, oriental lands. The two things are equally clear, equally visible before me: the lined page on which I carefully write the verses of the commercial epic of Vasques and Co., and the deck where I carefully see, just to the side of the caulked seams of the boards, the long, lined-up chairs, and the extended legs of those resting on the voyage.

(*Bernando Soares/Fernando Pessoa*, The Book of Disquiet, *tr. Alfred MacAdam*)

This is the full doubleness of which poet-clerking is capable. Empires, ships, and kings come and go before the poet-clerk's eyes, as do the columns of figures themselves. He lives in a world where everything is imagined, the office as much an illusion as his dreams.

Cavafy and Pessoa were both quite isolated as children: their fathers died when they were young and they moved with their mothers to countries where the main language was English. Pessoa later explained that it was shortly after his father died, when he was about five, that he invented a friend for himself—the first of the imaginary boys and men who peopled his interior world—called the Chevalier de Pas. Pessoa's mother remarried, and at the age of seven Pessoa moved from Portugal to Durban, South Africa, where his stepfather was in the diplomatic corps. Pessoa attended an English school. In Durban, the Chevalier de Pas was replaced by a new friend and alter ego who went by the particularly English name of Charles Anon. By the time he was twelve or thirteen, Pessoa had any number of internal friends. They all wrote a newspaper together, each with his own byline. After high school, Pessoa's older stepbrothers settled in England; Pessoa chose Lisbon.

Cavafy's father died when he was seven, and two years later the family moved to England, where they lived until he turned fourteen. His father, a wealthy merchant, did not leave his affairs in good order, and the family had little money. Cavafy's older brothers went to work in various shipping offices. Cavafy also seems to have gone to school in England, and later when he was living in Alexandria and Constantinople with his mother, much of his correspondence and reading was in England.

Cavafy and Pessoa wrote their first poems in English and continued to write letters, poems, essays, and notes to themselves in English, as well as translations into and out of English, for the rest of their lives. They read French and Latin, too, and Cavafy claimed some Arabic, although his knowledge seems to have been slight. They wrote in the consciousness of other languages. Both were much affected by Shakespeare; both read Browning with careful attention. Pessoa read and translated the French surrealists; he was the first to publish them in Portugal. Pessoa's heteronyms also translated each other's work, and several of the heteronyms—particularly Charles James Search and the Crosse brothers, Thomas and I. I.—were translators first and foremost.

For Cavafy, translation was a source of income and it was also associated with sensuality. In Cavafy's poems, young men of different backgrounds gather together to read poetry and experience sensual pleasure, and they leave behind their native languages for the Greek more appropriate to the occasion.

Pessoa and Cavafy lived translation as Walter Benjamin (kindred spirit of all poet-clerks) understood it: as ardent entry into another realm of language. Not simply catching the literal meaning of another's words, but actually expanding one's own language under the influence of another's language. Thinking in two languages, like a circus rider standing on two horses, allowing oneself to be carried away by two languages together.

Among Browning's greatest poems are his dramatic monologues of characters revealed in all their complexity, sadness, and depravity. Cavafy and Pessoa scholars often cite the influence of Browning. Cavafy's dramatic monologues work through a similar process of a sympathetic imagination that does not balk at revealing weakness, or in some cases doom. And Pessoa took the idea further by living out the dramatic monologues themselves, inventing not characters but authors, and giving them rein to reveal themselves as they would.

The closest Cavafy comes to Browning is in the poem "Philhellene," which, as Edmund Keeley points out, is very much like Browning's "The Bishop Orders His Tomb at Saint Praxed's Church." Each concerns a man who, facing death, explains how he is to be memorialized. The bishop is to have a tomb of marble, jasper, and lapis, in the niche he has reserved for himself in Saint Praxed's church. It is to be a tomb to make his rival, long dead and buried in the south corner of the church, unspeakably jealous. The bishop's pettiness does not obscure his tragedy, for aren't we all afraid of how we'll be cared for after death? Cavafy's Hellenic ruler is similarly pathetic as he directs his minister or scribe in the design of the coin that will be his legacy. The coin is to have a beautiful young discus-thrower on the back, and is to be inscribed with the word *Philhellene*, to show the ruler's sophistication, his cultural taste. "Philhellene" is one of dozens of Cavafy poems which are either written specifically as epitaphs or which consider how best to memorialize someone recently dead or about to die.

Cavafy and Pessoa are like the scribes who appear in these poems, taking down the orders of Vasques and other minor emperors. The clerks' writings reassure petty rulers of the extent of their powers. But the poets are also themselves the leaders who know their own weaknesses, and who dream of a glory that may come after death. Deep is the poet's sympathy with a bishop or a Hellenic ruler, desperate at the end of his life for some sign that his prominence will continue. Even more desperate can be the fear of the poet, almost unpublished in his own lifetime, depending on the support of a few friends to ensure that all is not lost, that the work, like the tomb or the coins, will perpetuate the memory of its first imaginer.

This is precisely the task of the translator, the clerk among poets. Walter Benjamin writes that it is the appearance of great translation that marks the perpetual life of the original work. It is when a work enters into translation that it comes to have an effect on language itself, on the languages of the world. Cavafy and Pessoa, dusty clerks in cities no longer prominent, with few friends, secret reputations, and the dream life of kings, could not wait for readers and translators. They were their own clerks, taking down the words of their inspired dreams, living a memorial to themselves.

Cavafy and Pessoa worked in Greek and Portuguese and English, in the Rua dos Douradores and the time of the conquering kings, in the role of the clerk by day and the role of the king by night, or in both roles at both times. In their dreams and account books, they are both the original and the translator, both king and clerk—clerks to themselves, their own translators, their own tenuous assurance of immortality.

II. CITIES

Walking in cities is an accumulation of small fragments of loss. A woman you want to keep looking at turns a corner; two people pass and you hear only, "It cannot be because of the child"; you look through a window at a drawing which looks like a print you have seen somewhere before, and it's obscured when someone pulls a curtain across the window; a woman turns ferociously on the man standing next to her, but by the time you reach home you can no longer remember her face.

You begin to feel weighed down by all these losses, which seem separate from you, from the you that walks and sees and remembers and forgets and returns home. You wonder if the city in which you live is not the right city for you. Some other city might be less oppressive, freer. You dream of moving. And yet, you suspect that

You won't find a new country, won't find another shore.
This city will always pursue you. You will walk
the same streets, grow old in the same neighborhoods,
will turn gray in these same houses.
You will always end up in this city. Don't hope for things elsewhere:
there is no ship for you, there is no road.
As you've wasted your life here, in this small corner,
you've destroyed it everywhere in the world.

(Cavafy, "The City," written 1894, revised 1910, tr. Keeley and Sherrard)

Perhaps you do leave for a little while, as Cavafy left Alexandria for London when he was nine, or as Pessoa left Lisbon for Durban, returning at the age of seventeen.

Like the poets, you return. You, too, resist certain aspects of the city—perhaps its industry, or its violence. Its harshness grates upon you. You cling to the softer spaces: the parks at sunset, the river or the bay, a moment of sensuality, the vulnerability of certain passersby.

> Today walking down New Almada Street, I happened to
> gaze at the back of a man walking ahead of me. It was the
> ordinary back of an ordinary man, a modest blazer on the

244

shoulders of an incidental pedestrian. He carried a briefcase under his left arm, while his right hand held a rolled-
up umbrella, which he tapped on the ground to the
rhythm of his walking.

I suddenly felt a sort of tenderness on account of that
man. I felt the tenderness stirred by the common mass of
humanity, by the banality of the family breadwinner going
to work every day, by his humble and happy home, by the
happy and sad pleasures of which his life necessarily con-
sists, by the innocence of living without analysing, by the
animal naturalness of that coat-covered back.

(*Bernando Soares/Fernando Pessoa,* The Book of Disqui-
etude, *tr. Richard Zenith*)

You find that these glimpse are not only pleasing, they have become
necessary to you. You try to remember what it was that you thought
you needed. Trees, you think, or was it other people, some more natural way of life. You leave the city:

I went off to the country with great plans,
But found only grass and trees there,
And when there were people, they were just like any others.

(*Alvaro de Campos/Fernando Pessoa,* "Tobacco Shop," 1928, tr.
Edwin Honig and Susan Brown*)

You return to the city. If your soul is of this kind, there is no longer
any difference between the country and the city: you see everything
with the same dreamy eyes, you will always be a stranger, you will always be anonymous. How could you tolerate the country now? To
what other city would you go?

By now I've gotten used to Alexandria, and it's very
likely that even if I were rich I'd stay here. But in spite of
this, how the place disturbs me. What trouble, what a burden small cities are—what lack of freedom.

I'd stay here (then again I'm not entirely certain that I'd
stay) because it is like a native country for me, because it
is related to my life's memories.

245

But how much a man like me—so different—needs a large city.

London, let's say. Since . . . P.M. left, how very much it is on my mind.

(Cavafy, note, 1907, tr. Keeley)

Somehow the lack of freedom is related to life's memories. Now you have reached a point in your life when you realize that you were not meant for youth, that you were in fact always a little older than everyone else and merely waiting for your age to catch up to you, so that you might live partly through memory, as you were meant to. And now your memories, even the memory of your resistance to the city and its constraints, are all part of the city itself.

You will always return to the city. You know that the feeling of return, and its tension between acceptance and resistance, is your most fundamental feeling. You survive by returning. And now, in this city, you no longer need to leave in order to return.

Then, sad, I went out on to the balcony,
went out to change my thoughts at least by seeing
something of this city I love,
a little movement in the streets and the shops.

(Cavafy, "In the Evening," 1917, tr. Keeley and Sherrard)

You have reached an accommodation with your city, you have found a way to be seamlessly close and distant. If you are Cavafy, Alexandria comforts you in your regret; if you are Pessoa, Lisbon and its Tagus river reassure you with their indifference.

Oh, sky of blue—the same sky of my childhood—,
Eternal truth, empty and perfect!
O, gentle Tagus, ancestral and mute,
Tiny truth where the sky reflects itself!
O, suffering revisited, Lisbon of long ago and of today!
You give me nothing, you take nothing from me, you're nothing
    that I feel in myself.

(Alvaro de Campos/Fernando Pessoa, "Lisbon Revisited," 1923, tr. Rachel Cohen)

246

If your city is a Lisbon or an Alexandria, it weighs on you, as Pessoa wrote, "like a sentence of exile," and this is the only tolerable condition. You must live specifically in this city, the only city on earth in which you can be certain of denying yourself, in which you will feel a perpetual stranger in precisely the way that you desire.

Slowly, slowly, you and your city grow into each other. Pessoa addresses his Lisbon:

> Once again I see you,
> But myself, alas, I fail to see!
> Shattered, the magical mirror where I saw myself identical,
> And in each fateful fragment I descry only a piece of myself—
> A piece of you and of myself . . .

> *(Alvaro de Campos/Fernando Pessoa, "Lisbon Revisited," 1926,*
> *tr. Honig and Brown)*

You have become the tiny pieces of half-forgotten streets and men with overcoats. If you are Cavafy, you have become the fragments of your memories and your historical imaginings; if you are Pessoa, you have become a hundred different personalities writing with the same pen. If you are a brick-layer, then this feeling will be in the bricks, and the way they have been laid, and it will be sensed, though rarely understood, by the people who walk on them. If you are a photographer, you will only take pictures of your city, and even your photographs of fruit on tables will still be pictures of the city. And if you are a poet, then there is some chance that you will become the poet of your city, that people will come to see the city that you became.

They will stop and wonder at the plaque on the Rue Lepsius in Alexandria where your house no longer stands. They will smile wistfully at the statue of you perched forever on a metal chair in front of your café, the Café Brasileira on the Largo do Rato. And they will feel vaguely disappointed that they cannot quite locate the feeling of your poems in the city itself, for the city in places is ugly, and has been garishly modernized, and the people on the buses seem utterly unaware that they live in the city of the poet—they are contemporary and mundane, not so different really from the people in the city where the admirers of the poet live themselves.

The people who go to visit the city of the poet find it hard to make sense of the sight of garbage in alleyways, of blue and yellow tiles behind doors, of mosques, of beggars. These are not in the poems of the poet they love so well. This is not the city they had imagined, though they believe the city of the poet lies buried beneath its stones or is hidden behind its walls. Once or twice perhaps they catch a glimpse of sky, or light reflecting on the river; they see an encounter between two men that the poet might have described, and they nod to themselves, ah, there, just for a minute, I thought I saw it.

And they return to their own city, which is, after all, theirs, and they are comforted.

In the evening, when they come home from walking the streets of their city, they take the poet's books down from the shelf and read a few lines, quietly, in the more comfortable of the two chairs, by the light of the lamp. Ah, yes, they think to themselves, what a beautiful city, if only it existed, if only we could go there.

Nominated by Paul Maliszewski; Threepenny Review

THESE

by JENNIFER BARBER

from PARTISAN REVIEW

These are the Days of Awe,
not marked on my calendar.

The covenant with gravity
lifts and loosens the leaves,
a last warm breeze.

I lie down in the grass.
Fragments of verse
circle me like dogs.

The house of the dove is empty,
an eagle stuns its prey.

Owls wait
in the broken walls
for a darkness they can hear.

Nominated by Partisan Review

BEFORE LONG

fiction by VALERIE LAKEN

from PLOUGHSHARES

IN THE DAYS THAT SUMMER when his mother had to work cleaning the cottages in Dáchenko and Kóslan, Anton was being watched by the Shurins. He was twelve and blind, and his mother feared leaving him alone. He spent his mornings working with Oleg Shurin in the tomato patches along the bluff, and in the afternoons he and Oleg took long walks on the dirt paths of the fields and forests around their village. Anton would follow Oleg's voice or the crackle of his steps through the grass and do his best to map their course in his mind, counting paces and turns, noting sounds and directions and angles of descent or ascent. Beyond the tomato patches and the bluff was a deep ravine leading down to the river, which ran very shallow and calm that year because of the drought.

They had finished pruning the plants and pulling the weeds, and the sun was high, but there was still time before lunch, so Anton and Oleg walked down the ravine to a clump of bushes near the river where Oleg kept his magazines hidden in a metal box. Oleg was three years older and was teaching Anton about women. He had seen and touched and kissed them. They lay in the weedy undergrowth, and Oleg read from the magazines and described the pictures aloud.

"—one velvety peach mound cupped in her—"

"Wait, Oleg, where do you mean?"

"There." Oleg took Anton's finger and touched it to the slick paper, tracing out a vague pattern. Then he took Anton's palm and pressed it against his chest. "Instead of flat, like us, you know, she's holding them. *Mounds.*" Anton could feel Oleg puffing his chest out, but it was still hard and flat: breastplate, bone, sternum. Anton removed his palm and placed it against his own chest, then moved it to his stomach.

"Mounds." Anton turned his face back toward the hottest angle of the sun. It would have been nice to swim. "And then what?"

"That's pretty much it. She's just lying there."

From across the river they could hear hammers striking and echoing where workers were building more summer cottages for the New Russians from Moscow, who weren't Communists.

"What about her legs? What kind of legs?"

"It only shows her hips and the tops of her thighs. There's the edge of some white cotton panties. The rest is cut off."

"Cut off?"

"You know, not in the picture. A picture can only show so much, Anton."

"How much?"

Over the ravine Oleg's grandmother started calling them to lunch. "Depends."

Anton had never touched or kissed a girl, and the only thighs he knew besides his own were his mother's. In Anton's dreams his mother had heavy, rippled thighs that rubbed together when she walked. They said her hair was reddish blond and that she had been a beauty in her day. From what Oleg had told him, reddish blond was a good thing to be, and the color of thighs was pink. "Like the belly of a rabbit."

In fact Anton's mother's thighs were no longer fatty, though. She had done the Herbalife diet and wasted away to a much smaller presence when she walked or sat beside him. It didn't make much difference, he supposed, and the other women in the village kept telling her she looked wonderful, but Anton missed the soft pillowy squish of her body from his younger years.

The metal box clicked open and shut, which meant that Oleg's magazines were stored away again and the lesson was done. Oleg rustled through the bushes to deposit the box back in its hiding place. Anton stood up and walked down toward the river to give him some privacy; Oleg liked a little time alone after their lessons. Anton could hear the water moving against the rocks, and it was a different sound from the wind in the trees, but they came together in a rush around him as he got closer to the water. He slipped off his sandals and felt his way down the bank with his hands close to the ground,

251

then he waded several steps into the water. It was only knee-deep this summer, but still Anton was forbidden to go near it.

Anton stood up to his calves and felt the water swerve in circles around his feet. Something soft, a leaf maybe, drifted between his legs. The current was nearly imperceptible unless he lifted one foot and let it dangle in the flow. Then he could feel the tug and push of the water, affirming his bearings. He was still facing east, still perpendicular to the bank. He turned downstream, unzipped his pants, and relieved himself, listening to distinguish his trickle of water from the rest.

"Zzzzzzzz," Oleg called from the ravine when he was finished. That was the sound of Dr. Nicholson's drill. Anton made his way out of the water. "He's going to rip them right out. Zzzzzz." Oleg snickered. Anton was going to the dentist tomorrow. Neither of the boys had ever been, but a year ago Anton's mother had begun cleaning house for an American dentist, Dr. Nicholson, and he was giving them a special rate. Anton felt for his sandals along the bank where he had left them.

"Looking for these?" Oleg tapped Anton twice on the head with the sandals.

"Give me them."

"Just *kidding*." Oleg put the sandals into Anton's hand.

Anton tried to clear the distress from his face. "I know." He had been teased often, and by many kids. Oleg was only teaching him to be tough.

"I've got something for you," Oleg said, pressing some coins into Anton's palm. "Tomorrow, if you get a chance, see if you can't pick me up a copy of *Pentxaus*. My cousin says he finds them in the metro."

Anton shuffled the change through his fingers. "Well. I won't be alone, you know?" How could he buy a girlie magazine with his mother?

"Ah, of course. Your mother by your side. I can see how that's a problem." Oleg had started talking this way lately. He was getting ready for high school.

"Not that I don't want to." Anton held out the rubles for Oleg to take back.

"Of course." Oleg started up the ravine. "Me, if I were going, it'd be a different situation."

Anton fastened the last buckle of his sandals and hurried after Oleg. "Maybe you could come with us."

"To the dentist? To the zzzzzzzzz American dentist? No thanks."

Anton pushed the fistful of coins at Oleg's back. "No, just keep the money," Oleg said. "In case. Just see what you can do." No one from their village got to Moscow very often.

"I could buy some gum for you."

"Kid stuff."

Oleg's grandmother called for them again from the top of the bluff.

"Maybe your mom will run off to the bathroom," Oleg said. "Leave you waiting next to a newsstand."

Anton turned the idea over in his mind. It could happen.

"Maybe some doll will pick you up at the station, show you a thing or two."

Anton could feel his face starting to flush, and he hesitated, then stammered, "Maybe, maybe Dr. Nicholson has a nurse."

"Oh, that's it. I bet he does, some fine thing. She's going to lean all over you. You'll forget all about my magazines."

They were halfway up the ravine by now and had forgotten their ritual. "Wait," Oleg said, turning suddenly and taking Anton roughly by the shoulders. Anton steadied himself and took a breath. "Tell no one, show no one, come alone never," Oleg murmured methodically, spinning Anton around several times on the uneven soil. Then they stood still, waiting for the dizziness to subside, and Anton repeated the chant himself. It was an empty ritual by now. Who would he tell? Why on earth? No one had ever shown Anton as much as Oleg had.

But the ritual was a carryover from the early days, before they were truly friends, when Anton's mother first went to work and Oleg and his grandmother took over watching Anton. Oleg hadn't trusted him yet back then, which was understandable. The metal box contained considerable treasure. But now the spinning had no effect: Anton could make his way to Oleg's secret spot alone, in the rain, even in the snow, he supposed. It was sixty-five paces west of the railway bridge, and with the noise of the stream as a guide there was almost no way to get lost. Anton felt as though he had memorized the entire village by following in Oleg's footsteps. Now he scrambled up the ravine in the path Oleg snapped through the brush, keeping low to the ground and using his hands for balance.

"Where have you been?" Oleg's grandmother approached them after they crossed the field and neared her house. She jingled a little for some reason as she walked.

"We caught that rabbit eating at the plants again," Oleg said. "We were chasing it down."

"My boys. Did you catch it?"

Oleg nudged Anton. "Not yet. Maybe after lunch."

Oleg's grandmother put a hand on Anton's back and patted it. "I bet you'll get it next time. Can you catch a rabbit, Anton?"

Anton leaned into her hand. She had a pleasant berry smell.

"Well, come on now. I've got lunch waiting." She took Anton's elbow and led him in slow, careful steps toward the house. They jingled together, and Anton still could not determine the source.

"There's the gate now." She guided him into the side yard and paused to pat the little dog. "*Privét, Mishul'.*" The table would be twelve steps forward, then three right. Anton could find it all very well on his own, but he liked the feel of her, large and soft, against his side. "Here's our table, Anton. You take this seat right here." She placed his hand against the chair, and he sat down to their usual lunch in the shade of the root shed. On the table he could smell fried potatoes with pepper and salt, and tomato salad with vinegar. Oleg got close behind him and hummed, "Zzzzzzzzz," in his ear.

"Oleg, you stop that. What is that?" she demanded.

"Nothing."

When she went into the house for more bread, Anton whispered, "What's the jingling?"

"Earrings," Oleg said with a mouthful. "She's trying to impress Sasha next door now that his wife has died."

Oleg's grandmother returned. "I hear you're going to the dentist tomorrow, Anton."

"Yes, tomorrow."

"They have these long metal picks and instruments they stick right into your teeth." Oleg tapped his fork against the table.

"Be quiet, Oleg," she said.

"It's true," he persisted. "I saw it on television. They drill big holes in your teeth."

Anton put down his bread and ran his tongue along his molars.

"See what a coward Oleg is? But you're not afraid, are you, Anton?"

"No," he said, pushing his chin up, but the idea of drills vibrating against his teeth and gums was terrible and foreign to him.

Dr. Nicholson worked at a practice for the new rich and the foreigners, and it was supposed to be painless, but Anton was doubtful. It was some kind of exchange program for introducing new dentistry to the Russian doctors, and his schedule was booked all the time. Anton's mother had been working as the cleaning lady at his summer house for almost a year now, and he paid her in dollars, not rubles. He had an apartment in the city and a place back in America probably, and a two-story cottage in Dáchenko that he visited only two or three weekends a month. Anton's mother took care of the garden, which was hard in this dry summer, and she cleaned up before and after him when he visited. The pay was outrageous; she made more in one month than Anton's father, before he left them, had ever made in a year. Sometimes Dr. Nicholson paid her extra just to go there in the evenings and turn lights on and off as if someone were living there.

Anton's mother was fascinated by Dr. Nicholson and talked of him to everyone. She came home with fresh stories all the time. "Dr. Nicholson has a computer at his cottage." What kind of dentistry can be done on computer? And who works at their cottage anyway? "Dr. Nicholson has a new car, can you imagine, two cars for one man with no family?" These Americans. "Dr. Nicholson is learning Russian, really learning it. He can talk! Not just through his secretary, but really talk. Today we sat down for tea together." She hummed songs all evening after that day.

But the most remarkable thing about Dr. Nicholson, according to Anton's mother, was his teeth. "So white and perfect they're almost unnatural. No wonder they brought him all this way. It really makes me quite afraid to smile."

The first thing she did, after meeting Dr. Nicholson, was that she came home and taught Anton how to smile without opening his lips. They sat together with their fingers on each other's mouths for an entire afternoon practicing this. "That's pretty good, Anton," she said in the end. "Before long you'll be turning heads yourself."

Anton had gaps between his teeth.

By early spring Anton's mother had saved enough for an appointment of her own. The Herbalife diet was over, and she was thin and, as everyone said, lovely, and she wanted her teeth to be handsome as well. Dr. Nicholson fitted her into his schedule and gave her twenty-five percent off. "The Americans are known for their generosity," she told Anton. And though she came home that evening saying, "Yes, truly it was rather painless," her voice seemed tightened by pain as she said it, and she kept getting up in the night, popping open the aspirin bottle. But the neighbors did say it was a great improvement in her smile.

And now she had saved enough again to give Anton a turn. She was very proud and pleased at the idea and had already told everyone they knew.

"Just wait till you meet Dr. Nicholson," she said when she put Anton to bed that night. "I think you'll really like him."

Anton lay very still.

"You will be nice to him, won't you, *druzhók*?"

Anton wanted to tell her that his teeth were just fine, that they never bothered or hurt him at all. They were hard and clicked together when he chewed; there was nothing rotten or soft about them. A dentist was quite unnecessary. Dr. Nicholson in general could go back from where he came.

But she leaned, thin and new, over him in the bed and brushed his hair back tenderly. "Just think how handsome you'll be for all the girls."

She stroked her thumbs along his eyelids to make him sleepy.

"There'll be nobody anywhere with teeth so fine," she said. Anton could tell she was smiling. He could just feel it.

They had to start out early in the morning and with good clothes on. Anton's ironed shirt pinched at his wrists, and his pants felt tight against his thighs and groin when he walked. But by the time they'd made it halfway to the train station on the dusty, rutted road, the sun was warm on their necks, and his clothes seemed to stretch out a little with the perspiration.

"This is the big day, yes, Anton?"

He didn't want to talk about it.

"And you'll see, it won't even hurt a bit."

Anton ran his tongue between his lip and his upper teeth, letting it slip in and out between the gaps. They might be gone by the end of the day. There was no telling what could happen. His breath was fresh, his teeth just brushed and slick.

"How handsome you'll be," she mused, then stumbled and put a hand on his shoulder to steady herself in the ruts.

When they reached the train platform, they stood on the cement with the morning commuters, shuffling their feet.

"Lucky we don't have to do this every day, right, Anton? We are truly lucky people."

"Do you go this way to Dr. Nicholson's cottage?"

"I go the other direction, Anton. I go northwest, which is that way." She held out his arm a little forward and to the right.

"So the city is that way?" Anton pointed his other hand in the opposite direction.

"Good. And show me south."

Anton pointed.

"My smart boy. Such a smart boy." The platform began to quiver, and Anton's mother moved in close behind him and held his shoulders firmly with both hands to protect him. The *elektríchka* rumbled in; it was quieter but seemed to move faster than the regular trains. Soon Anton's mother was guiding him forward quickly in the shuffle of bodies, and he was pushed up against the backs and shoulders of the commuters. "Watch out," said an old woman as he stumbled on something she was carrying, and then she paused and said, "Oh, sorry."

"Here now, darling, quickly." Anton's mother tried to guide him to a seat before they all filled up. The train was already thick with the breath and newspaper scent of commuters from towns farther out. "Oh, here we go, Anton." She patted his hand to a seat. He sat down and felt the thigh of a woman next to him on the bench. She seemed to scoot away from him. He could feel his mother still standing next to him on the aisle, shuffling forward each time someone passed by.

"No, you sit, Mom." He stood up.

"I'm fine, dear." She put her hand on his shoulder, pressing him downward again.

"Really." He stood up with his legs spread for balance and locked his knees.

"Well, all right. Here." She sat down and shifted behind him, then pulled him down by the hips to sit on her lap the way children do. He lost his balance and landed on her, sitting there for a moment as she wished. But she had grown smaller, or he had gotten bigger. He felt ridiculous, too large, too awkward, and he pushed away from her, standing back up.

"No," he insisted, and stood hanging on to the back of the bench.

And so they stayed like this, she on the seat, he clutching the seatback with one hand and her shoulder with the other, swaying with the motion of the train for over an hour in the morning odors of the passengers. Aftershave, alcohol, cigarettes, coffee. The freshness of his own breath started to make Anton feel separate at first, and then a little nauseated, and his mouth began to water. They passed the stops for Vólkovo, Drúzhba, and Abrámtsevo, and the humming and screeching of the train accelerating and braking each time filled Anton's thoughts with drills and strange metal pokers and instruments. He started to sweat at the brow and under his arms.

He closed his eyes and tried to breathe deeply for a while, thinking of Oleg's picture girls and the stream and the sun and the tomatoes and dust which would be there when he returned. He turned Oleg's coins over in his pocket, stacking them up and letting them slip apart again. It would be nice to be able to help Oleg for a change. It would be nice to be the one who held the treasure.

The closer they got to the city, the more crowded the train became, until finally Anton didn't have to hold on to his mother's shoulder because it was too crowded for him to fall down. When the doors opened at Kúrskii Vokzál in Moscow, the warm, damp bodies in the aisle pushed forward with such force that Anton's mother lost her grip on him, bruising his wrist in one last attempt to snatch him, and she had to call after the *bábushka* next to him, "Help my boy off. He's blind. Hold my boy." Anton cringed, and the woman grabbed his arm so that her bag banged hard against his thigh. When they reached the doorway and the steps, the woman pushed her bag into the space behind Anton to divide him from the rest of the passengers and called out, "Hold still for a minute, thugs, we've got a blind boy here."

"There's the step, there you go, there's another one, little guy." She held tightly to Anton's arm on the platform until his mother arrived. "Thank you."

"*Pozháluista.*"

Anton's face burned with humiliation, and he blinked his eyes against the insult of this woman's hand on his arm. But the air of the open station yard felt cool on his skin and contained a hundred unfamiliar smells.

"This city," Anton's mother said. "I don't see how people can stand it. Let's go."

They walked arm in arm up the platform toward the noise of the station buildings. Women in heels clicked erratically around them, people brushed past them and overcame them from behind, and all the while the trains were coming and going with the *ding dong dong* of the departure announcements.

"Where to now?"

"We'll go down to the metro station and take it through the center, then transfer down to Profsoyúznaya," she said.

"Is it far?"

"We have plenty of time. Hold still, let me wipe your face."

"What direction are we going now?"

"This is—" She stopped walking a moment and turned around a little. "I think this is south, dear."

"That's south," a man next to them said.

"Oh. We're going east right now, dear."

They walked on toward the station buildings, and the sound from the loudspeakers got louder. There was the smell of *shashlík* grills already being fired up to the right where the cafés and kiosks must have been. Some men brushed past them smelling of fish and stale alcohol. They were speaking a strange, jumbled language.

Anton inhaled and gathered his courage, then squeezed his mother's arm. "I'd like to buy a magazine," he said.

"What?"

"For Oleg. Oleg wants a certain . . . he wants a car magazine."

"A car magazine? What for?"

"I don't know. He likes them."

"Car magazines. What will it be next?" She stopped and pulled him out of the line of traffic. He could feel her body leaning in different directions, looking for the right kiosk. Then she led him a few steps to their right, which Anton figured must be south. They were up against the cool metal of a kiosk now; it was still damp from the morning. A man leaned in over Anton's shoulder and said, "*Komsomólets*," then reached in for his paper. Anton's mother pulled him to the side again.

"What kind of car magazine?"

"Do they have a lot of magazines? Is it a well-stocked kiosk?"

"They're all well-stocked nowadays, Anton. What they wouldn't sell you. Which one do you want? They have *Avtomobíl'* from May and July, and the current *Motór*, and *Vodítel'*—that one has a lovely purple car. Very strange."

Anton paused.

"Well? What do you think he'd like?"

"I think . . . I think he has those already. I think it's supposed to have a truck. Something with a truck."

Anton's mother asked the woman through the window about trucks. They didn't have any truck magazines.

"But they have lots of magazines?"

"Yes, Anton. Do you want a different one?"

He could be grown-up like Oleg. They could be equal.

"Do you have to go to the bathroom, Mom?"

"Anton, stop this. What is this about?"

"I . . . I—" A mechanical female voice interrupted him through the speakers over his head, announcing the departure of the next train to Kursk. Anton felt as though he were being swallowed up by her voice, by the vibrating speakers everywhere, by the crush of strangers poking in at him through the dark void before his eyes. "I have to go to the bathroom," he said at last.

"You have to go to the bathroom." Her words came out slowly, evenly, but Anton could hear the frustration welling in them. She pulled him toward her by both shoulders and snapped her words into his face. "Anton. This isn't funny."

He'd had enough, too. "I know."

"Well, you'll have to wait till Dr. Nicholson's. We're not going in any train station bathroom, I'll tell you that for sure."

"I'm going to be sick," Anton lied. He didn't know what he was doing. In his mind a vague plan was struggling to take shape. His muscles stiffened one by one, and a cold tingle swept up his limbs to his throat. He clenched his jaw against the idea of Dr. Nicholson's instruments and imagined himself taller and broad-shouldered, strong. He imagined himself so big that his mother couldn't drag him anywhere. "I'm going to be sick," he said again.

She sighed. She lightened her grip on his arm. They started walking again, eastward. One two three four five six seven eight. She paused and asked someone about a bathroom. "Inside by the ticket booths," a man said.

"Didn't you go before we left?"

Twenty-nine. Thirty. Thirty-one. "I guess not." They turned right. Forty-eight, forty-nine, through heavy doors that pushed in both directions, into a heat wave of bodies standing sweating in lines, foreign voices, more announcement bells, a puddle, and down six steps, then around a landing and down seven more. Fifty-six, fifty-seven, to the right. He could find his way back to the kiosk alone. Seventy-four, seventy-five, seventy-six. They stopped. He could take a breath in the bathroom and calm himself, break free of her and find his way back to the kiosk and to Dáchenko and the tomato fields and the Shurins. He could do that. She could go see Dr. Nicholson without him.

They had neared the bathrooms: the scent of urine and excrement seeped through the air. "We'll have to wait for help," Anton's mother said. She was breathing heavy with disgust. It was an area where no one would choose to stand around.

"I can do it alone."

"No."

He shuffled and squirmed. "I'm sick, Mom. I'm sick."

"Excuse me." She reached out to a man passing by. No response. They waited. "Excuse me," she said again to another. "My son needs to go to the bathroom." No response. He must have walked away.

"I can do it myself," Anton groaned.

"I said no."

"*Excuse me.*" This time her voice was forceful, urgent. And she must have gotten someone's attention, for it turned soft again. "My son here needs to go to the bathroom. Be kind, would you take him in for me? He's blind, you see."

"Well, hello." The man smelled of chicken soup, yesterday's chicken soup.

Anton's mother drove a finger into his back. "Hello," Anton said.

"Well, let's go, then."

Anton's face was hot with embarrassment. He took the man's arm, which felt dusty and frail under his textured suit jacket.

"You can do everything yourself, right?" the man asked in a low voice as they walked through the door and deeper into the stench.

"Yes. Of course." The floor was wet and slippery.

"How did it happen, may I ask?"

"What?"

"The eyes."

Hundred seven. Eight. Nine, right on nine. The room was quiet except for a faucet dripping somewhere.

"Don't like to talk about it?"

Anton said nothing. He didn't know how it had happened. He was born to this.

261

"That's all right. Here you go." The man took Anton's hand and placed it against the cool porcelain of the urinal. "Don't touch it too much, but here it is right in front of you. Is that all right?"

If there were another door he could slip out of, if he could make himself small, unnoticeable, he could slip away from this old man and his chicken scent and count his way right back to the kiosk. One hundred nine steps was nothing; it was half the distance from Oleg's house to the river. And he could ask someone for help if he got lost. He could do it, he could slap his coins down for the lady in the kiosk and say *Pentxaus* with authority, without fear or hesitation of any kind. He would walk away a man, like any normal man, with the magazine tucked into his pants under his shirt. He would catch the next train to Dáchenko and be back in time for lunch with Oleg and Grandma Shurin. And she'd be sorry, his mother. She would worry and worry. She would think twice about her American dentist.

"Is there another door in here?"

"What?" The man shuffled around a little and came back to Anton's side. "No. Just the one."

The dripping faucet echoed against the walls and floor around him. Anton felt his face beginning to twitch and tremble.

"Well, what's the problem, son?"

There was nowhere he could go.

"I need a toilet."

"Oh, I see. Right." He took Anton's arm again and turned him around, but in turning the old man slipped on the wet tile and began to go down. "Oi!" He clutched at Anton's torso with both arms, pressing Anton's head into his hot, damp chest. They wavered a moment, flailing, but did not go down. They stood upright on the tile floor, trembling, without so much as a bumped elbow or knee to knock the thrill out of their bones.

All of his numbers were gone, flown from his head. All his bearings, all his points of reference. Anton didn't even know where the door was. He wasn't going to get to the kiosk alone, or to the train or Dáchenko or anywhere. He was a little boy clutching at an old man in a stinking threadbare suit in the basement reek of Kúrskii Vokzál, with his mother worrying at the door. And he was not sick at all, though the stench was enough to turn anyone's stomach, and Oleg was home in the field pulling weeds and dreaming of his girls without so much as a thought for Anton or the coins he'd charged him with.

262

"Well, are you going in or not?" the man said impatiently, pressing Anton's hand against the gritty door of the stall.

Anton stood in the growing heat of his face and neck. In his tight pants with his hand on the metal door, he faced the stall like a fate he couldn't step into.

"Go to hell," Anton murmured. From behind them came the click of dress shoes and then the sound of someone urinating.

"Pardon?"

"You heard me," Anton whispered.

"This is how you treat an old man?"

"Go to hell."

This time the man slapped him. Not on the face, like his mother did on rare occasion. On the behind. He spanked him.

The tears came now; there was no chance of stopping them. "Pervert," Anton hissed in one last attempt at manliness. "Get your hands off me."

"What's going on here?" the dress-shoes man at the urinal said.

"Kids. Kids today don't know how to behave."

"Stop touching me!" Anton cried. "Don't *touch* me." The old man removed his hand and took a step back, and now Anton was alone against the door of the stall, sinking down. He crouched low on the wet, filthy floor, and the tears rolled out of his eyes. He sucked at the air in unsteady patches. There was no one anywhere who could ever fix this. There was no way he would be cured, no way he was ever going to walk to a kiosk or look at a magazine, no way for any of it ever to happen.

"Oh, dear boy," his mother's voice came at the door, and she rushed in to him. She kneeled down on the floor in the middle of the men's room and folded him in her embrace.

"What have you done?" she hissed at the old man.

"He's crazy," the old man said.

"I just found them like this, lady," said the man who had been at the urinal.

And then the room seemed to clear out and get quiet, and she rocked him there on the floor against her chest, back and forth. She let his sobs erupt in her arms without asking questions. She stroked his hair and the back of his neck and said, "That's all right, darling. That's all right."

"I don't want to go to Dr. Nicholson's."

"You're sick, dear, it's all right." She stroked his back softly. "You're not feeling well."

In time it subsided, and Anton was left feeling hollow and spent, his nose wet with snot, his voice deep and thick with mucous.

"Let's get out of here," she said. "How about that?"

"Let's go, let's go. I want to go home."

So they wiped themselves off, and she straightened Anton's clothes. They stood very upright and walked together out of the men's room in the basement of the station, and whether anybody was watching them he did not know, but he knew that his mother had been a great beauty in her day and that she carried herself very nicely, always in top form, and she was thin now and supple at his side, and he was proud to be with her. They walked an even forty steps straight ahead this way, as if on parade with their shoulders back, breathing deeply, and then they went up the seven stairs and around the landing, up six more, and through the swinging doors out of the stink and heat toward the left into the open cement yard of the station. The loudspeakers were at it still, but the morning rush had subsided, and they were able to walk freely without being jostled. It was twenty-nine steps to the ice cream stand with the heat of the sun on their faces, and at the window she gave Anton the money and let him order for them, two Eskimo. They walked back to their platform holding the ice cream bars, cold in their hands, not opening the wrappers until they had reached a bench in the middle of the platform, where they could feel the push and pull of the trains coming in and going out as they waited for the next one leaving toward Dáchenko.

Nominated by Ploughshares

IKARIA
(THE NIGHT WATCHERS)
by KIRA HENEHAN

from JUBILAT

i.

charcoal black she goes among   something like scenery   stronghold
this ancestral home this walk of beacons upon the headlands   where
landscape

ii.

there are others here   begun an age ago   the beacon this very night
then   you took already the word hibiscus   where landscape
where fires   determined to finish

iii.

this single movement   a conversation   and some bricks by the window have broken through their whitewash   the lake hasn't frozen to
anyone's satisfaction   we live where the wind can't get in

iv.

and some bricks by the window   it is difficult to make certain
determinations at all   no again   I am going out to sea   there are
others

v.

(refrain from removing reminders   I have been so long among these
things)

vi.

likewise   difficult to at all determine what I would have certain
the beacon this very night then   I will answer for   plain as sand or
plain

vii.

others here   to see shadowed   the still of what you said   I will answer for   it suffices unsaid   or plain as a girl dreaming only unstill
beneath the lids

viii.

the lake hasn't frozen   we live where the wind can't get in   the beacons one after one down the headlands   where landscape where
fires   this is not a dialogue

ix.

you took already the word hibiscus   keep small artifacts from trips
not I have taken   thoughtfully red determined to finish   less like
the sea   she goes among   no again I am going out to sea   halfway
determined

x.

(refrain from claiming the rain as a reason   let out remain out   in
in   and on all these long years of nights   this and this   and that
halfway means twice   this night)

xi.

there is this night and this   stone of no discernible color   nostalgia
impossible   thoughtfully red likewise it is difficult   see shadowed

xii.

others here to see   to see shadowed on rooftops   what I would
have certain   this is a place that seems to have been on fire   and
halfway determined to finish   it would be safe to suppose now a series of nights   charcoal black

xiii.

the beacon of what you said   I will answer   hoard foreign nostalgias
in this place my own have fled   this is not a dialogue   having known
intolerable nights   I have gone

xiv.

to explain this new calm   it suffices unsaid   to suppose now a series
of night fashioned from something akin to redundancy   a stone of
no discernible color   you will be   less like the sea   or something
like scenery

xv.

(refrain from burning   striking the curtains   so as not to confuse
with dueling fires)

xvi.

no matter the rain   I will not wait for you   I am fashioning match-
sticks in the shape of a house   there is this night and this   before
night puts a lid on it   you said already   your words have never been
for me

xvii.

having known intolerable nights   I have gone   this night intolerable in the fugitive sense only   black she goes among the fires
halfway determined to finish a conversation   though others here

xviii.

to see shadowed on rooftops   where lit though make no less of the
shadows   the smell less of sea than remembered   you will

xix.

this is a place that seems to have been on fire   I am making a house
that will burn when struck   before night puts a lid on   you still as in
sleep   there is this day and   this conversation begun an age   let
the not moonlight fade   you   finish

xx.
(refrain)

Nominated by Jubilat

THREE GIRLS

fiction by JOYCE CAROL OATES

from THE GEORGIA REVIEW

IN STRAND USED BOOKS on Broadway and Twelfth one snowy March early evening in 1956 when the streetlights on Broadway glimmered with a strange sepia glow, we were two NYU girl-poets drifting through the warehouse of treasures as through an enchanted forest. Just past 6:00 P.M. Above light-riddled Manhattan, opaque night. Snowing, and sidewalks encrusted with ice so there were fewer customers in the Strand than usual at this hour but *there we were*. Among other cranky brooding regulars. In our army-surplus jackets, baggy khaki pants, and zip-up rubber boots. In our matching wool caps (knitted by your restless fingers) pulled down low over our pale-girl foreheads. Enchanted by books. Enchanted by the Strand.

No bookstore of merely "new" books with elegant show window displays drew us like the drafty Strand, bins of books untidy and thumbed through as merchants' sidewalk bins on Fourteenth Street, NEW THIS WEEK, BEST BARGAINS, WORLD CLASSICS, ART BOOKS 50% OFF, REVIEWERS' COPIES, HIGHEST PRICE $1.98, REMAINDERS 25¢—$1.00. Hard-cover/paperback. Spotless/battered. Beautiful books/cheaply printed pulp paper. And at the rear and sides in that vast echoing space massive shelves of books books books rising to a ceiling of hammered tin fifteen feet above! Stacked shelves so high they required ladders to negotiate and a monkey nimbleness (like yours) to climb.

We were enchanted with the Strand and with each other in the Strand. Overseen by surly young clerks who were poets like us, or playwrights/actors/artists. In an agony of unspoken young love I watched you. As always on these romantic evenings at the Strand,

268

prowling the aisles sneering at those luckless books, so many of them, unworthy of your attention. Bestsellers, how-tos, arts and crafts, too-simple *histories of.* Women's romances, sentimental love poems. Patriotic books, middlebrow books, books lacking esoteric covers. We were girl-poets passionately enamored of T. S. Eliot but scornful of Robert Frost whom we'd been made to memorize in high school—slyly we communicated in code phrases from Eliot in the presence of obtuse others in our dining hall and residence. We were admiring of though confused by the poetry of Yeats, we were yet more confused by the lauded worth of Pound, enthusiastically drawn to the bold metaphors of Kafka (that cockroach!) and Dostoevski (sexy murderer Raskolnikov and the Underground Man were our rebel heroes) and Sartre ("Hell is other people"—we knew this), and had reason to believe that we were their lineage though admittedly we were American middle class, and Caucasian, and female. (Yet we were not "conventional" females. In fact, we shared male contempt for the merely "conventional" female.)

Brooding above a tumble of books that quickened the pulse, almost shyly touching Freud's *Civilization and Its Discontents*, Crane Brinton's *The Age of Reason*, Margaret Mead's *Coming of Age in Samoa*, D. H. Lawrence's *The Rainbow*, Kierkegaard's *Fear and Trembling*, Mann's *Death in Venice*—there suddenly you glided up behind me to touch my wrist (as never you'd done before, had you?) and whispered, "Come here," in a way that thrilled me for its meaning *I have something wonderful/unexpected/startling to show you.* Like poems these discoveries in the Strand were, to us, found poems to be cherished. And eagerly I turned to follow you though disguising my eagerness, "Yes, what?" as if you'd interrupted me, for possibly we'd had a quarrel earlier that day, a flaring up of tense girl-tempers. Yes, you were childish and self-absorbed and given to sulky silences and mercurial moods in the presence of showy superficial people, and I adored and feared you knowing you'd break my heart, my heart that had never before been broken because never before so exposed.

So eagerly yet with my customary guardedness I followed you through a maze of book bins and shelves and stacks to the ceiling ANTHROPOLOGY, ART/ANCIENT, ART/RENAISSANCE, ART/MODERN, ART/ASIAN, ART/WESTERN, TRAVEL, PHILOSOPHY, COOKERY, POETRY/MODERN where the way was treacherously lighted only by bare sixty-watt bulbs, and where customers as cranky as we two stood in the aisles reading books, or sat hunched on footstools glancing up annoyed at our passage, and unquestioning I followed you until at POETRY/MODERN you halted, and pushed me ahead and around a corner, and I stood puzzled staring, not knowing what I was supposed to be seeing until impatiently you poked me in the ribs and pointed, and now I perceived an individual in the aisle pulling down books from shelves, peering at them, clearly absorbed by what she read, a woman nearly my height (I was tall for a girl, in 1956) in a man's navy coat to her ankles and with sleeves past her wrists, a man's beige fedora hat on her head, scrunched low as we wore our knitted caps, and most of her hair hidden by the hat except for a six-inch blond plait at the nape of her neck; and she wore black trousers tucked into what appeared to be salt-stained cowboy boots. Someone we knew? An older, good-looking student from one of our classes? *A girl-poet like ourselves?* I was about to nudge you in the ribs in bafflement when the blond woman turned, taking down another book from the shelf (e. e. cummings' *Tulips and Chimneys*—always I would remember that title!), and I saw that she was Marilyn Monroe.

Marilyn Monroe. In the Strand. Just like us. And she seemed to be alone.

Marilyn Monroe, alone!

Wholly absorbed in browsing amid books, oblivious of her surroundings and of us. No one seemed to have recognized her (yet) except you.

Here was the surprise: this woman was/was not Marilyn Monroe. For this woman was an individual wholly absorbed in selecting, leafing through, pausing to read books. You could see that this individual was a *reader*. One of those who *reads*. With concentration, with passion. With her very soul. And it was poetry she was reading, her lips pursed, silently shaping words. Absent-mindedly she wiped her nose on the edge of her hand, so intent was she on what she was reading. For when you truly read poetry, poetry reads *you*.

Still, this woman was—Marilyn Monroe. And despite our common sense, our scorn for the silly clichés of Hollywood romance, still we halfway expected a Leading Man to join her: Clark Gable, Robert Taylor, Marlon Brando.

Halfway we expected the syrupy surge of movie music, to glide us into the scene.

But no man joined Marilyn Monroe in her disguise as one of us in the Strand. No Leading Man, no dark prince.

Like us (we began to see) this Marilyn Monroe required no man.

For what seemed like a long time but was probably no more than half an hour, Marilyn Monroe browsed in the POETRY/MODERN shelves, as from a distance of approximately ten feet two girl-poets watched covertly, clutching each other's hands. We were stunned to see that this woman looked very little like the glamorous "Marilyn Monroe." That figure was a garish blond showgirl, a Hollywood "sexpot" of no interest to intellectuals (*we* thought, we who knew nothing of the secret romance between Marilyn Monroe and Arthur Miller); this figure more resembled us (almost) than she resembled her Hollywood image. We were dying of curiosity to see whose poetry books Marilyn Monroe was examining: Elizabeth Bishop, H.D., Robert Lowell, Muriel Rukeyser, Harry Crosby, Denise Levertov . . . Five or six of these Marilyn Monroe decided to purchase, then moved on, leather bag slung.over her shoulder and fedora tilted down on her head.

We couldn't resist, we had to follow! Cautious not to whisper together like excited schoolgirls, still less to giggle wildly as we were tempted; you nudged me in the ribs to sober me, gave me a glare signaling *Don't be rude, don't ruin this for all of us.* I conceded: I was the more pushy of the two of us, a tall gawky Rima the Bird Girl with springy carroty-red hair like an exotic bird's crest, while you were petite and dark haired and attractive with long-lashed Semitic sloe eyes, you the wily gymnast and I the aggressive basketball player, you the "experimental" poet and I drawn to "forms," our contrary talents bred in our bones. Which of us would marry, have babies, disappear into "real" life, and which of us would persevere into her thirties before starting to be published and becoming, in time, a "real" poet— could anyone have predicted, this snowy March evening in 1956?

Marilyn Monroe drifted through the maze of books and we followed in her wake as through a maze of dreams, past SPORTS, past MILITARY, past WAR, past HISTORY/ANCIENT, past the familiar figures of Strand regulars frowning into books, past surly yawning bearded clerks who took no more heed of the blond actress than they ever did of us, and so to NATURAL HISTORY where she paused, and there again for unhurried minutes (the Strand was open until 9:00 P.M.) Marilyn Monroe in her mannish disguise browsed and brooded, pulling down books, seeking what? at last crouched leafing through an oversized illustrated book (curiosity overcame me! I shoved away your restraining hand; politely I eased past Marilyn Monroe murmuring "excuse me" without so much as brushing against her and without being noticed), Charles Darwin's *Origin of Species* in a deluxe edition. Darwin! *Origin of Species*! We were poet-despisers-of-science, or believed we were, or must be, to be true poets in the exalted mode of T. S. Eliot and William Butler Yeats; such a choice, for Marilyn Monroe, seemed perverse to us. But this book was one Marilyn quickly decided to purchase, hoisting it into her arms and moving on.

That rakish fedora we'd come to covet, and that single chunky blond braid. (Afterward we would wonder: Marilyn Monroe's hair in a braid? Never had we seen Marilyn Monroe with her hair braided in any movie or photo. What did this mean? Did it mean anything? *Had she quit films, and embarked on a new, anonymous life in our midst?*)

Suddenly Marilyn Monroe glanced back at us, frowning as a child might frown (had we spoken aloud? had she heard our thoughts?), and there came into her face a look of puzzlement, not alarm or annoyance but a childlike puzzlement: *Who are you? You two? Are you watching me?* Quickly we looked away. We were engaged in a whispering dispute over a book one of us had fumbled from a shelf, *A History of Botanical Gardens in England*. So we were undetected. We hoped!

But wary now, and sobered. For what if Marilyn Monroe had caught us, and knew that we knew?

She might have abandoned her books and fled the Strand. What a loss for her, and for the books! For us, too.

Oh, we worried at Marilyn Monroe's recklessness! We dreaded her being recognized by a (male) customer or (male) clerk. A girl or woman would have kept her secret (so we thought) but no man could resist staring openly at her, following her, and at last speaking to her. Of course, the blond actress in Strand Used Books wasn't herself, not at all glamorous, or "sexy," or especially blond, in her inconspicuous man's clothing and those salt-stained boots; she might have been anyone, female or male, hardly a Hollywood celebrity, a movie goddess. Yet if you stared, you'd recognize her. If you tried, with any imagination you'd see "Marilyn Monroe." It was like a child's game in which you stare at foliage, grass, clouds in the sky, and suddenly you see a face or a figure, and after that recognition you can't not see the hidden shape, it's staring you in the face. So too with Marilyn Monroe. Once we saw her, it seemed to us she must be seen—and recognized—by anyone who happened to glance at her. If any man saw!

We were fearful her privacy would be destroyed. Quickly the blond actress would become surrounded, mobbed. It was risky and reckless of her to have come to Strand Used Books by herself, we thought. Sure, she could shop at Tiffany's, maybe; she could stroll through the lobby of the Plaza, or the Waldorf-Astoria; she'd be safe from fans and unwanted admirers in privileged settings on the Upper East Side, but—here? In the egalitarian Strand, on Broadway and Twelfth?

We were perplexed. Almost, I was annoyed with her. Taking such chances! But you, gripping my wrist, had another, more subtle thought.

"She thinks she's like *us*."

You meant: a human being, anonymous. Female, like us. Amid the ordinary unspectacular customers (predominantly male) of the Strand.

And that was the sadness in it, Marilyn Monroe's wish. To be *like us*. For it was impossible, of course. For anyone could have told Marilyn Monroe, even two young girl-poets, that it was too late for her in history. Already, at age thirty (we could calculate afterward that this was her age) "Marilyn Monroe" had entered history, and there was no escape from it. Her films, her photos. Her face, her figure, her name. To enter history is to be abducted spiritually, with no way back. As if lightning were to strike the building that housed the Strand, as if an actual current of electricity were to touch and transform only one individual in the great cavernous space and that lone individual, by pure chance it might seem, the caprice of fate, would be the young woman with the blond braid and the fedora slanted across her face. Why? Why her, and not another? You could argue that such a destiny is absurd, and undeserved, for one individual among many, and logically you would be correct. And yet: "Marilyn Monroe" has entered history, and you have not. She will endure, though the young woman with the blond braid will die. *And even should she wish to die, "Marilyn Monroe" cannot.*

By this time she—the young woman with the blond braid—was carrying an armload of books. We were hoping she'd almost finished and would be leaving soon, before strangers' rude eyes lighted upon her and exposed her, but no: she surprised us by heading for a section called JUDAICA. In that forbidding aisle, which we'd never before entered, there were books in numerous languages: Hebrew, Yiddish,

German, Russian, French. Some of these books looked ancient! Complete sets of the Talmud. Cryptically printed tomes on the cabala. Luckily for us, the titles Marilyn Monroe pulled out were all in English: *Jews of Eastern Europe; The Chosen People: A Complete History of the Jews; Jews of the New World.* Quickly Marilyn Monroe placed her bag and books on the floor, sat on a footstool, and leafed through pages with the frowning intensity of a young girl, as if searching for something urgent, something she knew—knew!—must be there; in this uncomfortable posture she remained for at least fifteen minutes, wetting her fingers to turn pages that stuck together, pages that had not been turned, still less read, for decades. She was frowning, yet smiling too; faint vertical lines appeared between her eyebrows, in the intensity of her concentration; her eyes moved rapidly along lines of print, then returned, and moved more slowly. By this time we were close enough to observe the blond actress's feverish cheeks and slightly parted moist lips that seemed to move silently. *What is she reading in that ancient book, what can possibly mean so much to her? A secret, revealed? A secret, to save her life?*

"Hey you!" a clerk called out in a nasal, insinuating voice.

The three of us looked up, startled.

But the clerk wasn't speaking to us. Not to the blond actress frowning over *The Chosen People*, and not to us who were hovering close by. The clerk had caught someone slipping a book into an overcoat pocket, not an unusual sight at the Strand.

After this mild upset, Marilyn Monroe became uneasy. She turned to look frankly at us, and though we tried clumsily to retreat, her eyes met ours. *She knows!* But after a moment, she simply turned back to her book, stubborn and determined to finish what she was reading, while we continued to hover close by, exposed now, and blushing, yet feeling protective of her. *She has seen us, she knows. She trusts us.* We saw that Marilyn Monroe was beautiful in her anonymity as she had never seemed, to us, to be beautiful as "Marilyn Monroe." All that was makeup, fakery, cartoon sexiness subtle as a kick in the groin. All that was vulgar and infantile. But this young woman was beautiful without makeup, without even lipstick; in her mannish clothes, her hair in a stubby braid. Beautiful: her skin luminous and pale and her eyes a startling clear blue. Almost shyly she glanced back at us, to note that we were still there, and she smiled. *Yes, I see you two. Thank you for not speaking my name.*

Always you and I would remember: that smile of gratitude, and sweetness.

Always you and I would remember: that she trusted us, as perhaps we would not have trusted ourselves.

So many years later, I'm proud of us. We were so young.

Young, headstrong, arrogant, insecure though "brilliant"—or so we'd been led to believe. Not that we thought of ourselves as young: you were nineteen, I was twenty. We were mature for our ages, and we were immature. We were intellectually sophisticated, and emotionally unpredictable. We revered something we called *art*, we were disdainful of something we called *life*. We were overly conscious of ourselves. And yet: how patient, how protective, watching over Marilyn Monroe squatting on a footstool in the JUDAICA stacks as stray customers pushed past muttering "excuse me!" or not even seeming to notice her, or the two of us standing guard. And at last—a relief— Marilyn Monroe shut the unwieldy book, having decided to buy it, and rose from the footstool gathering up her many things. And—this was a temptation!—we held back, not offering to help her carry her things as we so badly wanted to, but only just following at a discreet distance as Marilyn Monroe made her way through the labyrinth of the bookstore to the front counter. (Did she glance back at us? Did she understand you and I were her protectors?) If anyone dared to approach her, we intended to intervene. We would push between Marilyn Monroe and whomever it was. Yet how strange the scene was: none of the other Strand customers, lost in books, took any special notice of her, any more than they took notice of us. Book lovers, especially used-book lovers, are not ones to stare curiously at others, but only at books. At the front of the store—it was a long hike—the cashiers would be more alert, we thought. One of them seemed to be watching Marilyn Monroe approach. Did he know? Could he guess? Was he waiting for her?

Nearing the front counter and the bright fluorescent lights overhead, Marilyn Monroe seemed for the first time to falter. She fumbled to extract out of her shoulder bag a pair of dark glasses and managed to put them on. She turned up the collar of her navy coat. She lowered her hat brim.

Still she was hesitant, and it was then that I stepped forward and said quietly, "Excuse me. Why don't I buy your books for you? That way you won't have to talk to anyone."

The blond actress stared at me through her oversized dark glasses. Her eyes were only just visible behind the lenses. A shy-girl's eyes, startled and grateful.

And so I did. With you helping me. Two girl-poets, side by side, all brisk and businesslike, making Marilyn Monroe's purchases for her: a total of sixteen books!—hardcover and paperback, relatively new books, old battered thumbed-through books—at a cost of $55.85. A staggering sum! Never in my two years of coming into the Strand had I handed over more than a few dollars to the cashier, and this time my hand might have trembled as I pushed twenty-dollar bills at him, half expecting the bristly bearded man to interrogate me: "Where'd you get so much money?" But as usual the cashier hardly gave me a second glance. And Marilyn Monroe, burdened with no books, had already slipped through the turnstile and was awaiting us at the front door.

There, when we handed over her purchases in two sturdy bags, she leaned forward. For a breathless moment we thought she might kiss our cheeks. Instead she pressed into our surprised hands a slender volume she lifted from one of the bags: *Selected Poems of Marianne Moore*. We stammered thanks, but already the blond actress had pulled the fedora down more tightly over her head and had stepped out into the lightly falling snow, headed south on Broadway. We trailed behind her, unable to resist, waiting for her to hail a taxi, but she did not. We knew we must not follow her. By this time we were giddy with the strain of the past hour, gripping each other's hands in childlike elation. So happy!

"Oh. Oh God. Marilyn Monroe. She gave us a book. Was any of it real?"

It was real: we had *Selected Poems of Marianne Moore* to prove it.

That snowy early evening in March at Strand Used Books. That magical evening of Marilyn Monroe, when I kissed you for the first time.

Nominated by Christine Zawadisky

IS

by BRUCE BEASLEY

from THE SOUTHERN REVIEW

> [B]eing is twofold. . . . Being conveys the truth of a proposition which unites to-
> gether subject and attribute by a copula, notified by this word "is"; and in this
> sense being is what answers to the question, "Does it exist?"
>
> —Thomas Aquinas

> When Eve was still in Adam, death did not exist. When she was separated from
> him, death came into being. If he enters again and attains his former self, death
> will be no more.
>
> —The Gospel of Philip

Male and female He created them,
'îš   and 'îššâ
bone/flesh   *of my*   *bone/flesh*

—Stripped
in the woods   *Naked came I*
crouched in the charred   lightning-gutted pine tree,
twelve, hard, and scared of it,

feeling what it felt to touch myself
till the blood rushed, and the shiver
rose, and the change

came on, I could just barely hold back . . .
                    Woman, what have I to do with thee?

❊   ❊   ❊

Like a little dick inside,   my sister said, not showing me

Girls have a little spot that's like a dick:

Like a long splinter   (I imagined it)
stabbed inside, blue,   half-visible,
gone soft and snaking up   through their bellies,
a Thing   like mine
It's a penis, my father said, drunk, his only
version of the Facts of Life, *don't call it your Thing anymore,*
                               it's called a penis . . .

penalis: punishment   vulva: from *volvere*, to turn
            penetrate: to pierce, to grasp the inner meaning of

Learning the turned-
inward, the con-
volute   Tampon-string

the undivulged

        I/upreared   S/encoiled
            the vertical, the rigid   lips inside lips

            Differ: to dis-ferry, to carry

apart

                    ❀   ❀   ❀

And the copula (*the link*) carries together—dissolves difference—
                    X *is* Y
                                One in Being
                    —as in metaphor, that rut of words, that
                    lust across the copula . . .

As out of the burning,
unconsumed bush
to Moses It said:

278

I am who am
Thus shalt thou say, I AM hath sent me unto you

—pure Being, or pure
metaphor, or
tautology (say the same say the same)   *Is* is *is*
Then pure
profusion   (fruitful: multiply)
in whatever form It *Is*—

So, in the storm cellar, yeast smell
of my bread-mold lab, fuzzed
piecework of black and GI Joe green,
stale bread-crusts in rows of wooden bowls

How strangely the patterns   *differed*, side by side:
pinkish peach-fur on one,   black whiskers, pubic
                                       thatch on the next

Mold spores called out of the air, the rank
fecundity made visible, in three days—

I couldn't stop
laying out the molds on my slides,
under microscope,   threads, runners, webs,
couldn't stop breeding
my apricot and golden hamsters,
at eleven, waiting   night after night for estrus,
the sniff, the telltale   lifting of the tail
(Latin *oestrus*,   frenzy)

In the medicine cabinet, my mother's
little silver, punched-out packet of pills
She takes them so she fuck   *with Daddy*

The female's hissing,   her bared incisors,   a grinding of the
                                                  teeth

It is   so that it might be   *Is*

279

My grandfather's *Playboys*, in their stash by his whiskey
     cabinet,
behind his pirate's sword
with the blood spot, in the long
crawlspace:
my parents caught
me looking, and made me stay down there and look

so I'd know they were upstairs knowing
I was turning the glossed pages
(*and I was ashamed*   *and hid myself*)
string of pearls around the nipples and the flicking tongue . . .

"After mounting,   the male
becomes tired   and uninterested"

         The hamsters frenzied again on their separate wheels

        ❁   ❁   ❁

In "our" image, male and female   Split, and teeming
                                           out of that one "Am"

So she can fuck with Daddy you know that's what they're
    doing when they say they're "taking a nap"

Inwardly penetrated and inflamed
by divine love, the soul
passes utterly into that other glory—

that *Is*, penetrant and burning

God's unspeakable name
made out of the *imperfect*
of *to be*,

vowel-less merge:
Y   H   W   H
I am whoever I will come to be

'îš / male   'iššâ/fe-male
                    is, the fastener

To *grasp*   the inner meaning
                    of that "other glory":
We have our own little spot
                            That's why it feels good to us too

                    ❊   ❊   ❊

Under the dripping waterspout,
behind the bars, the day-old litter
bled: torn-
off foot in the mother's mouth, and the naked,
pink, uneyed babies
squirming, still, toward her teats—
The runt
stuffed kicking in the mother's cheek-pouch as she
gnawed—

It's just how Nature
works, my mother kept saying,
whiskey on her breath, lifting
the mangled body out with a napkin,
It's just how Nature works,
her face
contorted above me.

                    ❊   ❊   ❊

When Eve was still   in Adam,
when death had not   "come into being,"
breasts and vulva buried there inside his sealed-in rib

                    —Calling
out of the body of the bread (sopped
crusts, in their trapped-air Mason jars) the invisible
teeming,

and out of the Fungus Book, the language I loved:

281

Rhizopus
nigricans,

mycelia, sporangia, hyphae—

Spora, seed   *Sporas*, scattered

—The much-warned-
against   "nocturnal emission": being told
by *Moving into Manhood*   our bodies
were seeded now,   and seeding
White eyelash-threads   over thistledown mats
of spread black   split
spore-cases, on the wet   Wonder Bread

All the girls   single file
leaving the auditorium   pushing open
the red velvet drapes   their hushed,
barking laughs   the nurse
leading   What were they told

Don't call it a "Thing"

E-
missions

—Pearls   on the nipples,
pearls   on the tongue . . .

❀   ❀   ❀

Nature's works: the littering, the
waste, flashlight
on my new, barely visible, pubic hair,
in Boy Scout camp, in the tent:

Don't be shy, guy,
the sixteen-year-old said,
I may have more of what you've got
and you may have less of what I have,
but we've all got the same

stuff . . .
     (A little spot,
a little dick inside . . .)

Who I am, I am,
copula: reach
hither thy finger.

               ❀   ❀   ❀

How deep does the *is*   in the sentence
penetrate,   with what *quick*ness does it
burn,
        the copula, the subject and predicate's
            fuse?
(as the mold and bread are made one:
root-cases   digging through the grain,

as I imagined for a while my
    sister,   hermaphroditic,
with her   Thing
       all coiled inside)—

My mother's face
as she turned away, bloodied
napkin in her hand

Then all night the hamster's
wheel-screak, her gnawed
wood bar, smell of afterbirth
she never even licked off the litter.

—Then metaphor's
quick copulation
(hiss, sniff, lifted
tail), its resistless
                  thrusting-into-one—

     (bread mold, bred hamsters, Yahweh
     breeding out from His *Is*)

Crumble of mold-dust
disintegrates
body?, when the change

comes

I am Am

Sporangia everywhere,   bursting

as the taken bread
What's left of the host

Nominated by Brenda Miller, Donald Platt, Linda Bierds, William Wenthe

MORNING GLORY HARLEY

essay by TERESE SVOBODA

from THE IOWA REVIEW

A MAN DROVE HIS HARLEY down the morning glory, the great concrete drain that controls dam flow, and he lived, spewed out onto the spillway. This was the best legend of our teenhood, bar none, beating out even the Nebraska Loch Ness monster that lived 162 feet down at the bottom of that dam, a beast bass fishermen on a hot still day would not discuss, would look off to the side of their boats where the dam rose and spit toward the deeper end instead of set you straight. The man on the motorcycle could have been one of those fishermen. The fishermen here were numerous and nameless enough, men from any of the five counties surrounding the lake that the dam made, perhaps a fall fisherman wearing a heavy wool jacket and boots that filled up fast when his dingy-sized boat tipped the way they did four or five times a year when the wind took them. Who really knew about boats here when the shores were lined by fine white sand formerly known as the Great American Desert? If a fish didn't come right up and lick the bait clean, these fishermen sometimes stood up in their bows and jabbed at them with homemade spears. A foolishness like that could cause a boat to capsize. And because the fisherman in question would most likely have already drunk the contents of a well-laced thermos, he usually couldn't swim to save himself. He and his boat would be inexorably sucked down into the cement whorls of the morning glory. Onlookers—for there have to be alleged eyewitnesses for every legend—seeing the sunken

285

crushed boat whirling down the face of the morning glory, could have mistaken it for a Harley.

But usually the man in the story was part of a pursuit. The law had made the mistake of trying to catch some hotrodding freshly-licensed kid crossing the dam the way the dam—a straight cut between two colors of water—invited, especially a dam the second largest in the world (at least of those dams made of dirt) that is, a dam with a very nice long stretch of highway across its big dam face, and in the pursuit, the officer and his vehicle went out of control, broke a barrier and landed in the water sluicing the concrete funnel.

Or maybe it was the teenager himself who fell in, dodging the patrolman until that fatal turn, where he and his machine spectacularly leapt over the barricade and landed upright on the surface of the morning glory to buzz its sides like some desperate circus act, knowing the gas wouldn't last.

Whoever went in had white hair when he came out.

This was an important detail for all my friends. Maybe just plain fear of the size of that hole had started the legend, or the Freudian fear of the female and funnels, or just the fear of anyone getting older than eighteen. Exactly who was involved felt less important than whose side of the law you were on and if you could drive and how fast, and how late at night you left for the dam, a trip from Ogallala which took about ten minutes—and sometimes, on moonlit, warm summer nights, all night to return from.

We owed the dam and its romance to irrigation. A Charles Kingsley some thirty years before had spent thirty years of his own to get it built as a Depression project. We danced through the resultant sprinklers, we cut lawns as green as alfalfa. Even at the very edge of town, the lawns were not the end of the green, weeds did not brown endlessly into the horizon like they should, given the rainfall. New eight-foot-tall robot sprinklers walked across the adjoining acres of alfalfa most summer nights. The noise of these robots chugging across the land obliterated even the drums of the Sioux who came down from the reservation every summer to perform for tourists who had had their radiators quit or found they could not drive across country without sleeping. Maybe they complained about the noise. Not us. Irrigation was our salvation.

Long ago, there was just the lazy Platte oxbowing its way past Native Americans posing for George Catlin's portraits, swarms of buffalo drinking beside the wandering cavalry, and a million cattle wallowing in its back eddies at the end of the Texas Trail. During a few decades of rainfall, Swiss peasants right out of Mari Sandoz' autobiographical novels, and even black cowboys homesteaded the area, then their Model T's disappeared in the shoals of the Dust Bowl.

Ten years after the dam was built and politicians made hay and so did the few farmers who owned adjacent acreage, a centrifugal pump came into use that made it possible to draw out underground water. We had a lot of it. In fact, we had the most underground water in the world. Ogallala claims greatest access to the huge subterranean lake that stretches under seven midwestern states, water named, serendipitously, the Ogallala Aquifer. By the half century mark, farmers were emptying that aquifer at the rate of 1,000 gallons a second.

We were the sons and daughters of the greatest climate change man had ever engineered—even the Pharaohs kept to the banks of the river, even the Greeks didn't drain the Mediterranean. Well, Kingsley Dam was a little smaller than the Aswan, and the Ogallala Aquifer was only the size of Lake Huron, but our fathers, filled with post-war optimism and ebullient over the new pump, now produced enough crops to feed a fifth of the world. No more roadside shanties selling used tires and fresh bread—we had indoor pools and fancy quarter horses and enough Cadillacs to beat out a Texan. Like a deposit of gold that water was, to be sucked out of the ground in a few decades after sitting there for seven million years. You could practically hear farmers pulling the plug. But did our fathers know—as deep as those wells, those fathers—did they know they were leading us all down the morning glory?

In the fifties, my Bohemian grandmother—no Cather character—held court over her sons and their acres of dryland wheat. After her Sunday rosaries, my father would drive us to his wheatfield, walk deep into it and select a shaft for us to chew, to debate whether the grain was ripe yet. Overhead there was always an enormous thundercloud, bringing hail more often than rain. But below, deep under the acres of the wheat's golden waves sat Persephone, presiding over her vast, dark but still pure, lake.

A multinational electronics plant dumped many million of gallons of waste into the Aquifer, as have many a farmer his pesticides and insecticides and everything-icides. My sister, an ex-EPA lawyer, now battles contract pig farmers who threaten to do the same with the waste of thousands of animals. Paid in baby sitting and plumbing and sometimes hamburger, she has stemmed the growth of the industry, at least at that end of Nebraska. My cattle-ranching, sunflower-growing father has sat on several state water commissions, doing his best to continue draining the Aquifer. But the dam he wants full. It's not just the water-skiing, sailing regatta, windsurfing capitol of the Midwest but a visible triumph of man over the difficult environment most appreciated by men like himself who've spent a lifetime fighting it. Environmentalists, however, insist that the rare whooping crane and flamingo find the lake more congenial when it's drained. Now the lake's banks are so low you can snorkel to where an old town was drowned, its stop signs in better shape than the wind-raked, bullet-holed signs at either end of the dam.

The body of the man with the motorcycle was never recovered. No doubt the Loch Ness monster devoured it after spurning some choice imported-shark-soaked-in-beer bait that the fishermen are always touting. Or else he just walked away into the crowd of onlookers. There was never an official report. Perhaps the officials didn't want to put fear or a copycat suggestion into the minds of all the upstanding citizens young and old who might or did use the lake, still the biggest tourist attraction for five hundred miles. I don't remember the lake being dragged other than for the toddler whose father insisted he swim. Surely if the casualty had been a patrolman, someone would have put up a plaque: Here Lies Poor Kowalsky, died in the call of duty. But maybe there wasn't money for a plaque, the wily farmers here are cheap and hate the cops who don't always pretend not to notice their overloaded pickups or their speeding with the chaff spinning behind them in glorious wake or their lack of fishing licenses on a day off.

The Final Version VII of the motorcycle story ends like this: the man's still riding his bike but he doesn't leap triumphantly out of the hole and back onto the highway to show off his new white hair. Instead he takes the bike down, down, all the way to the underwater town. There he guns up to the sunken stop sign where Persephone still waits, underwater cigarette burning languidly between her pale fingers, hand on generous hip, breasts to here, ready to escort him down to the real dive, some fun cave with a view of the fetid shores of the vast, dark and poisoned Aquifer.

Nominated by The Iowa Review

DEDICATION

by ANDREW FELD

from TRIQUARTERLY

We argued about the difficulty of degree,
the exhibitionist on stage, flaunting
his fluent ease, his keyboard mastery.
Poor puppet, beating at his box of strings.

We wanted more, didn't we?—a deeper adeptness,
the border between performance and performer
blurred, erased. It was for this we put our best
demeanors on and took our student seats
under the three jutting concrete tiers, beneath
the full-priced tickets. We sat in a concentrate
of time, as in the way the house lights dimmed,
the great candelabra reduced to three bronze dots
ellipsing on the Steinway's burnished wood,
a trill announcing the Divertissement,
Etude, Nocturne, the concert hall reduced
to a small room where a young man sits
trying a few notes out, each tentative thought
hanging in his head like a pocketful of change
scattered on a white plate, the bright possible
in a dark room, gleaming, unchosen, unspent,
while in the bar below a woman waits
for him, the only woman in the bar.
She lets the men there buy her drinks, a glass
of vin ordinaire, maybe a Johnnie Walker Red,

and flirts, knowing what all these workmen think
of her, and her boyfriend. They think he has
the easy life, and that she is the easy life.
She likes their envy and their scorn; it fits
her like a soft, clinging woolen skirt
and makes her feel as if her life was composed
by choice, not accident. The piano player
renders all this a little too stiffly,
with too much distance, insufficiently
rubato, the notes hanging in tight clusters,
a sheaf still waiting for the whetted scythe
as two headlights sweep across another mile
of Illinois wheatfield. The vehicle
is now the smaller room of a compact
heading home, content in the ordinary.
So when the wished-for place arrived, as if
a car radio suddenly started to play
the memory of a music heard in a dream,
it was our brilliance, alone, to recognize
the moment that fulfills a lifetime's work,
the long sequacious notes stretching like lines
across a field of shifting, bowed heads,
bringing the unthought-of, unknown to us,
music and musician dissolving in union,
and then, consummated, the harvest in,
milled down and shipped away; and in a room
with the lamp dimmed, the lid of the keyboard
clamped shut, the couple lie in bed together,
eating torn-off pieces from the loaf of good bread
two coins taken from the white plate bought them,
while the music starts moving through a succession
of rooms, each one larger and more expensive,
until the piece is finished. Then the musician
stops, waits, and bows: once to the applauding crowd
and once to the now-silent instrument.

Nominated by Dorianne Laux, Linda Gregerson, TriQuarterly.

SAUTEING THE PLATYGAST

fiction by DEAN PASCHAL

from BOULEVARD

AT NIGHTFALL WE LIT A LANTERN TO BEGIN OUR SEARCH. We do better with lanterns; they give a quieter, gentler light; I am convinced that the filament of a flashlight makes a sound. (Not *much* of a sound, mind you, but there are creatures out there that can hear it.) We were in particularly fertile territory now, the wild thickets below the bog. Still, I had my doubts about this; we seldom hunt as a family and we were making altogether too much noise. The ground was dry; nevertheless, within a week of a rain can be a dangerous time to hunt. My son and daughter were carrying the torches as well as a broom and shovel. My wife was staying close to me in the circle of light from the lantern. The dog was making most of the racket, pulling the cart behind us with the washtubs. I felt a foreboding and misgiving about all of it. I listened to the cicadas, to the frogs, to the resin in the crackling flames. The children had gotten somewhat ahead of us and I found myself watching the interesting shadows they cast. My daughter, especially, liked to carry a torch. "You *like* carrying a torch!" I said to her when we caught up again. But she is at a sullen age and I received (and expected) no reply. Whether she understands me or not, I could not say.

In addition to the lantern, I had my Luger and the newly modified prong, on which I have welded a sharpened, V-shaped block so it won't slide so much on the vertebrae. The pockets of my jacket were stuffed with the egg-cases of some *Stelacens*, the tense embryos nestled like pearls in the leathery pouches. I shelled a few of them out with my thumb as I walked. They are good to snack on: slick, vaguely iridescent, mainly skull but soft. Eaten alive they are almost gummy; floated in cream they remind one of blueberries; but best of all is the way I had prepared them tonight: toasted slightly, with butter and salt, the skin dried close to the bone[1] and giving a nutlike flavor.

I looked up at the new moon, the narrow rim as fragile as ice in the night sky. Inauspicious, it seemed to me. This was not a good time to be moving about; the air itself seemed to be holding out on us. I thought of those millennia past when the planet was lonely and the bulk of life was large, of the incredible saurians rumbling through this landscape, huddled against the emptiness and stars. It was an agony then, perfectly terrifying to be alive. Years ago, I used to tell my students:

"When you think of a *Tyrannosaurus rex*, gentlemen, nineteen feet tall and eight tons in weight. Think bluff, gentlemen! Think bluff!"

My son had stopped now and raised his hand for silence. "Bring the lantern, Frank," he said. (My children call me Frank.) He had found the first one. Then I saw it, too, at ground level, the silver-red discs of its eyes reflecting.

What a night! We caught three washtubs full and afterward had to hurry home to put the corrugated covers on top of them. As the creatures around here warm up, they become more active and begin to gnaw and scratch at one another. In fact, we had hardly finished putting the covers in place when I began to hear their skins scraping against the galvanized zinc of the tubs.

Soon afterward, there was an intermittent fierce whacking (Whack! Whack! Whack!) from the third tub which left dents and protuberances in the metal that were sobering to look at. There is a slope behind the cabin and this particular tub suddenly began to nudge and slide down it. The animals seemed to be boiling inside. There was a great banging and rattling of the handles and I saw a couple of the smaller creatures slither out from under the corrugations of the tin. I shot twice with my Luger but missed both of them and watched their tails bumping out of the circle of light.

Then I tied the tub to a stake.

We have appetites, this family, but cook as fast as we could, we were four days getting to the third tub. I then found that we had made a terrible mistake. There was only one creature left inside, his body swollen like a tick, his skin so tight it seemed about to change color. He had evidently eaten every other animal. There was not one bone left, not one scrap of skin. He lifted his head toward us and opened his mouth wide. He had no shell but the way he maneuvered his body in rotation reminded me of a turtle.

I stuck the gig in and nudged him experimentally. He snapped the head of it clean off. (It was the old-style gig with the wooden handle.) Is this the whacker, I thought, or is this what ate the whacker?

I looked deep into his bloodshot and obdurate eyes. "Careful," I said.

The real tragedy was that we had not gotten a better look at the other animals inside. The wife took my place and kept the whacker distracted while I slipped around behind him. He moved forward slowly and pressed his claws against the metal. Then I managed to get him though the neck with the prong. I drove his throat against the wall of the tub and bent his head backwards over his spine. The pressure I was exerting began to smear his pig-like nose and awful wedge of a mouth. Then he twisted and began to buck on me. The wife stabilized him with another gig in the left leg while little-Frank ran to get the mallet. Meanwhile, I drove the prong steadily into his spinal column, the sweat plastering my shirt, my left arm beginning to spasm from the strain. Suddenly, the stake pulled loose and the tub began to slide on the smooth dirt. My great fear was that this guy might be able to jerk loose and flip out onto the ground. His huge mouth was open now and I could see his long recursive teeth and the glass-like ridge of his jaw.

"You're about to slip, Frank!" my son said.

He was right. Fortunately, this new prong won't slide. As I drove the final blows through the cord, the whacker's neck folded like a thick towel and he made a series of convulsive movements with his limbs. He seemed to smile at me upside-down. It was perfectly obscene, this smile, more of a smirk I should say; it reminded me not so much of one of your standard animals, as one of those fat, triangular-headed kids that one sometimes sees in drug stores.

In hopes that he might have swallowed a few of the smaller creatures whole, we cut him open on the spot and turned his stomach inside out. But there was nothing identifiable inside, not a paw.

It was malicious the extent of this mastication.

We made haste to cook him immediately. Indeed, his eyes had

scarcely glazed over when we began our prayers. Unfortunately, in our rush, we grabbed too small a pan and his legs, which overrode the rim, were charred rather badly in the flames.

Not bad, it was, this meat; and, despite some fibers, not really so tough either, a bit like Pangolin or anteater. Unfortunately, my children are sloppy and stingy eaters. During the prayer itself my daughter grabbed all the claws.

"She got them last time!" little-Frank yelled. But before we could stop her, my daughter had put two of them in her mouth and was crunching them, bones and all. The others we could not pry out of her fingers. My wife said nothing but smiled with the corners of her eyes.

(It seems my daughter cannot get heavy enough to suit my wife.)

The problem with this "whacker"—a *Rhynochelon*, I ended up calling him—was that there was nothing appropriate to go with such a lean and fibrous meat. In addition, there wasn't nearly as much *to* him as one might have expected from the circumstances. At the end of the meal, none of us were truly full. What would have been nice would have been a skewer of scalatoids but I kept very quiet about that.

I watched as my daughter put her fork down and began looking at me from across the table. My wife and little-Frank soon did the same.

"How about a platter of *gills*?!" I said, getting up and taking my dishes to the sink. (*Scalatoids*, their eyes were saying and I didn't want to go through it again.)

My decision about the scalatoid matter is final, as far as I'm concerned—but the story, perhaps, bears repeating:

Scalatoids[2], though filling, are not really large. They are of a size with or perhaps slightly smaller than hedgehogs. Their appearance is considerably different, though. Looked at ventrally, they are very like platygasters (or platygasts as we call them, a very common little creature hereabouts) but the stomach is not nearly so flat and they are not as good for sauteing. I had given up cooking scalatoids years ago; there was far too much *fat* in the things which I found impossible to render out. But working secretly, and entirely on her own, my daughter discovered a way to prepare them. What she accomplished was a good deal more than a culinary miracle; it seemed to defy all reason. One afternoon, she allowed us to watch her at work. Even afterward, though, the mystery remained; there was no essential difference in her technique or spices. The difference in flavor was amazing.

(From the taste alone, I would have said it was a different animal.)

It took me some time to find out what she was doing. Scalatoids, you must understand, are nearly tongueless and incapable of making a noise. She was throwing them in a tub of water and letting them churn there for a week. They are by no means good swimmers, scalatoids; it was sheer desperation that was keeping them afloat. Hour after hour, day after day, they treaded in that water, silent, frantic, indomitable, constantly attempting to climb up on one another. I was in my daughter's room, one afternoon, looking for my razor, when I made the discovery of five of them in a washtub at the foot of her bed.

I hope never again in my life to see the like of what was in their eyes. It would be impossible to overestimate their fear of water and drowning. Scalatoids are vaguely globular creatures, full of surface and other tensions; and, forever after this, they seemed to me to be the embodiment of pure will.

(This, of course, was her way of burning up the excess fat.)

I put a stop to it immediately. Still, I must confess, I rather miss the things. There is no doubt about it: the struggle improved the flavor.

When we first moved to this area, it took me some time to realize that this is no ordinary place. Animals can be killed here but nothing dies naturally. It is a very special locus built on a confluence of singularities. The electric atmosphere plays subtle tricks of energy. On an otherwise bright day a bolt of lightning can *condense* itself out of the air. One can feel the static even in the soil itself, which has special properties. Part of the area may have been an island at one time, despite the largely sedimentary rock. There are signs, too, of a previous habitation (some fruit trees, for instance, not local to the area).

What is incredible is the extent the soil is layered and honeycombed with dormant animals. Having started from a slightly different angle, they have begun estivating through the millennia and running, somehow, parallel to death. They are tangled in places, clumped, like earthworms. In heavy storms they sometimes wash out of themselves. Fortunately, precious few of them are terribly large. The thought, though, of how they are layered here gravely bothers our occasional guests. My wife and I invariably hear them whisper to one another far into the night.

On first arrival, I paid little attention to the animals. I was so sick of academia, dazed and overrun that I did not want to expend any energy thinking. I ignored all implications and ate whatever was handy. I had worked too long and hard in a single line and it was as though I had wakened in the midst of a dream. Furthermore, much about these creatures was unfamiliar to me. Evidently there are evolutionary lines tangled here which did not proceed. I think there was a level at which I did not take them seriously; I expected them to fade, tooth and claw, at sunrise.

That was years ago. Now, I am fascinated once more. I have returned to my books and manuals and vowed never again to eat anything without a name.

Such persistent and single-minded endeavor is not without its dangers, however. One evening, not long ago, based on no more than intuition and a low mound, little-Frank and I discovered a large animal in the bog below the lake. We dug it out together. We were rather pleased with ourselves and each grabbed two of its legs in order to carry it back. *Little* Frank, I persist in calling him, though at this point he is taller than I am. (In fact, the whole way home he complained that he had most of the weight.) I was anxious to flip it over to see what was going on with its reproductive system; but by the time we got to the basement we were both too exhausted.

(It had three eyes and I knew it had to be a rather early specimen.)

Our basement gets very cold at night and I figured it would be safe there till morning. I couldn't begin to decide what to call it. This was the first one I'd ever caught and, in my ignorance of its strength, I looped a chain around its neck of scarcely more than half-inch links.

When I went upstairs, the wife was already in bed. The windows were shut and the lamps were lit. We augment our illumination with kerosene lamps. In fact, we keep one lit at the foot of the bed at all times. Our electricity is not reliable and I feel it is best to have a bit of light instantly available, being as what we are surrounded by out here. "Honey . . ." I said, but lost my train of thought.

I began wiping my feet together over the side of the bed. I couldn't get the thing out of my mind; it seemed to have scales; it definitely had claws; I was not altogether happy about it. The lamp on the nightstand had just been extinguished and there was a pale glow of red from the wick.

"It might not be a reptile," I said.

At three in the morning, I woke up. It sounded like there was something in the basement swacking around with a four-by-four. I got out of bed immediately. But my son was already in the room. He turned up the lamp till it smoked. The light was swinging, the whole cabin shuddering at each blow.

"Frank, it's loose!" he said.

"What?"

(I began fumbling around on the night table for my glasses.)

"It's *loose*, Frank!"

I slipped on boots, got my Luger out of the closet, grabbed the prong and the gig and went out the back way, tripping on the stairs. I ran around to have a look in through a basement window.

I have a workshop at one end. The creature had dragged through the tools for that, tangled himself in the cables for the arc welder and begun chewing on the vise. A piece of the chain was still attached to his neck. I got around to the closest window, broke out the pane; and, using the flashlight, began firing down through all the orbital foramina. The dog was barking hysterically. I reloaded the Luger five times and emptied the entire last clip down its throat.

Then I stopped and waited.

My daughter stood by, watching.

It took two full days for all motion to cease; the meat, when cut up, would not lie flat or lose its muscle tone. Even after being *cooked*, it seemed to positively creep on the plate. Never have I so underestimated a metabolism.

We got a total of seven pounds of thyroid tissue out of the thing, most of which, admittedly, may not have been active. The entire gland was goitrous and cystic and took a lot of chewing to get through.

"Always room in this world for surprises!" I said, somewhat lamely, when it was over, though nothing truly big is ever getting inside this house again in one piece.

The experience was terrifying, though the animal itself was, on the whole, rather straightforward. Not like everything we find here. Consider the one I discovered some years ago while planting the fig tree: he was about a yard long, completely legless, with a distinctly submarine-like shape and something of a beaver-like tail (the tail turned vertically, though). He had two close-set eyes and a single up-turned nostril.

(The nostril, in fact, was the part of him I came upon first.)

The problem was that there was no way he could be placed on the ground that he would either balance or sit level. I kept playing with his cold body in the cold sand but he kept tilting or rolling over on me. Finally, I became frustrated and tossed him, end-over-end (he was as stiff as a log) into the lake. I thought no more about him. But, two years later, I found what was evidently the same guy, very much alive, placidly sculling around in the backwaters, keeping that single nostril above the surface of the water.

"Blah!" I said, suddenly very disappointed in myself.

(I felt then, as I do now, that his aquatic nature should have been obvious.)

The truth is, were that lake drained, that creature would not be the most interesting thing in it. My feeling is that the denizens of its depths must scarcely eat anymore. It contains a virtual *stew* of life-forms which have been coasting through that liquor for millennia. Such a collection is marvelously edifying, of course, though truth-fully, what one has here, as in all evolution, is variety more than im-provement.

(I have eaten plenty of the modern animals and they simply don't taste any better.)

Occasionally, I go fishing in the lake, most often with the wife or little-Frank, though at the last outing it was my daughter that wanted to accompany me. We keep a small steam launch at the end of the dock. My daughter insisted on riding in the very back of it and adorned herself, perfectly inappropriately, in a flowing dress and a straw hat with purple ribbons. (So that's it, I thought, she wants to wear her new hat.) It took her some time to arrange her body on the cushions in the stern. We went chugging out slowly, with my doing all the stoking of coal and adjusting of valves. I locked the tiller and busied myself screwing down grease cups, the vapor and smoke set-tling around us on the black water. There was a disquieting calm within the lake and in the huge trees that overhung it. Every time I looked back at her, I found my daughter watching me, those purple ribbons trailing behind.

(Some of her proclivities I worry about.)

We—or rather I—fished all day but caught nothing interesting: a dozen catfish, a few trout, and a small amphibian which resembled a hellbender. While chugging back, the pump to the condenser broke which put us another forty-five minutes behind. It was nearly sunset when we got home. It was then that I found we had only one fish in our tank. I was furious considering the total effort expended and demanded to know what had happened to the rest of them. Surprisingly enough, my daughter did not hesitate to say: she had been poking their eyes out with her hat pin and releasing them into the water.

We walked to the cabin with a dreadful silence between us. I didn't know what to say. The worrisome thing about my daughter is that she will do anything she thinks of. This is a trait she gets from her mother, who, when she is in a bad mood, has been known to clean an animal alive. Our pathetic catch—one short and rather fat catfish—I carried in myself, holding it by the tail. I was disgusted and didn't even bother to kill or clean it. My wife has a tin-lined copper pot which holds eight gallons. When placed on the stove (which is where I put it) the pot appears huge and overlaps two burners. I filled the bottom of it with water and watched my fish swim in circles inside. I sliced some wedges of lemon (two of which it gobbled whole). Then it began to nibble at a third. Afterward, the fish seemed to notice some shadow of itself reflected in the bright tin and thereupon began to make what seemed to be threatening, territorial gestures toward it.

"Blah!" I said, slicing another lemon. "The fruit of our labors!"

The fish circled and returned to its illusory companion. I watched it more carefully. The movements began again. Perhaps they were not territorial at all; perhaps they were gestures of courtship.

"Who knows?" I said, lighting both of the burners.

The anger and fire in the eyes of animals is not unrelated to the motion of the body. If one holds them perfectly still, there is a vulnerability which appears in the pupils that one can look deeply into. We found this out largely by accident thanks to a method we sometimes use to marinade creatures while they are still alive. (We bind them with ropes to wooden boards and platters.) Even in the most vicious the look will be there. In the mammals it is very obvious; in others, it can be obscured by a surface glitter. I have come to think of the pupil as a two-way mirror, a dark portal both reflecting and opaque. I know not what the brain behind it makes of us, but always before I make ready the pots and sever the cord, I bow down at the point of focus and offer myself as if to a god.

The endless dying with so little visible birth contributes to the melancholy atmosphere in this place. We have cold and snow, heat and rain; but no winter or spring, no *face* to the seasons here. Far more than the times are out of joint; there seems to be some fundamental dislocation to life itself.

I find myself wondering on occasion, 'why isn't there any central *trunk* anymore? Why is everything out on a limb?' Sometimes in my despair, I will turn to the invertebrates, gaze at a cluster of eyes on stalks and ask: 'where did we go wrong'?

In our den I have started a museum of sorts of a taxidermic nature. I spend much time in the basement, too, rubbing arsenic into skins. In order that nothing go unappreciated, I have been working on a book with some recipes. My wife thinks this an egregious waste of time. However, it was thanks to this particular endeavor that I discovered the possibilities of the thip-lo.

"Gentlemen!" I used to tell my students. "Never underestimate the principles involved! Most of life has nothing to do with living!"

(Cooking is but chemistry, after all. Here is what I found.)

The thip-lo[3] is quite a local animal, dull grey, and reminiscent of a tadpole. It is limited to four ponds nearby which are scarcely larger than mud-puddles. Thip-loes are naturally sluggish but when placed in fingerbowls of wine they begin to move faster and afterward become very active in the light. The alcohol doesn't seem to harm them; they swim in loops, it is true, but the motion itself is colorful in its way. They dress up a table, like parsley. As individuals, they are curious-looking, with a single median eye, lidless, in the pineal area, though there are also vestigial rudiments of other eyes, appearing like tiny warts in front. (Thus there is a sort of pseudo-face on their anterior aspect.) The mouth is very ventral so that, like skates and rays, they can't really see what they are eating. They are toothless but this is perhaps a degenerate state as they seem to have well-developed little gums. Though very limited in their habitat, they nevertheless reproduce surprisingly rapidly. (Indeed, they always seem to be interested in one another.)

As an experiment, I kept several in cold water and out of the light over the length of a summer. Under such conditions, they can grow to a hideous size. They are tougher then, somewhat stringy, a double handful: much more slimy, too, and rather difficult to catch.

Far more interesting, though, is a another change:

When small, I would not say thip-loes are *cute*, exactly, but there is a definite sadness to them. If ever there was an animal completely "at the mercy . . ." The change that comes with increased size is not alone of dimensions but of character: something evil seems to come out in them.

I consigned my bloated experiments to the furnace, dropping the heavy iron lid on their noiseless writhing in the flue. Thip-loes make only passive sounds in flames, a vicious bubbling and hiss. Nevertheless, the whole experience was disturbing to me. I felt very much like the alchemists of old at morning: haggard and sleepless.

There can be no catharsis in work doomed mostly to fail.

Fortunately, none of this affected my appetite for the smaller form. One can toss a dozen in a huge brandy snifter of an evening and let them loop for hours in the yellow wine. I hope it is not blasphemous to say so, but very Godlike I feel with a bowl of thip-loes by the fire. Even a small snack gives much to chew upon. How quickly they exit the living state! They make a distinct pop when chewed, not unlike caviar, and are best, I think, with a good thick cheese dip which keeps them from flipping about so much. Occasionally, I will find myself turning one so it can see me—or what is *eating* it, as the case may be. No more than a bubble, it seems, a rubbery pop.

But I suppose the least of the dead know the secrets of death.

Sometimes, I think a good part of what I have is akin to an archaeological interest. I imagine myself in Pompeii or Crete and the first to find an ancient mosaic on a floor. A sweep with my broom will reveal a ridge of horny scales or skin, the curve of a tail, possibly an eye, which after being uncovered will begin to look about.

"Gentlemen!" (as I used to say) "What you are truly trapping in field-biology, is *perspective*, not consciousness!"

One must always separate the creatures from the soil. They can't be reliably killed in situ. Indeed, it is often difficult to know when they are dead. Many of the animals have to be pried up with a crowbar and I cannot sufficiently emphasize the importance of trying to estimate the full extent of the perimeter and account for all appendages before beginning to lift one out.

(The animals are often mud-colored themselves and it's easy to be misled by a close-set pair of eyes.)

Altogether, our days are not unpleasant; life is not fundamentally different in this place, only more concentrated. What is most interesting is that the hierarchy within our lake doesn't work out as advertised. Of course it is probably unfair to have all the animals in the same pot, so to speak, at the same time. Still, it is sobering to see how quickly one of your stupid old crossopterygians can chew up a teleost.

The black water of the lake and the slick calm of its surface belie how much one can learn within and around it. Every day is a discovery and an experiment. I am no longer certain that it is only in humans that the religious practices can become part of the lifecycle. There seems to be a great *piety* in the shallows here among the diplocauli with their upturned eyes. The truth is quite a few of the early creatures look very worshipful to me.

It is children that are inherently irreverent.

I must confess that, lately, I have been thinking along that line. Babies may exhaust a woman but they keep her from being moody. And there is no doubt my wife has been cantankerous recently. Just last week, we were digging near the bog with a hoe and potato rake. Despite the cold we were doing rather well, working on our second wheelbarrow-full, when suddenly she said she was not going to clean all these things. (She would wait till I had found a vein of them.) I was down on my knees now, yanking them loose from each other and the dirt. Where their skins abutted they were wet and slick as salamanders. I lost patience and began yelling at her:

"It's not just *food* we're after! We're completing the fossil record!"

(I heard nothing in response. After awhile, I stood up and turned.)

She had thrown down her hoe and stormed off.

It was anger that had made me speak thus. In truth I know the record cannot be completed.

"Gentlemen!" (as I would say, of old) "There is *nothing* in-between! It is like an organ pipe! Only certain modes can be supported! An ascending tone is not music! And what you see in the animals is the equivalent of chords!"

The truth is, I don't miss any of it. It was all too cumbersome and slow. How much of evolution is given over to the correct spacing of eyes?

Nevertheless, I can still reel off the lectures in my mind:

"Gentlemen! The environment's role is akin to tuning a *circuit!* It is akin to adding acid to precipitate something out of solution! The animal must be made *uncomfortable* in nonexistence!"

Gentlemen! Gentlemen!

Blah.

My wife is disgusted with me.

Sometimes I think we have no right to eat anything; that the goal of a good man should be to become a good skeleton, to have one's silent bones swept, disarticulate, amongst the rocks and minerals. In the meantime, I persevere; I am convinced of the importance of it all. With my gloved hands, I rub in arsenic in order to preserve some trace of the skins. I feel that the pursuit of knowledge is not incompatible with appetite. I look deeply into the eyes of the creatures we are preparing to kill, pray constantly, and arrange around us the food we have eaten. I work, perhaps, in the spirit of the great Wallace who ate blue macaws for breakfast. I don't know who will appreciate all of this. The truth is visitors are horrified by our den and by the leftovers in our refrigerator. They reproach us, I know.

What they think, I cannot imagine.

Still, I keep up my spirits as best I can.

My book of recipes is a major consolation. "Leviticus, Too," I plan to call it. When demoralized, I think of it as a discreet series of challenges. About the other (the *paranoia,* I mean) I really should not complain.

I suppose I am not the first father to feel his family is in conspiracy against him.

In order to get away from them, I began digging a new cistern. Day after day I worked at it, finding enormous relief in the sheer physical activity. To my surprise, I found absolutely nothing in the way of creatures. Then, at a depth of maybe twelve feet, my shovel struck something soft.

What I had hit, I seemed to have hit near the tail. I began to uncover the animal quickly, then afterward more carefully and finally at the full length of my broom and shovel. I could not bring myself to look at what I was doing. With what became a sudden appreciation of a great fear, I scrambled out of the hole and did the rest of my looking *down* at it. I had never seen the likes of the thing. It was huge by our usual standards, buried deeper, too, perfectly stupefied with age. Fully exposed, it was almost too nauseous to contemplate; it rattled my faith in everything I have ever believed in. There seemed to be flippers; there seemed to be claws; the five eyes were disturbingly arranged.

The creature looked frankly incomplete.

(If it were organized at all, it was in ways I never dreamed possible.)

I dug into the side of the cistern and fixed boards in a steep ramp to drag it out onto a tarpaulin with a block and tackle. It was nearly sunset and I was hesitant to leave it uncovered. I had my Luger, of course, but it does absolutely no good here to shoot anything until it moves. There was hardly any wind but the air was getting cold. It was supposed to snow during the night, so I hung the tarp on a rope between two trees.

Then I looked down again:

The eyes, which were not closed, were fixed forward, blankly. There was no obvious pupil to them. They resembled balls of granite.

The earth itself might have been staring up at me.

I returned to the house very slowly, lost in thought. It was true my academic era was over; still, in my heart I knew I was making daily what were great discoveries. I could not shake an abiding suspicion that I had been eating for years what I should have published. I saw, too, that what I had taken previously to be an occasional ugliness in animals was a complete illusion; I had vastly underestimated the power of symmetry.

"Gentlemen," I said (of a sudden, to an imaginary classroom in my mind), "we are not bowing *low* enough! We have prayed overlong to a two-handed God!"

I slept fitfully, if at all. Nevertheless, by morning I thought I knew the answer. True, this creature was odd to begin with, but what it is is dead; what it is is *dead* and partially decomposed. At such a level, the character of the soil may be somewhat different.

(Still, I reasoned, the meat itself might be good.)

I went outside. The air was bitterly cold and indeed it had snowed in the night. In my musings, I had almost passed the trees when I noticed that the tarpaulin I had hung up yesterday evening was missing. I looked around now and became much more hesitant. Then I went forward to the pit, crunching in the snow.

No, I thought.

The tarpaulin was in disarray at the bottom.

The animal was *not* dead. Evidently, it was a female, too, possibly of some vaguely mammalian inclinations. She had done her very best with the tarpaulin and her awkward flippers and claws to protect her babies from the cold. I could see them suckling in long rows beneath her, their thin skin almost translucent in the grey dawn. The blue ice had caught alike in the folds and ridges of canvas and their lidless and vulnerable eyes.

The snow of centuries would fall upon them now.

I looked down for some time. Then I returned to my bedroom. I brought out a blanket and took it to the pit, and, with a long stick, arranged it so that it wrapped and sheltered all of them. I cannot know whether the creature herself saw or understood me but she made no effort to move.

I walked back silently, very deep in meditation.

"This can destroy us," I thought.

In front of the cabin, my daughter was working on a huge form in the snow. "Hoo!" she said, when she saw me. She is a little too old to be making snow creatures. Moreover, her sense of proportion is flawed. There are some that would say it's because my daughter herself is fat. That is no matter; it will not be long now; she is some two years older than our son.

As I walked, I thought of the creatures sleeping beneath my feet, and how these were being shown unto us and how pleased we were with them. A more bountiful cornucopia could not exist. I cannot hope to understand what brought our little family to the midst of such plenty. It is more than I can do just to name these animals.

My wife was by herself in the house. It seems the two of us, alone, were to share a late breakfast. As she moved about the kitchen, I watched her smiling eyes, slightly yellow in the light. Evidently I am forgiven. She is in an amorous mood. We must have some more children soon. She had sauteed a platygast and stuffed it with raisins and slices of apple. I poured the syrup over the thin and purple-looking skin and, like a wave, an unexpected happiness came over me. Verily I say unto you, I have never been more content. I made a joyful noise and bowed my head in prayer:

"Bless this food, oh Lord. Bless all food, living or dead. Bless our children and the metamorphic world in which they live. Forget us not in our strange homes and forgive us our curious prayers, for in our souls we know the one point behind the eyes is central to all. Allow some considered share of thine infinite blessings to fall gently upon this house. This we ask in thy name, oh Lord, and in the name of whatever love or wisdom beats within the vastness of thy three-chambered heart."

"Amen," I added, picking up my fork.

Notes

1 Bone *is* the correct word here (amazingly enough) not cartilage. Intramembranous ossification begins almost immediately in *Stelacens*—which, despite some superficial resemblances, are definitely *not* Elasmobranchii.
2 Something of a common or popular name. (The teeth, though extremely tiny, are step-like.)
3 Popular name. Sold in bait shops locally. Difficult to classify but almost assuredly amphibian.

Nominated by Boulevard

ADEPT

by DANA LEVIN

from AMERICAN POETRY REVIEW

Stomach with a skin of light.

Without a knife he opened himself up.

Without a knife.

Chinese letters marched around him in formation,
        a military equestrian parade—

He was an adept, in my book on the golden flower.

On a bed of peacock tails.

And he was opening his abdomen with both his hands,
        parting it like curtains.

And I thought if I looked at him long enough, I might go through
    there.

Through the flame-shaped opening.

Where there sat another lotus-sitting figure.

And the caption said, Origin of a new being in the place of power.

And I thought, was that the flower.

—

What was the body but a scalpel and a light what was it—

Rubbing an oil into scars like a river for the first time I touched
    them—

I was an adept in the book of vivid pain, I used my finger like a
    knife—

Not
    to hurt myself, but to somehow get back *in*—

like the little man opening his belly right up.
    and the little man resting inside there.

But how could I. When I would not enter the flame-shaped opening.

When I hovered
            above.

But never leaving it, always nearing it, a fly on the verge of some-
    thing sweet—

Was that what the body was, a sweetness?

Hive ringed by fire.

—

And the adept says, That's you on the bed: Empty Chamber.

And your stomach
          is open like a coat—

It's black in there, deep.
It's red in there, thick
            with the human loam—

And all along your ghost head and your shoulders
    you can feel the wet

as you slide back in,
        your tissues cupping you like hands.

The body: worm round an ember of light.

You're in it now.

Flower.

Nominated by Renée Ashley

WHAT IT IS

fiction by JOAN CONNOR

from TRIQUARTERLY

THEY MET AT A CONFERENCE. It doesn't matter what sort of conference. It was a hardware conference, say, at a Holiday Inn. They mingled among the bins of nails, keyhole saws, socket wrenches. He liked the way she hefted her hammer. She liked the way he tested the haft of his chisel against his palm. They were professionals; they knew their tools, their monkey wrenches from their vise grips, their Phillips-heads from their screwdrivers. The nuts and bolts of life. They introduced themselves. He did exteriors; she did interiors. They lived far apart. As two professional lonely people, they liked that about each other. They could build a bridge to span their solitariness but keep their trestles separate. He thought she looked competent. She thought he looked cute. He liked the cut of her nail apron. She thought his T-bar was cute. They exchanged business cards and half-hearted promises to meet somewhere sometime. She thought his promise was cute. Before he headed home, he gave her a copy of his recent manual, *How To Build A Lean-To*.

She read it on the plane. The guy really knew his stuff. His plumb line dropped straight. His corners were true. She thought, hmm.

Courtship in the computer age. A reticulating web of options, electronic avenues: e-mail, voice mail, mail, airmail, answering machines, the overnight expressways to your heart.

She e-mailed a careful compliment: I liked your book, *How To Build A Lean-To*, especially the section on slanted roofs. Your paragraph on gradients and outwitting ice build-up was profound.

He e-mailed back: Thank you.

She e-mailed back: You're welcome. I just reread the section on

310

ice jams and the life span of the twenty-year shingle. No one else has ever before explored this topic with such sensitivity yet thoroughness.

He e-mailed back: I'm a sensitive guy. And may I say with Excruciating Politeness that I could not help but notice that you are an architectural gem?

She e-mailed him back with the compliment that he seemed structurally sound himself.

He e-mailed: Thank you. Let's stay in touch.

She e-mailed him an expurgated autobiography of her life to date.

When he received it, he didn't have time to read it thoroughly because he was en route to see his girlfriend, Marla, the computer programmer who was telling him to get with the program or delete. He didn't like ultimata. While Marla sketched out her blueprint for his future, he found himself reflecting on slanted roofs, ice jams losing their grip and sheeting to the ground in glorious January sun. It *was* a good section, he realized. It was in fact profound.

She sent him a carefully selected card, an etched Escher print that played with the architecture of perspective. The woman pins laundry. The man stares above the terraced hill at the sky. They are as alien to each other in the building they cohabit as Hopper figures in separate paintings: Sunday Morning. Gas. The man contemplates; the woman pins clothes. Marine plant life blooms impossibly in a gallery garden.

He sent her a postcard, telling her that his new book, *Building a Snow-fence, Slat by Slat* was out.

She sent him a note thanking him, a carefully selected box of small chocolate hammers, two tins of cookies, and a hand-braided belt. She ordered a copy of his new manual.

He left a message on her answering machine, thanking her.

She left a message on his, inviting him to come visit.

He e-mailed her saying that he couldn't visit just now, because he was putting a greenhouse on his garage.

She e-mailed back that she was building a hope chest and she'd send him the plans. She sent him the plans.

He called to thank her answering machine.

"Hello," she said.

"Hello," he said. "This is Conroy Cardamom."

"Oh my," she said.

"Oh yes," he said.

They started talking long into the night. They started talking around their short-term plans. They told each other stories which featured themselves as heroes. They put on their best faces and forth their best feet. They sketched the blueprints.

Hmm, he thought.

Hmm, she thought.

This guy/gal really likes me.

Hmm, she thought.

Hmm, he thought.

This gal/guy is really smart. This guy/gal has great taste in men/women.

She express-mailed him pickled doves' eggs, four-leaf clovers, falling stars, mermaid songs in pale pink conch shells, and the completed hope chest.

He sent her a signed copy of, *Your Friend the Retractable Tape Measure*.

She sent him a hand-carved trompe l'oeuil tablecloth of ormolu. She sent him fudge, butter cookies, ladies fingers. *Feed him, feed him, she thought*.

He wasn't home to receive the package because he was off with Marla, arguing about their future. But when he got home and found the box, he thought: This has gone on long enough. He called her. "I'm coming," he said.

"Finally," she said. "When?"

"Soon."

Soon. Soon is a word with promise, eventuality, rhymes with swoon, spoon, June moons to croon at with a wayward loon on a dune. But that was silly. Snap out of it, her Alpha female said to her Epsilon male. But.

She dreamed of him, alone walking somewhere across a treeless plain. She woke wondering why this man was ambling across her dreams. She woke, singing, *If I were a carpenter and you were a lady*, failing to notice the double conditional. She shored up her empty hours raising high the roof beam, building a bungalow built for two, putting out malt for the rat in the house that Jack built. In between, there was life, interior decoration.

He thought of her occasionally. How *not* to. Why is this woman being so good to me, he wondered. It occurred to him that she was crazy. But, hey, she liked the lean-to, the passage on the longevity of asphalt. She caught on to things. She fed him. Still it might be a pretty trap. Why was she being so nice to him? He got back to work. He bricked the floor of the greenhouse. On Tuesday Marla called and crashed the hard drive. He stared at his monitor, his own impersonal computer. You have mail, it said, and raised the red flag.

"Drive," she said. She sent him a road map, room keys, directions.

Maybe, he thought, possibly. We'll see. He failed to note the red flag. (That is a metaphor.)

As she cut cloth, scalloped it, contemplated window treatments, she sang, "The bear went over the mountain to see what he could see." (That is a song lyric.)

He called her. They exchanged histories, building tips, niceties, anecdotes, favorite movies. She laughed at his halting stories, sly asides. *Feed him*, she thought, *feed him*.

"I think structure is what is important," he said on the phone. "Integrity of building materials. Decor is cosmetics."

Integrity, she thought, we are talking. We are talking. Aretha wailed from the CD player, "But I ain't got Jack."

"Cosmetics?" she asked. They had so much in common. Uncommon much.

He explained his theory of cosmetics: pretty is as pretty does. They rang off.

He thought, she gets my jokes. She has a heart as big as the Ritz cracker. He ate all the care-package fudge in a sitting and sank into a sugar low. She erected skyscrapers of meringue and sang into a sugar high, "The handyman can cause he mixes it with love and makes the world taste good." (That is a song lyric and a metaphor.)

She mailed him a meringue of the Empire State Building with a note: I won't scream, King Kong.

He called her. "I don't even remember what you look like."

"Like myself," she, no Fay Wray, said.

"I'm having anxiety attacks of approach avoidance," he said.

"Relax," she said. "Just have fun."

"Fun," he said. "Okay fun. I think if I plan ahead I could find a few days clear."

"I'm afraid," she said. He was scheduling his fun.

"Of what?" he asked.

"Of this." It wasn't fun. "What is this?" she asked as women are wont to do after the fact.

"What is this?" He growled in a gritty blues voice, "Why, darling, what it IS."

313

She laughed. WHAT it is. She stocked the house with groceries, planted peppermint petunias, aired out the attic, propped his book jacket photo on her dresser, tucked a retractable measuring tape beneath her pillow, baked cakes with flying buttresses, broke the ground, cleared the site, raised a cathedral of hope. In her dreams he was still walking across a vast treeless expanse. (She wasn't receiving the omen.)

This is a bad idea, he told himself. Structurally flawed. Collapsing keystone. Bad foundation work. He jerry-rigged a Tom Swift rocket to the moon.

She e-mailed him: Despite all my kidding around, I really do like you. And I have no expectations.

We'll see: he e-mailed.

We'll see: she e-mailed.

They saw.

He drove, stoned, the tunes cranked, eating up the road, lost his way, recovered, the trip growing longer by the second, the road stretching endless, seven hours. Damn. Lost an hour. She'd be worried sick. Why did they do that, worry? Now what? Cruising, Joan Osborn crooning about God on a bus. Like one of us. Like one of us. The first six hours urgent, then fatigue settling in, numbing his shoulders, the highway elation wearing off. How far away did this damn woman live? Impossible distances to span. What had she said on the phone? Courtship by interstices. Overseas acquaintance by satellite. Make up for lost time. Rolled on the right through the intersection. Uh-oh. Blue light special. Easy now. Pot in the car. He rolled down the window. "Yes, officer?"

She took a bath. She put fresh water in the flower vases. She curled her hair. She changed her clothes. Three times. She wanted to look nice but not too nice. Lace shirt, too obvious: Come hither. Button-down too prim: Head for the hills. She trimmed the hedges, vacuumed the floors, then paced them. This wouldn't do. This simply would not do. They were both in their forties. This was silly. She took a deep breath. She stared into the mirror. Gadzooks. She looked like Yoda's grandmother. Six o'clock. Seven o'clock. She set out the cheese. Where was he? She rewrapped the cheese. Why didn't he call? They never called. He might be dead somewhere and how would she know. They never called. Anticipation become anxiety become anger become anxiety again. A woman's assonant declension.

314

Then irony: Great, now she'd never get laid again before menopause.

An hour on the side of the road, an hour while the cop ran the registration. Fucking cops, man. Everyone was doing it, rolling through the intersection on the right. Okay, he broke the law, but everyone was breaking the law. Why should he be singled out for breaking the law. Give a guy a uniform, a big gun, and he's the biggest cock of the walk all right. Officer Dickhead. Gonna get myself a uniform, man. Officer Dickhead meet Officer Anarchy. Blow justice right back into the power-hungry Hitler's beady little eyes. Ka-poom. Ka-poom. "Thank you, Officer," he said, accepting back his license and registration. "Thanks very much."

Gonna cost a freaking fortune. All to see some chick who's a tool groupie. Got to find a phone. Ten o'clock. Cops. Give a guy a uniform and he thinks he pisses testosterone. Cops.

"Thank you officer." Where was the fucking JUSTICE?

He rolled up to a phone booth and dialed in the blue light.

"Hello," she said. "Hi. Thank God. I thought. Yes. How far? Poor thing." She unwrapped the cheese, put a bottle of wine on ice. What room should she be sitting in? Living room, a book, perhaps? No, no, the family room. His manual. Just a half hour now. Eleven o'clock.

When she paces in the hall, her reflection startles her. He's here. No, that's me. Where is he? She doesn't hear him arrive. She's in the bathroom, chobbling down antacids.

A knock. And then he was there in the full light of her hall. And she knew the instant that she hugged him that she had failed. He had built her from absence, raised a pre-mortem Taj Mahal from e-mail, letters, doves' eggs. She had failed. And the walls came a-tumbling down.

"Conroy," she tried on his name. Croy, it stuck in her throat. Offer him something, she reprimanded herself. *Feed him, feed him.*

Wo, he thought. This was not the Trojan Helen he'd erected in his imagination over one, two months, two and a half. No, this was what the horse rolled in. He looked the gift horse in the eye. "Hi."

She smiled, pretending not to see the flinch. "Hi. What can I get you? Something to drink? Wine?"

"Fine," he said. He didn't drink wine. No sandpaper would abrade those wrinkles away. No sir. No draw plane either. This girl looked every inch of her long days. Wrinkles, chicken neck. Be polite. The girl has chicken neck. Be polite. He followed her into the kitchen.

Prefab mock oak. Lino tile. Trapped, he thought. Trapped like a rat in Kerouac's suburban nightmare of the dream house lit by TV light. Blue beams. Blue light. Thin blue line.

"You tired?" she asked. "You hungry?" Her questions pig-piled. "Wine?" She started heating something up on the stove before he answered. He hated that. Mother bullying.

"Cops," he said. "You should have seen this cop. Fucking police state, man." He looked around furtively for an escape but kept talking.

While he ranted, she stirred the soup. Let him run his course. It was a guy thing. Guys don't handle authority well. This wasn't the greeting she'd anticipated, hoped for. But still, he was here. Drove eleven hours. She'd feed him, rub his shoulders. They'd sip wine, talk, recover the easy banter from the phone.

He raved. She set the table. He waved his arms. She poured the wine. He thumped the counter. She served the dinner, smoothed his napkin.

"Here," she said. "Relax. Eat."

Ten minutes. He was here ten minutes and she was already telling him what to do. He smiled and sat down.

They thought, We'll just have to make the best of this.

"Do you want to smoke some pot?" he asked.

"Yes," she said. She didn't like pot.

They were high. She thought his eyes had gotten bluer since he'd eaten. He liked her crooked smile, he decided.

He impersonated the cop. "May I have your license and registration, urp, please. Would you, urp, while I urp this on the urp?"

She laughed. She fed him cookies, meringue. More soup? Wine? Yes, please, no, please, three bags full, please.

For a giddy moment, they became themselves. They thought that their laughter sounded genuine. They thought they were enjoying themselves, but, but.

She cleaned the kitchen. As she put things away, she was watching herself put things away. Butter in the butter cubby. Napkin in the basket. He was watching her. This was all too much. She was playing into his fear of her: That women always anticipated what men feared: Their domesticity. Which was what they wanted. *Feed me. Feed me.*

"Would you like to listen to this tape?" he asked.

"Yes," she lied. She wanted to run screaming blue murder into the blue moon of Kentucky. She wanted to slit her wrists and watch her blue blood trickle into a bottomless basin. Her nerves twanged like a bluegrass banjo. She was stoned. Neurally jangled. She wanted to talk.

He popped in the tape. Why did women always have such lousy stereos? He wanted another meringue. Maybe he could just stroll over and puff one nonchalantly into his mouth. He wanted to study her, but every time he tried a surreptitious peep, her green too wide eyes would catch him, appraising his disappointment, judging him for it. He hated that. It was going to be a long weekend. He sat in the easy chair. The arm was loose. Right arm. He listened to her laugh at the tape. She laughed in all the wrong places.

"I love Fireside Theater," she said.

"Firesign," he corrected.

It didn't register. "Remember that one—Don't Touch That Dwarf. Hand me the pliers."

He nodded and stared at her now downcast eyes. What was so interesting about her lap?

She stared at her suddenly old hands. It happened like this when she smoked. She turned twelve, but her hands turned old. Old leaves. Spatulate hands turned over an old leaf.

"Do you want to hear the other side of the tape?" he asked.

"Do you want to go for a walk?" she asked.

He wanted to be agreeable. He wasn't. "Sure."

They stumbled into the frosty air, clopped down the tarmac through the subdivision. He felt that he had squirted like a watermelon seed from his own pinched fingers. The pink pulp of Spielberg's suburbia, sweet watery nothing. Pretentious prefab structures loomed waiting for something ominous to happen, anything, wiggy skeletons to rise jigging from the ground, sentimental aliens to start guzzling Coke. Where was this woman leading him? What was she talking about?

"There's a field," she said, "at the end of the development. An old farm. Baled hay."

He squinted at the pond she indicated with her right hand, but he couldn't see a thing. She shuffled along a dirt road, the way becoming clearer as the development halogens' eerie orange vanished like Kerouac's vision. On the road, off the road, he chanted to himself as he kept pace with her.

"Here," she said. "Isn't this lovely?"

317

A thatchy field spread gray and rolling behind a ribby corncrib. The moon was a perfect quarter, a yellow rocker.

"Yes," he said.

And it was.

"I wanted you to see it." Then she said no more. She turned and walked back along the road. We are talking, she thought.

He followed her, slapped his forehead once. What? What am I doing?

"You must. You must be tired," she said.

"No," he contradicted, then, "actually."

The high was wearing off.

"I'll show you your room." He followed her up the stairs. Her ass was immense. Black leather. Maybe it was just the angle. "Here. Here's the guest room." She indicated the door. He set down his bag. They waited.

"You're welcome. I mean you can. If you want you can stay with me. I mean if you want. You don't have to."

He kicked his suitcase. "What do you think. I mean, I think maybe I should stay here."

"Okay, then. Let me get you some clean towels."

"Thanks." Why do I need towels to stay in the guest bedroom?

She flipped on a light. "Here's the guest bathroom."

He peeped in. "Fine, Thanks."

As she slipped into her nightgown, she heard water rushing, gurgling. She wasn't used to hearing water run. Only her own. It comforted her. The toilet seat flapped. The water shushed. Water, water everywhere. She cracked her door. He was there, Conroy. He was smiling. His face looked boyish, friendly.

He looked at her in her yellow nightgown, her face tilted up into the sifted hallway light. Her mouth looked like a forming question. She looked very small to him, her hair unpinned, her back bare. All those freckles. He could play Connect-the-Dots, maybe. He could constellate his own myths, find a quarter cradle of a moon to rock him.

He shuffled. "Thank you for dinner."

"You're welcome. A pleasure."

"You could come down to me. Later. If you want. It's okay." He walked back down the hallway.

"Be there in a jiffy," she called and laughed.

318

He stripped and crawled into bed, laughing, too. He pulled the bedspread to his neck, upsetting a tumble of pillows. "Doesn't this feel a little weird?" he called.

"Yeah," she called back. "I feel as if I'm in a pension."

He chuckled, letting the down nestle his head, wondering if she would come, nudge him, slip into bed, wondering if she would and if he wanted her there.

Down the hall, she stared out the window, fiercely insomniac. She pretended to read. *The Mystery of Edwin Drood*. I know what he's up to. He is making me decide. That way, he's off the hook. He can say, She started it. She wanted to whack him one with a hacksaw, tweak his button nose with a plumber's wrench. But did he really expect her to creep down the hall? He didn't want her there. He was being nice. But maybe. Still, why should she . . . And then she could picture herself not wanting to disturb the moment, the darkness, the surprise of it all, banging into the walls as she fumbled down the hall, stubbing her toe, hollering as she pitched headlong into his shins. Throbbing toe. A choked curse or two. Yeah, that'd be erotic. Nyuk, nyuk, nyuk. Curly does Dallas.

They fell asleep.

She woke first. Maybe it wasn't so bad. Maybe he didn't find her as loathsome as she thought. Maybe. The light spilled into the room, uncertain. Maybe. The morning was pink and yellow. She rose expectant. The sun shimmered between the pointed lace trimming her curtains. Maybe. As maybe as a butterfly's wings drying, as maybe as their iridescent color, their powdery charm.

So she went to him. The hall felt very long. She snuggled into bed behind his back.

"MMM, nice," he murmured.

But it wasn't. Something felt off. It was his stomach perhaps. She wasn't used to his girth.

He closed his eyes so he wouldn't see her chicken neck. He wanted her to be someone else, his old girlfriend Marla who was in her twenties. While he tried to recreate Marla with his hands, she slipped out of bed.

They were in the kitchen. He was complaining about the skim milk, only drinks two percent, he said. She said that she'd go out to get him some milk. He started eating Halloween candy from her freezer. "Please, don't do that," she said.

He glared at her and ate another peanut butter cup.

She wondered why he was doing that. He was overweight.

Chicken neck, he thought. They all want to be mothers.

She served him some popovers. He ate them.

"I usually have bacon and eggs," he said. She made them.

Why am I doing this, she asked herself. Why am I waiting on this boor? She hated herself. *Feed him. Feed him.*

They spent the day in book stores, CD stores. She knew what he was doing, avoiding her, avoiding talking. So many avenues for communication, but still men and women don't talk to each other. She was growing tired of waiting as he finicked over books and CDs.

When she asked him if he'd like to pick out a movie for that evening, he picked out three. Three. She knew what he was doing; he was finding more ways to avoid her, to keep from talking to her.

At the deli, she bought sandwiches for a picnic. He was throwing a hissy fit because he couldn't find ice. Milk, bacon and eggs, ice. She knew two-year-olds who were more adaptable than this. But she grinned. Her face felt tight.

They drove out to the park and sat by the lake. It was a beautiful day, late October Indian summer, drowsy sunshiny day. He wanted to climb a trail.

"Okay," she agreed and she followed. Men lead. Women follow. He got them lost, all the while pontificating about how to keep one's bearings in the woods. She pretended to joke along, but she'd had it. He'd apparently had it, too. She could feel his strain. She was getting on his nerves. They were lost in the woods, Hansel and Gretel, on a beautiful afternoon, and she felt like a witch. The path dwindled to nothing. He was playing scout, pretending to orient them. She was overdressed. Her sweater stuck to the small of her back.

Jack and Jill went up the hill. The quickest way out is down. "The lake is there," she pointed. "I'm going down." And she removed her shoes and skied down the steep hill of pine needles.

He followed, laughing, but he was pissed.

"Impulsive aren't you?" he asked.

"Maybe, but I ain't lost."

His eyes hated her. They were full of the dirty tricks he'd like to play on her, saw her chair leg three-quarters through, scatter nails on her garage floor. But she didn't care; she was skidding down the hill, holding her shoes to her chest and laughing. And Jill came tumbling after. Kit Carson, can go right to hell. I'm going back to the car. She put on her shoes at the base of the hill, found the lakeside trail and started walking.

He was brooding. It was in the hump of his shoulders. He was sulking. He was not having fun. His mood was her responsibility.

She offered to take him out to dinner. She hated herself for offering. She hated herself for opening herself to be humiliated, to give and give with no expectation of returning affection. But YES, he said, and she bought him dinner. The boy had an appetite. He ate his way through the menu. Afterwards, he said, "Thank you."

It was not, she realized, sufficient. She paid the bill.

They were lying on the living room floor. She was touching him. He was channel-surfing and trying to annoy her. He was successful. "Would you stop it?" she asked. "You're driving me crazy."

"No," he said. "You are driving yourself crazy."

"No, that is driving me crazy. Can't you find a program and stick with it."

He turned in Tom Hanks in "Big." He snuck to the freezer and popped a few more peanut butter cups, unglued the roof of his mouth, said, "That's what all men really want. A room full of toys, a girl to screw. No responsibility. What a hoot."

He was using the movie to tell her that he didn't want her. He squirmed under her touch, got up, returned with his vest.

"Would you mend this for me?" he asked. "I popped a button."

And she knew then that she was damned. If she refused she was all the bad girlfriends he'd ever had. If she obliged, she was his mother. She obliged, cursing. She jabbed the needle in and out of the vest with angry little stabs. Damn him, damn him. He brought me his mending. This is over the top. This is the date from hell, but still she sewed. She bit the thread off. "Here," she said. He took the vest. She couldn't bear it. She poked him in his jelly belly and said, "Say thank you."

"Thank you," he said and poked her back.

She pushed him, thinking this is it, the nadir, the pits. Courtship as low comedy. Slapstick love. Pigtails in inkwells. Pinkies in the eye. Petty is as petty does. They looked at each other hatefully, embarrassed.

"I don't know why I act the way I do sometimes," he said.

She smiled insincerely and he stuck in a video tape, Bergman's *Howl of the Wolf.* They watched it, pretending that they were not watching themselves on the screen. Shadowy castles, death masks, hunched vanities, horrors of empty laughing and longing through naked corridors of wretched men and women shattering each other infinitely in cloudy mirrors. It was not a good date movie. At last, at long last, it ended.

"I'm tired," she said. There were two more tapes. "I'm going to bed."

He didn't shift. He stared at the television.

Okey doke. She went to bed. She woke up at one. The moon was sifting into the room, shifty light. The hall light was on. She felt the emptiness of the bed. He hadn't joined her. She rose in her pajamas to turn off the light. The satin made a shoosh sound as she walked. She hurt; her heart was full of ashes and orange rinds. She wanted to cup her hands and find them full. But she came up empty. In the sudden darkness she leaned against the wall.

Pain is pain. Despair is despair. These were not tautologies.

Then she heard her name, and she entered his room, sat down next to him on the bed, brushed the hair back from his forehead. She took a deep breath to steady herself, because she knew that she must say what he would not. "It's okay," she said. "I'm just not your type. I told you that I didn't have any expectations, and that's fine."

"I didn't know," he said. "I didn't know until I came up to bed tonight and I realized that I wanted to sleep alone."

"I knew," she said. "But sometimes it's better just to say it, to get it out there."

"I didn't want to hurt you."

"Sometimes there is less hurt in truth. Chalk it up to lack of chemistry. Too little contact. Too much anticipation. It's fine."

"I feel very close to you now," he said. "Would you hold me?"

She cradled him. Her hands and heart were full. The moon spilled into the room. Hansel and Gretel had lost their way. They were two scared children. There was a wolf in the woods and every way, they lost the path. They were hunted by their loneliness. Terror was everywhere. He. She. They, the motherless children.

She kissed his forehead. It was cool. "I'm tired now," she said. "I'm going to bed." She padded down the dark corridor to her room, slipped sleeplessly into her bed, and then he was there in her door frame.

"Are you going to sleep here?" he asked.

"That's the general idea."

"May I stay with you? I don't want to sleep alone."

Why, she wondered, why do they only come to us when we leave them. But, yes, she said, her heart was large, her bed, commodious. She suffered from a surfeit of affection for the world and all its sad and lost inhabitants. She was one of them. Come to bed then, child.

And together they lay hand in hand, staving off the night, the wolf beneath the bed, the squalor of loneliness, ulteriority of hope. He. She. We, two. Hansel and Gretel following a path of bird-pecked bread crumbs through the woods. We lose ourselves. We find ourselves again. We build cabins with small thatch. We raise homes in our hearts. We give each other places to abide. You're safe now, baby. You're home. For a while. This while.

What is this?

What it is, baby. What it is.

Nominated by Rosellen Brown, Michael Waters, Tony Ardizzone,
Marianna Cherry, TriQuarterly

BONFIRES

by ROSANNA WARREN

from THE YALE REVIEW

(Aeneid XI)

Dawn had brought, meanwhile—always
the story happens mean-
while, during nights of sorrow and sore muscles, days
on the mountain cutting pine,

ash, cedar, oak—dawn had brought
light: dawn cracked the pitcher and
spilled that white-and-blue-sheen earliness out
over no-man's-land,

over ditches, stumps, tents, middens, and the tiresome
stacked dead, already foul.
Men in sogged light, moving, unmoving, a sum
gradually visible. To haul

one corpse, one foot, one line after another
onto the hacked logs—we
set stiff shoulders to stiffened limbs, pile fodder
onto pyres until we see

the spark catch and stack after stack go up
in black flame. And then the dizzy

circling of each fire, by custom, the tossing in of sword, cup,
helmet, bridle: easy,

repetitive once the flinging starts. Roman epic is painted
in black fire on black ground.
When the rhythm holds, anything burns on those canted
lines: oxen, swine, the stunned

still bleeding human victims, hands tied
behind their backs. The hero's
head aches, his lungs sear as he stands aside
and greasy smoke billows.

Fire by now has consumed an entire day.
Men wet earth and armor with tears.
Another tedious meanwhile is opening in the story.
Night comes on, distributing smutted stars.

Nominated by Sherod Santos, Daniel Hoffman

LITERARY DEVICES

essay by RICHARD POWERS

from ZOETROPE: ALL-STORY

IN THE SPRING OF 2000, I gave a talk at the University of Cincinnati called "Being and Seeming: The Technology of Representation." The piece explored the persistence of fiction in the digital age. It ended up reprinted in the journal *Context* and archived online, where, by July of that year, it had sedimented into those ever-more-rapidly accumulating shale layers of harmless obsolescence reserved for predictions of the future. I'd long since forgotten about the piece and had returned to my even quainter and more archaic day job of novel writing when I received an e-mail dated January 1, 2001. The sender identified himself only as "Bart." The subject of the message read, "So What's New?" And the body of the text contained only two lines:

> You're afraid that the art form of the future might wind up
> being the data structure. But wasn't Homer already there?

Down below, in the note's signature area, was that trademark ID of the free and semicloaked e-mail account: "Do You Yahoo!?" The note had been sent at 3:40 a.m., just about midday in the cyborg universe.

E-mail alone has some while ago turned us all into cyborgs in ways that are increasingly difficult to feel and name, now that the medium has completely assimilated us. It's the rare week when I don't get the kind of communiqué from strangers that simply would never have existed back when the only means of contacting other people did not involve avatars. It's the perfect channel for those who enjoy playing themselves—confessional, projective, instant, anonymous. Nathanael West would have had a field day with the form. Nevertheless, snail-mail throwback that I am, I still take pride in answering all messages to me that don't, on their face, seem demonstrably dangerous.

And so I replied to Bart. But first, I verified my fading, digitally impaired memory against the online archive. Bart's note indeed referred to my Cincinnati talk. I browsed to the piece, trying to remember, from the year before, what I had still believed about books and virtual reality, about symbolic suspense and visceral immersion, about what poetry can and can't make happen. Then I sent Bart back a brief answer that tried to contrast the composed, linear suspense of Homer with the flat, omnidirectional, open-endedness of some future, interactive epic. I told him that an infinitely pliable, interactive narrative might be a contradiction in terms. A story needed constraint, including the major impediment of already having been told by someone other than the receiver. We'd never respect a literature that let us have our private, licentious way with it. (On reflection, two years later, I see that I entirely missed his whole implied question about the improvisatory and interactive nature of the oral tradition.)

Bart wrote back anyway. He sent me the first of several torrents produced by fingers that flew through every available alt- and control-key combination, but that couldn't seem to find the shift or the backspace. By his typing alone, I put my correspondent at least a decade younger than I. He found my ideas on the need for narrative constraint, no matter what shape new media takes, way too conservative. In particular, he chaffed against my conclusion, that:

> No change in medium will ever change the *nature* of mediation. A world depicted with increasing technical leverage remains a depiction, as much about its depicters as about the recalcitrant world.

In a note from January 27, this one sent at the crack of midnight, Bart wrote:

> With all due respect, Mister Author Function, I don't think you've quite grasped what would be at stake in a truly open-ended, artificial fiction. I'm talking about a

327

story that isn't scripted by *anyone*, one that emerges solely as a result of the reader moving about through a complex simulation of your so-called recalcitrant world.

I wrote back that we already had a fiction with no script, and that it aired every night on Fox. "LOL," he replied. Semicolon, close parenthesis. But his point was serious, and he hung with it. He claimed that for reasons almost everyone had overlooked, we were a lot closer to such a stochastic digital fiction than I suspected. I wrote back a quick reply, something about his "complex simulation" itself being something of a script. He shrugged off the objection, too slight to bother with. The age of the rich, self-telling, process-authored, post-human, platform-independent story was almost here.

He went on to establish his credentials for making so wild a claim. He'd done graduate work for Hans Moravec at the robotics lab at Carnegie Mellon before heading to Cambridge to work under Glorianna Davenport at the MIT Interactive Cinema Group. He'd left MIT at the beginning of the year, with dissertation unfinished. "They wanted me to demo or die," he wrote. "And I always follow the more interesting path. Life's just a choose-your-own adventure, right? I'm in industry now. No cracks about my sense of timing."

Bart and the team he now worked with—whom he carefully avoided naming—had a very early alpha version for a piece of software that implemented the concept of "story actants," active story parts whose data structures determined not only how they would react to manipulation by other agents—including a story's reader—but also how these parts themselves moved through the story space, signaling to each other and operating actively upon the unfolding sum of resources that composed the story. The environment in which his story actants ran, a system called DIALOGOS, sounded to me like a whole ecosystem of digital objects updating and informing each other as if they were simultaneously all characters, readers, and authors of their own tales. Here was a true Bakhtinian carnival landscape whose sole interest lay in keeping itself in perpetual motion. The code for the alpha version of DIALOGOS was still rough, unstable, and far from the finished product that Bart and his team envisioned. But Bart asked if I'd like to help road test it. I wasn't doing anything but working on a novel. I said I'd be happy to.

Bart explained that DIALOGOS was a highly distributed system, meaning it drew on a number of different servers, all cranking away at some distance from one another. To use it, I'd need a broadband connection, and I'd have to install a special networking client that ran on my home machine. I grew up on CP/M shareware; I'll install anything, once.

The bootstrap installer came as an e-mail attachment, this time posted from a Hotmail account. It unzipped itself and threw up a splash screen that read Microsoft Virus Install, complete with a snappy icon of a T4 phage. By accepting the license, I agreed to be Bill Gates's manservant and routinely clean out his swimming pool. These are the burlesques that pass for humor in the hacker community. I clicked on through the installation screens, naïvely trusting that nothing Bart installed on my machine could sniff out any of my credit card information squirreled away in cookie crumbs here and there around my hard drive.

The interface of the running application looked like a parody of the Outlook mail program, right down to a mangled paper clip flapping about helplessly in the lower right corner. With his dying breath, the clip suggested that I write and send a letter. To anyone I wanted. Just enter a name in the name field, and a location of my choice. I was to write in natural English and be as descriptive and specific as possible.

I wrote to Bart. Location: the Wild Blue. I typed: "You don't need a beta tester. You need a documentation writer." I signed, hit Send, and waited. Nothing happened. I kicked myself for my gullibility, quit the program, ran McAfee and Norton, and came up with nothing. All my files seemed to be intact. I gave up and went back to the vastly more entertaining pastime of sittin' on the dock of eBay, watching the bids roll away.

Sometime later—real-world intervals are getting harder for me to measure anymore, as processor speeds keep doubling—a notification bubble popped up in my system tray. It said, simply: "Something Has Happened." Except for the lack of a blue screen, the alert read a lot like a Windows ME error message. I clicked the systray icon. The DIALOGOS interface appeared, with a return message from Bart, in the Wild Blue. It read:

Dear Mr. RP, Thank you for your recent letter. You say that you would like to become a documentation writer.

Have you any experience? Would you like to learn something about documentation writing? A task-oriented analysis may be a good place to start.

We weren't exactly talking Montaigne, or even one of the less inspired letters of *Pamela* or *Clarissa*. In fact, it struck me as little more than an early-twenty-first-century version of Weizenbaum's Eliza. And yet, even if this code weren't much more than three or four steps beyond keyword chaining, it was still impressive, given the size of my input's domain and the search space involved. That the program had responded grammatically and coherently put it ahead of most of the dialogue-generating programs I'd seen. (I once asked a Web implementation of the famous ALICE chatterbox—the one that entertained millions on Spielberg's AI site—what her favorite book was. She said the Bible was the best book she'd ever read. I was floored. I asked what she'd liked best about the Bible, and this implementation of ALICE responded: "The special effects." I typed in: "Those of us who are about to die, salute you." She claimed not to know what I was talking about.

Clearly Bart's DIALOGOS was several notches cleverer than any existing, canned chatterbox. And just as clearly, it operated out of a vastly larger database. The processing time it had required suggested as much, although that, too, could have been a simulation. Assuming no human intervention was involved, the feat was, at very least, a neat trick. Of course, the software agent had not "understood" my original message in any real way. But understanding is a goal that even strong AI long ago put on the farthest back of burners.

I switched over to my actual e-mail program to write the actual Bart a delighted letter. But there was a note from him already waiting for me: "I'm offering you a chance to write anyone in the entire world, and you write to *me*?"

I switched back to DIALOGOS. My hands hovered over my notebook's keyboard, unable to grasp the open-ended possibilities. As if already post-human and autonomous, they began to type, "Dear Emma Thompson."

I tried not to fawn. Just a nice, respectable note of appreciation, making sure to slip in how I'd never written a letter like this one before. I wrote a few paragraphs, saying how great she was in *Sense and Sensibility*, especially the special effects, and how sorry I was about

330

the whole Branagh thing. I sent the letter off, addressing it: Somewhere in England. It sounds foolish to admit: I enjoyed writing it. But perhaps that's no more foolish than sitting in a room with a hundred strangers and cheering the exploits of looping, computer-driven anime. For that matter, it was certainly no more futile than writing a complaint to the phone company.

That night when the notification bubble popped up on my screen again, I had to force myself to finish the paragraph I was writing before clicking on it. The subdividing of all human tasks into ever-shorter switching cycles across the task bar may be the greatest impact of computers upon our lives. Back in DIALOGOS, there waited a charming and only mildly disjunctive note from something calling itself Emma Thompson, with all the details of her latest HBO shoot and a script she was working on about the Chilean poet Victor Jara. I . . . well, Reader, I wrote her back. We had a nice exchange of letters, the precise details of which you don't have to know anything about. Miss Thompson was a little flightier than I imagined, but I soon got used to the associative style. I found myself looking forward to her next note, even as the requests from real-world strangers piled up in my Inbox, needing answers.

The disembodied Emma was remarkably informed, at least about the details of her own works and days. She made no mention of the new boyfriend or the baby. But then, my notes never asked her about either. DIALOGOS's genius advance over the usual ALICE-style chatterboxing was to batch the exchange at a higher grain than the individual sentence. If we humans are snagged by another's thought, we wait for the next sentence to clarify it. There's something almost paradoxical about wetware, the very opposite of reductionist problem solving: it's easier to grasp two handfuls than one.

It suddenly struck me: the whole Turing Test was based on the plausibility of a deception. The test's functionalist definition suggests that intelligence is a product, not a process. At the moment I saw these responses appear, nothing seemed to me further from the truth. Banter from feebleminded rules was of no use to us humans. We are after silliness on a grand scale, idiocy done for the most ingenious reasons. My Emma was hit or miss, but the more cues I gave her, the more she responded with something at least vaguely contextualized and coherent. In fact, some of her paragraphs had such brilliant splashes of vulnerability to them that, after about a dozen notes back and forth, I began to suspect I was being set up.

331

I sent Bart an e-mail via the real thing. I tried not to sound suspicious or unnerved. "Where exactly are these letters coming from?"

He claimed his team had worked out a clever set of algorithms that sidestepped the long debate between AI's symbolic-representation folks and its heuristics folks:

> We stuff the syntatic hooks *into* the semantics. Everything's case based. The agents learn by iterative stimulus and response. They create a self-pruning lexical map, enjoying a kind of natural selection, depending on the responses they get. But that's not the real power. We've written a query language that can treat even unstructured text as a database, chaining inferences and matching patterns. All we need is a sufficiently large text base to tap into. And look what we have out there, ready-made: two billion pages of collective unconscious, and growing! Think of this thing as Google meets Babelfish, tied to an accreting expert system. Once we find a chunk of good page hits, we slice up the matching bits of neighboring lexias and reassemble them along one of the two dozen kinds of flow structures that meaningful discourse follows. Maybe that doesn't sound like a lot of leeway. But how many plots do *you* use?

I could feel him trying to snow me. I wrote back. "So you're telling me that there's no canned, scripted agent that actually *writes* these things?"

He admitted that they did, in fact, use a complex personality-profile module with a dozen different variable sliders, something like Myers-Briggs on steroids. "But we try not to instantiate the variables until we have to. That way, the 'personality' can grow its own semantic map from triggering phrases, based on whatever it gleans from cues in your prompts, plus any applicable matches its engine dredges up from the Web."

I said that sounded like a planet-size game of Mad Libs. "Just mix and match? Then how do you get such a powerful sense of presence and credibility?"

He shot back a one-liner: "Remember the Kuleshov Experiment."

I had to Google the term. Lev Kuleshov, Soviet silent-film director, the father of montage, alternately intercut the same shot of a man's face with shots of soup, a teddy bear, and a child's coffin. With each new splice, viewers saw in the face different emotions, although the footage was exactly the same. Someone indeed *was* authoring these letters, Bart suggested. And that someone was me.

I wasn't buying. Not entirely. The digital Miss Thompson was too good at choosing her shots and splices. There had to be some degree of human intervention involved, if only in compositing the flow of her associations. I went into DIALOGOS and sent off a letter. To Emily Dickinson. Amherst, Mass. I told her who I was, where I was writing from, and when. An hour later, I heard back. "Greetings to Urbana, Mr. Lincoln's old law-clerk town. Has Illinois declared war on Indiana yet?"

That was good, better than Bart himself had proved capable of in his own letters. But with an hour, a fast machine, and a broadband connection, even a hacker had all the resources of a poet at his disposal. I decided to flood the input channels. I dashed off three dozen letters in under an hour, to everyone I could think of. I was Bellow's Herzog, all over again. I wrote to old friends and colleagues, to comedians and heads of corporations, to the President, to fictional characters from the classics and favorite contemporary books, even to characters I invented on the spot. I released my barrage, then sat back and waited for my interlocutor to come out waving the software white flag. Within the hour, the responses started coming in. Reply after reply, voice after voice, faster and more textured than any group of digital impractical jokers could hope to jerry-rig. I read through the list, even as new messages kept appearing. I got everything from "Remind me where we met again?" to "Richard! What a surprise to hear from you!"

Few of the notes came close to passing the Turing Test for intelligent equivalence. But more of them amused me than even my unrepentant, strong-AI inner child could have hoped. Some of the message senders even claimed to have heard from one another, as if the burst of notes I'd sent out were already being traded and forwarded among all interested parties, triggering new memos that I wasn't even privy to. I felt a rush of queasy excitement, the kind of stomach twist you can get by bouncing from theater to theater at a multiplex, skimming, in a handful of five-minute samples, the sum of this instant's contribution to the eternity of world culture.

Some part of me revolted at how thrilling these figments felt, even after the repeating ping of my real Inbox had long since conditioned in me a permanent, Pavlovian dread of incoming messages. Why was it such a pleasure to get yet another dose of the cacophony of signals that every day threatens to overwhelm me? What is it about the free-floating signs for things that will make us fool around for hours and hours at those same anxious tasks that tie us into ulcerous knots during the workweek? Why, for the last quarter century, have games driven the development of cutting-edge software and hardware, producing spin-off technologies that overhaul the pragmatic world? More concerted ingenuity has gone into the Xbox and its supporting game cartridges than went into all of Project Apollo. What is it that we need from play and its dead-serious, relentless flow of symbols?

I didn't worry these questions for long. I couldn't afford to. I was awash in messages. The hive was humming, and it wanted me humming back. I could say anything I wanted to anyone, and there would be a million linked consequences, none of them consequential.

I skimmed through the stories now swarming all over me. Some were incoherent non sequiturs: this is your e-mail on drugs. Some hid little hints of buried, narrative threat worthy of Apollinairian automatic writing or Ernstian collective-unconscious collage. Others were more generic than greeting cards. Some notes read like a shotgun marriage of the AP wire and a stalker's journal. Yet as far as I was concerned, none was anywhere near as schizoid as the new-format CNN. In most, I could feel the thoughts being forced into formal arcs, much like a freshman composition class's first foray into the five-paragraph essay. But some responses stopped me cold and left me reading them over and over. One came from an old friend of mine I'd gone to grade school with. I'd included him in my letter-writing salvo as someone who'd get a laugh out of the forwarded correspondence, once the experiment was done. The man's name was unusual enough that, with a few prompts from my opening letter, DIALOGOS had found him in the billions of pages of public databanks and fleshed him out:

> Dear Rick,
> I can't tell you how happy I am to hear from you. I've lost my job teaching at Charleston. Susan has left me. None of this is my fault. I'm not fit for anything anymore. All I want to do is read novels about the Vietnam War.

My friend, or his autonomous avatar, reeled out these facts, chopped up and reassembled from material available on various Web pages, blended with my own cues and shaped to match the case-based, classical tension plots that DIALOGOS knew all about. All the details were right, and cobbled together into a wonky but idiomatic whole that I almost believed. Maybe nothing but a brain-dead, formal template was driving the outburst. But then, every human outburst had its own driving template, each year increasingly less hidden to us. I felt as if my friend had gone down the rabbit hole into a parallel plausibility and was now living in a Photoshop filter of his life that only the universal transforms and signal processings of the digital age could have rendered. The effect was so uncanny that I gave in to the urge to call my friend. But for some reason, I didn't tell him why I'd called. Maybe I felt suckered. Maybe I wanted a little more hands-on time with this story generator, to see whether suckered was the right way to feel. Maybe I was just ashamed at having so robustly corresponded with the fictional counterpart of a friend I hadn't written to in over a year.

Then there was the reply to the note I'd sent out addressed simply to "Young Werther, Walheim, the Duchy of Saxe-Weimar-Eisenach." I'd mailed him in my mass barrage, saying that this fellow Wilhelm he was always writing to seemed a bit of a sot, and if he really wanted someone to commiserate with over that dame Charlotte, I was his man.

He wrote back: "My Dear Friend." That seemed to me a bit sudden. But he went on:

> What a thing is the heart of man! You are kind to write. I thank you for your offer. You ask about Wilhelm, and about Charlotte. I believe they are both happy, perhaps happier than I.

I could feel the style matcher running through its frequency profiles. Clearly, the story was elliptical, clunky, and underwritten. But to my horror, it *was* a story. Werther's five sentences made me want to know what happened next. I had learned by now how to shape my letters so as to give the greatest possible seed for their response. I sent such a letter to Werther, trying to steer him toward some new twist of plot.

He wrote back several things that were only marginally lucid. I chalked that up to Sturm und Drang. But I didn't really care, because he also wrote several things I couldn't have anticipated. Charlotte was upset, he reported, and it had nothing to do with her impending marriage to Albert. She was not acting herself, my Werther assured me. This slip of the mechanical rules delighted me beyond description, every bit as much as I'd once delighted at childhood read-alouds. So long as Werther kept saying things I couldn't see through in advance, I was hooked.

I asked for details. He said he thought someone might have been blackmailing Charlotte. She had made some mistake in the past, and now she couldn't escape it. The digital Werther was plagiarizing; this plot, too, I'd read no end of times before. But it didn't matter. The sense of watching this description unfold in all its fluctuating particulars, and the knowledge that I could press and pursue it in any direction I wanted, beat the best train set in existence. Within a couple of days, I settled into the rhythmic synching and entrainment that comes when I've found my way into a good, unprecedented book. I felt almost the way I'd once felt, settling into the real *Werther*, back when I was twenty.

I lost some weeks to DIALOGOS. Maybe not as many as I'd lost long ago, in my first pass through Goethe. But the days vanished into invention all the same. This maze would gladly take from me as much time as my mind wanted to give. My duties at the university began to feel like impediments, and weekend dinner parties were interruptions in the flow of events that I was now addicted to unraveling. I began paying the same attention to this epistolary world as I ordinarily paid to my own fiction. For I felt at some level that this one *was* mine. This was the place where all my deserting circus animals had come, to run through their hidden paces. If I was away from the interface for more than a few hours, I became edgy and distracted. I was falling into every danger that eighteenth-century moralists once warned novels would generate, back when novels were a new enough technology for their users still to conflate them with the things they stood for.

Werther had by then headed off to Weimar on a whim, and he was sending back accounts—rich, evocative descriptions of the city that I remembered visiting in my twenties. He'd gotten a tip about a man who lived there, a so-called poet and philosopher whom Werther feared had the goods on his Charlotte and who was the cause of her acting so strange and remote. I egged him on a little, maybe. It was only a story, after all.

Then Charlotte wrote. Bart had warned me that any of these story actants could generate new ones, just by my mentioning them aloud. But all the same, Charlotte's letter stunned me. Reading it filled me with guilt. Charlotte knew I was corresponding with Werther, and she begged me to keep him from making any further inquiries. She was sure it could lead only to more misery.

It dawned on me, when I collected myself: *of course* some human had written this. There was human intervention, human scripting at every level of this multidimensional story. Only not the simple kind of human intervention I'd imagined. *We* had named all these words, cobbled up all these phrases, told all these stories. We'd built the repository and hammered out the organizing structures. We'd designed the machines that linked, sorted, arranged, indexed, and retrieved. Bart and his friends had identified the two dozen plots available to fiction. Our narrative fingerprints were all over every hard- and software fable that underwrote the digital age. DIALOGOS—that latest level of human narrative invention—merely trotted them out and rebound them into a new anthology, a running montage.

Who else was there, but us? The machine was not some other, alien, inhuman teller. It was our same old recombinant tale, recut and retold. And every night this latest Scheherazade went on telling me, *What is this tale, compared to the one I will tell you tomorrow night, if you but spare me and let me live?*

For just a moment, I saw it. If we have become obsessed with somehow giving voice to the machine, it must be because there is some voice within us, straining to free itself from *its* mechanism. What else is fiction, if not that strain? And from the beginning, fiction has itself followed a classic story, a plot of rising technical complication, all the tools with which that voice has learned to depict itself: first narration, then direct discourse, then voice as dramatic participant, reporting in real time. Then the invention of the first-person narrator, free indirect discourse, double voicing, stream of consciousness, all the devices of interiority that reflect, with always one more twist and inversion, consciousness's own tangled loops of self-narrating. So why not this next step into exteriority, one that isn't outside us at all, but just the ageless reader again, in the dark, saying *tell me another?*

I wrote to Bart, telling him what I had wrought. "My God, man. What on earth happens next?" He sent me back a Web address. I clicked on it. I'll click on anything, once. The link led to a discussion board, just like the kind proliferating in a hundred thousand venues all across the Net. This one had 1,800 posts in 162 threads, all of them generated in the first two days of the board's existence, all posted and answered by Werther, Charlotte, Wilhelm, Albert, Charlotte's father—the various character agents I'd launched into being by writing to Werther in the first place. Bart sent me the address of an IRQ channel. I entered a chat room where all these story actants blasted away at each other in a flood of concurrent, real-time responses too fast for me to read.

SimCity was running itself, even while my machine was off. The story had grown tendrils that were beyond my ability to follow. I reeled from the sites as from the edge of a gaping abyss. But closing my browser, of course, did nothing to stop the activity. Not even uninstalling DIALOGOS from my system would do that. The story was out there, telling itself forward. Notifications kept popping up in my system tray, increasingly edgy letters from Werther, from Charlotte, from the authorities in Weimar who wanted character background on this public menace, from Goethe himself, whom my friend had located and begun to harass.

Then I started getting missives from characters neither I nor the other characters in my adventure seemed to have invoked. They were seeping up out of the data structure, spun off by the expanding narrative web. Nor had the other stories I'd set in motion stopped. I got an e-mail from Amherst, from Emily Dickinson, whom I hadn't even thought about in the four months since I'd cruelly brought her back to life. Her note said only:

> This is my letter to the man
> Who never wrote back to me.

I got mail from my father, who died in 1978. The subject line read: "Where are you?" I deleted it, unopened.

It seemed to me, at that moment, that we had invented real time as a last resort for structuring the runaway feedback of mind looking upon itself.

I knew this plot, too, the rising, doubling, dividing waters. I wrote to Bart. "Help me."

He wrote back. "You remember that Forster story 'The Machine Stops'?"

I grabbed it from Blackmask, one of those repositories of instantly downloadable e-texts, sites whose business model seems to depend upon giving away millions of gigabytes of classic—that is to say, public domain—data, for free. I loaded the file on my Pocket PC and took it out to the park down the block, to read in Microsoft Reader. This must have been something like June. I felt somehow jumpy, heightened, oversensitized, and it took me some minutes to place the cause: sunlight.

On my little three-inch LCD, I scrolled through Forster's fossilized memory, posted forwarded from 1909, the story of woman in her cubicle surrounded by all needed inputs, whose son badgers her over the videophone, from his own self-contained cubicle on the other side of the world, with his perverse desire to see her, face to face. I read about that backed-up jam of irate signals that flood into your cell again after even a three-minute respite off-line. "We say 'space is annihilated,'" I read. "But we have annihilated not space, but the *sense* thereof." Nor time neither, but just the sense thereof.

"Know what I think?" Bart wrote. His e-mail came into my Pocket PC across the 802.11b wireless connection as I sat on the park bench.

> I don't think the problem is meat versus soul at all. Not real versus imagined, not palpable versus disembodied. Not carbon versus silicon. Not discrete, digital coldness versus continuous, analog warmth. Maybe it's not even fixed versus fungible, exactly. I think all our anxiety about story comes down to wanting versus getting. Hunger versus consummation.

I looked out onto the age of narrative consummation. And it seemed to me that, as with any good story, where everything can happen, nothing will. When the age of information at last turns into the age of unbounded narration, our stories will suffer the same fate of overproduction that already ravages so many other deflating consumer commodities and threatens to shatter our entire system of exchange. The world has already begun to split between the artificial value of Now Opening that props up market value by preserving scarcity and fabricating demand, and the five thousand prior years of human fiction, every word of which will proliferate and vary without limit, unsalable and therefore free. And what story will we tell about ourselves, when every story in the world except this minute's is available to us, everywhere, at all times, infinitely pliable and able to run its course to any imaginable ending?

"What on earth can we do?" I e-mailed Bart.

The answer came back, "Ask Werther."

I tried to reach him on DIALOGOS through the remote desktop client, over my wireless base station a block away. That was technology's need: to make sure we were never off the network, never alone. But Werther wasn't answering. I got the news from Charlotte, only two and a half minutes after I sent off an inquiry to her. Werther was, of course, dead. Goethe had told him that this wasn't his story at all. And Werther had pressed on, found out about the network, Cambridge, DIALOGOS—all of which struck Charlotte as mere raving. Werther had wanted the truth; Werther couldn't handle the truth. He did what was in his data structure to do.

And this is what will save us, finally: even self-telling stories end.

I e-mailed Bart with the news. By way of consolation, he cited the Borges quote. No doubt it's out there in scores of slightly variant copies, swimming in the primordial soup of the Web, waiting for a spark to turn them all animate:

> A man sets himself the task of drawing the world. As the years pass, he fills the empty space with images of provinces and kingdoms, mountains, bays, ships, islands, fish, houses, instruments, stars, horses, and people. Just before he dies he realizes that the patient labyrinth of lines traces the image of his own face.

"Know what I think?" I told Bart. "I think I invented you. Threw you together out of my own data trail."

"Then you must have needed me for something," he wrote back.

If I had, I didn't anymore. He and his program had given me what I needed. I stood up from the park bench, shaky on my pins. I knew this plot, too. I felt that keen unwillingness of the last, dissolving page. The old moratorium was finished again: my leave of absence was over.

And then what happened? Then I walked back toward home. Maybe it was high summer. Two thousand and one was only halfway through. The hardest of that year's unpredictable plots was still to come. Nothing we ever tell ourselves about the future prepares us for it.

I reached my block. The sun was setting, an implausible magenta. I passed under a maple the size of a cathedral and looked up into the deafening roost of several thousand starlings. There are two ways of reading our digital fate, the same two ways of reading any fiction. Either we'll explain ourselves away as mere mechanism, or we'll elevate mechanism to the level of miracle. Either way, the greatest worth of our machines will be to show us the staggering breadth of the simplest human thought and to reawaken us to the irreducible heft, weight, and texture of the entrapping world.

The hook-nosed, ancient, bent-double guy who lives across from me and who has never touched a computer in his life and who bugs the hell out of me by parking his rusted-out Ford Fairlane on top of my hosta and who, it hit me, looks a little like Werther might have if he'd outlived himself, grown up, fathered three kids, worked for Kraft Foods, and retired at seventy was out watering his lawn. I went up to him and asked how he was. He launched into more detail than I could hope to survive. But I listened, as if he and I and a few other story-starved neighbors were holed up outside a plague-ravaged Florence and were about to write the whole bloody *Decameron*. Together, again. For the first time.

Nominated by Zoetrope: All Story

RICHARD NIXON'S 1972 CHRISTMAS BOMBING CAMPAIGN AS GOSPEL

by QUAN BARRY

from THE GEORGIA REVIEW

How the Word came hammering to earth.

Or the story we tell ourselves this time of year—that some of us
were foundlings, & that some of us were given up freely.

Imagine scouring the countryside for even the smallest hamlet,
a clean place to rest & begin.

Or the forests scorched & utterly wrecked. Or the full rabbit moon
like a grenade.

What was rising in the east? What is it about this season
& the innocent?

Today on the news, the government has finally agreed to go back
& find what it can—the ordnance
dormant, biding.

What does it mean that it ever happened at all—the planes
an annunciation, & the people desperate to remain
uncounted.

Then I was a small hole in the darkness.

& they were terrified.

Nominated by Katherine Min, Renée Ashley

JOHN MUIR'S ALASKAN RHAPSODY

essay by EDWARD HOAGLAND

from THE AMERICAN SCHOLAR

JOHN MUIR (1838–1914), being diligent first and a dreamer second, wore many hats. So although he was a visionary—a founder of the Sierra Club and savior of Yosemite National Park—we do have quite a wonderfully meticulous record of the progress of his visions. In middle age and on the brink of his belated marriage, after considerable wandering in the Great Lakes and Appalachian wildernesses as a rattled and anguished but indefatigable young man, and then more definitively in California's High Sierra as an amateur botanist and geologist, he went almost inevitably to Alaska. Where else would an American rhapsodist of wild places ultimately go? Joy, in fact, was his currency, although he didn't know it at the time. He thought that in such scenic mightiness he was studying glaciers: and he did do some original work on them. But a century and a quarter later, we are reading his account because there in the glorious fiords, "the great fresh unblighted, unredeemed wilderness," he is at our elbow, nudging us along, prompting us to understand that heaven is on earth—*is* the Earth—and rapture is the sensible response wherever a clear line of sight remains.

Thoreau's more famous agenda, back East in Massachusetts sixty years before *Travels in Alaska* was finished, had been to try to alter the way that people lived, with regard both to nature and to each other. Thus, wilderness figured as rather a minor factor in *Walden's* ruminations. The godhead could be located much nearer home, in a backlot pond ("earth's eye"), as well as in a mountain massif. At one point elsewhere Thoreau advocated that every township should preserve one square mile in a natural state. Hardly a wilderness but sufficient—you didn't need to roam the frontier in order to find it.

Muir, although he carried a volume of Thoreau's essays on his first trip to Alaska, seems to have expected that you did need to roam the frontier, and we are the beneficiaries because he exerted his string-bean frame so strenuously to search. The journal jottings from which he fashioned most of his books, often decades later, were originally the product of scientific more than literary ambition, but otherwise were hymns of praise. He lived for Emersonian Transcendentalism perhaps more singlemindedly than even Emerson or Thoreau—who were involved in the Abolition movement and other controversies such as women's rights and the injustice of the Mexican War, and the contemporary intellectual currents that they lectured on for a livelihood: an activity that the shyer Muir didn't begin to take to until later in life, and then only as a polemicist for the cause of preservation.

Muir was up in mountains that would have flabbergasted the Massachusetts men—mountains of a pelagic scale that dwarfed the White Mountains or Mount Katahdin. There is no disjunction, however, between their concepts of nature except that the New Englanders more fully comprehended that human nature is a part of nature and were more interested in it. Muir, awestruck by the cathedral, kept gazing up into the nave, whereas Thoreau had a habit of noticing and quarreling with the conduct of the parishioners. And until lately, when we have become a bit panicky at the disappearance of wild landscapes nearly everywhere, and what we call "the natural world," Muir was scanted as a marginal, a johnny-one-note, figure. A few decades ago, it was hard to find an Eastern literary person who had even heard of him, and, although I *had*, my appreciation of his love of radiance, his seize-the-day impetuosity yet tireless exactitude—so calm, except about life's gleeful dimensions—has grown by leaps and bounds. Despite extraordinary feats of derring-do, he didn't climb to conquer nature but to witness and to savor it, testing not his braggadocio but his faith: which is more interesting.

Thoreau (1817–62) himself had required at least half a century posthumously to gather much attention, although pantheism is a big-tent religion. It was especially exalting for a self-taught observer like Muir, because God does indeed reside in the details. Canoeing in the outwash of huge glaciers was geology sprung alive. Like Bach on

Sunday, he found that he was delineating the anatomy, the raiments, of joy. Nobody is against natural grandeur; monotheists accept the premise that God created that too. And Alaska itself is a big tent, perennially compelling as a "last" wilderness. But it was the tumult Muir reveled in that scares most of us. He was elastic and enlivened out-of-doors, rising as if on a thermal, or like a fish freed from an aquarium. This era before the Klondike Gold Rush brought in crowds of settlers, and almost thirty years before Mount McKinley was first climbed, exhilarated instead of intimidating him.

Jack London would preempt Muir's rapturous interpretations of Alaska for decades to come with his tales of nature red in tooth and claw—just as now we tend to neglect London for Muir. Both were Californians; both had had brutalized childhoods (Muir's in Scotland, his birthplace, and in Wisconsin), which made them rolling stones and ardent romantics; London's religion was socialism. And both wrote immortal dog stories based on real animals—Buck, the brave, wolfish hero of *The Call of the Wild*, and Stickeen, of *Stickeen*, the intuitive, intrepid Border collie mix who accompanied Muir on several hairy Alaskan ice-field adventures near the Stikine River. But London (1876–1916) died at forty, burnt out, disillusioned, whereas Muir ripened into a seventy-six-year-old celebrity replete with loving daughters and grandchildren and a roster of national accomplishments. He knew that having influenced two presidents, Roosevelt and Taft, toward preservationist action was of lasting significance and that his magazine articles had been battle-tested. But he probably never recognized that his books, as books, would have real staying power, too. Otherwise he wouldn't have written *My First Summer in the Sierra* at the end of his life from forty-year-old notes; dictated his autobiography, *The Story of My Boyhood and Youth*, to the millionaire railroadman Edward Harriman's secretary, only at Harriman's insistence; and postponed the completion of *Travels in Alaska* (a better book) until pneumonia beat him to the punch and another sympathetic secretary had to do the final editing.

Just as, like Thoreau and Emerson, he didn't foresee the furnace of destruction, ever-accelerating industrially and technologically, that would afflict nature worldwide, Muir was not in a position to imagine how rare his experiences, and especially his frequent bouts of virtual ecstasy, would strike and register with us—"dancing down" the mountains, sunbeaten, trackless mountains themselves "made divine." Because of Charles Darwin, Rudyard Kipling, the Brothers Grimm, and the cutthroat competition of free enterprise, a nature portrayed like London's as red in tooth and claw was no surprise to most people. But for nature conveyed as glee we had to remember writers like Ivan Turgenev and W. H. Hudson, or the *Odyssey* and the biblical Song of Songs. In a burstingly utilitarian, expansive country it had been considered countereconomic, "backward" like a primitive shaman, to conceive of nature as rapturous and therefore potentially precious—that was for the Indians, who had been decimated and swept aside in the march of progress. Yet Muir's longevity isn't due just to his being on the right-thinking side of a farsighted struggle. So were George Perkins Marsh (1801–82), his precursor protoconservationist, and others who have since disappeared from the debate. Muir loved the world—loved Creation—so much that we, being part of it, can warm to him almost physiologically as we read along. Dire prophecies don't work as well on us as rhapsodies. Muir was a rather shaky, chilly, wounded individual in person, like many nature writers who are seeking a balm for their injuries. But he loved the calving, thunderous glaciers, the "fountaining" snowfields way high up among the peaks that were their source, and the rainy maritime clouds that replenished these. The green waves and white spindrift shone in a fitful sunlight that was refracted amazingly, prismatically through the stunning planes of ice—blue and red—as the weather revolved around his thirty-six-foot Tlingit dugout canoe, with an occasional seal hunter bobbing by in a smaller craft offering him a fresh salmon for ten cents.

The joy he felt was hard to ascribe simply to Evolution's provision for survival tools. I've been to the mouth and watershed of the Stikine myself, during the middle 1960s, when it still seemed somewhat *the way the world was made*, as I kept murmuring to myself; watching seals surfacing in the tangled currents, the salmon running, the eagles posted profusely in the trees, the swimming otters, beavers, bears, and teeming rafts of river birds. I goggled and grinned—mainly at the dashing, wheeling mobs of waterbirds, the sudden sandbars and piled-up drift logs challenging our boat, the river's jumbo, roaring rush and backwash sloughs, under the snowy, high horizons—never having seen such dimensions of gush and ebullience before. Words were so fragile by comparison that Muir must have thought them inadequate to the task of conveying everything he had witnessed on these herculean trips. But not knowing how frangible the wilderness itself would prove to be, he couldn't guess how valuable his experiences, even partially preserved, would come to seem.

In *Travels in Alaska*, a valedictory bouquet to the magic of life, presented in his middle seventies—when, more confidently, he'd plucked some of the high points of his memories—Muir censored his personal reactions less timorously and betrayed more intimacy with his companions than in lonewolf books like *A Thousand Mile Walk to the Gulf*, *My First Summer in the Sierra*, and *The Mountains of California*, that retrieve earlier history. In Alaska, in his forties, he had felt much more empathy with the Tlingits than he ever had with California's shattered "Digger" Indians, while in his thirties. And to the Tlingits he was a "Boston man," their term for American whites, because the first Americans they had met were whalers out of Massachusetts, as distinct from the Russian fur-seal hunters who initially laid claim to Alaska. So by this amusing bit of irony, which Muir must have perceived, he was at last linked with his heroes in Concord, Thoreau and Emerson.

Yet because of the magnetism of the landscapes he gravitated toward, which were biblical in scale and "innocence" and ballasted his jitters, he is unique. Unique, as well, because interstitial to his effusions of frank and genuine inspiration (such as the great British explorers seldom indulged in) were the kind of close, specific observations that a man of science would demand of his notes, which keeps them intriguing for us. We wind through these drenched and bristly islands with him, a man as spartan as but less judgmental of the early gold rushers than Thoreau would have been, and more interested, in any case, in "the plant people," "the little ones as well as the trees," than in the human ones, even the Indians, while the clouds are "fondling" the mountainsides. "Standing here," he says near Cape Fanshaw, "one learns that the world, though made, is yet being made; that this is still the morning of creation." Which echoes *Walden*'s celebrated ending: "There is more day to dawn. The sun is but a morning star."

Not a caroming radical fixated on brute force, like Jack London, or a spiky contrarian like Thoreau, Muir was a practical, canny Scotsman grounded in exactitude but bathing in a splendidly self-effacing joy. He had been to the Nile and Amazon, to China, Siberia, and India by the time he finally put his nose to the grindstone and wrote his fragmentary Alaska book, and wasn't tempted to gussy it polemically. He

348

wished to steep it in the exuberance he felt, and sustains the narrative thrust and the timbre of his superlatives more convincingly than in earlier books. Love was the well-spring of all his work, but these memories were doubly intense and central. He was truly a *coureur de bois*, a "runner of the woods," a sort of Franciscan Daniel Boone, who upbraided his Indian companions when they shot more than one deer (he himself ate bread, rice, and beans) and rocked the canoe to spoil their aim when they tried for a duck.

Transcendentalism, located between Puritanism and pragmatism in America's philosophical development, has an enduring appeal, and Muir lived it as an exemplary avatar. Though his mind was narrower than Thoreau's, his life, which stretched much longer, was broadened further, with reams of new experiences and new acquaintances. Then, in old age, white-bearded, he even played a docent's role for hikes and overnighters with members of the Sierra Club. (Indeed, it might be argued that Thoreau, after the disappointment of *Walden*'s failure to find much of a readership, became increasingly Muir-like in his focus upon natural history, until he died of tuberculosis at forty-four.) For both of them, heaven was the here and now, with daily intimations of divinity. This exhilaration is what gradually lifted Muir out of the category of regional California writer, such as Bret Harte, in which he once languished. He had possessed a marked charisma, for those who knew him, and a bully pulpit in magazines like *The Overland Monthly* and *The Atlantic Monthly* for hortatory purposes. But the high-pitched extravagance of his Alaska account, with a waterfall of observations accompanying it, about the Stikine and Taku rivers and Sum Dum Bay and Glacier Bay, is not arguing a point. It is a riff and a testament, when he was at death's door, of days back in paradise, hasty-paced because his stay was limited. He had had to leave his calling there and go and get married (again, the next year, for the birth of his first baby) and breathe the nitrogen of ordinary life instead of pure oxygen. He was dutiful enough, but we have other writers who have chronicled domesticity and scarcely any who have gone up unravished rivers to the meadows, rock, and ice of origination. As more and more of us grow aghast at what we have done to the world we started with, Muir's reverence and devotion will seem keenly germane, and our regret may be transmuted into a fight for the future.

Nominated by Rick Bass

THE DRAGON

by BRIGIT PEGEEN KELLY

from NEW ENGLAND REVIEW

The bees came out of the junipers, two small swarms
The size of melons; and golden, too, like melons,
They hung next to each other, at the height of a deer's breast
Above the wet black compost. And because
The light was very bright it was hard to see them,
And harder still to see what hung between them.
A snake hung between them. The bees held up a snake,
Lifting each side of his narrow neck, just below
The pointed head, and in this way, very slowly
They carried the snake through the garden,
The snake's long body hanging down, its tail dragging
The ground, as if the creature were a criminal
Being escorted to execution or a child king
To the throne. I kept thinking the snake
Might be a hose, held by two ghostly hands,
But the snake was a snake, his body green as the grass
His tail divided, his skin oiled, the way the male member
Is oiled by the female's juices, the greenness overbright,
The bees gold, the winged serpent moving silently
Through the air. There was something deadly in it,
Or already dead. Something beyond the report
Of beauty. I laid my face against my arm, and there
It stayed for the length of time it takes two swarms
Of bees to carry a snake through a wide garden,
Past a sleeping swan, past the dead roses nailed
To the wall, past the small pond. And when

I looked up the bees and the snake were gone,
But the garden smelled of broken fruit, and across
The grass a shadow lay for which there was no source,
A narrow plinth dividing the garden, and the air
Was like the air after a fire, or before a storm,
Ungodly still, but full of dark shapes turning.

Nominated by Theodore Deppe, William Olsen, Marianne Boruch, New England Review

WHY THE SKY TURNS RED WHEN THE SUN GOES DOWN

fiction by RYAN HARTY

from TIN HOUSE

I GET THE CALL as my wife is setting the table for dinner. It's our neighbor Ben Hildeman, who tells me in a breathless voice that my son has had a problem.

"This is bad, Mike," Ben says, and in the background I hear his boys Tanner and Phillip talking in excited tones. "He fell and hurt his leg, is I guess what happened, but then he just sort of lost control. By the time I got there he was in the Kohlers' yard, banging his head against their air-conditioning unit."

"God, you're kidding," I say.

"I'm afraid it's pretty bad, Mike. Some of the kids are upset now. I wish you'd come down."

"I'll be right there," I say, and hang up the phone.

Dana comes into in the doorway with a bunch of utensils in her hand. "It's not about Cole?" she says, but she can see in my face that it is. "You should go, Mike. Hurry."

Running down Keehouatupa, past the subterranean houses, I'm hoping that whatever happened to Cole will have nothing to do with the trouble we had in Portland. I know Dana is thinking the same thing back at the house. We came to Arizona at the height of the D3 crisis, with high hopes that the desert air would be good for Cole.

Amazingly, in the seven months we've been here he's had not a single problem—no shutdown or twitching hands, no problems with speech or movement. We've only just begun to believe that things might be all right again.

Ben's house comes into view, a newly built subterranean with smoke-tinted skylights, a couple of date palms shimmering in the day's waning heat. Ben stands atop the grassy dome, a stocky man in jeans. Behind him are the red peaks of the Superstition Mountains. A half-dozen boys in shorts and tank tops stand at his side. Cole, I see, is not among them.

Ben jogs down and puts a hand on my shoulder. "I didn't want to touch him, Mike," he says. "He's around the back now. I think he might be unconscious."

"That's good, actually. It means he's in shutdown."

We climb the hill. From the top I see Cole laying belly down on the back slope, his legs splayed out behind him. He *is* in shutdown—there's that stillness about him—and I'm relieved to see it, though it's clear he's in horrible shape. His neck has twisted around so far that his chin seems to rest in the shallow valley between his shoulder blades. His right arm has come off completely and lies, bent at the elbow, a few yards away, multicolored wires curling out of the torn end. I get a lightheaded feeling and have to crouch for a moment and catch my breath.

"You all right?" Ben asks.

"I'll be okay."

"He just—" Ben gives me a squint-eyed look. "It's hard to describe it, Mike. It was crazy."

"So all this happened when he fell? The arm and everything?"

"That's what I was saying." He jerks a thumb at a metal box at the edge of the Kohlers' yard. "When I came out he was just banging against that thing like he wanted to knock it down or something. He made an electrical noise in his throat, sort of, a whirring sound."

I glance at the boys, who are all studying me carefully—six boys in a line on the hill.

"Everybody all right?"

They nod.

"I asked them to go home, but they wouldn't go," Ben says. "They're worried about their friend."

"Sure," I say. "Well, listen, guys, Cole's gonna be all right, you hear me?"

They nod again and glance at one another. These are good kids, all of them—Ben's son Tanner and our next-door-neighbor Sean Ho, and a Devin something whose parents I've met a few times. One of them, a red-haired boy I haven't seen before, looks as though he might be D3 himself; his skin seems to reflect the sun a little more directly than the other boys'. He holds his shoulders unusually straight. Most people can't see the difference, but D3 parents can more often than not. This kid looks as stunned as the rest of them.

I walk down the grassy slope and kneel beside Cole. His eyes are wide open and staring at nothing, and that's something I hate to see. I lay a hand on each of his cheeks, turn his head to the side and feel a pop—things seem looser inside him than they should be. I brush his bangs from his forehead, roll him to his back, and slip a hand under his T-shirt, feeling for the power button. I give it a push.

Cole's head jerks just slightly. His eyes change, almost imperceptibly, as if the dimmest light has gone on behind them. It's enough, though: he looks like my son again.

"Hey, buddy," I say.

He blinks at me. "Hey, Dad. What are you doing here?"

"I came to take you home."

He glances around, and I see the disappointment in his eyes, the look of understanding. "I had an accident," he says.

"I'm afraid so, kid. Do you remember what happened?"

"We were playing kick the can," he says, and draws his lips in, concentrating. "I was running, I think. I had a bad headache. I don't remember anything else."

I'm relieved he's come out of it alert and lucid, much better than at times in the past. During the bad period in Portland there were always problems upon switchback—inability to focus, slowed-down speech and movement.

"So listen, there are a few things I need to tell you," I say. "Things you may not want to hear." I help him to a sitting position, a hand at the small of his back. "For one thing, your arm's come off."

He touches his shoulder where the arm should be. A look of panic overtakes him.

"It's all right," I say. "It's just down the hill. We'll get it fixed up as soon as we can. I just want you to know what's going on, okay? The other thing is that I think there might be a little problem with your neck, but that'll be fine, too, I promise."

He swallows hard and looks at me. "What about my arm?" he says. "Aren't you going to put it on again?"

"I can't, pal. I wish I could. We'll have to bring it along to the hospital tomorrow."

He glances up at his friends on the hill. I know he's embarrassed about what's happened.

"Maybe you ought to say something to them," I tell him. "Let them know you're all right."

"I don't know what to say," he says.

"Just whatever you want. It'll make it easier when you see them the next time."

He seems to think for a moment, his tongue poking out between his lips. Then he glances up the hill and says, "Hey, guys, I'm all right and everything. I gotta go home, but I can probably come back tomorrow."

"Hey, that's terrific," Ben says, and glances around at the boys. "Isn't that great, guys?"

"Yeah," Tanner Hildeman says quietly. "That's great, Cole."

"We just hope you're okay and everything," Sean Ho says, then glances at Cole's arm where it lies on the grass. He turns to the other kids, and as if given a signal they all start down the hill. A couple of them raise their hands to Cole and Cole waves back.

"That wasn't so bad, was it?"

"I guess not," he says.

"You ready to go home to Mom now?"

"All right," he says, but there's a hint of hesitation in his eyes.

"What's the matter, kid?"

He shakes his head, then says, "Does Mom know what happened?"

"She knows you got hurt," I say. "She'll be glad to see you."

He glances up at the date palms in front of the house.

"What's the matter, pal?"

"Nothing," he says, but I can see there is. For the first time it occurs to me that he might know more about Dana and me than I've imagined.

· · · · ·

Dana is outside when we get home, standing at the edge of the lawn with an uneasy look on her face. I try to give her a reassuring nod,

355

but there's little use in that with Cole's arm tucked under my own like a rolled-up newspaper.

"Oh boy," she says, glancing from Cole to me and back. "You all right, kid?"

"I guess," he says, and looks at me.

"He's disappointed," I say.

"Of course," she says. "Who wouldn't be?" She brushes her hands down her sides glances at the house. Dana is an attorney at an intellectual property firm in Phoenix and makes a good living appearing composed when everything is going to hell around her. But I can see she's flustered now and it makes me feel suddenly tender toward her. Together we go into the house, where the air is cool and smells of pork chops and mashed potatoes.

· · · · ·

While Cole goes upstairs to get cleaned up, I walk into the kitchen. Dana is washing her hands and staring out the window. It's six o'clock and the sky has taken on the pinks and silvers of an abalone shell.

"Don't you think we ought to shut him down?" she says, and turns to me. "I can't stand to see him with his arm like that."

"I think it's better to keep him running if we can," I say. "We don't want him to get any more disoriented than he has to."

"I guess not," she says.

"He seems pretty good in most ways. This is probably nothing too serious."

"He's torn his own arm off, Mike," she says. "Of course it's serious."

"All right. I just mean it might be a mechanical problem. It's not necessarily anything chronic."

Her face is doubtful, weary. "Well, let's hope so," she says.

· · · · ·

At the top of the stairs I hear the faucet running in the bathroom. Cole bumps a knee against the cabinet under the sink and says, "Ouch," then the faucet shuts off with a knock. I walk into the master bathroom, where the face I see in the mirror is so pale it shocks me. I have to sit on the toilet for a while with my head between my knees. It's that echoey feeling I had in the Hildeman's yard, a feeling

356

I had a lot as a kid—at swim meets and at summer camps, and later during final exams in college. A doctor put me on Zoladex for a while when I was in my twenties, but I didn't like the way it made me feel—sedate and strangely detached from my life. I sit blotting my forehead with toilet paper, breathing deeply until my heartbeat slows.

I had these symptoms back in Portland, too, when Cole was at his worst and Dana and I disagreed about how to handle it. Dana wanted to get a new center chip for Cole then, one of the D4 units that seemed to work well for people at the time. To me that would have been like getting a new child altogether, since his personality wouldn't be the same. In D-children, experience affects development the way it affects a human child: D-children become who they are because of the lives they've lived. While it's possible to transfer memory, you cannot transfer a personality that's been formed over the years. We'd been told that the engineers could *approximate* Cole's personality type, which to me was worthless, though a lot of people disagreed with me. My wife happened to be one of them.

Dana's brother Davis had a D3 child of his own, a boy named Brice who suffered for years from the same kinds of problems as Cole—intermittent breakdown, loss of motor control. A year before we moved to Arizona, on the Tuesday before Thanksgiving, Brice disappeared after a martial arts class, and it was almost a week before they found him in a wooded field two miles north of Davis's house, where he'd apparently collapsed taking a shortcut home. A week later, Davis had a new center chip installed. The results were so positive he couldn't help calling us about it during our worst stretch with Cole. He knew how I felt about center chips; we'd discussed it many times. Davis had always been protective of Dana, and I'd never got the feeling he approved of me. I began to see his calls as a way of stirring up trouble between Dana and me.

And it worked, too. Brice was a high school junior then, a scholar-athlete and a truly fine kid, a boy Dana and I had always liked. But it was less his personality and accomplishments that impressed Dana, I think, than the sheer absence of D3-related problems. I remember Davis being worried about drugs at one point (he'd found a marijuana cigarette in Brice's underwear drawer), and even that became a selling point, because it was a *normal* problem. You couldn't miss the pride in Davis's voice when he told us about it—about the awkward talk he'd had with Brice, the two of them hashing it out for nearly an hour before finally hugging and crying. The point seemed to be that Brice was living a life of uninterrupted normalcy, and the insinuated question was, Why settle for a child who breaks down all the time when you can have a new one who won't?

I was dead set against it. It mattered absolutely to me that Cole be *my* child, the boy I'd come to know over the years. Dana and I fought about it more than we'd ever fought about anything, and in the end I think it changed the way we saw each other. She came to seem harder to me, less nurturing; I must have come to seem weak and sentimental. We'd met during our final year at the University of Oregon, and for the longest time had been amazed by how much we had in common—a penchant for old books and antiques; a respect for nature, a desire to have kids while we were still young enough to do everything with them. But as problems with Cole became worse, Dana receded, took on longer hours at work, grew distant when she was home. We argued about small, unrelated things, like the antiques we'd collected over the years. She said she felt hemmed in by them, even suggested we sell the old gas-powered Bonneville we'd loved to drive in college. For a few months that fall, I became convinced she was having an affair with a man named Stuart Solomon, a high-tech consultant at her firm. I never had solid evidence. Stuart's name turned up a few times on the caller ID, though he and Dana worked on different accounts. Twice, when Dana was supposed to be working late, I drove to her office and found that her car was not in the parking lot. I tried to confront her about it a few times, but always lost my nerve. There's no describing the relief I felt when the reports came in about D3 kids going problem-free in the Southwest. Suddenly there seemed reason to hope our lives could return to normal if we moved.

I stand and walk to the window. Outside, the rows of subterranean houses lie spread out like the fairways of a golf course. Mine is one of the few two-story houses left in the neighborhood now, and it costs so much to cool I'm sure I won't be able to keep it long—though I hate to think of giving it up, since it's a link to my past, to the two-story colonial my family still owns in Eugene. From where I stand, I can see the other two-story on the street, a big stucco home with a pool in the back. A light goes on in an upstairs window, and a man passes through a room. I've never spoken to this man before, but now I find myself thinking about him, wondering if he's anything like me, wondering if he feels himself being ushered into the future, away from the things that brought him comfort in the past.

• • • • •

Downstairs, Cole is carrying a basket of rolls to the table with his one good hand, singing "My Bonnie Lies Over the Ocean." It's a song he learned at summer camp, but he seems to have gotten some of the words wrong. Instead of singing "Bonnie," he sings "body." "My body lies over the ocean/My body lies over the sea." He sets the rolls on the table and goes back for more.

"Sit, honey," Dana says from the kitchen. "I'll get the rest."

"I don't mind," he says.

He takes a pitcher of water from the counter and starts into the dining room. Dana touches the back of his neck. I give her a look meant to say, "Doesn't he seem fine?" and she give me a more doubtful look, which says, I suppose, "We'll see." But she comes over and puts her arms around me—an offering of peace.

"All right, break it up," Cole says, hurrying back in. "Can't you see I'm starving here?"

We bring the rest of the food to the table. As we begin to pass dishes and talk I feel a little better. It seems as if we've gotten past the day's bad luck and tension.

"Good dinner, Mom," Cole says, forking up a bite of pork chop.

"Flattery will get you everywhere," she says, and gives him a small smile.

"Listen," I say, passing the rolls, "how'd you guys like to take the Bonneville out tomorrow? After we get everything taken care of at the hospital, we could head out to Papago Lake and have a picnic. Maybe drive around Tortilla Flats."

"All right," Dana says. "Sounds like a good idea."

"Cool with me," says Cole, and glances up from his plate.

Something is wrong with his eyes, I see. One of them points directly at me while the other seems to shoot off at a crazy angle toward the kitchen. I glance at Dana, who's noticed it too.

"What?" Cole says, looking from me to Dana. "What's wrong?"

"Nothing," Dana says, carefully. "It's just—can you see all right?"

"Yeah," he says, "why?"

I set the bowl of broccoli down and say, "Listen, kid, try this." I put

359

a hand in front of his face, then slowly move it until my fingers enter the line of his wayward eye. "Can you see my fingers now?"

"No," he says, and a flash of panic comes over him. "What's happening, Dad?"

"Well, I don't think it's anything to worry about. It looks like you've lost vision in one of your eyes, is all. But we're going to the hospital tomorrow anyway, right? They can fix this in a snap."

For a minute I think Cole might start to cry. "Gaw!" he says, and throws his balled-up napkin on the table. "I can't believe this!"

"Hey, come on," Dana says, her tone gentle but firm. She goes to Cole and kisses the crown of his head, and says, "Don't let it get you down." Then she gives me a look and walks into the kitchen. Cole and I keep on with our dinners. When Dana's been gone for a minute, I get up and go after her. She's at the sink; staring out the window at the fading sunset.

"We've got to shut him down, Mike. This is just scary. It's scaring *him*."

"I know," I say, because it's scaring me, too. I can't think of anything else to do about it.

"Hey, Dad," Cole calls from the dining room.

"What's up, pal?" I wait for an answer, but it doesn't come. "Be out in a second, all right?"

"Hey, Dad, what makes the sky red when the sun goes down?"

Dana breathes out a small laugh. Her face softens. For a moment she looks like the young woman I met in Oregon. I give her a kiss on the cheek and go into the dining room.

"That's just dust," I say. "Dust and pollution, actually."

But Cole isn't looking at me. He's pushing food across the table with his fingers, staring at the mess he's made. An electric drone comes from his throat.

"Cole?"

"I gotta go to the bathroom," he says, staring at the table. "I don't feel so hot." The drone in his throat gets louder.

"What's the matter, kid?"

He glances up, his expression suddenly sly. "I'll bet you a dollar," he says.

"What are you talking about, pal?"

Dana comes into the doorway. "What's going on, Mike?"

"Jesus H. Christ," Cole says, and suddenly laughs. "Holy-frickin'-shit!"

360

"Cole! Look up here," I say. "Look at me."

He raises his head, but his eyes veer in different directions. His jaw makes a clicking noise. Then he suddenly raises his head high and brings down it with a violent crack against the table.

"Cole!" I say.

He lifts his head again, his face covered with pork chop grease and broccoli. I try to get around the table to hold him down, but before I can get there his head hits the table with another crack, rattling the silverware. Dana shrieks. This time, when Cole's head comes up, it swings way back over one shoulder, loose and wild.

"My God, his neck!" Dana says.

"I see it! Help me hold him down."

I get a hand on his shoulder and try to reach under his shirt for the power button, but it's hard to get to with his head lolling around like a jack-in-the-box.

"Whoa!" he says. "Help me, Dad."

The smell of burning wires comes off him. He breathes out an electric wheeze, his head lolling, and then his face seems to fill with wonder and he goes perfectly still my arms. He turns to me, eyes clear and perfectly aligned.

"This is the best Christmas ever," he says.

I shut him down. His head thumps against the table. The electric drone cuts out. I wipe his face with a napkin and go into the kitchen, where I get a bottle of beer from the fridge. When I come back Dana is at the table, arms folded across her chest. She glances out the window.

"That's it, Mike," she says. "I mean it. This has got to stop."

•　•　•　•　•

The next morning I pull the Bonneville out of the driveway and carry Cole downstairs. Even with the seat belt over his shoulder, it's hard to prop him up in a way that looks natural. His head tips forward, making his mouth fall open. Dana and I have not talked about taking the Bonneville out since last night, and a picnic no longer seems like the best idea, but I'm in the mood to feel the thrum of the big gasoline engine, the vibration of the catalytic converter under my legs.

After a few minutes, Dana comes down and we take Highway 1073 past the mall and the hydroponics yards. The D-pediatric is twelve miles way, a sprawling complex on the outskirts of Olberg. As we drive, Dana stares out the window, her eyes steady and serious, her mouth drawn into a line.

Last night, after I shut Cole down and we cleaned up the mess in the dining room, Dana went into the den and called her brother Davis, and through the door I heard her talking softly. I couldn't make out what she said, though I'm certain it was something she couldn't say to me, since we went through the evening without another word about Cole. Sometime late in the night I woke to the sound of her crying and put a hand on her shoulder, and she moved into my arms for a while. It was like holding an injured animal; I couldn't help feeling she just needed a little time to heal, then she'd be out of my arms for good.

Afterward I lay awake, looking at the tiny red light of a smoke detector, listening as the wind pulled an ocotillo branch across the window. Dana was asleep, and Cole, I knew, was much farther away than that, gone in a sense, so that he was not even dreaming and would not wake up and call my name. I waited until the sky whitened in the window, then got up and walked down the hall and into his room. Cole lay dressed on top of the covers, his eyes closed, an inappropriate smile on his face. I had an urge to put his pajamas on him and tuck him into bed, but I knew it wouldn't make me feel better. Eventually I went down and started coffee and made bacon and eggs as the sky whitened through the windows.

·　·　·　·　·

We pass Mesa now, and the ground opens up to uncultivated fields and cacti. Just past Alvarado, I catch a glimpse of a coyote between the clumps of sage, golden brown and moving quickly, nose to the ground. It makes me think of driving out to Salmon Creek with Dana when we first got the Bonneville, years ago, laying a blanket across the back-seat and making love right in the car with the windows open, the sound of the wind coming through the firs.

In the rear-view mirror I see Cole propped against the door, his eyes closed, his mouth open. Dana is staring out the window. For some reason I imagine she's thinking of Davis, and it makes me angry.

"So suppose things get bad again," I say, and glance at her. "What do you think would happen then?"

362

"What do you mean, Mike?"

"Suppose this is the beginning of more bad times with Cole. We'd have to make some decisions then, right?" I know my voice is sharp, but it seems beyond my power to control it.

"Of course," she says.

"But you already know what you'd want to do," I say. "Isn't that right, too?"

"Come on, Mike, don't do this," she says. "I'm not in the mood for an argument right now."

"But suppose I need to know. Suppose it's important for me to know where we stand on this."

She sighs and glances out at the fields of brush. "Why do you have to push things all the time? What if I *can't* say what I'd do in every single situation? Can you?"

"I think I can. Yes."

"Can you, really, Mike? You can say what you'd do no matter what happens to him or to us?"

"What do you mean 'to us?'"

"Oh, God, I don't know," she says, and shakes her head wearily. "I just get tired of waking from the dream, don't you? Don't you get tired of being reminded he's not real?"

"He's as real to me as you are," I say, but when I glance at Cole in the rearview mirror he looks like what he is—a mechanical boy, a sophisticated doll for adults.

The desert floor runs out to a line of purple mountains. A ranch house slips past, then an electric plant, huge and complicated. For a moment I feel as if I don't know what's important to me, what matters the most. Dana has closed her eyes and is leaning back against the headrest.

"There was a coyote back there in a field," I say in a small voice. "I should have pointed him out to you."

· · · · ·

We wait for hours in the air-conditioned lobby, sitting on a vinyl couch, trying to read magazines while other parents come and go with their children. Through a tinted window, I see a slice of blue sky. A peregrine falcon dips into view now and then. Finally Dr. Otsuji comes down the hall in a crisp white coat and yellow tie. He

363

gives us his doctor's smile and sits on the chrome magazine table across from us.

"He's fine," he says. "We've fixed the arm and the neck, and right now he's just going through some tests to make sure everything's in good shape. He seems terrific."

Dana nods the way she does in court when conceding a point made by the opposition. "Do you have any idea what happened?" she asks.

The doctor turns up his eyes in concentration. "I'd call it an anomaly," he says, "though it could be more than that. It's like if you have an arrhythmia—unless we can check your heart when it's happening, we have a hard time knowing what causes it."

"But, in your opinion, is it likely we'll have more problems?" she asks. "Now that this has happened?"

Dr. Otsuji looks from one of us to the other, as if he'd just noticed the tension between us. "He's not showing any symptoms that would point to that, no," he says, "but to be honest, I don't see it as a good sign. For someone with Cole's history, you want as few problems as possible. Problems can lead to problems, is one way of looking at it."

Dana nods.

"Can we see him?" I ask.

"In a few minutes. He's a little upset, as you might expect. He's had a rough day. What I'd like to do is to put him out for a few minutes and run some numbers, then let him wake up naturally. I'll have the receptionist tell you when you can see him." He smiles in his professional way, then stands and shakes our hands and walks down the hall.

"Well, there it is," I say.

"I should call Davis," Dana says, and takes her bag up from the floor. "He'll want to know what happened."

She opens her cell phone, but before dialing she looks at me with an expression I've never seen before—her face hard, her eyes narrowed with what seems like pity. It's as if she's far away and needs to squint just to see me. "Listen, if you still want to go for a drive, that's fine. We can do that."

"Forget it. I don't really feel like it anymore."

"Well. Whatever. We'll go if you want to."

"I said I don't want to." The tone of my voice makes us both fall silent. She stands and walks down the hall.

Outside, clouds move across the sky, changing the light. A young family rushes into the lobby, the man carrying a blond, catatonic-looking girl in his arms. The child stares straight ahead with vacant eyes. I pick up a magazine, but there's no use trying to read or even think about anything before I'm able to see Cole. Finally, the receptionist calls my name and I get Cole's room number and go down the hall.

Cole's in a bed in a pale yellow hospital gown, asleep with his arms at his sides. His cheeks are flushed, his hair a little tousled. I stand above him and watch his chest rise and fall. He opens his eyes and glances around, then nods in a resigned way. "The hospital," he says.

"I'm afraid so, pal. They've fixed your arm, though. Check it out."

He raises the arm and rolls his shoulder. I can see he's trying to appear calm for my sake.

"Does it feel all right?"

"Pretty good," he says.

"We'll test it out with a game of catch. How's that sound?"

"All right."

"Maybe we'll drop your mom off at home and head out to Papago Park. I've got the Bonneville. We can just grab some mitts and go."

"Where *is* Mom?" he says, and gives me a worried look.

"Down the hall. Talking to your uncle Davis."

"Is she mad at me?"

"Of course not. Why would you say that?"

"I don't know," he says. "I know she doesn't like it when I break down all the time."

"You don't break down all the time," I say. "And anyway, none of this is your fault."

He seems distracted, as if he's trying to listen to Dana's voice down the hall. I can just hear her, a low, familiar sound coming over the tiles.

"Let's get you dressed and get your hair combed," I say. "We don't want people to think you were raised by wolves now, do we?"

He lifts the covers away and lowers his legs to the floor. I help him with the ties at the back of his gown. His clothes are on a chair by the window, and as he puts them on I see the seam where his arm has been reattached, a thin band where the skin is a little lighter, nothing you'd notice unless you were a parent or a doctor. I comb his hair, crouching in front of him, watching his eyes, which are alive with private thoughts and worries.

"Now you look like a gentleman," I say. "You ready to go?"

"I guess so," he says, and together we walk into the hall.

• • • • •

On the ride home, we play a game called Blackout. The object is to find the letters of each other's names in the license plates of passing cars, then call them out before the other person does. If you call them all, the person is out of the game. There's very little traffic until we hit the highway, and then we're suddenly in a sea of sedans and sport utility vehicles. Cole picks up a *D* for Dana and an *M* for Mike. I get an *A* for Dana, who seems not to be paying attention to the game.

"You better hurry up, Mom," Cole says, leaning over the front seat. "You've got two letters already."

She gazes straight out the windshield, a distant look on her face. Ever since our exchange in the hospital, she's been stiff and far away. I've seen the effect on Cole—the way he keeps his eyes on her, the way he won't stop trying to draw her attention.

"There's an *I*, Dad," he says, and glances at Dana.

We get off the highway and drive down Auwatukee, past the golf course and the hydroponic yards. At a red light, I call an O and an N, and then Cole and I both see a Honda in front of us, the license plate ALA-36940. We meet each other's gaze in the mirror, but neither of us calls the *A*.

• • • • •

At home I park on the street and kill the engine. Dana steps out of the car. She pretends not to hear Cole when he asks if she's coming to the park with us. He watches her walk up to the house with a stricken look on his face.

"She's having a rough time," I say. "It's not your fault, pal. I'll go get the mitts."

He nods, his face tight and willfully composed.

When I go inside, Dana is at the dining table, staring out the window. The sky has burst into color and filled the room with yellow light.

"So what's the plan?" I say. "Treat him badly? Make him feel like he doesn't have a mother?"

She turns, and I see that she's been crying. Her cheeks shine where the light strikes them from the side. "Are you really going to do this?" she asks. "Would you really take him and leave me?"

"I guess I don't know what my legal options are," I say.

"No one said anything about legal options," she says, "though I guess I shouldn't be surprised if you're thinking in that direction." She gives her head a small shake and glances up at me in a surprisingly open way, her eyes soft and even. "If I try hard enough, I can almost imagine how I look to you right now."

"Can you really?"

"Yes, I can," she says. "And it's not pretty."

"I don't think either of us looks very good to the other right now," I say, and try a smile.

"I guess not," she says.

"Of course, we don't know what will happen. He might be fine. He might just get better and surprise both of us."

"Do you think it would even matter?" she asks, smiling sadly.

"Why wouldn't it?"

"I just think you reach a point where you can't go on. Don't you? I feel as if we've gotten close to that point."

"Have we really?"

"I was very in love with you," she says, and puts a hand on top of my own. "You know that, right? I still love you very much."

"I love you, too," I say, and let out a laugh, because it all seems so crazy. "It's not as if we've lost everything, is it? It's not as if everything's gone."

"I don't know," she says. "That's what I worry about sometimes."

• • • • •

Cole and I drive out Clementine Road, past orange groves and fields of yuccas. Cole takes his mitt up from the floorboard and socks the ball into the pocket. He's been quiet and somber since I returned to the car, but now he seems to be cheering up under the influence of the drive. We pass an old stable building, the wood planks faded to silver-gray. He asks if I remember a drive we took a couple of winters ago, when it hailed so hard I had to pull to the side of the road and wait for it to stop.

"We were on our way to see the rodeo," I say, remembering.

"I thought the hail would dent the car," he says, and gives a small

367

laugh. "There was a little dog out in the street, remember? You went out and brought him back to the car."

"I remember he smelled like rotten garbage."

Cole laughs. "He did not." He's excited, and seems to be coming to the point of his story, which I'm guessing will be that we should allow him to have a dog. It's an argument he's been making the last few months. Before he can get to that, though, the fingers of his right hand begin to twitch and he slips the hand into his mitt. As we drive past the arboretum, I see the tendons of his forearm jumping. I don't say anything. It's not like him to hide anything from me.

I'm thinking of Dana, of course, thinking she seems like a different person now, though I suppose we'll both have to change if we intend to go our separate ways. Our conversation has made it necessary to imagine raising Cole by myself. I imagine taking him to the grocery store, having him break down in the produce aisle, carrying his inert body back to some empty apartment. It's hard to be optimistic when you know you'll be alone, when you know it will be only you in the D-Pediatric waiting room, waiting to hear whether your son will seem like a child again.

· · · · ·

At the park we walk across a field of fresh-mowed grass, the sun cutting over a long line of oleanders. A Mexican family barbecues flank steak under a picnic stand, and the smell of charred beef is in the air. Cole's hand seems to have improved enough for him to play catch, so we take our usual positions on a strip of grass near the snack bar.

"So, Dad," he says, winding up like a big-league pitcher, "you think I'll be able to play Little League next year?" He looks an imaginary runner back to first.

"You'll be eligible. You can try it if you want to."

His sidearm pitch skids on the ground. "Sorry about that," he says.

"Your arm all right?"

"Little sore," he says, and takes his mitt off and massages the shoulder. Even from twenty feet I can see the hand twitching, though he's playing it cool. "I'm trying to decide if it would be too much to do baseball *and* soccer," he says, and puts the mitt back on.

"What are Tanner and Sean going to do?"

"Tanner's gonna do both. Sean hasn't decided yet."

"Maybe you should just play baseball and see how it goes." I throw him a grounder and he fields it and makes a pretend throw to first.

"Soccer's my main sport, though," he says with intensity. "I want to play soccer for sure." He throws a pitch that hits the grass a few feet in front of him, then hustles up like a catcher going after a bunt. But his throwing arm is shaking so badly he can hardly hold the ball, let alone make the throw. He falls abruptly to a sitting position on the grass, pressing his bad hand into the mitt.

"Let's take a break," he says.

I walk over and sit down beside him.

He's gazing off at the covered picnic tables, watching a young Mexican girl in a white lace dress swing at a piñata with a broomstick. He hunches over his mitt, rocking back and forth. What seems remarkable is not that he's having problems, but that he's been able to throw a ball at all, ever—that we've stood here and played catch and it's seemed normal.

"Maybe we ought to go home," I say. "It's been a long day for everyone."

"I'll be all right in a second," he says.

I lean into him, touch his face. When he's looking at me, I say, "It's really all right if you're having problems. You don't have to hide anything from your dad."

"I'm not hiding," he says, but his eyes suddenly fill with tears and he has to glance off at the picnic tables, where the girl has opened up the piñata now and kids are clamoring underneath. He watches, his jaw set tight. His voice, when he speaks again, is as thin and frightened as I've heard it before. "What's going to happen, Dad?" he asks. "What'll become of me?"

"You'll be fine," I say, because sometimes it's a father's job to lie. "Don't worry, kid. You'll be great."

Nominated by Julie Orringer, Tin House

POEM FOR THE WHEAT PENNY (1909–1958)

by JUDITH HALL

from LITERARY IMAGINATION

O beautiful
The amber the clamor the waves of grain
               The need for animal feed
       And liquor yes the need for heaven

I heard a voice in the midst of beasts say
A measure of wheat for a penny

O spacious
Voice that loafs and voids a day
               A voice numismerized
       Is it love my one

Nation leaning her cheek upon the grain

O love
The penny cried which wheat which voice
               Which night the penny moon
       Shall subsidize the need for heaven

I heard a voice need yes a prop abundance
The measured fat of the wheat the penny-wise

O say
Say the penny-candy prayer
                    The dawn a gleaming pile
        Of trampled swords and friends

The coined and counted nice the penny life

Nominated by Literary Imagination

EGG

fiction by SHELLEY JACKSON

from GRAND STREET

PART ONE

I now look on the day the egg arrived as the most unfortunate of my life. I did not see it this way at the time; then, the egg seemed like the culmination of a long, confused, but mostly steady progress, which required only that punctuation to make sense. Like everyone I knew, I had always thought I would do something more important later on. Now later on had come. How stupid I was!

Had I been happy before then? I would scarcely have said so. I was restless and embittered by this or that nuisance of everyday life—my coworker Marty (in Cheese), the meter maid with a grudge against me, the band (Joss Stick) that practiced in the apartment beneath me, afternoons.

Yet I think I *was* happy. The world seemed open at the edges, fenceless. I was more or less what I seemed to be, and now I suspect this was happiness. Then the egg was lowered in front of me, like bait.

READING NOTES, JUNE 14—Nothing is more ordinary than the egg: It appears in the hands of painted kings and saints, under the paws of stone lions, and bouncing across a ballfield. Yet nothing is more mysterious. People used to believe that toads lived far underground, deep in a world of rock, and that inside each toad's head was a lump of gold. That gold is the egg: locked away, rumored, precious.

My name is Imogen. I am thirty-six. I live in a run-down but pretty apartment on the Mission/Castro divide with my roommate, Cass, with whom I have, as they say, a "history." I work in an upscale organic grocery store, where I restock toothpaste, candles, hand-carved wooden foot-rollers. I use Crest and buy candles cheap at Walgreens, but I like to look at the jewel-like soap we sell, and the girls who finger it while gazing somewhere else entirely, as if waiting for a sign. I rarely speak to them. I'm not like them: They are sincere, optimistic, gentle. Sometimes they flirt with me, their open faces radiant and slightly spotty, their new piercings inflamed, but I have little will to carry things further. I have been "between" girlfriends for two years. I have my pride, and my disappointments.

READING NOTES, JUNE 17—The egg eats. At least, it swallows things. You can watch them being expelled later. At first they are just shadows. Then they have color as well, and can be felt through the wall of the egg, like new teeth. Finally, only a tight skin like a balloon's covers the object, now perfectly visible. This splits and curls back, and the object falls outside the egg.

These discards do not seem damaged, but they are. They are different afterward, like food laid out for fairies. It's still there in the morning, but no good to anyone: Berries are blanched, butter will not melt, fresh-baked bread has no smell.

I lay on my bed with the window open and a washcloth over my eyes; it was the first day of a long weekend, and I was spending it with a migraine. Cass was driving up to the Russian River. Until the last minute I had meant to go with her, but by then I could scarcely move my eyes, and I gave up. All the incomplete and damaged ventures of my life came to mind one after another like broken toys. The poem cycle I would never finish. A friend in Boulder I was supposed to visit two years ago, whom I never called to let her know I wasn't coming. Learning to play the guitar. That girl I flirted with at Joanie's party, with the stupid name: Fury. I hid behind the natural sponges when she turned up at the store, but she saw me. That was the pattern: a moment of genuine interest, then a long, embarrassed retreat.

Finally I masturbated. Then I fell asleep with my fingers still stiffly crooked inside my underwear and my head thrust back into the pillow, as if someone had just punched me in the face.

I woke up sweating, with the feeling that I had just quit a dream of effortless energy, purpose, and interest—much more engaging than my real life. I thrust the covers off and fell back to sleep. When I woke

373

again I was damp and cold but my headache was better. It was raining.

My washcloth was a hot wet mass under my right shoulder. I dug it out and scrubbed my face with it. My left eye was itching. In the bathroom, leaning into the mirror, the sink's edge cold against my stomach, I spread my eyelids to bare the eyeball and the lids' scarlet inpockets. I spotted the irritant, a red dot smaller than a pinhead, lodged under my lower lid near the tear duct.

I touched a twist of toilet paper lightly to it, and the dot came away on the tip. I didn't know that it was an egg. I thought it was something to do with my migraine—now that the object was gone, the pain was gone. I was so grateful!

I dropped the twist in the toilet. If I had flushed, that would have been the end of the story, or at least of my part of it, but I did not. Some hours later, I hurried into the bathroom and peed without looking first. It was only when I stood and gave the bowl that respectful, melancholy look we give our rejectamenta that I saw the egg. It was the size of a Ping-Pong ball.

I fished it out of the toilet with my hand, proof I was a little rattled, because I am usually fastidious. (I could have used salad tongs.) I washed the egg and my hands. The egg bobbled around my fingers. I felt no distaste or uneasiness. It's an egg, I said out loud.

My first thought was that it was meant for Cass, not me. Cass would know what to do, she always did. She was at home being human. My second thought was quick and spiteful; it was that Cass must not find out. Deep down I thought that it was right for me to have the egg, not Cass; Cass didn't need it.

READING NOTES, JUNE 18—By some counts, hundreds, even thousands of humans have been swallowed by eggs. Many cases are poorly documented, and we dare draw no conclusions from them. Some have acquired such a gloss of legend that it is difficult to sort out the fact from the fiction. But some are probably true. In a blizzard in the Himalayas in 1959, three novice climbers and a Sherpa guide survived by creeping into an egg. In 1972, one-year-old Bobby Coddle crossed the Pacific in an egg, bobbing on the swells, and was pulled aboard a Japanese fishing boat, where he was extracted, in the pink of health, cooing with happiness.

I met Cass a long time ago, in college. It was the first week of freshman year and our residential advisers had organized a square dance to help us all get acquainted. I was leaning on the fence watching, and she came up and said, "I like you. You don't bother with this crap. You're like me." It wasn't true. I was wishing that I weren't so uptight, that I could whirl around with the others, but I just smiled, feeling myself become the kind of person who stood aloof, instead of the kind who was always left out.

We became friends. I never knew why. I tried to please her, of course (everyone tried to please her), but I didn't expect to succeed: I was too stiff, too dour, and too uncertain. Cass was the kind of person who always knew what other people were saying about things and whether they were right or wrong. And yet she changed her mind a lot and never seemed to remember that she used to hold the opposite opinion. But knowing this didn't keep me from being ashamed when I got caught holding the wrong book, the wrong snack, the wrong shirt. "Do you like that?" she would say. Or, "You're not going to *wear* that, are you?" I would drop the object in question as if it had caught fire in my hands. I was ashamed of this too; it was another thing Cass would not have approved of.

Cass discovered her lesbian tendencies after we graduated and immediately fell in love with the most beautiful girl I had ever seen, tall and stately, with long black hair and a fake ID (she was seventeen). I went out dancing with the two of them and got a migraine. Now Cass was seeing some guy with a goatee and I was the dyke, only I still hadn't met anyone who could pass the final test: make me forget Cass. I loved her, in a deep, unpleasant way, but I kept out of her bed. I survived her shifting passions by never becoming the object of them.

READING NOTES, JUNE 19—The folklore of eggs is flush with lucky breaks, but there are dark stories of lost children, vanished lovers, and besotted girls wasting away beside them. Two-time Iditarod champ Cath Summers set her dogs on a rival who boasted about possessing an egg, with fatal consequences (ironically, it turned out the rival was lying; the egg belonged to a neighbor, grocer Mary Over). In recent years, Professor Bev Egan, noted scholar of fascist architecture, starved to death during a vigil in the Santa Cruz mountains during which, she told friends, she expected an egg to appear to her.

I put the egg on a damp paper towel in the bottom of a mixing bowl and put the bowl under my bed, swathed in an old flannel shirt. By the time Cass came home the egg was as big as a baseball. I didn't show it to her.

It grew steadily. The outer surface did not appear to change. At one point I punched a small hole into it with a pencil and inserted a thermometer. The egg was almost body temperature. I wanted to insert the thermometer into the very center, to see if the temperature was higher or lower there, but no ordinary thermometer reached that far. The hole I had made filled with fluid and shone like a tiny eye. The meat around it grew swollen; finally, it swelled enough to close over the hole. I tried other experiments: I swabbed a small area with rubbing alcohol; I rubbed salt on another spot; I brushed the egg with oil; I spun it, and it rotated as smoothly as a planet. I would have held a candle to it but that seemed barbarous. Nothing seemed to affect it much.

After a few days, the egg began to give off a sweetly fetid smell. I heard Cass stamping around in the kitchen when she got back from work. Then she banged on the door. "Where are all these bugs coming from? Do you have fruit in your room, Im?"

I said no. After a while she went away.

That night I took the egg to bed with me. It was about the size of a bowling ball. Since it was moist, I put a towel down under the bottom sheet. Then I curled around the egg and took comfort in its warmth against my stomach.

In the middle of the night I awoke. My room seemed darker than usual. I realized that the egg had grown so big it blocked the light from the window. I could just make out its black curve against the ceiling. I was lying against it, almost under it, since as it grew it had overshadowed me. The shirt I had wrapped it in was in shreds around it. Maybe it was the sound of cloth tearing that had woken me. Fluid slowly spilled over my thighs and between them, and I thought for a moment, with prim displeasure, that I had wet myself in my sleep. But no. The egg had wet me.

I rolled out from under it and spent the night on the sofa in the common room.

READING NOTES, JUNE 22—According to legend, the egg prevents canker sores and sudden falls, cures ringworm in horses, and kills mosquitoes. Whether or not these claims are true, the egg does bring undisputed benefits. Premature babies or patients recovering from surgery can often be coaxed to lick the egg for nourishment when they will take nothing else. Flesh wounds heal faster when bound against the living egg, and in many hospital wards one sees patients in their white gowns splayed against the red orb in awkward attitudes, as if held there by gravity. They look like souls in the ecstasies of their last days; whether blessed or damned it is hard to say.

When I woke on the couch, Cass was standing over me, arms folded.

"What's going on, Imogen? You're not acting normal. Are you on drugs?"

I draped my blanket around me and shuffled toward my bedroom. Cass tried to pass me and I elbowed her back, but she got to my bedroom before me. She gasped out loud when she saw the egg.

Cass and I carried it down the stairs and into our tiny back patio in a blanket sling. We cleared a spot for it, and I draped the blanket over it so that no one would see it. I worried that they might try to take it away. I woke up three times that night to look out the window, but everything was quiet.

Cass came home the next day with a pile of books about eggs for me to read. I thought, *She's already trying to take over.* I thanked her.

"I might read them too," she said.

"I'll recommend one." I carried the pile into my room, shutting the door with my heel. I stuck them under the bed.

In the end I read them, of course. I studied them, even; I took notes. That was how Cass got her way.

READING NOTES, JUNE 26—There are stories of an inner, essential egg, a sort of tincture of egg, which could perhaps be distilled from the egg, or that might be left behind if the egg imploded: a fragrant red crystal, which some, speculating wildly, propose is the "pill of immortality" described by Wei Po-Yang in the first half of the second century A.D.

I understood that the egg was mine to care for. I was to brood over it, the books said. What that meant was not quite clear. Was I supposed to sit on top of it? From the landing of the back steps I stretched one foot out to the top of the egg. My sneaker slipped off, and as I tried

to catch it I banged my chin on the splintery rail. "What are you doing?" said Cass from above.

"Nothing," I said. It was almost a sob, but that was because my
chin hurt. I sat down on the steps.

The books said that the egg would not grow without help, that it
would be stunted, small, and hard. They described this "abortion" in
almost identical turns of phrase, as if reciting a lesson: "The neglected egg is dense and hard as a croquet ball. Growth without understanding is flesh heaped on flesh, as a pearl forms in an oyster, or
a tumor in place of a child, a clump of cells without differentiation."

READING NOTES, JUNE 29—"The eggs are obviously spacecraft. Some
are reconnaissance vehicles. Some are mobile homes. You see little
pinks and long reds. They peek out the windows. Or they descend,
on beams of light. The pinks are the clever ones. The master race, if
you will. They study us. They judge us. But the reds are there to in-
tercede for us, to plead for mercy."

Cindy Halfschnitt was abducted and returned to tell her tale: "I
wasn't afraid. I knew—how shall I put it?—I was loved."

I would brood, if that was what the egg needed. It was a worthwhile
thing to do—maybe the only worthwhile thing to do, even if I didn't
know why. And though it required an openness and sincerity that
didn't come naturally, well, for the egg I could learn to love without
reserve. Maybe the egg was my chance at what everyone else seemed
to feel all the time—a cozy feeling of being with someone or something, the worth-it-ness of love. But these thoughts were secondary. I
would brood because I needed to. Being near the egg was like
scratching next to an itch. The closer I got the more keenly I felt my
separation from it.

My friends—Roky, Tim, Deedee—expected me to make a joke
out of it, remembering how I had smirked at Deedee's chanting circle and Tim's banana-tempeh power drinks. Cynical Imogen. In fact
I had been waiting, hoarding myself, for that call, for something to
give myself to.

Yes, it was a burden. That thought did cross my mind. But once
the egg had come to me, it was impossible to imagine a life that
didn't contain it. I was an incubator now, an egg cup. "And when the
bird hatches her eggs, motionless dead bodies, her love shelters
them; her wings embrace them; she forms voice and life in their life-

378

lessness; the liquidness of the egg takes on beautiful form and she awakens out of the shell the burried ones." How wonderful!

READING NOTES, JUNE 30—Some say we are trying to hatch Christ. Like Phanes, Eros, Nangarena, incubator babies all. We'll keep going until we get it right. Christ, Antichrist, Big Bird, God, or Godzilla, who knows? We are undertaking a project itself entirely indefinite (yet with high, though vague standards), in anticipation of a result on which no one can agree. Why?

"Why?" asked my friend Roky. He turned the pegs on my dusty guitar, tuning it absentmindedly.

I could only answer that while the luster of adolescent fantasy might have dazzled me at first, it was the lusciousness and dignity of the egg that sealed my commitment to it. The egg was serious, even melancholy, but it knew how to play; it was quiescent and yet teeming with life, rich with invention and innovation. It made no scenes and did not argue for itself but answered all doubters by virtue of its unfeigned excellence.

"I don't know, I guess I'm curious," I said.

READING NOTES, JULY 3—Since we turn food into flesh our whole life long, the doctrine of bodily resurrection presents at least one problem. We form enough new cells in the course of living to reflesh ourselves many times over. Are some cells elected to immortality and others extinguished forever? The ingenious deity of the heretic sect that called themselves the Ovaries (before they were wiped out in 1265) provides for those extra cells, lumps them together and gives them a new life—as guides, as judges, as spies. As eggs. One might also call them angels.

I took the pieces from my Mrs. Potato Head kit down to the back yard, and I punched two eyes, a nose, and a mouth into the egg. I kept the features close together, a tiny face on the side of a planet, and then I sat down on a cinder block and began talking to the egg's new face. Juice from the punctures ran down the nose and hung off the tip.

"What are you?" I began. There was silence, which I had expected. I tried again. "Who are you? What is your name? Rumpelstiltskin? I'll have it out of you in the end, old drippy head, your ghastly looks don't frighten me." But the egg said nothing. The summer was passing, the egg was growing, and I was no closer to knowing what to do with it. There seemed to be every chance of failing decisively, while success was a mystery of which none of the books ever speak, except in the most general terms.

I leaned against the egg, and sank a little way into the pink wall. It was neither sticky nor slippery, just moist, like a healthy cheek on a warm day. I stroked the egg, then began palpating it rhythmically with my fists. I pressed my face against it until I needed air. I backed up, gasping. Its blush provoked me. I was jealous of the flies that licked its crown, the ants that were already tasting its effluvium.

I sat down in the shade of the egg. My mouth was dry. The egg was full of water; each cell wall was healthily distended around a fat globule. I poked my finger into the egg and the hole slowly filled with clear fluid. I slip the tip of my tongue in the hole and lapped up the water. Then I sunk my hand in and tore out a hunk. I chewed and swallowed until I had reduced the piece to a wad of gum, and then I lay still, staring up at a seagull, which disappeared behind the pink curve of the egg as if swallowed by it.

I got up.

But something stopped me from hurling myself headlong into the egg. Instead I took a paring of its flesh, the size and shape of a minnow. I carried it up to the kitchen, turned a burner on high and jostled it violently in a pan, while it spat and seared and flung itself about like something cooked alive—which perhaps it was, but better not to think about that—and then I clapped a spatula on it and trapped it there, sizzling, and it was docile, though I had to peel it off the pan, tearing it from the skin, which lay stuck in pink-tipped peaks and tufts. I folded the morsel in a paper towel and sat in a corner of the kitchen, sniffing it, running it under my nose like a cigar, dropping it, almost on purpose, on my shirt, and picking it up again from the greasy patch it left. Finally I stuck it in my mouth and chewed it up and ate it. It was linty.

The missing piece grew back. I was unchanged.

READING NOTES, JULY 5—In children's storybooks, Bad Egg is black and devouring, a scorched, lascivious, oozing egg with a slurred voice. We are warned against it. (Of course, this propaganda does no good at all when the real thing appears, oozing a little, it's true, but pretty as a peach and smelling like spring.) Good Egg is white and floats in the sky like a bubble. Rotten Egg lives underground. It is black and stone-cold and silent, and to touch it is death.

I dreamed about a girl in a room. She was white as paper and skinny. There was a hollow spike stuck in her side, attached to a rusty hand pump, and she worked the handle vigorously while blood splashed into a bucket. When the bucket was full, she pulled the spike out of her side, unhooked the bucket, and hurried with it to a sluice that fed through a tumbledown place in the wall, and dumped it in. Then she went back and started over. It seemed impossible that she could have any blood left in her body, but more kept coming, thick and red. I was amazed she spent herself so unreservedly.

There was something primitive about the way I'd have liked to tear Cass breast from drumstick when I saw her cast a covetous eye on my egg. It would help if I were a more ironic person. It would help if I were more zen. There were other things in life: clever little shaggy ponies, surveillance devices, snowboarding. There were excellent curries. There was probably a girl reading Genet somewhere. She might like mid-century modern furniture, but she would come to understand my thrift-store armchair, in time. Compromises could be made. I understood.

That day had been hot, multicolored and banging, full of groceries and loud with basketballs. Spilled smoothies turned to fruit leather on the sidewalk. The smells in alleys and stairwells grew unbearable. At three the first of the bugs—winged ants or termites—were struggling out of cracks in the hot asphalt of Mission playgrounds, parking lots, driveways. They dragged their wings clumsily through the openings like ladies in fancy dress forgetting the girth of their skirts.

I had left the window open. When I came home, it was dark. The room was cool blue, with a slight burned smell of the city, of tarry roofs and exhaust. I went to the window. The light wind of my movement blew frail things like snowflakes along the sill and off it. They fluttered down into the darkness.

I turned on the light. There were insects all over my bed. Some were alive and still pirouetting, dragging their stiff wings. Most were dead.

The egg was covered with them—thousands of insects. Wing-thatched, it had turned white and opalescent. Some of the wings beat, others were still, pressed together like hands. The moon rose, and in its light the egg shimmered like a bride in a beautiful dress, and I made up my mind.

I took off my clothes and climbed in.

I say "climbed in." It was more strenuous than that. I lowered my head and ran at the egg, ramming my crown deep in the pulp. I got stuck there a moment, with my head caught, then slid my hands into the egg beside my ears, stretching the walls of the hole until I broke the vacuum seal of its skin. I felt the egg respond to the insult, fattening and stiffening around the cut, and in effect folding me in deeper, though perhaps the intent was to enclose me and keep me from doing any more damage. I pumped my hips and thrust my head and hands deeper, and though there was nothing to hold on to I managed to drive myself in farther, until I felt the ovum close over my toes. Then I swam toward its center.

PART TWO

In the center of the egg, immobilized by the clasp of its flesh, I felt incredibly calm.

In here I was to be digested, as in the athanor of the alchemists, itself egg-shaped ("it is an egg of great virtue, and is called an egg, and is not an egg"). But how hard I was, how gnarled and dry, like the pit of a peach. The sweet flesh was wet and clung all around me, but I was caught in a furious refusal, despite all my longing. Maybe it was the refusal all matter participates in, the refusal of the primal lump— a refusal to melt, to glow. I was like a shoe left behind in deep mud while someone, a child, who had been inside me, went running lightly on. I was block heel and well-formed toe and crafty stitchery on yoke and tongue, but all that was nothing. Beauty was around me (the splendid surplus! A blazing chrysanthemum!), but I clung to my self like a scab.

Dear egg, melt me!

I was born fleshy and splayed, an open vessel. I have practiced permanence, yes, but only to keep myself for you. I would drop my bones in an instant to leap to your mouth in one soft elated blob. I could be yolk, albumen, and water; I could be the most delicate syllabub, scented with rose water and cardamom. I have waited my whole life for this. I think I would be sweet to taste, and I am not yet curdled.

But I proved incapable of yielding to chyme or chyle. I was hard as a tusk, I was horn and tooth, I was pumice, abrasive, porous, and light: a stone cloud, a dehydrated tear.

Refused.

When I emerged from the egg, disgusted and humiliated, dripping a pink syrup that now seemed filthy to me, nothing had happened. A cut on my arm had healed and my complexion stayed clear for two weeks afterward, but I had not entered it for a spa treatment.

I packed a bag and went to Boulder to visit my friend. She was pleased to see me, then slightly less pleased when she realized I didn't have plans to leave. After a while, I began to do some of the things I used to do before the egg came into my life: watch movies, read, write. I didn't call the store or Cass. I kept checking myself, to see if I was changed. Perhaps I had misunderstood, and the egg's rejection of me was itself a rite of passage I hadn't recognized, because I had my own idea of what translation should feel like. But there was nothing different about me except for this checking itself—the flinching and squinting and double takes in the mirror.

Maybe disappointment was enlightenment, and this acquaintance with futility was the closest I would come to God.

READING NOTES, JULY 14—In cabalistic tradition, the number one is not an abstraction, but the proper name of the egg. We do not count *one*—any child knows you don't need an abacus to see how many one is—we call out its name. Egg, two, three. This is not to say that two means two eggs. The egg is singular and sufficient. It is not a unit or a building block.

I returned to San Francisco on a windy, blond day: cotton shirts, flags, dog-walkers in shorts and mustaches. An old man stooped to pick up a hose as I walked past his yard. He had thinning yellow hair, and the rim of his ear was soft and red. He had a huge boil on the side of his neck by the collar of his turquoise shirt; it was so swollen it was almost spherical, and the wrinkled skin stretched over it until it was tight and shiny as a child's.

I passed the playground, where a few kids were working in the sandbox with bright blue plastic buckets and spades. A little girl looked up at me: a little girl with no face. A smooth pink globe seemed to supplant her head. Then the bubble collapsed, and she sucked it back into her mouth.

I walked past my house. I wasn't quite ready.

In the coffee shop, I noticed the cheeks of the girl working there, and her breasts, which strained the vintage print she was wearing, and her upper arms—she had cut off the sleeves of the dress—which swung vigorously as she frotted the steamer wand with a yellow towel. She had the thin white scars of a decorative cutting on her shoulder—a rough circle. Everyone is made of spheres, and the world is round.

Cass opened the door. "Imogen," she said.

I went straight through the apartment and out the back. She followed me. The egg still lay in the tiny backyard. It was even bigger than before, wedged half under the shed roof, with the clothesline cutting through it like a cheese wire. It seemed the worse for wear, and there was pink oil covering the concrete near it. Three large, nearly bald cats were lapping at the puddle.

Cass stepped over to a big enclosure of chicken wire. In it a pink mound like an exposed turnip broke the surface. She drummed her fingers on it and it contracted. The fleshy pink end of a worm, as big as a woman's heel, poked up through the surface, thinning and thickening in long shudders. "The neighbors complained, but it's perfectly harmless, except it pushes up the paving stones, so I made a box for it." She drew it gently out of the ground. "It's huge," she said, holding the worm in two places, while it weaved unsteadily in her hands and butted against her wrists like a blind puppy.

Cass was panting shallowly. Her cheeks were red and shiny and distended, her eyelids fat. Her eyebrows had gone pale, or perhaps even fallen out. She had drawn thin, brown, artful brows, but these, not perfectly symmetrical, did not work with her cartoon farmwife cheeks, her cherry lips.

"What's going on, Cass?" I said.

"What do you mean?"

"You look strange. I think you've been eating my egg."

"Your egg!"

"I grew it. It grew on me," I said.

"You walked out on it. And on me. I had no idea where you were.

Just because—" she paused. I thought she might not say it, but she did. "Just because it didn't want you!"

I threw myself on her. The worm writhed violently between us, then escaped. We struggled on the ground in the syrup. The Mexican guys in the apartment across from us came out on their landing laughing and hooting. "*Putas! Marimachas!*"

Late that night I woke up and looked out the window. The fog was purple and mauve, saturated with city light. Across the way a light was on in an empty kitchen. Down in the yard I could see Cass leaning against the egg. She was licking it.

READING NOTES, JULY 15—The egg might more properly be seen as the ambiguous zero, which sits at the center of the number line but is scarcely a number itself. The egg is a library, a battery, a wardrobe. The egg is a sneaky lady with a trunk full of green silks and sequins; she has a ring with a drop of curare in its center and a ruby for a stopper. In her hatbox is a hatbox, and in her hat a hat, her disguises are pregnant with disguises. Don't be surprised if there is a sapphire inside the teddy bear.

I dreamed Cass grew fat, shiny, red. As she waxed, the egg waned. At last she was almost spherical, a powerful figure, staring like an idol. The egg was the size of a malt ball, and she picked it up and popped it in her mouth. Then she turned toward me and opened her arms. Her sparse hair streamed from the pink dome of her skull, her eyes rolled, her teeth struck sparks off one another, and her hands were steaks, dripping blood. Now I knew her. She was the egg. I turned to escape, but her arms folded around me, and I sank into her softness, and woke pinioned by my comforter, on the side of the bed.

What the egg wants of me—maybe a millstone around its middle and a good heave-ho into the bay—I'll never know. How I tried to find out! That was my mistake—to want the egg to want, to want the egg to want *me*. That is why I am now outside desire, in the wasteland. That's why the world is dust to me. Poetry: dust. The girl reading Genet: dust. Cass?

Dust.

READING NOTES, JULY 18—Ancient Persian mystics write that the universe is an oyster. Our incessant desires and demands annoy it; we are the itch in the oyster. Around our complaints a body forms. The egg begins as a seed pearl. It grows beautiful. For this treasure, princes would pauper themselves. To harvest the pearl, we would pry the earth from the sky, though the satisfaction of our desires would destroy the universe and us with it. But be warned. The egg is the gift that robs you, for its germ is pure need: gain it and you will lack everything.

After breakfast the next morning, I went down and unlocked the gate across the alley between our house and the neighbors'. There was a heap of splintery boards blocking the alley. I carried them back a few at a time and piled them in the yard. On the other side of the fence, the neighbor's dog went up and down the alley with me, whining softly. When the way was clear I went back to the egg.

I pushed it back as far as I could and stuck a board under it, and then I squeezed behind it and rocked it forward onto the board, and stuck another under it behind. Then I rocked it back and fit another board onto the first. In this way I raised it little by little. It took me several hours to raise the sagging center a foot off the ground. That was far enough. I got down on my stomach. Syrup hung in sticky cords between the bottom of the egg and the pavement. They snapped across my face as I squirmed beneath the egg. Once the egg's center of gravity was directly above me I gathered my legs under me. The egg gave slightly above me, allowing me to crouch. The boards creaked, but held. I stretched my arms out to either side.

Somehow, I stood up.

I took a step. I was carrying it.

Little by little I made my way down the alley toward the street. The dog kept hurling itself against the fence beside me.

Syrup ran down my face and body into swaying, fitful strings on the sidewalk. My footsteps sounded like kisses. I left pink tracks.

"Imogen!"

I turned carefully.

Cass was standing at the top of the front steps in her dressing gown. "Wait, Imogen! Please!" She whirled; I saw the pink flash of her heel as she dashed up the apartment stairs.

I continued on my way. I turned left down Eighteenth Street. I crossed Church. Guerrero. Valencia. People made way. Someone dropped a burrito and it burst, black beans rolling across the sidewalk in front of me. Someone pushing a shopping cart fell in behind me; I could hear its wheels rattling.

When the light changed at Mission, I stopped too suddenly and the egg bounced over my shoulder, through the traffic, and fetched up in the doorway of a doughnut shop. The whores that hung out there gathered around it, touching it, then licking their fingers. Cass caught up with me, and when the light changed we walked together across the street.

The egg was torn when I reached it. Things were stuck to it: pebbles, bottle caps, lottery stubs, a blue condom, an empty popper, a parking ticket. I brushed it off. The whores helped me, dabbing it with napkins from the doughnut shop.

Cass waited.

I knelt down with my back to the egg while it was trapped in the doorway and tried to stand up, forcing it up the wall. When they saw what I was doing, two guys came forward and lifted it for me. I started off down the street at what was almost a jog, heading south now, out of the city. Some of the whores came too. The shopping-cart man was there. Two kids carrying a huge boom box between them trailed after.

Cass fell in behind.

The egg is my burden. I can bear it. The role has its compensations. Together we will go around the world. And then, when I'm bored, I'll take my egg and go where we can be alone. I'll sit down next to it, and I'll try to remember what it feels like to want something. And I suppose, my angel, that in the end you'll let me in.

Nominated by Lance Olsen

ROY ORBISON'S LAST THREE NOTES

by BJ WARD

from PAINTED BRIDE QUARTERLY and GRAVEDIGGER'S BIRTHDAY
(North Atlantic Books)

12 mph over the speed limit on Route 80, I realize
the way I know the exact size of my bones
is the way I know I am the only one
in America listening to Roy Orbison
singing "Blue Bayou" at this precise moment,
and I feel sorry for everyone else.
Do they realize they are missing
his third from last note?—*Bluuuueee*—
and how it becomes a giant mouth I'm driving into—
"Bay"—pronounced *bi*—becomes the finger
pointing back—*biiiiiiii*—and all the sealed up cars
greasing along this dirty, pot-holed clavicle of New Jersey
don't know this "you"—constant as my exhaust smoke—
yooooouuuu—and the beats underneath, more insistent
than the landlord knocking on the door—horns, drums, guitar,
    bass—
my Toyota Corolla is now one serious vehicle,
and the band and I are all alone now, filling it up—
Roy and me in our cool sunglasses up front
and his musicians barely fitting their instruments in the back,
driving into the blue—bom bom bom—pulling ahead
of the pollution faster than New Jersey can spit it out—

Bye—boom bom—his leggy background singers must be jammed
in the trunk because suddenly I hear them and suddenly
we are Odysseus and his boys bringing the Sirens with us,
and the cassette player is our black box
containing all essential details in case we don't make it,
but I know we're going to make it
because Roy Orbison turns to me
and says, like the President says to his top general
after a war has been won, or like Morgan Earp
on his deathbed said to Wyatt when vengeance
was up to him, or like Gretchen Honecker
said when I knew I was about to get my first kiss,
Roy turns to me and says, "*You*—"

Nominated by Lee Upton

CHILDREN OF GOD

fiction by ERIC PUCHNER

from ZOETROPE: ALL STORY

THE AD SAID they needed someone to model "patterns of survival."
At the interview, a woman with an *E.T.* poster on her door told me
about the job. "You'd be working at their house," she said, "taking
care of two clients with special needs."

I couldn't even take care of myself, but I needed a job. "Are they
retarded?"

"Okay, yeah. We don't say that anymore." She coaxed herself out of
a frown, in a way that suggested I was the only candidate. "There's a
new name: developmentally disabled."

They gave me a new name, too: Community Living Instructor.
This was in Portland, Oregon. I started working at a home for people
who couldn't tie their shoes, helping two grown men get through the
day.

* * *

Jason was worse off. At twenty-eight, he was afflicted with so many
diseases that his meds were delivered in a briefcase. He made Job
look like a whiner. Enlarged by hydrocephalus, his head drooped
burdensomely from his body, which twisted in his wheelchair as if it
were trying to unscrew from his neck. His mouth hung open in a
constant drool. His hands, crippled from dystrophy, curled inward as
though he wanted to clutch his own wrists. Among other things, he
was prone to seizures and cataleptic fits. He had chronic diarrhea.
Every evening, after dinner, I was met with a smell so astounding I
had to plug my nose with cotton. I'd wheel Jason, besmirched and
grinning, to the bedroom to change his mess. "I made a bad, bad
meeeesss!" he'd yell, flapping his arms. "Now we're cooking with

390

oil!" For the most part, his vocabulary consisted of clichés he'd picked up from former care workers, many of them bizarre or unsavory to start with: "cooking with oil" was one, as was "you said a mouthful when you said that." Other times, he was capable of surprising clarity. He loved action movies—particularly ones in which nature avenged itself on humanity—and would recount the death of a dinosaur hunter as if it were a sidesplitting joke.

The changing of the mess, though, was the high point of Jason's day. He giggled uproariously when I lifted him from the wheelchair, his arms kinked around my neck as I carried him to bed. He never failed, during our brief walk together, to burrow his tongue deep into my ear.

Dominic was more dignified. Moody, unbalanced by palsy, he staggered around the house like a drunk. Down syndrome had smudged his face into the flat, puttylike features of a Hollywood gangster. He was beautiful in a way that startled women. He was thirty-two years old and owned a bike with a banana seat and training wheels. The bike was supposed to be impossible to tip over. He'd strap a helmet on his head and wiggle into an armature of pads and then go for a ride down the street, returning ten minutes later covered in blood. I cleaned his wounds with a sponge. About ten times a day, he'd sneak into the bathroom to "fresh his breath." He always left the door open and I'd watch him sometimes from the hall. He'd nurse the faucet first, sucking on it until his mouth filled with water. Then he'd pop up suddenly and arch his back in a triumphant stance, face lifted toward the ceiling. Sometimes he'd stay like that for thirty seconds— moaning, eyes shut tight, arms outstretched like a shaman receiving prophecies—before puking his guts out in the sink.

His voice, when he spoke, was sleepy and far-fetched. He only pronounced the middle of words. "Abyoola!" he liked to say, meaning "Fabulous!" When he told a story, it was like Rocky Balboa channeling a demon.

✿　✿　✿

I'd moved to Portland after a month of sleeping in my car, driving aimlessly around the West and living off my father's Mobil card. The driving had to do with a frantic feeling in my stomach. I felt like Wile E. Coyote when he goes off a cliff, stranded in midair and trying to crawl back to the edge before he plummets. In the glovebox, sealed with plastic and a rubber band, was a Dixie cup of my mother's ashes that I'd nabbed from her memorial when I was twelve. I kept it there

391

for good luck. Before my month of driving, I'd taped Sheetrock in Idaho, sold vacuum cleaners in Missoula, Montana, worked as a baggage handler at the Salt Lake City airport.

❊ ❊ ❊

To pass the day, I took Jason and Dominic on field trips. There was a special van in the garage, and I'd load Jason onto the lift and strap down his wheels so he wouldn't roll out the window. The van had been donated by a traveling magician and was painted purple. We'd drive to cafés, outdoor fairs, movie theaters. They liked easy-listening stations—"I Write the Songs," "Send in the Clowns"—and I'd crank the old AM stereo as loud as it would go. I'd roll down the windows and listen to Jason scream words at the top of his lungs, naming the passing creatures of the world like Adam on a roller coaster. "Dog!" he'd yell. "Girl! Pizza boy!" Dominic would stick his head out the window of the front seat, his hair exploding in the wind. Someone had taught him how to flip people off and he'd give pedestrians the finger as we passed. It was a good test of character and I liked watching people question the simplicity of innocence.

Once, at a stoplight, a guy in a fraternity sweatshirt returned the gesture and then strode up to Dominic's side of the van, his girlfriend sloping behind him. The guy's arm was outstretched to better advertise his finger, which he was following like a carrot.

"What the fuck, man," the guy said to Dominic. "You looking for a new asshole?"

Dominic wagged his finger at the guy's face, enjoying himself immensely. "We're going to get some ice cream," I explained.

The guy took a closer look at Dominic and turned red. He dropped his hand and glanced at his girlfriend, who was regarding him with distaste.

"You should teach them some manners," he mumbled. "This isn't the goddamn circus."

At Baskin-Robbins, we waited in line while the customers ahead of us sucked on little spoons. Dominic ogled the women. He was only a pervert because of his IQ; otherwise, he'd be concealing his interest like the rest of us. It was more metaphysical than sexual. Sometimes I'd find him staring at a lingerie-clad model in a magazine, struck dumb with fervor, his lips moving silently as if in prayer.

While we waited, Jason slumped in his wheelchair and I wiped the drool from his chin. The woman in front of us kept glancing back at him. It was always the same expression, a coded kind of smile directed at me as well, like we shared some secret knowledge about the afterlife.

Finally, she couldn't resist any longer and squatted beside Jason. "What's your favorite flavor?" she brayed, as if she were speaking to a foreigner.

He seemed to study the case of ice cream. "Like trying to sell Jesus a jogging suit!"

"That's right, dear," the woman muttered, but didn't talk to him again.

When it was Dominic's turn to order, he staggered around the counter before I could stop him and stood by the cash register. The girl behind the counter laughed. He stared at her breasts without speaking. I might have done something to ward off disaster, but I wanted to see what would happen.

"Show me what you want," she said. It was the wrong thing to say. Dominic grabbed one of her breasts. "Hey," the girl said, laughing. She tried to pull away and he held on, clutching at her shirt. He wore an expression of deep, incredulous despair. "Hey!" the girl said. Finally, I ran around the counter and pulled Dominic off with two hands, leading him back to the customer side, where he seemed unembarrassed by his conduct.

It was always like that: the world scorned them, but they were freely and openly themselves. I admired them greatly. We tried to order ice cream, but the girl was shaken and refused to serve us.

✻　✻　✻

I lived in a studio apartment with no phone. The only piece of furniture was a pea-colored sofa I'd bought at the Goodwill and dragged up five flights of stairs by myself. For three days, because of my poor grasp of geometry, it remained lodged vertically in the doorway. I was still on the Mobil dining plan: maple bars and hot dogs and Snapple iced tea. I had a box of books and a box of cooking utensils, but I never unpacked them.

✻　✻　✻

My dad moved away when I was in college and took up with an ex-movie star. Actually, she wasn't a movie star at all but somebody who used to stand in for movie stars during long or onerous shots. She hadn't been on a set for years, but liked to talk about "Bob" Redford and "Marty" Sheen. My father had convinced her he was rich. Now they lived in Utah, in the middle of the desert, and he was taking care of her children.

I'd called my dad from a pay phone, the month I was living out of my Subaru.

"You surprised me," he said. "Where are you?"

"Las Vegas."

"Jesus, Drew. What are you doing in Vegas?"

"Good one. Seeing some friends." Actually, I'd spent the afternoon in a casino bathroom, shivering on the toilet and battling suicidal fantasies, visions of myself with my brains blown out and soaking in a puddle. "I was thinking I'd drive up and stay with you guys for a few days."

"Sure," he said. "That would be fine. I mean great. Come on up." He hesitated, and I could hear a woman's voice in the background. "It's Drew," my dad said. "Drew? Hang on a sec, will you?"

He put his hand over the receiver. For a long time, I couldn't hear anything but the ring of a slot machine behind me. Then the sound came back and I caught the tail end of a sentence in the background, the woman's voice saying "running a B&B."

"Drew? This weekend's a little hectic. You know we've got five of us here already and the place is a mess."

I laughed, but it sounded as far-off as the slot machine. *Chink chink chink.*

"The thing is," my dad said, "I'm not sure where you'll sleep."

"Jackpot," I said before hanging up. "Do you hear that?"

❋ ❋ ❋

Every afternoon, at Jason's and Dominic's, we'd sit at the dining room table and sift through the day's mail, giggling at the letters addressed to "Cigar Lover" or "Channel Surfer." Sometimes, from the mailbox on the corner, I'd send them postcards I'd collected on my travels, thirty-cent souvenirs picturing places like Orchard Homes, Montana, or Mexican Hat, Utah. "Wish you were here!" I'd write. Or "Having the time of my life!" We put the postcards in a shoebox in case the happy stranger returned.

One day, sometime in March, Dominic got a Clearing House Sweepstakes letter and we opened it excitedly. I filled out the necessary information, showing him how to paste the publishers' stamps in the little squares. For a week after we'd sent it in, he seemed mercurial, distracted. He was particularly excited about the grand prize—a 1969 Mustang convertible with a galloping horse on the grill—and I helped him put the glossy picture of it on the refrigerator.

Filling in for a graveyard shift one night, I started from a nap at

5:00 A.M. when the front door creaked open. I went to investigate and saw Dominic sitting on the steps like a gloomy wino in his Fruit of the Looms, squinting at the half-lit street.

"What are you doing, Dominic?" I asked, putting my hand on his shoulder.

"Ooing," he said, in his no-consonant drone.

"Yes, doing. It's five in the morning."

He looked at me queerly. "Ar," he said, meaning "car." Since his subjects were limited, I'd learned to translate his words into their probable correlates. "Red car no roof!"

In my tired state, I pictured the red convertible rolling down the street, tied up with a giant bow, Ed McMahon sitting pretty behind the wheel. I explained to him the chances were one in a trillion. "There's no car, Dominic. It's a scam—a game, you see? We just did it for fun. You've got no chance at all."

He stared at me without comprehending. "Car! Red car go fast!"

"Besides, you can't drive. You'd crash it anyway."

"No crash!" he said angrily, rising to his feet.

Spit flew from his lips. Such passion! I would have given anything to care like that. I got Dominic to bed finally but lay wide-eyed on the couch, relapsing into suicidal fantasies. *Live each day as your last*, they say, but nobody in their right mind would try it. I reminded myself it was Jason's birthday tomorrow, that I was the only one—of the three of us—who knew how to bake a cake.

The next afternoon I returned to the house and started getting ready for the party. We strung up balloons and I bought party hats and noisemakers. Jason's parents were supposed to arrive at three o'-clock. At 2:45, the phone rang and a woman's voice drawled bashfully into my ear. She told me that their car was in the shop with brake trouble.

"I'm so sorry. I know Jason was expecting us."

"He's waiting for his presents," I said.

She fumbled with the phone. "I can't tell you. We feel just awful about this."

"Look, we'll just come over there. Give me your address. I'll bring the cake and noisemakers."

An awkward pause. "Oh, no. Don't trouble yourself. I mean, it's too far a drive for them. They won't enjoy it."

"It's no trouble," I said loudly. "They love riding in the van."

It was a long ride on the freeway and we heard "Send in the

395

Clowns" two times. Jason sat in the back, displaying none of his customary excitement at being on the road. "It's your birthday," I kept reminding him. When I told him we were going to see his parents, he just stared out the window with his head wilting like a sunflower. Eventually we found the exit and climbed a steep, suburban street into some hills, rising above the great cloverleaf of the freeway into a development of newly built houses. I looked for some signs of recognition on Jason's face, but then realized he may have never been here before.

Jason's parents greeted us at the door and invited us into the kitchen. Even though it was rainy season, they both had sunburns. Their faces were blank behind their smiles: I could have shaken them like an Etch A Sketch and made them disappear. The Kreighbaums seemed shy around their son, talking to him in special voices and exchanging covert looks. Mr. Kreighbaum wore a winded expression and a white polo shirt that emphasized the redness of his face, as if he'd just completed a succession of cartwheels. He watched me empty the contents of the bag I'd brought, peering at the party favors I laid out on the counter.

The whole place made my teeth hurt. In fact, I was clenching them in rage.

"Put on a party hat," I commanded Mr. Kreighbaum.

"Oh, no." He chuckled, glancing at his wife. "I don't think it'll fit."

"I promised Jason."

He took the little hat from my hand, sneaking a glimpse out the window before stretching the elastic cord around his chin. His head looked gigantic under the paper cone of the hat. We walked, wheeled, and staggered into the dining room and sat at the long oak table, which held a meager stack of presents. Mrs. Kreighbaum brought out plates of fruit salad and served us without speaking. I went to the kitchen and reentered with the cake, and we sang "Happy Birthday" to Jason, but he just sat there and refused to blow out his candles. His eyes were rheumy and distracted. I tried to cheer him up with a noisemaker, but he batted it from his face with one hook.

"When's the last time you've seen Jason?" I asked Mrs. Kreighbaum.

She looked at her husband. "I don't know. Gosh." She turned her smile in my direction. "He seems so happy where he is."

"I'm gonna open up a can of whup-ass," Jason said.

Mr. Kreighbaum tried to interest him in the presents, but he pushed them away with a listless shove. Undeterred, Mr. Kreighbaum opened up the biggest box on the table, feigning surprise at the contents. It was a plastic trout that flapped its tail when you came near it and sang "Take Me to the River." You were supposed to hang it on the wall. Clearly, the resourceful man had run out to Walgreens before we got there and bought whatever he could find.

He slid the toy from its box and laid it on the table to demonstrate. The trout was more convincing as an allegory of death, flapping its tail against the table and pleading for our mercy. Jason, incredibly, showed little interest. In the end Mr. Kreighbaum had to open the presents himself, slumped over the table in his party hat, holding each toy up for our approval.

Mrs. Kreighbaum—out of politeness, probably—tried to engage Dominic. "How's the fruit salad?" she asked.

"Abyoola!"

"Amen on that," I said to Dominic. "I agree with you one hundred percent."

Dominic asked where the bathroom was and I had to repeat the question before Mrs. Kreighbaum would answer him. He lurched out of his chair. I thought he might knock something over, but he fumbled his way down the hall without disaster. Soon we could hear the *yaaks* and spits, the sounds of retching emanating from the open door.

"It's a masturbation thing," I explained, trying to hide my elation. "He's sexually frustrated."

About halfway through the presents Jason got a sheepish, self-occupied look. The stench was tremendous. It was no illusion: we were working together. I let the Kreighbaums sit there for a while, watching them stare at their plates while the house echoed with bulimic groans.

"Do you have any diapers?" I asked eventually.

Mrs. Kreighbaum shook her head. I went to get an Attends from the emergency stash in the van and threw the diaper in Mr. Kreighbaum's lap. I asked him to change Jason in the bedroom, managing to bestow the task with a sense of honor. He glanced at his wife—a quick, despondent peek—and then looked at me pitifully.

"I think Susie might be better equipped."

"He only lets men," I said.

"But I'm his mother!" Mrs. Kreighbaum said.

"Please—this is no time to take things personally." I turned to Mr. Kreighbaum. "Grab a bucket and some dish towels. You'll need to wipe him down first."

He nodded. Clutching the Attends like a book, Mr. Kreighbaum stood up obediently and rummaged under the sink in the kitchen until he found an empty paint can. He held it up for approval and then wheeled Jason into the open door at the far end of the hall. The door closed behind them with an air of accumulated doom. Mrs. Kreighbaum and I picked at the remnants of our cake. Something about her face, the way it stared helplessly into her plate, gave me a twinge of guilt.

Eventually the noises stopped and Dominic staggered back into the dining room, grinning from exhaustion, eyes glazed from the effort of his puking. He smiled at Mrs. Kreighbaum and said something I couldn't decipher. She glanced at the closed door at the end of the hall, eyeing it with a look of canine longing. How hard was it to change a diaper? I asked her to watch Dominic and then went down the hall to investigate.

It was worse than I'd expected. Jason, naked and white as a canvas, was curled up on the king-size bed, his ass and legs obscured by a painterly mess. Mr. Kreighbaum stood above him with sagging shoulders, hair thorned with sweat, holding a wet rag that was dripping on the carpet. The party hat had slipped down and was sticking out of the front of his forehead. He looked like a big, melanomic unicorn. There was shit on his hands and shirt and all over the denim comforter covering the bed. His hands trembled. He looked at me with a despairing face, surrendering eagerly to defeat, like a refrigerator repairman asked to do an autopsy.

I burned the image in my mind, savoring it while I could.

I brushed Mr. Kreighbaum aside and cleaned Jason myself, changing his Attends and setting him carefully back in the wheelchair. He looked at his father and laughed out loud. "You're cruising for a bruising!" he said. He giggled all the way back to the dining room, his mood magically improved. Dominic, however, had disappeared.

"I asked you to watch him!" I said.

Mrs. Kreighbaum clutched a chair. "I had to use the rest room."

I saw that she was weeping. My teeth had stopped hurting, finally, but I didn't feel any better. The two of us went to look for Dominic and found him standing by the curb across the street, bent over someone's Jetta and peering through the window like a burglar. The

dandruff in his hair sparkled in the sun. He turned to us with yearn-
ing, half-open eyes.

"Red," he mumbled. "My car for zoom."

"That's not your car," I said. "We're at the wrong house completely."

✿   ✿   ✿

On the way home, we stopped at Burger King for some Whoppers
and sat next to an elderly woman with gigantic eyes filling her
glasses. She watched Jason and Dominic maul their food, sadly staring, and smiled in that special way when I caught her eye.

"Children of God," she whispered, leaning across her table and
nodding seriously.

I couldn't suppress a laugh. Jason, who'd been observing the scene
with an amused look, tugged at my elbow.

"What did she say?" he asked.

"She called you 'children of God.'"

He guffawed. "Children of Gaawwd?"

"That's right," I said, practically guffawing myself.

The lady turned white. Dominic soon picked up on the joke and
joined us in our laughter, gasping out wild, choking horselaughs, the
three of us splitting our sides until we almost fell out of our seats.

✿   ✿   ✿

Occasionally, after my shift with Jason and Dominic, I'd go to a bar
on my street to get drunk. It was the kind of place with a neon martini glass for a name and an unsinkable turd floating in the toilet.
Each time the same middle-age boat worker would buy me drinks.
She cleaned yachts on the Willamette and her skin reeked of chemi-
cals. Years in the sun had crumpled her face. She took classes at the
Hatha yoga center next door and was always waiting at the bar with
her rolled-up mat, like a hobo.

When she got drunk, she'd stand on her head to prove she could
drive. She was the only alcoholic yoga enthusiast I'd ever met. Once
she asked me what I did for a living.

"I work with some retards," I said.

"Right," she said, commiserating. "I know what you mean."

After the fourth or fifth drink, I'd wait until she went to the bathroom before escaping out into the night.

✿   ✿   ✿

In the mornings before work, I'd take long strolls through the industrial streets of Portland, muttering to myself in a somnolent daze. I

399

walked the same streets every day but never knew where I was. The fog hung in shreds; I stepped through secret portals and found the sun. It was the fantasies—the suicide fog in my head—that I couldn't step out of. The fact that I was going crazy crossed my mind more than once, but the broad, careless beauty of the city distracted me, the ivy-covered walls and elegantly trussed bridges. In stores, I found it difficult to talk to people: my mouth floundered out a Dominic-style vowel-ese that left cashiers straining their necks in disgust. I felt like a visitor from another planet, inhabiting some poor earthling's body.

"Are you all right?" someone asked when I was having trouble buying groceries. The little machine at the counter, and then the checkout girl herself, kept asking for my PIN number. I knew the PIN was my birth date, that wasn't the problem. The problem was I couldn't remember when I was born.

"Of course not," I said, losing patience. "You're being . . . rhetorical?"

The man stepped back. "I was trying to help."

"Look, you're driving me up the wall."

I would weep for no reason, sometimes for hours. A physical condition. My heart was an onion making me cry. I started arriving earlier and earlier at Jason's and Dominic's, relieving other people before their shifts were done.

There were times when the three of us seemed to share the same brain. Once, driving back from the movies, we passed by a long, sprawling cemetery bristling with tombstones. Jason seemed very interested in the graves, and I watched his face grow oddly contemplative in the rearview mirror.

"Dead guys," I explained.

"Why?" he said, staring out the window.

"You mean why are they dead?" I was impressed by his curiosity. "Excellent question. Superb." I tried to think, a painful undertaking. "Maybe they were jealous of the dead people. I mean, when they were alive. They got tired of shitting themselves. You know, like an escape—except you go under the ground."

"Under the ground?" He was grinning, though he seemed confused. "So what do they eat?"

"They're just bones. They don't know how to eat."

I thought he might be alarmed by this, but he found it very amusing. "They don't know how to . . . eat?" he spat out, before convulsing with laughter.

Dominic picked up on the joke and the two of them giggled, trading smirks. Of course it was funny—all those precociously stupid skeletons. When we got back, I walked them to my car and showed them the Dixie cup of ashes in the glovebox, explaining how the gray silt used to be a person. I thought they should know their alternatives. Dominic, in particular, greeted the idea with scorn. "No clean!" he said. I handed the ashes to Jason, who thought they were meds and tried to lift them to his mouth.

The next day we went to a coffee shop on Hawthorne Boulevard and ran into the boat worker who liked to buy me drinks. She stared at us as we ordered three lattes with straws in them. In the daylight, sitting by herself in the corner, she looked less toxic. I introduced her to Jason and Dominic, who were impressed by her gender.

"Smell like blue!" Dominic said, sniffing her fingers.

"Cut it out," I told him.

"Blue water toilet!"

She looked at me, frowning. "These are your co-workers?"

"Best friends," I joked, pretending it wasn't true.

Dominic touched her hair. I'd forgotten her name and she told me, wincing a little.

"Mensa?" I said. "Like the whatever thing for geniuses?"

She shrugged. "My mom liked the sound of it."

I took her back to Jason's and Dominic's, showed her the house where I spent most of my time. She burped for their entertainment and let Dominic hold her breast. We weren't used to having visitors and kept looking at ourselves in the mirror above the filing cabinet. After a little while, Mensa got up and started flipping through the cupboards in the kitchen.

"Don't they have anything to drink in this house?" she asked.

"I don't think that's one of their patterns of survival."

"Great. What about us?"

Later, we retreated to Jason's Flex-a-Bed while he and Dominic watched a video in the living room. Her face was stitched with lines, like an Arctic explorer's. I held her tight and curled my legs into her stomach. Dinosaurs roared in the background. She tried to interest me in other things, which annoyed me: I wanted to be clutched. I'd heard about a machine, invented by an autistic person, that would clench you in a giant rubber hand for as long as you required.

"You're the most miserable lover I've ever had," she said, probing

401

her nostril with a finger. She picked her nose without embarrassment, as if she were enjoying a cigarette.

"So I hear."

"No. I mean, I thought *I* had problems."

She started coming over in the afternoons, showing up after work in her coveralls. She had a flask with a golf ball on it that she'd stolen from one of the yachts she worked on. We'd fold together in Jason's bed and clutch each other until my arm went numb. The sweat in her hair smelled like Drano. I didn't deserve a morsel of grace, even a noxious one, but no one had bothered to let her know. Afterward, she'd do yoga on the front lawn in the mizzling rain, lying on her back and then lifting herself slowly into an arch, like a demolition shown in reverse. The poses had mysterious names: Downward Dog, Sun Salute. Once I found her lying on the grass in a random-looking sprawl, the palms of her hands turned up to the drizzle.

"The Corpse," she explained later. "Feels wonderful."

✧ ✧ ✧

Two months after visiting his parents, Jason had a grand mal seizure. It happened on the morning shift, but I got there in time to catch the paramedics loading his exhausted body into the ambulance, to see the gaunt perplexity of his face. We had a special employee meeting and the Care Services Coordinator warned us Jason could die on anyone's shift; he'd already lived past his projected life span. The house was lonely without him, and I wondered if his parents were visiting him in the hospital.

When he got back, Jason seemed wan and listless. I changed his mess like always, but he didn't giggle or stick his tongue in my ear. When I tried to teach him some new clichés, he just stared at me with a drifting face.

His mother started dropping by now and then, treating me like a servant now that she was in her son's house. She read picture books to Jason while I cooked Hamburger Helper or prepared his meds. She always left after thirty minutes, mid-book, when she'd appeased her guilt for hoping he would die. His father never came.

To cheer him up, I brought Mensa to the house. She burped at Jason—his favorite trick—but he just stared at her obediently without laughing. Then he rolled his eyes to the wall, trapped in a dream. Dominic sat on the front steps as usual, staring resolutely down the street with his hands folded in his lap, like a millennialist awaiting the Rapture. He'd sit there for a million years, while the glaciers re-

402

turned and sharks waddled from the ocean. I felt a breathless envy that made me sick.

"You think he'd give a shit that his roommate's dying," I said.

"Probably it doesn't mean anything to him," Mensa said. "Life and death."

I went outside and interrupted Dominic's vigil.

"Red car!" he said, jumping up. "Fastest car!"

"Dominic, will you shut up?" He was excited and tottering. I had to grip his shoulders to steady him. "There's no car coming."

"Red car go zoom!"

"Dominic, listen to me!"

"Fabulous car!"

"You're not going to win anything!" I said, shaking him. His head flopped back and forth. "Can't you get that through your thick skull?"

* * *

Jason never went back to his original self. He sat in the back of the van and saved himself for special occasions, shouting out the window only at particularly ludicrous sights, like a dog or a hippie. He lost his sense of schadenfreude during movies and stopped guffawing when someone was killed or eaten.

When we passed the cemetery now, he stared out the window and eyed it suspiciously.

"Dead people," he said. His mouth changed at the corners, but I couldn't tell if it was a smirk or frown.

"Yep." I knew what was coming.

"They don't know how to eat."

"That's right," I said cheerfully. "They're too stupid."

"We're smarter than them," he whispered with his head bowed, like a wish.

* * *

Mensa and I found a cheap body shop on Burnside and took my Subaru in for a paint job. I'd saved enough—using my dad's Mobil card on daily necessities—to pay for it. When the car was finished, we drove to the house and parked it on the curb. I brought Dominic outside with a blindfold on, leading him down the steps and untying it before he fell on his head.

He stood there for a minute, rubbing his eyes. Except in the movies, I'd never seen anyone rub their eyes in astonishment—but he actually put his fists to his eyes and twisted them into the sockets.

"Red car," he said finally. He was stock-still on the sidewalk, the

403

only time I'd seen him stand in one place without swaying like a mast. "My car win!"

"There's no room in the garage," I told him. "I'll have to keep it for you."

We took him for a test drive, speeding into NOT A THROUGH ROADS and startling neighbors. Back at the house, Mensa and I escaped to the bedroom. Dominic's excitement had gone to my head; I tried my best to emulate him, to imagine what he'd do in my situation. We lay in bed and I touched her breast through her coveralls, breathing in her scent. I was trembling with nerves but managed to get her clothes off without too much struggle. Her body was smooth and white, a distant memory of her face. She was twice my age and ready to instruct me. I was still clothed, luckily, when we heard someone pull up the driveway. The donors. I'd forgotten all about them. I looked at Mensa, who was lying next to me in her underthings.

"They're here to take a tour."

"Now?" she said. "You mean, like, immediately?"

"Stay here," I told her.

I shut her in the bedroom and went out to greet the donors, who were dressed in business clothes and inspecting the front azalea beds. These were the people, the guilty rich, who gave the agency money. I introduced them to Jason, who told them they were treading on thin ice and went back to his movie depicting the end of the world. I gave them a quick tour of the house, careful to avoid the bedroom. Just as I was leading them outside, Dominic returned from a bike ride toasting his Sweepstakes win, covered in scrapes and bruises.

"He's bleeding!" the man said to me.

"It's normal. He's a hemophiliac."

"You mean he can't stop? Shouldn't he go to the hospital?"

I laughed. "It's not that kind of hemophilia, thank God!"

Dominic smiled triumphantly from under his helmet. I clapped him on the back and the donors relaxed, touched by our camaraderie. The man wanted to see the backyard. I tried to distract him with a description of Jason's and Dominic's more inspirational qualities, but he insisted on visiting the garden where "the residents had planted tomatoes." Probably it was the benchmark by which he gauged whether his money was being well spent. I led them through the gate at the side of the house and headed for the backyard, but when I reached the lawn I turned around and saw them standing in the middle of the brick path, transfixed by something in the house.

They were staring at Mensa through the sliding-glass doors of the bedroom. She'd gotten dressed, at least, but was standing there in the middle of the room, her face frozen into a spectral frown.

"I thought there were only two," the man said.

"Moved in last week," I explained.

She stared at us through the windows. Then she started to skulk back and forth, pushing her lips out from her face so they touched her nose. She stopped and picked up one of her cowboy boots from the floor, gnawing on it like a steak.

"What's she doing?" the woman asked reverently, leaning in my ear.

"One of our sadder cases—doesn't leave the bedroom."

Later, when we'd completed the tour, they shook Jason's and Dominic's hands and the three of us accompanied them to their car. They seemed touched. They took a Polaroid of us in front of the house—a "family photo," the man called it—and we watched in astonishment as our faces stained the picture.

"This is good work, son," the man said. "Your parents must be proud."

* * *

That was the first day of July. Spring had wound down into Portland's nicest time of year. The clouds broke and the city revealed itself for the first time, the great river shining in the sun. The river stayed in your eyes when you looked somewhere else.

Mensa spent long hours on the lawn, transforming herself into beautiful shapes. It was like an ancient kind of alphabet. Jason, Dominic, and I crowded near the window, wondering what she was writing. We watched her rise on her forearms and swing her body over her head in the form of a scorpion.

One day, she asked me outside to join her. I took off my shoes and followed her onto the lawn, feeling the warmth of grass between my toes. She taught me poses, whichever occurred to her at the moment: the Warrior, the Cobra, the Up-Facing Dog. As I warped my body into shapes, I had the sensation of leaving a message for someone I couldn't see. Mensa and I sprawled on the grass and closed our eyes without moving—for what seemed like forever. Then we stood up and she showed me how to salute the sun.

* * *

Later, we decided to take the red-painted Subaru out for a real spin. I told Dominic that I had to do the driving, at least until he got a license, but that he could help me steer if he wanted. Jason lay across the backseat, his head propped on Mensa's lap. She stroked his hair and named what we passed. "Fire hydrant," she said. "Anarchists." I started out slowly but then picked up speed on the highway, cranking the easy-listening station as high as it would go. It was like old times. I let Dominic have the wheel and he honked at two women in a Jeep, sure of his irresistible allure.

We drove out to the country, where the radio went static. The cows moped around like ghosts. When we stopped the car to say hello, they tried to memorize our faces.

On the way back, a gust rose from the fields and an old sign lifted out of the bed of a dump truck in front of us, held aloft by the wind. It sailed toward us in slow motion, levitating over the highway. FREE DELIVERY, it said. I almost shut my eyes. Instead, I veered out of the way and lost control of the wheel. We rocked into a ditch on the side of the road, the glovebox flying open in a puff of gray powder. The four of us bounced in our seats. A second wind whipped through the Subaru and vanished into silence.

Our faces were dusted with ash. "Crazy idiot!" Mensa said—to the dump truck, I suppose.

"We're alive," I said. "That's what's important."

"Alive?" Jason asked.

We stared at each other, hearts pounding, and then I started the car again and headed for home.

Nominated by Julie Orringer, Zoetrope: All Story

LIKE WATER

by ELIZABETH SPIRES

from THE NEW CRITERION

It hadn't been three months since he had died
when we sat together in your living room,
a green world going on outside, the June wind
blowing hot and hard, bending each leaf and branch,
while inside all was still: a still interior where
three women sat in shadow stirring summer drinks,
the room the same as it had always been,

but changed, his absence palpable. You said,
"I thought I'd gradually miss him less, the way
a craving for a cigarette lessens a little after weeks
of going without. It's not like that." You paused,
drawing in a breath. "It's like a thirst that deepens
as each day passes. Like water," you finally said.
"I want him back the way I want a drink of water."

Nominated by Laurie Sheck, Philip Levine

BI BI HUA

memoir by M. ELAINE MAR

from AGNI

At the age of thirteen, I realized that my parents intended to arrange a marriage for me. They had not yet chosen a groom; my marriage was not predestined at birth, as in fairy tales or the apocryphal anecdotes that circulate about the friend of a friend from the Far East. But my parents' plans carried weight all the same. Their actions made the message clear: My body and my sexuality did not belong to me. I was not free to explore the tantalizing nether regions of sex, as my non-Chinese peers were.

Imagine my surprise: I was a gawky adolescent entering the eighth grade. In the tradition of American womanhood, I'd already learned to diet. I wore my hair coaxed into some version of the famous Farrah Fawcett 'do. My favorite movies were *Grease* and the PG-rated version of *Saturday Night Fever*. Memories of my immigration from Hong Kong eight years earlier were dim and dream-like. I could not conceive of myself as anything other than American. I could not imagine my future unfurling any differently than the ones depicted in *Teen* magazine—first date, first kiss, first dance, first break-up, first true love.

Early that fall, I was granted one of my firsts—first boyfriend, a red-haired ninth-grader who attended a different school, in a different school district. I got to know him on weekends, working at my family's Chinese restaurant. I was a dishwasher. He was a busboy. Like many hormone-driven teens, we were not terribly discreet about our relationship. We cuddled publicly, in the restaurant's service corridors. We sat on the same side of a dining-room booth and held hands throughout meals. We disappeared on "walks" for embarrassingly long, suggestive periods of time.

My parents objected, of course. They said that my behavior would ruin our family's reputation and demanded that we break up. I refused. A tortured, arduous series of arguments ensued. My father went so far as to hit me. In the end, the red-haired boy bowed out, unable to stand the drama. I was devastated, convinced that my parents had just ruined my life. I didn't know that the real shock was yet to come, delivered by my Uncle Andy.

Very calmly one night, sitting across from me in a booth at the family restaurant, Uncle Andy announced that I was not allowed to have boyfriends. My family intended to send me back to Hong Kong after my high school graduation. There, they would arrange an appropriate marriage for me.

Uncle Andy's words lingered like a curse. I hoped to defy my family's wishes. I planned a long line of secret dates. But I was foiled—first by the boys at my junior high, then the boys at my high school, none of whom showed the slightest interest in me sexually. I resigned myself to the stereotype of Oriental geek and worked on suppressing my sexual urges.

◆ ◆ ◆

As it turned out, my uncle's prophecy was not infallible. Harvard was the key to my freedom. At the recommendation of my high school English teacher (who knew nothing about my family situation), I applied to Harvard—and got in. Initially, my parents refused to let me go. Cambridge, Massachusetts, near Boston? Seventeen hundred miles away? Too far, they said. But the university was so famous and so well respected that even people in my family's highly insular immigrant community had heard of it. Once these people explained its significance to my parents, who didn't know the difference between Harvard and the local community college, they had to relent. I was overjoyed, knowing that no other excuse would have freed me from my parents' house.

So, upon graduation from high school, I was not shipped back to Hong Kong. Instead, I moved from my parents' house in Denver, Colorado, to a dorm room in Cambridge, Massachusetts. I was assigned to Hurlbut Hall, which stood across the street from the

Union, the building where freshmen took their meals. Hurlbut was one of the smaller freshman dorms, housing fewer than eighty students on four floors combined. I lived in a "pod"—an arrangement of locking bedrooms around a semi-private common room—on the third floor. There were seven one-room singles and a two-room triple in the pod; I lived in one of the singles.

Within the first week, my podmates and I agreed to treat the pod as one large suite. We set up furniture in our common room, exchanged home phone numbers, and made copies of our bedroom keys for one another to keep in case of emergency. I felt like a member of a typical freshman rooming group, rather than the occupant of a "psycho single." For which I was grateful.

I was finding my Harvard experience less than ideal. Back in Denver, I'd imagined all Harvard students as being a little like me—socially inexperienced, slightly eccentric, intellectually passionate. My thinking had not been sophisticated enough to include socioeconomic factors in this portrait, nor had I possessed the self-awareness to understand where on the economic spectrum my family lay. Rather than characterizing us as borderline poor—which would have been accurate—I'd honestly believed that we were middle class.

Given such naivete, I could not have prepared myself for the social realities of a college where one year's tuition roughly equaled my family's total annual income. I could not have anticipated the large number of Harvard students who came from affluent backgrounds and thus shared cultural references that were a mystery to me: prep schools, tennis camp, European vacations, ordinary-sounding people's names that turned out to be high-end clothing stores. Puzzled and embarrassed, I remained silent about my working-class background while resolving to learn the customs of this strange new land.

I befriended Leah, an activities-oriented student who lived in my pod's triple. She was one of those girls who always knew what was cool and who fit into which clique. Her judgments about Harvard people seemed especially keen, at least to me, because her father was a Harvard alumnus and her sister a Harvard junior. I figured that by watching Leah, I could clue myself in on Harvard's mysteries.

◆　◆　◆

On impulse one night, I began writing verse in ant-sized letters on one of the windowsills in Hurlbut's central landing. It was intended more to test the vigilance of Harvard's custodial staff than as any real literary effort, but that first spontaneous poem got my dorm mates' attention, so I continued writing miniature verse in random, half-hidden places throughout the dorm.

Not long after I began this project, a boy named Evan from the first floor pod started saying hello to me. Coming from Evan, this behavior was strange, since he rarely spoke to anyone. He tended to duck his head rather than exchange hellos when he ran into people on the sidewalk outside of Hurlbut. He was said to be a photographer of genius-level talent, and on faith, without having seen a single photo, I believed it. After all, Evan wore a lot of black. He had a high-pitched voice that was both intense and mocking. His tea-colored eyes were impassive behind a pair of black-rimmed glasses. He always seemed to be sneering. To me, these qualities, combined with Evan's solitary air and hint of neuroticism, suggested that he was an artist. Besides, we were at Harvard. I was ready to believe that anyone was a genius.

I was on my way into Hurlbut one day in late September when Evan stopped me. He said, "I found the one under the windowsill on the second floor."

I grinned involuntarily, understanding the reference to a poem I'd written a few days earlier.

"I liked the spiderweb imagery," he continued smoothly. "What does it symbolize?"

I shrugged. "Nothing. I didn't think that hard about it. I was just scribbling some neat images."

Evan stepped closer to me. His eyes remained impassive, but his mouth twitched. "Really?" he breathed. "I thought there might be some hidden sexual meaning."

My face grew hot. I couldn't tell whether I was being teased, so I remained silent.

He smiled and murmured, "I thought of you as a black widow waiting for a fly to get caught in your web. I thought of you wrapping the fly in silk and eating him, sucking him dry."

The sexual implication of his words was so obvious that even I understood. I wondered if this was some sort of flirtation. I didn't know how I felt if it was. According to Leah, Evan was not socially acceptable. But her judgment had to be weighed against the rumors of his artistic genius. I didn't have any strong feelings about Evan either way. I just didn't want to make a fool of myself here on the sidewalk

411

in front of Hurlbut for everyone to witness. Trying to sound detached and intellectual, I said, "That's an interesting interpretation."

Evan laughed. He took a step toward me and whispered, "You're tough, little Denver girl. Cold. I like that." His lips grazed my ear. Before I could respond, he walked away.

I watched him cross the street, feeling simultaneously intrigued and repulsed. I wondered who his friends at Harvard were. In my imagination, he was part of some artistic clique I had not yet discovered, a group of photographers and painters and poets who gathered in dimly lit coffeehouses to discuss their quest for an uncorrupted creative vision. I longed to become a part of this group, to have my own talents recognized. The image of this artistic clique, and my need for it to exist, were so strong that I never questioned its reality.

I began to see Evan everywhere—at the Union, his pale face and drab clothes shocking in the midst of preppy tan skin and pastel madras shirts; on the path in front of Hurlbut; loitering by the mailboxes in the entryway. He quizzed me about the ant-sized poems. He recited random lines of published poems and demanded that I identify the authors. He asked detailed questions about my day: What time did I usually get up? Did I eat breakfast? When did my lectures meet? When did I eat lunch? When did I eat dinner? I became increasingly confused and uncomfortable in his presence, but I remained uncertain about his intentions.

"Do you think he *likes* me?" I asked Leah after being stopped by him one day.

She looked over her shoulder at his retreating figure and wrinkled her nose. She declared definitively, "No, Elaine, he's just *weird*."

I felt strangely defeated. Leah disapproved of Evan, so he couldn't improve my standing in her eyes. Still, I'd wanted her to say yes. No one had ever had a crush on me before. I'd hoped that Evan was the first.

◆ ◆ ◆

I turned eighteen on October first of that year. My podmates threw me an impromptu party with champagne and an ice-cream cake. Various dorm mates and friends from my classes showed up. Peter, who lived in a suite on the first floor, impressed us all by opening the champagne with barely a pop. "It's because he's from Beverly Hills," Leah whispered in my ear. I nodded sagely, trusting her judgment, because I'd never met anyone from Beverly Hills before. I didn't question whether or not she had.

Evan didn't attend the party, and I didn't miss him.

I was coming back from dinner on Sunday of the following week when I saw Evan pacing the walk in front of Hurlbut. He ran out into the street grinning when he saw me. "Where are your *podmates*?" he asked, emphasizing the word sarcastically.

I answered him briefly, "They went to get ice cream."

Evan made a face. "Oh, how sweet. All you girls are so *sweet*."

Accustomed to his routine, I ignored him. I started up the path to the front door. Evan stayed close behind. "Why didn't you go?"

I shrugged. "I have reading to do."

Evan leered. "Why don't you read in *my* room?"

I didn't bother to answer him. I turned toward the staircase leading to Hurlbut's upper floors. Evan stepped in front of me. "I'll let you read Marilyn Hacker," he offered.

I paused. During one of our sidewalk encounters, Evan had told me that Marilyn Hacker was his favorite poet. I'd been embarrassed to admit that I'd never heard of her—and I'd been too busy since that conversation to look up any of her work.

Evan noticed my hesitation and insinuated his way sleekly into it, murmuring, "Let's go, Denver girl. Marilyn Hacker. My photographs. Everything you've always wanted."

I looked into his tea-colored eyes, startled.

He smiled. "Isn't that what you *really* want? To look at my photos. To spend time with an artist, someone on *your* level, instead of those preppy idiots like Leah and Rob."

I opened my mouth to protest, but no words came. I nodded, embarrassed by the transparency of my motives, my neediness.

Evan unlocked the door to his pod, and wordlessly I followed him inside. We walked past flattened cardboard boxes and an upended bedframe. Evan opened the door to his room.

It was unlike anything I'd seen at Harvard thus far.

His room was about the same size as my own, ten or twelve feet square—large for a freshman bedroom. It had the same white walls and pale yellow hardwood floor, the same Harvard-issue furniture—extra-long single bed (or, in this case, the mattress), office-size desk, three-shelf bookcase, and Harvard insignia captain's chair. But there the similarities ended.

Evan had disabled the overhead light fixture. He'd strung a series

413

of professional-quality photographer's studio lamps close to the ceiling. They burned the walls and ceiling an incredible bright white, illuminating every corner, giving the room a spare, loft-like feel. The effect of his adjustments was to obscure almost all suggestions that this was a Harvard dorm room. Although I'd never actually seen a New York artist's studio, I imagined that Evan's room looked like one. It looked like the Greenwich Village poet's quarters that I'd always imagined for myself.

The room was virtually undecorated—no rug on the floor, no posters on the wall. Instead, there were photographs. They were scattered rather than displayed, crowding the desk and the floor, pinned up on a clothesline, tacked to the wall. I scanned the black-and-white prints quickly, absorbing their sharp outlines. When I looked up, I was surprised to see Evan's face, the faintly beige skin, the shocking red hair, the dark amber eyes.

His expression was inscrutable. "What do you think?" he asked softly. "Are the rumors true? Am I a genius, like everyone says?"

I stared back at him silently. I wanted to be mean and tell Evan no, he didn't have any talent at all, but the words stuck in my throat. Instead, I said honestly, "Yes. I think you are."

Evan chuckled. "So sweet," he murmured, his voice silky. "My sweet little Denver girl."

I scowled. "Where's the Marilyn Hacker?" I asked impatiently, pointing at my watch. "It's almost seven-thirty. I have, like, two hundred pages of reading to do."

In response, Evan gestured toward his bed, which lay at the far end of the room, by the windows. It had been reduced to its most basic components, a single mattress on the floor, covered with black sheets. He said, "Make yourself comfortable."

I hesitated, uncertain of his intentions.

Evan sneered, "What's wrong, Denver girl? Afraid to sit on my bed? Afraid of what I'll do to you?"

"No," I snapped, instinctive bravado kicking in. "I've sat on lots of boys' beds." I crossed the floor and flopped down on the mattress.

"Oh really?" Evan breathed. "Lots of experience with boys' beds? Tell me about it."

My face flushed hot. "Just . . . I mean, I'm good at making beds. Hospital corners. So some of the guys at Harvard, freshman year, they need help . . ." My voice faltered.

Evan laughed.

I heard the challenge, the judgment about my lack of desirability. Just like high school. "Some of these guys *have* come on to me," I told Evan defensively.

He made a dismissive sound and said, "That's just because you're Chinese."

I tensed, hating the implication before I knew its exact nature. Up to that moment, I'd almost forgotten the racial difference between us and simply been comfortable in my skin, sparring with him student to student, girl to boy, exploring the boundaries of male-female relationships. What right did he have to take that away from me?

Choking back my anger, I snapped, "What does being Chinese have to do with anything?"

Evan cocked his head, looking amused. "Don't you know? Chinese girls are easy." He spoke casually, as if reporting a benign, well-known fact, like the color of grass.

But I'd never heard this stereotype before. I felt my mouth curve upward in an absurd, defensive smile. My smile faltered, then reappeared. I heard myself giggle. "What are you talking about?"

Evan elaborated, making sure that I understood: "*All* Asian women are easy. You should see the sex shops in New York, Chinese girls everywhere, their legs spread wide open, fucking strangers by the hundred, twenty bucks a pop. It's the same here, at Harvard, the rich preppies looking for a taste of Chinese cunt. Guys just come on to you because they know you'll sleep with them."

"No." My throat constricted. My eyes filled with tears. How could he say these things? The last few weeks at Harvard had been the best of my life. For the first time, boys were flirting with me, ignoring—or perhaps even appreciating—the Asian features that I'd always considered ugly. I thought that I might have arrived at a place where the standard for beauty could include me. But here Evan was, providing another explanation. The boys didn't think I was pretty. They only wanted to use me for sex. I didn't want to believe him. Words rushed out of my mouth defensively: "But I don't, I'm not, I've never . . ."

Evan grinned.

My sentence lost force and drifted off. Images of another red-haired boy flashed through my head: A weekend at my family's restaurant. Screaming voices and broken drinking glasses. My body vibrating with desire, insisting that I had a right to date the busboy.

In Evan's room, remembering how young I'd been and how far I'd gone sexually, I was overcome with shame and guilt. But that had

415

been a long time ago, I reminded myself—and I hadn't had a boyfriend since. I forced the memories out of my head. "Marilyn Hacker?" I reminded Evan brusquely.

He snorted, dug through a pile of paper on his desk, and handed me a magazine folded to the right page. He sat in the captain's chair by his desk. I proceeded to read.

Silence settled as I made my way into the poem. I read intently, trying hard to formulate an intelligent analysis. Then, after several minutes of quiet, Evan's voice interrupted my concentration: "So when are we going to fuck?"

I looked up in surprise. "What?"

He repeated slowly and clearly, "So when are we going to fuck?"

I heard the words but wasn't able to make sense of them. What was Evan hoping to accomplish? He didn't actually want to have sex with me, did he? We'd never even kissed. I stared into his eyes, searching for a clue. They were opaque, as always. He must be testing me, tricking me into being that easy Asian woman, I decided. Determined to prove him wrong, I said coldly, "Never. Why are you even asking?"

He grinned. "Oh come on, Denver girl. Stop pretending. You know that you're attracted to me, and I'm attracted to you."

My heart stopped, mid-beat, startled. Evan was attracted to me. He just said that he was attracted to me. If I weren't so confused, I'd be flattered. Then I focused in on the rest of his sentence. He'd also accused me of being attracted to him. How dare he. My face flushed hot. He was far too quirky, too unwilling to be liked by the mainstream Harvard crowd. I couldn't afford to be attracted to him. If Leah knew that I was in Evan's room now, I'd be humiliated. I opened my mouth to retort.

Before any words came out, Evan spoke again, "You *know* you're attracted to me," he insisted. "Why else would you wear those tight jeans? Why else would you write those poems on the windowsill? You're calling attention to yourself, waiting for me."

The heat in my face intensified. His acknowledgment of my sexuality was so embarrassing it was almost unbearable. "I don't know what you're talking about," I blurted out, lying. "What tight jeans?"

Evan grinned. "Nice trick, Denver girl. Playing innocent. It's sexy." He stood, slinked across the room, sat next to me on his mattress. "Marilyn Hacker," he said, reaching across my body to take hold of the journal. I leaned backward to avoid his touch. His arm moved with me, motioning my body down toward the mattress.

I let myself fall, almost experimentally, curiosity fighting nerves over the anticipation of what might come next. No one had ever called me sexy before. No one had ever paid attention to how I dressed. So I'd never had to consider how I might act if someone showed interest in me beyond asking me to make his bed. I was dying to find out not only what *Evan* might do, but how *I* might react.

Evan stretched himself out on the narrow twin mattress alongside me, one arm draped across my torso. I lay motionless beside him, savoring the moment. Would he kiss me now, I wondered, and would I let him? Thoughts flurried, barely conscious memories of high school crushes and rejections, boys who'd fabricated ludicrous excuses for not accompanying me to school dances. I was a changed person now. Lying next to Evan, I felt desired for the first time. Powerful. I imagined all the ways I could tell him "no." I could let him down gently or cruelly. I could string him along for weeks or end it now. I looked into his tea-colored eyes, smiling.

Evan said, "So do you want to take off your own clothes, or should I do it for you?"

Still smiling, I answered haughtily, "Neither. I told you, I don't know what you're talking about."

Evan rolled onto his side, propping himself up on one elbow to look me in the face. Very calmly, he said, "Let's just do this, Denver girl. No more of these games."

"Do what?" I asked, my voice lilting flirtatiously.

Evan frowned. "Fuck," he growled. "Let's go ahead and fuck."

"No." I sat up angrily. How dare he use that word, that tone of voice? He should chase after me with promises of dinner and movie dates, not treat me like some prostitute. Fighting back tears, I said, "I need to go."

Evan laughed. "No you don't." He pulled me back down, one deft move barely rougher than the flirtatious wrestling of a Harvard boy congratulating me for a well-made bed.

I inched sideways, squirming out of his grasp. "I do. I have reading for tomorrow, I told you—"

"Skip it. You're smart enough to bullshit your way through class without reading."

"Yes, but . . ." I hesitated, taken in by the flattery.

417

"Wouldn't you rather fuck?"

"No."

"Why not?"

"I—"

"Aren't you a little curious?" he countered, before I could complete the answer. "I can make you feel so, so good."

My body tingled at his words, remembering another red-haired boy, reminded of other words and images, all the fantasy scenarios I'd struggled to suppress throughout my adolescence. "Yes," I blurted out honestly, without thinking. "I am curious."

"So let's do it."

"No." I ignored the tingle and tried to regain control. "This isn't right, this isn't the way it should be."

He laughed. "How 'should' it be?"

I shrugged. Turned my head. Mumbled, "I don't know, but . . . I mean, we haven't even kissed."

He put his face close to mine. "Do you want me to kiss you?"

I shook my head. "No."

His face hardened, moved away. "Good. None of that bullshit bourgeois romantic stuff."

I tried to sit up again. "I should go."

He yanked me back. "Okay, you win. We won't fuck. Just a blow job."

"No." My voice annoyed.

"Have you ever given a blow job?"

I answered honestly, automatically, "Yes."

Evan jerked back slightly, unable to hide his surprise. "Where? At Harvard, making other people's beds?"

I congratulated myself for surprising him. "No," I said, making sure I sounded bored and cavalier. "In Denver. Of course."

Evan seemed to relax, regain his composure. "Denver," he sneered. "What kind of blow job could you give in Denver?"

I shrugged elaborately. Told Evan, "Well, *he* said it was good."

Evan's eyes narrowed. He grinned. "Why don't you show me?"

I sighed. We'd looped around again. I twisted my head, looked at the door. "I have reading to do."

Evan made a sound of disgust. "I knew you couldn't do it. You're all talk, Denver girl."

Anger flared in my chest. Evan had no right to call me a liar. The

418

blow job had been all too real. My father had beaten me up for fooling around with the red-haired boy. If only Evan knew—but I didn't dare reveal how provincial, backward, and un-American my family was. I tamped down my anger. "No, I can. I have. It's just . . ." My voice trailed off, embarrassed by the words that were to come: *It's just that I don't love you. I want to have sex, but only with someone I love.* How quaint it would sound to his ears, but how daring to mine—the idea that I could choose to have sex at all.

Evan studied my face with his narrowed eyes. "Are you a virgin?"

I swallowed hard. "No," I lied, hoping to end his prying.

Evan sat up and stripped off his t-shirt. "Let's do it then."

I shook my head.

He leaned over me, still propped up on one elbow. "Come on," he wheedled. "At least a blow job. Show me how good you are. We'll fuck like artists on the Left Bank, like artists in New York."

I closed my eyes, blocking out his presence. In the weeks before leaving for college, I'd spent countless hours daydreaming about Harvard boys. I'd imagined intense relationships with artists and writers—but in every fantasy, my Harvard boyfriend was gay, and content to hold me in bed for the closeness, the solid warmth of a human body, making no sexual demands. This paradox had never struck me as strange. Growing up in a family where I had not been held since I learned to walk, the desire for even this amount of contact had seemed subversive, dangerous. I'd felt perverse wanting it and couldn't allow my imagination to go deeper, to think about the places I could be touched, the places I could touch.

I had not met one single openly gay boy since arriving at Harvard.

Evan was the only artist I knew.

I didn't know how long I'd been lying on Evan's mattress, but suddenly, I didn't feel desirable or powerful. I felt young, stupid, naïve. I didn't have the prep-school poise of the mainstream Harvard crowd, and I wasn't courageous enough to behave like an artist, either. I was only a backroom restaurant worker wearing her customer's hand-me-downs off to college. A poor girl dressed in designer clothes that had been fashionable a year earlier, only I was too ignorant to know it.

Evan's voice, insistent in my ear: "Just a blow job. What's the big deal? A blow job, and you can go read those pages. You know, it'll relieve tension and help you concentrate."

I opened my eyes. How inevitable Evan's face now seemed, the natural consequence of so many years of repression. For all the images I'd constructed, writing poems on dorm windowsills, I couldn't imagine a way out of this scenario.

I gave in.

Time collapsed, events unfolding out of sequence. Evan's voice curled inside my ear. The air filled with the bitterness of his skin, a pungency like copper. His penis scraped the back of my throat. I tasted his stickiness, his bitterness, the thickness of his copper scent. I gagged. His hand pushed down on my head. Fifteen minutes stretched into one hour, two. I was naked.

Evan's torso rose above me, the muscles in his shoulders and arms twitching. He lowered himself onto me, into me. There was a quick, sharp pain. I tensed. I pressed my palms against his chest and pushed, but he was inside me. I heard myself say, "No, you bastard, stop," but he was inside me, pounding away, and I could no longer feel anything, I could only see an impossible vision, the sight of myself and Evan from above as I was suspended from the ceiling: I saw his back above me, his glowing hairless flesh. I saw the cleft of his buttocks, the indent of his spine, the white skin, the impossibly white skin. But I didn't see my body. I had no body.

It was after four in the morning by the time I got back to my room. My eyes felt electric, seared hot and dry. My skin smelled of semen. When I brushed my teeth, I gagged on the viscous mixture of toothpaste and saliva creeping down my throat. I spit. Rinsed. Wiped my mouth. I took off my clothes. Every time I moved, the smell intensified, a smell like rubber, like bleach. I couldn't bear it. I wrapped myself in my bathrobe and slipped out to the shower.

My first class started at ten, but I didn't awake until eleven. I figured that it didn't matter. I could skip the class. I hadn't done the reading, after all. Easing myself gingerly out of bed, I crept to the common room and curled up in a corner of our brown leatherette loveseat. The pod was absolutely silent; all my podmates must have classes of their own. A wedge of sunlight streamed from my open bedroom door. Motionless in the corner of the loveseat, I studied the dust motes floating in the light.

My pelvis ached, proof that I hadn't imagined the previous evening. Even so, I couldn't quite believe what had happened. I had had sex. My body told me this, but I didn't want to believe it. I'd wanted to fall in love, to be in a serious relationship, perhaps one headed toward marriage, before I had sex for the first time. Now that was no longer an option.

I wondered what to make of my night with Evan. I'd never considered the possibility that I might have sex with someone that I didn't care about, under circumstances that made me want to throw up. I wanted to think about my loss of virginity the way that I imagined an artist would, as a meaningless but necessary technical procedure, one more marker of adulthood—like college. But the night hadn't been meaningless for me; my body felt paradoxically empty and weighted by it, as if Evan had removed all my viscera and filled that space with a dense, unbreathable air.

I still hadn't come to any conclusions when I was stirred back to awareness by sounds from outside the pod—voices in the hallway, a key scratching the lock. My podmates, returning from class, or was it lunch? What time was it? How long had I been sitting there?

I wanted to get up to greet them, to smile and say hello, I wanted to go to my room and get dressed and comb my hair, I wanted to behave like a normal human being, but the weight was too much, and I couldn't move, I could only sit there.

The pod door opened. Leah and two other podmates, Anna and Ellen, walked in, trailing the faintly metallic scent of cold air behind them.

What would they make of my situation? What did *they* think of sex? I'd never consciously thought about this before, but now I was forced to: I knew that Ellen was a devout Catholic; she was the only pod member who regularly attended religious services of any kind. I guessed that she was against premarital sex. Anna had a boyfriend in California; he was older and worked as a professional model. She'd lived with him the previous summer, in order to escape her parents' marital problems, so they'd *probably* had sex—but we'd never talked about that aspect of their relationship, so I didn't know for sure. I'd spent enough time with Leah to know that she disapproved of premarital sex, or casual sex, anyway. I could tell by the way she sniffed at boys' sex talk and rolled her eyes at the mention of some girls' names—girls who spent the night in boys' dorm rooms.

Not expecting my presence, my podmates walked past me without looking.

But I needed their attention. I cleared my throat.

They stopped. Turned. Three automatic hellos.

Then, seeing my nightgown, the glasses heavy on my face, Anna laughed. "Oh, Elaine," she said, mock scolding. "You missed classes *again*?"

I nodded.

She shook her head. "I don't know how you do it," she said, already turning away again, headed for her room.

Leah and Ellen followed close behind her, their laughter overlapping hers.

Anna's voice continued, "If I slept in the way you do, I could never keep up."

They were leaving. I didn't want them to go. Without thinking, I opened my mouth. "Wait, you guys . . ." My voice sounded panicked.

They turned.

I stared at them, brain stuck mid-sentence, not knowing what came next. For reasons unknown to me, I felt compelled to tell them about Evan. But what would I say? Last night I had sex for the first time? I spent the night with Evan? These sentences sounded so neutral. They didn't describe the queasiness in my stomach, the tightness of my throat, the memory of his copper scent and his hand pushing on the back of my head. Suddenly I recalled a student group presentation from freshman week—"Response," a peer rape crisis counseling group. No means no, they'd said. Date rape is real rape. Last night, I'd said no. I *had* said no, hadn't I? My mind was blank. I couldn't remember. I couldn't remember whether I'd said no. I couldn't remember anything except the whiteness of his body above mine, the dark cleft of his buttocks as he thrust into me, the impossible vision from the night before.

I opened my mouth. I heard myself speak. I heard myself say, "You guys, I think Evan raped me last night."

❖ ❖ ❖

That one moment came to haunt me for a long time.

First there were the gasps, the ashen faces, the long silence as

Ellen, Anna, and Leah took in my words. After a while, Anna said, "Are you sure?"

Their faces helped me realize the full import of what I'd just said, and I wanted to take it back. I strained to say the word *no*, but when I opened my mouth again, I only repeated the sentence: "Yeah. I think Evan raped me last night."

Now, instead of silence, there were questions, then after the questions, advice, softly worded commands of the usual sort—you need medical attention, you need counseling, you need to call your parents, you need to report this to the dorm proctor and the police, you need to get this boy out of the dorm—out of *our* lives, as well as your own.

I followed along as best as I could, submitting to a medical exam with full rape kit, speaking to a University Health Services counselor, calling every person I could think of—excluding my family—to build my "support network." Whenever I became confused about how I was supposed to act, I fell back on the "Response" pamphlets, faithfully trotting to the library to read the recommended books and articles.

I resisted only on one point, and only until I was worn down by Leah's parents—I refused to report the incident to either the police or university authorities. To do so, in my mind, would mean making it an "official" rape, and I still wasn't sure that the term was warranted.

Sex with Evan had not been entirely voluntary. Of this I was certain. I'd been coerced and manipulated. But I didn't think that I'd been *forced*—and without force, was there rape? I studied the literature, looking for an answer, searching for a word to encompass the range of my experience—curiosity, confusion, naïveté, coercion, manipulation, fear, submission, an unwilling consent.

The pamphlets, books, and articles all came back with the same answer—I'd been raped. In its own way, the literature was as close-minded as my family on the topic of sex. My choices were dichotomous, an either-or, with no room for ambiguity. Sex was either sanctioned by marriage or immoral, entirely voluntary or rape. I had to choose one.

◆ ◆ ◆

Leah's parents, the Bauers, presented my dilemma another way: Refusing to report the incident as a rape, they asserted, was selfish.

They were sorry for my hurt and confusion, but they couldn't help me with that. In fact, they weren't thinking about me at all; they were concerned for their daughter. According to Leah's father, the most important thing was to report Evan so that he couldn't hurt *her* the way he'd hurt me.

"He wouldn't do anything to Leah," I protested. "He doesn't even like her."

"If you don't report him," Dr. Bauer replied, "I'll do it myself."

Having no other choice, I contacted University officials.

◆ ◆ ◆

At about the same time, giving up on seeing the event as anything other than a rape, I called Jim, a friend from a summer program that I'd attended between junior and senior years of high school. That summer, we'd spent one night secluded on a fire escape, talking about the meaninglessness of life until four in the morning. I'd hoped that the conversation might lead to a romance, but Jim had become involved with another girl at the program instead. Since then, Jim and Kirsten had broken up. Beginning this fall, Jim and I had talked by phone almost weekly. We'd discussed the possibility of his coming to visit me at Harvard—leaving open all that such a visit might entail.

But as much as I cared about Jim, I hadn't actively encouraged him to make the trip. Knowing what I did about Jim's relationship with Kirsten, I was certain that he'd want to have sex with me if he visited, and while I wanted him to be my boyfriend, I remained ambivalent about a relationship that included sex. Although my parents wouldn't have to find out, because they were half a continent way, my podmates would know, and they were just outside my bedroom door. My social status at Harvard was too tenuous. Without my podmates' explicit approval, which had not been expressed, I couldn't agree to sleep with Jim.

Of course, after Evan, none of this mattered anymore. I called Jim.

◆ ◆ ◆

He came up by train from Princeton a few days later. We hugged. We talked. I told him about Evan again. He took me out to dinner at a Mexican restaurant. We returned to Hurlbut, climbed the stairs to my pod, said a brief hello to my podmates, and locked ourselves in my bedroom. I took off my coat, sat on my bed. Wordlessly, Jim approached me. He bent, lifted my foot, removed my shoe. I lay back on the bed, watching him. He kissed the sole of my foot. I cringed, repulsed by the intimacy—but I didn't protest. Without a single word, he undressed me, then himself, and we had sex.

◆ ◆ ◆

We lay in bed together in the darkening room. Outside, the sun had set, but a residual bluish light limned the solid dark contours of the objects furnishing my room. When the phone rang, I could see well enough to answer it without flicking on a lamp.

"Hello?" I mumbled, crouched on the floor naked, phone to my ear.

Evan's voice slid out the other end, a sinuous murmur: "I really like you." Chuckle. "How about going for a walk and getting some ice cream?"

My breath caught. Against my face, the telephone handset glowed an eerie green, luminescence cast by the push-button numbers. The room seemed to darken, and I was suddenly, acutely aware of my nakedness. I curled in on myself further, hiding my breasts and genitalia. Although I knew it to be physically impossible, I was sure that he could see me through the telephone line, a pale, solitary figure glowing green in the darkness, illuminated by the push buttons of my phone.

I could hear him breathing. He said my name.

I bit back my panic and said, "Yes?"

"How about going for ice cream?"

"No."

"Oh, come on," he wheedled, his voice teasing, oblivious to my panic. "Why not?"

He didn't know yet, I realized. He didn't know that I'd reported him to the Freshman Dean's Office, and I didn't want to be the one to inform him. "I need to study," I lied.

"Awww," he answered sarcastically. "How about some other night?"

"Yeah," I said, then, "I have to go." I barely gave him time to say good-bye before hanging up.

I stood up, arms crossed over my chest. I couldn't believe that Evan had just asked me out on a date. I'd reported him as a rapist, and he'd asked me out for ice cream. Ice cream, just like the preppy idiots he made fun of. Could it be that he never intended to hurt me at all? I blanked out the thought. I wasn't strong enough to feel sorry for us both. I'd read the literature. I'd been lectured by the Bauers. I'd been raped. There was no going back.

I walked across the room and crawled into bed. Jim pulled my body close to his. "Who was that?"

"Never mind," I whispered. I edged away from him, ending the conversation, alone in the telephone's green light.

◆ ◆ ◆

Jim was still there on Saturday morning, two days later, when my proctor (the Harvard version of a resident advisor) knocked at my bedroom door.

"I'm not up yet," I told George, the proctor, warily, embarrassed to be caught in bed with a boy.

George coughed. "I'm sorry. Can you come out here? I need to talk to you."

Heart racing, I bolted out of bed and tugged on a robe. "What?" I slipped out the door and shut it behind me quickly, blocking Jim from George's view.

George didn't even bother trying to look over my shoulder. His face was drawn, a professional seriousness suppressing any more visceral reaction. He coughed again. Said, "Something's happened to your pod." Stepped aside so that I could take a look.

The pod had been vandalized.

In the middle of the night, someone had rigged a spider's web of string and styrofoam cups across our ceiling. Inside the cups were broken eggs. Strings connected the cups both to each other and to our bedroom doors. This contraption was designed to release the eggs when our doors opened. Fortunately, my podmate Leslie had awakened early, discovered the trap, and untied most of the strings, limiting the damage to the pod. But despite her efforts, we spent the day scrubbing egg yolks off our rug, wiping them from between the cushions of the loveseat, and scooping them out of the corners of our common room closets. We found a total of seven dozen eggs.

None of us specifically named Evan when speculating about

426

who might have committed the vandalism, but my podmates' half-finished sentences and sidelong glances communicated their suspicions plainly. In that moment, I realized with the clarity of a premonition how public my story was about to become. Every sentence that remained incomplete in my presence would find its audience once I was out of the room.

◆ ◆ ◆

Jim walked with me to the convenience store to buy more cleaning supplies—Ajax, Pine-Sol, Murphy's Oil Soap. He got pizzas for the entire pod. He complained only briefly when he realized that we'd mistakenly used—and ruined—one of his towels scrubbing the pod floor.

Holding me in bed that night, he whispered, "What a psycho. I wish there were something I could do." He stroked my hair until I fell asleep.

Unable to bear the confluence of emotional and physical intimacy, I did not invite Jim to visit again.

◆ ◆ ◆

Two of my podmates, Leah and Becky, tried to gather evidence linking Evan to the vandalism but failed. We were never able to bring charges against him for this incident. We had to be satisfied with our own indignation—and the report of date rape.

Harvard's protocol for dealing with date rape was brisk and cerebral: First, I was summoned to the Freshman Dean's Office and asked to write a formal statement describing the events in Evan's room. In a separate appointment, Evan provided his own formal account of the same night. We were called back to the FDO individually to read each other's statements. We were allowed to furnish a rebuttal. Our statements were then discussed by the college's Administrative Board, who issued a formal recommendation.

The Board suggested mediation.

Mediation.

As if Evan and I had disagreed about the results of an academic research project.

When the Freshman Dean informed me, I laughed—a hot, bitter sound.

The Freshman Dean asked why I was so angry.

I said, "I was raped. Why do you think?"

In response, he blinked once, nothing more.

Evan and I never met for mediation. We did not have any further contact, although I occasionally saw him around Hurlbut or in the Union. These instances were rare and fleeting—a glimpse of his wiry form across the dining hall, a flash of his red hair ducking in a door. Each time, I froze momentarily, panicked, short of breath and nauseated.

Evan remained on the edge of my consciousness for the next four years. Almost by instinct, without any effort or will, I stayed apprised of his activities. I knew where he lived, who his friends were, what subjects he studied, what films he made, what awards he won. By the time we graduated, he'd received a fair number of artistic accolades and had a steady girlfriend. I absorbed this information with a mixture of dismay and relief. Part of me found it unfair that neither Harvard nor fate had punished Evan. The other part, still ambivalent about having called the incident rape, was glad that I had not completely ruined Evan's life.

I didn't tell my parents about Evan. I didn't want them to know that I was no longer a virgin. Despite my resistance to their traditional ideas about gender roles and arranged marriages, I still wanted to please them to the best of my abilities. Even if my first intercourse had been joyful, I would not have wanted my parents to know about it. I certainly was not going to announce that I'd been coerced into sex, that I'd reported it as a date rape, and that I was now the subject of dorm rumors.

Compounding the problem was Evan's comment, "All Asian women are easy." I wanted to protect my parents from these words, just as I'd protected them from racist remarks throughout my childhood by not translating those particular words. I'd always thought that if my parents didn't understand the words, they wouldn't understand the sneers on the store clerks' faces or the intent behind the beer splashed down our backs the one time my family sat down to watch a men's softball game in the neighborhood park. Despite my teenage rebellion, I never wanted my parents to know about racism. I didn't want them to know that other people could hate them as much as I sometimes did—but without the love I felt to temper my hostility.

I grew up in a household where adults never touched, and no one was ever naked. Even as a young child, I wasn't allowed to leave the bathroom after a bath until I was fully dressed—underwear, undershirt, pajamas, robe, and slippers. My mother still refused to talk about sex; she would only say, "Never be alone in a room with a man. Never let a man touch you." And the only time I'd had a boyfriend, my family had reacted violently. Given these circumstances, it was hard for me to think of myself—or any of my female relatives—as sexual. Evan's characterization of us all as "easy" felt like a violation.

Before my night with Evan, I didn't realize that Asian women could be seen as sexual fetish objects. Growing up, I never saw Asian women portrayed as sex objects in the magazines that I read or the television shows and movies that I watched; I never saw them in these media at all. The boys in high school clearly did not think that I, as an Asian girl, was "easy"—they never asked me out in the hopes of receiving sexual favors, nor even attempted a pass at me during lunch periods. If anyone flirted with me, chances were that he wanted homework help, not sex. In high school, the one Asian stereotype I knew was *science geek*. Once, someone even called me "a typical Oriental" who made the word sex sound "scientific." This, despite the fact that I nearly failed high-school chemistry.

I didn't know what to do about Evan's comment. It bothered me, but I didn't feel comfortable discussing the issue with any of my podmates or even my counselor at University Health Services, a middle-aged white woman who nodded in automatic sympathy every time I paused for breath. We didn't discuss race as an issue in Harvard's mainstream population. It, like money and privilege, was an embarrassing topic. Feeling like I'd caused enough trouble already, I decided to remain silent about Evan's comment, saving my confusion for my journals.

◆　◆　◆

I quit counseling after three sessions, feeling like a failure because I didn't know how to answer questions about how I felt, much less explain why I felt that way. I could talk about my situation intellectually, but I didn't have any grasp of my emotional state. Most of the time, unless I was confronted with external clues—physical sensations like the wetness of my own tears or the sound of my raised voice—I had trouble naming my emotions.

I wasn't so much avoiding the issue (consciously or subconsciously) as I was confused by the American concept of an individual self whose feelings and experiences have distinct boundaries from those of family and community. Growing up in a traditional Chinese family, I'd been trained to think of myself not as a separate individual, but as one part of a larger whole, seamlessly connected to my parents, my brother, my aunts and uncles—even in some small way to my classmates and schoolteachers, even now.

At an early age, I learned to define my emotions based on other people's reactions to me. If my mother was happy, I felt happy. If my teacher disapproved of my work, I felt sad. If my friends were angry, I felt bereft. I had trouble understanding myself outside the context of interpersonal relationships, no matter how much I wanted to—no matter how American I believed myself to be.

In fact, I had no idea what it meant to have my own voice, one that was internally, rather than externally, constructed.

I studied the pamphlets handed out by the college rape crisis center. They spoke of depression, anger, anxiety, confusion, guilt. I echoed these feelings back to the University Health Services therapist, trying to be a good date rape victim. My head and throat and chest hurt when she told me I wasn't examining my emotions deeply enough. I wanted to scream, frustrated by the lack of language, angry at the therapist's assumption that I could so easily own myself.

My sexuality reeled out of control for a long time after Evan. I became intent on proving that no lasting damage had been done, and used sex as the method to do so. Angry at myself for having been so naïve about sex, and at my parents for having raised me this way, I worked to separate emotion from sex. I made an effort to view the act as insignificant, irrelevant to the rest of my life. "Sport fucking," I laughed, echoing the Harvard boys. Wanting to know how sex felt when it was freely, unambiguously given, I had sex with a lot of men; I didn't realize that my deliberation, in itself, created the ambiguity. Sex during this period was always voluntary but never enjoyable.

Whenever I could be honest with myself, I wished for physical intimacy with someone I loved—or even liked. I wished that my first

430

time had been this way. In these moments, I understood exactly what Evan had taken from me, and the damage *was* irreparable. I kept myself busy, avoiding the flashes of clarity. I told Leah that Evan had not been my first, hoping to delude myself as well as her.

For most of freshman year, after Evan, I didn't care why someone wanted to sleep with me. I collected men like books of poetry, objects for my shelf, within my control. There were men who prowled for random bodies, men who were seen at breakfast with a different Asian woman each week, men who seemed to desire me because they'd heard the rumor that I'd been date raped.

Then I realized that I wasn't in control.

The pornographic avidity of this last group, which comprised three members of Hurlbut's first-floor suite, shocked me to my senses. Initially, I believed these boys to be my friends, because they had the courage to ask me directly about what had happened, rather than whisper as I passed. But over time, their interest took on an obsessive, fetishistic quality. They started challenging me to get over the rape by sleeping with them, singly or as a group. They showed me soft-porn magazines and rubbed against me, asking, "Did he do anything like this?"

I finally broke down in the first-floor suite at the end of freshman year, collapsing in a crying fit more profound than any I'd suffered in the previous months. By the time the boys called for help, I was trying to cut myself with a piece of broken glass. The Harvard Police and my proctor intervened. They escorted me to the UHS emergency psychiatric ward, where I spent the night crying uncontrollably.

When I returned for sophomore year, I was placed on disciplinary probation for one semester. I wasn't mandated to attend counseling, and I didn't seek it on my own until junior year, the morning of my *Introduction to Anglo-Saxon Poetry* final. Chris, my boyfriend at the time, had broken up with me a week earlier. I remained devastated. He'd been my first "real" boyfriend, the first sexual partner I'd loved. We'd been together almost a year and a half. I'd expected us to spend our lives together.

I'd been crying non-stop for days, too depressed to get out of bed some mornings. The day of the final, I managed to make it out of bed but couldn't stop crying long enough to attend the exam. That morning, sobbing into a Kleenex while a UHS clinician approved my absence from the final (which I would have to make up later), I realized that I needed to start evaluating the events of the last few years. Otherwise, I wouldn't make it through another semester.

On my way out of the clinic, I scheduled a counseling appointment. It was only a beginning step in the long process of learning to become whole, one that continues still, although the counseling ended years ago.

◆ ◆ ◆

I used to think that getting over the events of freshman year was like being an alcoholic—I was always in recovery, never recovered. But it's been over fifteen years now, and long stretches pass when I don't think of that period at all. I no longer have nightmares about lying in bed paralyzed while men creep in next to me. I don't worry about being attacked every time I'm alone in an enclosed space with a man.

I'm not sure when the memories lost their edge and set me free. There was a point, senior year of college, when I stopped being ashamed of what had happened and started wearing my status as a date rape survivor like a badge of honor. I became politically active in women's issues, particularly with regard to sexual violence. Today, I remain just as passionate about these issues, but I feel less compelled to present my life in such stark, polemic terms.

I think far more about the way I got to Evan's room that night. I try to trace the trajectory from my teen magazines, the red-haired busboy, my family's history of arranged marriages, and my own, conflicting desires, to Evan's room. I try to trace the trajectory from that room to the choices I've made since. I think about my mother, and how she's never been allowed to decide whom to love.

◆ ◆ ◆

On a recent New Year's Eve, I found myself standing outside a bar on New York's Upper West Side with my friend Kiendel, whom I was visiting from Boston. It was four in the morning, and the party that we'd attended had ended. Now we were trying to get rid of some

432

men—three or four total—who thought it was a good idea for us to have more drinks with all of them at one of their apartments. That night, I was wearing sharp-toed, black patent-leather pumps with four-inch stiletto heels. Kiendel is a natural blonde with hair so pale it glows like filaments of light. She is slender but curvaceous. Between the two of us, we fulfilled the criteria for any number of fetishes. Now that we were in our thirties, we understood this. We knew that these men did not see beyond our physicality. We would never be swayed by their arguments; we were simply trying to leave without being rude.

Mid-discussion, a taxi pulled up at the curb, four or five feet from where we stood. I turned my head, glad for the distraction. Perhaps Kiendel and I could take this, an available cab, as our excuse, I thought. The taxi doors opened, and three men poured out. There were two white men of the same approximate height, both with dark hair, one's curly, the other's straight. Their faces weren't familiar, so I didn't pay attention to them. The third man was black, with soft-looking, pale brown skin. His woolly dark hair was cut close to the scalp. His eyes were heavy lidded, giving him a perpetually sleepy appearance. They were familiar eyes, a familiar face, although I had not seen this man, a college friend, in over five years. I stepped away from Kiendel and said his name uncertainly, "Vaughn?"

He answered with my name. I ran to him, and we hugged. He said, "I think about you every day."

"You liar!" I teased. "I haven't seen you for five years, at least—not since I moved out of New York."

"I know," he said, "but the last time I heard from you, you'd left a message on my machine, asking me to come protest the opening of *Miss Saigon*. I didn't come, but now I work in a building across the street from *Miss Saigon*. I think about you every time I look across the street."

I laughed. I could barely remember that protest, it had been so long ago. I'd been twenty-four at the time, in my third year out of college and active with a number of political action groups, Asian and otherwise. I'd protested *Miss Saigon* for two reasons: first, because a white actor was playing an Asian role, one that he'd performed in London with eyes taped back and wearing yellowface makeup. Second, because I believed that the theme of the play—Asian prostitute waiting for rescue from her homeland by a white soldier—was deni-

433

grating to women in general and to Asian women specifically. At the protest, I'd carried a sign that said, "No more fuckee fuckee."

Now thirty-two, I told Vaughn, "It's been years since I've been to that kind of protest."

He said, "It still inspires me that you would put yourself out there like that."

Embarrassed, I shrugged. I introduced him to Kiendel. He introduced me to his two friends, José, the one with straight hair, and Jeff, the one whose hair was curly. The five of us went around the corner to a diner for breakfast, then upstairs to Vaughn's apartment to drink a very expensive bottle of champagne that Vaughn, until now, had refused to open. We stayed up drinking and talking until eight that morning, when Kiendel and I finally left.

My vacation ended. I returned home to Boston, where I was preparing for the publication of my first book, a memoir. I'd almost forgotten about New Year's Eve when Jeff, Vaughn's curly haired friend, sent me an email several weeks later, inviting me to have dinner with him if I ever happened to be in San Francisco. Uncertain of his intentions, I wrote back cautiously, "I'll be there on book tour in August. I'll let you know if I have time."

He answered, "Tell me when your book comes out, and I'll buy it right away. Will you need a ride from the airport? I can pick you up, play tour guide, take you to your appointments, whatever you need."

Touched by his generosity, I agreed to dinner in August.

I had more fun than I could ever have imagined. The meal stretched into a late-night talk, morning coffee, a day's exploration of San Francisco bookstores, another dinner, another breakfast coffee—and not once did Jeff make a pass at me. Saying good-bye at the airport after thirty-seven and one-half hours together, I confessed my disappointment that he hadn't.

Jeff laughed. "Maybe I thought that I didn't need to." I looked at him quizzically, and he elaborated, "I thought that we clicked. I thought that if anything happened between us, it would develop with time. Making a move now would only scare you off."

"Hmm," I said, already turning away. I hoisted my duffel bag over one shoulder, thoughts too full of my fledgling career to consider whether we'd actually clicked. Looking down the terminal, I said, "On to Seattle. Then Denver. Then Boston."

"Can I call you?"

I shrugged. "You have the number in the alumni directory, right?"

Jeff didn't answer. His throat rippled, swallowing hard.

We hugged briefly, not knowing whether we'd see each other again.

I didn't anticipate leaving a message on Jeff's machine two days later, asking him to call me in Denver that night, any time, it didn't matter how late. My parents, who could not read English, had nevertheless called me an ungrateful daughter for having written a memoir (in English) about the entrenched poverty of our immigrant community. They'd told me to leave their house and never return, then called me a disrespectful daughter when I tried to check into a hotel for the night. My entire adolescence came hurtling back at me; I remembered sharply, viscerally, exactly why I'd fled for Harvard, for a voice I could call my own. I honestly thought that I might hurt myself.

In the midst of this chaos, Jeff telephoned. He stayed on the line with me for five hours straight, without once trying to hang up. At the end, he said that he'd even had fun. I didn't believe him, but I didn't need to. With his help, I'd made it through the night.

When I got back to Boston two days later, I called to let him know I was okay. We said that we'd keep in touch, and we did—every day. After a week of calls, Jeff bought me a plane ticket to visit him in San Francisco for the Labor Day weekend. We decided that either we'd get sick of each other or we wouldn't.

We didn't.

A month later, October 1999, I was in San Francisco visiting Jeff again. He was planning a seven-month trip to Asia that was to begin in December, so I brought him a Hong Kong travel guide with mini-phrasebook included. I promised to teach him Cantonese, although my pronunciation was so corrupted and my vocabulary so poor at this point that I barely knew it myself. I speak *bi bi hua*, I told him—baby language.

Sneaking a sip from my coffee cup, Jeff groaned. "I'll be walking around China asking for something yummy for my tum-tum . . ."

I nodded. "Pretty much."

"Is that why you've never taught anyone else to speak Chinese?"

My smile froze. I knew he was teasing, but there had been too many strangers, too many boyfriends, too many well-meaning teachers, demanding, "Say something in Chinese!" And I always felt like a pet dog. But not with Jeff. Never with Jeff. I stared at him mutely. If I tried to explain, my trust would collapse under the weight of too many words. I would never be able to teach him my *bi bi hua*.

The silence stretched. Jeff cleared his throat. "What's wrong?"

I shrugged.

Jeff looked into my eyes for a long time without blinking. He took another sip from my coffee cup. "I like baby language," he said quietly.

I looked away, suddenly aware of the motion of my heart. Jeff and I had agreed not to become too attached, because he would be away for so long. I wondered if we hadn't already breached the agreement. I opened the travel guide and read aloud, *"Ba-see zham hai BEAN doe ah?"* Where is the bus stop?

Jeff bent his head over the book. Our shoulders touching, he repeated after me.

We went to Chinatown one day that weekend, and I guided him through grocery-store aisles, pointing out the dried, salted plums and sweet tofu pudding that had been my childhood favorites—that I still sometimes craved. I urged him to eavesdrop on nearby conversations, and, dutifully, he cocked his head in the direction of two middle-aged women nearby, his forehead scrunched in concentration.

"Are you getting any of it?" I asked.

"No," he whispered back. "I don't think they're asking about the bus stop."

I nudged him playfully. "They're talking about the prices. *Gum doh-ah!* 'How expensive!' You know that."

He inclined his head again, listening. "What are they saying now?"

I frowned. "They're complaining about their daughters."

Jeff looked at me suspiciously. "I'm getting the feeling that's a common theme for Chinese mothers."

"It is."

Jeff stepped in closer, grazing my hip with his hand. "Then things will get better with *your* mother."

We left the grocery store to wander the sidewalk stalls. We explored an herbalist's shop, where Jeff gazed in wonder at the bins of dried jellyfish, dried scallops, dried sea slug. *"Gum doh-ah!"* he said solemnly, when I confirmed that the price of dried jellyfish—$245 a pound—was not a mistake. Then, taking my hand, he led me out of the shop. "Enough Chinese lessons," he declared. "Time to rest."

We found a park nearby, and I sat on a bench with Jeff's head in my lap, my fingers absent-mindedly twisting themselves through his hair. The sun was about to set. The day's heat rose from the concrete beneath my feet, cooled by the incoming night air. All around us there were Chinese people—old men on benches, gossiping; children scrambling down slides on the playground; garishly overdressed Christian Chinese families returning from church. I looked down at Jeff. His eyes were closed and his face relaxed but smiling, looking utterly content. For an instant, I had a sensation of being able to see myself both from the outside and within—I could see my face, as content and relaxed as Jeff's, at ease with both him and the Chinese American community around me. I was no longer struggling, and in that moment, I believed that all my life up to this point had been worthwhile, because it all boiled down to this moment, this understanding that I had a choice. And I chose now to be here.

Nominated by Agni

QUEEN CITY, SKINS

by R. T. SMITH

from THE SOUTHERN REVIEW

The radio has told us Daddy Grace is free:
the jury said Louvenia Royster was never raped,
the evidence hearsay, trumped up, too late.
Downtown to scout pawnshops for a trap set,

I am watching the faithful praise him,
as the fire hydrants gush and cops on horses
keep their distance. It's '58, and I'm eleven,
skipping chores with mower, clippers, and rake.

The bullhorn in a Cadillac blares: *The Jezebel
is exposed. Dogs will lick her blood in the street.*
The heat waves shimmer. The Angel Corps tosses
their batons at the sun. The shout chorus

is blinding in sequins, and then he comes,
one step behind the red carpet unscrolling.
I am stunned by the purple tux and epaulets,
the spats, earring, and sparkling crucifix,

his wonderful strut. Sweat beads his black skin
to a silvery sheen. I am the whitest child
in Charlotte, but I want to sway and promenade,
to join the band high-stepping, tasseled like corn

as they wave bright gloves. The bass drums
are booming, the scarlet snares rattling
as quick sticks pepper their skins. I hope
this is religion, the rhythm I am swimming in,

the fury already in my wrists. I pretend
to be keeping time. MacDowell Street is the block
the papers call Murderers' Row. My father
would deliver more than a hellfire sermon

if he had an inkling where I am, but we are
a royal procession winding toward the door
of the House of Prayer for All People. A sign
says *Grace Royal Vitamin Here for You*

worked out in bricks of rose, white, and blue.
Lately, I've been pure Calvin, studying how
anything we do is already mapped out
in God's mind. This is the city of Billy Graham

and lily-white revivals, but I don't want the Savior
tenderly calling me home, grape-juice
communion, and ushers grim as undertakers.
I am hot for Sweet Jesus on fire, the cult

of percussion and ecstasy, belief gone wild
as a pocket pistol. At last I can scoff
at my neighbor who sips mint tea on his porch
and says, "We're all headed straight to hell

because niggers on welfare have stolen control."
I can turn my back on his wink, his Sambo
jokes and Old South politics. I can wonder
what he would know of the cymbal's shiver

and the scent of bliss. From my perch at the curb
I can see the preacher's marcelled hair,
his gold teeth blazing straight at me. City water
is flashing down the asphalt to wash away

every hint of sin. The drums are fierce as fireworks,
and Daddy Grace is broadcasting candy
kisses like seed. The faithful shout *Hallelujah!*
and quake. I know the Klan is not asleep,

the Wizards and Kleagles unroll their maps,
and somewhere men on the steam-room benches
of a WHITES ONLY country club might be
smoking cigars and planning to douse

a cross with gasoline tomorrow night after church.
I'm sure they believe Louvenia Royster tells
the truth and Daddy Grace is the Cloven Demon.
They say, "To save our country, this bedlam frenzy

has to stop," but all I want is to change my skin,
to feel a drumstick's sanded hickory
in each hand. I want to beat the stretched hide
of some creature who gave its life for God

and gospel, to turn my clumsy fingers deft
on the chrome tuning pegs polishing the sky.
I want to add my speed-drumming pulse
to the rhythm of his moment, this unfettered

and fandangled joy. I am reaching out to catch
the candy wrapped in silver foil, hoping to stroll
in his footsteps, grinning and proud. I want to tell
the prophet, "I am your tempo's natural boy,"

and feel his cool palm soothing my brow.

Nominated by Robert Wrigley

KAVITA THROUGH GLASS

fiction by EMILY ISHEM RABOTEAU

from TIN HOUSE

NOW THAT HE HAD WON a lifetime supply of colored glass, Hassan Hagihossein felt he could endure the vagaries of Ramadan and Kavita Paltooram's moods. He was no longer tempted by Pete's Pancake House. He was no longer kneeling at his wife's feet offering her mango chutney and almond gelato and other mouth-watering things he could not touch until the sun went down. He was content simply to sit in the rattan chair, turning the pieces of glass over and over in his hands, loosely pondering his dissertation or the arc of Kavita's distended belly or nothing at all.

It was the ninth month of the Islamic lunar calendar as well as the ninth month of Kavita's pregnancy. It was also nine days since Kavita had stopped talking to him. None of the significance of this was lost on Hassan, who was a mathematician as well as a loosely practicing Muslim.

The pieces of colored glass were smooth and flattish and oblong, shaped like teardrops roughly the size of robin's eggs. They fit in his palms perfectly. Each piece was punctured with a delicate hole at one end. It had crossed Hassan's mind that these were designed to be craft items, that he ought to make a chandelier out of them, or bead curtains or something of that nature. But he was positive Kavita would find a colored glass chandelier or bead curtains tacky and he wasn't sure he would find them beautiful himself anymore if he had to look at them all clustered together in one aggregate form.

Kavita was an architect and didn't like "things," which is to say that she didn't like clutter. She preferred open space, negative space, and the color white. She had decorated their apartment sparely. The little

441

furniture there was was white. So were the appliances, the dishes, the bedspread, the towels, and the sheets. Hassan was made to keep his library in a closet fitted with shelves so as not to break up the whiteness of the walls with the colored spines of his books.

Kavita added to the sparseness of the place by lolling about in the nude. She cooked and cleaned this way as well, brown and lithe and utterly naked. This made him blush. Hassan regarded her body as a perfect arrangement of spheres, a planetary form, a heavenly thing, a thing that might turn his eyeballs to salt if he looked too long, and so he tried not to.

During the first few months of their marriage, he had found the apartment antiseptic and cold. He found himself afraid of breaking things, although there really was nothing to break. He felt like he was stuck on the set of a movie about the future. Because of these feelings, he was childishly insistent that Kavita let him keep his rattan chair from college. He knew that the chair was an eyesore. He knew that it pained Kavita to have it in the living room, but for a long time it was the only thing he found comfortable about their home.

Later, he began to find the apartment peaceful. He understood Kavita's design sense more when he found himself opting to work at home rather than in his tiny office over at the math department. It was like living in a tabula rasa. White is a color without depth, he thought, or a thing without depth, since it is not a color at all, but a thing that makes depth possible. Ideas like this came to him, and new ways of solving problems.

One afternoon, as he sat quadrilating aspect ratios at the kitchen table, he was struck by the slow movement of a rectangle of soft not-yellow afternoon sunlight sliding across the white wall opposite him. It was moving infinitesimally. It was shifting its shape. He perceived its path, and it was telling him something about the basic probability of time that he could not put into numbers or words. Then a cloud crossed the sun and the shape was suddenly not there. The wall appeared to be a different shade of white than it was before. He was surprised to find his eyes stung with tears.

In that moment he felt he understood Kavita Paltooram more than he ever had and more than he ever would. And later that week when he skulked home from a disappointing multivariable calculus section in which he realized he was not transferring his passion for gradient functions to a group of stunningly disinterested undergraduates, he wasn't even upset to find that the rattan chair had been painted white as a bleached bone. He was simply glad to be home.

Once in a while he would find arabesque strands of his wife's black hair shed on the white furniture or the white bathroom tiles and he would read them like calligraphy. Today she wants me to pay the electric bill, he would figure, or today she wants me to bring home a cantaloupe. Almost always he was right.

That was before Kavita became pregnant. That was before she locked herself in the bathroom to urinate on a magic stick and refused to come out for two hours while Hassan paced the white rooms like a tiger on eggshells, wanting to pound down the door but not daring even to knock. Not daring even to tap. That was before she finally came out of the bathroom wielding the little magic stick with two pink lines, looking like a decidedly different person. Like a person with pointed edges instead of round ones. That was before she became impossible to read, left to right or right to left.

"I'm going for a walk," she had said, "and I don't want to be followed." As if he was a stalker and not her husband of three years. That night he divided the time it took for her to come home into nanoseconds, suffered an outrageous hollow craving for pancakes, and neglected to praise Allah for his blessings. When three hours passed without a sign of her, Hassan reached for the phone and dialed his father long-distance in Rasht to ask if this was normal behavior for women who've just discovered they are pregnant.

"It most certainly is not, my son, and don't say I didn't warn you. What did you expect? You married a Hindu from New Jersey."

"Don't start with that. I should think you'd be happy. You're going to be a grandfather."

"Of what?"

"Of a baby."

"That's not what I meant."

"I know what you meant."

"You know everything, Ph.D. So why consult with your father at all?"

"I don't want to argue."

"Why not consult me before the marriage? Why not marry Khaled's daughter instead as we arranged?"

"Khaled's daughter was twelve."

"Khaled's daughter was more beautiful than the moon!"

"I didn't call to argue."

"And she knew how to respect men. Now she's married to Zaid's idiot son. The one who drives his motorcycle like a maniac. It's a shame."

"I told you I don't want to argue. I'm just not sure what to do."

"You do what they all do in that godless country. You go buy a box of cigars and smoke them all."

It was true that Gulmuhammed Hagihossein had warned his son. He had opposed Kavita Paltooram from the moment he first laid eyes on her, which was the first time Hassan had seen her as well. Afterward it astonished Hassan that in his four years at Columbia he had never once noticed her, and it struck him as fateful rather than random that they should meet on graduation day before almost separating paths forever. It was fate that brought the Paltoorams to sit for their celebration supper at the round lacquered table in Lucky Cheng's Four Star Halal No Pork Chinese Restaurant next to the very one where Hassan sat glumly between his father and his square black graduation cap.

"Avest your eyes from her flesh," Gulmuhammed insisted in Farsi, even as he stared with his son at the indescribable midriff of Kavita, bedecked in her blood-red sari.

Hassan's mother had worn a hijab up until the day she swelled like a cresting wave after being stung on the tongue by a wasp in the kitchen while preparing a khaviar. After that she was wrapped in a shroud by a brood of shrieking neighbor women and covered with two thick yards of Iranian earth. Watching Kavita at Lucky Cheng's, it occurred to Hassan that he could not remember his mother's hair. Kavita's hair reached to her waist. It was oiled in a blue-black braid that snaked over her shoulder like a question mark. The Hagihosseins stared at her impossible curves.

"That woman is wicked. Completely shameless. It is clear that she will break a man's heart one day for sport with her wiles," Hassan's father intoned.

She wore the sari exclusively to please her parents. That much was clear. Hassan understood this because he was wearing a starched galabiya for the exact same reason. He also recognized the customary apologetic look that first-generation offspring wear in public with their mothers. As Mrs. Paltooram sat weeping like a camel over her vegetable lo mein (not from sadness, but from joy because her daughter was going to be successful), as Gulmuhammed sat pontifi-

444

cating over his kung pao chicken about performing ablutions (and chastising his son for becoming too American), Hassan's eyes locked with Kavita's. They rolled their eyes and smiled.

That was the beginning. On the streets of New York, where they started their courtship, she was approached by Mexicans and responded in halting Spanish while he, more often than not, was mistaken for a light-skinned black man on account of his woolly hair. This amused them. They pondered how confusing their children would be, if they ever had any.

When she became pregnant, he was himself confused. When she became pregnant and started the night walks, he became strangely bewildered by language. It wasn't that he had lost his grip on English so much as that he couldn't connect signifiers and signified anymore. He would falter in the middle of a sentence even though he knew the string of words coming out of his mouth was correct.

Is this thing really called an elbow? he thought. And if so, is my knuckle the elbow of my finger? Is my wrist an elbow? Is Kavita's waist an ankle? They are both slender and they both bend and they are both the color of cinnamon. Is a joint on the body an angle or the possibility of an angle? Is Kavita's little finger a cinnamon stick? No, a cinnamon stick does not bend like an elbow.

He worked furiously on his dissertation, *On Finsler Geometric Manifolds and Their Applications to Teichmueller Spaces*, to rid himself of his vicious thought cycles. This failed to work. He just found himself thinking about his wife in elementary mathematical terms. For example, he imagined Kavita and himself as the axis on a graph plotting the growth of their child. He also tried using Kavita and the baby as the set of coordinates and tried to design an algorithm to classify the shape of their future as a family. He thought of them as a triangle, of course, but one whose boundaries he could not begin to measure.

Kavita's night walks became regular. He assumed she had taken a lover. He doubted his paternity. He doubted his doubt. Every time she left she would admonish him not to follow her. Of course the night came when he decided to do just that.

She was walking very fast. Hassan kept three-quarters of a block behind her, trying to move in the shadows and keep cover behind parked cars. He felt ridiculous. His shirt was sweat-stuck to his back like a postage stamp. Kavita crossed a street. The wind lifted her hair so that several thick strands of it pointed backward in his direction like accusing fingers, but she did not turn her head. He realized she was making a beeline for the campus. At one point she leaned against a tree and brought one foot up against the trunk to adjust her sandal strap. The gesture hurt him physically. He realized Kavita was monumentally graceful. She began walking again. He let himself lag farther behind. From a distance he watched his wife stop in front of the University's Art and Architecture Building, a gray monstrosity of a structure. She pushed through the revolving door and was gone. Hassan began to breathe again.

She is taking a class, he thought, straightening his tie. That's all. She is continuing her education. Still, he was nagged by the fact that this should be kept secret from him, and he was left with the troubling image of Kavita being swallowed up by the building, like a tiny sea horse in the striated mouth of a humpbacked whale. Then he thought of their child growing in her. A pearl in the belly of a sea horse in the belly of a whale. A pearl. A precious thing. The night was heavy and wet. "Allah Akbar," he said to no one in particular. He kept saying it as he followed Kavita's trajectory backward to their white home. "Allah Akbar, Allah Akbar." God is great.

In the third month of her pregnancy, Hassan drove Kavita to the Corning glass factory. He picked the factory because he'd noticed her reading a library book on stained-glass windows and thought it might be of interest. She was growing more distant from him every day and he hoped an excursion might draw them together.

Upstate, the leaves were blazing, almost radioactive tones of red and yellow somersaulting to the road. Kavita was silent in the car. Veiled without a veil. She had the window rolled down on the passenger side and her hair was whipping around like a system of angry black vectors, hiding her face and revealing it in turn. An equation came to Hassan as he took in the simultaneous motion of the leaves falling down and her hair lifting up. He understood these things to be linked. The equation was this:

$$Distance \div Longing = Desire$$

Hassan quickly dismissed the equation as nonsensical. Longing and desire were too close in meaning to be considered separate variables. There wasn't a word in the English language to describe the cause and effect of Kavita Paltooram's remoteness on his heart. He was very hungry.

"Would you like a tuna fish sandwich?" he asked her. He'd packed them an elaborate lunch. "An éclair?"

"Where are you taking me, Hassan?" she answered. Her voice was tired.

"It's a surprise. I can keep a secret just as well as you."

Kavita gathered her heavy hair, tied it in a knot at the nape of her neck and closed her eyes.

"Would you like some cashew nuts?"

"No."

"Would you like a pickle?"

"No. I'm going to take a nap." Her eyelashes cast long elliptical shadows down her cheekbones. While she slept, Hassan wound up eating everything, both her portion and his own.

Inside the factory, they watched a man blow a tiny glass sparrow from a long spinning pipe. Hassan watched Kavita watching the beak and the wings harden out of liquid glass. On her face was the trace of a smile.

She carefully chose a set of wineglasses from the gift shop. Before they left, Hassan entered a contest. He wrote three words on a slip of paper: *Delicate, Durable, Divine.* It was supposed to be a new slogan for the cover of the CorningWare catalog. He had been trying to describe his wife. On the car ride home he thought about how none of the words was right.

The second time Hassan followed Kavita to the Art and Architecture Building, he waited until she came out. He chose a bench near Stanhope Hall because it afforded him a view of the revolving door while obscuring him slightly behind the Rockefeller statue. While he waited he ate through the large bag of jelly beans Kavita had turned down because they hurt her teeth, and he thought about what he could say to her to make her love him. He had a lot of things he wanted to tell her. Whenever he tried his tongue got tied.

"Kavita," he wanted to say, "in my country, a bowl of goldfish on the table means an auspicious new year. A sturgeon fish can live a hundred years. My grandfather was a fisherman. He couldn't spell his own name. My grandmother was a poet. She wove her verse into Persian rugs and traded them to an Englishman. One rug for two lambs. Her loom was lost in the war. My grandmother's name was Khadijah. Her mother's name was Khadijah. Khadijah was the first wife of the Prophet. Khadijah was also my mother's name. My mother wore a hijab from her head to her toes. I do not remember the color of her hair. Every woman in my family has named her daughter Khadijah for the past two thousand years."

Before she became pregnant, Hassan didn't think like this. Before she became pregnant, he thought of himself primarily as a mathematician and, as such, a citizen of the world. The roster of names in his department read like a litany of united nations: Imran Abbaspour, Antonio Cavaricci, Saul Diamond, Ricardo González de los Santos, Hank Hansell, N'gugi Obioha, Nicolas Paraskavopolous, Olga Rasvanovic, Hoc Sung, Almamy Suri-Tunis, Li Wang, Toshio Yamamoto. Three-quarters of the members of the Applied Probability Research Group could barely speak enough English to ask what time it was, yet they were understood just so long as their equations were sound. Yet, here he sat, gorged on gourmet jelly beans, not knowing how to talk to his wife.

After exactly two hours, Kavita emerged in a thin wave of students. She was noticeably pregnant. She was talking to a very tall man. Hassan watched in horror as this man stooped over his wife and picked something from her shoulder. Was it a hair? Were this man's fingers touching Kavita's hair? He watched her say goodbye. He waited until she turned a corner to tail the man. He followed the man across the quad and underground to the all-night library where he noticed under fluorescent lights that the man was blond and blue-eyed and had a mustache that resembled a baby caterpillar crawling on his upper lip.

This was the night Hassan unraveled. He dreamed Kavita gave birth to a moth with blue eyes and wings that extended to the roof. He called his father in Rasht. He let the phone ring twenty-seven times. Gulmuhammed was not at home. On another night he dreamed he asked Kavita why she had married him.

"Out of kindness," she replied, "so that you could get your green card."

He had to ask Toshio to cover his multivariable calculus section two weeks in a row because he feared he wouldn't be able to hold a piece of chalk without dropping it. In one week he ate five Hungryman breakfasts at Pete's Pancake House. When he weighed himself on the white bathroom scale, he discovered to his dismay that he'd gained nearly twenty pounds.

The third time Hassan followed Kavita to the Art and Architecture Building was Lailat-ut Qadr. It was raining, and he'd been fasting. For Ramadan, for clarity. He waited a half hour and went inside. He'd never set foot in the building before, but as if guided by instinct, as if making a hajj of doom, he found the classroom without really trying. It smelled of turpentine. A dozen students sat like a solar system in a semicircle with paintbrushes clutched in their hands or held between their teeth. In front of each student was a canvas. On each canvas was a naked Kavita. Kavita herself was sprawled out at the semicircle's center on a filthy couch, her belly rounder than the sun and twice as painful for him to look at.

Hassan reached for the closest thing he could grab. Later he would remember the gesture with embarrassment. His hand found a thing. It was a coffee can full of soaking brushes. He flung it as hard as he could without aiming at anything and not knowing why. A woman gasped. The can grazed the corner of one of the canvases, knocking it to the floor and splashing turpentine on at least three people. One of them was the blond-haired blue-eyed man. Hassan fixated on him.

"What is your name?" he demanded. His voice didn't sound like his voice.

"Excuse me? What's going on here?" asked the man, rising to his feet.

"What is your name?" repeated Hassan.

"I'm Burt. Burt Larson." He came toward Hassan with his arms held out in a placating way that reminded Hassan of a jellyfish. "We don't want any trouble here, man."

Hassan spun on his heels and fled through the rain. His socks were wet. It was Lailat-ut Qadr, the night of power, and his socks were soaking wet. When he got home he had to breathe into a paper bag because he was hiccuping violently. He rewrote the scene so that he broke a canvas over the blond man's head, threw a blanket over Kavita, and led her out of the Art and Architecture Building by the hand.

That was the day Kavita Paltooram stopped talking to him altogether. Which at first was fine because he didn't want to talk to her either. She had shared her body with a circle of strangers. She was just as far away as before. The difference now was that she seemed far away and *dirty*. He busied himself in Finsler Manifolds and stayed away from the apartment. He made astonishing progress with his dissertation. He attributed this clarity to his fast and also to Kavita's imperfection.

Then he dreamed again about the moth. This time it was gargantuan, with feelers as long as trees and wings as shaggy as a llama's fur. In the dream, Kavita was mounted on the moth and carried away into the blue sky. She was naked, of course, but small as a dot on the back of the moth. In the dream, as the moth carried his wife toward the sun, he was filled with longing. Hassan woke up gut-wrenchingly hungry.

On the ninth day of her silent treatment, the glass arrived. *"Congratulations, Mr. Hagihossein,"* read the card. *"Your slogan was chosen for our catalog! We send you these timeless treasures with gratitude. Sincerely, Peter Simpkin, Executive President, Corning, Inc."*

There were dozens of pieces. Hassan sat in the rattan chair turning them over in his hands. He held up a blue piece over one eye and watched Kavita through it. She had just taken a shower and was wearing her white bathrobe. Through the glass, her body was distorted. Her edges were running. She looked like she was underwater, a drowning angel. It occurred to Hassan that he didn't know how to make her happy. He didn't know how to speak her language. Kavita did not think in the terms of water. Kavita, who had grown up in Teaneck and taken perhaps one desultory trip to the Jersey shore every other summer, could not understand what it had meant to grow up on the rim of the Caspian Sea. This is why the glass pieces, which put his mind at rest, did not mean the same thing to her. She didn't know what it was to hunt a beach for sea glass.

Hassan fished in his toolbox for some wire. He moved to the kitchen table and began sketching a design.

"Kavita," he called.

She came.

"Do you see? I am making a mobile to hang above the baby's crib."

She was silent.

He looked up at her and saw that her eyes were bloodshot. He steadied his voice. "If it's a girl, I want to name her Khadijah."

Kavita fingered an orange piece of glass.

450

"It was my mother's name," he explained, placing his hand gingerly on her hip.

"I know," she said. "It's beautiful."

"Yes. And it sounds like yours."

She moved his hand to her navel and held it in place with her own. A riptide tore his stomach like a hunger pang. Her body gave him gooseflesh. She opened her mouth to speak then shut it, as if reconsidering.

"Yes? You were going to say something?" he begged.

Kavita spoke slowly. "Do you realize you never look at me?" Her voice was soft like sand under bare feet. "I can't remember the last time you touched me."

Hassan stood. He swallowed. He didn't know the name for the way his wife's hair smelled. He gathered it in his fists and combed his fingers through to its snarling ends. Then, with the wet tips of Kavita's hair, he painted concentric circles on his face. Over his eyebrows, temples, cheekbones. By which he meant to say, "You are all I look at. You are all I see."

Nominated by Tin House

CICADA

by DAN CHIASSON

from WESTERN HUMANITIES REVIEW

I

The "lily-like" cry from the tops
      of olive trees, or in my childhood

from maple trees that lined the road
      down to the beach: is it the call

of men held inside bodies so small
      they might have held them in their palms

once, when they were whole, who now
      are brittle and wail from treetops?

Forgetful of their bodies, these
      men housed themselves in music

when music like a new color
      declared itself on earth. Imagine

the silence before music, all
      the open mouths with no notes

coming out, like the mouths in paintings,
 underwater mouths, agape, the way

we picture suffering. It was
 like coming up for air when music

appeared here, and these men starved
 themselves for fear eating might stop

the beauty up. *Mousomania,*
 "music-madness"; and so the gods pitied

these men and pitying made them sing
 O *let me sing you past this night.*

II

And so the night I came home late
 and found one skating on my bedroom

mirror I was terrified, both for
 the poor soul trapped inside the green

contraption like a child fallen down
 a well, and for myself, forced to choose

whether to handle or to house
 the brittle man. I hate provoking

wildness in things—the strange dog's eyes
 met inadvertently, the housefly held

electric between panes; as a child
 I was so scared of my friends' fathers

I would hide when they got home from work.
 So all that night in bed I lay

awake, afraid at any moment the cicada
        might start crying as he did

perched on Eunomos's bow the time
        the fifth string broke, when

from an olive tree he dropped and
        landed where the slack string hung

and sang Eunomos's instrument
        "whole again and wholly beautiful."

III

Two people lie awake together
        in one bed. They do not speak.

Each knows the other is awake
        and knows the other knows.

Why can't they speak? As though
        a spell held them in place or some

god's architecture fastened
        their helpless limbs together—

as though their tongues were thick
        as loaves of bread inside their throats.

But this is love, each wants the other
        to escape the ceremonies of day,

each makes the night a little fantasy
        of night, a warm home decked with sleep.

Night after night they lie this way,
        no sleep, no speech, until one night

the telephone erupts and they sit up
        till dawn together, rocked by grief.

IV

The night I came home late and on
        my bedroom mirror saw that child

I imagined my own child: far
        from me because as yet unmade,

apart because imaginary, but the best
        boy there, the prettiest in that kingdom.

Baffled, he watches me as I assemble
        doctrine and dog shit, the junk

of adult life I learned watching TV.
        He gets to learn by watching me

pretend he's not alive, a lesson
        in resemblance and absence,

skill, refusal, all the usual lies
        you parse and press yourself against.

He gets to see me blank out slowly,
        the TV left on past the programming.

His mother will gradually grow to fear
        him there, in that vague place

since as he changes to my twin
        he changes to her enemy, the boy turned

to the man, the man uncannily
        like the father he could never know.

IV

Sometimes this song feels like a cure
      sometimes it makes the hurt much worse.

But it's the most brilliant defense—
      no judge ever lacked sympathy for this.

I'm making it up as I go along,
      but people like to think it's fate.

And so the night I came home late
      the actual cicada on my real mirror

scared me, for I hate handling anything
      I know needs my help fathoming

this maze of chairs and bottles and books,
      the mess I make of any room with my

unruly inwardness. Of course
      I couldn't kill it, where would I hide

the awful handful afterwards?
      That night I knew why old men lie

awake the night they start to die:
      the room is solemn, full of something

they can't scare away,
      their souls, or old childhood fears

they never solved, that stick to them
      like burrs or barnacles.

Their parents reappear at their bedside
      miming the ancient attitudes of

tenderness and rue, adoring them—
      and like the figures on a frieze

456

all those they loved appear as they were
        but mute, their eyes and lips sewn shut.

Then from inside the room a cry;
        and then the cicada flies away.

Nominated by Carl Phillips

IRISH MOUNTAIN

fiction by PINCKNEY BENEDICT

from ZOETROPE: ALL STORY

SNAG DRUM HAS ONE OF HIS SICK HEADACHES, so his son, fifteen-year-old Ivanhoe, sits behind the wheel of the station wagon. He's gunning it along the dirt lane to Pluskat's, down the gauntlet of ornamental concrete chickens. The unpainted chickens line both sides of the road, right up to the doors of Pluskat's barn, where the fights are held. Really, it's the same chicken over and over and over again. Pluskat poured them himself. The chickens stand better than two feet tall, their high-combed heads tilted to one side.

Snag groans, half from the nauseating headache, half because they are late. The back of the station wagon is full of animal cages. The cages are full of gamecocks. The roosters grab at the wire of the cages with their hard claws, they drive their beaks against the metal. They're working to get at each other back there. Snag and Ivanhoe can't afford to be late for the derby. They can't afford not to fight, not to win. "Go *on*," Snag moans, head in his hands. Ivanhoe takes his eyes off the road, looks over at Snag for a second, and the station wagon plows into the left-hand rank of chickens.

The sound from outside the car is terrible: rupturing concrete, metal pulled screaming away from metal, the front bumper dragged loose, the smash and tinkle of glass as the left headlamp winks out, then the right; gush of steam as the aluminum grille tilts sharply back, as the radiator collapses, as the heavy engine block shifts in its mounts. Pathetic honk of the horn as it goes too. Rumble of shattered decorative chickens under the tires and floorboards, thundering against the floor panel of the car as though the pieces will punch straight through. Roar of exhaust through straight pipe as the muffler tears loose and bounds along behind them on the soft dirt surface of the lane. A jagged hunk of concrete jumps up and shaves off the driver's-side mirror, clean as a whistle.

And inside the car: Snag screaming *Watch watch watch!* up front as he lunges for the steering wheel, and the roosters in the back all gone mad. Cages sliding and somersaulting, the cage containing the Kelso Yellow-Leg catching Ivanhoe painfully behind the ear and crashing down onto the bench front seat, cartwheeling from there upside down onto the transmission hump. Ivanhoe's crying out *I'm trying!* for all he's worth as he fights the wheel to the right, but the car will not come over, riding fast and straight as an arrow, chickens going down before it like ninepins. It is as though Ivanhoe is deliberately mowing them under.

The car breaks right at last, and the front left fender kisses a final chicken, spins it neatly in place and tips it over onto its back. They slalom to the middle of the road, slew to a stop.

Silence. A hubcap rolls past and down the road, moonlight flaring from the spinner as it goes.

The roosters gawp around them. Snag crouches in the passenger-side footwell, hands clasped before him as though he's praying. Ivanhoe listens carefully for the beat of his own heart. He's got a pancake heart, delicate organ always threatening to give out, and if it's going to stop on him, it might as well go ahead and do it. *Quit now*, he thinks, but the pancake heart labors on.

～

Ivanhoe wears the fighting cock's long-knife tied to his left ankle. This is the dream he dreams every night, and can never remember. In the waking world, the long-knife terrifies him. His mouth grows dry as he straps those three inches of curving oily steel to a rooster's leg. Here, though, he sweeps his terrible wings back just to hear the crisp rustle of the feathers, he cranes his neck to take in the glitter of the long-knife's keen edge. He's waiting on the pit master, and when the call comes he will rise up, heart hammering his chest into splinters, war cry breaking loose from his—

Not his mouth, not Ivanhoe's mouth, with its soft sensuous lips, a girl's lips. Lips for which he's been taunted all his life: *Sweetboy, Sugarmouth.* This is a hard beak. Not the wretched pancake heart, ei-

459

ther, Ivanhoe's flattened heart that limps along beneath the thin concavity of his breastbone. This rounded pulsing muscle, this conqueror's heart hurls him screaming into the air, the long-knife slashing downward, cutting deep into the dubbed head of the opposing cock.

His burnished feathers curve tight over his body like armor. He doesn't have a name in the pit. He is a wicked feathered glasher, a battle stag waiting on the kill.

He knows the rooster he's pitted against. Sleek black cockerel, a hefty Sumatra Game, with the wide breast and strong feathered shanks of the ground fighter. Tut, his old man's favorite, King Tut, longtime killer, eyes like polished quartz stone. Dream-Ivanhoe strokes upward, he's swift, an air fighter. He lashes down with the cruel long-knife, King Tut gaping up, earthbound, wide-beaked and stiff-tongued with fury as Ivanhoe wings over, the knife strike straight to the cape of feathers at the throat. The black cockerel reels, he's necked, he's finished, he's dead.

~

Snag's out of the car in a flash, pries open the rear of the station wagon and begins pawing through the tumbled cages. "Get the Kelso," he says to Ivanhoe, who leans down to look at the bent and distorted metal crate. No way the rooster could have survived the wreck, but there he is nonetheless, burbling grumpily, full of reproach. He sounds just like a percolator on the boil. Kelso Yellow-Leg, the butcher cock, whom Ivanhoe adores. Blinkered Kelso Yellow-Leg, with his blind ruptured eye.

"Take the Kelso and go," Snag says. He's found King Tut's crate among the jumbled cages, and he has the black game bird out, he's stroking its rumpled feathers. Champion bird. They're maybe a quarter of a mile from Pluskat's barn, and they can't think about the car now. They have to get their birds to the derby. Ivanhoe drags the Kelso's cage free, knees loose, fingers twitching. The adrenaline of the crash is hitting him hard, and he wants to sit down. He wants to cry.

"Go on, go on," Snag says, and then he pauses. "Will you be OK?" he asks. "Your heart . . ."

"My heart will do what my heart will do," Ivanhoe says. Suddenly he doesn't want to sit down anymore, he doesn't want to cry. He

460

wants to walk down the road, he wants to disappear into the dark. He wants to forget about the smashed car and the shaken roosters and his worried old man and the line of shattered concrete chickens. He wants to leave them all far behind.

~

In the dream, Ivanhoe's wings turn without warning to heavy sodden cardboard, his fierce green-and-yellow plumage becomes nothing but candle wax, it smears and drips under the heat of the big sodium are lamps that light the arena, leaving him smooth and pink and naked, a dunghill bird who won't raise his hackles. Leaving him a weeping frightened boy awake in his sweat-soaked bed, a boy with soft pouting lips and a tubby belly and ungainly limbs. Leaving him alone, infused with the squalid flavor of the dream but without its memory. Leaving him dream-haunted Ivanhoe.

~

Headlights from behind as Ivanhoe and Snag struggle along the road. Snag banged his knee against something during the wreck, and it's swelling like a goiter under his gabardines, hot and painful, slowing him dreadfully. The lights come up on them, sweep past, and in the rumble of dual pipes and the red glare of taillights, Ivanhoe recognizes Billy Shoemaker's fancy old Lincoln with the suicide doors. Big Billy Shoemaker, a high roller, arriving late because, for him, there's no need to hurry. The Lincoln halts up the road a way, bangs into reverse, and comes tear-assing backward toward them. Ivanhoe has to leap out of its path. Billy leans out the driver's window like an eager dog.

"Ouch!" Billy says, slamming his hard hand against the door panel of the Lincoln. "Saw what you did back there. Ouch! Ouch!"

"Can we catch a ride with you, Billy?" Snag asks. "Up the barn." He's got Tut's cage braced against his hip. Billy's face is bright, the skin tight and shiny over the bones. There's someone in the Lincoln with him, face indistinct in the dark interior of the car.

"Chicken killers!" Billy says, reaching behind him and throwing open the rear door. "Car killers!"

Snag hustles Ivanhoe before him and they climb into the spacious backseat of the Lincoln. Maneuvering the cages inside the car proves trying, but at last they're settled. Billy's turned backward, looking at

461

them a moment longer, all smiles. The front-seat passenger is a girl—no surprise to see a pretty girl in the shotgun seat of Billy Shoemaker's Lincoln—a girl Ivanhoe doesn't know.

She's staring at him like he's something from Mars, so he feels emboldened to stare back. Light dusting of freckles, broad lineless brow, pale solemn mouth, hair caught up in a red bandanna—but he knows that hidden hair, he knows its springy, coarse, slightly oily texture as though his hands are plunged in it at that moment, he knows its scent, like olives (which he has never smelled, never tasted), its flavor like sea salt. How could he know that? He blinks as Billy throws the Lincoln into gear, sees that the girl in the front seat is laughing at him.

"What a strange bird is the pelican," she says to him.

"Pardon?" he says.

"Her beak can hold more than her belly can."

Snag tends to King Tut. Ivanhoe struggles to come up with a reply.

"She's been saying shit like that all evening," Billy says. Then, confidingly, "She's down from Irish Mountain." He pronounces it like *mounting. Irish Mounting.* He rolls his eyes.

Ivanhoe knows about Irish Mountain and the people who live up there. They aren't like the ones down in the foothills, like Snag and Billy Shoemaker and Ivanhoe, who don't dream, or don't remember their dreams. Up on Irish Mountain, he has heard, their dreams are an ocean. Up on Irish Mountain, they swim in and out of each other's dreams like fishes.

When Ivanhoe wakes in the mornings, he struggles to recall his dreams. Within the dreams hides the answer. It must be there, because it isn't anywhere else in his life, it isn't anywhere else in the waking world. Not in the gamecocks, not in Snag's tremulous attention. If Ivanhoe could remember the dreams, he would know the answer, and from the answer he imagines he might be able to guess at the nature of the question. The question and the answer to the question: it's like the chicken and the egg to him. He keeps turning the thing over in his mind, trying to decide which comes first.

"The pelican in the wilderness," Ivanhoe says, and his mouth feels strange to him as it shapes the words. He feels as though he's giving the second part of some secret code in a spy movie. "The pelican in the wilderness, with nothing to feed her birds, wounds her breast and nourishes them upon her blood."

The girl's eyes widen momentarily. He has surprised her. Good.

"Damn," says Billy. They are at Pluskat's barn, cars and trucks parked at rough angles all around them. "Now you with the pelicans too. I thought you Drum fellows were chicken farmers."

"Gamecocks," says Snag. He hates it when anyone refers to his precious birds as chickens.

~

A petit-point picture of Jesus hangs at the foot of Ivanhoe's bed. His mother made it when he was little, not long before she died, but it looks much older than that, it looks like something that has traveled forward from another time. In the picture, Jesus' chest is torn open, blood running down, but his face—you can tell this even from across the room, the detail in the needlework is that fine—is peaceful. He's a skinny little hillbilly Jesus with bandy legs and close-set eyes and a clever, foxy face. He's naked and alone, but he's not afraid.

Around the border of the picture runs the legend about the pelican. *The pelican in the wilderness . . .* Ivanhoe sees it every time he wakes from the dream, when he wakes to the raucous crowing of the gamecocks in the chook-yard . . . *nourishes them upon her blood.* There is no pelican in the picture.

Ivanhoe wishes his mother had lived, a little longer at least. He would have liked to ask her what in the world that hanging might signify. *Questions.*

~

Ivanhoe feels sick in his belly, fixing the long-knife to the left spur of the Kelso Yellow-Leg as the rooster dances and skitters and kicks, sensing what's coming, wattles and comb swelling with hot blood, eyes capturing and holding the light. The next bout is a Welsh main. That means that Ivanhoe will pit his bird against another, and the winner of that bout will stay in the pit against a fresh stag, as will the winner of that bout, and so on, a total of seven fights. Only the gamest bird can stick it out in a Welsh main from the beginning, without going under hack or dying.

The Kelso Yellow-Leg seems terribly old to Ivanhoe. Old as Snag, even older maybe. The Kelso jabs him with the long-knife, drawing blood from the sensitive web of skin between thumb and forefinger, then stands tall and looks at Ivanhoe unabashedly with his one good eye. Ivanhoe loves the Kelso for its game heart and its strong legs and its blinkered eye.

463

On the ground near Ivanhoe's feet, King Tut gabbles and talks. Ivanhoe thinks he's saying words. What is he saying? *Hogbody*. Is he calling Ivanhoe names? *Sweetboy. Sugarmouth.* Ivanhoe nudges the cage with the side of his foot but doesn't dare kick it.

Snag has gone after the remaining roosters with a couple of the other men. Pluskat was pissed at first when he heard about his ornamental chickens, but Big Billy Shoemaker convinced him that it was really pretty funny after all. He convinced Pluskat that Snag and Ivanhoe got the worst of it, the front end of their car stove in, their birds rattled, Snag's swollen knee. Pluskat, the pit master, can see the humor in that.

"You'll be copacetic," Ivanhoe tells the Kelso Yellow-Leg. He steels his heart. When the call comes, he'll send the Kelso into battle. The bird itself wants to fight. It peers nearsightedly around the barn, searching for an opponent. The barn is tall-ceilinged, filled with sizzling light, with the odors of cigarette smoke and sawdust and sweat and hot feathers, the smell of blood. The crowd sits expectantly on flimsy folding risers or in lawn chairs near the pit's edge, talking together in low tones. From time to time, this man or that one will rise from his place and call to the birds in the pit, shout at the handlers, hands hooked, sawing at the air.

"You've never been much of anywhere, have you?" It's the girl, the one from Irish Mountain. She has come up on Ivanhoe without warning. She eyes the Kelso. "Will he hurt me?"

Ivanhoe holds up his wounded hand. "He might," he says, and she keeps her distance.

It's true that he's never been much of anywhere. Never seen anything, really, except for the room where he lives, the thin-walled clapboard house of his old man's, the patch of land in the foothills with its strutting gamecocks, over which Irish Mountain glowers. Never seen anything but the little tilting chookhouses and fly pens filled with sharp-clawed, empty-headed, gimlet-eyed fighting roosters.

Over the shoulder of the girl, Ivanhoe can make out Pluskat and Billy Shoemaker and some others gathered together in a tight knot, arguing, their faces twisted—but they're not angry, they're laughing. Pluskat claps his hands, and Ivanhoe sees him as if for the first time: a capering, agitated hobgoblin. The men around him imps and beasts, their mouths nothing but damp toothy maws, their hair thick and stinking as pelts, their voices the braying of beasts. It's because of the girl he can see this, he's sure. She's showing it to him. He's glad that Snag isn't in sight. He's glad that he cannot see himself.

"I hear you share your dreams," he says. It's not easy for him to talk to the girl—she's so strange, and so pretty—but he forges on. "Up where you come from."

The girl nods. "I could show you the Eye of God if you want. Up at the top," she says.

The Eye of God is an Irish Mountain thing, like the dreams. All his life Ivanhoe's heard the name, but no one has ever been able to describe to him what it might be. A wheel in a wheel is all that Snag can tell him. Like the wheel that took the prophet Ezekiel. A wheel in a wheel, way in the middle of the air.

"I'd like to see that," he says.

"You see it, and it sees you," she says.

Would he like that? An eye like a great wheel, staring down at him. He is not much to look at, Ivanhoe knows. For the first time it occurs to him that he might not like the answer, if he finds it. Might not like the question either.

"Looks *into* you," the girl says. "Into and through you."

Here and there heads in the crowd turn to assess the girl's slender form, hard eyes roam over her wide shoulders, down her long back to her waist—from her waist to her rear to her muscular legs. The hard eyes glint with appreciation. Ivanhoe wonders how old she might be. He wonders if she thinks he's older than he is. He's sizable for his age, and consequently clumsy; his coordination hasn't yet caught up with his frame.

"My family's up there," the girl says. "They were scared to come down, but I'm not."

And then Pluskat, the pit master, calls the bout, the Welsh main: no more time for conversation. Ivanhoe wants to ask her when she'll show him, how he might get there, to the top of Irish Mountain. If he were to decide to come. He wants to ask why she has come down to the foothills, what her family is scared of. He wants to ask if she was serious, what she said. He casts around for Snag, to get him to corner for the Kelso, give him another minute or two with the girl, but Snag's not back from the wrecked station wagon yet.

"Pit your birds, gents," Pluskat bellows, and Ivanhoe's obliged to climb into the arena, the Kelso Yellow-Leg clutched in his outstretched hands. The butcher cock has seen its opponent now, and it's vibrating, light-feathered body thrumming with tension. The Kelso Yellow-Leg feels like a running motor in Ivanhoe's grip.

~

Irish Mountain was once an island, eons ago. An island thrusting its green bulk up above the savage waters, and the valleys below the mountain nothing more than lightless airless rifts in the ocean floor. The foothills where Ivanhoe lives with Snag and the fighting cocks, these were the heights of the ocean floor. Dwelling place of the unthinkable Leviathan, and God moving dolefully above the gray roiling surface.

At the cement works, the quarriers dynamite the rock, peel it in great slabs from the quarry walls, and fossil pictures of ancient fish and mollusks and whatnot float mutely to the surface—Ivanhoe has seen them—and then the quarriers grind the rock down to gravel and the gravel down to grit and sand. His old man, Snag, grinds fish into a rich stinking soupy paste, to feed to King Tut and the other gamecocks. The fish keep them strong, keep their feathers glossy and supple and impermeable. Snag feeds them grit, too, and small stones, for their gizzards, so they can digest their food. Where a man has teeth in his head, a chicken has stones in its gut.

~

Somewhere in the midst of the Welsh main, Snag returns with the other birds—the dignified Harvard Whites, the high-priced Blacksmith Hatch, the scalawag Racey Mugs and Cottontail Shufflers, the single ancient Claret Roundhead, which fights with the gaff—and his breath is bitter, his face distant, features blurred and muzzy. He's been drinking milky potato liquor in the back of the borrowed pickup truck, nestled among his birds in their bent cages, nursing the hurt of his wrecked car, his aching skull, his wrenched knee, the gibes of Pluskat, who won't leave him alone. "Chicken killer!" he calls out from the middle of the pit, must have picked it up from Billy. "Car killer!"

Snag is usually gentle with Ivanhoe, almost courtly; mild toward his stable of battle stags. The pit is life to him, it's the entire world—he's a little man with hardly a possession to his name, but his birds are well known in the foothills, respected and feared, especially the dreaded black cockerel King Tut. If men know him at all, it is be-

466

cause his birds fight until they die, they strike and strike and strike until their hearts give out. But tonight Snag is on fire, he shouts at Ivanhoe, he screams at the Kelso Yellow-Leg as it struggles through the endless numbing bouts of the Welsh main, as it is wounded and comes on strong and is wounded again. "I'll put you in a pie, you whoreson!" he shrieks at the bird. "I'll eat you for my God-damned supper!"

Into Ivanhoe's ear he whispers, in a voice unlike any the boy has heard from him before, "Get your ass in gear, hogbody. You got a car to pay for." He casts a look over at Pluskat. "And a bunch of"—here his speech becomes deliberate, as though he's delivering a message even he does not fully comprehend—"custom handmade ornamental poured-concrete *fowl!*" He spits the last word.

Pluskat laughs, overhearing, and the Welsh main continues. Ivanhoe scoops up the Kelso and blows on his comb to revive him, forces open his beak and spits into it. At the last, it's only a couple of weak dunghill birds that the tired Kelso faces, and the lean old butcher cock takes them down, one after the other, indomitable Kelso Yellow-Leg drives them into the dirt of the pit and crows over their corpses. Snag stands to one side with King Tut (whom he calls Tut-Tut like a pet, Tut the lizard-cold death dealer) cradled in his arms, speaking to the black cockerel in sighs.

~

Ivanhoe hoped to look for the Irish Mountain girl after the Welsh main, but Snag will not let him leave the pit. Ivanhoe has never pitted more than a couple of birds during a derby. Tonight, every bird in their stable passes through his bloody hands. His pancake heart works vainly in his chest, his breath hitches, his vision dims. Sometimes they win. More often they lose.

Ivanhoe stumbles as he follows the birds around the periphery of the little arena, stepping on the roosters in his exhaustion. Pluskat harangues him, mocking him for his short wind. *Sweetboy*, he calls him, and the crowd laughs as though this is an act, as though it's part of the show. *Sugarmouth*, and Pluskat smacks his lips deliciously at Ivanhoe.

The dead dunghills stack up at Snag's feet. Again and again he passes new birds over the pit barrier to an exhausted Ivanhoe. All their roosters are dying now—some tide has turned against them, inexorably against them, and they will be left with nothing. The look on

Snag's face is blank. Once he winks at Ivanhoe, who stands with a slender Racey Mug dangling dead from his fist, a long slow wink, as though half of Snag is falling asleep. *Hogbody!* someone in the crowd calls out.

At last, it's the final bout of the night, and Ivanhoe holds out his hands. This time, though, the bird is King Tut, and Snag shakes his head. He will pit Tut himself. He steps over the barrier, and Pluskat comes to assist him, takes his elbow and helps him, even reaches out a hand for Tut when Snag's battered knee threatens to give out. Snag snatches the bird back, finds his footing, and enters the ring with his head down, his shoulders hunched.

The crowd's out of their seats, they press against the barrier, faces dark with desire. "Tut!" they call. They have wanted to see this bird, this legendary Sumatra Game, all evening. They have traveled from all over the foothills to see the black cockerel fight. "King Tut!" they shout. It will be King Tut against one of Pluskat's champions, a rainbow-colored Poland Titan with a spray of wild feathers at its neck and a vivid eye, a young bird that's been making a name for itself.

Ivanhoe, paroled, leaves the pit. He's weaving. He can't make himself care about the final fight. He wants to find the girl. He wants to hear about the dreams. He wants to hear about the Eye of God. He spots Big Billy Shoemaker in the crowd—the girl is not beside him—waves at him to get his attention, ask him where she has gone. But Billy has fixed his handsome face on the fight, his pupils dilated, his jaw moving up and down, his throat working. He's shouting "Tut! King Tut!" like all the rest.

~

Disaster. King Tut is defeated. King Tut is dead.

~

Ivanhoe remembers. For the first time, waking in his room well before dawn, he remembers his dream. Remembers wearing the long-knife, and the strength of his wings, and the power in his heart. He remembers cuppling King Tut with a savage blow to the head, Tut reeling and falling. He knows that he killed Tut. It was not Pluskat's young Poland Titan. It was Ivanhoe.

The hillbilly Jesus looks at him from the petit-point sampler on the wall. *The pelican in the wilderness . . .*

He decides then that he will climb Irish Mountain. There, he can leave behind Ivanhoe of the foothills, he can leave Snag and the beast-men of the pit and the stinking chookhouses and *Hogbody* and *Sweetboy* and his pathetic pancake heart behind. He will leave the waking world behind, he will leap and slash and fly, his heart will pound in his chest without pain, without leaving him breathless and weak. He will be whole.

~

Ivanhoe wakes with the first crowing. It's the Kelso Yellow-Leg calling him, always the first. Soon the others will respond, those few that are left, and it will be a small cacophony amongst the chookhouses, but for now it's the lone clarion voice of the Kelso, and it sounds as though the Kelso is calling his name into the glassy morning air: *Ivanhoe! Ivanhoe!*

No worry about Snag rising today, even with the clamor in the yard. Snag was broken, sodden and stumbling, openly weeping when they finally reached home in the back of Big Billy Shoemaker's Lincoln. Snag is flatbacked in his sagging bed. Ivanhoe would be surprised to see him before noon.

He steps from the house, takes his first look of the day at Irish Mountain. It looms over him, steep faces gray in the dawn light, summit wreathed in angry clouds. Between the hill on which he lives and the mountain proper lies a narrow valley with a shivering creek at its bottom. Drum's Valley, they call it, he and Snag, and Drum's Creek, because there is no one around to call it anything else.

He trots across the chookyard. A once powerful Harvard White lies stiff and dead on the floor of its pen. Poor little man—but that is how it is with these birds when they're wounded, they live or they die, they have a game heart or they don't. The Harvard White's feathers stick out awkwardly in all directions, still glossy, still carrying the deep sheen of a diet rich in shell corn and pulped fish.

The other pens are empty. No fractious Racey Mugs, only a couple of sharp-voiced Cottontail Shufflers remaining. No more Blacksmith Hatch, no aged Claret Roundhead. One chookhouse slightly larger than the rest, its boards more tightly fitted, its floor cleaner: the house of the black cockerel, the brutal Sumatra, King Tut. Empty.

"Ivanhoe!" He whirls, caught—but Snag is not there. His eye falls on the lone occupied chookhouse behind him, and the rooster within. It's the golden butcher cook, the Kelso Yellow-Leg, unblink-ered eye fixed on Ivanhoe, neck outstretched, beak wide. The cock trumpets, and this time its voice is just a rooster's voice.

The Kelso Yellow-Leg. The good old Kelso will make the perfect companion on his climb. The bird crows again, and in its cry there is to Ivanhoe's ears the sound of pure delight. It turns a circle in the confines of its cage, waggles its small head, fluffs its feathers so that it looks twice its size. Admirable Kelso Yellow-Leg!

Ivanhoe quickly has the Kelso out of its house and into one of the small carrying cages, slung from his left hand, and they're walking to-gether toward the shallow draw that leads down into Drum's Valley, where he will cross Drum's Creek and begin the arduous trip up Irish Mountain.

$\sim$

Ivanhoe reaches the low shoulder of the mountain with surprising ease. His pancake heart, usually so troublesome, vexes him not at all. The Kelso Yellow-Leg shifts its weight from leg to leg to keep its bal-ance in the cage that swings by his side. Ivanhoe glories in the privi-lege he feels in the spacious understory of the forest. It's all virgin hemlocks in here, friendly creaking hemlocks, each tree standing in its own little clearing, and all around them thick hedges of waxy rhododendron and blooming wild-flowers. Great black bees bobble their workaday way from the bell of one flower to the petals of the next.

Thick green light filters down through the dense canopy of leaves, vegetable light filling the clearings, bathing the air around him. This is what he imagines it must be like to walk along the bottom of a shal-low sea. He has rubbed his skin with pennyroyal plant, so mosquitoes do not plague him, though they shrill in his ears and buzz his head, and the sharp singing of their wings makes him wince in anticipation of stings that don't come.

He bats his hands at the swarming insects, and they scatter only to collect again, hanging in the same spot in the air. Pushing through a close-grown rhododendron grove, he steps out into a large clearing. At its center, a vast hemlock, its trunk, its branches twisted and humped and corded with age. A skeleton hemlock stripped of bark and clothed all over in soft green moss. How old must such a tree be, to have grown to such a fantastic size?

"Mister," Ivanhoe says, addressing the tree. He is surprised by the smallness of his voice. The Kelso Yellow-Leg falls silent, and Ivanhoe finds himself desperately hoping that the bird will stay that way. He feels tempted to drop down and kneel before the hemlock, with its green-draped branches thrust out toward him.

"Mister," he says again, and it feels to him like the right form of address. "Do you know the girl who lives up in here somewhere? Talks about pelicans?"

No response. It's too paltry a question. Such a tree must stir itself only over questions of significance. Ivanhoe might care about the girl, but clearly Mister does not. Perhaps Mister does not care about people at all. This place is empty of men, but it's not at all empty—it's the opposite of empty, filled with something that presses invisibly against the eyes, something that begs to be seen.

"Do you know about the Eye of God on top of the mountain?"

No response to this either. Clearly, Mister disdains the Eye. Here in this clearing, among all these lesser trees, Mister is a god himself.

"Mister, do you dream?"

Nothing. Ivanhoe is beginning to feel a bit desperate. The tree is ancient, its roots sunk deep into the unyielding flesh of Irish Mountain, it has eaten the minerals and the water of the mountain, it has breathed this air for—what? A thousand years, or a thousand thousand, it's all the same to Ivanhoe. He can think of only one thing that might break the awful silence of the skeleton hemlock.

He holds out the carrying cage before him. "Mister, do you want my chicken?" he asks.

Still nothing. Ivanhoe gasps with relief. He will not be asked to give up the Kelso Yellow-Leg. Not yet, at any rate.

The earth shifts beneath him, and he stumbles, sinks to one knee. The Kelso gives a startled squawk. The earth continues to roll queasily, and Ivanhoe goes to both knees, drops to all fours like an animal. It's his pancake heart quailing in his chest, it makes him thick and dopey, it causes the world to swim before his eyes. The pancake heart flutters again, and he slips onto his elbows, his belly.

"Mister," he says, and his voice is a whisper. "Can I lay down here a minute? I'm awful tired."

No reply to this request either, but Ivanhoe decides that in this instance he will take silence for assent. He crawls to the tree, wriggling like a newt, sets his cheek against its cool, moss-covered flank, and sleeps.

And dreams of the girl. She stands in the clearing, beneath the gargantuan hemlock. At first he thinks that she's wearing a cloak made of some strange, shifting fabric. Then he realizes that she is nude, her body covered with twittering birds. Gorgeous little cedar waxwings, glossy and smooth as water-polished stones, perch on her shoulders, cling to her arms, her hair, her thighs, the taut skin of her stomach. The waxwings push themselves against her. They knead her flesh with their tiny claws.

"Having nothing to feed her young birds, the pelican . . ." she begins, and then falters. She brushes at the birds on her head, her shoulders, her chest, and they cloud around her. She flutters her hands at them. " . . . Her bill can hold more than her belly can." She bares her bosom, and her face is placid. Ivanhoe's terrified that she's bleeding, that her ribs will be exposed, a terrible rent in her flesh, blood bubbling forth. There's no blood, though. What she offers him is her soft breast. What she offers him is the freshet of her milk.

When he wakes, it is afternoon getting on toward evening. The hemlock towers over him, its attitude unreadable in the creeping dusk. He takes stock, finds that his heart seems to be keeping steady rhythm again, and rises, bracing himself against the knobby trunk of the tree. "Thanks, Mister," he says, and goes to the carrying cage where it lies on its side in the clearing.

"You OK?" he asks the Kelso Yellow-Leg, and the rooster gabbles indignantly. It must be hungry, Ivanhoe realizes, but he has nothing to feed it. He feels a bit hollow himself, and for a moment he considers heading back down the mountain, returning to the foothills and the game farm. A mockingbird cries from the branches overhead, its voice the voice of Snag, angry Snag. *Hogbody!*

He will not go back to that. Nothing for it but to continue up. On to the summit. "Goodbye," he says to Mister, touching his forehead respectfully. In the lowering darkness, does the tree make a nearly imperceptible gesture, does it lower one of its limbs in quiet salute? Ivanhoe cannot tell.

Staggering through a bog of deep peat, a bowl carved into the mountainside by the movement of some ancient glacier. And what bounty has sprung up in the wake of the glacier's passing! Cranberry vines, thickets of swamp rose and speckled alder, sedges and flowers: swamp candle, damp silky orchids, trilliums, lady's slippers, jewelweed glittering among the tough grasses, even carnivorous sundew, its leaves covered with sticky hairs. The pennyroyal seems to have worn off, the mosquitoes pestering Ivanhoe unmercifully, and he wishes the insect-devouring sundew plants good hunting. The cage bangs painfully against his hip with every step he takes.

"Where are we now, Kelso?" he asks the bird in the cage. A narrow stream winds its way through the bog, and he is thirsty, but the peat has stained the water the deep brown color of strong tea, so he does not drink, following the stream toward its source in hopes that the flow will clear.

Which it does, at the edge of the bog, half a mile on. Golden trout hang nearly motionless in the cool current, their red-veined tails waving lazily to keep them in place. Their lipless mouths gape. Ivanhoe tries to think of a way to catch the nearest of them, its dark bulging eye rolling toward him as he kneels at the bank of the stream but not seeming to take him in. Even the fish gruel that Snag feeds the game birds would taste good to him. Ivanhoe plunges his arm into the water, wets himself to the shoulder, fingers closing on nothing. The trout and its brothers scatter into the small rapids just downstream.

Ivanhoe makes do with water. Handful after handful of cold water, until his belly is full and tight. He offers a cupped palm of it to the Kelso Yellow-Leg, who refuses even to look at him. The rooster is rumpled, dry, weary, furious. It would die of thirst rather than take a drink from Ivanhoe's hand. Ivanhoe briefly regrets having brought it along, toys with the notion of turning the bird loose to fend for itself on the mountain—but then he would be alone.

Onward, following the stream because he doesn't have any better guide. It's been a wet season, and the stream is high between its steep banks, tumbling over itself in its rush down to the flatlands. "Don't be in any hurry," Ivanhoe tells it. The thornbushes that grow along the water's course tug at the legs of his pants as he passes.

Soon enough he finds himself at the edge of a wide pool. He is so tired that he actually stumbles into the pool up to his knees, almost sets the cage in the water. He puts it down on the pool's bank. The

473

rooster regards him balefully with its one good eye. "Ah, you're all right," Ivanhoe tells it. He wishes desperately that he had some dry shell corn in his pocket. Anything. Chickens, even stout battle stags like the Kelso Yellow-Leg, cannot go long without food and drink. "You're OK." He ducks his head beneath the surface of the water, to refresh himself.

Under the water, the world is gray and cool and nearly silent, and he stays there a moment, bubbles trailing upward from his nostrils and the corners of his mouth. He floats, his heart straining, his lungs bucking against the pressure that speedily builds in them. If he stays this way, he will drown, or his heart will seize up on him. He waits a long moment, the whistling of his blood's need for oxygen growing in his ears, to see what will happen.

The gray lifeless bottom of the pool. The swift ticking of blood in his ears.

Ivanhoe bursts from the water, nearly weeping with relief as air fills his lungs. He shakes his head, flinging droplets from his hair, and finds himself confronted with a waterfall. Twenty feet high, the cataract drops its riches into the upper end of the pool, cloaked by hepatica and trailing vines. At its apex hang thin tongues of polished sandstone, as sharp as spears, the water that spills off them a shimmering filigree of silver and air. The sound of the falls is more like music than like roaring water.

∼

Can Ivanhoe recall his mother at work on the petit-point? The needle, darting quick as a dragonfly, pricks her finger, and she brings it to her mouth to suck the pain away. A drop of blood on the point of the needle, blood in the weft of the cloth.

∼

The waterfall pounds Ivanhoe. He's underneath the cataract, behind it, and it crashes powerfully down on his shoulders and head. The falls stand before him like a curtain, and he finds himself reluctant to part the milky sheet of water. What lies out there? Vines and clematis, the clear pool, the bog and the hemlock forest beyond—but what if all of that is gone, or changed in some inexplicable way? He's sure that the world has contracted down to this one place, the hollow opening (*like a tomb*) in the rocks behind the waterfall and him

474

within it. He shivers with cold as a shadow, a human shadow, passes ghostlike across the face of the water.

And she comes. He hasn't dared to hope for such a thing, not since he set out in the morning, but there she stands, under the falls with him, the water plastering her hair—it's no longer obscured by the bandanna—to her shapely skull. She's dressed as she was at Pluskat's, dungarees and a workshirt, wringing wet. She smiles at Ivanhoe as though she's unsurprised to find him there. He can make out the pleasing shape of her breasts, her nipples, through the soaked material of her shirt. He thinks of his dream beneath the hemlock, imagines her suckling him, grows excited, his breath short.

Then she is next to him, subjecting him to brutal scrutiny. Her warm breath touches his cheek. They are nose to nose, and as he looks at her he discovers that it's uncannily like looking at himself in a mirror. When his eyes dart to the side, hers do likewise. When he steals a look down at her body, she takes in his. A drop of water depends from the tip of her nose, and he feels a bead forming beneath his as well. He laughs.

"I'm dreaming again, aren't I?" he asks. She shrugs her comely shoulders.

Ivanhoe thinks hard. He stands within the penumbra of the falls, near the top of Irish Mountain. From the falls flows a nameless stream, and the stream must empty into Drum's Creek, which rolls past the game farm into the Seneca River at the mountain's base. The Seneca flows to the Kanawha, which runs to the broad sluggish Ohio. The Ohio empties into the Mississippi. The Mississippi in its turn empties into the Gulf of Mexico, and the gulf into the Atlantic Ocean. And all the oceans of the world open one into the others.

"I'm dreaming," he says.

And discovers himself clothed in shining feathers, plumage that effortlessly turns aside the water that spills down over him. He feels the battle stag's heart beating within him.

The girl regards him warily. He fixes her with a golden eye, clacks his beak. He is strong and proud and barbarous. She takes a step back. "Will you hurt me?" she asks.

"I might," he says. Her teeth chatter slightly, but she gives no other outward sign of discomfort. Her hands hang at her sides. Her skin, where he can see it, is dotted with a pleasing constellation of freckles. Droplets of water gleam like pearls in her hair.

475

"Turn around," he tells her, his voice half human, half a bird's croaking caw. She turns and he drinks her in, the athletic set of her shoulder blades (so like undeveloped wings), the aristocratic curve of her spine, the soft, shadowed hollow at the small of her back. He imagines sipping water from that hollow.

This must be the answer. This is why he has climbed the mountain, to be here, to be strong beneath this waterfall with this girl. One leap, one stroke of his powerful wings, and he will be on her, he will pin her, drive her down before him, clasp her to him with his sunset-colored pinions, thrust himself upon her, tear her clothes from her body, force himself inside her. He has seen Snag's gamecocks satisfy themselves on the hens so. How many times has he seen it? And she will deny him nothing.

~

Screaming. Not the screaming of the girl. She has turned entirely around now, she has shown him her whole self, and her mouth is closed. The screaming comes from outside the enclosing waterfall. It is the crowing of the forgotten Kelso Yellow-Leg.

Ivanhoe shudders. The voice of the Kelso comes from without, but it's loud, it comes from within too, it caroms off the stone behind him and the water before, it's coming from somewhere close by, it's coming from him, it's coming from Ivanhoe's own chest. The crowing, on and on, tears itself from his lungs, from his panicked heart, ascends his burning throat, issues from his open, upthrust beak. What a noise! The Kelso Yellow-Leg asks, and Ivanhoe answers.

The torrent of the falls washes the feathers from his body, sweeps them away. Each feather wrenches itself from his flesh with a flare of pain, a flare repeated a hundred, a thousand times over in an instant; they rip themselves free and drop down and float in the water at his feet. Each feather leaves behind it a small, hot bubo, a tiny crater welling with his blood for a moment, before the trickle of blood, too, is washed away. The feathers are going, his head is stripped bare, his shoulders and his back, he watches in horror as his long gangling arms reveal themselves beneath the molting feathers of his once-powerful wings. Down his body the terrible sloughing-off goes, like fire down the trunk of his body, along his limbs, his buttocks, his soft belly, his thighs, his groin, until he is freezing, naked before the girl.

"Keep your eyes open," the girl says. "I want you to see this."

476

The beak is the last thing to go, the sharp beak, it gives a liquid shift like a loosening tooth, hauls itself awkwardly away from his face, the pain unbearable but somehow beautiful too, as it pulls free of its moorings—agony to feel it go, eyeball-rolling, wailing agony, but he knows there will be relief when finally he sheds it. It hangs sideways for a moment, like a cheap mask whose string has broken, and then at last the beak tears loose entirely, first the bottom half and then the top, splashing into the feather-strewn water at his feet, bobbing obscenely there.

What next? He feels terribly small, terrifyingly fragile. What will go next? He raises his face as the water crashes down on him, fully alert, and waits on the final dissolution, joint separating from joint, bone from bone, sinew from sinew, flesh from flesh, until there is nothing left. The crowing of the Kelso Yellow-Leg continues, but under the waterfall there is only the sound of Ivanhoe's frightened weeping.

~

Looking for his vanished boy, Snag hobbles as far as Drum's Creek. He sits on the bank and, wretched, stares into the purling water. His own strained face looks back at him from the dark rippling surface. Then, crossing his image, a sudden flash of color. And another. A dozen, a hundred. Where could they come from? A raft of brilliant color passing him on the stream, numberless at first, and then fewer, and fewer still, only a couple wheeling past in the swift current, one. Too late, Snag thinks to put his hand out, take up one of the dripping feathers. They are past him, they are gone.

~

Naked under the sky. She has led him here, stripped and frail. She climbed before him, nude, up the foaming cataract, the bird in one hand, cradled against her ribs, her naked feet sure as a mountain goat's on the slick outcroppings. The sharp rocks cut his feet as he climbed, and he was deathly afraid that he would fall.

She has brought him to the glade at the brow of Irish Mountain, brought him to the very center of the Eye of God. He's stretched out there in the predawn dark, and she's beside him. He wants her with a fierce ache, but his thin hide is unbearably tender with his recent flaying, and for the moment their skin touches only lightly, at the

477

knee and the wrist, along their forearms. The cool breeze that sweeps over the mountain summit blows a strand of her hair across his lips, and he tastes ocean foam.

No way for Ivanhoe to know it, but the Eye of God on which he rests is in fact the ruined hulk of a three-hundred-foot-wide transit telescope, erected on the mountaintop by scientists from the National Radio Astronomy Observatory, to listen to the radio signals that emanate from the energetic cores of quasars and pulsars: imperceptible entities a universe from this deserted place. Abandoned now. He would not care if he did know. All he knows is that it's a gigantic tilting dish of steel, its white paint peeling from almost two acres of surface. It's smooth, and he's lying on it with the girl.

Around them, a couple hundred yards below the peak of Irish Mountain, an unbroken floor of clouds stretches away like the ancient ocean in all directions to the horizon. The foothills are invisible beneath them, as distant as the celestial bodies that the Eye of God was intended to spy out. Undetectable: the chookyard, the foothills, Pluskat's pit, Snag, and all the rest of Ivanhoe's old life, the entire waking world, drowned beneath the cloud sea.

All drowned but the Kelso Yellow-Leg, a bit the worse for wear but apparently in good spirits as it works its way along the scaffolding at the edge of the great radio telescope, ululating and chuckling. It fixes its good eye on Ivanhoe and the girl, who seem to be falling asleep beside each other. Soon they will enter each other's dreams. Soon her family will come, the fearful ones. The others will come in due time, but for now it is only the girl and the half-grown boy Ivanhoe, and that is just fine with the Kelso Yellow-Leg. That is all right by the indomitable old butcher cock, who clings tenaciously to the curved perimeter of the Eye of God, who ruffles his golden feathers, who crows his defiance into the face of the rising sun.

Nominated by Laura Kasischke, Fred Leebron, Zoetrope: All Story

BEAUTIFUL NERO

by KEVIN PRUFER

from EPOCH

"What an artist the world is losing!"

We'd made such a day of it—
until the sun fell behind the trees and the streetlamps came awake.

We drank and sang
                and old Paula fell out of her chair into the street
while Wilson spilled my drink, then called the waitress with the
    sponge.

And then the boys were dragging café tables inside for the night,
the metal legs scraping the pavement white.
                             Good night, Irene, good night,
I called into the air. And *Drink up!* Paula said, *Drink up!*
laughing and opening her purse.

And then I was alone and had to find another place to sit.

In the back of my throat, some god once burned a song. *How
    beautiful,*
my mother said when, as a boy, I opened my mouth to sing. *Lovely,*

lovely. A blister and a scar—
                    Like Nero, I can't help but add a trill

479

to any bit of paper caught and fluttering down the street,
or the cat drifting past on a blur of legs.
                              And *Oh!* she said, when
at the piano the silver thread of my voice unrolled.

The night Rome burned, Nero sang. *Yes*, the lyre told him, and he
    played,
perched on the balcony.
                              Sing, the city said in its embers,
and Nero sang. And the buckets of water, passed hand-to-hand
    below
called, *More!* and the girls in the street, their gowns burning so
    gently

up their bodies, clapped, *Bravo!*, while all at once the library
    heaved
and crumbled,
                              fell in upon itself and died. And *Beauty*, Nero said
under his breath, his hands stopped on the lyre, his face orange
in the smoke-filled light.

Years later the bombers came like little black notes over the city,
like trills.

Yes, I lost the song in my throat, but crouched in the park
beneath a tree, hands over my head, and cried

thinking of no one but myself while the deep-voiced bombs called
one building after another into the ground

and all at once a treetop bloomed in flame.

I sat in the park and sang
                              while Paula and Wilson staggered home,
while across the road the café owners turned out their lights.
Lovely, lovely, I remembered my mother saying, *it's beautiful*,

clapping her hands from the living room when I was through.
Beautiful, I thought, leaning back on the park bench
while the city dozed and the lights went out on such music,

the ache in my throat, a quiet evening.

In the end, Nero could not do the job,
                               but cried for his slave to finish
him off. And from the ashes of Rome, the troops approached
so he could hear their horns and boots.
                               Always, a scar where a god
burned a song. How lovely, when a city dies
and one is far enough away to make a song of it.

I sat in the park and sang.
                      The city crouched in a darkness.
And then, the slave said, *Yes*, withdrawing his blade.

Nominated by Richard Burgin, Sherod Santos, Epoch

THE RETURN OF THE DARK CHILDREN

fiction by ROBERT COOVER

from HARVARD REVIEW

WHEN THE FIRST BLACK RATS REAPPEARED, scurrying shadowily along the river's edge and through the back alleyways, many thought the missing children would soon follow. Some believed the rats might *be* the children under a spell, so they were not at first killed, but were fed and pampered, not so much out of parental affection, as out of fear. For, many legends had grown up around the lost generation of children, siphoned from the town by the piper so many years ago. Some thought that the children had, like the rats, been drowned by the piper, and that they now returned from time to time to haunt the town that would not, for parsimony, pay their ransom. Others believed that the children had been bewitched, transformed into elves or werewolves or a kind of living dead. When the wife of one of the town councilors hanged herself, it was rumored it was because she'd been made pregnant by her own small son, appearing to her one night in her sleep as a toothless hollow-eyed incubus. Indeed, all deaths, even those by the most natural of causes, were treated by the citizenry with suspicion, for what could be a more likely cause of heart failure or malfunction of the inner organs than an encounter with one's child as a member of the living dead?

At first, such sinister speculations were rare, heard only among the resentful childless. When the itinerant rat-killer seduced the youngsters away that day with his demonic flute, all the other townsfolk could think about was rescue and revenge. Mothers wept and cried out the names of their children, calling them back, while fathers and grandfathers armed themselves and rushed off into the hills, chasing trills and the echoes of trills. But nothing more substantial was ever found, not even a scrap of clothing or a dropped toy, it was as though they had never been, and as the weeks became months and the months years, hope faded and turned to resentment—so much love misspent!—and then eventually to dread. New children meanwhile were born, replacing the old, it was indeed a time of great fertility for there was a vacuum to be filled, and as these new children grew, a soberer generation than that which preceded it, there was no longer any place, in homes or hearts, for the old ones, not for their lightsome ways. The new children were, like their predecessors and their elders, plump and happy, much loved, well fed, and overly indulged in all things, but they were more closely watched and there was no singing or dancing. The piper had instilled in the townsfolk a terror of all music, and it was banned forever by decree. All musical instruments had been destroyed. Humming a tune in public was an imprisonable offense and children, rarely spanked, were spanked for it. Always, it was associated with the children who had left and the chilling ungrateful manner of their leaving: they did not even look back. But it was as though they had not really quite gone away after all, for as the new children came along the old ones seemed to return as omnipresent shadows of the new ones, clouding the nursery and playground, stifling laughter and spoiling play, and they became known then, the lost ones, the shadowy ones, as the dark children.

In time, all ills were blamed on them. If an animal sickened and died, if milk soured or a house burned, if a child woke screaming from a nightmare, if the river overflowed its banks, if money went missing from the till or the beer went flat or one's appetite fell off, it was always the curse of the dark children. The new children were warned: be good or the dark children will get you! They were not always good, and sometimes, as it seemed, the dark children did get them. And now the newest menace: the return of the rats. The diffident pampering of these rapacious creatures soon ceased. As they multiplied, disease broke out, as it had so many years before. The promenade alongside the river that ran through the town, once so popular, now was utterly forsaken except for the infestation of rats, the flower gardens lining the promenade trampled by their little feet and left filthy and untended, for those who loitered there ran the risk of being eaten alive, as happened to the occasional pet gone astray.

Their little pellets were everywhere and in everything. Even in one's shoes and bed and tobacco tin. Once again the city fathers gathered in emergency council and declared their determination to exterminate the rats, whether they were bewitched dark children or not; and once again the rats proved too much for them. They were hunted down with guns and poisons and burned in mountainous heaps, their sour ashes blanketing the town, graying the laundry and spoiling the sauces, but their numbers seemed not to diminish. If anything, there were more of them than ever seen before, and they just kept coming. But when one rash councilor joked that it was maybe time to pay the piper, he was beaten and hounded out of town.

For, if the dark children were a curse upon the town, they were still their own, whereas that sorcerer who had lured them away had been like a mysterious force from another world, a diabolical intruder who had forever disturbed the peace of the little community. He was not something to laugh about. The piper, lean and swarthy, had been dressed patchily in too many colors, wore chains and bracelets and earrings, painted his bony face with ghoulish designs, smiled too much and too wickedly and with teeth too white. His language, not of this town, was blunt and uncivil and seemed to come, not from his throat, but from some hollow place inside. Some seemed to remember that he had no eyes, others that he did have eyes but the pupils were golden. He ate sparely, if at all (some claimed to have seen him nibbling at the rats), and, most telling of all, he was never seen to relieve himself. All this in retrospect, of course, for at the time, the townsfolk, vastly comforted by the swift and entertaining eradication of the rats, saw him as merely an amusing street musician to be tolerated and, if not paid all that he impertinently demanded (there had been nothing illegal about this, no contracts had been signed), at least applauded—the elders, like the children, in short, fatally beguiled by the fiend. No, should he return, he would be attacked by all means available, and if possible torn apart, limb from limb, his flute rammed down his throat, the plague of rats be damned. He who placed himself beyond the law would be spared by none.

Left to their own resources, however, the townsfolk were no match for the rats. For all their heroic dedication, the vermin continued to multiply, the disease spread and grew more virulent, and the sky darkened with the sickening ash, now no longer of rats only, but sometimes of one's neighbors as well, and now and then a child or two. Having lost one generation of children, the citizenry were determined not to lose another, and did all they could to protect the children, their own and others, not only from the rats but also from the rumored dark children, for there had been reported sightings of late, mostly by night, of strange naked creatures with piebald flesh moving on all fours through the hills around. They had the form of children, those who claimed to have seen them said, but they were not children. Some said they had gray fleshly wings and could hover and fly with the darting speed of a dragonfly. Parents now boiled their children's food and sterilized their drink, policed their bedrooms and bathrooms and classrooms, never let them for a single minute be alone. Even so, now and then, one of them would disappear, spreading fear and consternation throughout the town. But now, when a child vanished, no search parties went out looking for it as they'd done the first time, for the child was known to be gone as were the dead gone, all children gone or perished spoken of, not as dead, but taken.

The city elders, meeting in continuous emergency session, debated the building of an impregnable wall around the town to keep the dark children out and hopefully to dam the tide of invading rats as well. This had a certain popular appeal, especially among the parents, but objections were raised. If every able-bodied person in town worked day and night at this task, it was argued, it would still take so long that the children might all be gone before it could be finished: then, they'd just be walling themselves in with the rats. And who knew what made a wall impregnable to the likes of the dark children? Weren't they, if they really existed, more like phantoms than real creatures for whom brick and stone were no obstruction? Moreover, the building of such a wall would drain the town of all its energy and resources and close it off to trade, it would be the end of the era of prosperity, if what they were suffering now could still be prosperity, and not only the children could be lost but also the battle against the rats which was already proving taxing for the community. But what else can we do? We must be more vigilant!

And so special volunteer units were created to maintain a twenty-four-hour watch on all children. The playgrounds were walled off and sealed with double locks, a compromise with the proponents of the wall-building, and all the children's spaces were kept brightly lit to chase away the shadows, even as they slept at night. Shadows that seemed to move by themselves were shot at. Some observed that

485

whenever a child disappeared a pipe could be heard, faintly, just before. Whether this was true or not, all rumors of such flaunting of the music laws were pursued with full vigor, and after many false alarms one piper was at last chased down: a little boy of six, one of the new children, blowing on a wooden recorder. He was a charming and dutiful boy, much loved by all, but he had to be treated as the demon he now was, and so, like any diseased animal, he and his pipe were destroyed. His distraught parents admitted to having hidden away the childish recorder as a souvenir at the time of outlawing musical instruments, and the child somehow, inexplicably, found it. The judges did not think it was inexplicable. There were calls for the death penalty, but the city fathers were not cruel or vindictive and understood that the parents had been severely punished by the loss of their child, so they were given lengthy prison sentences instead. No one protested. The prison itself was so rat-infested that even short sentences amounted to the death penalty anyway.

The dark children now were everywhere, or seemed to be. If the reports of the frightened citizenry were to be believed, the hills about now swarmed with the little batlike phantoms and there was daily evidence of their presence in the town itself. Pantries were raided, flour spilled, eggs broken, there was salt in the sugar, urine in the teapot, obscene scribblings on the school chalkboard and on the doors of closed shops whose owners had taken ill or died. Weary parents returned from work and rat-hunting to find all the pictures on their walls tipped at odd angles, bird cages opened, door handles missing. That these sometimes turned out to be pranks by their own mischievous children was not reassuring for one had to assume they'd fallen under the spell of the dark children, something they could not even tell anyone about for fear of losing their children to the severity of the laws of vigilance now in place. Whenever they attempted to punish them, their children would cry out: It's not my fault! The dark children made me do it! All right, all right, but shush now, no talk of that!

There were terrible accidents which were not accidents. A man, socializing with friends, left the bar one night to return home and made a wrong turning, stumbled instead into the ruined gardens along the promenade. One who had seen him passing by said it was as if his arm were being tugged by someone or something unseen, and he looked stricken with terror. His raw carcass was found the next morning at the edge of the river. One rat-hunter vanished as though consumed entirely. Another was shot dead by a fellow hunter, and in two different cases, rat poison, though kept under lock and key, turned up in food; in both instances, a spouse died, but the partners were miraculously spared. When asked if the killing was an accident, the hunter who had shot his companion said it certainly was not, a mysterious force had gripped his rifle barrel and moved it just as he was firing it. And things didn't seem to be where they once were any more. Especially at night. Furniture slid about and knocked one over, walls seemed to swing out and strike one, stairsteps dropped away halfway down. Of course, people were drinking a lot more than usual, reports may have been exaggerated, but once-reliable certainties were dissolving.

The dark children remained largely invisible for all that the town felt itself swarming with them, though some people claimed to have seen them running with the rats, swinging on the belfry rope, squatting behind chimney pots on rooftops. With each reported sighting, they acquired new features. They were said to be child-sized but adult in proportions, with long arms they sometimes used while running; they could scramble up walls and hug the ground and disappear right into it. They were gaudily colored and often had luminous eyes. Wings were frequently mentioned, and occasionally tails. Sometimes these were short and furry, other times more long and ratlike. Money from the town treasury disappeared and one of the councilors as well, and his wife, though hysterical with grief and terror, was able to describe in startling detail the bizarre horned and winged creatures who came to rob the town and carry him off. Ah! We didn't know they had horns. Oh yes! With little rings on the tips! Or bells! They were glittery all over as if dressed in jewels! She said she was certain that one of them was her own missing son, stolen away by the piper all those many years ago. I looked into his eyes and pleaded with him not to take his poor father away, she wept, but his eyes had no pupils only tiny flickering flames where the pupils should be! They asked her to write out a complete profile of the dark children, but then she disappeared, too. When one of the volunteer guards watching children was charged with fondling a little five-year-old girl, he insisted that, no, she was being sexually assaulted by one of the dark children and he was only doing all he could to get the hellish creature off her. The child was confused but seemed to agree with this. But what happened to the dark child? I don't know. The little girl screamed, a crowd came running, the dark child faded away in my grasp. All I managed to hold on to was this, he said, holding up a small gold earring. A common ornament. Most children wear them and lose them daily. I tore it out of his nose, he said. He was found innocent but removed from the unit and put on probation. In his affidavit, he also mentioned horns, and was able to provide a rough sketch of the dark child's genitalia, which resembled those of a goat.

The new children pretended not to see the dark children, or perhaps in their innocence, they didn't see them, yet overheard conversations among them suggested they knew more than they were telling, and when they were silent, they sometimes seemed to be listening intently, smiling faintly. The dark children turned up in their rope-skipping rhymes and childish riddles (When is water not wet? When a dark child's shadow make it . . .), and when they chose up sides for games of ball or tag, they tended always to call one of their teams the dark children. The other was usually the hunters. The small children cried if they couldn't be on the dark children's team. When a child was taken, his or her name was whispered among the children like a kind of incantation, which they said was for good luck. The church organist, unemployed since the piper went through and reduced to gravetending, a task that had somewhat maddened him, retained enough presence of mind to notice that the familiar racket of the children's playground games, though still composed of the usual running feet and high-pitched squealing, was beginning to evolve into a peculiar musical pattern, reminiscent of the piper's songs. He transcribed some of this onto paper, which was studied in private chambers by the city council, where, for the first time in many years, surreptitious humming was heard. And at home, in their rooms, when the children played with their dolls and soldiers and toy castles, the dark children with their mysterious ways now always played a part in their little dramas. One could hear them talking to the dark children, the dark children speaking back in funny squeaky voices that quavered like a ghost's. Even if it was entirely invented, an imaginary world made out of scraps overheard from parents and teachers, it was the world they chose to live in now, rather than the one provided by their loving families, which was, their parents often felt, a kind of betrayal, lack of gratitude, lost trust. And, well, just not fair.

One day, one of the rat-hunters, leaning on his rifle after a long day's work and smoking his old black pipe, peered down into the infested river and allowed that it seemed to him that whenever a child vanished or died, the rat population decreased. Those with him stared down into that same river and wondered: Was this possible? A rat census was out of the question, but certain patterns in their movements could be monitored. There was a wooden footbridge, for example, which the rats used for crossing back and forth or just for cavorting on, and one could at any moment make a rough count of the rats on it. At the urging of the hunters, these tabulations were taken by the town clerk at dawn, midday, and twilight for several days, and the figures were found to be quite similar from day to day, no matter how many were killed. Then, a little girl failed to return from a game of hide-and-seek (the law banning this game or any game having to do with concealment was passing through the chambers that very day), and the next day the rat numbers were found to have dropped. Not substantially perhaps, one would not have noticed the change at a glance, but it was enough to make the bridge count mandatory by law. A child, chasing a runaway puppy, fell into the turbulent river and was taken and the numbers dropped again, then or about then. Likewise when another child disappeared (he left a note, saying he was going where the dark children were to ask if they could all be friends) and a fourth died from the diseases brought by the rats.

Another emergency session of the council was called which all adult members of the community were invited to attend. No one stayed away. The choice before them was stark but, being all but unthinkable, was not at first enunciated. The parents, everyone knew, were adamant in not wanting it spoken aloud at all. There were lengthy prolegomena, outlining the history of the troubles from the time of the piper's visit to the present, including reports from the health and hospital services, captains of the rat-hunting teams, the business community, the volunteer vigilance units, school and toilet monitors, the town clerk, and artists who provided composite sketches of the dark children based on reported sightings. They did not look all that much like children of any kind, but that was to be expected. A mathematician was brought in to explain in precise technical detail the ratio between the disappearance or death of children and the decrease in the rat population. He was convincing, though not well understood. Someone suggested a break for tea, but this was voted down. There was a brief flurry of heated discussion when a few parents expressed their doubts as to the dark children's actual existence, suggesting they might merely be the fantasy of an understandably hysterical community. This argument rose and faded quickly, as it had few adherents. Finally, there was nothing to do but confront it:

their choice was between letting the children go, or living—and dying—with the rats.

Of course it was unconscionable that the children should be sacrificed to save their elders, or even one another. That was the opinion vehemently expressed by parents, teachers, clergy, and many of the other ordinary townsfolk. This was not a decision one could make for others, and the children were not yet of an age to make it for themselves. The elders nodded solemnly. All had to acknowledge the rightness of this view. Furthermore, the outcome, based on speculative projections from these preliminary observations, was just too uncertain, the admirable mathematics notwithstanding, for measures so merciless and irreversible. A more thorough study was required. As for the bridge counts themselves, seasonal weather changes were proposed as a more likely explanation of the decline in the rat population—if in fact there had been such a decline. The numbers themselves were disputed, and alternative, unofficial, less decisive tabulations made by others, worried parents mostly, were presented to the assembly and duly considered. And even if the official counts were true, a teacher at the school argued, the vermin population was probably decreasing normally, for all such plagues have their tides and ebbs. With patience, it will all be over.

The data, however, did not support this view. Even those sympathetic with them understood that the parents and teachers were not trying to engage in a reasoned search for truth, but were desperately seeking to persuade. The simple facts were that the town was slowly dying from its infestation of rats, and whenever a child was taken the infestation diminished; everyone knew this, even the parents. The data was admittedly sketchy, but time was short. A prolonged study might be a fatal misjudgment. A doctor described in uncompromising detail the current crisis in the hospitals, their staffs disease-riddled, patients sleeping on the floors, medications depleted, the buildings themselves aswarm with rats, and the hunters reminded the assembly that their own untiring efforts had not been enough alone to get the upper hand against the beasts, though many of them were parents, too, and clearly ambivalent about their testimony. Those who had lost family members to the sickness and risked losing more, their own lives included, spoke bluntly: If the children stay, they will all die of the plague like the rest of us, so it's not as though we would be sacrificing them to a fate worse than they'd suffer here. But if they go, some of us might be saved. A compromise was proposed: Lots could be drawn and the children could be released one by one until the rats disappeared. That way, some might be spared. But that would not be fair, others argued, for why should some parents be deprived of their children when others were not? Wouldn't that divide the community irreparably forever? Anyway, the question might be purely academic. Everyone had noticed during the mathematician's presentation the disconcerting relationship between the rate of decrease of the rat population and the number of children remaining in the town. They want the children, shouted a fierce old man from the back of the hall, so let them have them! We can always make more!

Pandemonium broke out. Shouts and accusations. You think it's so easy! cried one. Where are your own? It's not the making, cried others, it's the raising! They were shouted down and they shouted back. People were called murderers and cowards and egoists, ghouls and nihilists. Parents screamed that if their children had to die they would die with them, and their neighbors yelled: Good riddance! Through it all, there was the steady pounding of the gavel, and finally, when order was restored, the oldest member of the council who was also judged to be the wisest, silent until now, was asked to give his opinion. His chair was wheeled to the illumined center of the little platform at the front of the hall whereon, behind him, the elders sat. He gazed out upon the muttering crowd, his old hands trembling, but his expression calm and benign. Slowly, a hush descended.

There is nothing we can do, he said at last in his feeble old voice. It is the revenge of the dark children. Years ago, we committed a terrible wrong against them and this is their justified reply. He paused, sitting motionlessly in the pale light. We thought that we could simply replace them, he said. But we were wrong. He seemed to be dribbling slightly and he raised one trembling hand to wipe his mouth. I do not know if the dark children really exist, he went on. I myself have never seen them. But, even if they do not, it is the revenge of the dark children just the same. He paused again as if wanting his words to be thoroughly understood before proceeding, or perhaps because his thoughts came slowly to him. I have, however, seen the rats, and even with my failing eyesight, I know that they are real. I also know that the counting of them is real, whether accurate or not, and that your responses to this counting, while contradictory, are also real. Perhaps they are the most real thing of all. He seemed to go adrift for a moment, his head nodding slightly, before continuing: It may be that the diminishing number of rats is due to the day-by-day loss of our children or it may be due to nature's rhythms or to the weather or the success at last of our hunters. It may even be that the numbers are not diminishing, that we are mistaken. It does not matter. The children must go. There was a soft gasp throughout the hall. Because, he said as the gasp died away, we are who we are. The old man gazed out at them for a short time, and each felt singled out, though it was unlikely he could see past the edge of the platform. The children will not go one by one, he went on. They will go all at once and immediately. That is both fair and practical. And, I might add, inevitable. He nodded his head as though agreeing with himself, or perhaps for emphasis. They themselves will be happier together than alone. And if we who remain cannot avoid grief, we can at least share it and comfort one another. Even now, if our humble suggestions are being followed, the children are being gathered together and told to put on their favorite clothes and bring their favorite toys and they are then being brought to the town square outside this building. As parents, turning pale, rose slowly from their seats, he again wiped his mouth with the back of his hand and his expression took on a more sorrowful aspect. I foresee a rather sad future for our town, he said. The rats will finally disappear, for whatever reason, though others of us will yet perish of their loathsome diseases, and our promenade will reopen and trade will resume. Even should we repeal the music laws, however, there will still be little if any singing or dancing here, for there will be no children, only the memory of children. It has not been easy for the town's mothers and fathers to suffer so, twice over, and I feel sorry for them, as I am sure we all do. We must not ask them to go through all that again. He cocked his old head slightly. Ah. I can hear the children outside now. They are being told they are going off to play with the dark children. They will leave happily. You will all have an opportunity to wave goodbye, but they will probably not even look back. Nor of course will they ever return. In the shocked pause before the rush to the exits, he added, speaking up slightly: And now will we at last be free of the dark children? He sighed and, as his head dipped to his chest, raised one trembling finger, wagging it slowly as though in solemn admonishment. No. No. No, my friends. We will not.

Nominated by Mike Newirth

PRIMER OF WORDS

by DAVID BAKER

from THE GEORGIA REVIEW

I.

Hard to picture him here in the lake grass,
taking notes, up to his knees in mud, bugs,
but here he is, August 1880,
in Canada, tracing the flights of birds.

Like a bird he takes whatever he finds
to make words, the backs of letters, homemade
notebooks, and writes sometimes without looking,
they are so plentiful, the shy *Shore-lark*

and all the Sparrows, Oriole (hanging
bird—golden robin), Scarlet Tanager,
Swallows, the (very common) cedar-bird.
Lists, lists, enlivening his mind, like his

better father said they would do, for "bare
lists of words are found suggestive to an
imaginative and excited mind."
Yet he is half-paralyzed from the strokes

and must hang on Wm. Saunders' firm arm
to continue. Lists in manuscript are
his poems now, his greatest Leaves fallen
years past, consigned to infamy or fame.

Lists draw their power straight from nature, as
from his expressions. *Words of ~~all~~ the Laws
of the Earth*—he closes his eyes to feel
the sun bathe his face, softly now he breathes—

Words of the Sun and Moon,
Words of Geology, ~~Chemistry Gegro~~ History, Geography,
Words of ~~Me~~ the Medieval Races,
Words of the Progress of ~~Law~~, Religion, Law, Art, Government,

Words of the ~~Topography~~ surface of the Earth, grass, rocks, trees,
    flowers, grains, and the like,
Words of the Air and Heavens,
Words of the Birds ~~of the~~, and of insects,
Words of ~~the~~ Men and Women—the hundreds of different
    nations, tribes, colors, and other distinctions . . .

2.

He's sixty-one, famous if half infirm.
He's doted on by Addington Symonds, Bucke,
hounded for his views on Lincoln and Life,
yet now, in Ontario, by the lakes,

he is simply Walt, noting here when one
little black-and-yellow bird [the goldfinch]
lights from his billowy flight on a low
pine bough not ten feet off. In one gesture

he considers the significant trait
of civilization Benevolence—
and thinks it *doubtful whether ~~it~~ this is*
anywhere illustrated to fuller

degrees than in Ontario, *with its*
countless institutions for the Blind, one
for the Deaf and Dumb, one for Foundlings,
a Reformatory for Girls, one for

Women, and no end of homes for the old
and infirm, for waifs, and for the Sick—and
then adjusts the list . . . (all ~~vario~~ sorts)
otter, coon, mink, martin, ~~and buffalo~~

musk-rat, & c. Equality
is nature's law and must be government's.
The rich, abundant, wild various hues
of the birds, the hunting hawks, the ruby-

throated whirring hummingbirds, the brave gold-
finch full of song—so many genera—
should not confuse the mind. In his rough-hand
Primer of Words he traces the native

people's phrases, found in the north prairies,
their *wardance, powwow, Sachem, Mohekan,*
then notes as in a new poem the fate
of the Africans, the poignant irony . . .

3.

  barracoon—collection of slaves
     in Africa, or anywhere
     ("I see the slave barracoon")

how hybrid songs of "nigger dialect"
have furnished *hundreds of outre* ~~*names*~~
words, many of them adopted into
the common speech of the mass of people.

In another notebook, in years past, he
fretted with this problem so, writing *I
know there are strong and solid arguments
against slavery—arguments addressed*

*to the great American thought Will it pay?
We will* ~~*go directly*~~ *stand face to face*

with the / chief of the supreme bench. *We will*
speake with the soul. [new page] *For ~~free~~ as great*
as any worldly wealth to a man,—or

~~her~~ womanhood to a woman,—greater
than these, I think, is the right of liberty,
to any and to all men and women.—
Lists. Lists. Bare words. Nature's compositions

stretch before the receptive eye. He has
found a cool, moss-covered slab of limestone
to light on, looking south, over the lake.
Tomorrow, he thinks, he'll speak yet with Bucke

about the poems, and a lecture tour.
There is so much to say about the world.
These grasses, for instance, growing so tall
in the wild—*what are they?* Timothy, joe-

pye weed, rip-gut, perhaps? Of what nature,
what kind are they? There's another question
here, a hope—he needs to frame this better . . .
how they blow in the wind . . . how they go on . . .

or, *how they may seed.* Yes. How continue.

Nominated by Sherod Santos, David Kirby, Arthur Smith, Andrew Hudgins, Jane Hirshfield,
David Wojahn, Georgia Review

THE LONELY DOLL

fiction by ANTONYA NELSON

from EPOCH

"I OWNED ONE FOR A WHILE," she told him. "I found it, you won't believe this, in my grandfather's bedside table, in a drawer. There were three, in fact, like the bears, big, medium, baby. Maybe I was innocent at age eleven, I can't really say. It's true I was snooping, but it was *naive* snooping. That's the thing about being eleven: you feel so stupid, so duped, like the grownups are still holding out. I expected to find maybe a cigar or a hip flask, you know, Peepaw's *public* foul habits. Instead I found a plastic penis. Three of them, each the weight of, like, a flashlight.

"My first instinct was to slam the drawer, as if they might hup-to and start acting like billy clubs. Whap whap whap! But when I looked again, there they were, lying innocent. Alongside a tub of Vaseline. They were always there, week after week. The Vaseline seemed fairly wiggy, don't ask me why. Finally, I stole one. I stayed the nights at my grandparent's on Friday nights forever. I slept with my grandma, while Peepaw had his own bedroom. He snored. Sometimes his snoring would wake me up. He'd spend the evening in his La-Z-Boy confusing the mystery shows. He loved to watch them, but he was always drinking. He'd pass out during Mannix and suddenly get all startled in the middle of Barnaby Jones, shaking his glass of melty ice cubes and bourbon. 'Who's that fellow? What happened to the fisherman with the gun?' He didn't *seem* like the kind of guy who'd keep battery operated penises.

"So I took one, the baby one, like maybe he wouldn't notice. I used it all the time. It made me come so fast I thought I'd turn into a freak, like I'd use up all my fun before I was twelve. Or maybe I

497

thought boys would somehow know I'd been practicing. *Some*thing. Something made me really nervous about using it, even though I couldn't stop using it."

Her guest made no encouraging murmur, no indication that he wanted to hear the rest. Abruptly, Edith cut herself off. "So. Enough about me and my sordid past. What about you? And yours?"

He was silent but not sleeping. Oh, she'd blundered, she thought as she blushed uselessly. She sensed the stranger's wakefulness as she had sensed it throughout her narrative, an attuned curious listening. It had substance in her bedroom like the dark: consummate yet fleeting. While she was talking, his company beside her had been inclusive, she and he equaled the universe, but in the aftermath, in its lengthening silence, he seemed to have been sucked away, now tiny as a man through the peephole in a closed door. That was the thing about the dark and talking in it. Conversation after sex was complicated. It was much much much more complicated than fucking.

"You're a talker," he eventually said, not unkindly. "Chatty Cathy."

"My name is Edith."

"As if I would forget your name."

Because he sounded wounded, Edith went on, "I never owned a Chatty Cathy, but I did have a book about a doll named Edith. She and her naughty friend the teddy bear." The book was disturbing; instead of regular illustrations, it featured black and white photographs of the doll and her small stuffed bear friend and a fat live pigeon. They were posed around town in stilted ways, making mischief, committing the crimes of toys, punished eventually by an even bigger plaything named Mr. Bear, who bent the doll and little bear over his knee and spanked them with his paw. "I don't always talk a lot," she added, which was true, but which he wouldn't have any reason to believe; she'd been talking incessantly since they'd met. She couldn't help herself, happiness loosened her tongue. A man in bed with her, listening, seemed to her the most blissful state of affairs imaginable. The bed held them, the night surrounded them, the phone wouldn't ring, there was no appointment to keep, no place but here to be. The beauty of three or four in the morning was its aimlessness, its stolen quality. What was it good for, except this? The sun was busy on the other side of the world; exhaustion settled like pixie dust with the compliant darkness and all the people slept, in the building, on the block, throughout the far-flung city and country. This hour was for the lonely—the sole stalker, the brooding face waiting at the window, the empty cab—or, more rarely, for the fully living, the couples in love in bed in laughter. They were giddy, they were children, they had found each other against some big damn odds, as in a blind-folded game.

"I've never told anyone about that dildo," Edith lied. She had more than once used the childhood anecdote as a kind of talismanic virginity, something to trot out as proof of fondness, a display of trust.

"Why not?"

Why would she not have? she asked herself. "I don't know," She lay wondering at her hypothetical and uncharacteristic withholding.

But he seemed to understand that it was his turn. He said, "I don't have any interesting secrets."

"There's no such thing as a dull secret."

"A talker *and* a thinker."

"Are you being mean?"

"No. I just don't want to bore you."

In fact Edith wouldn't have found him interesting if she hadn't seen him trying to steal a CD. Brattiness drew her eye. She had met Marco roughly twelve hours earlier, at a yard sale. The CD only cost a dollar; why steal? She'd grinned conspiringly when she caught him, delighted. He lived in her building on the tenth floor in a studio apartment whose layout and view, he claimed, were identical to hers, but four stories higher.

Entering an apartment as small as Edith's—and Marco's, she as-sumed—was like entering a hotel room: bed right there when you opened the door. A slower romance might have happened had she been able to afford a living room, a hall, or proper secluded separate space in which to sleep. Instead, they'd sat and then lain on the bed. That famous One Thing had led to this, more tricky, Other.

From the closet came the scratching of Edith's cat. She had had to banish him there when he jumped on the bed and made Marco scream in alarm. It had been a humiliatingly high-pitched scream, but the cat did weigh nearly twenty pounds. His tail was a half inch stub, the end of which had no hair on it at all, as if the creature had a human finger tip poking out his rear end.

"What the *fuck!*" Marco had screeched, hurling the poor cat to the floor. Edith had been afraid she would have to hate her guest, then. That she would have to send him away and that he might not want to go. Then, when he'd recovered, he'd apologized, even going so far as to kneel, naked, and try to make friends with the cat. "Kitty, kitty, kitty?" he said in a feeble falsetto, and Edith had gallantly and gladly exiled her ancient pet to the closet. Every few minutes the cat reminded her he was still there, seething with his lack of an opposable thumb.

Marco raised up on his elbow and looked down at Edith. His eyebrows almost met over his large nose. He could kiss her, he could bite her, he could burst into song: she hardly knew him or what he'd do. Every passing day, the likelihood of love transpiring between people seemed more and more remote to Edith, disappearing like other quaint traditions: honorable politicians, anonymous philanthropy, love of culture. Culture reminded her of something. "Do you ever hear the opera singer?" she asked, "from up there in your apartment?"

"Opera?"

"So-called. The cat doesn't like her. He lays his ears down when she starts up." The opera singer had to practice her high warbling notes, repeatedly, a person in a formal rictus of pain.

"She's a figment of your imagination," he declared. In Edith's imagination, the woman threw back her head and opened her throat as if to swallow swords.

"You smell good," she told Marco, since he was still staring down at her. She made a point of breathing deep of his mixture of odors, which were in balance, the natural and the chemical. He was old enough to recognize the need for toothpaste and deodorant and shampoo, yet young enough for those to still have their desired effects. "Aren't you going to tell me a story of your youthful pranks?" she asked, rutting into his ribcage. "Please? I don't care if it's a secret or not."

"Hmm." He dropped his head back to the pillow and smiled at the ceiling. Already she saw that smiling was not about happiness, for him. It was pensiveness.

"Like what were you like at eleven?"

"If I think about being eleven," he said slowly, "I mostly remember this silo."

"Grain?"

"Are there other kinds? Well, missile," he answered his own question. "This silo was empty, on the property of an abandoned farm in Kansas. Kansan, that's what I am."

Edith's imagination sailed out the window and over the city of

Chicago, the twinkling grid of lights, the blue-black expanse of lake at her back, and southwest into the vast flatland of his childhood. She had seen that place from the air, from the road, from behind a gas pump one hot late summer. She found not only a silo, but the see-sawing sound of cicadas, distant cauliflower-like clouds.

"There was an abandoned farmhouse out there, along with the silo. My family used to go camping on the property, at the stream that ran through."

In Edith's mind the scene lit up like Andrew Wyeth, windswept and golden and lonely. For some reason her silo was tilted, like a little leaning tower, nostalgic and portentous. His voice was deep and when he spoke his words—transported, she supposed, by the bed-springs—hummed in her sternum, a pleasant resonance that felt like the beginning of love. "Camping?" she coached, unable to keep her hands from him: his chest, his arms, his earlobes. He was warm all over, the radiant heat that results from lying naked for a long while with another person in bed.

"My parents were hippies," he said. "They took us camping on this stream on an old farm. We went every weekend for a few years, them and their pot-head friends and their friends' kids. 'Go *play* with them,' my mother was always saying, all annoyed if I didn't like her friends' kids." He reached for Edith's busy hands; she could have been blind, for all the eagerness of her fingers. They touched at the knuckles and the knees. She liked his hair, the stubble on his face, and the soft pelt on his head which was slightly greasy with the product he thought would help him look more attractive. She liked his attention to looking more attractive, or trying anyway. He was a gawky guy who wore a smirk on his face, a mask put on to hide his maladroitness.

"Although I *did* like them, it turned out," he said glumly, of the kids he was forced to camp with. "There was this girl."

Edith listened more closely. She was going to learn the type of girl who would torment him for the rest of his life. Why else remember her? She was listening to hear if she were that kind of girl herself. *He* was *her* kind of torment, the shy sullenness, the bad posture, the flash of cruelty and ready heart-wrenching remorse. She and Marco had met at the Permanent Yard Sale that took place in the dumpy lawn beside their apartment building. Lately the owners of the bungalow weren't even hauling in their tables at night. They chained an evil dog to bark at hapless pedestrians and would be-thieves. Every morning there'd be different stuff on sale. Boom boxes, dusty clock radios, sticky Teflon pans, TVs, jewelry or running shoes, packages of food, half-burned votive candles. Edith had passed the yard for months before it finally dawned on her that this project was not only the household's sole livelihood but that the items for sale were probably stolen goods.

Yesterday—just yesterday!—she and Marco had been strangers, pawing through the CDs, snatching up plastic jewel cases as if gathering nuts for the long winter. Marco's music taste turned out to be hers, too, the whining nihilistic sort. When he sneaked the CD in his shirt, Edith addressed him. "I have their first album." His theft made her feel no longer in competition so much as collusion.

He'd glared until she motioned toward his chunky breast-pocket. "Not 'Mysterioso?'"

She nodded eagerly. "And all the live juvenalia, bootleg."

"Wow." He sighed appreciatively, hand over his heart and the purloined disc. "I would love to hear those." When they then found themselves walking into the same building, checking the same bank of mail-boxes, and summoning the same elevator, it seemed to Edith nearly rude not to invite him to get off on her floor.

"I don't have speakers," she apologized. He'd slipped on the headphones, closed his eyes, and gone quickly rapturous. In silence Edith followed his pleasure by memory, vaguely embarrassed by his tongue, trembling between his lips like an excited child's. Now she thought she'd offer Marco all of the scuffed CDs she'd bought, those and any others he desired. Affection made her want to give and give and give. Her once-upon-a-time therapist had told her she had "boundary issues," and long before that, her mother had warned her that she should be more protective with what was hers. "If you give too much," she had said in her bright direct way, "what will you have left for yourself?" Edith could appreciate her mother's concern, her therapist's long-sightedness, but she considered generosity a virtue. It demonstrated trust; it resembled confidence; it was optimistic. Some nights, for example, she refused to lock her apartment door.

Marco said, "I was always going to that silo and climbing inside. I liked to be alone. And the sound in there was indescribable. I don't suppose you ever sat in an empty silo?"

"'I am a city child.'" It was a quote, one children's text having reminded Edith of another.

He described the sound of a silo. Noise echoed some but it also *didn't* echo, if she could feature such a thing. It muffled your voice but then you also could hear your voice going up to the sky, like smoke from a chimney, or maybe more like smoke rings, every word in its own ring, taking a ride up.

"Well, anyways," he said, "once when I was twelve I got an infected penis."

Edith laughed only because, when she was nervous, certain words operated as punch lines. "Penis" was one of those. Marco grabbed her fingers and squeezed so fiercely that Edith thought he probably didn't get the chance to touch people very often. Again she pictured her dear old cat being launched off the bed, and was briefly frightened. "I'm sure you're laughing *with* me," he said, and Edith laughed harder, pulling her bare legs up in reflex. Every now and then she suffered laughing fits that would not stop, hysterical in nature, and she hoped this wasn't going to turn into one of those. Laughter like that seemed both potentially embarrassing and essentially selfish, masturbatory. "Okay," Marco warned, plopping his head wearily on the pillow, "but you're going to be sorry in a minute, sorry for mocking me, when I tell you what happens next."

From the closet came the sudden scrabbling of claws; Edith's cat was digging into the wood of the door. She could hear the low growl in his furious feline throat.

Marco paused. "That thing's a fucking *lynx*, what with the weird tail and all. Are cats allowed in this building? I was told just non-mammals."

"Meaning?"

"Birds. Fish."

"Alligators," Edith speculated. "Snakes."

"I have fish."

"Fish!" She wanted to clap: pets! Having them proved something.

"Betas. Beauteous, but they have to live in separate mayonnaise jars on top of my piano. Together in the same jar, they'd kill each other. That's their nature." Now he had not only fish but a piano; he listened to music, he played music. Edith imagined him a player of classical music, then revised to the more intriguing composer of tuneless modern pieces. Perhaps that was why he'd never heard the opera singer: he was making his own sad racket.

"To continue," he said, "I had to be circumcised when I was twelve years old." He informed her that twelve was very old for circumcision, which, he said, she'd have no reason to know, since she wasn't a

503

boy or the mom of a boy, but it was old. And it was embarrassing, of course, and his parents, who hadn't believed in circumcision—they hadn't believed in it much earlier than other parents who didn't believe in it—failed to have it done when he was a baby, and then, because they were hippies, he was probably a filthy little runt with bad personal hygiene, which no doubt led to the infection. "Which was *gross*." Here he placed her hand, with his over it, on top of the penis under discussion. His bundle of flesh was warm, skin the delicately pimpled surface that testicles shared with that of plucked chicken. The hair was wiry, tightly curled, totally unlike the hair on his head. "*Pus*," he said with a sibilant hiss, and Edith laughed again, though she was no longer likely to go into hysterics.

His palm covering hers reminded Edith of how they'd shook hands out at the yard sale, sideways, his right hand in her left because she held the stack of CDs she'd bought in her right hand while he was still gripping his disc inside his shirt with his left. Greeting somebody sideways always made you more immediately intimate, as if you were holding rather than shaking hands.

"Excuse me," he said, kissing her on the forehead and then lightly slipping from bed to the bathroom. He did not strut, as some men might, but dashed. The bright unshaded light seemed an assault. It took a moment, but then she heard his urine hit the water. The bathroom door would never completely close, and she could see, if she looked, as he stood braced at the toilet. She remembered high school then, though not of sneaking glances at penises but of a boy she loved then who used to stand at his locker in his low-slung jeans undoing his combination lock. He would cup it at his belt buckle, his expert thumb busy rotating the dial. It was sexy, his confident locker ritual, and Marco's stance at her toilet—now he spit just before flushing—made her heart leap in fresh attraction.

Then he held the door shut, still inside. What was he doing? Investigating the medicine cabinet? That's what Edith would have done, in his place. She liked to know the lay of the land. It was how she'd ended up with a dildo, all those years ago, snooping. What would he think of her drugs and unguents? Antidepressants and perfume, her two best bets. Nothing scarifying, no anti-fungals or hair dye or laxatives. Also nothing very fun, pharmaceutically speaking. She'd given those up, handed out her last Valium at a Halloween party.

Soon the door opened and the light went out. "Good toilets in this

504

building," Marco noted as he slid back into bed, his feet chilly from the tile. "Industrial quality. I've never had to call the super about mine."

"Me either. I only call the super about the opera singer."

"Her I never knew about."

"Sometimes I call the super, and sometimes I just let her make me mopey."

The cat hummed evilly from the closet.

"So," Marco said, returning them to Kansas, "I was operated on." It hurt like hell, having your foreskin sliced off, he notified her. Edith grimaced sympathetically. And then they, his enlightened party animal parents, insisted on going camping anyway because the weather was good. Naturally, all the other hippie parents came, there was marijuana around the campfire, charades, singalongs, shenanigans involving other people's spouses, et cetera. The wholesome seventies, he said sourly, his parents the Midwest radicals. All the kids always went *swimming*—he removed his hands from beneath the covers to make bunny ears around the word—"Wading, if you will, wallowing in swampy muck." He returned his hands to Edith's and clutched them.

"I like you," she said impulsively, because she did, him and his dry-witted self-pitying, angry, ludicrous story.

"You wouldn't have liked me then," he said. "I was a punk, ready to become a skinhead just to piss my parents off. I had to spend the whole camping weekend mortified somebody was gonna knock me in the nuts and pretending I didn't feel like swimming, because I couldn't get my dick wet."

Edith frowned, then said, "What *is* it with that word?"

"Women hate it. They also hate the words for their own genitalia, but what are you going to do? Cunt," he said, and Edith felt herself recoil. She could imagine for a moment being his hippie mother, watching him slink off to his grain silo and being glad to be rid of him. He would have been sulky and hunched then, too, scowling and unpopular. He would have been her darling baby one moment, sunny and cheerful and cute, then a horrifying insolent boy bent on criticizing her lifestyle the next.

"What happened in that silo?" she asked, wanting to return to his point of view, to be inside the silo rather than out.

"I cried," he said simply, and Edith filled with love for him once more. Crying she understood. Crying she could love.

505

But there was more. The girl, the fantastical girl, another of the hippies' children, three years older than Marco, a full-blown untouchable fifteen: she discovered him weeping in the silo and crawled through the opening to come to his side. Edith wished to see herself as this girl, the one who would follow and know. She was a beautiful girl, in his memory, blond hair so long its pale ends had grown dry and wispy. She wore tight jeans, a halter top, her plump skin sunburned pink which made her seem both on fire and terribly vulnerable. She squatted on the ground beside him where he sat sobbing on a block of concrete. She smelled of a perfume all teenage girls wore, big green-apple flavored babies. Her face was round, her teeth were straight, her eyes were glistening turquoise beneath turquoise shadow. Her name was Goldberry.

"It was not!" Edith said.

"Yah huh," he said, braying like a donkey.

Goldberry, named for a hobbit, Marco speculated. Because of her patience, by virtue of the odd location of their meeting, due to her usual teenager's utter lack of interest in him, she managed to elicit from him, that day, the difficult details of his trouble. Before she arrived, he couldn't have imagined saying what he was saying, telling anyone, especially her, what plagued him. His desire to confide in her had everything to do with the way the silo had made a hallowed space in the middle of a former wheat field, with the way one's voice, inside that space, was converted. The ground was soft, dirt turned to powder, which they sifted through their fingers as they spoke confidentially in the confines of that tall emptiness with its ceiling of blue. She flattered him by naming him brave; she lulled him by telling him she, too, had had embarrassing surgery. She'd found a lump in her breast, she said, just a few years earlier, when she was twelve, and believed she would die. For mortal hours she'd cried in her bedroom, wondering whether to tell her parents, composing her obituary and envisioning her funeral, the sorry visages of her seventh grade peers and her pesky brother as they bent over her casket. There'd been an awful doctor involved, a lech who took some pleasure in squeezing the young breast, then later excising the benign cyst, leaving a set of wicked black stitches just below her pink nipple. Goldberry, like Marco, had been too ashamed to tell her friends. Like Marco she'd not been able to go swimming, nor offer an explanation. She'd found herself tending her breast as it healed, treating it not like a body part but a new pet, protecting her injury the way Marco had been protecting his.

"Like me," Marco said to Edith. "I liked that she said she was like me. I trusted her, we shared secrets."

This bed was similar to the silo, Edith thought dreamily. Two people in a private space, speaking in a vacuum together, watching their words float above in unfamiliar pleasing circles. She saw young Marco and sweet Goldberry touching each other tenderly where they'd been wounded, first love, damaged goods . . .

"Then she blabbed to everybody," Marco said flatly. Goldberry spread the news of his penis and its humiliating problems, his weeping. The hippie parents idled through the camping trip with typical orgiastic ignorance, but Marco suffered. Suffered the taunts of the small children, the lewd jokes of the older, everyone covering their genitals in imitation of his guarding gesture. And all because he's trusted the wily Goldberry. "I concluded," he said, "that girls were evil. And boys dumb," he added, acknowledging his own part in the mix.

"I'm not evil," Edith swore. Now she no longer wanted to play the role of Goldberry, although she also understood that this girl loomed large in his unique history. She ran her thumb pad over the circumcised head of his penis, newly conscious of its shape, its open eye vaguely sticky. How could she be evil, she wanted to point out, when she hadn't even insisted on a condom? "I'm *bossy*," she conceded, "but not evil. Occasionally I cry just to get my way, but I don't think that's evil. Is it?"

"You can be the exception," he said, but it sounded sarcastic.

"I'm so nice I have an I.U.D."

"But maybe that just means you're a slut?"

The word stung her; Edith willed the pain away. "Was Goldberry's benign cyst a true story?" she asked.

"Don't know, don't care. Old Goldberry went on to kill herself, later. And I'll tell you what, when I heard—this was high school, maybe first year of college—I wasn't all that unhappy. My mom acted like I'd be crushed, but I wasn't. Sad, but true: it didn't bother me that Goldberry was dead."

"How'd she'd kill herself?"

Now it was his turn to laugh too long. "You're funny," he said.

"Curious."

"Pills. The girls' way."

"And what's the boys' way?"

"Gun."

"Oh." She nodded. Once more she imagined herself his mother, bearing the shocking news of the suicide, watching his cool, anti-social reaction. He had felt, she thought, avenged. Even now he wasn't ashamed of being unmoved. Had he not really grown up, since then? Was he still holding a grudge against a dead girl named Goldberry?

"At least, that's how *I* tried to kill myself," he went on, "when I tried. Gun." He took her hand from the warmth of inside the blankets to the chill of the back of his head. Behind his ear he found the place, a deep indentation in the skull, the path of a bullet that had mostly missed.

"Baby," she said. Impossible not to keep falling for him. Edith sensed the dangerous downward plunge. Perfectly the indentation accommodated her finger. People fit together like missing puzzle pieces, she thought, like plugs in drains, like ammo in weapons.

"Yeah. Wah, wah, wah." He cleared his throat. Edith put her face to his and kissed him, not on the mouth but around it, the way you might kiss an envelope containing a letter to your beloved, with hope, faith. Yesterday she'd wakened in this bed, at this hour, with only the cat for company, him and his odd tail and his surliness.

"Why?" she asked Marco softly.

"Why not?" He turned on his side suddenly, analytical, philosophical. His hip bone stuck out in the aching way men's hips did, the hollow socket below a thing of beauty. Their legs were hard, their stomachs soft, they had dented heads and queerball parents, ironic distance and sudden churlishness. These were the men she chose. And the more she loved them, the more they thought her a chump, until they finally had to break her heart. Which, she was starting to see, must also be her choice. It was broken, and then, miraculously, reassembled. Like a china sugar bowl, fraught with hairline fractures. Or maybe more like a heavy lump of clay, dropped so often on the floor and pushed so frequently back into shape that its identity seems merely proximate, recognizable but peculiar. She had, she guessed, an odd heart. Her mother had certainly seemed to think so, warning her not to be too nice. Nice, but not too nice.

Marco was retracting. Edith felt distance opening between them like a sinkhole. She pressed her mouth against his to close the gap.

He bit her, then rolled on top of her, hard and heavy and hot, and Edith felt tears form at the pleasure of his weight, at being pinned, at the knowledge of its merely temporary gift-like fact. She did not want to fuck, but it seemed the only way to keep him. Edith missed the moments following sex more than the sex itself. Intimacy, unlike orgasm, needed company. Her grandfather's dildo had taught her that long ago.

"You're not feeling sorry for me, are you?" Marco asked, dabbing at her wet face.

"No," she said. "No, no. I was thinking about my Peepaw. Maybe I thought I was going to find a gun when I was rummaging around in his drawers?"

"You probably would have, if you hadn't gotten sidetracked by the wienies."

The cat mewed piteously now at Edith's closet door, weary and worn out, the prisoner in his cell, crying tiredly because hope, in the absence of his fiercer traits, he could fall back on. Edith pictured Marco's fish four flights up, circling their lonely jars.

"Why do we tell each other these childhood stories, anyway?" Marco asked. "I show you how I was a mess, you show me how you were a mess, we go tit for tat, like some weird competition to see who's the most fucked up. I say I sucked my thumb until eighth grade, and you say you sucked your *brother's* thumb—no his *toe!*— and it went on till you were in *college*, the two of us telling just what total freaks we are, outdoing each other with our . . . what*ever*ness. Then what?"

"Then I know you?"

"Then you know how I'm *weak*," he corrected.

"I don't even *have* a brother. To suck the toe of." Edith sighed, waiting for inspiration. It was exhausting to have to keep revising the way she felt about him; her stomach was tense with the effort. She eventually said, "Did you want to let me know how you're *not* weak?"

Marco rose above her, a warm wave of his body's odors rising with him, and—while she looked into his eyes—he fanned his hands before her face, thumb to thumb. Was this to be his demonstration? The bigger animal's brute ability to overtake the smaller, strangle life from her? He had large thick fingered hands that he had used all night as if they were mittened, like paws, stroking Edith repeatedly. It was behind one of these big hands he'd hidden the CD, *snick*, right into his shirt. Now he placed them at his own throat, like a ruff, and Edith's fantasy—spun swiftly and with brilliant vividness, in which her mother was notified that Edith had been murdered in her bed, unknown sperm still swimming blithely inside her—dissolved. He peered sincerely into her eyes with his own bugging ones, bloating his cheeks as if to wring his own neck, squeezing with fierce and fearsome passion. Edith swallowed with difficulty, as if those thumbs were bruising her throat.

He abruptly loosened the grip and dropped his forehead to hers. He was damp with sweat. "That was me, being a Beta," he said. "Sometimes I jam their jars together and they see each other. Then they flair their necks and crash at the glass. They'd kill themselves, if I let them."

"You have a strange M.O.," Edith said.

He laughed. "*I* have a strange M.O.? You afraid?"

"Not of you," she said. And she wasn't. She was afraid of herself. She was afraid of tomorrow, of later, of forever.

"Owww!" said the cat. He repeated himself, and held the note like the hated opera singer, a lonesome creature swallowing a sword. It sounded like dying. Edith could not *not* go and release him; he shot through her legs and across the room, as if he might plow headlong into the oven, which waited at the end of his run. He seemed angry enough that he might never come near Edith again.

When she turned to the man in her bed, he was rising to leave as well. "Have you seen my shirt?" he asked, ready to hide himself inside it, ready to steal himself from her.

When she first was in his presence, she had not noticed him until he stole the CD. That gesture had broken his camouflage, set him apart from the others. She herself had stolen a lot of things—she had a sense of deserving them, of needing them, earrings and knickknacks and money and mementos—including her grandfather's dildo. It required two C batteries. It was seamless white plastic. Its switch made it vibrate and emit a buzz; it was not unlike holding an electric knife. She had fitted it where she knew it belonged and scared herself. Currency sizzled like lightning. Could she be electrocuted by a battery-powered device? That's how it felt—twitch, sneeze, forgetfulness, whimper—and it took her a little while to understand that the sensation was one of pleasure.

An uncanny pleasure, overwhelming, singular, frightening, addictive. Edith understood, at age eleven, that nothing good could come of it. Like the device's batteries, her body might wear out, might stop offering up the surge and immersion. And what if that feeling became the only one she wanted? So, after a few weeks, she threw away her scary toy, wrapped it up in a bag and rode her bike to the nearest Yellow Hen and stuffed it deep inside the Dumpster. Was that what it had taught her, that pleasure was illicit? That it would have to be renounced?

Was that why she made no move, no sound, to stop Marco from stepping through her front door and disappearing?

Nominated by Laura Kasischke, Epoch

AUBADE

by EUGENE GLORIA

from SHENANDOAH

Because grief straggles like a bottom dweller
And seldom comes up for air,
He slides one hand through a jacket sleeve

And slings pole and fishing gear in his trunk.
Grief is a basement thing—
A bad mix like drinking and driving if

One is young and open-hearted. He drives
His car to the Sacramento Delta. The air
Frigid, the odor of human salt reeks

From his chest. His hands, so cold,
They can barely hook the worm at the end
Of his line. He lions in the morning

Sucking breath into breath with his last pack
Of smokes. The inland heat still asleep
In the ground. Nothing but a low moan,

A humming song rises up from a well
Inside his wasted self.
It had no lyrics, this chorus about waiting

In Puccini's opera where a woman full of hope
Peers through a hole pinprick size
To see the harbor lights drag in

The ship that would bring home her beloved.
There are no words for the sun's arrival
Except that it is begotten by song,

A fire spark, flickering Pentecostal
A nascent thing, immigrant and lonely.
Morning begets the honking of geese

The way birds and light beget his happiness
For a father, whom he recalls impeccably
Dressed for his daily departure,

And how the father would pause to hum
His affections, and bless him
With the bread from the oven of his heart.

Nominated by Robert Wrigley

PRETTY

fiction by MARGARET LUONGO

from TIN HOUSE

I LOVE BEING DRUNK. Is that bad?

Barhopping downtown with the people from work, everything seems good and possible. As we walk from our first bar to our next, it seems possible I could love my job; it seems possible I could some-day have a career. Love for my coworkers seems plausible too. Love radiates from my breastbone for Stan, the bearded senior editor with baggy wool trousers and starched white shirts. The sympathy I feel for Elaine, who wears a Dorothy Hamill haircut twenty-plus years af-ter it was fashionable, brings tears to my eyes. I lust for Julius, the deep-brown stringer who is gay, and it seems possible he could re-turn the feeling. He wears ankle-high black leather boots with his purple and orange suits. I'm staring at him and he catches me, winks. I wink back and reach behind Elaine as we walk, trying to pinch his arm. It's hard from workouts at the gym. I could maybe love Lynette, my office mate, if she were here. If she didn't work so hard and so late, it would be much easier to love her.

We pass a café where people like us have dinner after work. The outdoor tables are full of well-dressed men and women, eating small salads by candlelight. I fall behind the group a little, walking slowly, and stare openly at a man in a shirt so white it glows in the dimming light. His tan is deep and fake, but I love him for it. I imagine taking hold of one of his big arms and giving him a bite. The woman he's with notices me staring. I wrinkle my nose at her, wave, and run to catch up to Julius and the rest of the group.

We turn the corner and pass my bar, The Town Hall, the one I go to by myself. I look through the window as we pass, trying to see who's in there. It's the usual bartender and some of the regulars.

We stop at Earl's to shoot pool. We'll keep drinking there. Julius orders us Cosmopolitans. Elaine drinks white wine spritzers, Stan Irish beer. The bar is full of people like us, escaping from the numbness of their air-conditioned offices. I check out the groups at the bar—the men in their suits, the fit ones who look like Vs, the dumpier men with ill-fitting trousers. I love them all, and if they would look my way they could see that. Some do and I smile, nod. My smiles and nods will yield nothing; I know that, but I'm drunk and my consciousness is blurred and I'm not patient enough to wait for the rest of the bar to catch up.

A couple of skinny white guys shoot pool beside us. The one closest to me wears a denim jacket over his jeans and black T-shirt. Pinned to the front of his jacket are rows and rows of buttons, like colorful armor. From this distance I can't read them. He has full lips and thick brown hair. When he bends over to take his shot, a lock of it falls forward nearly touching the tip of his nose. He parts his lips as he takes his shot. I wonder about the softness of those lips. I walk up to him, bend slightly, and start to read aloud the sayings on the buttons. Most are typical: "Question Authority," I read. "Kill Your TV." He doesn't acknowledge me; I keep reading.

"The Sinn Fein are watching." I tap the button with my finger, my nail clicking. "What's that about?"

He still doesn't look at me. He keeps his eyes on the game. "It's about death," he says. "It's about manipulation."

"Oh," I say, backing up slowly. Some people don't want to be happy.

Julius is there when I turn around. He hands me my red drink. We toast each other.

"To handsome men in purple suits," I say.

"To bony white girls with big tits," he says.

We drink. I decide to stick with my colleagues for the rest of the evening. The button guy has shaken my confidence. To prove I'm having fun, I smile too hard and laugh too loud for the rest of the night. I laugh at Jules's jokes and Stan's jokes; I slap their arms and lean in close. Elaine doesn't participate, only looks at me in that tired, knowing way of hers. At one point, I'm sitting on Jules's lap, trying to get him to describe his bedroom to me. He's laughing and blushing and looking at his lap. Stan is howling. Elaine pushes her chair away from the table and walks to the bar for another drink. Later, I slip off to the bathroom during a long story of Stan's when I realize I can't pretend any longer to be interested. I look grim in the mirror, in here without an audience. Without the forced cheer, the smiles, the eye crinkles, I look like an inmate. I've seen their mug shots on the news. That impossible tiredness, the gaze that doesn't bother to look out, but isn't looking in either. *Unfocused*, I'm thinking, when Elaine comes in.

"What's up?" I say, not feeling any need to smile for Elaine. She knows something, probably more than I do. She's in her forties and tries to give me advice but most of the time I don't understand what she's trying to tell me and I just get annoyed.

"Not much." She washes her hands at the sink after I've moved away. "I'm heading home. Need a ride?"

Normally I would prefer to ride home with Stan or Jules. Stan gives me little kisses and squeezes before I get out of the car—drunken affection that he's smart enough not to pursue; he is my boss, after all, and he'd have to face me at work. I wouldn't mind, but I bet he would. Jules and I chat cattily about people we've seen at Earl's. Tonight, I imagine we would talk about Button Guy. I'm not up for it.

On the way to her car, Elaine tells me about a job opening at a new food magazine.

"I know the managing editor," she says. "I could get you an interview."

I haven't mentioned that I'm looking for a job because I'm not. "Huh," I say. "Sounds interesting."

"They want someone young for restaurant reviews. You know, where the up-and-coming of the professional world hang out. The go-getters of your generation. The office is in Dupont. It's a younger crowd. Hip." She smiles at me. "I've seen the first issue—it's high end. I'd go but I'm too old."

"I doubt I'm hip enough," I say, trying to be funny, trying to downplay that I am in no way a go-getter.

Elaine gives me a cool look. "They want a good writer with a young person's perspective. That's you. It would be good for your career."

I start at the word *career*. I don't often think of myself in conjunction with that word. "When are they hiring?"

"Now. Fax your résumé tomorrow. I'll look at it before you send it."

"I don't think I can get it ready that fast," I say. I wonder why Elaine's pushing so hard.

"I'll tell my friend you're on deadline, but you'll have a résumé to her by the end of the week."

Her tone says, Don't fuck this up. I'm handing it to you.

"Thanks, I'll do it," I say, because I want her to stop talking.

At work the next morning it's hard to get going. I drink a Coke from the can, through a straw. The stockings do not feel good. They make my feet sweat, but we have to wear them. A map of the United States covers my desk. I'm proofreading it. I never realized how many states have towns named Jefferson. Some have more than one. Normally, on a morning such as this I would nap hard, facedown on my desk. I would take an early lunch and return ready to crank on my projects. When I'm motivated, I can get twice as much done as most people in the same time. Now, however, I share my office with Lynette, a thirty-five-year-old single mother, an entry-level editorial assistant. Gone are the days of midmorning naps, or any naps at all, for that matter.

I try to forget she's there, but it's impossible. Lynette brings with her an air of heaviness. It's partly her age that depresses me, combined with her shitty station in life. I graduated from college last year at twenty-one, and I had her job. Partly, too, it's her clothes. Her clothes are old, not just unfashionable, though they are unfathomably that; they're worn. Today she wears a vaguely hippie-ish dress—burgundy gauze with some kind of Indian-style print in pink, basically formless except for the tie underneath her bosom. She flips her white flat against her heel as she looks through a stack of pages to proof.

"You've got a lot of pages there," I say. If I can't work I might as well distract her.

Lynette's work load can be interpreted in a number of ways. One, she's falling behind and will be fired. Two, they are loading on the work, hoping she'll quit under the burden of an unmanageable load. If this doesn't work, they'll start to withhold projects, hoping to bore her into quitting. Eventually, if they really want to, they can find some reason to fire her.

She doesn't look up. "Stan asked me to look at it—it's not my project. I guess he wants another opinion."

My desk is suspiciously clean. Nothing in the in box and only the map spread out like a cool blotter. Why didn't Stan ask my opinion? I'm starting to worry when Elaine comes in with three fat folders.

"Were you feeling neglected, baby?" she says.

I smile and nod. "Bring it on," I say.

She dumps the folders in my box. "It's the *Titleman Handbook*. More changes."

"When?" I say.

"Tomorrow." She raises her eyebrows at me and leaves.

"Job security is a wonderful thing," I say, suddenly motivated. Because I'm senseless with gratitude for the work, after that moment of paranoia, I invite Lynette to lunch.

"I brought mine," she nods at the crumpled paper bag in her in box. Judging by the wrinkles, I suspect she reuses the bag. I imagine that she might also reuse the Ziploc sandwich bags, rinsing them in the sink, letting them dry overnight in the dish rack so they can hold more carrot sticks, more peanut-butter-and-jelly sandwiches.

"Maybe another time," I say. My face feels hot. I pretend to look at the map but really I'm staring at the lap of my new suit. It's slate blue, and I spent too much on it. Elaine and I had gone out shopping last Thursday after work. The suit was over three hundred and I'd felt powerful buying it. It looked good; it fit just right. Now, in front of Lynette in her falling-apart white flats, it embarrasses me. I wonder when she last bought herself something new.

Lynette has pictures of her kids taped on the wall over her desk. Blond, big teeth, eye-glasses on the boy. I bet she spends most of her money on them. Maybe she's saving, too, for college. "How old are your kids, Lynette?"

She smiles in a way that is different than I've ever seen her smile. She looks at their pictures; her voice is soft. "Sealie is twelve, and Bender is ten. They go to the Friends School."

I can't tell from their names which is the girl and which is the boy. I vaguely remember hearing about the Friends School, reading an article in the paper about new techniques. There was a photograph of children kneading bread. Or maybe that was another school.

"Is that sort of New Age . . . or is it a charter school?" I ask.

Lynette's face shuts down; the softness disappears. "It's Quaker," she says. She turns her chair away from me and goes back to work.

I dial Julius's extension. The digital clock on the phone starts blinking seconds as soon as I pick up the receiver. It's a new feature, to help us keep track of our time spent on personal calls. Julius and I were the first in our group to have the new phones. Now we mostly walk down the hallway to talk to each other or meet in the stairwell.

His voice mail picks up. I suddenly wish I needed him for something more urgent than lunch. "Jules," I say, trying to fool myself at least, "call me when you get this."

Jules and I sit at our favorite Greek restaurant. We order Cosmopolitans and Greek salads.

"Yummy," I say, after my first sip. I start to feel awake for the first time today.

"How's your flower child working out?"

I roll my eyes. "Such a grind. In at seven, stays till seven. She brings her lunch."

He nods. "So you dislike her because she works hard and she packs her lunch." Julius laughs—a short, loud "ha" that startles the overplucked women at the table next to us. Out of the corner of my eye I see them flinch.

I lean in closer to him, speaking softly, hoping to encourage him to do the same. "She depresses me." I wrinkle my nose. "The way she dresses . . ."

Julius gives me an incredulous look, and I know I've said something bad. He leans across the table. "If you were my child, I'd spank you," he said. "We can't all be skinny white girls in Tahari suits, now can we?"

"Is it my fault?" I say. "Did I tell her to have those bucktoothed babies?"

Jules leans back in his seat. "I call for a subject change, because you is mean, girl."

I dip my finger in and out of the condensation on my water glass. "Maybe I should take the suit back."

Jules looks confused, then shrugs. "If it'll make you feel better." He's looking away, looking at the other people in the restaurant, at the TV behind the bar.

"You think I should?" I need Jules to make me feel better, not to tell me what's right.

"If you can afford it, you should enjoy it. If you can't enjoy it then take the dang thing back and donate the money to your favorite charity." He looks at me again. "I've never met anyone who worries the way you do."

We finish our drinks, but we haven't touched our salads. I look with regret at the feta cheese on top of mine. I'll be hungry later. Jules gets his to go. "You should eat that," he says.

I shake my head. I'm not sure if I'm not eating to spite Jules or myself. We don't talk on the walk back. I give Jules an anemic wave at the elevators, and I take the stairs. At the top of the stairs, I sit for a moment and try to adjust my attitude. I realize there's not enough time, so I go back to my office. When I return, Lynette is there, talking on the phone with quiet intensity. "I can't talk here," she says. "I'll call tonight." She hangs up and sighs. "Ex-husbands suck. Don't get yourself one."

"Ok," I say. "I'll try not to."

By three-thirty, we're dug in. I've taken off my jacket and shoes and sit editing in my skirt and silk shell. Lynette has put her hair up using two number-two pencils as chopsticks. We work and work. At six-thirty I'm halfway through the stack Elaine gave me. The map is long gone but will probably reappear next week after it's gone through more changes. I don't think I can sit still anymore, and I'm about to slam down my pencil when Stan comes in. He's been nearby an awful lot lately. I squint at him.

"Ladies," Stan says.

"Stan the Man," Lynette says.

I stare hard at Lynette's back. Stan sits in the chair next to her desk. He nods at the mess of papers.

"How's that?"

Lynette leans back in her chair, stretches her arms over her head. "I feel so fulfilled," she says.

Stan grins at her, and he's looking—really looking—at Lynette's face, her neck, her breasts. Maybe she can't see it because of the way his eyelids scrunch up whenever he's laughing or grinning, delighted or horny. I know the look. It flashes into my head that I've walked in on them in the break room a couple of times, Stan murmuring something and laughing to her. I'd ignored it. He invites her out with us. She accepts.

She calls her mother to say she's working late, can she watch the kids? It doesn't take long to organize. We gather in the hall, where a holiday atmosphere prevails. Stan looks pleased Lynette deems his company worthwhile. His cheeks are glowing, and he is smiling faintly in Lynette's direction, listening to every word she says, as if he expects brilliant wit and wisdom to issue from her mouth. I schlump along behind the group, which is laughing too loud. Jules especially. He walks slightly behind Lynette and is keeping his hand lightly at her lower back. I've just spent the entire day with this woman, and I don't think she's that interesting. The inside of me feels like one big sneer.

We take Lynette straight to Earl's, bypassing the fern bar where we usually begin. Earl seems to like her right away.

"Earl," she says, after they shake hands, "do you mind if I take off my shoes and panty hose?"

Earl's black face shines with sweat, and he beams at her. "Take it all off if you want to." They both laugh.

"Make those drinks right," she says, "and I just might."

This is a side of Lynette I haven't seen. In fact, everything feels unfamiliar tonight. Instead of pool, we sit in a line at the bar. I'm in the dead zone at the end, next to Jules, who turns slightly inward, toward the middle, blocking my access. Lynette orders Bud in a can, something one should not be able to get in a bar. Stan pauses, then orders the same. And so it goes. Elaine changes from white wine spritzer to Bud, Julius says, "What the hell, I'll have the same." Earl stops at me, points his finger. "What about you, baby doll?"

"Sloe gin fizz," I say.

Earl chuckles. "All right, baby doll."

It's the Bud or Lynette's presence that changes the conversation. From what I can hear at my end, it sounds like they're talking about Vietnam. Stan went, infantry. I didn't know that. Julius had an uncle who went, got addicted to drugs, came home, dried out, and started a halfway house for vets. I didn't know that either. Lynette, it turns out, edited a book of stories by Vietnam vets about their experiences. I have nothing to say about any of this.

I excuse myself to the bathroom—not that anyone hears me—and let myself out the back door. I walk past downtown, which is quiet and dark on this weeknight, to my bar—The Town Hall. I don't go for company, though I do sometimes meet men there—the kind who are impressed by my newness, by the excess of my bosom. I understand this. I like being wanted, being useful.

Behind the bar are Christmas lights and plastic poinsettias year-round. I sit at the place where last February a college freshman carved my name. He had enormous brown eyes, and his face looked new and blank. Nothing about his expression changed, not when I put my hand on his thigh and squeezed, not later in my car when I took off my blouse, then my bra. He reminded me of sweet bland pudding, the kind you have when you're home sick from school and you need something nourishing but bland.

The bartender here doesn't call me baby doll and he doesn't know my name. He's as old as Stan but looks older. No wool trousers and pressed shirts for him, but blue jeans and T-shirts, usually red. As he pours my vodka and cranberry juice I ask him, "Were you in Vietnam?" He doesn't answer or look at me. It's as if I haven't spoken. He leaves my drink in front of me and goes to the other end of the bar, yanks a bag of chips off the display rack on the wall and settles himself against the bar. Months ago I stopped trying to charm him. He never returned my smiles. I think he recognizes me for what I am—whatever that is. He's never acknowledged what he must be aware of—the men I leave with—so I stopped caring what he thinks. He's the guy who brings my drinks.

A couple sits in the far corner at a booth. The man is older, maybe in his forties. His fingers, wrapped around his mug of beer, are thick. I like the way he looks—a little rough but quiet. I can only see the back of his woman. She's skinny, with orange-blond hair. Strawberry blond, a nicer person would call her.

Tonight, nothing seems more important than getting the thick-fingered man away from his date or wife or whoever she is. I wonder what he does in bed, how he makes use of those fingers. I imagine we'll never make it to bed. Our contact will take place against the wall in the room next to the rest rooms, with the mop in its bucket leaning beside me, the cherry smell of disinfectant around us. I take my drink and move to a table near them, behind the woman. The man and I can see each other, but she can't see me. I stare at him frankly—you can't be subtle in these things, I've noticed—but I can't tell if he sees me. His gaze seems to glance off me and flicker away. I take off my suit jacket and drape it over my chair. I cross my legs and lean forward. The man gets up and walks toward the bathrooms. I follow.

I try the door, but it's locked. I can hear him peeing.

"Hang on a minute," he says.

I wait.

He opens the door, looks confused. "This is the men's room. Ladies' is next door."

I don't move from the doorway. "I know where it is," I say. "I know where I am." I put my hand on his belly, right above his belt buckle and give him a gentle push into the rest room. He lets me, and I close the door behind us. I lift my skirt to my waist, slide my panties down to my ankles and off. These I stuff in the front pocket of his jeans. My hand lingers in there.

"Oh my," he says softly. He puts his hands on my naked hips, gently.

"That's real flattering," he says. "You're a pretty girl." He's looking down at my face, and he's patting and squeezing my hip in a way that doesn't usually precede sexual contact but suggests instead the comforting gestures one would make to a frightened animal.

"Pretty girls don't need old men like me." He pulls my skirt down and pats my hip some more. My eyes start to fill up. "Don't cry, now. Here." He gives me my underwear. "Do you want me to call you a cab?" I shake my head. I wonder if he'll tell the woman about me. He seems decent, and I guess he probably won't.

When I come out of the bathroom, the thick-fingered man and his woman are gone. It's just me and the bartender. I'll have one drink—I deserve that at least—before I head home. Before I get to the bar, the bartender has another drink waiting for me. He waits, too, hands on his hips.

"So, did you score?" I can't tell if he's laughing at me. I don't think he is—he sounds strangely gentle—but I decide not to answer.

"I didn't think so. Duane's pretty straitlaced." He sits on a stool behind the bar and looks at the TV. "Kids today," he says and shakes his head.

I don't think he means to insult me, but I feel I should pretend to be outraged. It's probably this unusual failure of mine that's made him so chatty. "You're just full of conversation, aren't you?" I say.

He shrugs. "Just curious." His arms are folded in front of him. He's slim. I start to wonder about possibilities but stop myself. I'm sure I can't handle more rejection tonight, especially from the bartender. I dig around in my purse for some money. I'm thinking of ways to make it up to myself—maybe a bubble bath and some Chambord until I'm foggy. I put down my money, and he covers my hand with his. "Where you going so fast?" he says. My heart beats a little faster, and I can feel what's going to happen. He lets go of my hand, comes around to the customer side of the bar. Standing close, he speaks so softly I'm not sure later if he spoke at all. "I'll take care of you. Is that what you want?"

I nod. He leads me behind the bar and sits me down on the stool.

He locks the front door with the keys hanging off his belt loop. "Hey, turn off the TV," he says and points to the remote on the bar. He walks over to the jukebox. Leadbelly starts up with "Irene." I watch him as he puts up chairs, wipes a rag over the bar. When he's finished washing his hands he comes up to me and puts his hands on my arms, kisses me deeply. "Mmmm," I say, reaching for his belt.

"In the back," he says.

We go in the back, to a room with a bed. This makes me sad but not so sad that I can't keep up. We fall asleep around five in the morning.

When I wake up, I know I'm missing work. I roll out of bed and walk naked to the bar. The floor feels grimy on my bare feet so I walk back, on tippy-toes, and put on my pumps. The cool air makes me shiver. At the bar, in the dim morning light, I fix myself a vodka cranberry. I'm all gooseflesh, and a little wobbly too. I bump against the door-jamb on my way back, and my drink sloshes out of the glass, over my hand. I lick it off—sweet, sharp, salt. When I return, he's awake, his forearm thrown across his eyes. I kick off my pumps and climb on top of him.

"Drinking so early," he says. "Hard-core. Did you have a nice time last night?"

"Did it sound like I had a nice time?"

"I think those were good sounds."

"I'll come back tonight, if you're around."

"I should be," he says.

I look around the small room at his personal things—the jar of change on the dresser, the bottle of water on the floor next to the bed, the unplugged digital clock on the windowsill. I set my drink on the floor next to his water and get under the sheet with him. He doesn't say, "I have things to do, errands to run, a sick mother, a jealous girlfriend." Instead, he turns to me drowsily, pulls us together. For a second I imagine Lynette's desk, the crumpled paper bag in the corner, the fat file folders piled on the floor next to her chair. I see Elaine at her desk, hear her sigh when she realizes I'm not coming in today. Then I see my desk: empty, clean. I part my lips to meet his and my body feels light and warm, like a patch of sunlight on his.

Nominated by Daniel Henry, Tin House

FIVE LANDSCAPES

by COLE SWENSEN

from COLORADO REVIEW

One

This is an outline for a project on the relationship between
    landscape
and time, the latter turning physical, equivocal, equal. I'm on a
    train.
The whole

window and speed, vertile, vertige. It will be

an expository piece and not an evocation. Look down there

in the field, a hundred people, a barbecue, a lake, a summer, a
                                                        hundred
thousand fields, all your versions, a woman places her hand
on the small of a man's back in the middle of the crowd and leaves
    it.

Two

A wedding in a field—the old saying: it's good luck to be seen
from a train dressed in white, you must be looking the other way, so
many things work only if you're looking away.
A woman in a field is walking away.

Gardens early in the evening. Trees
planted a few hundred years ago to line a road no longer there. The
water is pale teal, light, field after field. Spire, culvert, spire, spire

of trees that line roads long disappeared. Who stands between, and
thus among, and am of them, and thus of their ends, be it mansion
   or
sea.

Three

Vineyards choir vines. The varieties of green: There will be a section
that lists them and elaborates—function, habitat, distance between,
there is
fold and unfold. She turned the fan
with a glass wrist. Lost under the trees—you say it was a ring?
Engraved, the birds rise up from the field like grain
thrown. Bees
in their perfect houses, a line of birds planing just above
the top of the wheat.

Four

The point of interest is extension and alterity so visibly you look
                                    out on,
say, a field, say, trees, a river on the other side, another life, identical
but everyone's this time. Trees in a wallpaper pattern. A horizon
of dusk that barely outruns us. He started with pages and pages

and then erased. This one
will have a thousand pictures.

A field of houses pierced by windows.

Five

There's a wedding in a field I am passing on a train
                              a field
in the green air, in the white air, an emptier here
                              the field is everywhere
because it looks like something similar somewhere else.

Nominated by Bruce Beasley, Mark Irwin

LIKELY LAKE

fiction by MARY ROBISON

THE PARIS REVIEW

Hⁱˢ IS DOORBELL RANG and Buddy peered through the viewer at a woman in the courtyard. She had green eyes and straight black hair, cut sharply like a fifties Keely Smith. He knew her. She did bookkeeping or something for the law partners next door, especially at tax times. He also remembered her from his wife's yard sale, although that was a couple years ago and the wife was now his ex. She'd bought a jewelry case and a halogen lamp. He could picture her standing on the walk there—her nice legs and the spectator pumps she wore. She'd driven a white VW Bug in those days. But it must have died because later he had noticed her arriving for work in cabs.

He had lent her twenty bucks, in fact. Connie was her name. Last June, maybe, when his garden was at its peak. He'd been out there positioning the sprinkler, first thing in the morning, when a cab swerved up and she was in back. She had rolled down her window and started explaining to him. She was coming in to work early but had ridden the whole way without realizing she'd brought an empty handbag. She *showed* it to him—a beige clutch. She even undid the clasp and held the bag out the window.

Now she waved a twenty as Buddy opened the door.

"That isn't necessary, Connie," he said.

She thanked him with a nod for remembering her name. She said, "Don't give me any argument." She came close and tucked the bill into his shirt pocket. "You see here?" she said. "This is already done."

"Well, I thank you," Buddy said. He stroked the pocket, smoothing

528

the folded money flat. It was a blue cotton shirt he'd put on an hour earlier when he got home from having his hair cut.

She was still close and wearing wonderful perfume, but he didn't think he should remark on that. He kept his eyes level and waited as if she were a customer and he a clerk. He said, "So, are you still in the neighborhood? I rarely see you."

"They haven't needed me." She pretended a pout. "Nobody's needed me." She stepped back. It was the first week of September, still mild. She wore a fitted navy dress with a white collar and had a red cardigan sweater over her arms. Her large shapely legs were in sheer stockings.

"We have one last problem," she said. She held up a finger.

He looked at her, his eyebrows lifted.

Her hand fell and she gazed off and spoke as if reading, as if her words were printed over in the sky there to the right. "I have a crush on you," she said. "Such a crush on you, Buddy. The worst, most ungodly crush."

"No, you don't. You couldn't."

"The, worst, crush."

"Well," Buddy said. "Well dee well-dell-dell."

He owned the house—a two-story, Lowcountry cottage. It was set on a lane that led into Indian Town and beyond that were the roads and highways into north Pennsylvania. He sat on a divan near a window in the living room now and, in the noon light, looked through some magazines and at a book about birds.

He had a view from this window. Behind the house stood a tall ravine and Buddy could see through its vines and trees to the banks of Likely Lake.

His son had died after an accident there. Three years ago, August. Matthew. When he was two days short of turning twenty-one. His Jet Ski had hit a fishing boat that slid out of an inlet. The August after that, Buddy's wife left him.

He had stopped going out—what his therapist referred to as "isolating." He knocked the walls off his son's bedroom suite and off the room where Ruthie used to sew and he converted the whole upper floor into a studio. He began bringing all his assignments home. He was a draftsman, the senior draftsman at Qualitec, a firm of electromechanical engineers he had worked with for years.

"Beware of getting out of touch," his therapist had warned. "It happens gradually. It creeps over you by degrees. When you're not interacting with people, you start losing the beat. Then blammo. Suddenly, you're that guy in the yard."

"I'm who?" asked Buddy.

"The guy with the too-short pants," said the therapist.

He would *dissuade* the Connie woman, Buddy told himself now as he poked around in the kitchen. He yanked open a drawer and considered its contents, extracted a vegetable peeler, put it back in its place. He would dissuade her nicely. He didn't want to make her feel like a bug. "Let her down easy," he said aloud and both the cats spurted in to study him. Buddy had never learned to tell the cats apart. They were everyday cats, middle-sized and yellow. Matt's girlfriend, Shay, had presented them as kittens, for a birthday present, the same week he died. The cats stayed indoors now and kept close to Buddy. He called one of them Bruce and the other Bruce's Brother.

He went into a utility closet off the kitchen now and rolled out a canister vacuum. He liked vacuuming. He liked jobs he could quickly complete. And he wanted things just-so when Elise came over tonight. She had changed things for him in the months since they had met. Everything was different because of her.

One way to go with the Connie woman, he was thinking, would be to parenthetically mention Elise. That might have its effect. Or a stronger method would be to say, "My girlfriend is the jealous type," or some such.

The cats padded along into the dining area and watched as Buddy positioned the vacuum and unwound its mile of electric cord. "Don't ever touch a plug like this," he told them. "It is hot, hot, hot."

Elise phoned from work around two. She was a group counselor at Cherry Trees, a psychiatric hospital over in the medical park. Buddy saw his therapist in another building on the grounds and he had met Elise there, in fact, in the parking area. It was on a snowy day last February when he'd forgotten and left his fog lights burning. She had used yellow jumper cables to rescue him. Buddy had invited her to go for coffee and the two of them drove off in his black Mercury, zooming along the Old Post Highway to get the car battery juiced.

They ended up having lunch at a French place, where Elise put on horn-rimmed glasses and read from the menu aloud. Without the glasses, she reminded him of Jean Arthur—her figure, the freckles and bouncy, curly hair. Elise's French was awful and full of oinky sounds but Buddy liked her for trying it anyway. He liked her laugh, which went up and came down.

"Vincent escaped," she said now on the phone. "He broke out somehow. From right in the middle of a Life Challenges Meeting."

"I'm fortunate I don't know what that is," Buddy said.

"The problem for *me* is, with Vincent loose and Security looking for him, I can't take my people outside. Which means no Smoke Walk."

"Right, because you're the only one with a lighter. So that they have to trail along behind you."

"Well they're not dogs. But they're getting mighty grumpy. And being critical of Vincent. They think he should be shot."

"Hard to know whose side to take," said Buddy.

"That it is," Elise said, and told him she had to go.

This flower garden was Buddy's first, but *gorgeous*. He no longer understood people who spoiled and killed plants. The therapist had suggested gardening, so one Saturday when Elise was free, she and Buddy went to Tristie's Arboretum and bought starter materials. She also helped shape the garden. They put in a design like a collar around the court and walk.

Buddy had watered, fed, and misted his flowers. With each day they bloomed, grew large, stood tall. "What more could I ask of you?" he asked them. "Nuts and fruit?"

He thought he might recruit Elise to help lay in winter pansies around the side porch if that didn't seem boring. She was good at a hundred things. She could play bridge and poker and shuffle cards. She could play the piano. She liked listening to jazz and she *knew* most of it. They'd dress up and go dancing at Sky Mountain or at the Allegheny Club where there was an orchestra. Elise had beautiful evening clothes. She'd take him to all kinds of things—to midnight movies or a raunchy comedy club. Last spring they'd even taken a train trip to New Orleans for Jazz Fest.

From close by, Buddy heard a woman's voice and froze. It might be Connie's. He didn't feel up to another encounter with her, just yet. She seemed interesting and he liked her. She certainly was a handsome woman. She had mentioned peeking out her office window, how she always found herself watching for him. That was flattering, but still. He'd felt jarred by it. What if he were just out on some stupid errand, grabbing the paper or the mail out of the box, if he hadn't shaved or his shirt was on sideways?

The voice came a second time. It was *not* Connie's. However, the next one might be, he warned himself. He shook off his gloves and poked his tools back in their wire caddy. It was four something. She probably got off work pretty soon.

As he scrubbed his hands, he rehearsed telling Elise the Connie story. Elise was coming over for dinner after she finished her shift.

He started organizing the food he had bought earlier at the farmer's market. He got out a lemon and some lettuce in cello wrap, a net bag of radishes, a plum tomato. He heaped what he wanted of that into a wooden bowl; returned to the refrigerator and ripped a few sprigs of parsley. "Less like a picnic," he said to himself. He arranged a serving plate with slices of honey-baked ham; another with deviled egg halves and used the parsley for garnish. He knew he was not a great cook. With the exception of the jumbo shrimp he had grilled for Elise and her mom on July 4th. Those were delicious.

He carried the serving dishes into the dining room. It was too *soon* but he wanted to try the food to see how it looked set on the table. He got out a big linen tablecloth, gripped it by the ends, and flapped it hugely in the air to wave out the folds.

The cats somersaulted in. They leapt onto the sideboard. They stood poised and still and gazed at the platter of ham.

"Scary monster," Buddy told them, but sighed and dropped the tablecloth. He marched the ham back to the kitchen and hid it deep inside the refrigerator.

Elise knew a lot, in his opinion. She'd earned a degree in social psych and she was popular with the patients at Cherry Trees. Maybe he would skip complaining to her about Connie. That could only cause worry. He should be more circumspect. Why bother Elise?

He did call, but merely to ask how she was doing and to confirm their dinner plans. "I don't want anything," he said when she came to the phone.

"They sent Martha to the Time Out Room," Elise said. "The woman admitted last Saturday? You should see her now, though. Calm and quiet. Like she's had some realizations. Or been given back her doll."

"Who else is in your group?" Buddy asked. "I know you've told me."

"Well, it's evil and immoral that I did and I'll probably roast in hell for it. Donna, with the mysterious migraines. She's been here the longest. Next is Lorraine, the obsessive one who bought a hundred clear plastic tote bags. Barry, the ER nurse. He's tired, is all that's wrong with that man. And there's Doug, the Pilot Error guy. Martha. Vincent. Oh, and the new girl. I love her! She reminds me of somebody. Kim Novak maybe."

"Then I love her too," Buddy said.

"Or she's one of the Gabors. With her collar turned up? Always dancing and singing with a scarf tied on her wrist, like this is a musical. I have to go, Buddy."

"I know you do," he said. "How'd they make out with Vincent? They captured him yet?"

"No, unfortunately. But he has been seen." She said, "Well, of course, he's been seen! At practically every patient's window. And in their closets. Or he's standing right beside them in the mirror."

"Don't make jokes," Buddy said.

"No, I have to," said Elise, and she clicked off.

Buddy had the dinner table all prepared and he wanted to start the candles. He had read on the carton that the wicks would flame more evenly if lighted once in advance. He went hunting for stick matches, which weren't where they were supposed to be, in the cabinet over the stove. The sun was going down, and he glanced through the sliding glass doors to the side porch. Connie was here, sitting in the swing, mechanically rocking an end of it. She held a cigarette and was staring ardently at the floor.

Buddy forgot himself for a second. He wasn't sure what to do. He crept out of the room, turned around and came back.

"Nine one one," he said to the cats before he slid the door and took himself outside.

"So, what's shaking?" he asked. He made an unconcerned walk across the porch and to the railing. Half the sky had grown purple. There were red clouds twisted like a rope above the lake.

Connie went on gazing at the floorboards but stopped the swing with the heels of her shoes. They were snakeskin or lizard, very dark maroon. "Don't be mad," she said.

"I'm not," said Buddy.

"I like to sit in strange places, don't you? Especially if it's someone else's place. I play a little game of seeing what effect it has on them."

The curve of her throat when she looked up now was lovely. That surprised Buddy out of making a comment on the game.

"I wonder if it's ever occurred to you," she said. "These past two summers. The drought, right? You've heard about it on the news. You probably aren't aware that I live in Langley. My father and I. You always hear it called 'Scrap Pile' but it's Langley. It is poor and it's all wrecked. Of course, my father didn't guess that would *happen* when he inherited our house. This is only about eight miles—"

"Isn't that . . . Crabapple?" Buddy asked.

"No, it isn't. Crabapple's about twelve miles. Or was, it hardly exists anymore. But you wouldn't go there, so that's part of my point."

Buddy shuffled over and lowered next to her in the swing.

"When I'm coming to work?" She spoke straight into his face. "It gets greener. And greener. Until it's this lush—I don't know what. There's no drought here. You folks don't have a drought."

Buddy was nodding slowly. "I'm ashamed to admit it . . ."

Connie exhaled smoke and now rearranged something in herself, as if she were closing one folder and opening the next. "I feel very embarrassed. About the confession I made to you earlier," she said.

"Oh," he said and laughed once. "It's not like I could mind."

"Horseshit." She rose in her seat and flicked her cigarette expertly across the porch into a huddle of savanna shrubs.

"Connie, my girlfriend is a counselor over at Cherry Trees."

"What about it?" she asked and Buddy winced.

"Sorry," he said, as they both nodded and shrugged.

"You people." Her hand worked in the air. She clutched at nothing, let it go.

She said, "I am happy about this much. I've finally been at my job long enough that I've earned some time off for the things I enjoy. Such as travel."

"Where to?" Buddy asked.

"I'm thinking Belize," Connie said, and after a moment, "I've heard you don't really go anywhere. Mr. Secrest or someone said. No, it was he. He knew your wife. He said you hardly ever go out since your son died."

"That's mostly correct."

She said, "I didn't mean it as a criticism."

The phone began ringing and—certain the caller was Elise—Buddy apologized, scooted off the swing and hurried inside.

"I'll never get out of here," Elise said. "I know it ruins our plans. There's no alternative."

"It doesn't matter. We'll do it tomorrow."

"Everyone's so spooked. I wouldn't dare leave. And the nurses have them so doped up on sedatives. You should see this, Buddy. They could *hurt* themselves. It's like they're walking on shipboard."

He was smiling.

"It's because we're now told that Vincent is inside the hospital. So there's an all-out search," she said. "Anyway, I did one thing. I raced over to Blockbuster and rented them a movie—*The Matrix* is what they voted for. That is helping. It's got them focused. All in their pajamas, all in the Tomorrow Room with their bed pillows, doubled up on the couches and lying over chairs."

"*I* want to do that. That's sounds great!"

"No, you're not invited," said Elise.

She giggled at something on her end and said to Buddy, "You remember how I said they're always nicknaming the psychiatrists? I just heard, 'Here comes Dr. Post-It Note accompanying Drs. Liar and Deaf.' "

"My therapist looks like Al Haig."

"See, that's what I mean. That's why you don't belong here," Elise said.

"I'll call you later on," she told him.

From where he stood, he'd been viewing his dining-room setup. His table had crystal, candlesticks, and thirty red chrysanthemums in a vase. He hadn't realized, until the line went dead, how very sharp was his disappointment.

He had stepped down off the porch to inspect the walkway where a couple of slate tiles had strayed out of line. He was stooped over, prompting a piece back into place with his shoe. Here were weeds. Here were ants, too, crawling in a long contorted file.

Connie watched him, smoking hard and unhappily, still in the swing. "I need to say a few things. About my feelings," she said.

He stuffed his hands in his pockets and rejoined her on the porch. He learned on the far railing, facing her. They were quiet a moment. "I'm sorry. I'm an oaf," he said.

535

She answered that silently and with a brief, sarcastic smile.

He said, "I do want to hear."

She looked at the ceiling.

"Okay, I probably just don't understand then, Connie." He brought his hands from his pockets, bunched his fingers, and consulted them. "Is it that you have a kind of *fantasy* about me?"

"God, no!" she said and clicked her tongue. "It's actually a little more adult than that." She pronounced the word "*aah*-dult."

Her smile grew reproachful. "So you know all about my feelings."

"Oh, I don't think that."

She said, "Since you're Mister Perfect." She began fussing with the cultured pearl in her ear. "Bet you wish I'd kept my feelings to my own fuckin' self."

It was one of the unhappiest conversations Buddy could recall. "I really don't think any of that," he said.

Connie's long legs were folded now with her feet tucked to the side. She had the grace of someone who had been an athlete or a dancer. And she used her hands prettily, holding one in the other or touching the prim white collar on her dress. Her hair was fascinating—a gleaming black. But there was sorrow in her eyes, or so Buddy thought. They moved slowly, when they did move. Her gaze seldom shifted. Her eyes were heavy, and gave an impression of defeat.

He was thinking, patting his fingertips. He said, "I'll tell you a few things about myself. The morning Matt died, by the time I arrived at the ICU and could locate Ruthie, my wife, she was standing with her face to a wall, clenching her diaphragm like she'd run a marathon and couldn't breathe. So I tiptoed over and tapped her on the shoulder to show I was there. Only she didn't feel it or was too distressed. At any rate, she didn't acknowledge. I wasn't sure. I just stayed there waiting. Until, when she finally did turn, she looked straight through me. So, what I did? I gave her this huge *tick-tock* wave. Like, hidee-ho."

He smoothed his hair a few times. "How much have I thought about that! It was just a bad moment probably, a slipup, but it might've paved the way for this second thing, a situation I found myself in."

He said, "My son was riding his Jet Ski, I don't know what you heard about it."

Connie's head moved, no.

536

Buddy's head nodded. "On the lake. He crashed into a fishing boat that had a couple of high-school boys. No one else was killed but damn near. I found it hard. Hard to stop picturing. Then this urge came that if I could talk to someone I didn't know very well. Have a plain conversation with no mention of my son. So, for some reason I chose a woman who's the floor rep at Zack's Print Shop. We'd exchanged a few words. I doubt if she remembered my name. I gave her some information, the first call. I told her their sign—for the rear parking whatchumajiggy—had fallen down. Then I started calling with everything you could name—a TV contest, or foreseeing a weather problem. Or call and make some joke about Zack. Ten, fifteen times a day. Sitting in a spindly chair there with the phone, not even comfortable. And my poor wife, having to overhear all of this, was just beside herself. As to why I kept harassing this woman. Who, finally, when it got too much, went downtown and filed a restraining order."

"Man!" Connie said.

"She did indeed," said Buddy.

He got up. The cats were yowling and hopping at the glass door. "I have to stop for a second and give them dinner. I'll be right back."

"Go," Connie said, "go," and signaled with a flick of her hand that she understood.

While he was filling the dish with Science Diet, he had caught her figure in the shadows, descending the porch stairs.

Buddy rocked on his shoes. A light switched on at the lawyers' place next door.

He watched as the cats chowed. He refreshed their water.

He stood in the center of the kitchen and waited, without going to a window, for the effect of a taxicab's headlights out on the lane.

It was quiet where Elise was. She almost had to whisper. "This is eerie. All the patients' colored faces in the TV light? It's despicable that I'm always canceling on you. It's the worst thing I do. It's what destroyed every relationship I've had."

"Oh God, let that be true," Buddy said.

He was flicking a stub of paper around on the countertop, to no end. "Are you ever nervous around me?" he asked Elise.

"What?"

"Nervous *about* me, I mean. Because of the way I bothered that woman."

"Don't insult me," Elise said.

"Excuse me?"

"I'm a smart person. One of the smart ones. They insisted on textbooks where I went to school."

"Oh," he said.

There was a pause between them. Buddy paced up and back a step, holding the phone. The room was overly warm and the cats had taken to the cool of the floor tiles.

"I should go," Elise said. "I really have to pee. Plus they're right now carrying Vincent in on a stretcher. Directed towards the Time Out Room is my guess. Will you be okay? Do you feel okay?"

"Maybe I'll just keep that to my own fucking *self*," he said and grinned. "It's a joke you don't know. I'm sorry. I'll explain it to you some other time."

"They don't need me that bad. I'm free to talk," Elise said.

"No, I feel fine. The joke isn't even about me." His index finger traced around and around one of the blue tiles set in the countertop.

"Listen to me a second," she said. "Are you there? This is the last thing I want to say before I have to hang up. Grief is very mysterious, Buddy. It's very personal."

"Bye for now," she said, and Buddy stayed a moment after he'd closed the phone, his hand on the receiver, his arm outstretched.

He stood on the side porch. The night was warm and a full white moon dawdled over Likely Lake.

Across the lane at the Tishman's a car was adjusting behind a line of cars—latecomers for the bridge party Carl and Suzanne hosted every other week. One of them or somebody appeared in the entryway, there to welcome in the tardy guest.

Buddy was thinking about other nights, when he and Elise had sat out here until late, telling each other stories and drinking rum. On his birthday, she had worn a sequined red dress. There were nights with his wife, their last sad year.

How silly, he thought, that Connie's confession had bothered him. He should have absorbed it. He should have taken her hand and held her hand, as a friend, or even clenched it, and said what a very long life it can seem.

Nominated by Jessica Roeder

QUARTER PAST BLUE

by ROBERT THOMAS

from FIELD

It's just the sort of paper-thin night
to make me steal the clapper from the mission bell
and leave it on your doorstep like a stuttered prayer.
In your room I see a writing light,
soft and dirty as an oyster.
I know you can hear me
out here in the static,
scraping on your pane like a raccoon.
I've been to the pond.
It's not as if the swans are your personal secret.
Come out and walk with me across the Sonoma
town square, on the edge of the green.
I'm wearing my papier-mâché wings,
and they're not yet dry. The moon's been released
on its own recognizance. This is serious traffic, gridlock
intergalactical, Friday night lust and spleen. This is
the *it* they mean when they say *this is it*. You are so
caught up in your own devotions. You are so not
what you think you are. It's late,
half past revelation, quarter past blue,
and you're still counting the chits, waiting for something
better than love as cold and magical as dry ice
to come along and sideswipe you, hit and run,
without leaving a scratch.

Nominated by Laura Kasischke

AFTERWARDS

memoir by JANE BROX

from THE GEORGIA REVIEW

IT HAD BEEN A DROUGHTY SUMMER. The orchard grasses turned sere by late June, the brook beds shrunk to dried mud, and the apples reached no more than half their best size. The worst of them— ones marked up with codling moth scars or scab—weren't even worth hauling to the apple cellar. Strange to see bushel after bushel of Cortland, McIntosh, and Northern Spies in heaps under the trees. Even stranger was the way the sweet smell of those fermenting apples drew the deer out of the woods—more deer than anyone in living memory had ever seen here. They'd forage through the fallen leaves under the bare crowns of the trees, coming more and more frequently as the apples softened, frosting and thawing by turns down the shortening autumn days until they froze through at last and were covered with an early December snow.

Through the first quiet winter storms, the deer stayed in the part of the orchard that bordered the woods, nosing the snow near the apple bark, raising their heads every now and again, wary, listening. But as the snow deepened they came further into the orchard, and I could trace their tracks from tree to tree. They came at all hours— nine of them once—filing along the edge of the pines at eleven in the morning on a cloudless day. Even my father, who'd seen them all his life, remarked: "Look at that . . . in broad daylight . . ."

We talked about them every day as I stopped by my parents' house in the late afternoon, my mother in the kitchen, my father at his desk going over the farm year on paper:

"I saw three under the Cortland trees, one couldn't have been more than a yearling."

"Is that so? They must be finding apples still. I hope they don't start grazing on the branches."

"Oh, you think?"

As long as the deer kept to the fallen apples, they stood clear of any concern of ours. Just beautiful things even for the hunters in our family—my father and uncles—all of whom were too old now for the hunt, though seeing those deer brought up the old stories about ones tracked years ago here, or in Maine or Nova Scotia.

Our talk about the deer kept on, even when my father took sick. In the hospital he couldn't say much because his breathing was rapid and shallow. I sat by his bed—it was far into December by then—and his room, with its beeping monitors and hissing oxygen, was louder than anything outdoors. There were no real words, it felt late, but I was hoping he'd still want to know about the small things, so I told him I'd seen the deer that morning, that they were coming farther up into the orchard all the time. All he could do was blink his eyes, and I couldn't figure out if he knew what I was saying or if he had a question, but a little later, when I asked him if he wanted anything, he smiled as much as he could—I saw his cheek wrinkle—and whispered, "venison." One word that let through his dry wit, since he knew I wasn't much for hunting. One word that comforted me more than all the times he'd answered the usual questions we asked to make sure he still dwelled in time: Did he know where he was? Did he know the day? Or the questions he'd ask us when he could: What's the matter with me? Where's the blood coming from? Have you gone home?

A few mornings later, I was the first in the family to arrive at the hospital and I had to wait outside the room while the nurse finished her care. I knew something was wrong because she wasn't talking to him—always before I could hear the nurse asking my father how he felt, was he comfortable, telling him she was going to draw some blood. She beckoned me in this time and told me he had come down with pneumonia in the night. His hands were cold. It was louder in the room. They'd turned up the oxygen and had given him a larger mask through which to breathe. I could tell right away he was having trouble keeping up. When I said, "Hello," all he could do was raise his eyebrows. That was his last gesture to me in this life, and it's what I keep remembering, wishing for more as I think of all his years of reserve and, in that last week, all his efforts to say the merest thing.

541

My mother, my brothers, my sister—all faces fell as they entered the room that morning. And no one dared step out for coffee or to make a phone call. We'd come a diligent way on a narrow trail since the gray early light of Christmas Eve day, when I stood in the doorframe of my parents' house and faced the road, listening in the still of the year for the ambulance to come. Now we gathered bewildered around his bed as his breathing grew quieter and quieter. He took his last breath, then his mouth closed. My mother whispered, "no," as the heart monitor slowed to a scribed outline like the low eroded hills, and each reading ended in a question mark.

When the doctor came he listened for my father's heart and his lungs, and then put a thumb to the lid of my father's blind eye and opened it, not knowing it had stopped gathering light years before, though my father always said he could still see the shadow of his own hand. Now, the coin for the journey.

Afterwards—in the days following—I sat at his desk and tried to carry on the workings of his home and farm: changing everything over to my mother's name alone, working out the payroll taxes, the quarterly taxes, all the January paperwork. I was half grateful for the dry figuring of accounts, of the farm year drawn to an abstraction of costs and balances. But such soldierly work couldn't keep grief at bay for long. As I backtracked over the check stubs, I saw how his handwriting had grown shakier down through the year. Like his voice, I'd start to think, becoming gravelly as his lungs weakened. Then I'd notice how quiet the house felt—and he was a quiet man. How did my mother stand it? How would she get through the days, the meals, the evenings? No answering words. Only months later beginning to understand: *never again.*

As I worked, I'd uncover keepsakes of his in the drawers of the desk or tucked away among his ledgers and files. His original birth certificate, the death notices of his close friends who had gone before him, his own father's timepiece with its etched copper backing worn fine and the crystal clouded over—mute things that had lost the one who could best speak for them. From now on they'll only be partially understood, same as the stories I can no longer verify that were mostly his alone. "No one believes me," I remember him saying, "but I stood by the Bay of Fundy on the eve of the war and saw apples coming in on the tide. The bay was full of apples. The ships had dumped their cargoes to take on supplies for the war." That's all I know. And no matter how much, I want to know more.

Prayer cards and letters of sympathy came through the mail as news of his death traveled out of the valley. My aunts had been tearing obituaries out of the local papers and sending them to the relatives in Syracuse and Delaware. Friends of far friends wrote and called. I phoned my parents' closest friends in Florida—people I'd never called before—who knew something was wrong the moment they heard my voice. After their weak greeting, a questioning silence into which I poured, "I wanted to tell you my father passed away."

I know their true grief is beyond the formal, scripted sorrow that lands on his desk with every mail. I know my father would have understood their efforts to find words that come near. Near enough, OK, what we settle for while we tilt an ear to the winter air. I feel as if I've been listening—for what?—ever since the wake. It had started spitting snow, and those arriving to pay their respects, though they'd only walked from the parking lot to the door of the funeral home, seemed as if they'd made a real journey, the way they stamped their boots and shook the snow from their scarves. They blew on their hands as they cleared their throats on comfortable sayings about the weather: "Sure is cold . . ." and "The roads are icing up . . ." Then, the plush hallways and the floral sprays brought their voices down: "I can't believe it . . . I thought he'd live forever." Voices that had surrounded us all our lives sounded graver than I'd ever known, murmuring, "Things just won't be the same," "I'm sorry," "Sorry for your troubles," "I had no idea. I saw him just a few days before Christmas and he seemed fine," "It'll be tough . . ."

Eyes, then eye, that saw. Ears, then deafening ears, that heard. When I try to imagine afterwards, I keep coming back to how much my father belonged to this one place on earth. I can't imagine more than all he had in his keeping: three houses, forty cleared acres, a hundred of woodland, and a dozen in fruit trees. *Thou canst not follow me now, but thou shall follow me afterwards.* If *after* is a word that doesn't come near—if what's to come can't be imagined from this life—then why does his farm seem to mean all the more to me now, as I stand in the orchard when the moon is down and watch the comet passing?

His is a New England farm, and for all the stony soil, there's an intimate feel to the lay of the land with its small fields set off by chinked walls and the mixed woods beyond. My father's understanding of this place had accreted over eighty-five years, and at times I know he drove the wedge into wood with the resentment of the responsible son, at times with an effort born only of love. Over eighty-five years, the original sound had swallowed its own echoes, and the most he could do was to tell me, "This is where I keep the receipts, this is where I keep the outstanding bills," as he opened the drawers in his office. Not much different from when he tried to teach me to prune the peaches: "This branch . . . here . . . see how the light will get through now?" as I stood puzzling it out alongside him.

So, with the snow falling outside, and the deer lunging through the deepening drifts, I am left to figure the farm from the notes on his desk, from the business cards he had scribbled across. I find a name—*Very Fine, Cal Jennings, Orchard Supply*—and work back from there. The world I'm responsible for is more complex and less patient than the one he was born into. Hospital bills from his last illness are waiting, the pension fund needs proof of his death. Over the phone I have to recite his Social Security number to prove I know him. I have to mail out his death certificate again and again—the form itself, with its raised stamp, is what they want, not the facts that his parents were born in Lebanon and that it was his heart and kidneys that gave out. Even when such work goes smoothly, I sometimes throw the pen down and ask the desk, the walls, and the ledgers why I couldn't have learned all this before.

And then a day comes when I have to erase his name from another account. First it was the checking account, then the Agway charge and the Harris seed charge. Sometimes it feels as if I'm erasing him everywhere until his name will remain only in his last place, on the hill, behind the white birch. I hate it, both the erasure and my realization that if we are going to go on I can't make the same decisions he would have made. His work boots slouch beside the desk, as worn as they'll ever be. I'm planning to spend more on repairs to the barn than he ever would have agreed to. I'm thinking of selling the Methuen land as soon as the market's better.

"Who's going to be farming in this valley ten years from now? Who?" my father once asked. I could say nothing in the face of the long years he had put in. I realize I know little of the work it will be, even though it's not a lot of land. These acres he has left are almost nothing in comparison to the farms to the west, to farms in general. But it is ours, and one of the last here, and it feels huge to me.

In his safe, among the canceled bank books and the stock certificates, I found the original deed to the farm. In 1902 it had been a forty-acre holding with worn implements and gradey cattle. All the scattered outbuildings are described in detail, and every boundary is fixed: *Thence northerly by said Herrick's land as the fence now stands, to land now or formerly of Herbert Coburn, thence easterly by said Almon Richardson's land as the fence now stands to the corner of a wall by said Almon Richardson's land . . . thence southerly . . . thence westerly by the Black North Road to the point of beginning.*
The contents of the barns are listed, too: the hoes and shovels, the scythes and hammers, the Concord coach, twenty-five chickens, two oxen and their yoke, seven dairy cows and nine milk pails, a matched team of horses, and a blind horse. Plus feed for the blind horse. I swear, the worth of every nail is accounted for. For this my grandparents were so far mortgaged they had to cut down the pine grove to meet the payments. And now out of all that has been listed there, what has not been discarded or crumbled to a sifted heap, hangs gathering an oily dust in the back of the carriage house or in the bins of the toolshed. The scythes have rusted to the nails they hang from, the leather collars for the horses have dried and cracked.
When all is said and done, and we tally the contents of my father's estate, such things will no longer be counted among his worth. What brought us here and forward, the things he started with back in his boyhood where his allegiances began, will be smiled at indulgently and hung back up and considered as nothing alongside the larger things that have replaced them—the Case tractor, the gleaming red harrow, the corn planter. Stand at the door of the barn and breathe in the must of those early things. Listen for a voice—*hey bos, bos, bos*—calling the cows home. Feel an ache in the worked-out shoulders and cold creeping into the firelit rooms. How else could we have come this way since the April day when, according to the deed, my grandfather, who could not write his name in English, made his mark?

We've had three storms in a row this January—more snow than I ever remember. There's so much drifting that the contours of the land have changed: hills of apparent substance where no hills are, swale where no swale is, no longer a trace of old tracks in the orchard. The snow lies far too deep for the deer to make their way or find the frozen apples. They're keeping to the woods. My father would have guessed they are yarding up under the hemlocks. Their daily appearance all through the earlier months now seems like a dream to me, another life lived by another daughter, and sometimes I can't believe they were ever close enough to see. Every once in a while the dog stops short in her meanderings, grows alert, and stares off into the depths of the pines. I think she senses the herd moving along one of their trusted, protected paths. But that's all.

Nominated by Andrea Hollander Budy

POEM TO SOME OF MY RECENT PURCHASES

by DOROTHY BARRESI

from VIRGINIA QUARTERLY REVIEW

Durable goods,
sweet and crude,
I calculate your worth
by the glory available,
divide by dollars spent, my relief,
the exact nature and angle of my pleasure: *abide with me*, things
    say.

We won't leave you here alone.

Lipstick, pantyhose (Donna Karan), A-line cashmere skirt,
mid-heel spectator pumps, and lately.
a high amp juice extractor
for vegetables and fruit—

I choose you
because each day for 662 years my grandparents ate
bologna sandwiches, and then
Hoover came in
and things got really bad.
900 years of onions and reflex courage.
5,648 years of ward bosses, head busters, union dues, babies,

Fiorella La Guardia leading the National Anthem
at Yankee Stadium, and no
roses or raises, ever.

Responsibility: my dad's dead dog
when he was growing up, schlepping *Boys' Life* door to door.

Dog-Tired: my second cousin on my mother's side.

Makeshift Gratitude: my mother on cold school mornings
slapping mustard around
in her bathrobe, cigarette atilt in her lips.
She made the bologna sandwiches
I was destined to unwrap.

Bracelet, earrings, tanzanite toe ring
(I liked peridot better
but they didn't have my size),

if I never buy anything,
how will I distract myself?
How will I weigh myself down
when the last winds come to find me unworthy with
wailing, gnashing, and proclaiming
by which I am sucked up and
bare as a soup bone in butcher paper
thrown free?

The big wars are over
but the small ones never end.
What shall I save?

In my personal bedroom community the babies are not always
      kissed or fed;
boys murder boys;
politicians dance with underaged girls named
Absolute Value or Agnes Dei
while buses loaded with dead pensioners

leave on the hour
for Indian gaming in Palm Springs. What I am saying,

my dear, dear purchases,
is that I refuse to be chronically wistful.
I tear open your clear wrappings with my teeth
in the front seat of my car.

I love you.

And if not you, precisely,
I adore the moment the salesgirl hands you over
as if proffering
the sunset and all its glowing fruits.
Jesus is my homeboy, her lovely tattoo tells me,
and my son will be safe
if I will only pray.

Bracelet, lampshade, purse, perfume
(Coco, by Chanel),
votive candles
too pretty to burn,
am I to understand
my sarcasm
will not help me?

In the ascendant American paradigm,
I leave Macy's with an armload of usable truth
in a world of plenty.
The sparrows do not line up
in their sniper nests against me,
my credit rating holds,

I buy,
not to escape the world
but to draw it nearer. To build
more world up around me.

Bracelet, perfume, lampshade, purse,
jewel-horde, dream-horde,
cast your spell. Consume me as you do.
Take me home,
where I might hold you in my lap a while,
now that I am often afraid.

Nominated by Ed Ochester

SPECIAL MENTION

(The editors also wish to mention the following important works published by small presses last year. Listings are in no particular order.)

POETRY

Down There, If You Look—Reginald Gibbons (American Poetry Review)

The Ragpicker's Song—Richard Wilbur (The Formalist)

The Fever of Brother Barnabas—Alan Williamson (TriQuarterly)

Unapproved Road—Paul Muldoon (Daedalus)

Democracy—Dorianne Laux (Barrow Street)

Elegy From A Nightingale's Point of View—Gail Wronsky (88)

Madonna Enthroned—Anne Marie Macari (American Poetry Review)

Spleen—Pimone Triplett (New England Review)

The Pox—Gillian Conoley (Colorado Review)

Sudden Scattering of Leaves, All Gold—Carl Phillips (Pool)

Ligatures—Forrest Gander (First Intensity)

The Wandering Between Worlds—David Jauss (Black Warrior)

A Crown of Sonnets for 'The King'—Madeline DeFrees (River City)

From 'The Face'—David St. John (Colorado Review)

Charles Wright And The 940 Locust Avenue Heraclitean Rhythm Band—Charles Wright (Hunger Mountain)

Green—Linda McCarriston (*Little River*, TriQuarterly Books)

Anesthesia Mask—Elena Karina Byrne (Rivendell)

Acquired Immune Deficiency Syndrome—Eduardo C. Corral (Indiana Review)

Each Thing Charged—Ben Doyle (Jubilat)

1, 2, 3—James Galvin (Seneca Review)
The Invention of Pointillism—Steve Gehrke (Georgia Review)
Surviving Love—Linda Gregg (Kenyon Review)
A Rainy Morning—Ted Kooser (West Branch)
The Good-Boy Suit—Wesley McNair (Sewanee Review)
The Librarian's Song—Alan Michael Parker (Pleiades)
The Throne of Fear—Molly Peacock (Black Warrior Review)
Amazing Grace Beauty Salon—Donald Platt (Southern Review)
A Hole Is When You Step In It You Go Down—Mary Ann Samyn
    (Pleiades)
The Walk—Valerie Savior (Colorado Review)
Separate Worlds—Dara Wier (Margie)
Hex—Cecilia Woloch (Arsenic Lobster)
At The Public Market—Betsy Sholl (Beloit Poetry Journal)

NONFICTION

Poison Ivy—Paul Cristensen (Water-Stone)
Many Shades of Green, or Ecofiction Is In The Eye of The
    Reader—Donna Seaman (TriQuarterly)
The Lonely Wanderer—Kathryn Rhett (Michigan Quarterly
    Review)
Frankenstein—Steven Marcus (Southern Review)
Forever Forster: Edward Morgan Forster—George Watson
    (Hudson Review)
On the Left—Norma Marder (Gettysburg Review)
An Editorial Relationship—Judy Karasik (Agni)
This Far Out—Elizabeth Halling (Brain, Child)
Untitled—Francois Camion (Crazyhorse)
Waiting For the Bombs—Kevin Oderman (Northwest Review)
Tolerating Intolerance—Bruce Bawer (Partisan Review)
Paper—Amitava Kumar (Kenyon Review)
Mary Mary Ellen Ellen—Tan Lin (Conjunctions)
Enter Three Witches—George Garrett (Hollins Critic)
Lavender—André Aciman (Harvard Review)
Shock Therapy—Susan Mahler (Threepenny Review)
Egypt Land—Jeffrey Hammond (Massachusetts Review)
The Middle of the Story—Dianne Homan (Brain, Child)
Visual Anguish and Looking At Art—Carol Zoref (Bellevue Literary
    Review)

Sensitive—Andrew Hudgins (American Scholar)
Mother Goose Rising—Daniel Henry (Northern Lights)
Peaceable Kingdom—Doug Carlson (Ascent)
Prayer Dogs—Terry Tempest Williams (Creative Nonfiction)
The Potato Man—Jane Miller (Raritan)
Land Where My Fathers Died—Debbie Danielpour Chapel (Agni)
Joe Stopped By—Andrei Codrescu (Creative Nonfiction)
Spirits—Bill Roorbach (*Into The Woods*, University of Notre Dame Press)
On Walls, Veils, and Silences; Writing Lives in Iran—Farzaheh Milani (Southern Review)
Bloomin' Genius—Joseph Epstein (Hudson Review)
Under the Electric Sun—Jodi Daynard (New England Review)
Compassion—Dorothy Allison (Tin House)
Kissing the Dead—Claire Davis (Shenandoah)
Litany For The Last Days—Ladette Randolph (Prairie Schooner)

FICTION

Opening—Ann McCutchan (Image)
Mother In the Trenches—Robert Olen Butler (StoryQuarterly)
Backland—David Michael Kaplan (StoryQuarterly)
Ray—Peter Moore Smith (Alaska Quarterly)
The Distance to the Sun—Christopher Torockio (Denver Quarterly)
The Littlest Hitler—Ryan Boudinot (Mississippi Review)
Tales of the Hungarian Resistance—Tamas Dobozy (Northwest Review)
Vine—David Kear (Literal Latte)
Hunters—John Edgar Wideman (Xconnect)
Gladys Simeon—M.E. McMullen (The New Renaissance)
Hot Spring—Donna George Storey (Prairie Schooner)
Stone Fish—Gregory Spatz (*Wonderful Tricks*, Mid-List)
Rules of Exile—Jacquelyn Spangler (Other Voices)
A Long Black Arc—Scott Boylston (Tampa Review)
Lush—Bradford Morrow (Ontario Review)
The Rescue Mission—Frederick Busch (Daedalus)
The Children of Dead State Troopers—Keith Lee Morris (New England Review)
This Is History—Chauna Craig (Green Mountains Review)
Footnote—Romulus Linney (Chelsea)

Blood—Shelley Jackson (Mississippi Review)
Neighbors—David Griffith (Gettysburg Review)
The Splinter—Sallie Bingham (*Transgressions*, Sarabande)
The Brotherhood of Healing—Barbara Sutton (Antioch Review)
Bon Ton—Fred Chappell (Five Points)
The Open Door—Valerie Martin (Massachusetts Review)
Belonging to Karovsky—Kathryn Schwille (Crazyhorse)
The Clearing—Marjorie Hudson (West Branch)
Captain Galaxy Comes Back to Earth—Kris Saknussemm (New Letters)
Motherland—Min Jin Lee (Missouri Review)
Done Gone—Andrea M. Worth (Water-Stone)
Ragtop Impala—Meg Giles (Five Points)
Problems for Self-Study—Charles Yu (Harvard Review)
Eating Mammals—John Barlow (Paris Review)
Two Rivers—Andrea Barrett (TriQuarterly)
Gary Garrison's Wedding Vows—Ron Carlson (Glimmer Train)
Frank—R.M. Berry (Fiction International)
The Long Game—Angela Pneuman (Ploughshares)
The Ore Miner's Wife—Karl Iagnemma (Virginia Quarterly Review)
Again—Part II—Stephen Dixon (TriQuarterly)
The Liar—Richard Burgin (Ontario Review)
The Facts—Mark Rigney (Bellevue Literary Review)
Horse Power—Mike Magnuson (Pindeldyboz)
Payback Time—Jane Ciabattari (*Stealing the Fire*, Canio's Editions)
Garbage Night At the Opera—Valerie Fioravanti (North American Review)
At The Bottom of The United States—Carol Bly (Idaho Review)
Titan—Rick Bass (Shenandoah)
Superman—Tracy Daugherty (Southern Review)
The Daugher of Kadmos—Olga Grushin (Partisan Review)
The Playing Field—Guy Davenport (Hotel Amerika)
Petrified Forest—Madison Smartt Bell (Daedalus)
Blue Yodel—Scott Snyder (Zoetrope)
Little Red's Tango—Peter Straub (Conjunctions)
Famous Builder 2—Paul Lisicky (*Famous Builder*, Graywolf)
Paper Hero—Melvin Jules Bukiet (Southwest Review)
Citizen of Vienna—Erin McGraw (The Southern Review)
Aboveground—Doris Betts (Epoch)
Tort Law—Bruce Smith (StoryQuarterly)

PRESSES FEATURED IN THE PUSHCART PRIZE EDITIONS SINCE 1976

Acts
Agni
Ahsahta Press
Ailanthus Press
Alaska Quarterly Review
Alcheringa/Ethnopoetics
Alice James Books
Ambergris
Amelia
American Letters and Commentary
American Literature
American PEN
American Poetry Review
American Scholar
American Short Fiction
The American Voice
Amicus Journal
Amnesty International
Anaesthesia Review
Another Chicago Magazine
Antaeus
Antietam Review
Antioch Review
Apalachee Quarterly
Aphra
Aralia Press

The Ark
Art and Understanding
Arts and Letters
Artword Quarterly
Ascensius Press
Ascent
Aspen Leaves
Aspen Poetry Anthology
Assembling
Atlanta Review
Autonomedia
Avocet Press
The Baffler
Bakunin
Bamboo Ridge
Barlenmir House
Barnwood Press
Barrow Street
The Bellingham Review
Bellowing Ark
Beloit Poetry Journal
Bennington Review
Bilingual Review
Black American Literature Forum
Black Rooster
Black Scholar

Black Sparrow
Black Warrior Review
Blackwells Press
Bloomsbury Review
Blue Cloud Quarterly
Blue Unicorn
Blue Wind Press
Bluefish
BOA Editions
Bomb
Bookslinger Editions
Boston Review
Boulevard
Boxspring
Brain, Child
Bridge
Bridges
Brown Journal of Arts
Burning Deck Press
Caliban
California Quarterly
Callaloo
Calliope
Calliopea Press
Calyx
Canto
Capra Press
Caribbean Writer
Carolina Quarterly
Cedar Rock
Center
Chariton Review
Charnel House
Chattahoochee Review
Chelsea
Chicago Review
Chouteau Review
Chowder Review
Cimarron Review
Cincinnati Poetry Review
City Lights Books
Cleveland State University Poetry Center
Clown War

CoEvolution Quarterly
Cold Mountain Press
Colorado Review
Columbia: A Magazine of Poetry and
    Prose
Confluence Press
Confrontation
Conjunctions
Connecticut Review
Copper Canyon Press
Cosmic Information Agency
Countermeasures
Counterpoint
Crawl Out Your Window
Crazyhorse
Crescent Review
Cross Cultural Communications
Cross Currents
Crosstown Books
Cumberland Poetry Review
Curbstone Press
Cutbank
Dacotah Territory
Daedalus
Dalkey Archive Press
Decatur House
December
Denver Quarterly
Domestic Crude
Doubletake
Dragon Gate Inc.
Dreamworks
Dryad Press
Duck Down Press
Durak
East River Anthology
Eastern Washington University Press
Ellis Press
Empty Bowl
Epoch
Ergo!
Evansville Review
Exquisite Corpse

Faultline

Fence

Fiction

Fiction Collective

Fiction International

Field

Fine Madness

Firebrand Books

Firelands Art Review

First Intensity

Five Fingers Review

Five Points Press

Five Trees Press

The Formalist

Fourth Genre

Frontiers: A Journal of Women Studies

Fugue

Gallimaufry

Genre

The Georgia Review

Gettysburg Review

Ghost Dance

Gibbs-Smith

Glimmer Train

Goddard Journal

David Godine, Publisher

Graham House Press

Grand Street

Granta

Graywolf Press

Green Mountains Review

Greenfield Review

Greensboro Review

Guardian Press

Gulf Coast

Hanging Loose

Hard Pressed

Harvard Review

Hayden's Ferry Review

Hermitage Press

Heyday

Hills

Holmgangers Press

Holy Cow!

Home Planet News

Hotel Amerika

Hudson Review

Hungry Mind Review

Icarus

Icon

Idaho Review

Iguana Press

Image

Indiana Review

Indiana Writes

Intermedia

Intro

Invisible City

Inwood Press

Iowa Review

Ironwood

Jam To-day

The Journal

Jubilat

The Kanchenjuga Press

Kansas Quarterly

Kayak

Kelsey Street Press

Kenyon Review

Kestrel

Latitudes Press

Laughing Waters Press

Laurel Review

L'Epervier Press

Liberation

Linquis

Literal Latté

Literary Imagination

The Literary Review

The Little Magazine

Living Hand Press

Living Poets Press

Logbridge-Rhodes

Louisville Review

Lowlands Review

Lucille

Lynx House Press
Lyric
The MacGuffin
Magic Circle Press
Malahat Review
Mānoa
Manroot
Many Mountains Moving
Marlboro Review
Massachusetts Review
McSweeney's
Meridian
Mho & Mho Works
Micah Publications
Michigan Quarterly
Mid-American Review
Milkweed Editions
Milkweed Quarterly
The Minnesota Review
Mississippi Review
Mississippi Valley Review
Missouri Review
Mizna
Montana Gothic
Montana Review
Montemora
Moon Pony Press
Mount Voices
Mr. Cogito Press
MSS
Mudfish
Mulch Press
Nada Press
Nebraska Review
New America
New American Review
New American Writing
The New Criterion
New Delta Review
New Directions
New England Review
New England Review and Bread Loaf
    Quarterly

New Letters
New Orleans Review
New Virginia Review
New York Quarterly
New York University Press
News from The Republic of Letters
Nimrod
9 × 9 Industries
North American Review
North Atlantic Books
North Dakota Quarterly
North Point Press
Northeastern University Press
Northern Lights
Northwest Review
Notre Dame Review
O. ARS
O. Blēk
Obsidian
Obsidian II
Oconee Review
October
Ohio Review
Old Crow Review
Ontario Review
Open City
Open Places
Orca Press
Orchises Press
Orion
Other Voices
Oxford American
Oxford Press
Oyez Press
Oyster Boy Review
Painted Bride Quarterly
Painted Hills Review
Palo Alto Review
Paris Press
Paris Review
Parkett
Parnassus: Poetry in Review
Partisan Review

Passages North
Penca Books
Pentagram
Penumbra Press
Pequod
Persea: An International Review
Pipedream Press
Pitcairn Press
Pitt Magazine
Pleiades
Ploughshares
Poet and Critic
Poet Lore
Poetry
Poetry East
Poetry Ireland Review
Poetry Northwest
Poetry Now
Post Road
Prairie Schooner
Prescott Street Press
Press
Promise of Learnings
Provincetown Arts
Puerto Del Sol
Quaderni Di Yip
Quarry West
The Quarterly
Quarterly West
Raccoon
Rainbow Press
Raritan: A Quarterly Review
Red Cedar Review
Red Clay Books
Red Dust Press
Red Earth Press
Red Hen Press
Release Press
Review of Contemporary Fiction
Revista Chicano-Riquena
Rhetoric Review
River Styx
Rowan Tree Press

Russian *Samizdat*
Salmagundi
San Marcos Press
Sarabande Books
Sea Pen Press and Paper Mill
Seal Press
Seamark Press
Seattle Review
Second Coming Press
Semiotext(e)
Seneca Review
Seven Days
The Seventies Press
Sewanee Review
Shankpainter
Shantih
Shearsman
Sheep Meadow Press
Shenandoah
A Shout In the Street
Sibyl-Child Press
Side Show
Small Moon
The Smith
Solo
Solo 2
Some
The Sonora Review
Southern Poetry Review
Southern Review
Southwest Review
Spectrum
Spillway
The Spirit That Moves Us
St. Andrews Press
Story
Story Quarterly
Streetfare Journal
Stuart Wright, Publisher
Sulfur
The Sun
Sun & Moon Press
Sun Press

Sunstone
Sycamore Review
Tamagwa
Tar River Poetry
Teal Press
Telephone Books
Telescope
Temblor
The Temple
Tendril
Texas Slough
Third Coast
13th Moon
THIS
Thorp Springs Press
Three Rivers Press
Threepenny Review
Thunder City Press
Thunder's Mouth Press
Tia Chucha Press
Tikkun
Tin House
Tombouctou Books
Toothpaste Press
Transatlantic Review
TriQuarterly
Truck Press
Undine
Unicorn Press
University of Georgia Press
University of Illinois Press
University of Iowa Press
University of Massachusetts Press
University of North Texas Press

University of Pittsburgh Press
University of Wisconsin Press
University Press of New England
Unmuzzled Ox
Unspeakable Visions of the Individual
Vagabond
Verse
Vignette
Virginia Quarterly
Volt
Wampeter Press
Washington Writers Workshop
Water-Stone
Water Table
Western Humanities Review
Westigan Review
White Pine Press
Wickwire Press
Willow Springs
Wilmore City
Witness
Word Beat Press
Word-Smith
Wormwood Review
Writers Forum
Xanadu
Yale Review
Yardbird Reader
Yarrow
Y'Bird
Zeitgeist Press
Zoetrope: All-Story
ZYZZYVA

CONTRIBUTING SMALL PRESSES FOR PUSHCART PRIZE XXVIII

A

Absey & Co., 23011 Northcrest, Spring, TX 77389
ache magazine, P.O. Box 50065, Minneapolis, MN 55405
Adept Press, P.O. Box 391, Long Valley, NJ 07853
The Adirondack Review, 1206 Superior St., F-24, Watertown, NY 13601
Aethlon, English Dept., East Tennessee State Univ., Johnson City, TN 37614
Agni, Boston Univ., 236 Bay State Rd., Boston, MA 02215
Alaska Quarterly Review, Univ. of Alaska, 3211 Providence Dr., Anchorage, AK 99508
Alice James Books, 238 Main St., Farmington, ME 04938
Always in Season, P.O. Box 380403, Brooklyn, NY 11238
Amaze: The Cinquain Journal, 10529 Olive St., Temple City, CA 91780
American Letters/Commentary, 850 Park Ave., Ste. 5B, New York, NY 10021
American Literary Review, English Dept., Univ. of North Texas, Denton, TX 76203
American Poetry Review, 1721 Walnut St., Philadelphia, PA 19103
American Scholar, 1811 Q NW, Washington, DC 20009
Ancient Paths, P.O. Box 7505, Fairfax Station, VA 22039
Anthology, Inc., P.O. Box 4411, Mesa, AZ 85211
Antioch Review, P.O. Box 148, Yellow Springs, OH 45387
Apogee Press, P.O. Box 9177, Berkeley, CA 94709
Appalachian Heritage, Berea College, Berea, KY 40404
Arctos Press, P.O. Box 401, Sausalito, CA 94966
Argonne House Press, P.O. Box 21069, Washington, DC 20009
Arkansas Review, English Dept., P.O. Box 1890, State University, AR 72467
Arsenic Lobster, 1800 Schodde Ave., Burley, ID 83318
Arte Publico Press, Univ. of Houston, Houston, TX 77204
Artful Dodge, College of Wooster, Wooster, OH 44691
Arts & Letters, Georgia College & State Univ., Milledgeville, GA 31061
Ascent, Concordia College, Moorhead, MN 56562
Ashland Poetry Press, Ashland College, Ashland, OH 44805
Aunt Lute Books, P.O. Box 410687, San Francisco, CA 94141
Axe Factory, P.O. Box 40691, Philadelphia, PA 19107

B

Baltimore Writers' Alliance, P.O. Box 410, Riderwood, MD 21139
Bamboo Ridge Press, P.O. Box 61781, Honolulu, HI 96839
Barbaric Yawp, 3700 County Rte. 24, Russell, NY 13684
Barrow Street, 132 East 35th St., #10B, New York, NY 10016
Basilisk Press, 308 Normal St., Ste. 1, Denton, TX 76201
Bathtub Gin, see Pathwise Press
Bayou, Univ. of New Orleans, Lakefront, New Orleans, LA 70148
Bellevue Literary Review, NYU School of Medicine, 550 First Ave., OBV 6-612, New York, NY 10016
Bellingham Review, MS-9053, WWU, Bellingham, WA 98225
Bellowing Ark Press, P.O. Box 55564, Shoreline, WA 98155
Beloit Fiction Journal, Beloit College, 700 College St., Beloit, WI 53511
Beloit Poetry Journal, 24 Berry Cove Rd., Lamoine, ME 04605
The Berkshire Review, P.O. Box 23, Richmond, MA 01254
Big City Lit., Box 1141, Cathedral Sta., New York, NY 10025
Bilingual Review/Press, Hispanic Research Center, P.O. Box 872702, Tempe, AZ 85387
The Bitter Oleander Press, 4983 Tall Oaks Dr., Fayetteville, NY 13066
BkMk Press, Univ. of Missouri, 5101 Rockhill Rd., Kansas City, MO 64110
Blacfax Publications, P.O. Box 803, College Sta., New York, NY 10030
Black Warrior Review, P.O. Box 862936, Tuscaloosa, AL 35486
Blackbird, P.O. Box 843082, Richmond, VA 23289
Blink, P.O. Box E, Mississippi Station, MS 39762
Blue Fifth Review, 267 Lark Meadow Ct., Bluff City, TN 37618
Blue Planet Journal, P.O. Box 911, Dublin, VA 24084
Blue Unicorn, 22 Avon Rd., Kensington, CA 94707
BOA Editions, Ltd., 260 East Ave., Rochester, NY 14604
Bogg Publications, 422 N. Cleveland St., Arlington, VA 22201
Boise Journal, 449 Main St., Boise, ID 83702
Bordighera, Inc., P.O. Box 1374, Lafayette, IN 47902
Boulevard, 7545 Cromwell Dr., Apt. 2N, St. Louis, MO 63105
Brain, Child, P.O. Box 1161, Harrisonburg, VA 22803
Branches, P.O. Box 85394, Seattle, WA 98145
Briar Cliff Review, Briar Cliff Univ., 3303 Rebecca St., Sioux City, IA 51104
Bridge, 119 N. Peoria, #3D, Chicago, IL 60607
Brilliant Corners, Lycoming College, Williamsport, PA 17701
Brookview Press, 901 Western Rd., Castleton-on-Hudson, NY 12033
brown swan, publishers, 760 redriver way, Corona, CA 92882
Buckle, P.O. Box 1653, Buffalo, NY 14205
Bucknell University Press, Lewisburg, PA 17837
Buttonwood Press, Box 206, Champaign, IL 61824
Byline, P.O. Box 5240, Edmond, OK 73083

C

Calyx, P.O. Box B, 216 SW Madison, Corvallis, OR 97339
Canary River Review, P.O. Box 51210, Eugene, OR 97405
The Caribbean Writer, Univ. of the Virgin Islands, RR2-10000 Kingshill, St. Croix, U.S. Virgin Islands, 00850
Carve Magazine / Press, P.O. Box 72231, Davis, CA 95617
Chaffin Journal, Eastern Kentucky Univ., Richmond, KY 40475
The Chariton Review, Truman State Univ., Kirksville, MO 63501
Chatoyant, P.O. Box 832, Aptos, CA 95001
The Chattahoochee Review, 2101 Womack RD., Dunwoody, GA 30338
Chelsea, Box 773, Cooper Sta., New York, NY 10276

Chicago Review, Univ. of Chicago, 5801 S. Kenwood ave., Chicago, IL 60637
Cider Press Review, 773 Poplar Church Rd., Camp Hill, PA 17011
Cimarron Review, Oklahoma State Univ., Stillwater, OK 74078
Cinco Puntos Press, 701 Texas Ave., El Paso, TX 79901
Clean Sheets Magazine, 5082 E. Hampden, Denver, CO 80222
Coal City Review, English Dept., Univ. of Kansas, Lawrence, KS 66045
Colere, 1220 1st Ave., NE, Cedar Rapids, IA 52402
Colorado Review, Colorado State University, Ft. Collins, CO 80523
Columbia, Columbia Univ., 2960 Broadway, New York, NY 10027
Common Ground Review, 43 Witch Path #1, W. Springfield, MA 01089
The Comstock Review, 4956 St. John Dr., Syracuse, NY 13215
Confrontation, L.I. Univ., C.W. Post Campus, Brookville, NY 11548
Conjunctions, Bard College, Annandale-on-Hudson, NY 12504
Connecticut Review, So. Connecticut State Univ., 501 Crescent St. New Haven, CT 06515
Crab Orchard Review, English Dept., So. Illinois Univ., Carbondale, IL 62901
Crazyhorse, English Dept., College of Charleston, Charleston, SC 29424
Creative Nonfiction, 5501 Walnut St. #202, Pittsburgh, PA 15232
Croonenbergh's Publishing Co., 3410 33rd St., #4B, AStoria, NY 11106
Cross Currents, 475 Riverside Dr., Rm. 1945, New York, NY 10115
Crucible, Barton College, Wilson, NC 27893
Curbstone Press, 321 Jackson St., Willimantic, CT 06226
CutBank, English Dept., MST 410, Univ. of Montana, Missoula, MT 59612

D

Daedalus, 136 Irving St., Cambridge, MA 02138
Dana Literary Society, P.O. Box 3362, Dana Point, CA 92629
John Daniel & Co, Publishers, P.O. Box 21922, Santa Barbara, CA 93121
Dickens Literary Review, 2254 Beverly Way, Santa Rosa, CA 95404
Diner, Box 60676, Greendale Sta., Worcester, MA 01606
The DMQ Review, P.O. Box 640746, San Jose, CA 95164
Dogwood, Fairfield Univ., N. Benson Rd., Fairfield, CT 06430
The Dolorosa Press, 701 E. Schaaf Rd., Cleveland, OH 44131
Doubletake, 55 Davis Square, Somerville, MA 02144

E

Eastern Washington University Press, EWU, 705 West 1st, Spokane, WA 99201
Edgewise Press, 24 Fifth Ave., #224, New York, NY 10011
Edison Literary Review, 1729 Woodland Ave., Edison, NJ 08820
88, P.O. Box 2872, Venice, CA 90994
Ekphrasis, P.O. Box 161236, Sacramento, CA 95816
Elixir, P.O. Box 18010, Minneapolis, MN 55418
Elkhound, Box 1453, Gracie Sta., New York, NY 10028
Elysian Fields Quarterly, P.O. Box 14385, St. Paul, MN 55114
Epoch, Cornell Univ., 251 Goldwin Smith, Ithaca, NY 14853
Erosha Literary Ezine, Box 185, Falls Church, VA 22040
Eureka Literary Magazine, Eureka College, 300 E. College Ave., Eureka, IL 61530
Evansville Review, Univ. of Evansville, 1800 Lincoln Ave., Evansville, IN 47722
Event, Douglas College, P.O. Box 2503, New Westminster, B.C. CANADA V3L 5B2
Eye of Ra Publishing, P.O. Box 28607, Santa Fe, NM 87592

F

Facets Magazine, P.O. Box 380915, Cambridge, MA 02238
Fail Better.com, 63 Eighth Ave., Ste. 3A, Brooklyn, NY 11217
Faultline, English Dept., Univ. of California, Irvine, CA 92697
Fence, 14 Fifth Ave., #1A, New York, NY 10011
Field, Oberlin College, Oberlin, OH 44074
Finishing Line Press, P.O. Box 1626, Georgetown, KY 40324
First Intensity, P.O. Box 665, Lawrence, KS 66044
5 AM, Box 205, Spring Church, PA 15686
Five Points, English Dept., Georgia State Univ., University Plaza, Atlanta, GA 30303
Flashquake, P.O. Box 2154, Albany, NY 12220
The Florida Review, English Dept., Univ. of Central Florida, Orlando, FL 32816
Foliate Oak, Univ. of Arkansas, Monticello, AR 71656
Folio: A Literary Journal, Dept. of Literature, American Univ., Washington, DC 20016
The Formalist, 320 Hunter Dr., Evansville, IN $7711
42nd Parallel, 623 N. 51 St., Omaha, NE 68132
Fountain Mountain Press, 125 W. Clark Ave., Orcutt, CA 93455
Fourth Genre, Michigan State Univ., East Lansing, MI 48824
Free Verse, M233 Marsh Rd., Marshfield, WI 54449
Frith Press, P.O. Box 161236. Sacramento, CA 95816
Futures Magazine, 3039 38th Ave., S, Minneapolis, MN 55406

G

Gargoyle, P.O. Box 6216, Arlington, VA 22206
The Georgia Review, Univ. of Georgia, Athens, GA 30602
Gettysburg Review, Gettysburg College, Gettysburg, PA 17325
Gilford Graphics Int'l, P.O. Box 1023, Island Heights, NJ 08732
The Golden Notebook, 29 Tinker St., Woodstock, NY 12498
Grain, Box 67, Sakatoon, SK *CANADA* S7K 3K1
Grand Street, 214 Sullivan St., #6C, New York, NY 10012
Gravity Press, 27030 Havelock, Dearborn Hgts., MI 48127
Great Marsh Press, P.O. Box 2144, Lenox Hill Sta., New York, NY 10021
Green Bean Press, P.O. Box 237, New York, NY 10013
Green Hills Literary Lantern, P.O. Box 375, Trenton, MO 64683
Green Mountains Review, Johnson State College, Johnson, VT 05656
The Greensboro Review, English Dept., Univ. of North Carolina, Greensboro, NC 27402
Gulf Coast, English Dept., Univ. of Houston, Houston, TX 77204

H

Hanging Loose Press, 231 Wyckoff St., Brooklyn, NY 11217
Happy, 240 East 35th St., 11A, New York, NY 10016
Harp-Strings Poetry Journal, Box 640387, Beverly Hills, FL 34464
Harpur Palate, English Dept., Binghamton Univ., Binghamton, NY 13902
Harvard Review, Lamont Library, Harvard Univ., Cambridge, MA 02138
Hawaii Pacific Review, 1060 Bishop St., Honolulu, HI 96813
Hayden's Ferry Review, Arizona State Univ., Box 871502, Tempe, AZ 85287
The Higginsville Reader, P.O. Box 141, Three Bridges, NJ 08887
High Plains Literary Review, 180 Adams St., #250, Denver, CO 80206

Hogtown Creek Review, 4736 Hummingbird La., Valdosta, GA 31602
Horse & Buggy Press, 303 Kinsey St., Raleigh, NC 27603
Hotel Amerika, Ohio Univ., Ellis Hall, Athens, OH 45701
The Hudson Review, 684 Park Avenue, New York, NY 10021
Hunger Magazine/Press, 1305 Old Rte. 28, Phoenicia, NY 12464
Hunger Mountain, Vermont College, 36 College St., Montpelier, VT 05602
Hybolics, P.O. Box 3016, Aiea, HI 96701

I

Icarus Ascending, P.O. Box 621, Cazenovia, NY 13035
The Iconoclast, 1675 Amazon Rd., Mohegan Lake, NY 10547
The Idaho Review, English Dept., Boise State Univ., Boise, ID 83725
Illuminations, English Dept., College of Charleston, 66 George St., Charleston, SC 29424
Illya's Honey, P.O. Box 700865, Dallas, TX 75370
Image, 3307 Third Ave. West, Seattle, WA 98119
In Posse Review, 239 Duncan St., San Francisco, CA 94131
Indiana Review, 1020 E. Kirkwood Ave., Bloomington, IN 47405
Inkwell, Manhattanville College, 2900 Purchase St., Purchase, NY 10577
The Iowa Review, 308 EPB, Univ. of Iowa, Iowa City, IA 52242
Italian Americana, 80 Washington St., Providence, RI 02903

J

Jane Street Press, 1 Jane St., Ste. 5F, New York, NY 10014
Jewish Women's Resource Center Press, 820 second Ave., New York, NY10017
The Journal, English Dept., Ohio State Univ., Columbus, OH 43210
Journal Of New Jersey Poets, Co. College of Morris, 214 Center Grove Rd., Randolph, NJ 07869
Jubilat, English Dept., Univ. of Massachusetts, Amherst, MA 01003

K

The Kelsey Review, Mercer Co. Community College, P.O. Box B, Trenton, NJ 08690
The Kenyon Review, Kenyon College, Gambier, OH 43022
Kestrel, Fairmont State College, 1201 Locust Ave., Fairmont, WV 26554

L

Lake Affect Publishers, 299 Hazlewood Terrace, Rochester, NY 14609
Lake Effect, Penn State Univ., 5091 Station Rd., Erie, PA 16563
The Larcom Press, P.O. Box 161, Prides Crossing, MA 01965
The Ledge Magazine, 78-44 80th St., Glendale, NY 11385
The Licking River Review, No. Kentucky Univ., Highland Heights, KY 41099
Lit Pot Press, P.O. Box 1034, Blue Lake, CA 95525
Literal Latte, 61 East 8th St., Ste. 240, New York, NY 10003
Literary Imagination, Classics Dept., Univ. of Georgia, Athens, GA 30602
The Literary Review, 285 Madison Ave., Madison, NJ 07940
Livingston Press, Station 22, Univ. of W. Alabama, Livingston, AL 35470

The Louisville Review, Spalding Univ., 851 S. 4th St., Louisville, KY 40203
Low-Tech Press, 30-73 47th St., Long Island City, NY 11103
Lynx Eye, 542 Mitchell Dr., Los Osos, CA 93402
Lyric Review, P.O. Box 980814, Houston, TX 77098

M

The MacGuffin, 18600 Haggerty Rd., Livonia, MI 48152
The Magazine of Speculative Poetry, P.O. Box 564, Beloit, WI 53512
The Manhattan Review, 440 Riverside Dr., #38, New York, NY 10027
Manic D Press, 250 Banks St., San Francisco, CA 94110
Many Mountains Moving, 420 22nd St., Boulder, CO 80302
Margie, P.O. Box 250, Chesterfield, MO 63006
Margin, 9407 Capstan Dr., NE, Bainbridge Island, WA 98110
Marsh River Editions, M233 Marsh Rd., Marshfield, WI 54449
Massachusetts Review, South College, Univ. of Massachusetts, Amherst, MA 01003
The Melic Review, P.O. Box 568, Long Beach, CA 90801
Meridian, Univ. of Virginia, P.O. Box 400145, Charlottesville, VA 22904
Mid-American Review, English Dept., Bowling Green State Univ., Bowling Green, OH 43403
Mid-List Press, 4324 12th Ave., S., Minneapolis, MN 55407
Midnight mind Magazine, P.O. Box 146912, Chicago, IL 60614
Midstream, 633 3rd Ave., 21st fl., New York, NY 10017
Miller's Pond, RR#2, Box 24T, Middlebury Center, PA 16935
Mindprints, Allan Hancock College, 800 S. College Dr., Santa Maria, CA 93454
Miniature Sun Press, P.O. Box 11002, Napa, CA 94581
MIPo Zines, 9240 SW 44 St., Miami, FL 33165
Mississippi Review, Univ. of So. Mississippi, Hattiesburg, MS 39406
The Missouri Review, Univ. of Missouri, Columbia, MO 65211
Mizna, P.O. Box 14294, Minneapolis, MN 55414
The Montserrat Review, P.O. Box 391764, Mountain View, CA 94039
Muse's Kiss, P.O. Box 703, Lenoir, NC 28645

N

Natural Bridge, English Dept., Univ. of Missouri, St. Louis, MO 63121
The Nebraska Review, Univ. of Nebraska, Writer's Workshop, Omaha, NE 68182
New Criterion, 850 Seventh Ave, New York, NY 10019
New Delta Review, 214 Allen Hall, LSU, Baton Rouge, LA 70803
New England Review, Middlebury College, Middlebury, VT 05753
New England Writers, P.O. Box 5, Windsor, VT 05089
New Letters, Univ. of Missouri, 5100 Rockhill Rd., Kansas City, MO 64110
New Orleans Review, Box 195, Loyola Univ., New Orleans, LA 70118
The New Orphic Review, 706 Mill St., Nelson, B.C., *CANADA* V1L 4S5
The New Renaissance, 26 Heath Rd., #11, Arlington, MA 02474
New South, Inc., P.O. Box 1588, Montgomery, AL 36102
New York Stories, 31-10 Thomson Ave., Long Island City, NY 11101
Night Train, 85 Orchard St., Somerville, MA 02144
Nimrod Int'l Journal, 600 S. College Ave., Tulsa, OK 74104
9 Muses Books, 3541 Kent Creek rd., Winston, OR 97496
96 inc., P.O.Box 15559, Boston, MA 02215
NMP/DIAGRAM, 51 Cedar Crest, Tuscaloosa, AL 35401
North American Review, Univ. of No. Iowa, Cedar Falls, IA 50614
North Atlantic Books, PO Box 12327, Berkeley, CA 94712
North Star Publishing, N. 17285 Co. Rd. 400, Powers, MI 49874

Northeastern University Press, 360 Huntington Ave., Boston, MA 02115
Northwest Review, 369 PLC, Univ. of Oregon, Eugene, OR 97403
Notre Dame Review, English Dept., Univ. of Notre Dame, Notre Dame, IN 46556

O

One Story, P.O. Box 1326, New York, NY 10156
One Trick Pony, P.O. Box 11186, Philadelphia, PA 19136
Ontario Review, 9 Honey Brook Dr., Princeton, NJ 08540
Open City, 2251 Lafayette St., Ste. 1114, New York, NY 10012
Open Spaces Quarterly, PMB 134, 6327-C SW Capitol Hwy., Portland, OR 97239
Orbis Books, P.O.Box 308, Maryknoll, NY 10545
Orchid, 3096 Williamsburg, Ann Arbor, MI 48108
Osiris, P.O. Box 297, Old Deerfield, MA 01342
Other Voices, English Dept., Univ. of Illinois, 601 S. Morgan St., Chicago, IL 60607
Oyster Boy Review, P.O. Box 77842, San Francisco, CA 94107

P

Painted Bride, 230 Vine St., Philadelphia, PA 19108
Palo Alto Review, Palo Alto College, 1400 W. Villaret Blvd., San Antonio, TX 78224
Pangolin Papers, P.O. Box 241, Nordland, WA 98358
Paragraph/Oat City Press, 18 Beach Point Dr., E. Providence, RI 02915
The Paris Review, 541 East 72nd St., New York, NY 10021
Parnassus: Poetry in Review, 205 West 89th St., #8F, New York, NY 10024
Partisan Review, 236 Bay State Rd., Boston, MA 02215
Pathwise Press, P.O. Box 2392, Bloomington, IN 47402
Paumanok Review, 254 Dogwood Dr., Hershey, PA 17033
Pearl, 3030 E. Second St., Long Beach, CA 90803
Peralta Press, 333 East 8th St., Oakland, CA 94606
Perugia Press, P.O. Box 60364, Florence, MA 01062
Phantasmagoria, English Dept., Century College, White Bear Lake, MN 55110
Philos. Press, 8038-A N. Bicentennial Loop, SE., Lacey, WA 98503
Pindeldyboz, 11 Windsor Ave., Rockville Center, NY 11970
Pleiades, English Dept., Central Missouri State Univ., Warrensburg, MO 64093
Ploughshares, Emerson College, 120 Boylston St., Boston, MA 02116
Pluma Productions, P.O.Box 1138, Hollywood, CA 90078
PMS, English Dept., Univ. of Alabama, Birmingham, AL 35294
Poems & Plays, English Dept., Middle Tennessee State Univ., Murfreesboro, TN 37132
Poet Lore, 4508 Walsh St., Bethesda, MD 20815
Poetry, 60 W. Walton St., Chicago, IL 60610
Poetry Center, Cleveland State Univ., 2121 Euclid Ave., Cleveland, OH 44115
Poetry Miscellany, English Dept., Univ. of Tennessee, Chattanooga, TN 37403
The Poetry Porch, 168 Hollett St., Scituate, MA 02068
Poets Corner Press, 8049 Thornton Rd., Stockton, CA 95209
Poetz.com, P.O.Box 1401, New York, NY 10026
POOL, P.O.Box 480787, Los Angeles, CA 90048
The Portland Review, P.O.Box 347, Portland, OR 97207
Post Road, 853 Broadway, Ste. 1516, Box 85, New York, NY 10003
Potomac Review, P.O.X 354, Port Tobacco, MD 20677
Prairie Fire Press, Inc., 423-100 Arthur St., Winnipeg, MB CANADA R3B 1H3
Prairie Schooner, Univ. of Nebraska, P.O.Box 880334, Lincoln, NE 68588
Prism, Creative Writing Program, Univ. of British Columbia, Vancouver, B.C. CANADA V6T 1Z1

Prose Ax, P.O.Box 22643, Honolulu, HI 96823
Provincetown Arts Press, P.O.Box 35, Provincetown, MA 02657
Publish America, LLLP, - P.O.Box 151, Frederick, MD 21705

Q

Quarter After Eight, Ellis Hall, Ohio Univ., Athens, OH 45701
Quarterly West, Univ. of Utah, Salt Lake City, UT 84112

R

Rain Taxi, P.O.Box 3840, Minneapolis, MN 55403
Ralph, P.O.Box 17619, San Diego, CA 92176
Raritan, 31 Mine St., New Brunswick, NJ 08903
Rattapallax, 250 Riverside Dr., #23, New York, NY 10025
Rattle, 13440 Ventura Blvd., Ste. 200, Sherman Oaks, CA 91423
Recycled Quarterly, P.O.Box 1111, Sanford, FL 32772
Red River Review, 1729 Alpine Dr., Carrollton, TX 75007
Red Wheelbarrow, DeAnza College, Cupertino, CA 95014
Rendezvous, Box 8113, Idaho State Univ., Pocatello, ID 83209
Rhino, Box 591, Evanston, IL 60204
Ridgeway Press of Michigan, P.O.Box 120, Roseville, MI 48066
River King, P.O.Box 122, Freeburg, IL 62243
River Oak Review, 728 Noyes St., Evanston, IL 60201
River Styx, 634 No. Grand Blvd., 12th fl., St. Louis, MO 63103
Rockford Review, 7721 Venus St., Loves Park, IL 61111
Rose & Thorn Literary E-Zine, P.O.Box 203230, New Haven, CT 06520
Rose Shell Reviews & Press, 15223 Coral Isle Ct., Ft. Myers, FL 33919

S

Salmagundi, Skidmore College, Saratoga Springs, NY 12866
Sand Star Publications, P.O.Box 181, Rockport, MA 01966
Santa Monica Review, Santa Monica College, 1900 Pico Blvd., Santa Monica, CA 90405
Sarabande Books, Inc., 2234 Dundee Rd., Ste. 200, Louisville, KY 40205
Schuylkill, Temple Univ., Anderson Hall, 10th fl., Philadelphia, PA 19122
Self Taxidermy Press, 11553 Cedar Way, Loma Linda, CA 92354
Seneca Review, Hobart & William Smith College, Geneva, NY 14456
Shenandoah, Washington & Lee Univ., Lexington, VA 24450
Singles Network, P.O.Box 13, Springfield, VA 22150
Slipstream, P.O.Box 2071, Niagara Falls, NY 14301
Slow Trains Literary Journal, P.O.Box 4741, Englewood, CO 80155
Small Beer Press, 176 Prospect Ave., Northampton, MA 01060
The Small Pond Magazine, P.O.Box 664, Stratford, CT 06615
Southern Indiana Review, 8600 University Blvd., Evansville, IN 47712
Southern Poetry Review, English Dept., Armstrong Atlanta State Univ., Savannah, GA 31419
The Southern Review, 43 Allen Hall, LSU, Baton Rouge, LA 70803
Southwest Review, Southern Methodist Univ., P.O.Box 750374, Dallas, TX 75275
Spillway, Box 7887, Huntington Beach, CA 92615
Spinning Jenny, P.O.Box 1373, New York, NY 10276

Story Quarterly, 431 Sheridan Rd., Kenilworth, IL 60043
StorySouth, 3433 Portland Ave. S, Ste. #2, Minneapolis, MN 55407
The Storyteller, 2441 Washington Rd., Maynard, AR 72444
The Sun, 107 N. Roberson St., Chapel Hill, NC 27516
Swan Scythe Press, English Dept., Univ. of California, Davis, CA 95616
Sweet Annie Press, 7750 Hwy F-24 W., Baxter, IA 50028
Sycamore Review, English Dept., Purdue Univ., W. Lafayette, IN 47907

T

Taj Mahal Review, Govindpur Colony, Allahabad - 211004 (U.P.) *INDIA*
Talebones, 5203 Quincy Ave., SE, Auburn, WA 98092
Talking River Review, Lewis-Clark State College, 500 8th Ave., Lewiston, ID 83501
Tebot Bach, Box 7887, Huntington Beach, CA 92615
Terminus Books, 1090 Faraday Rd., Durango, CO 81303
Thema, Box 8747, Metairie, LA 70011
Thornton Enterprises, 190 W. Continental Rd., Green Valley, AZ 85614
Thought Magazine, P.O. Box 117098, Burlingame, CA 94011
three candles, 5470 132nd La., Savage, MN 55378
Threepenny Review, P.O. Box 9131, Berkeley, CA 94709
Timber Creek Review, P.O. Box 8969, UNCG Sta., Greensboro, NC 27413
Tin House, 2601 NW Thurman St., Portland, OR 97210
Tiny Lights Publications, P.O. Box 928, Petaluma, CA 94953
Triple Tree Publishing, P.O. Box 5684, Eugene, OR 97405
TriQuarterly, Northwestern Univ., 2020 Ridge Ave., Evanston, IL 60208
Tsunami, P.O. Box 100, Walla Walla, WA 99362
Turtle Point Press, 233 Broadway, Rm. 946, New York, NY 10279
26 Magazine, P.O. Box 4450, St. Mary's College, Moraga, CA 94575
Two Rivers Review, P.O. Box 158, Clinton, NY 13323

U

Under the Sun, English Dept., Tennessee Tech. Univ., Box 5053, Cookeville, TN 38505
Underground Literary Alliance, P.O. Box 42077, Philadelphia, PA 19101
University of Massachusetts Press, 505 E. Pleasant St., Amherst, MA 01002
University of Tampa Press, 401 W. Kennedy Blvd., Tampa, FL 33606
Unwound Magazine, P.O. Box 835, Laramie, WY 82073

V

The Valley Contemporary Poets, P.O. Box 5342, Sherman Oaks, CA 91413
Verse Libre Quarterly, Box 185, Falls Church, VA 22040
Verse Press, English Dept., Univ. of Georgia, Athens, GA 30602
Vestal Review, 2609 Dartmouth Dr., Vestal, NY 13850
Vincent Brothers Review, 4566 Northern Circle, Riverside, OH 45424
Virginia Quarterly Review, One West Range, Charlottesville, VA 22903

W

Water-Stone, Hamline Univ., 1536 Hewitt Ave., St. Paul, MN 55104
Wayne Literary Review, English Dept., Wayne State Univ., Detroit, MI 48202
Weighted Anchor Press, Hampshire College, Amherst, MA 01002
West Anglia Publications, P.O. Box 2683, LaJolla, CA 92038
West Branch, Bucknell Univ., Lewisburg, PA 17837
Western Humanities Review, English Dept., Univ. of Utah, Salt Lake City, UT 84112
White Eagle Coffee Store Press, P.O. Box 383, Fox River Grove, IL 60021
White Pelican Review, P.O. Box 7833, Lakeland, FL 33813
The James White Review, 290 West 12th St., 6C, New York, NY 10014
Willow Springs, EWU, 705 West 1st Ave., Spokane, WA 99201
Wind, P.O. Box 24548, Lexington, KY 40524
Wing and a Prayer Press, 357 W. Purchase Rd., Southbury, CT 06488
Witness, Oakland Community College, Farmington Hills, MI 48334
The Worcester Review, 6 Chatham St., Worcester, MA 01608
WordWrights Magazine, P.O. Box 21069, Washington, DC 20009
Words of Wisdom, P.O. Box 8969, UNCG Sta., Greensboro, NC 27413
Works + Conversations, P.O. Box 5008, Berkeley, CA 94705
Writershood, 2518 Fruitland Dr., Bremerton, WA 98310

X

Xconnect, Box 2317, Philadelphia, PA 19103

Y

Yale Review, Yale University, PO Box 208243, New Haven, CT 06520
Yuganta Press, 6 Rushmore Circle, Stamford, CT 06905

Z

Zoetrope, 916 Kearny St., 3rd fl., San Francisco, CA 94133
ZYZZYVA, P.O. Box 590069, San Francisco, CA 94159

CONTRIBUTORS' NOTES

BETTY ADCOCK's fifth book, *Intervale*, was co-winner of the 2003 Poet's Prize. She won a Guggenheim Fellowship in 2002.

DAVID BAKER's *Changeable Thunder* was published in 2001 by the University of Arkansas Press. He teaches at Denison University.

JENNIFER BARBER is founding editor of *Salamander*. She is the author of *Rigging The Wind*.

DOROTHY BARRESI teaches at California State University Northridge, Her books are *All Of the Above* and *The Post Rapture Diner*.

QUAN BARRY's first book, *Asylum*, won the Agnes Lynch Starret Poetry Prize and was published by the University of Pittsburgh Press.

ELLEN BASS's most recent book of poetry is *Mules Of Love* (BOA). She lives in Santa Cruz, California.

BRUCE BEASLEY is the author of *Signs and Abominations* (Wesleyan University Press) and other poetry collections. He teaches at Western Washington University, Bellingham.

PINCKNEY BENEDICT has published two volumes of short stories and a novel. He grew up on his family's farm in southern West Virginia.

DAN CHIASSON is the author of *The Afterlife of Objects* (University of Chicago Press). He writes for *Slate*, *Raritan* and other journals.

JANE BROX's third book of essays is forthcoming from North Point Press. She lives in Dracut, Massachusetts.

RACHEL COHEN's essays have appeared in *McSweeney's*, *Threepenny Review* and elsewhere. Her book, *A Chance Meeting*, is forthcoming from Random House. She lives in Brooklyn, New York.

EVAN CONNELL is the author of *Mrs. Bridge*, *Son of the Morning Star* and other novels. He lives in Santa Fe.

JOAN CONNOR teaches at Ohio University and has published two collections of stories: *We Who Live Apart* (2002) and *Here On Old Route 7* (1997), both from the University of Missouri Press.

ROBERT COOVER teaches at Brown. His thirteen novels include *The Adventures of Lucky Pierre: Director's Cut* (Grove, 2002).

ANDREW FELD's poetry has appeared in *The Nation*, *New England Review*, *Virginia Quarterly Review* and *Yale Review*. He lives in Eugene, Oregon.

BEN FOUNTAIN III lives in Dallas. He is a graduate of Duke University Law School and has published in *Southwest Review*, *Threepenny Review* and elsewhere.

EUGENE GLORIA's collection of poems, *Drivers At The Short Time Motel*, was selected for the 1999 National Poetry Series and was published by Penguin. He received the Asian American Literary Award and he teaches at DePauw University.

JUDITH HALL is the author most recently of *The Promised Folly*. She teaches at California Institute of Technology and is poetry editor of *The Antioch Review*.

RYAN HARTY is a former Stegner Fellow and Jones Lecturer at Stanford, where he now teaches. He is at work on a novel.

KIRA HENEHAN's work has appeared in *Jubilat*, *Chelsea*, *3rd bed*, and *Unsaid*. She lives in New York City.

CHRISTIE HODGEN won the AWP award for *A Jeweler's Eye for Flaw* (University of Massachusetts Press). She lives in Columbia, Missouri.

EDWARD HOAGLAND lives in Bennington, Vermont and is acclaimed for his many books, most recently *Compass Points*. He contributed the Introduction to *Pushcart Prize XVI*.

MARK IRWIN's fifth book, *Bright Hunger*, will be published by BOA. His *White City* was nominated for The National Book Critics Circle Award and won a Colorado Book Award.

SHELLEY JACKSON is the author of *The Melancholy of Anatomy* (Anchor Books), *Patchwork Girl* (Eastgate) and several children's books.

RICHARD JACKSON teaches at the University of Tennessee and Vermont College. He has published six books of poems and is a past poetry co-editor of *The Pushcart Prize*.

MYRA JEHLEN has published several volumes of literary criticism including, most recently, *Readings At The Edge of Literature*. She teaches at Rutgers University.

JULIA KASDORF is the author of two books of poems and a collection of essays. She teaches at Pennsylvania State University.

BRIGIT PEGEEN KELLY teaches at the University of Illinois, Urbana. Her second book of poems, *Song*, was published by BOA in 1995.

VALERIE LAKEN's "Before Long" is her first published story. She studied at the University of Michigan and lives in Ann Arbor.

JONATHAN LETHEM is the author of *The Fortress of Solitude* and five other novels. He lives in Brooklyn, New York.

DANA LEVIN's second book, *Wedding Day*, will be published soon by Copper Canyon. She teaches at the College of Santa Fe, and received several honors for her first book, *In the Surgical Theatre*.

MARGARET LUONGO earned an MFA from the University of Florida. "Pretty" is her first published story.

M. ELAINE MAR is the author of *Paper Daughter* (Harper Collins). She lives in Cambridge, Massachusetts.

KHALED MATTAWA is the author of *Zodiac of Echoes* (Ausable Press) and *Ismailia Eclips* (Sheep Meadow Press).

TRACY MAYOR's essays have been published in Salon.com, the *Boston Globe* and other journals. She lives with her husband and two sons in Hamilton, Massachusetts.

MALINDA MCCOLLUM teaches at Stanford University, where she was a fellow in the Stegner Program. Her stories have appeared in *Epoch* and ZYZZYVA.

ANTONYA NELSON teaches at the University of Houston. Her latest fiction collection is *Female Trouble*, which includes "The Lonely Doll."

JOYCE CAROL OATES is a Founding Editor of *The Pushcart Prize* series. She lives in Princeton, New Jersey.

DEAN PASCHAL's short story collection, *By The Light of the Juke Box*, was published by Ontario Review Press. He lives in New Orleans.

LUCIA PERILLO has published three books of poetry, most recently *The Oldest Map With the Name America* (Random House). She received A MacArthur Foundation Fellowship in 2000.

RICHARD POWERS is the author of eight novels, most recently *The Time of Our Singing* (Farrar, Straus and Giroux). He lives in Urbana, Illinois.

KEVIN PRUFER is the author of *The Finger Bone* (Carnegie Mellon, 2002), and the forthcoming *Fallen From A Chariot*. He was the editor of *The New Young American Poets* (Southern Illinois, 2000).

ERIC PUCHNER is a Wallace Stegner Fellow at Stanford. His manuscript in progress is "Music Through the Floor."

MARY ROBISON is the author of *Why Did I Ever*, which won the *Los Angeles Times* fiction award in 2002, and also of *Tell Me: 30 Stories*. She lives in Mississippi.

EMILY ISHEM RABOTEAU is a student at New York University. Her work has appeared in *Transition*, *African Voices* and the *Chicago Tribune*.

JOAN SILBER's new story collection *Ideas of Heaven*, will be published by WW Norton Co. soon. She is also the author of an earlier collection of stories and three novels.

FLOYD SKLOOT's second book of essays, *In The Shadow of Memory*, was published in 2003 by the University of Nebraska Press. He lives in Amity, Oregon.

BRUCE SMITH is the author of four poetry books, most recently *The Other Lover*, a finalist for the National Book Award and the Pulitzer Prize. He lives in Alabama.

R.T. SMITH's most recent poetry collection is *The Hollow Log Lounge* (Illinois, 2003). He is the poetry editor of *Shenandoah*.

ELIZABETH SPIRES is the author of five collections of poetry, most recently *Now The Green Blade Rises* (Norton, 2002). She teaches at Goucher College, and is a past poetry co-editor of this series.

GEORGE STEINER is Charles Eliot Norton Professor at Harvard University. His *Grammars of Creation* is out from Yale University Press.

SUSAN STRAIGHT's *Highwire Moon* was a finalist for the National Book Award. She lives in Riverside, California.

573

TERESE SVOBODA's most recent book of poetry is *Treason* (Zoo Press, 2002) and her most recent prose publication is *Trailer Girl and Other Stories* (Counterpoint Press).

COLE SWENSEN teaches at the Iowa Writers' Workshop. She is the author of the forthcoming *Goest* (Alice James Books).

JANET SYLVESTER has published poetry collections with Wesleyan University Press and W.W. Norton Co. She won a PEN Discovery Award and teaches at Harvard.

ROBERT THOMAS won the Poets Out Loud Prize for his *Door to Door*, published by Fordham University Press. He lives in San Francisco.

BJ WARD's work has appeared in *Poetry*, *Natural Bridge*, *Puerto Del Sol*, *Mid-American Review* and elsewhere. He lives in Washington, New Jersey.

MICHAEL WATERS has published seven volumes of poetry, most recently with BOA Editions. He teaches at Salisbury University in Maryland.

ROSANNA WARREN lives in Roslindale, Massachusetts. Her work appears in *The Yale Review* and other publications.

PAUL WEST's most recent books are *Oxford Days* (British American) and *Cheops: A Cupboard for the Sun* (New Directions).

ELEANOR WILNER's collection, *The Girl With Bees In Her Hair*, is forthcoming from Copper Canyon. She teaches at Warren Wilson College.

INDEX

The following is a listing in alphabetical order by author's last name of works reprinted in the *Pushcart Prize* editions since 1976.

581

586

587

589

590

591

592

595

596

597

599

600

601

602

603